RING OF FIRE III

Baen Books by Eric Flint

The Ring of Fire series:

1632 by Eric Flint
1633 by Eric Flint & David Weber
1634: The Baltic War by Eric Flint & David Weber
1634: The Ram Rebellion by Eric Flint with Virginia DeMarce
1634: The Bavarian Crisis by Eric Flint & Virginia DeMarce
1634: The Galileo Affair by Eric Flint & Andrew Dennis
1635: The Cannon Law by Eric Flint & Andrew Dennis
1635: The Dreeson Incident by Eric Flint & Virginia DeMarce
1635: The Eastern Front by Eric Flint
1636: The Saxon Uprising by Eric Flint

Ring of Fire ed. by Eric Flint
Ring of Fire II ed. by Eric Flint
Ring of Fire III ed. by Eric Flint

Grantville Gazette ed. by Eric Flint
Grantville Gazette II ed. by Eric Flint
Grantville Gazette III ed. by Eric Flint
Grantville Gazette IV ed. by Eric Flint
Grantville Gazette V ed. by Eric Flint
Grantville Gazette VI ed. by Eric Flint (forthcoming January 2012)

1635: The Tangled Web by Virginia DeMarce

Time Spike by Eric Flint & Marilyn Kosmatka

**For a complete list of Baen Books by Eric Flint,
please go to www.baen.com**

RING OF FIRE III

EDITED BY
ERIC FLINT

RING OF FIRE III

This is a work of fiction. All the characters and events portrayed in this book are fictional, and any resemblance to real people or incidents is purely coincidental.

A Baen Books Original

Baen Publishing Enterprises
P.O. Box 1403
Riverdale, NY 10471
www.baen.com

ISBN: 978-1-4391-3448-1

Cover art by Tom Kidd
Map by Gorg Huff

First printing, July 2011

Distributed by Simon & Schuster
1230 Avenue of the Americas
New York, NY 10020

Library of Congress Cataloging-in-Publication Data

Ring of fire III / edited by Eric Flint.
      p. cm. — (The ring of fire series)
   ISBN 978-1-4391-3448-1 (hc)
  1. Fantasy fiction, American. 2. Alternative histories (Fiction), American.
3. Europe—History—17th century—Fiction. 4. Americans—Europe—Fiction.
5. West Virginia—Fiction. I. Flint, Eric. II. Title: Ring of fire 3.
III. Title: Ring of fire three.
   PS648.F3R554 2011
   813'.0876608—dc22

                                                                2011015813

10   9   8   7   6   5   4   3   2   1

Pages by Joy Freeman (www.pagesbyjoy.com)
Printed in the United States of America

To the memory of
Jim DeMarce and Betsy Boyes

Contents

RING OF FIRE III

Preface

Eric Flint

Short fiction has always been an integral part of the 1632 series. The third volume in the series was an anthology of short fiction: *Ring of Fire,* which came out after *1632* and *1633.* More than a decade has gone by since *1632* was published in February of 2000, and seven years since the first *Ring of Fire* anthology was published in 2004. Over the course of that time, to date, nine novels have appeared in the series and the same number of anthologies.

The anthologies fall into three categories: the *Ring of Fire* volumes; the paper editions of the *Grantville Gazette,* whose stories are taken from the electronic magazine by that name; and braided-story anthologies. Only one volume has so far appeared in that last category, *1634: The Ram Rebellion.* The second one, *1636: The Wars on the Rhine,* is being put together at the moment.

Roughly, the distinction between the three types of anthologies is as follows:

The *Gazette* volumes represent the traditional type of anthologies connected with popular series. The stories are all set in the 1632 universe, but have no particular relationship to each other and may or may not have much impact on the series as a whole. Some do, but they are not chosen for that reason. They are included simply because Paula Goodlett and I think they're good stories. (Paula is the editor of the magazine from which the stories are selected.)

The braided-story anthologies like *1634:The Ram Rebellion* are collections of short fiction that share a common story arc. The "short" fiction involved always includes at least one short novel.

The *Ring of Fire* anthologies are more loosely organized. But, with a few exceptions, every story in the anthology is either closely connected to existing story lines in the series or opens up new story lines for later development. And each volume ends with a short novel written by me.

In this third *Ring of Fire* volume, my short novel ("Four Days on the Danube") provides the sub-plot hinted at in *1636: The Saxon Uprising* and serves as a bridge to the next novel in the series centered on Mike Stearns.

Chuck Gannon's story "Upward Mobility" comes just before mine because it provides some of the background for my story.

Mercedes Lackey's story "Dye Another Day" lays some of the basis for a novel she and I will be writing later in the series.

Walter Hunt's story "Les Ailes du Papillon" is connected to a novel that he and I are working on at the moment. And, as with Chuck Gannon's other story, "Birds of a Feather," it starts to bring the New World into the series.

Panteleimon Roberts' "Mir Arash Khan" and Kim Mackey's "Salonica" do the same thing for the Ottoman Empire, which will also come to play a prominent role in the series as time goes on.

The Far East has so far been almost completely absent in the 1632 series. Garrett Vance's "All God's Children in the Burning East" begins to change that situation. Other stories develop the series in still different ways. Gorg Huff and Paula Goodlett's "Royal Dutch Airlines" illustrates the ongoing development of air travel—as does Gannon's "Upward Mobility." David Carrico's "Sweet Strings" continues his exploration of the impact of the Ring of Fire on music—and, at least indirectly, helps lay some of the basis for a novel he and I are writing entitled *1636: Symphony for the Devil*. Aspects of Jewish history have been an important part of the series since the very beginning. Tim Roesch's "Falser Messiah" continues in that tradition.

In one way or another, all of the stories in this volume open up or further develop various themes in the 1632 series. And, at least in my opinion, all of them are good stories in their own right.

I hope you enjoy them.

Dye Another Day

Mercedes Lackey

Prague was remarkably pleasant for a city that had been the subject of a Defenestration slightly less than twenty years ago. Tom Stone had not retained a lot of facts from his old college classes at Purdue, especially not the History electives he'd taken, but that one—"The Defenestration of Prague," had stuck with him all these years. He loved that phrase—of course, all that it meant was that three people had been thrown out of a window and had lived because they had landed in a manure pile, but it *sounded* as if some great catastrophe had taken place. Not so amusing was the fact that the act had been central to the start of the Thirty Years' War that the up-timers had landed right smack in the middle of.

At any rate, Wallenstein had been a good steward of the place. He'd done a damn fine job of keeping most of the mayhem out of the city.

Morris and Judith Roth, who had moved there to expand their very profitable jewelry business, were hosting Tom and his down-time wife Magda—which meant a certain amount of up-timer comfort amidst the down-timer "ambience." Upholstered furniture, for instance. Backless wooden benches, hard wooden chairs, these were the norm down-time. There was *some* upholstered furniture, but it wasn't what he would have called "padded," and the older he got, the more he appreciated cushioning. The heavily cushioned chair he was sitting in now was luring him into a discussion he ordinarily would have steered clear of. It was almost political.

Tom didn't like politics at all, and he especially didn't like down-timer politics.

The subject at hand was the king of Bohemia himself, Wallen-stein, who was an ally of the United States of Europe. He was very clearly sick and his nurse, a former hardscrabble Grantville native, was afraid he was dying. The problem was that Wallenstein had some very decided notions about physicians and what they could and could not do with, to, or around him, and that was making diagnosis... difficult. To say the least. Of course, when you lived in a time when you didn't surrender as much as a hair off your head because someone might use it to curse you with, you could understand his point. A sick king would not want to disrobe in front of a crowd, because *someone* in that crowd would surely pass on information about his condition to his enemies—but he also would not want to disrobe in front of a physician, alone, because that would be the ideal time for an assassin, perhaps even in the person of that physician, to strike.

And as for up-time medical instruments being used on him—well, how was *he* to be sure they would do what the up-timers *said* they would do?

"On the one hand, Wallenstein should have been dead already," Tom Stone mused to his wife and youngest son. "He should have been assassinated over a year ago. I mean, you could say, like, I dunno, karma? Or maybe the timeline trying to correct itself or... something?" He wished his son hadn't dragged him into this. All he'd wanted to do was to get back to Grantville for a while and forget about parading around Italy as if he was some sort of genius, like Galileo, when he wasn't. He was just an up-time dope farmer with most of a pharmacy degree and a knack for the sort of herbal-slash-pioneering style of medicine that the hippies of his commune had used instead of the real doctors none of them could afford.

Gerry Stone sighed. "You read too many science fiction books," he replied.

Tom raised a bushy eyebrow. "We're *living* in a science fiction book," he pointed out. "Just in case you hadn't noticed." He pon-dered the situation with Wallenstein a little more. "On the other hand, I haven't seen a lot of evidence of other people dropping dead that should have been dead already, so it's probably not that. What's Edith say?"

Morris snorted. "That she's not a doctor."

"Well neither am I!" Tom protested, feeling extremely uneasy.

"But Tomas, you are *ein Doktor*," Magda corrected him. "Universitat of Padua makes you vun."

She insisted on speaking English in the presence of notable up-timers like the Roths, instead of the Amideutsch she was more comfortable with. Her speech was comprehensible enough, though, if a bit garbled and heavily accented.

"I am *Frau Doktor* now," she added proudly. "I haf married a *Doktor*! Papa is so pleased!"

Tom groaned. Although being granted the title of "Doctor" by the university in Padua had added considerably to his social status, by his own estimation, given the general level of knowledge among the down-timers, it was pretty much the equivalent of buying your doctorate from a diploma mill, or being ordained as a High Priest of Zen Druidism.

"All hail the tree that is not there," he muttered. Magda looked puzzled, but Gerry jumped on what he'd said.

"See, now *that* is exactly why you're what Edith needs right now!" he exclaimed. "You know all that New Age crap! Shoot, I think Lothlorien Commune probably had one of every crackpot out there, given some of the stories you've told me!"

"But I don't *believe* that New Age crap!" Tom protested feebly.

Gerry merely fixed him with a stern gaze that looked remarkably like the one his father used to nail him with when he didn't want to mow the lawn. "You can come up with some mystical sounding garbage that will let you do *some* kind of tests, and if you can do that, you can probably figure out what's wrong with him. And then you can figure out how to wrap the treatment in more mumbo-jumbo that will ensure he actually follows what's been prescribed."

Gerry wasn't backing down, but neither was Tom. "I'd have to go back to Grantville. I'd need to dig into the stuff in the commune library. All the way back to Grantville, then dig through all those boxes of books in storage." He nailed Gerry with the same look. "I'd take months."

"No, you don't," Gerry replied, just as stubbornly. "You don't have to convince another believer that you know what you're talking about. You just have to convince Wallenstein enough that he'll take whatever meds he's advised to take—or whatever it is Edith and Doc think he needs to do. You just have to give him something that sounds plausible so he'll stop listening to the

astrologers. And now he's listening to Gribbleflotz too, since he
showed up in Prague."

"But why *me*?" That was what he didn't get.

"Because you're the only living hippy in Grantville," said Roth.
"Logic and science aren't going to work on Wallenstein. We need
something as kooky as Kirlian auras, and you're our expert on
crazy religions."

What made *him* the expert? He was almost agnostic, for crying out loud! He'd seen so many flakes with religion come and
go at Lothlorien that—well, he was only sure of one thing. God
was probably laughing Her socks off at humankind. "Did you see
what they came up with *this* week? Holy Me!"

"I spent the Harmonic Convergence in bed," he reminded them,
sinking a little into the chair and hoping that Magda would not
ask "and with whom?" "I didn't do Channeling. I refused to have
my Chak—"

He stopped.

"You haf thought of something!" Magda exclaimed. "I am
being know that face you are being make!" She clasped her hands
together gleefully.

Tom groaned. "It's quackery," he said.

"*Ja, und?*" Magda dismissed that with a wave of her graceful
little hand.

"It's—I don't remember a lot of it—"

"So you make it up. Or you borrow from other stuff." Gerry
was just as dismissive. Judith and Morris leaned forward.

Tom sighed. "Chakras," he said, reluctantly. "I'm going to go
to hell for this, I just know it."

Judith and Morris looked at each other. "I vaguely recollect
something about chakras—isn't that some acupuncture thing?" she
asked, worriedly. "Wallenstein will believe in a lot of nonsense, but
I am fairly sure he won't sit there and be made into a pincushion."

Tom shook his head. "No, I mean, some acupuncturists used
the whole chakra thing as another explanation for their stuff, but,
no, acupuncture is Chinese and chakra healing is Indian. There's
supposed to be seven energy vortices up your spine, each one a
different color. And that's why I'm going to hell."

Gerry tilted his head to the side. "I don't get it—"

"Colors. Energy colors, aura colors. It works *with* the Kirlian
aura nonsense. Which is why I'm going to hell. I'm not going

to convince him to stop listening to Gribbleflotz. Edith tells me the Kirlian stuff is actually an improvement over the crap the astrologers were feeding Wallenstein. I'm just going to convince him that Gribbleflotz is right. In fact, I am probably going to end up giving Gribbleflotz even more ideas."

"Does it matter?" Morris demanded. "For God's sake, Tom, even if we were only talking about extending a man's life, here, *I'd* put up with Gribbleflotz! But it's not just that, we need to keep Wallenstein alive to protect his son for as long as possible, we're extending the stability of the region and the relationship we have with—"

"I know, I *know*," Tom interrupted, rubbing his temples. "Dammit, I hate politics. I *really* hate down-timer politics. They can get you killed."

"Not dis time, Tomas," Magda said, reaching out and patting his hand comfortingly. "Dis time ve make life, not var."

Tom might be "Doctor Thomas Stone of the University of Padua," but if he was going to convince Wallenstein to talk to him—and get diagnosed and treated by him—he was going to have to look the part. The part being—he was going to have to look the way a seventeenth-century Bohemian thought a Tibetan guru would look.

Which was to say . . . colorful. As if he was his own best customer at the dye works. It started with a turban the size of a small country house, moved down through a caftan and floor-length vest with a wide sash, and ended with bright red felt boots.

"I look ridiculous," he grumbled, adjusting his turban. It was huge, and centered with an enormous brooch. He had the feeling that he looked just like Johnny Carson playing the phony fortuneteller, Carnac the Magnificent.

"*Nein, nein,* you look *ausgezeichnet!*" Magda replied, her eyes dancing. "So impressive!"

"Your mouth says 'no' but your face says 'yes,'" he muttered.

At least he could take comfort in the fact that if he looked ludicrous, his assistant looked worse.

He'd decided early on that if he was going to be able to pull this off, he was going to need some help, and it wasn't going to be Edith, devoted to the royal family though she might be. It had taken his assistant five days on fast horses to get here, and he hadn't been happy about his costume, but—well, he was a reservist in the State of Thuringia-Franconia's National Guard, and he was under orders. The orders had come from Ed Piazza himself, the SoTF's president.

"Are you ready yet?" Tom called into the next room.

"I hate you, Stoner," came the growled reply.

Tom sighed. "Look, I'm doing the best that I can. It could be worse."

"I'd like to know how." George Mundell shuffled into the room, glowering. "First off, I am never going to get this crap off my skin. It's gonna have to wear off."

"You look like George Hamilton."

"I look like Al Jolson in blackface." George bared his teeth in a grimace that did look startlingly white in his walnut-tanned face. "But I wouldn't mind that so much if I wasn't wearing clown shoes, I Dream of Jeanie's vest, my grandma's curler-turban, enough Mardi Gras beads for an entire float, and M.C. Hammer's pants."

It wasn't *quite* that bad, but he did look...colorful. And it was a good thing that they were down-time, or he would have seriously offended any native of India that happened to spy him. When he asked for George's help, Tom had also radioed Grantville's theater teacher. That was Shackerley Marmion, a young Englishman who'd emigrated to Grantville the year before. Marmion had a flair for such things, and at Tom's request he'd put together a costume for "a mysterious Hindu magician" and this was what had come with George. The pants were actually a pair of the infamous "parachute pants" from the eighties whose owner had allegedly donated them only on condition that no one reveal who he was. The vest had come right out of the Lothlorien attic. The "clown shoes" and the turban were the only actual costume pieces—they weren't actually "clown shoes," though they were very flamboyant with their up-curled toes.

"I guess it could be worse," George said, after a moment of surveying Tom. "You could smuggle a Humvee in that hat. And are you wearing a *dress*?"

"It's a *caftan*," Tom corrected, sourly.

"It's a granny-dress," George snickered.

Tom considered any number of responses and rejected them all. He needed George. Mundell was the only stage-magician in Grantville. He'd done it as a hobby for years before the Ring of Fire. Thereafter, once his sons Mike and Jim started working as apprentices with Philip Massinger's troop of actors, he'd begun doing stage magic on a semi-professional basis. He'd gotten pretty damn good at it.

"Let's get this show on the road," he said instead, and gestured to the two servants to pick up their bags and schlep them along.

He felt very uncomfortable, with a manservant following him with a bag he could very well carry himself, but *Herr Doktor* Thomas Stone, master of Akashic Magick and scholar of the Chakras would *never* demean himself by carrying anything. Even Gupta Rai Singh, his assistant, was too important to be burdened with a bag. And the farce absolutely had to begin at the front door of the Roths' palatial home. People would be watching. Word had been spread that the famous *Herr Doktor* Stone had come straight from Padua just to cure the king.

So, they made a spectacle of themselves, trucking down to the waiting carriage, which he and George occupied alone, for even their baggage handlers were so important that *they* required their own carriage. They proceeded through the streets of Prague to the palace, with plenty of rubberneckers along the way. Tom remained serene, upright, and enveloped in dignity, but George fanned the flames of their reputation by producing small plastic coins out of thin air and tossing them to the crowd. Tom had been worried that people would be angry when they realized George's coins weren't spendable and weren't even metal, but it seemed the opposite was the case. Once again, the exotic look of up-timer plastic fakery was valued as high as or higher than the real thing.

So by the time they got to the palace, there was a substantial buzz in the streets. Some people might have known that Tom was allegedly a physician, and some might have known that he was (in name anyway) one of the up-timer industrialists—but *no one* until now had known he was a magician.

George's sleight of hand was good—very good. It had to be. He'd been the go-to guy for kids' parties, and you had to be good to trick kids once they were old enough to suspect trickery. Big stage illusions—not so much, in no small part, he had told Tom once, because he didn't have the skills to build them himself, and couldn't afford the good ones. But he was good enough at close-up work that even when Tom knew *exactly* what he was doing, and when, and how, Tom still couldn't catch him. This was going to prove important, because Tom was depending on him not only to convince Wallenstein that he was seeing solid evidence of that chakra nonsense Tom was about to spout, but because George was going to perform most of a physical exam that Wallenstein had no idea he was going to get. The king had flatly refused anyone permission to do the sort of examination that would actually *tell* them something. Even Edith wasn't sure why, though Tom had a notion it might have less to do with either modesty or the concept of the King's Sacred Person and a lot more to do with a very rational fear of assassination. Who would be more in a position to do a man in than his own physician?

"No psychic surgery," George had said, flatly, when he'd heard what Tom wanted of him. "Absolutely, positively, no psychic surgery."

"What?" Tom had replied, shocked. "*No.* I just want a blood pressure check, get his temp and heart-rate, stuff like that."

"Good. Nobody is pulling that particular scam here down-time yet, and I'd rather they didn't get ideas," George had said, his grim tone conveying, even over the radio, the depth of his loathing for the sleight-of-hand charlatans that "removed tumors psychically" from the bodies of gullible victims up-time.

They descended the carriage and mounted the steps, followed by their entourage, and paused at the door for just a moment.

He and George exchanged a look. To his relief, he saw George smiling ever so slightly.

"It's *showtime*," George muttered out of the corner of his mouth, and as if that had been a cue, the doors swung open, and they stepped inside.

The king received them in a private audience chamber, and seemed quite impressed by their flamboyant outfits. Until Tom knew whether or not Wallenstein had high blood pressure or a dingy heart, he didn't want to put any stress on the man; that limited him quite a bit in what *he* could do. Not so George. Tom was the distracter so George could do his work. He'd commissioned seven hand-blown glass bowls in graduated sizes, and ordered seven framed panes of stained glass in red, orange, yellow, green, blue, purple and white, after getting the dimensions he needed from Edith. He positioned the king in a comfortable chair under the window that the sun was coming through, then mounted the red glass inside the window frame so that the king was bathed in red light.

"I fear, Your Majesty," Tom said, as Wallenstein peered at him through the ruddy light, "That the good Dr. Gribbleflotz is only partially correct in his interpretation of the aura. You see, he has not studied the secrets of the aura among the ancient sages of the Tibetan mountains as I have. They teach us that the aura is merely the outward reflection of the inward emanations of the seven chakras."

He then launched into a sermon on the chakras which owed as much to snake-oil medicine as it did to the little he remembered from the commune days. It really didn't matter anyway, his son was right about that. All that mattered was that he was consistent, that what *he* said didn't contradict Gribbleflotz so much as make Gribbleflotz look like the kid who had brought a baking-soda volcano to a science fair where other kids were showing off their dancing robots and osmotic sea-water purifiers. In this, he was helped immensely by George, who demonstrated a robust set of chakras by producing a "chakric resonator" in the form of a crystal wand that glowed the appropriate color when held over the appropriate spot on himself—and flickered and dimmed when held over the same spots on the king.

All except for the blue one—which corresponded to a spot right at the throat (and was the "auric color" that Gribbleflotz had told the king was his own. George made that one glow strongly. The king stared at the wand in fascination.

"Ah, now you see, all of your chakras are unbalanced," Tom told him. "The only strong one is the Muskogee chakra, the chakra of communication and intellect. You are a man of your mind, Your Majesty. Your mind is the most powerful part of you. But by strengthening that part of your energy exclusively, you weaken the rest of your etheric body, exactly as if you concentrated on strengthening only your hand, until you could crush a walnut with your fist, but your legs would not take you across a room unaided."

Since he couldn't remember the Indian names for the chakras, he had finally just used the names of the home towns of some of his old friends. The chakra at the top of the head he called "Sheboygan," followed by Mishawaka, Muskogee, Oskaloosa, Chillicothe, Oolagah and Austin.

The king nodded. "That is how I feel ever since *Doktor* Gribbleflotz was reading my aura and telling me it was blue!" he exclaimed. "I thought I was to be—" He broke off, looking perplexed.

"Now I will be examining your chakras with my colleague and assistant, Gupta," Tom carried on blithely. "Then we will know what is to be done to re-balance you."

So the king sat in the red light while Tom dipped his fingers in a little water and made the biggest bowl "sing" by running his wet finger around the top of it, chanting nonsense syllables the entire time. The king's eyes widened at that; evidently no one had invented the glass harmonica yet. Tibetan "singing bowls" were made of brass and made to sing in much the same fashion but using a wooden mallet—Tom had never quite mastered that, but he was pretty good at making wineglasses sing. George made mystical passes, made red silk handkerchiefs appear and vanish, did the same with glowing balls that he rolled around on his hands. Then they repeated the whole routine with orange light from an orange pane of glass, a higher pitched bowl, and so on right up to the white light. George meanwhile was getting a wealth of information.

By the time they were done, poor Wallenstein was exhausted and more than willing to go back to his bed while Tom and George "consulted" and "made their calculations and charts" to present to him the following day.

In reality they went back to the Roths', and Tom holed up with the radio and the closely-written pages of notes, consulting not with the stars, but with Dr. Nichols back in Magdeburg. Some things were obvious—Wallenstein had gout, for instance, a common complaint among nobles whose diets were worse than any American teenager who lived on fast food. His heart was definitely dodgy. By process of elimination, they figured he had a chronic infection somewhere.

"The heart's going to kill him eventually," Nichols said, "I'd say three, four years." Tom clearly heard the frustration in Nichols' voice, and he sympathized. Things that could have been treated with a couple generic prescriptions up-time were deadly now, and sometimes he could tell it grated on the Doc that Tom often knew more about what worked in the here and now than he did, with all of his experience and medical knowledge. "But you've got foxglove to keep him going, and the point is mostly to get the baby past the danger zone of infancy, according to Mike and Ed."

"We can improve his diet some, if I put enough mystical spin on it. Garlic and kelp might clear up that infection, especially if it's his tonsils; heck, I know I can make a Lister's Fluid he can gargle with. Or if it's in an infected tooth, maybe Edith can get him to get the tooth pulled." Tom rubbed his forehead with the back of his hand. "I'll see what I can figure out. He's a tough old bastard, and he might surprise us. Look how long Henry the Eighth lasted, and he not only had a lot of the same problems, he had an abscessed leg too."

"I hate this," Nichols said, after a long pause. "I hate knowing that I know what to do, if only I had a modern operating theater, if only I had the right drugs, if only—"

"Don't beat yourself up, Doc," Tom interrupted. "Look at it this way. You and me, we're still managing to save people no one down-time could before." He said that, and he knew as he said it that it wouldn't help much. Nichols was a real doctor; he had never been in medicine for the money, but because medicine was his calling. "And have patience. We're getting antibiotics. We've got chloramphenicol and even some small amounts of penicillin. We'll get there."

"Providing quacks like Gribbleflotz don't kill them first," Doc said sourly. "All right, I've used up my allotted time. Good luck."

Tom didn't even get a chance to say goodbye; the voice of someone else, calling another station, immediately filled the speakers. He turned off the set, gathered up his notes, and headed for bed. Enough for now; tomorrow they'd start treatments and see if their guesses were going to work.

The treatments had begun to work. Tom really had not expected such a quick result, but already Wallenstein's color was better, his breathing had eased thanks to the rosemary-infused steam he was inhaling, and Tom thought his BP might be going down. That might have been partly the placebo effect, partly the effect of just getting some of the king's other conditions under control.

Whatever, there was progress, and it was beginning to look as if he and George would be able to go back to Grantville and leave things in Edith's hands.

Which was, of course, the moment when everything went pear-shaped.

"I'm going to kill him," George said for the fifty-sixth time. "I am going to mug Gribbleflotz in a dark alley, tear out his liver, and feed it to him."

Dr. Gribbleflotz had been closeted with the king all morning, and the longer he was in there, the more convinced Tom became that things were not looking good for Chakras versus Kirlian.

Still. They had an ace in the hole, and that was Edith. Wallenstein trusted her as he trusted no one else.

But George was pacing up and down the antechamber they had been sent to wait in, muttering. Tom had never seen him this agitated before. Something more was going on here than Tom was aware of, obviously, but if George wasn't going to say anything—

That was when Edith entered the room, and she didn't even have to say anything; the expression on her homely face told both of them everything they needed to know.

George was already angry—but it was Tom who suddenly felt himself overcome with fury.

"Come on," he growled, "Follow my lead." And before Edith could say or do anything at all, he charged towards the king's private chambers. Fortunately, Edith managed to sprint ahead of them, or they might have gotten skewered on the halberds of Wallenstein's guards.

As it was, when they burst through the doors together, both Gribbleflotz and the king nearly jumped out of their skins.

"Thanks be to the Lord Jesus!" Tom bellowed. "I am here in time! Gupta! The violet ray! This is an emergency!"

And he leapt, not for the king, but for Gribbleflotz.

"Doctor, God save us," he shouted, pulling the first thing he could lay his hands on out of his sleeve—it was an atomizer full of Lister solution—and spraying Gribbleflotz liberally. "Your chakras are fluctuating so dangerously that we felt the effects in the antechambers!"

George meanwhile had fished out the little flashlight they'd put a tiny scrap of blue theatrical gel on and was playing it into Gribbleflotz's startled eyes.

"I beg your pardon, Majesty," Tom continued, waving a quartz crystal point all over Gribbleflotz's upper torso. "We dared not wait any longer. Your devoted doctor has put his own life in jeopardy by treating so many sufferers. His Mishawaka is utterly drained, his Sheboygan enlarged, and the rest of his chakras so muddled it is a wonder he has not collapsed before now!"

"They are?" Gribbleflotz managed, face stricken with doubt. "It is?"

Now George took over. "When you drink wine at dinner, do you sometimes feel dizzy when you rise, sahib?" he asked, earnestly, carefully mangling his German. "Do you find yourself waking in the night with a terrible need to relieve yourself? Do you find yourself stumbling over nothing? Do you sometimes forget a word or a name that you know as well as your own?"

Gribbleflotz paled. The doubt on his face was erased by slowly growing fear.

George had managed to palm one of his little lights, and he suddenly thrust it at Gribbleflotz's belly, where it began to flash most alarmingly. "Sahib! Dr. Thomas!" George screamed in panic. "The Mishawaka! There is no time! I must operate!"

Before anyone in the room could react, Tom shoved Gribbleflotz down into a chair, and ruthlessly yanked up or tore open his clothing, exposing a very pale belly. In an instant, George had plunged his fingers into that belly, as both the king and Gribbleflotz's eyes bulged and the king's guards backed away, making furtive signs against evil.

One of them fainted dead away as George pulled his hand back out, bloody and sticky, and opened them to reveal a mass of what looked like bloody hair and things best left unidentified. "You see!" George shouted. "You see! It was almost too late!"

Gribbleflotz fainted dead away.

Back in Grantville at last, Tom and George gave the president of the State of Thuringia-Franconia their reports in person. Ed Piazza had come up from the new provincial capital at Bamberg to hear their report, on his way to Magdeburg. He'd pass the information along to Mike Stearns and Rebecca Abrabanel later, when the current political ruckus settled down. The dynastic situation in Bohemia was important but not exactly an urgent matter.

"Although I thought you said no psychic surgery," Tom said. "I thought—"

"Look," George growled. "I'm not proud of myself, all right? I hate those bastards. But we needed something dramatic, something that couldn't be explained away as up-timer science, and we needed it right then. I had the feeling we might, so I helped myself to some stuff from the kitchen and a hairball one of the cats coughed up that morning. When I saw he wasn't falling for your crystal waving, I played my ace. Do *not* ask me to do it again."

"I won't," Tom replied. He didn't add that he was making no promises about Ed Piazza or Mike Stearns.

"So, the treatments are going well, then?" Ed prodded.

Tom nodded. "Wallenstein's actually making some improvement—he's not going on any long hikes, but he's able to do pretty much everything that a king needs to do on most days. Edith's pleased. She asked me about the dyes I used in his medicines. I just told her they're safe enough. I didn't have the guts to tell her that Doc Nichols said congestive heart failure is going to kill him long before the dye will."

Ed nodded with sympathy, then one corner of his mouth quirked up in a half smile. "And just what is this "special treatment" she keeps objecting to in her letters?

"Oh..." Tom blushed. "That..."

"Go on—" Piazza ordered.

"Well...you know that the 'root chakra' is supposed to be located in the...ah..."

"Goolies," George supplied helpfully.

Ed nodded. "Right, I follow you. And since you're balancing all the chakras you can't leave that one out."

"Right." Tom blushed further. "And the, ah...goolies...can't drink. So we can't exactly give them medicine. Except topically. But all the medicines are colored."

"And—"

"So the salve is colored. Blue, because the root energy is supposed to get boosted." By now Tom felt like his face was on fire. "Because a lot of impotence is psychological and I figured—well—"

"Right. And?"

"Well, besides coloring the salve, I really needed something that was going to, you know, remind the king that the stuff is working. So the...ah...the dye is kind of permanent."

Tom watched as Ed mentally went over everything he had just said, then stared at them both incredulously.

"You don't mean—"

"He does mean," George said, with a grin on his face. "Old Tom gave the king a case of blue balls."

Birds of a Feather

Charles E. Gannon

Owen Roe O'Neill started at the burst of gunfire, not because—as a veteran of the Lowlands Campaigns—he was unaccustomed to the sounds of combat, but because such sounds were now out of place near Brussels in 1635. Old habit had him reaching toward his saber, but the pickets at the gate leading into the combined field camps of the *tercios* Tyrconnell and Preston seemed utterly unconcerned by the reports. As O'Neill let his hand slip away from the hilt, his executive officer, Felix O'Brian, jutted a chin forward: never at ease atop a horse, O'Brian didn't dare take either of his hands from the reins to point. "So what would all that be, then?"

Ahead and to the right, a score of the men of *tercio* Tyrconnell were skulking about in the trenchworks surrounding the commander's blockhouse. So far as Owen could make out, they seemed to be engaged in some perverse, savage game of hide-and-seek with an almost equal number of troopers from *tercio* Preston. As he approached, the soldiers of the Tyrconnell regiment repeatedly bobbed and weaved around a sequence of corners, usually in pairs. One stayed low, training a handgun or musketoon on the next bend in the trenchworks while the other dodged forward. If one of Preston's men popped his head around that far corner, the man with the gun fired, immediately reaching back for another weapon. If the approach was unopposed, the advancing trooper finished his short charge by sliding up to the corner and—without even checking first—lobbing a grenade around it.

17

Of course, these "dummy" grenades simply made a kind of ragged belching sound as they emitted puffs of thin grey smoke: rather anticlimactic. But the training and the tactics were startlingly new. And quite insane.

"This is what comes of O'Donnell's visit to the up-timers," Owen grumbled to O'Brian. "Thank God he's given over his command."

"It's only *rumored* that he's resigned his command," amended O'Brian carefully.

"Well, yes," Owen consented. "Too much to hope for until we see the truth of it, eh?" But as soon as he'd uttered the saucy gibe, Owen regretted it: Hugh O'Donnell, Earl of Tyrconnell, was hardly a poor commander. Quite the contrary. And humble enough, for all his many admitted talents. Maybe that's what made him so damned annoying—

"Seems we've picked up an escort," observed O'Brian, glancing behind.

Sure enough, close to a dozen monks—Franciscans, judging from the hooded brown habits—had swung in behind their guards, who remained tightly clustered around the *tercio* banners of Tyrone and O'Neill. One of the monks was pushing a handcart through the May mud, prompting Owen to wonder: *had someone died* en camp? Or maybe the brown robes had come to seek used clothes for the poor? If the latter, then the monks were in for a rude surprise: the Irish *tercios* were no longer a good source of that kind of easy charity. They were in dire want of it themselves, these days.

As he approached the *tercios'* staff tents, Owen noticed that, in addition to the pennants of the staff officers, a small banner of the earl of Tyrconnell's own colors were flying. As he gave the day's camp countersign to the interior perimeter guards, he pondered the fluttering outline of the O'Donnell coat of arms. Strange: did this mean that Hugh was actually here?

A lean fellow, saber at his side, came bolting down the horse-track from the much larger commander's tent, perched atop a small rise. The approaching trooper was an ensign: probably Nugent, O'Neill conjectured, or maybe the younger of the Plunkett brothers. No matter, though: they were all cut from the same cloth and class. New families, all half-Sassenach; all lip-service Catholics. Some allies, those.

But Nugent or Plunkett or whoever it was had stopped, staring at the banners carried by O'Neill's oncoming entourage. Then he turned about and sprinted back up toward the commander's tent without even making a sign of greeting.

"Seems we've got their attention," muttered O'Neill through a controlled smile.

"See what you've done now?" O'Brian's voice was tinged with careful remonstrance. "They seen the earl of Tyrone's colors. They'll think John is wid' us! They'll think—"

"Let 'em think. They do so much of it as it is, a little more can't hurt. Aye, and let 'em worry a bit, too."

"But—"

"But nothing. Here's the Great Man himself."

Thomas Preston had emerged from the commander's tent. He was an older man, one of the oldest of the Irish Wild Geese that had flocked to Flanders after the disaster at Kinsale, thirty-four years before. And Irish soldiers had been flying to Flanders ever since: leaving behind increasing oppression and poverty, they had swelled the ranks of their four *tercios* now in the Lowlands. Mustering at slightly more than twelve thousand men, many of the newer recruits had been born here, grown here, learned the trade of the soldier here. And all knew that the recent consolidation of the Netherlands, and the consequent divisiveness amongst their Hapsburg employers, made their own future the most uncertain of all.

Preston did not look approving—or happy. After a few sharp phrases, he sent the runner back down the hill; he waited, arms akimbo, a dark scowl following the young ensign's return to O'Neill's honor-guard.

"Colonel O'Neill," the ensign panted before he'd come to a full stop, "Colonel Preston would have the commander's password from you."

O'Neill looked over the thin fellow's head—he was not much more than a *gossoon*, really—and stared at Preston. "Oh, he would, would he?"

"Yes, sir." A second group of pickets had come to flank the youngster. "Apologies, but Colonel Preston is most insistent. New security protocols, sir."

"Is that right? And those are his fine ideas, are they?"

"No, sir; they are Hugh O'Donn—I mean, the earl of Tyrconnell's, sir."

Ah, but of course. The ever-innovative earl of Tyrconnell's legacy lived on in the camp he had abandoned almost a month ago, in the first week of April. O'Neill's gaze flicked briefly to the small O'Donnell coat of arms fluttering just behind him. Or, maybe he had *not* abandoned it, after all ...

O'Neill urged his mount forward. "The commander's day-sign is 'Boru.'"

"Very good, sir, you may—"

But Owen Roe O'Neill had already passed, his entourage—including two officers from John O'Neill's Tyrone *tercio*—following closely behind. The monks, however, were detained by the guards at the staff tents.

O'Neill said nothing, gave no sign of recognition as he approached the commander's tent, with Preston's pennant snapping fitfully before it. Preston was equally undemonstrative. O'Neill stayed atop his mount, looked down at the older man and thought, *Sassenach bastard*, but said, with a shallow nod, "Colonel."

Preston was not even that gracious. "Where is the earl of Tyrone?"

"I expect he's enjoying a nap about now."

Preston's mustache seemed to prickle like a live creature. "Yet you fly his colors."

"I received your instructions to come without the earl. I have done so. But he is symbolically here with us in spirit—very *insulted* spirit—Colonel Preston."

"Damn it, O'Neill: the whole point of excluding him was so that you *wouldn't* be carrying his colors."

Owen, bristling reflexively at the profanity, found his anger suddenly defused by puzzlement: "You were worried about his—his colors?"

"Yes, blast it. And why did you bring those bloody Franciscans with you?"

O'Neill looked back down the low rise: most of the monks had moved past the first checkpoint, were drawing close to the second, where the commander's day-sign was to be given. Two lagged behind with the handcart, near the staff tents. "I assure you," muttered O'Neill," they're not my Franciscans. I'd not bring—"

The flap of Preston's tent ripped open. O'Neill gaped: Hugh Albert O'Donnell, in cuirass, was staring up at him, blue eyes bright and angry. "The Franciscans who came in with you—do you know them? Personally?"

"No, but—"

Hugh wasn't looking at him anymore. His strong neck corded

as he shouted: "First platoon, down the hill! Guards: take hold of those monks. Immediately!"

Owen Roe O'Neill was, by all accounts and opinions—including his own—excellent at adapting to rapid changes on the battlefield. But this was not a battlefield, or rather, had not been one but a slim second ago. And that change—from common space to combat space—was not one he easily processed.

Stunned, he saw the nearest monks pull wheel locks from beneath their robes and discharge them into the second set of pickets at murderously close range. Further down the slope, one monk pushed the handcart into Tyrconnell's staff tent while his partner drew a pistol on the guards there.

In the same moment, the grimy soldiers who had been skulking to and fro in the trenches came boiling out, not bothering to dress ranks. But stranger still, they seemed in perfectly good order, operating not as a mass, but in groups of about five men each. This chaotic swarm of small, coherent teams streamed downhill, several tossing aside practice guns and pulling real ones, others drawing sabers and short swords. O'Neill's own guards retracted, clustered tight around him, weapons drawn, as the leading infiltrators drew grenades and shortswords from beneath their robes and closed in—

Just as the first teams from the trenches caught the assassins in the flank with a ragged chorus of pistol fire. Snaphaunces and wheel locks barked while a strange, thick revolver—a "pepperbox?"—cracked steadily, firing five times. When the fusillade was over, only one of the monks was still on his feet; a few on the ground moved feebly. A second wave of soldiers—sword-armed—closed the last few yards and finished the bloody execution. An alert trooper kicked the one lit grenade down the slope and away from the cart-track, where it detonated harmlessly.

Down at the staff tents, the monk who had drawn a pistol had evidently not done so any faster than one of the guards. The two weapons discharged simultaneously and the two men went down—just as the monk who'd trundled the hand cart into the staff tent came sprinting back out. The other guard who'd been slower on the draw went racing after him—and went airborne as the tent exploded in a deafening ball of flame.

By the time O'Neill had his horse back under control, the whole exchange was over. Almost twenty bodies lay scattered along the cart track, small fires guttered where the staff tents had been, and men of the Preston *tercio* were carrying two of their own wounded off to where the Tyrconnell regiment's young surgeon could tend to them. With his ears still ringing from the explosions, and his veins still humming with the sudden rush of the humor the up-timers called "adrenaline," Owen could only feel one thing: that he was glad to be alive.

Then he turned and saw Hugh O'Donnell's eyes—and wondered if his sense of relief was, perhaps, premature.

"Why did you bring John O'Neill's colors, Owen?" O'Donnell's voice and eyes were calm now. But most of the others in the commander's tent—those belonging to the staff officers who would have been blown to bits if they hadn't already been summoned here—remained far more agitated.

Owen relied on the tactic that had always served him well: when your adversary has you on the run, that's when you turn and hit back—hard. "Maybe you should be asking yourself that question, Hugh O'Donnell. A Sassenach"—he glared at Preston, who glared right back—"tells the earl of Tyrone not to come to a council of the colonels? Well, let me tell you, even if John O'Neill is not 'permitted' to sit and talk with the regal likes of Preston—or you—I *will* come bearing his standard, and with it, the reminder of his authority—and that of his clan."

O'Donnell looked away, closed his eyes. "Owen, it wasn't Preston who excluded John. It was me. And I did it to protect him."

"Protect John? From what?"

O'Donnell cocked his head in the direction of the killing ground that led down to the gate. "From that ... or worse. It was folly for us to have too many tempting targets in one place."

O'Neill paused. Then, voice level: "What do you mean?"

"I mean, if John *had* come, the last two royal heirs of Ireland would have been in the same place, at the same time. And with politics in the Lowlands being what they are, signaling such a gathering was tantamount to inviting an attack. As we just saw."

O'Neill frowned. "But we've got peace—for now—so who'd want the two of you dead? And how would they—whoever they are—even know you're in the Lowlands at all, Hugh? The last any of us heard, you were off in Grantville."

O'Donnell nodded. "Reasonable questions, Owen. Will you listen to the answers, *before* you tell me how wrong I am?"

Owen nodded. "Of course; *that* I can do." And he grinned. O'Donnell returned the smile—and there were audible sighs of relief in the tent as the tension ebbed. "So let's have it, Hugh: who is trying to kill you and John? The English? Again?"

O'Donnell leaned back, hands folded firmly on the field table before him. "It could be them. But you also have your pick of new possible culprits. Local Catholics who feel Fernando has been too lenient with the Calvinists. Ministers in Madrid who want to topple Fernando as King in the Netherlands. Maybe Philip himself. In short, anyone who wants to give the Spanish crown a reasonable pretext for 'restoring order' in the Netherlands."

Owen shook his head. "I'm lost. How does attacking us achieve that?"

"We're a wild card, Owen—all of us Wild Geese. Four *tercios*, almost all full strength at three thousand men each. What happens to the Lowlands if we disband—or rebel?"

"Chaos. The Prince of Orange might try to take charge, but he hasn't the troops. The locals will try to oust the Spanish. Fernando, a Hapsburg of Spain, and his wife, a Hapsburg of Austria, will soon be surrounded and in peril for their lives."

"And what happens? Who comes in, if we disband or just stay in barracks?"

"France might try to take advantage. Or maybe the Swede."

"Exactly—and would Philip want either?"

"Christ, no!" And then Owen saw it. "So, with us no longer ready to be an independent spine for Fernando's army, the local Spanish *tercios* call for help, and Philip has no choice but to intervene. Decisively."

O'Donnell nodded. "There are many possible variations on the theme, but that's the basic dirge. Half the court in Madrid is already calling for a 'stern approach' to Fernando's recent actions: after all, he did take the title 'King in the Netherlands' without Philip's permission. And since then, Philip has let his brother fend for himself . . . and we've all felt the results of that."

"What do you mean?"

"I mean, what has happened to your salaries over the last few months?"

Grumbles arose from every quarter of the tent.

O'Donnell spoke over them. "That's not Fernando's doing: he's not the one holding the purse strings. That would be Olivares, either working independently, or at Philip's behest. The Lowlands have long been a drain on the Spanish; over time, they've invested far more in this patch of ground than they've ever earned back. So, while Philip may not yet consider his brother a traitor, why should he pay for his *tercios*? Particularly those which aren't Spanish?"

"So we Irish are like a redheaded stepchild between spatting parents."

"Something very like it, yes." Hugh looked around the tent. "Which means that, any day now, your allegiances may be questioned. And whatever you might answer, you can be sure of this: one or another of your employers will be very unhappy with your answer."

"You mean, as unhappy as they were when you turned in your commission and titles?"

O'Donnell's voice was quiet. "You've heard then?"

O'Neill shook his head. "Not officially, no: your officers have been keeping it quiet. But when your *tercios* came over here into bivouac with Preston's, talk started—particularly when your men started getting orders from the Sassena—from Colonel Preston. And there were some as claimed that before you left, you'd folded up your tabard and sash of the Order of Alcantara and sent them back to Madrid."

"That I did."

Owen kept his voice carefully neutral: "So are you wanting us to follow your example?"

O'Donnell waved a negating hand. "I'd ask no man to follow my path. And there's no need for you to declare your allegiance until you're asked."

"Then why didn't you wait to do so, yourself?"

"Owen, when I was made a Knight-Captain of the Order of Alcantara, a Gentleman of His Majesty's Chamber, and a member of his Council of War, I took my oaths before, and to, the king himself. In his very person, in Spain. I had my benefits and titles directly from his hand, and was, at his personal instruction, naturalized as a Spanish citizen. Honor demands, then, that if I know in my heart I can no longer be Philip's loyal servant, I must relinquish all those privileges and garnishments at once. I can't bide my time, waiting to be cornered into admitting that my allegiances have changed—even as I continue to enjoy the king's coin and favor. Given the state of affairs here, honor may be all I have left—so it was both right and prudent that I keep it untarnished."

"Fairly spoken," Preston said. Owen found himself nodding; the earl of Tyrone's officers were doing the same.

The flap of the tent came back. The young surgeon of the Tyrconnell regiment—blood still on his hands, some on his face—crossed the open center of the council ring and sat down next to O'Donnell. He said nothing, stared hard at nothing.

O'Donnell leaned toward him. "You've word on our worst wounded, Dr. Connal?"

"I do. Russell and Fitzgerald will live, but Nugent—" The young man dropped his head; O'Neill couldn't tell if it was out of anger or grief. Perhaps both.

"Easy, Shane, easy," soothed O'Donnell. "Have we lost him?"

"Not yet," the younger man snapped through gritted teeth. "But we will, and there's damn-all I can do to stop it. A gut wound"—he looked up, eyes narrow—"a small gut-wound. And I still can't save him. If I were an up-time doctor—even one of their nurses—then, yes, maybe so. Probably. But me? I'm just—just a damned butcher, I am." His head dropped again, neck rigid.

"It's not a bit of your fault, lad," put in O'Neill, seeking a moment in which simple kindness might also achieve some additional inter-clan mending. "And let's not hear any more o' this tearing yourself down because you're not up-time-trained. I'm sure those fancy Grantville doctors are not half as good as everyone says they ar—" And he stopped, transfixed by a baleful glare from Hugh's senior sergeant and old companion, O'Rourke—until a sudden, stinging chill of realization coursed through him. O'Donnell's young wife of barely a year had died in childbirth only six months ago—and it was universally held that her death could have been prevented by an up-time doctor or nurse. O'Donnell might have had access to one of them through his godmother, the Infanta Isabella, but he had known that Philip IV would have been sorely displeased. And so, Hugh had refrained. And so, his wife, and only child, had both died. Criticizing up-time medicine was, Owen concluded, probably the stupidest thing he could have done at such a moment. He surveyed the faces in the tent to see just how much damage he had done.

Almost no face was turned towards him: they were toward O'Donnell, who sat very still, eyes lowered. He spoke to the doctor without looking up. "Owen Roe is right, Shane, when he says there's no fault of yours in this. There are some things you can't fix." He looked up at the surgeon and smiled. "Not yet, that is."

Connal nodded—and O'Neill swallowed hard: looking at O'Donnell's smile, he could see—could almost feel—how much that had cost the earl of Tyrconnell. But Hugh kept that expression in place for a long moment, only allowing it to dim when he asked, "Dr. Connal, can you shed any light on our Franciscan visitors? Were they here to save our souls by hastening us to our reward?"

A few snickers underscored the surgeon's answer. "Not unless the Franciscans are sending disguised mercenaries to carry out their holy work, m'lord. And desperate ones, too, to take such a job as this. Judging from the grooming and the gear under the habits, I'd say most of them were part-Spanish mercenaries—mixed-bloods, born in the Lowlands—and the rest Germans or Walloons. Some may have been simple cutthroats: no military gear on those—and not even a hint of third-rate camp hygiene. Dirty as pigs and twice the stink."

Owen nodded and looked at O'Donnell. "So who do you think sent them?"

"I don't know—and right now, there aren't enough hours or facts to puzzle it out." He stood. "I've stayed too long. But before I go, I feel I must tell you all this: the *tercios* are dead."

Owen recoiled as if struck—in fact, felt as if he had been. "What fine, parting words of encouragement for all the men, Sir O'Donnell. I'm not sure the earl of Tyrone will agree to disband his *tercios* on your say-so, though."

"Owen, I'm not talking about the *existence* of our regiments. I'm saying that the concept of the *tercios*—of that kind of warfare—is dying on its feet. The first victories of the USE are just initial freshets of proof: soon, it will be an inarguable flood. The new muskets—and now, Turenne's breechloaders—are changing the battlefield. And those who do not learn to change with it will be the first to die upon it."

"So this is the reason for all the hide-and-seek I saw when I came in?"

"The up-timer manuals call it 'close quarters combat.' Or, 'CQC.'"

"And the USE forces train to use these tactics?"

"No, their equipment isn't right for it, yet—and there aren't enough up-timers who can teach them, either. But some special units—like Harry Lefferts and his group—use a simplified version. Granted, it seems their 'CQC' is based more on 'movies' than training manuals. But we can choose to do it *right*. We've got the discipline—and now the manuals—to genuinely learn these tactics, and then use them once we get our hands on enough revolvers and double-barreled weapons." O'Donnell paused, looked around the ring of faces focused on him. "And if we want to be the victors instead of the vanquished, we must start learning these tactics now—before they are used upon us."

O'Neill made as sour a face as he could. "They look more like tomfoolery than 'tactics.'"

"And so they might, but this is just one of the ways in which war is changing—and each change will spawn more. New weapons, new training, new skills, new organization: before long, we'll be revising everything we learned as our stock-in-trade. But we have to do it, even if it goes against our grain."

"Heh. It doesn't seem to go against *your* grain, Hugh."

O'Donnell nodded somberly. "I suppose it doesn't—not any longer. I've read their unit histories and accounts; I've seen up-timer military 'documentaries' that show how they—and before long, we—will wage war. Trust me, whether or not we're comfortable with it, our tactical doctrines *must* change." He looked around the tent. "And change is never easy. Never. Particularly not when one has to make *many* changes, and all at once.

"And that is what is sure to happen here in the Lowlands. Soon, you will all have a choice to make. And it can't be long in coming, because Fernando is running out of money with which to pay you. So, before that day comes, I counsel you: think upon your oaths, and listen to your hearts. Task them to answer this one, simple question: where is your loyalty? To Philip and Olivares or to Isabella and Fernando? To a distant king's coin, or to each other? For rest assured, that choice is coming—for each and every one of you."

O'Donnell stepped from behind the table, crouched down as if he were going to scratch a battle plan on the ground—but what it did was put him at eye-level with even the lowliest man in the room. "Always remember this, lads. We Wild Geese—we're all birds of a feather. We've been harrowed, but never broken—because we've always stuck together."

O'Neill wanted to sneer, but he couldn't—partly because O'Donnell hadn't parsed the old saw as doggerel, so it hadn't sounded trite. But mostly because he could see—could feel—all the men around him respond to the elemental honesty that shone out of Hugh's eyes. O'Neill wished he could look away, could be somewhere else—anything, just so he wouldn't have to see the indictment of his own clan laid out so plainly before him. The O'Donnells were leaders, always had been. They could touch hearts at a gesture, bond men to them with a whisper. Obversely, every O'Neill of note had made his name as a fighter, an intriguer, often a shrewd manipulator who might even conspire with an enemy, if it served his ultimate goals. They were renowned, feared, even respected—but never admired or loved. And that, Owen admitted, was probably the real reason behind the prickly *hauteur* of the Tyrones: a jealous envy after the natural nobility that they lacked.

Owen cleared his throat. "You've given us much to think about, Lord Tyrconnell. I wish you safe travels—and Godspeed. And now, I should be going."

O'Donnell straightened up. "And I've stayed longer than is safe. Until we meet again, Owen."

Who nodded, wanted to say—something—but could not decide what it should be. So he simply added a second nod and let a potentially bonding moment slip by.

Just as he had all his life.

O'Rourke made sure that Preston's tent was empty except for two orderlies, who stayed busy—and distant—moving gear to the newly completed blockhouse. When O'Rourke indicated that the young soldiers were out of earshot, O'Donnell muttered, "There's one person in particular who'll now be watching all of what you do here. Very closely."

"Who?"

"Isabella—my aunt." The earl paused, looked down. "Returning the honors I had from Philip was a shame, but leaving her service—that was a hard, hard step to take."

O'Rourke poured a small mug of half-beer for himself. "Huh. Now that's something I never did understand, m'lord."

"What?"

"Why you always doted on the Infanta, and she on you."

"Well, she's my godmother—and has looked out for me since I was a babe."

"Mebbe. But she also derailed the Killybegs invasion in 1627, and when at first she couldn't scuttle it herself, she insisted that it be led by John O'Neill—with you to be left behind in the Lowlands. Just the opposite of what Philip had called for."

"Oh, that. You misunderstand. She didn't pass me over."

"No? What would you call it, then?"

"She was protecting me. I was twenty-two, green as could be, and yes, Philip was going to put me over John—who'd no doubt have found some excuse to put me in my grave once we were in Ireland. Besides, she wanted me where she thought I'd do the most good."

"You'd do the most good *here*? Was she mad?"

O'Rourke looked away from the gaze Hugh fixed on him. "No, she was not mad. She remains amongst the most astute political minds of this era. She knew that if Philip did send us to invade Ireland, we would be underfunded and undersupplied. As it was, the closest we came to readiness—eleven boats waiting for a few thousand of us—would still have been suicide."

"Not if you and John O'Neill had gone together. The prat may be insufferable, but he's a competent captain and a bear in a fight. Together, the earls of Tyrconnell and Tyrone would have been invincible."

"Gaelic bluster, O'Rourke. Don't start believing the tales we tell to keep our spirits up during these long years of exile and waiting. Yes, I wanted to go. Yes, I wanted to lead. Yes, I agreed to Owen's and Father Conry's plan to create Ireland as a republic and to renounce any claim to preeminence. But unless wild luck had smiled on that project—instead of the death's head which has loomed over all our others—the only result of an invasion led by both O'Neill and O'Donnell would have been the loss of the last two royal Irish heirs that the English are really worried about."

"So your godmother was willing to let O'Neill to take the lead, and get himself strung up . . ."

". . . in the unlikely event the invasion occurred at all; yes."

"And you she saved out of love."

"That—and practicality."

"What practicality was that?"

"O'Rourke, how much trouble has our regiment had living side by side with the Walloons, even the Dutch?"

"Other than the occasional argument over the price of provisioning, none."

"And O'Neill and his regiment?"

O'Rourke nodded; he saw Isabella's logic now. "One incident after another. He's been hard- and high-handed from the start, right down to this very day."

Hugh nodded back. "Precisely. So if Isabella had to depend on mercenaries—and in particular, us Wild Geese—to protect her realm, she needed at least one loyal leader that enjoyed the trust of the locals and was not wholly subject to the manipulations of Madrid, nor the intrigues of her sworn enemies."

"In other words, she needed you. And us. Well, now I understand the past a little better, but I'm still in the dark regarding the present." O'Rourke lifted his mug. "So tell me, why skulk back into camp? And why not one word of what you're planning next? What's afoot?"

Hugh leaned forward. "For the nonce, O'Rourke, this is just between us."

"As always."

"Then here it is. I've hired on with the French. With Turenne. To work with an up-timer. To go to the New World. To take Trinidad from the Spanish crown. To sell it to the French. Because they want the oil."

O'Rourke put down his mug, which had been suspended midair during Hugh's brief, bulleted explanation. "You're serious."

Hugh nodded.

"And what do you get out of it?"

"*We*—all of us—get money, maybe enough to keep our men and their families in food long enough to find a more permanent billet."

"You mean the French would pay for our costs up here? They'd send ecus over the border to Isabella?"

"To Fernando," Hugh corrected. "And yes, that's the general idea. Subsistence costs only, of course. And some of the men—a few hundred maybe—would have to come down to France. Doing farm work for a few months, to help pay their keep. And then to travel—to serve—with me."

O'Rourke's response was a long, astonished whistle—which he abruptly ended when he noticed the puzzled stares of the orderlies, who then became conspicuously refocused upon their work.

O'Donnell was smiling. "You've a great future as a confidential agent, O'Rourke. A veritable master of undercover work."

"Funny you should mention undercover work, m'lord. Years ago, when I was courting Maureen Hennessy on the sly—"

"Spare me the tawdry details, reprobate. Now, about getting a few companies of the regiment over to France: here's the hitch—"

"There's just one?"

"Very well: here's the *first* hitch in that project: the companies joining me in Amiens must transfer over the border in one group."

"But the archduchess is seeing to that, no?"

"She's seeing to each unit's release from service, yes. Moving ourselves and our gear: that has to be up to us. And we have to make the transfer without any Spanish-owned equippage."

"Well, that will make the regiment look like the beggar's army on parade, but I can put a good face on it. We've enough of our own equipment that if we spread it out one weapon per man, there'd only be a few empty hands. And we'll keep those few in the middle of the formations. Also, we can march the swords and pieces separately to make it all look intentional—if absurd."

"Good. Then there's the approach to the border."

"The French know we're coming, right?"

"Yes, but the lads need to understand their weapons will have to go into French hands during the march to Amiens. And they won't like it."

"They don't have to," grumbled O'Rourke.

"That's the tick, O'Rourke: I'm sure there'll be no problems with you in charge of—"

But O'Rourke leaned far back. "In charge? Me? Not by Christ Almighty's toenails, m'lord."

"Who better to be in charge?"

"Someone who'll be with the regiment, sir."

"And so you shall be."

"With respect, I shan't. I'll be with you."

"With me? Now see here, O'Rourke—"

"'O'Rourke' me no 'O'Rourkes,' Hugh O'Donnell. You'll not be leaving me in France to tend a bunch of turnip-pullers while you sail into high seas and perdition."

"Sergeant O'Rourke, you are a man I can trust and a man who enjoys the respect of the entire regiment. You *will* see our men safely over the border, and then through their stay in France."

"With respect, sir, I will not. There's many as can baby-sit them better than I. Shane Connal is the one you've been grooming for this kind of work. Most of the men will hear and heed his voice almost as if it were your own. And m'lord, if fair speech is required in dealing with our French hosts, then let's speak plain and admit I'm not the man for that. But Shane's got your way with words and manners—and he'll oversee a just and proper succession of your title here, should something ill befall us out there."

Hugh considered the arguments. "You rehearsed that speech earlier, didn't you, O'Rourke?"

"I thought I might have occasion for words such as those, m'lord. I figured a man of genius like yourself often lacks a bit in the common sense department; he might leave his right hand at home if the right hand wasn't determined to stay attached all by itself."

Hugh smiled. "You're a pain in my neck, O'Rourke."

"And other parts of the body as well, I'd wager."

"Another bet you'd win. Now, for our trip to the New World, we'll need about a half of a company for the landing and defense— as well as repelling pirates, if we're unlucky. Recommendations?"

"I've been thinking about just that, m'lord, and the men that seem best suited to those purposes—"

O'Donnell clapped a hand on his shoulder. "I trust you, O'Rourke—in all things. Go get your list—and while you're at it, fetch Shane Connal from the blockhouse, as well. Let's not keep him in the dark on this any longer."

O'Rourke rose quickly. "In a trice, m'lord." And he was out the tent flap in a rush.

He had gone half the way to the blockhouse when a suspicion began to churn in his gut. Bt the time he had turned and sprinted back up the low rise to the commander's tent, his misgiving had become a certainty. Pulling the flap aside, he burst into the dim interior.

One orderly looked up from his tasks, startled.

He was the only person in the tent. Of course.

O'Rourke smiled and shook his head; it was sad to think that after all these years, he was still so easily conned. He should have seen it coming: O'Donnell would want to slip out of the camp as stealthily as he had come in. And he'd have—rightly—known that O'Rourke would have had none of that: two guards, at least, to escort one of the last two princes of Ireland. But O'Donnell had given him the slip.

Again.

O'Rourke went over to stand by the table they'd shared but two minutes earlier. He rested his hand on the back of his earl's chair. And smiled:

See you in Amiens, old friend.

Falser Messiah

Tim Roesch

Lost in Grantville, 24th of Av, 5394
(T minus 5 hours and 43 minutes)

"I am not the Son of God!" he screamed at the library.

At least he thought he was screaming in the direction of the library.

With eyes red with tears, Shabbethai Zebi ben Mordecai spun about, glaring at the world which was suddenly bright and out of focus, frightening and repulsive. The world he could not wait to see each morning and wept over as he closed his eyes every night was suddenly wrong.

Or, maybe, he was wrong.

Memories came; out of focus, silent, out of any order.

He remembered his mother crying on the dock in Smyrna as he left on a ship, a real ship, with his father and elder brother.

His mother had not waved at him.

He remembered how eager he was to learn everything and show his father what he had learned and how hard it was, all of a sudden, to get his father to simply look at him.

There was the trip to this magical place, Grantville. Here, he had forgotten how often his questions went unanswered, his small discoveries went unnoticed, how often his father and elder brother seemed to talk quietly to each other and occasionally looked at him as if he had done something wrong.

Here was the town of Deborah and an entire community of Jews who lived and worked amongst non-Jews and not once, not even once, had he heard a single bad word or seen an evil look directed at any Jew, and how exciting it was and how he wanted to ask questions.

No Sabbath had ever been so beautiful as his first in Deborah. Never had he sung the Torah so fervently, so fervently he did not remember, until now, how his singing caused so much silence.

"Why, Abba?" he whispered, sniffing. Grantville had been a magical place and now it felt like it was burning and he was the fire. "Abba!"

No answer. No one looked at him. They told him what to do and where to be and conversations stopped when he entered rooms and there was arguing but never did anyone look him in the eye or ask him how his day went or what new and magical thing had he learned today.

Silence.

Even the other children viewed him with suspicion. Games ended when he joined them. Meals were quiet and even during prayer he felt he prayed alone.

So, as he had learned in the schools in Smyrna, the Jewish ones with dour old men who were quick with a harsh word to those who seemed inattentive, he went to answer his questions. He went to the library at Grantville.

He listened and heard his father and his elder brother and rabbis, learned men, arguing about him, about little Shabbethai Zebi and how his name was in the library, the great library in Grantville.

In a place where Jews could move about freely, it had been simple for him to go to the library.

And now?

Silence.

He tried hard in the silence of the library to translate an entry in a book, an entry that had his name in English.

A girl saw him and, miracle of miracles, she spoke Greek and this English that not even his own father could understand well, let alone read, and she had told him.

"You are the Messiah? You are the son of God?"

What was he to do? What could he do?

The silence shouted at him as he ran from the library and out into the streets of Grantville.

Shabbethai Sebi: Son of God. Messiah.

"I am not the son of God!" Shabbethai shouted, though his voice had less strength. He spun about looking for something familiar, something to hold onto, something not silent.

Grantville was not silent but its voice was not familiar to him. There were people and magical things called "cars" and horses, and children screaming.

Shabbethai sniffed and looked about, hunting the source of the screaming.

There had been a time when he had screamed like that, screamed with the pure joy of play and running and jumping.

Now, since that last view of his home in Smyrna and his mother standing motionless, crying on the dock, there had been silence.

"I am not the Son of God." Shabbethai tried to smile, tried hard and the smile almost came to his face. His steps began tentatively, slowly but soon he was running again, running as if he was being chased or, maybe, he was chasing something.

He ran toward the sound of screaming, away from silence.

Grantville Public Library, 24th of Av, 5394 (T minus 5 hours 1 minute)

Julie Drahuta trudged up the steps of the Grantville Public Library.

The day hadn't been that long. It was just that it was Friday, the end of the week, and her thoughts had been on the weekend until the phone call.

The work of a social worker slash police officer who specialized in child welfare in a town filled with seventeenth-century Germans and twentieth-century Americans—West Virginians, to be more precise—meant her work was rarely finished, weekend or no weekend.

If there was a minor problem or a major one and if it involved children, which it often did, Julie was called in. She had earned a reputation of solving difficult and delicate problems, of translating cultural languages and norms from one century to another, from one religion to another, from one family to another.

Julie's Flying Mom Squad, made up of Protestant, Catholic, Lutheran and even Jewish mothers, multiplied her effectiveness but it also kept her on call twenty-four/seven.

Of course, what had truly brought her to the attention of almost everyone were the Pascal children; Blaise and his sister, Jacqueline. Their father had sent them to Grantville to protect them from their historical notoriety. Who would protect Grantville from them?

Julie Drahuta, of course!

The Pascal children were reminders to every up-timer just where and when they were. Blaise showed up in religious texts, math texts and almost every encyclopedia had an entry about him. Heck, even she knew of Pascal's Triangles before the Ring of Fire.

Blaise embraced twentieth-century tech with a passion that was frightening, if not life-threatening. Jackie liked to write and learn languages.

Were there more children hiding in the history books? Hopefully they would go somewhere else. The Pascals were enough.

It was Jackie Pascal who had called her. The girl's problems rarely required police or fire intervention. This was why Julie didn't bring backup with her as she trudged up the stairs.

Tina Jones, an assistant librarian, met Julie at the front door to the library; snapping Julie out of her daydreaming about the impending weekend and the relative dangers of the Pascal children.

Julie knew that the circulation desk was a throne to Tina and for her to come out from behind that desk meant something serious had occurred, something more serious than a misshelved book or an angry scholar who felt that his dignity had been assaulted because a child was often asked to translate for them. Jacqueline was really, really good at languages.

"What's up?" Julie smiled. Julie rarely smiled when she was happy. This situation had the makings of unhappy written all over it.

"It could be nothing, nothing at all. Or it could be everything. I don't know what to think." Tina Jones was the one Jacqueline Pascal went to for permission to use the phone to call Julie away from her nice, neat and tidy "end of the week" thoughts. Jackie's first two words over the phone were the words that brought Julie to the library.

"Officer Drahuta."

Jacqueline only called Julie "Officer" when it was real serious.

"I have done something bad. Come quick. Oh, come to the library. Please."

"Jacqueline is quite upset." Tina's voice shook Julie out of her thoughts.

"What did she do, Tina, misfile a romance novel, again? Was she loudly critiquing Chaucer or Melville?" Julie smiled. "Remember that time she was reading that Barbra Cartland novel? I thought we'd have to call the EMTs for a mass cardiac event."

Tina Jones, library aide, averter of eyes when Jacqueline Pascal roamed the stacks of books far away from the children's section, was not smiling. She was fiddling with her necklace, the one with the silver cross dangling from it.

"I hope it is nothing." Tina hurried across the library's main floor to the reference section. "I hope Jackie is wrong. She's only eight. Maybe she's imagining things. I hope she is. She does have an excellent imagination. Some of the books in this library will be authored by that girl, someday."

Julie followed Tina to a far corner of the reference section. There, before a large study table crowded with books, some open, some closed, stood Jacqueline Pascal. The girl was standing straight, as if asked by a judge to stand and hear judgment.

"Have you been in 'that' section of the library again, Jacqueline?" Julie asked, smiling. Jacqueline loved historical romances. Worse, she seemed to be able to memorize entire passages and repeat them in at least four languages, loudly. Worse, she knew exactly what she was reading.

"No." Jacqueline looked over at the table and lifted a large book. It was a volume from the Encyclopedia Britannica. There were other volumes from other encyclopedias on the desk as well. Jacqueline opened the book she had picked up and held it against her chest, the entries facing Julie.

"Right there." Tina pointed at one of the entries.

Julie looked at both Tina and Jacqueline then carefully took the book.

"Sabbatai Sebi?" Julie asked finally, looking up.

"Keep reading," Tina prodded.

"Sabbatai Sebi, born 1626, died 1676. That makes him forty years old when he died?" Julie asked. "Born in Turkey. So there's a kid in Turkey..."

"Fifty," Jacqueline whispered, correcting Julie.

"I'll keep that in mind." Julie frowned then continued reading. "Jewish mystic, whose Messianic claims produced an unparalleled sensation throughout the world, was born in Smyrna."

"That's in Turkey," Jacqueline whispered helpfully, looking at a nearby atlas, open on the table. That was Jackie, Julie thought, thorough to a fault. "I think I translated the word Messiah wrong. I looked it up. Oh, Julie . . . I translated it into 'son of God.' How could I?"

"It says he thought he was Jesus Christ," Tina whispered. "And people believed him. He was an 'unparalleled sensation.'"

"He was trying to translate this entry into Greek. I helped him. I'm sorry," Jacqueline added, close to tears.

Julie closed her eyes, hiding her face behind the open volume. "He's eight years old. Was he eating in the library, pulling loaves and fishes out of thin air? Making wine flow from the reference shelves? Was he talking to God too loudly?"

Had another "historical" child come to Grantville?

"Julie!" Tina snapped. "It isn't funny! Did you read the rest of it?"

"The boy would be, what, eight years old, Tina! It doesn't matter what the rest says. He is not the man this book says he is. He is an eight-year-old boy."

"And I told him he was the son of God." Jacqueline looked prepared to be led to the gallows right this moment.

"Simple mistake. Could happen to anyone. Okay, where's the kid? I'll talk to him, then to Rabbi Yaakov, though I am certain Rabbi Yaakov and even Rabbi Fonseca know they got a Messiah running around somewhere. If people just communicate, so many problems just disappear. I should have been in the loop."

"He said today was his birthday," Jacqueline added. "I should have been careful. When I translated the word Messiah . . . he ran. I wasn't thinking. I remember when Blaise found his name in that encyclopedia. I should have been more careful. Blaise ran away, too."

"Yeah, and he came back, didn't he? Why do you think it's this Sabbatai Sebi?" Julie asked. "Maybe the kid was doing research on False Messiahs for a school project?"

"He told me his name," Jacqueline said. "Why would he lie about that?"

Julie closed the book she held and set it down on the table. "Jesus Christ has the right to live in Grantville. Tina, let go of that cross before you bend it or cut yourself. Jacqueline, please go call Madam Delfault and tell her I am taking you out to Deborah to help me find the boy. I don't think we'll be disturbing their

Sabbath Celebration if we go now. Sundown isn't for a few hours yet. Sundown is like around 7:30 and it's about 2:30 so...what? Five hours? And, Tina? I would appreciate it if you didn't start a rumor that the Messiah has come to Grantville until at least I confirm that this boy is, in fact, the boy mentioned in this book. Okay?"

"I wouldn't dare." Tina looked like she wouldn't.

"I am serious," Julie added. "Jackie? Phone?"

Jacqueline ran off.

"I didn't know?" Tina whispered.

"What? About false messiahs?" Julie asked, pulling her radio out of her purse, "The Jews believe Jesus was a false messiah. That's one of the reasons they've been massacred all over Europe."

"I thought it was about having the Sabbath on Saturday or something. I don't know. I guess I never thought much about it. There weren't many Jews in Grantville. I just didn't think about it."

"Somebody should go through the entire encyclopedia, twice, and make a list of the famous people who might show up so at least I can prepare. I've read up on Blaise. Seems there's someone named Fermat who might walk into the library looking for a certain pain in the ass, but at least Fermat's an adult now. He's beyond my pay grade, thank God. Just a second, Tina. Central? This is Officer Drahuta, over."

"Go, Julie," came the answer over the radio.

"I'm heading up to Deborah with Jacqueline Pascal so she can help me ID someone. You heard anything about a missing boy, Mimi?"

"Not a word, Julie," Mimi Rowland, the dispatcher on duty answered. "I know Blaise has been with Steve behind the fire station in his disaster containment shed all afternoon. This isn't about that boy, is it? Do you need some backup?"

"No, Mimi, not *that* boy. Tell me if you hear anything about a missing child, okay? Over."

"Gotcha, over."

"What if it is, you know, Him?" Tina asked.

"Well, I will tell 'Him' to come back here and put away his books." Julie shrugged. "My quiet weekend destroyed by an act of God."

Somewhere in Grantville, 24th of Av, 5394 (T minus 5 hours 14 minutes)

"Hey! You! Come here!" A boy waved at Shabbethai. He was a good-looking boy with a welcoming smile, the sort of smile that did not suggest violence or cruelty.

Shabbethai had learned early to recognize that smiles were not merely smiles. Smiles required understanding as the word of God did. They were complicated and to misunderstand one could be deadly or worse.

Shabbethai approached with caution.

"You wanna play with us?" The boy who spoke now was smaller. Shabbethai could tell there was little in the way of cruelty in this younger boy.

The game seemed to involve a stick and a ball. That was comforting. Games with only sticks involved hitting and when hitting was involved, Jews got hit if they were available.

"He's too little," another, older boy said. This boy looked different from the one who had called him over. Shabbethai thought he would not like it if this boy smiled.

"He makes the teams even. So, you wanna play with us?" The first boy smiled and that settled it.

Shabbethai couldn't quite understand the words. He understood "you" meant him and "us" meant them. It didn't look like they meant to kill him. Besides, there were three girls watching. Boys rarely, in his wide experience of eight years, were cruel around girls.

So Shabbethai nodded his head and hoped for the best. Already the thoughts of being the son of God and curiosity and books being translated from English to Greek by some girl who had looked at him with wide eyes were receding.

"I don't think he understands English," one of the children said.

Shabbethai understood "English" and the head shaking meant "no."

"No English good." Shabbethai smiled hopefully, stringing some English words together.

"That's okay," the boy with the welcoming smile said. "My name is Joseph Drahuta. Call me Joe, okay? Joe." The boy pointed at himself and said "Joe" again.

"Shabbethai Zebi," Shabbethai pointed at himself.

"*Sprecken she dutch?*" the boy named Joe asked in very bad

German. Even his German was not that bad, Shabbethai thought, very much to himself. It would never do for a Jewish boy, lost in a non-Jewish part of town, to laugh at a non-Jew or criticize them, no matter how deserved it was.

"Your German is funny." One of the younger girls laughed and clapped. Shabbethai understood the "your" and "German" part. The word "funny" was not one his father had taught him.

"He doesn't look German," stated the other boy; the one with the smile Shabbethai knew he didn't want to see. "No German would wear hair like that."

"What does it matter what he looks like, Gabriel," one of the girls, the older one, snapped, her hands upon her hips. Shabbethai pretended he didn't see her hips or even know what "hips" were. You had to be careful how you looked at girls, especially ones who weren't Jewish.

"No Ger-man," Shabbethai tried in English.

"Easy game," Joseph said slowly, smiling at him. "Watch. I show you."

Shabbethai watched very carefully, completely involved in the game.

The boy with the smile Shabbethai liked held a stick and looked determined to hit something or someone with it. Shabbethai was determined to make sure he was not that something or someone to be hit.

Deborah, 24th of Av, 5394
(T minus 4 hours 15 minutes)

"He's the one who called me a boy when I asked him to teach me Hebrew. Rabbi Yaakov, him." Jacqueline pointed, indicating the elderly man who was pretending not to see Julie's car.

The fact that the good rabbi was doing a very thorough job of pretending that a car had not just appeared a few hours before the Sabbath with Officer Julie Drahuta inside told her a great deal. Maybe she would not need Jackie to identify the boy.

"Julie, where the hell are you?" the radio blared.

"Chief." Julie sighed. "I've got Jacqueline in the car and I'm about to talk to Rabbi Yaakov. You might want to modulate your vocabulary, Chief."

There was a long, tense pause in which Rabbi Yaakov finally looked over at Julie.

"What, Officer Drahuta, in the name of God, is your present location, if I might enquire?"

"Deborah, Chief. I'll leave the mike open. You'll probably want to hear this as it happens." Julie set the microphone on the dash and looked out of the windshield. Rabbi Yaakov looked back at her with a large smile on his kind face.

The old rabbi shared at least one common trait with her; they both tended to smile while under stress.

"I believe, Jackie, that the word he used was *goy*. It's Yiddish and it means a 'non-Jew,'" Julie said. "I guess their language hasn't changed as much as English has. Anyway, how you ask is as important as the question. Maybe if you talk to Chana first and show up at one of their Sunday schools, which are on Saturday, you might have better luck than just marching up to someone and telling them to teach you Hebrew."

"Chana just glares at me," Jackie said. "I don't think she likes me."

"Your recitations of Barbara Cartland are rather graphic, Jackie. Chana wants to make sure you are serious. Hebrew is an important language to Jews. It was still being spoken four hundred years from now. The language has survived a lot. Ask her respectfully, Jackie. Now stay in the car."

"Wow! I am told Jesus spoke in Hebrew. How many languages do Jews know, you think?" Jackie muttered. "'The boy spoke Greek.' I've never seen a Jew speak Greek."

Julie shrugged, opened the door and climbed out of her patrol car. "Good Shabbos, Rabbi Yaakov."

"Good Shabbos, Officer Drahuta." The man bowed slightly. Rabbis didn't bow easily to non-Jewish women in this century or in one almost four hundred years from now. This was looking more and more serious to her.

"Is there something special about this Sabbath, Rebbe?" Julie asked, smiling.

"All are special, Officer Drahuta." Rabbi Yaakov smiled back.

Shit, Julie thought. His smile was as good as a red flag. "So special that you have groups of children hunting down by the stream and looking along the road? You haven't lost something, have you?"

Rabbi Yaakov looked away from Julie for a moment.

"Or someone?" Julie continued. "Are you missing a Messiah, perhaps?"

Fire blazed for a brief moment in the elderly rabbi's eyes. "Julie, this is time for joke?"

"Purim is over, Rabbi Yaakov, so I am not joking. I don't smile when I am joking."

"Officer Drahuta... this is a difficult problem."

"Why didn't you come to me? Have we not worked well together? Have we not solved problems together? Have I not introduced you to the other men of God in Grantville? Have there been problems with the consecration of the new place of worship in Grantville? Have the Sephardim not been accepted? Non-Jews gathered money and helped Rabbi Fonseca to move here. Why do I have to learn of your problems from an eight-year-old girl?"

"Yes, and I thank you, Julie, but this is difficult. Yes, you have been very helpful. We have tried to be helpful in turn. For your help we have thanked God, Julie Drahuta."

"You wouldn't teach me Hebrew," Jacqueline interrupted. Like her brother, Jackie saw rules as something less "rule-like." The girl was, in this case, standing on the edge of the doorframe of the patrol car so, technically, she was still "in" the car.

"Jackie! Zip it!" Julie turned back to Rabbi Yaakov. She noted a loose ring of Jewish residents of Deborah standing just within earshot. "Jacqueline here had a little conversation with a young boy. I can have her describe him to you. She speaks Greek quite well. She and the boy had a short little talk. The boy seems to think he is Sabbatai Sebi and that name appears in a book or two in the public library."

Rabbi Yaakov closed his eyes for a moment.

"He's from Smyrna. That's in Turkey... or, well, Ottoman Turkey... or whatever. Doesn't that make him Sephardic? Am I missing something here? Are the boy's parents here or in Grantville? Your place of worship is Ashkenazi, I think, correct? Why would the boy be living here? You are looking for him, right?"

"Shabbethai Sebi's father and Rabbi Fonseca did not come to agreement on what was to be done about the boy. The father and elder brother are looking for him now," Rabbi Yaakov stated. "The boy was told not to go to Grantville, so the father and older brother look for the boy here."

"Ah. So the boy Jackie saw wasn't this Sabbatai person. Good, I will be going..."

"Julie Drahuta, please. This is a difficult matter," the man almost whispered. "God does not have a son. We must, first, be clear on this."

"So, while the adults argue, an eight-year-old boy wanders into Grantville and finds out he's the son of God all by himself?" Julie asked quietly, aware of the audience.

"God can not have a son! That is..." Rabbi Yaakov calmed himself. "...that is... that is not right, Julie Drahuta. Do you understand?"

"I understand, Rabbi Yaakov." Julie smiled. "I understand that Jews do not believe God may have children. Christians may not be so quick to deny God's paternity though. If I had known of our guest from Smyrna, I could have at least smoothed over any problems. Now he's running around in Grantville and you are spending time here in Deborah looking for him instead of thinking about the Sabbath because you told the son of God that he may not go to Grantville. I see."

"It is the reason we hoped to handle this matter among ourselves," Rabbi Yaakov sighed. "And I would like this very much if you do not call him the son... in my presence."

"That I can do, Rabbi Yaakov," Julie said.

"The Torah is very clear on who God is, Julie. This matter that you have brought with you from the future is one to be discussed carefully and completely. It is a matter of religion, not... the protection of children. The boy is safe... do you think? That is the important thing now. Right now. He is very smart. He is very smart, but he is a boy."

"I am pretty sure nothing has happened to him," Julie said.

"How to understand this matter of Messiah is a matter for men of God to determine," Rabbi Yaakov begged. "This should not be made into a joke."

"Yes. Theology is easy. Have faith and believe in God," Julie said carefully. "I have a Christian library aide thinking the son of God was in her library reference section. She calls a Christian dispatcher and now we have people in Grantville who are wondering if the son of God is wandering about Grantville. The chief is a bit upset. He feels someone should have at least discussed the appearance of such a boy, if for no other reason than crowd control. He wants to know what I was doing to allow this to happen. The people of Grantville wish to meet this boy who is not the son of, well, Him. This has become a problem of sociology and mob psychology and trust me on this one, sociology is much more complicated, Rabbi Yaakov. You can have faith in God, Rabbi, but to have faith in humans requires something like insanity."

"Will harm come to the boy?"

"Worse, the crowd may believe him." Julie shook her head and almost, almost, laughed. "And then what the Torah says or does not say about God and if He may have children or not will become a moot point. One of the little secrets of Christianity is that Jesus was a Jew. I learned early that to say that brought most religious arguments to an end. Sometimes the argument became centered on me, but I'm not eight, Rabbi. Next time, please, talk to me. Now I have to tell my chief that the Messiah is wandering around Grantville. He doesn't like his Friday afternoons to vary from the regular round of drunks and brawls."

Rabbi Yaakov closed his eyes and if he prayed then it must have been a very, very serious prayer, indeed.

"So, Chief..." Julie grabbed up the microphone and began, "about this 'Messiah' thing; you're gonna laugh so you might as well get it out of your system now..."

Somewhere in Grantville, 24th of Av, 5394 (T minus 2 hours 10 minutes)

"Shut up, everybody! It's the phone!" the boy named Joseph Drahuta shouted over the growing argument. "Hello? Mom? Yeah, we're all here. Kubiaks, too. Blaise came over, too. No, Mom, Blaise is fine. Where are you? Oh. Sure. Yes, Mom. I was making a snack. No, we won't make a mess. No. Sure. See you when you get home. Sibylla's right here. You wanna talk to her?"

There had been a time when Shabbethai would have been very curious about a "phone" but after the library and now the boy who could translate Greek into English, all he wanted to do was hide.

"Sibylla, Mom wants to talk to you," Joe shouted and Blaise translated. Shabbethai wanted very much to tell the boy to stop translating everything but Blaise wasn't Jewish so he remained silent.

"Yes, Mother?" the older girl, named Sibylla, said.

It took a certain kind of faith to believe that there was a real person talking back. Shabbethai hunched under the drone of Blaise's idle translation of almost everything being said in the room. It had been a rough and tumble game of stick ball. The smooth feel of the ball, made out of something called rubber and called a Pinkie, had almost meant that he had not thrown it in time for an out.

English was a curious language.

Shabbethai was curious about how the phone worked. He was curious about why the Jews of Deborah looked at him funny. He was curious about whether the French boy could understand Greek. Look where that curiosity had left him.

The boy named Gabriel, the one with the smile Shabbethai didn't want to see, asked if he was Jewish and Shabbethai said yes because lying never solved a problem and Blaise had translated his answer and now...

"Joseph, Mom wants me to make dinner," Sibylla stated very firmly to everyone present. "Mom won't be home until late and she put me in charge."

Sibylla placed the phone down on its cradle. Shabbethai looked sadly at the phone then glared at that boy, Blaise. What sort of name was Blaise? He sort of looked like that girl in the library who had translated that English book into Greek and destroyed his life.

"Did you tell your mom you have a Jew in your house?" Gabriel Kubiak asked, looking at Shabbethai, not smiling.

Blaise kept translating and Shabbethai kept wondering about the game of stick ball and how he was ever going to face his father and the Jews of Deborah...or any Jew for that matter.

"So what if there's a Jew in the house?" Joseph frowned. "What's wrong with being Jewish? Isn't like he's a Croat or something. Jews are nice people. I like Chanukah and the candles. One of Mom's friends is this lady named Chana. She's nice and she's Jewish. She comes to the house. She even ate here!"

Joseph Drahuta, once Blaise showed up to play stick ball and translate English into Greek, had introduced Shabbethai to Gabriel Kubiak and his sister, Dorothea. They both were orphans and their foster mother was Joseph's father's sister.

Once the French boy who knew Greek told everyone that he, Shabbethai Zebi, was Jewish, Gabriel started watching him almost like the Jews of Deborah had been watching him.

Shabbethai wondered if people back in Smyrna knew about him, too.

"Jews are worse than Croats," Gabriel muttered (and Blaise dutifully translated). "My father told me that Jews started the wars. Jews are evil."

Shabbethai didn't know what or who a Croat was. He hoped they weren't a type of Jew.

"Mr. Kubiak didn't say anything like that." Joseph laughed. "You're crazy! Your dad doesn't care if someone is Jewish. I have known him longer than you."

"I think he means his other father," Sibylla said quietly, glaring at Gabriel. "I think Gabriel means his German father. His dead German father. I think Gabriel forgets that it was not a Jew who killed his first father. I think Gabriel should forget more of the past and remember more of the future here in Grantville. He owes his new mother and father that much!"

"My father said Jews aren't to be trusted," Gabriel looked at Shabbethai and Shabbethai weighed the danger in that look. "He said Jews were witches and sorcerers. They poison water and steal babies."

Shabbethai flinched as the words were translated and wished, once again, that he hadn't met the French boy who knew Greek while at the same time thanking God that he had. This would be worse if he could understand none of it.

"It does not matter," Joe's younger brother Ulrich, who was adopted like Gabriel and Dorothea and Sibylla were, said. "Shaba is in Grantville. Everyone is safe in Grantville. And he plays stick ball well. You are mad that we beat your team, twice!"

"But he is a Jew."

"Shut up, Gabriel," Joseph said, defending him. Incredible! "The kid ain't a witch. You're just mad he hit that ball over your head. You thought you could win by letting me have the new kid and we beat your butt. You're just a sore loser!"

Shabbethai turned to look at the French boy who had ruined everything with his knowledge of Greek. He depended on that translation now. If he wasn't very much mistaken, things could go real bad at this point. Even if Gabriel were the only one who hated Jews, he probably had friends and would Joseph Drahuta defend Shabbethai Zebi, the Messiah, the son of God, when Gabriel brought friends who hated Jews, too?

"Gabriel Vogel Kubiak! I will tell your mother you said that!" Joseph's sister, Sibylla, shouted from her position of authority by the phone that was now lying on the small table near the door to the kitchen.

"You know it's true, Sibylla," Gabriel stated. "You were German once, too."

"Who says I am not now?" Sibylla shouted and the argument began, in German, fast and angry.

Shabbethai knew that arguments were rarely good things for Jews. Somehow, when there was arguing and there was a Jew, the Jew became a target. He had seen that in Smyrna. Would that happen here? He was, after all, the only Jew available and everyone knew that because of the French boy who knew Greek.

"There will be no food until you stop saying horrible things about people! And that includes Jews who play better stick ball than you!" Sibylla yelled.

Shabbethai needed no translation. A girl, now standing in front of the door leading to what could only be a kitchen, said two words that Shabbethai understood completely, no and food.

"He can't eat regular food anyway," Gabriel declared. "All I said was that he was a Jew. I heard you gotta be careful with Jews and food. They poison it."

"If you think you're going to be poisoned you can leave," Joseph shouted. Shabbethai noted that Joseph's younger brother, Ulrich, shouted encouragement to his brother. "You're just mad that Shabbethai helped us win! You're just a sore loser!"

"All I am saying is that he is Jewish and you should be careful around Jews. What do they plan in their secret meetings, in their communities set apart from good Christians?" Gabriel frowned.

"I see, Gabriel Vogel. Take your sister and go home to the Vogels, your first mama and papa, and eat there," Sibylla stated. Shabbethai wasn't sure why this seemed to strike Gabriel dumb. The older boy looked unable to speak. Dorothea looked ready to cry.

"Mama, our new mama, said we gotta stay here." Dorothea looked very upset. "Mama, the mama who took us in when we would have starved, said she'd come and pick us up after work. We gotta stay at Auntie Drahuta's house. And I don't care if he's a Jew. I want dinner. Our first Mama and Papa are dead and we can not go to them for dinner. That was mean, Sibylla. Your parents are dead, too. You go to them!"

Gabriel seemed unable to answer back. Shabbethai could see that there were words that wanted to come out but, for some reason, they did not.

"So, was it Catholics that killed your Protestant parents or Protestants that killed your Catholic parents? Or did anyone care to figure it out before they killed them? You of all people should know how foolish your words are, Gabriel. So what if he's a Jew? There is religious freedom in Grantville. Go. Leave Grantville with your 'he's a Jew' thoughts. There are people out there waiting for you, Gabriel Vogel. Just make sure you tell the right people the right religion or you may learn what it feels like to be a Jew. I have seen how Jews are treated and I will have nothing to do with that. Nothing!"

Blaise's translation into Greek extended into the silence after Sibylla stopped talking.

Gabriel looked at Shabbethai but without anger. Was there, perhaps, a touch of shame, Shabbethai asked himself?

"Come," Sibylla waved at Shabbethai and Shabbethai walked toward her as she opened the door to the kitchen. "Show me what you can eat and I will make it for you. Gabriel can watch, for all I care."

Were Jews truly welcome in Grantville? Would his welcome change if they discovered he was the son of God? But there was no son of God? Was there?

"I don't care if he's a Jew," Dorothea offered. "Can I eat too? I'll eat what he can't eat."

Former IOOF Building, Grantville, 24th of Av, 5394 (T minus 4 minutes 32 seconds)

"I don't care if he is the Messiah! Get those yahoos off the street!" Julie watched as Press tried to place the radio back in its holder with one hand and rub his forehead with the other. "We got a bunch of drunks wandering around with crosses made out of pool cues looking for the Messiah. We got a full house at both the Catholic and Protestant churches. Are you sure Blaise is at your house?"

"I don't think it is fair to blame the boy for everything. Besides, he's Catholic. Blaise wouldn't be playing at being the Messiah, Chief." Julie smiled at Rabbi Fonseca who was a few feet away listening politely to Jacqueline Pascal who was trying very hard to speak to the man. Julie wasn't so far away that she couldn't hear Jacqueline trying to speak Hebrew.

"What does Blaise being Catholic have to do with this?" Press demanded.

"Exactly, Chief. Exactly." Julie turned to Chana and Gertrude, two of the women in her Flying Mothers Squad. "Any word?"

"No," Chana sighed. "There is no sign of the boy. I am most appreciative of the help we have received. I can think of few places where a lost Jewish child would have this effect. People want to find him to protect him."

"We have seen the effect of religious bickering, Chana. I have lost family trying to find refuge in religion and being dragged out and killed anyway. Protestants killing Catholics. Catholics massacring Protestants and both killing Jews. Grantville has taught many the lessons we should have learned." Gertrude crossed her arms and dared any to argue. "If the boy is to be found, we will find him. Being Jewish will not stop us. God help the one who might harm the boy!"

"I better go and save Rabbi Fonseca." Julie sighed. "Hopefully her Hebrew is better than her Russian was at the beginning."

Rabbi Fonseca was listening politely as Jacqueline tried to hold open a book and speak in broken Hebrew to him.

"Jacqueline has not said something wrong?" Julie asked as simply as she could. The Sephardic community in Grantville was quite young and its rabbi was not much older. Rabbi Fonseca spoke many languages but English was still new to him.

"No," Rabbi Fonseca smiled at Jacqueline and gently pulled the soft covered book from her hands and looked at it. "Cannot think English word . . . Chana . . ."

There was an exchange of Hebrew and when it was over Chana nodded and turned to Julie.

"The rabbi is amazed to hold in his hand a book to teach Hebrew that was written many centuries from now. It gives him hope that great things can be done. He asks me to thank you for the things you have helped to be done. The idea of having a special place in the . . . synagogue for non-Jews was a good idea. Such a thing has helped much in bringing all together. He cannot think of a place in the world where a Jew can walk so freely amongst those who are not Jews," Chana translated.

"And the boy?" Rabbi Fonseca asked, with what little English knowledge he had, giving Jacqueline the book back.

"You didn't check the book out of the library, did you?" Julie sighed, looking at Jacqueline.

"We were in a hurry and I meant to. I will, Julie. I am sorry." Jacqueline clutched the book to her.

"The boy will be found," Julie assured Rabbi Fonseca.

"He knows where to come at sunset," Chana translated for the rabbi. "He is a good boy and will find his way here if he can. And the rabbi agrees with you, Julie. You should have been told and so should the boy. This might not have happened if the boy had been told. And he..."

There was a long pause.

"Chana?" Julie asked.

"He says..." Chana looked at Rabbi Fonseca for a long moment. "He says that he has sat in the library and contemplated that entry in the...encyclopedia. He says the knowledge, yes, knowledge should not have been withheld. It was wrong to let the boy discover this thing without those who love him around him. The boy is too smart, too full of his love of God, to be allowed to find this thing out by himself. He should have not been the object of...of...I do not know how to say. *Loshon Hora*, bad speech. The boy was looked at from the corner of the eye, whispered about. This should not have been done. I agree, too, Officer Julie Drahuta. Someone should talk to the boy's father. Possibly you?"

"I certainly will consider..." It was the prayer that caught Julie's attention.

"*Barukh ata Adonai Eloheinu melekh ha-olam*," Rabbi Fonseca began the blessing. Julie had heard blessings like that before the Ring of Fire when she worked in Wheeling, north of Grantville when it was still in the twentieth century and in America, and here, in Grantville, in 1634.

Who would have thought an IOOF building would have become a synagogue? Who would have thought a False Messiah would be something a social worker would have to worry about? What would they have done if the Ring of Fire had dropped them onto, say, Jerusalem in the year ten or fifteen?

God, a fifteen-year-old son of God...

Julie turned in the direction Rabbi Fonseca was praying in and, for a moment, didn't know whether to scream, cry or just remain silent.

"I know, I know, Mom, let me explain." Joseph had his father's impish smile. Julie found it hard not to smile back. "I locked up the house, Mom. Shabbethai said he was lost and needed to go to church and since he is a Jew I had to bring him here. He's too young to be wandering around by himself. Honest, Mom. That's why we left the house. I know you said to stay there until you got home, but there, I said it. It's my fault."

"I just translated into Greek," Blaise said. "I didn't do anything."

"*Ha-gomel lahayavim tovot sheg'malani kol tov*," Rabbi Fonseca finished his prayer.

"Ah-men," Chana added. Julie would find out later that this was the blessing for, amongst other things, surviving illness or danger.

"What's wrong, Mom?" Joseph, truly his father's son, had no clue what he had done, only that he had done something. "We played some stick ball. Is Shab in trouble?"

"I think you are," Sibylla whispered loudly.

"What did I do?" Joseph looked around, his eyes fixed on the chief of Grantville's police department.

"See? Blaise is involved!" Press shouted. "Is that the boy?"

There was a burst of strong Hebrew from the boy in the crowd of Drahuta and Kubiak children.

"He says—" Chana was trying not to laugh. "Shabbethai says we should all be glad of the Shabbos, not arguing. He wishes all a good Sabbath and that we should go inside. He tells us it is almost time of the Sabbath."

With that Shabbethai Zebi ben Mordecai led his friends into the former IOOF building which was now the first Sephardic synagogue of Grantville, though Julie heard the Portuguese Jews called it something else.

"And a little child shall lead them." Julie shook her head. "Is that him?" Julie asked Jacqueline, who was hiding behind her.

"How does he do that? How does my brother get in the middle of everything? Yes, Julie, that is the boy." Jacqueline nodded. "That is the False Messiah."

"Let's stick to Shabbethai Zebi for now, okay, Jackie?"

"Will come?" Rabbi Fonseca asked politely, indicating the front door with a smile.

"Certainly," Julie smiled. "Would it break the Sabbath if I drove him back to Deborah after the service?"

"It would be better if you walked," Rabbi Fonseca answered and Chana translated. "Or may he stay here for the night? There are certain laws to be followed, Julie."

"I could put him up in the guest room." Julie shrugged. "Would that tick off his father?"

"Yes." Chana smiled. "Maybe it will teach the father not to lose his son. Yes, Julie, it would be good for the boy's father to come to your house and speak to you about his son."

"Don't tell my father," Blaise muttered as the sounds of the Sabbath service began inside the building. "He is still angry that I called Descartes a dinosaur. What will he think if he knew I went into a Jewish church?"

Royal Dutch Airlines

Gorg Huff and Paula Goodlett

There is a King in the Low Countries

"His Majesty, Fernando I, King in the Low Countries wants us to come and visit," Herr van Bradt said. He hid a snicker as best he could. Really, the clothing women were wearing these days!

"What?" Magdalena van de Passe asked, ignoring the snicker. She knew what it was about, since she'd heard it all before. She was wearing a pair of the new bloomers, long puffy pants that tightened up again at the ankles. Also a leather flight jacket and leather flight helmet with goggles pushed up on her head. It wasn't a fashion statement. At least not an intentional one. The bloomers were warmer than the more common split skirt; the leather flight jacket was fur-lined and warm and the flight helmet kept her ears warm. None of that would be particularly necessary in one of the Jupiters, but the Neptune was another matter. The Neptune was a minimalist approach to carrying cargo, a two engine monoplane, with a seventy-foot wingspan. Like the Jupiters, they had a low air speed and a very good power-to-weight ratio. But they didn't carry passengers. The Neptune carried packages; it had no amenities that could be avoided. Anything to save weight and it got darn cold in them, two miles up, in the winter in Germany.

"His Majesty wants us to visit. And he wants us to come in one of the Jupiters."

"We can't. The schedule is messed up as it is."

"I know, but His Majesty insists and Frederik Hendrick added a note as well." Van Bradt paused. "Magdalena, most of my investments are there. I can't afford to have the two most powerful men in the Netherlands angry at me. The new engines are going to be ready in a month. Your young man already has the Jupiter Two and two Jupiter Threes sitting there waiting for them. This is politics. The schedule is just going to have to get a bit more out of whack."

Magdalena argued a bit more, but the decision was out of her hands. The Monster took off from Grantville International Airport at dawn three days later. On board were Magdalena van de Passe, Vrijheer Abros Thys van Bradt and three other major stockholders in TransEuropean Airlines.

Magdalena looked over at the copilot of the week. Most flights had one experienced pilot and one less experienced pilot. The idea was that by the time the new planes were ready they would have pilots for them. "You want to take a sighting, Karl?" They had just reached their cruising altitude so it was practice time.

"Sure." Karl bent over the periscopelike device and started fiddling with knobs as Magdalena held the plane straight and level. The knobs adjusted a couple of mirrors to align two images collected from almost ten feet apart on the front belly of the plane. When he got the best view, he looked at the dial on the knob and read off a number, which Magdalena wrote down. Some calculations with a slide rule would give them their height above ground. Those calculations would be done in a minute or so, after Karl took some more observations. He flipped a handle and looked in to the eyepiece again. This time he was looking for a landmark out in front of the plane. Anything recognizable would do; a tree, a barn, a really big rock. In this case he found a barn and called out "mark" as he clicked on a stop watch. He flipped another lever so that he was now looking straight down instead down and ahead at a forty-five degree angle, and waited for the landmark to reappear. How long it took for the landmark to show up again and how much it had shifted to the left or right would tell them, with more calculations, their true ground speed and how much drift they were experiencing from crosswinds.

"Mark!" Karl clicked the stopwatch again, then got out the

special purpose slide rule. Magdalena looked over his shoulder as he did the calculations.

"First check at 8:04 AM." Magdalena said. "What do you get for H over G? Remember, if we miss a major check point, you're the one that's going to have to get out and ask directions."

Karl looked at her like she was crazy.

"We land first," Magdalena reassured him. "But it's happened more than once. In fact, it's procedure if probable location permits and you're more than half an hour past a projected major check point without finding it. So what do you get for H over G."

After another minute with the slide rule, he gave her the answer.

"Okay. The angle is forty-five degrees so the leg that's on the ground is the same length assuming that the ground is flat as a pancake which it never is. So, what's our ground speed and drift?"

Magdalena watched as he set the slide rule, moved the slider, and got the numbers.

"Indicated airspeed is sixty-nine and compass heading is two eight three. So calculate the wind speed and direction, and give me our true heading." After he'd done that she continued, "Now we know what our speed and direction were a few minutes ago. We can guess that it's still close to that and make a guess about where we would end up if we continued on this course and the wind didn't change." Where they would have ended up was about seventy-five miles south of Kassel in just under ninety minutes. Since they would rather miss Kassel to the north they adjusted their course just a touch, then set about looking not so much for individual landmarks as for the general lay of the land. Patterns that would be recognizable from this altitude. Not a pond but a pond that was just to the right of a village with another village ahead of it. And a mountain peak in the background. They marked features on the map and made notes then made another set of sightings.

Aside from the sightings that they did every ten minutes or so, they took a bearing at Kassel. Which was done by looking out the window and finding Kassel, then comparing where it actually was to where they thought it should be. The sightings taken on random landmarks could give them a pretty good estimate of how fast they were going and in what direction, but couldn't tell them where they were. Not without better maps. They took another bearing at Dortmund, a third at Arnhem and landed near

Amsterdam not quite five hours after takeoff. They had been a bit off on their bearings at Dortmund and Arnhem, and had had a bit of a headwind for part of the flight.

"Now this is the way a princess should be rescued!" Maria Anna, the queen in the Low Countries, said with an arch look at her husband.

His Majesty didn't seem overly concerned with the reproach. "But where would be the excitement in that?" He grinned, looking like a naughty schoolboy. "Besides, there's altogether too much room. There's an aisle between the seats."

Magdalena looked back and forth between the king and his now blushing bride, and decided that this was not a conversation she wanted to get involved in. Luckily, His Majesty had other things on his mind. He turned to Magdalena. "It has a range of over three hundred miles?"

"Yes, Your Majesty. More still if it's lightly loaded and carrying extra fuel."

"And you've contracted for more of them."

"Yes, Your Majesty. We've committed to buying ten more as soon as they are ready. They won't be exactly the same as these. We've been providing feedback on the performance and some problems have come up. We have a Jupiter Two and two Jupiter Threes waiting for engines now. TEA also owns a Neptune, which would be a Jupiter except that we could only get two matching engines. It's good enough for cargo but not suitable for passengers. Also, it doesn't have the range of a Jupiter."

"Excellent!" King Fernando said.

They continued to discuss the ins and outs of the airline business, as well as the technology of the of the Jupiter-class passenger plane for a while. Then the king and queen took their leave. "It seems a very sound enterprise," King Fernando said in parting. "But I don't think the name is quite suitable. We'll call it Royal Dutch Airlines, I think."

It took Magdalena a few minutes to figure out the true import of the king's parting comment. Which was probably a good thing because it wouldn't have been a good idea to go off on King Fernando. Instead, as soon as she could find him, she went off on Herr van Bradt.

✧   ✧   ✧

"Have you lost your mind?" were the first words out of Magdalena's mouth when she found Herr van Bradt. "What is this business about renaming TEA Royal Dutch Airlines?"

"His Majesty wants an airline," Herr van Bradt said. "And the last time I looked my mind was right where it was supposed to be."

Perhaps going off on her boss and family patron hadn't been the best idea she ever had either. "But we're a USE corporation registered in the State of Thuringia-Franconia." Magdalena was trying to sound reasonable but even she could tell she wasn't doing a great job of it. "Look, Herr van Bradt. We've sweated blood getting TEA going. Now it's paying off, why should we move it to the Netherlands and change the name?"

"More than that His Majesty wants to buy the airline? He doesn't insist on owning every share, but he does insist on controlling interest."

"So why doesn't he start his own?" Maggie asked. "Why not pick on the Kitts? They're an airline and an aircraft manufacturer all in one. At least according to Vanessa Holcomb." She paused. *There might be a way out of this.* "I think aircraft may be one of the few technologies that the USE is unwilling to share. Would it even be legal for us to sell the airline to the Netherlands? After all, they're neutral and it wasn't all that long ago that they were the enemy. Can we sell airplanes to the Netherlands?"

Herr van Bradt grinned at her, but shook his head. "Nice try, Magdalena. But it won't work for a couple of reasons. First, His Majesty has already talked it over with Prime Minister Stearns and Emperor Gustav. Second, the reason they agreed is that Muscovy already has a dirigible and is working on a bigger one. France is working on aircraft in a little town south of Paris and Austria-Hungary stole one—well, a lot of the parts to one anyway. And your Herr O'Connor went with them and knows how the Monster was built."

"He was never my Herr O'Connor. I didn't much like him even when he was working for Georg and Farrell. And after he ran off we found that a bunch of our information on resins and putties, and on composites in general, had gone missing. If Georg or Farrell ever get to Vienna, Neil O'Connor is liable to get his lights punched out."

"As you've just pointed out, the cat, as they say, is already mostly out of the bag. There was, in fact, very little for the United States of Europe to gain by trying to tie a knot in the poor kitty's tail. On the other hand, there was a fair amount for them to gain in terms of trust and good relations by letting King Fernando have an airline. Especially in letting him have one before his brother got one on his own. The king of Spain and his advisors aren't happy with the king in the Low Countries and they are going to be even less happy with him when he one ups them by having a working airline before Spain has its first flight." Herr van Bradt shrugged. "His Majesty is aware of that, of course, but he really wants an air force. And this is the Netherlands. Our navy is merchant ships for the most part. It makes sense that the Netherlands Air Force should be an airline first. He wants to put off the final break with Spain as long as he can. But he is not willing to weaken the Netherlands to do it."

"You mean we're not just going to be a Netherlands airline but His Majesty's air force? These aren't combat planes. I'd rather do aerobatics in a 747 than in a Jupiter and I've never flown a 747 outside one of those computer simulations." The whole idea of trying to do a loop-the-loop in a Monster gave her the willies.

"The Netherlands aren't at war, Magdalena. Even if they were, His Majesty knows that the Monster isn't designed for combat. But neither was the DC3 and it was considered one of the most valuable planes in World War II."

"You've been talking to Georg, haven't you?" Magdalena sighed. She knew chapter and verse on the magical, mystical DC3. The way Georg talked about it, she sometimes imagined it in a miniskirt and high heels with really big engines falling half out of its blouse. Of course, other times, when she imagined flying it . . . Well, that was a different story.

"Yes, I have. And confirmed it with Hal Smith. I'd order a dozen of them if I could. The point is: even in war, there are other things a plane can do than bombing or strafing runs on enemy positions. And in peace, which we all hope for, the airline becomes both a money-maker and a status symbol for the Netherlands. That's what His Majesty wants and he is willing to pay for it."

Magdalena thought a minute. "Georg isn't going to like this. Not at all."

"Fat lot of good it's going to do him," Georg Markgraf muttered. "The aircraft are built here."

"Here is all of three hundred miles from Amsterdam, Georg," Magdalena said. "Granted, that trip used to take weeks. But you know we can do it in five or six hours."

"I didn't want a long-distance marriage."

Magdalena was stunned. While Georg had been, well, hanging around her a lot, he'd never mentioned marriage. Then she began to be a bit angry. Mostly at his assumption that she would agree to marriage. Which she wasn't at all sure about. She liked the life of a pilot, being free to go where she willed—or rather, where the schedule allowed.

"Oh?" Magdalena sniffed. "I wasn't aware that you'd engaged yourself, Georg? Who is it? One of the investors' daughters?"

"No! I thought you and I . . ." His voice trailed off.

"Nice of you to mention it to me." Magdalena threw him a look, then flounced away.

Farrell Smith sighed. "Georg, I've never met anybody who had such a bad case of foot-in-mouth disease. Not to mention that was just romantic as all get out . . . not."

Mary, his wife, shook her head. "Panic, dear, panic. I've got the strangest memory of somebody at this table"—she gave him a significant look—"getting rather tongue-tied, back in the day."

"Georg would be better off if he did get tongue-tied," Farrell pointed out. "Instead, he just blurts stuff out, usually stuff that's going to get him in hot water."

"I don't want Magdalena to move back to Amsterdam," Georg said. "I've just been waiting for the right moment to ask her to marry me. This wasn't the right moment."

"I'll say," Farrell said.

"You're being awful hard on him, Dad," Merton said. "Getting a girl is pretty hard when you're a nerd." Then he laughed. "Don't worry about it, Georg. Maggie's a nerd, too. She'll come around."

Farrell held his peace. Barely. He positively hated it when Merton said *nerd*. Merton had dropped out of high school, not exactly the best endorsement of a teacher. Farrell hadn't handled it well and Merton had moved out. Then he had that accident after the Ring of Fire and lost both legs above the knee. Merton had always been more of a physical kid than a mental one. The loss of his legs had been especially hard on him, and the Ring of Fire had had made it harder still, because it had turned back the clock in the field of prosthetics. It had never occurred to Farrell before Merton's accident that the switch from "disabled" to "physically-challenged" had been anything but political correctness. The difference between a peg leg and an up-time prosthetic limb was the difference between a disability and a challenge. At least in Merton's case. It was, for all practical purposes, impossible to walk on a couple of peg legs that started above the knee. That was not true with up-time prosthetics.

Farrell didn't peek under the table to see the fiberglass and resin prosthetics that his son now wore. But the knowledge that they were there and Georg had been instrumental in putting them there made it really hard for him to hold his tongue.

Georg snorted at Merton. "What would you recommend, O Great He-man?"

"Flowers, oh Nerdly Genius." Merton said, "Flowers and chocolates with a note telling her you're a jerk. The great truth of the universe is all men are jerks. The problem with nerds is they don't realize it."

"And the problem with jocks," his mother told Merton, "is you revel in it."

"And it's about time for me to get to my reveling," Merton agreed, pulling his walker to the kitchen table. He used the walker to lever himself up out of the chair, then reached down and adjusted the tension on the knee springs of his artificial legs, using the walker for balance. They weren't truly up-time artificial legs, but they were a great deal closer to what they had up-time than Europe had had before the Ring of Fire. With them and the walker, Merton wasn't limited to a wheelchair.

Wooden legs have the problem that they are heavy. And when you lose most of your legs, you lose that muscle mass as well. Aside from the limited ability to flex at the heel and knee, the fiberglass prosthetics were lighter than wood would have been. Merton still needed buns of steel to make them work, but physical labor had never been his trouble.

"Come on, Maggie. You knew he was going to ask you as soon as he got up the nerve," Merton said a couple of hours later. Merton was a pilot for TEA—RDA, he guessed it would be soon. It took some extra gear and the truth was that he probably wouldn't have been allowed to fly professionally up-time. The rudder controls were foot pedals after all. But while not a pilot before the

Ring of Fire, Merton did have flight time. He had gone up with friends of his grandfather and even considered it as a career. But he hadn't liked school.

"I know that. It was his blithe assumption that I'd say yes."

"From what I've seen, you've been going out of your way to give him that impression." Merton gave her a look. "Were you just leading him on?"

"Okay. I would have said yes but..."

"But he failed to suffer enough?"

"No. It's not that. But, why didn't he ask me?"

"Dowry."

"What?" Maggie looked up. "He wasn't satisfied with my dowry?"

"No. The other one, the one that the guy gives."

"He owns a big chunk of M and S Aviation!"

"Yep and you own a big chunk of TEA or at least you did. How's that going to work out, by the way? Is His Nibs buying you out?"

"Not entirely. He wants me to have an interest to make sure I don't jump ship. Actually, that was one of the things that a lot of the negotiations were about. TEA has two planes and a contract for eight more. But even more than the planes, TEA is the people. By switching off pilots we've been able to train more. We have eight pilots and twice that many maintenance people. We'll have more by the time we have planes for them to fly. All our pilots have experience on four-engine aircraft and most of them are cross-trained as maintenance people."

Merton nodded. He was one of those pilots; he got maybe three flights a month. And several hours stick time on each flight. And on every flight he was either training someone or being trained. While his legs limited what he could do in the way of aircraft maintenance, he spent time supervising that, too. Like most of the others, he was waiting impatiently for more planes to come off the line at M&S Aviation so that he could get more time in the air.

Maggie was still talking. "Herr van Bradt spent a certain amount of time explaining that to His Majesty. If the employees didn't like the deal, Royal Dutch Airlines would end up owning two cargo planes, two mail planes and having nobody to fly them, load them, or maintain them. He'd also probably have a new airline starting up here in competition with him. When you get right down to it, an airline is mostly its people."

"So what's he offering?"

"A ten percent raise across the board. Plus a bonus if you're willing to join the Dutch Royal Air Force Reserve. And he's going to want us to train Dutch pilots."

Merton nodded. It made sense if you looked at it from King Fernando's point of view, but he would have to think about it. Not that they were going to let him into the USE Air Force.

Moving the airline to Amsterdam wasn't that difficult. It was only some three hundred miles. But scheduling the move wasn't a picnic. TEA, now renamed Royal Dutch Airlines, had schedules to meet. One of which was with Claudia de Medici in Bolzano.

Claudia lifted an eyebrow when she saw the new logo on the side of the Neptune. "Royal Dutch?"

Magdalena shrugged. "A person has to do what a person has to do."

"And you have to move to Amsterdam. And delay what part of my cargo, pray tell?"

"None of it," Magdalena said. "We've been flying the wings off both planes to get caught up. Jupiter number three is ready for test flights. Once we've got it on the schedule, we'll open up a new route. The Brussels-Amsterdam-Grantville route will be a triangle, which will mean that you will be able to fly from Venice to Grantville, spend the night there, then catch a plane to Brussels, refuel there, then fly on to Amsterdam the same day. Just a day after you left Venice. Jupiter Four, when we get the engines for it, we're going to try and keep in reserve for when one of the other three is on its semiannual tear down and for the occasional charter. But it won't always be the Jupiter Four that is the reserve; they will rotate. The Brussels-Amsterdam-Grantville plane will reach Grantville, then fly the Grantville-Venice route while the Grantville-Venice plane is flying to Brussels. Then the reserve plane will get the Grantville-Venice route as the Brussels-Amsterdam-Grantville plane goes into reserve. All subject to change as one or another blows a cylinder or throws a rod. Which is happening a lot more than we'd like with the new engines in the testing phase. As we add more planes, we'll add more routes and more and more of those routes will be centered on Brussels."

"Why Brussels?"

"Mostly politics. Brussels is the capital, after all. But also, from

Brussels, London, Paris and Luxemburg are all short hops. Mostly short enough that the Jupiter Threes will be able to get there and back without refueling. Not that we plan on doing that. His Majesty is on relatively good terms with everyone just at the moment, so he's going to try to arrange for airports with fueling stations. Anyway, from Luxemburg it's a hop to Zurich then another here to Bolzano without a stop in the USE. We considered Basel, but with the city council's propensity for taking hostages . . . well, some of our passengers are fairly high profile."

Besides, Queen Maria Anna was still a bit annoyed with Basel and moving some of the highest-value trade to a competing city was just one of the ways she was demonstrating her displeasure. Maggie completely agreed with Her Majesty. Actually, almost all their passengers were pretty high profile, not all of them politically. Some were just rich. Some were princes of the church. The cardinal protector of the USE had flown on the Monster more than once, as had a couple of the great artists and scientists of the seventeenth century. Most of their passengers would make pretty good hostages for someone. And Maggy, like the queen in the Low Countries, felt that taking hostages was the sort of hobby that should be discouraged.

"What about Magdeburg?" Claudia de Medici asked.

"Not soon."

"Why not?"

"Again it's mostly politics and just a little bit of economics. You know as well as I that the planes rarely fly much under their max load. We have more passengers and cargo than we can carry and would on just about any route between major cities. There are hundreds of rich people in every major city in Europe. And thousands of tons of cargo that someone can make a fortune on, if only they can get it to their partner in days instead of weeks."

Claudia laughed. "When it absolutely positively has to be there on time. Yes, letters of transfer, bids ten pounds of gold coins because the person they are dealing with doesn't trust paper."

"Marijuana seeds so that the crop can be gotten in this year not next year. Dye because the ladies at court have to have the new colors for the party next week," Magdalena added.

"Fresh Italian oranges for Duchess Maria who is Frau Higgins' guest for the season and absolutely must have her freshly-squeezed orange juice or she'll die. Even though she has spent the last twenty years of her life without it."

And on they went listing some of the things that had been shipped on the Jupiter 1 and the Neptune since the Venice-Grantville route had opened. After they wound down Magdalena continued, "The same thing will be true in a route from Brussels to Paris or London, and almost as true on a route from Grantville to Magdeburg."

"Almost?"

"They have the train between Magdeburg and Grantville. Those oranges would have been just as fresh after a train ride as after a plane ride."

"The plane would be full anyway. You know there is a waiting list," Claudia insisted. "So why not Magdeburg?"

"His Majesty, so I am told, does intend to have scheduled flights to Magdeburg just as soon as we have enough planes for it. It's on the list right after Paris. But putting it at the front of the list would imply that the USE is more important than France or Spain. The point, as it was made to me, was that economically it's pretty much a wash whether the fifth plane we get goes from Brussels to London or Grantville to Magdeburg. But politically putting Magdeburg ahead of London makes the king in the Low Countries look like he's a vassal of the Emperor of the USE or at the very least like he's siding with Gustavus Adolphus against the League."

Claudia was nodding by the time Magdalena was finished. "If the Netherlands are to be effective as a buffer state they must, absolutely must, maintain an evenhandedness in their dealings with the nations that surround them. They already have scheduled flights to one city in the USE and Royal Dutch Airlines is owned by the crown."

"Please forgive me. Please, please, please?"

Magdalena looked toward the door. The voice had certainly been Georg's, but what was at the door didn't look much like him. Well, if you didn't count the feet. He'd apparently forgotten to put on the clown shoes. Or hadn't been able to walk in them, knowing Georg.

"Emmett Kelley was a silent clown," she pointed out.

Georg pulled three long-stemmed roses out of his sleeve. But he'd obviously forgotten to trim off the thorns, since he said "Ouch" rather loudly.

Magdalena couldn't help it. She began laughing. Georg's sad face didn't look so sad now. "What are you doing in that outfit, Georg?"

"Apologizing for being a jerk. Even if I didn't really know I was," Georg said. "I'm sorry. I just assumed...well, I'm not a very romantic type, I know. But I do love you. And I do hope you'll marry me. Even if you do go off to Brussels, I hope you'll marry me. Eventually. I'll move to Brussels, too. Anything."

"Hold off on that, Georg. Farrell needs you here." Magdalena thought for a moment. "You do realize I'll be back in Grantville at least twice a week, don't you?"

Georg looked hopeful. "We could maybe work something out, yes?"

"Yes. I imagine we could."

Merton looked at the maintenance checklist and flipped a switch to check the battery power. It was well into the green. *That's done. It's time to get some shuteye.* It was Merton's night in Brussels this week. He had spent one night a week here for the last month and never seen Brussels. Walking tours weren't his favorite type of entertainment. In fact, he wasn't looking forward to the walk to the Airport Inn. He turned in his chair and grabbed his walker.

Merton was hobbling back to the door of the Jupiter 3 when the guests arrived. There was Herr Quackenboss, a member of the new board of Directors of RDA and several other people, craftsmen of various sorts by their dress. "What can I do for you, sir?" Merton had met Herr Quackenboss just once. Several of the German board members had sold out and resigned when King Fernando bought the company. They had been replaced by members of Fernando's court and wealthy merchants from Brussels and Amsterdam. Herr Quackenboss was both a member of the court and a wealthy merchant from Brussels. But that didn't explain what he was doing bringing a bunch of people here in—well, not quite the middle of the night, but the sun had set.

"Ah, Herr Schmidt," Herr Quackenboss said, with what appeared to Merton to be false good cheer. Merton was sensitized to false good cheer as people saw his legs. But Herr Quackenboss had already seen them and had been mostly curious about how they were made. "Why are you still aboard?"

"Aircraft checkout." Merton tapped one of his fiberglass legs.

"It takes me a little longer to get it done. Speaking of which, what brings you..." Merton looked at the, yep, craftsmen, who had followed Herr Quackenboss onboard. "...and your friends out at this time of the evening?"

Quackenboss hedged a bit and blustered a bit, but eventually came clean. They were there to examine the airplane. In detail. Take measurements. Make drawings. Learn as much as they could about how to build it.

"Sir, you and your guests are free to take your measurements. You're on the board, after all. But I am going to have to be here. It's a safety matter. I have no desire whatsoever to fall out of the sky because something vital got broken." He motioned Quackenboss over, then whispered, "You know I'll have to report this, sir."

"I have His Majesty's approval." That was said rather huffily, so Merton figured he probably did. Otherwise he would probably have offered Merton a bribe. As it was, Merton figured that these guys were to be the guiding lights of the Royal Dutch Air Force, or whatever they ended up calling it. Not everyone in the Netherlands was thrilled with the idea of King Fernando spending so much money on airplanes and they were especially upset about his spending that money in the USE, not with good Dutch merchants and craftsmen. His Majesty ought to be spending his money on stuff they could make, like ships. Or at the very least give them a chance to make airplanes.

Georg wasn't going to be happy about this development. Neither was Maggy.

"Well, what the hell did you expect me to do?" Merton tilted his head up to look Georg in the eye. That was one of the most irritating things about his lack of legs. It made it really hard to stare someone down. "It's their plane, bought and paid for."

"But it's my, our, design. Royal Dutch Airlines didn't buy that."

"I'm not altogether sure of that, Georg," Farrell said.

"What? Show me in the contract where it said they could copy our design."

"No, Georg. I'm pretty sure that they are going to point to the contract and ask us to produce the clause that says they can't. Even worse, a clause that says that they can't let someone else look at it and copy it. After all, it probably won't be Royal Dutch Airlines that is making the Dutch knockoff Jupiters; it will be some other Dutch company that is also in large part owned by the crown." Farrell shook his head. "I don't know if the USE and the Netherlands have any agreement on the protection of patents and even if they do most of the Monst—Jupiters aren't patentable. The wing shape is right out of Dad's aeronautics text; the ACLG is from an article in *Time* ... even if we did have to figure out how to make it work. Don't get me wrong, there is some really brilliant engineering that we probably could patent. At least, we could have up-time. But none of it is stuff they couldn't work around."

"Well, I guess that means the king in the Low Countries won't be offering us tons of money to set up shop in the Netherlands," Farrell's wife Mary said. "What about that Magdeburg site?"

"Magdeburg!" Georg protested. "RDA doesn't even have Magdeburg on its flight schedule. They say there is no reason to compete with the rail line. I'll never see Maggie in Magdeburg!"

Captain Fredric van Moris had been with His Majesty when he was still a cardinal. He had a hundred hours in the Jupiters. He had taken off five times and landed three. He had flown left seat with Magdalena van de Passe and Merton Smith. He was the most qualified pilot in the Dutch Air Force. Based on what Fredric considered to be not very good advice, His Majesty had decided that the pilots that had come over to RDA from TEA were not to be involved in the flight of the first aircraft built in the Netherlands.

The Sea Bird looked like the Jupiter 3. In fact, from a distance you would think it was a Jupiter 3 rigged for two engines instead of four. When you got closer you could see other differences. After some difficulties with the composites, they had switched doped canvas and wood. That made the body and wings lighter than a Jupiter's, but also weaker. It had two straight six engines—made in the Netherlands at great expense—which together produced a bit over six hundred horsepower, but weighed over fifteen hundred pounds. To compensate for the weight of the engines, they had made the body of the plane as light as they thought they could get away with. However, the Sea Bird was still heavy compared to a Jupiter.

Fredric van Moris knew that the Dutch designers' knowledge of aircraft design was imperfect but he didn't know how significant the deficiencies were. One of the things that none of the Dutch designers realized was just how strong a shaped composite could be. It was also designed without benefit of a clear understanding of the laws of aerodynamics. Especially the cubed square law. The difficulty came from the fact that in an airplane some things scale up along a line and other things scale up along curves. Reynolds Number calculations derived from a one-twelfth scale model will work just fine for the full-scale model. Lift calculations work on the square which is nice. But weight and wing stress calculations work on the cube and that's not nice. Not nice at all!

Captain van Moris looked at the plane with a little trepidation but mostly with pride and excitement. It looked good to him. Of course, he wasn't an aircraft designer. He was, truth be told, barely a pilot. The Jupiters were a fairly forgiving type of aircraft. And a hundred hours was little more than twice the minimum to get a private pilot's license up-time. He went through his preflight checks with extra care, climbed aboard and spent a few minutes checking each of his controls. Finally, he started the engines, then inflated the bag and he was off. He sped along the lake as he neared takeoff velocity. Something felt different . . . the wings were flexing more than they should and the aircraft felt more like it was taking off overloaded. By now, the Jupiter would be telling him that it was ready to fly. But not this bird. It was still married to the lake. When the airspeed indicator reached the indicated speed, he pulled back on the stick and it tried. He could feel it reaching for the sky and not quite grasping it. He gave it more throttle and at sixty mph indicated airspeed, the Sea Bird crawled into the sky. Captain van Moris managed to get the aircraft almost thirty feet into the air, constantly just on the edge of a stall . . . and that's when the wings came off. The plane fell thirty feet onto the air cushion landing gear which compressed, taking some of the impact, then popped like a balloon.

Captain van Moris got out of the plane—barely. And swam to shore. He was very lucky. If the wings hadn't come off when they did, he would have hit the trees on the edge of the lake.

Farrell Smith looked at the fancy embossed letter with the royal seal. Then looked at his son.

Merton nodded. "They had a blow-up, Dad. Luckily Freddy van Moris wasn't killed. But His Majesty wasn't happy."

"What happened?"

"The wings came off at maybe thirty feet H over G. That's what Freddy van Moris said. Apparently they were flapping when he left the water. I didn't see it; the first I heard about it was when they called us in for the after-crash report. Anyway, it was a darn good thing Freddy's a good swimmer or there'd be another name on the tower out at Grantville Airport."

There were now forty-six names on the tower wall, each one for a person who had died in the pursuit of aviation since the Belle had flown in 1633. Thirty-seven of them had little silver wings painted beside to signify people who had died in crashes. People who had built planes that they thought would fly then tried to fly them. Apparently Freddy van Moris had come close to being number forty-seven. "Why?" Farrell asked. "Why did the wings come off?"

"Do I look like Georg or Grandpa? It was wood and canvas. I know that much. And Freddy said it looked very much like the J3. Before it came apart anyway."

That was enough to tell Farrell Smith what had probably happened. "Wood and canvas isn't the same as a composite. In a composite the load is spread pretty evenly. It stresses differently and needs fewer supports. Damn it, Merton, they could have asked us. We would have told them."

Merton nodded again with a half shrug. "It's the books. They tell you enough, enough so that you get high enough to kill you. No one is stacking eight wings on a bicycle and looking silly in a movie, like they did in our timeline. Instead they're building delta wings powered by black powder rockets and auguring in at two hundred MPH. Stuff that makes sense and seems like it'll work if you've read the books and only read the books."

"Where did they get the engines?" Farrell asked, trying to bring the discussion back to the Dutch accident.

"They built them themselves," Merton told him. "Big mothers. Bronze and crucible steel. I never saw them bright and shiny, just the one that they managed to fish out of the lake. That plane had to cost a fortune to build. The engines were, in essence, handmade by master craftsmen. Probably ten thousand man hours in each engine." Merton was shaking his head over it and Farrell understood why. To hand-make an engine was more than anyone could afford to do very often. Even kings could only do it occasionally as a proof of concept or proof of wealth, but it could be done and it didn't require the tiny industrial base that existed so far. What it did require was pot loads of money.

Farrell nodded and looked back at the letter. With the success of the Monster, orders had poured in to M&S Aviation. Unfortunately, planes had not poured out. The issue for M&S was the same as the issue for all the other aircraft manufacturers: engines or at least affordable engines. The tiny little wedge in the door that leads to the industrial revolution was producing goods, but not enough to go around. There weren't enough factory-made engines, not for airplanes and not for anything else either.

The Gustavs under government contract had first priority, especially in terms of up-time engines. The new down-time-built radial engines were just beginning to appear and were pretty darned expensive being partly handmade themselves. M&S was second in line, after the government, for those because of its involvement in their development. But that didn't mean that they got all the engines that the government didn't want. Radials were, in theory, being built by two companies in the USE, which were in turn getting several of their parts from other companies. Swartz Aviation was where M&S was getting their radials. The company had produced just eight engines so far. Four of the eight had gone to the air force; the other four had put the J3 into the air. Farrell didn't really trust them. They were prone to breakdowns, which was not a good thing in an aircraft engine. The J4 had had its design tweaked to suit the new radials after M&S's experience with the J3. So, once they got another set of four engines, they had the airframe ready for them.

"What's DKL saying?" Merton asked.

"More delays." DKL Power Systems had followed closely in Swartz Aviation's footsteps and had just finished its test engine. They insisted that they had most of the parts for the next half-dozen. But there were delays as people constantly underestimated the stresses that internal combustion put on engines. DKL had gone with a heavier nine-cylinder design that was supposed to deliver a bit over two hundred horsepower. Not that it mattered to M&S, because when Farrell had approached them he was informed that it would be six months at least before DKL Power Systems could start on new orders. Farrell didn't know which companies were ordering the new engines, but aside from the Kitts, the Kellys and the USE Air Force, there were three other aircraft manufacturers still trading on the Grantville exchange: one in Essen, one outside of Magdeburg and one in Brandenburg of all places. And that didn't count the privately-held companies or the government-backed programs in nations all over Europe. There had been a lot more right after the Belle flew, but most of them had folded since, finding the making of airplanes beyond their capability and all too often finding it out the hard way.

"What about Lufen?" Merton asked.

"No, absolutely not. I am not putting a jet engine near a composite wing. Even if they ever do get it to work without burning up." Lufen Jet Works was trying to build a jet engine using ceramics to handle the heat. They were using a small, low-horsepower four-cylinder engine to run fan compressors and force air into a combustion chamber. The jets would—if it ever worked—deliver thrust only, but—again, if it worked—it would let a twenty-five-horsepower engine produce thrust equivalent to around two hundred horsepower, because all the twenty-five-horsepower engine would actually be doing was providing air to the jet. From what Farrell had heard, it would be an amazing fuel hog, but would be able to use just about any liquid fuel in the main combustion chamber. There were quite a few groups like that, trying different things to see what would work. The combination of the information in the State Library and lots of bright people doing lots of different experiments was producing some weird results and an incredible number of expensive and sometimes fatal failures.

In any case, with the amount of work they had to do and the number of mostly finished aircraft components that were sitting waiting for engines and final assembly meant that M&S had simply run out of room. They had needed a new shop for months and since it looked like RDA was planning to go its own way, M&S was in final negotiations for a piece of land near Magdeburg. Georg was up there now looking over the shop. He was going to run the Magdeburg plant so that Farrell could stay in Grantville. Now this. The king in the Low Countries was offering to buy controlling interest in M&S Aviation for a fairly tidy sum—with the agreement that they move their main manufacturing facility to Brussels.

"So after stealing our designs didn't work, they want to buy us out?"

Merton just shrugged again.

Farrell wasn't surprised, really. Anyone that had something that might fly had three copycats by the end of the week and M&S had the Mercury, only a couple of which had been built and one had suffered a fatal crash. And the Saturn, one of which had been built and was flying. And finally the Jupiter, three in actual operation and another when they got the engines from Swartz Aviation. Of course, they had copycats. Hell, they probably had copycats in every major country in Europe, almost all of which were waiting on engines and most of which would crash within minutes of their first takeoff if they ever got them. "Well, what do you think? You own twenty-five thousand shares of the company."

"Get real, Dad. M and S Aviation is your deal. The shares you gave us when you and Georg started it . . . it was nice and all, but it's your baby."

Georg stared at the ribbons and seal. "King Fernando wants to buy us now, yes?"

"So I'm told," Magdalena said. "And this whole thing of landing in Grantville, then taking the train to Magdeburg is just silly. I'm going to mention that when I get back. Again." Once you were a flyer, trains were just plain slow.

"I only just got this operation up and moving, Maggie."

"You'd like Brussels," Magdalena coaxed. The more she thought about marrying Georg, the more she wanted to. Besides, the apartment in Brussels was just plain lonesome.

"Farrell doesn't want to leave Grantville."

"Have you asked?"

Nearly every up-time face in Cora's new outdoor eating area turned away from Mary. Which just really ticked her off.

"Well, the king is offering top dollar," she said loudly. "But that's not the reason we're considering it. We're mostly considering it because this place is a backwoods dive where everybody knows your business and isn't afraid to start bossing you around. For your own good, of course."

After weeks and weeks of remarks, Mary was at the end of her patience. She and Farrell had decided to vote against the sale. Right up to the moment she'd read an article in the *Grantville Times* that out-and-out accused Farrell and Georg of treason.

Flo Richards chuckled. "You go, girl."

"Easy for you to say, Flo. They're not accusing you of treason— *which it isn't!*"

The loudness of the last three words made Flo flinch. "I know that. And you never know. J. D. and I may go somewhere. You can't really raise that many sheep in these dratted hills. And I had a lot of fun on the trip to Amsterdam, you know."

"I'm stifled," Mary said. "This town is stifling. And it's getting worse, with all this publicity."

"It'll blow over. Nobody was fool enough to take up that bill and try to get it passed. Besides, you wouldn't have had to sell the company, anyway, if it did pass. Just dissolve it, then move as a private person." Flo snorted. "I can't believe some of those idiot politicians."

Cora bustled up with their coffee, including one for herself. "You know, Mary, I think you're right. There are too many people who are only too willing to tell a person what they ought to do these days." She raised her voice. "I'm thinking about selling out and moving to Bamberg myself. Get away from all these old fogies."

Then she winked at Mary and Flo. "See how they like that one."

"What's the matter, Mary?" Farrell had been wondering that for weeks. Mary had gotten quieter and quieter since her mother's death from flu in January.

"Grantville's just not the same anymore." Mary sighed. "Mom's gone. So many people have moved away. Judy and John are talking about moving down to Bamberg now that the capitol is there. Merton's moved to Brussels and we only see him twice a month or so. I guess I'm just...I don't know...stale. Just tired and stale and I'd like a change."

Farrell kind of felt that there had been plenty of change in the last five years, but in another way he did understand. It was sort of like empty nest syndrome, only different. He and Mary weren't exactly retirement age—and God knew there wasn't any kind of retirement system—but they'd often talked about what they'd do once they did retire. Most of that talk had been about getting out of Grantville, going someplace warm in the winter and cooler in the summer. Traveling in Europe, Canada and Mexico.

"Well, I think the 'buy an RV' idea has pretty much bitten the dust," Farrell said. "But we could try Magdeburg. Or Bamberg, if you want to be near Judy."

"I want something for us, babe," Mary said. "We always talked about what we'd do for us, once all the responsibilities were taken care of. About what we'd do when we weren't stifled anymore."

"Well, we did get that once-in-a-lifetime trip to Europe we talked about."

Mary grinned. "Indeed we did. Why don't we do something with it? We haven't seen London yet. We always wanted to go there. And Athens. Rome. Naples. And, well, everywhere."

"Ah..."

"Yes, dear. I know. We hadn't planned on it being the year 1636. But we do have planes now. It's just a matter of getting enough of them. Before you know it, there will be tourist traps all along the Med, just like back up-time."

Her husband gave her the "you're being silly" look. Mary knew perfectly well that "before you know it" in this case meant fifteen or twenty years.

"Well, maybe not tourist traps like we had up-time. On the other hand if you're one of the owners of Boeing... Which we are—" That look again. "—close enough. Magdeburg is a start, at any rate. We ought to be able to take a hop to Brussels and visit Merton. We're stockholders, after all. I can't see how RDA won't add a route to Magdeburg from Brussels, sooner or later. It's Gustav's headquarters. The pilots have to come pick up the planes, and dropping them off in Grantville to take the train is, well, silly, seems to me. And I bet they'll put Bamberg on a route, sometime. All those government functions, you know."

"We can get tickets if we want them," Farrell conceded. "Even do a charter if they don't open a route soon enough to suit us."

"Georg is going to run the Brussels plant. King Fernando made him an offer he couldn't refuse."

"Then it's doubly important for you to visit Brussels often. You know how Georg is. He'll be trying to handle the paperwork while covered in fiberglass."

Milton's Choice

Mark Huston

> The power of Kings and Magistrates is nothing else, but what is only derivative, transferred and committed to them in trust from the People, to the Common good of them all, in whom the power yet remains fundamentally, and cannot be taken from them, without a violation of their natural birthright.
>
> —John Milton

"I demand to be let out of here. There is no reason for you to keep me in this prison! I demand—" Milton's loud protestation was cut short. He didn't see the guard's fist streaking toward him in the half-light of the prison cell. The blow caught him in the side of the face, squarely on his cheek. The guard laughed as Milton fell back into the cell, stunned.

He lay sprawled half aware and bleeding on the floor. The floor smelled like a sewer, and was slippery under the rancid straw. It was the smell, combined with the surprise and the pain that nearly caused him to pass out. He was brought back to his senses by a kick in the ribs.

"Wake up, John Milton! Ye be here by royal order!" Milton half rolled on his side as the guard was flexing his fingers inside his weighted leather glove. The guard smiled down at him "Any more questions?"

Milton blinked a couple of times, and tried to stand. "On what grounds am I being held? Why am I here? Why was I grabbed on the road, minding my own business, and trussed off to this godforsaken Gatehouse Prison?" He used the wall as his support until he was standing, leaning against the back wall of the cell while he fought the dizziness from the blow.

The guard smiled at him again. "Why indeed? Why was ye caught makin' your way t' Kent, t' the sea? Per'aps to 'scape t' the continent? Carryin' your traitorous messages back to your masters? And don't disparage me prison. Gatehouse Prison ha' seen many a fine lord, finer than you. We not be as fancy as the Tower, but we be close to Whitehall."

Struggling to regain his equilibrium, Milton spoke quietly. "I have done nothing since I left Cambridge except study. This is ridiculous. You are an imbecile." He could no longer contain his temper, and he began to shout again. "Will someone with the ability to reason at a level above that of a dog come here soon to relieve you? You are tedious. Now be off and bring me some answers."

The guard swept Milton's feet out from under him, and he landed hard on the stone floor, crying out in pain and surprise. "Fer someone who' s'posed t' be so bloody smart, ye are one slow learner, ain't ye?"

"Why in the name of all that is holy are you doing this to me? By what right—" His words were cut off by another boot to the ribs. This time there was an audible *crack* as boot broke bone. Milton shrieked, clutched his right side, and rolled in the filth towards the wall, curling into a ball, whimpering.

"Ye got no such thing as a 'right,' you traitorous bastard. And soon ye will join the other 'fine lords' we have sent to the block already." Milton winced as he saw the guard pull his leg back to deliver another kick, when a command was shouted from the corridor. John risked a small turn of his head.

"Wilson! Hold! Wha' are you doing?"

The guard's head snapped around, and he smiled. "Jus' teachin' 'im some rules. Manners as it were, sir. That's all."

"They want to talk to this one." A squat man who looked like a bulldog, with a large square jaw and jowls to match, lumbered into the cell. "I 'ave 'eard the minister his own self is comin' down to talk to this one. So go a bit easy, Wilson. We want 'im a bit presentable, now don't we?"

"The minist'r?"

"Aye."

Wilson turned to the whimpering form on the ground. "I guess you is special, Mr. John Milton. And you're no' even a lordship like some of the others." Wilson knelt down to whisper. "I got nothi' fer traitorous bastards like ye. Just as soon see their heads roll. So be quiet, and behave yerself, so I don't have to teach ye any more manners. Do ye understand me?"

Milton managed a small nod.

"That's better." The guard straightened, and mockingly extended his right hand, and spoke a bit louder. "I don' think we have been properly introduced. Me name is John Wilson, and I be a guard in this part o' Gatehouse Prison. I will be expectin' proper payment from ye by tomorrow. Prisoners are expected to pay for their upkeep and treatment 'ere. It's clear to me that you never been in this sort of a situation before, so I am 'splaining it to ye all special and quiet like." Wilson looked at his still extended hand, then glanced at his supervisor with a half smile. "Not very p'lite. Didn't even shake me 'and."

The bulldog supervisor laughed. "Roll over and pay attention. This is simple. Who in London can pay for your keep 'ere? Give us an address where someone lives who can pay for you. Otherwise the conditions go downhill. D'ye understand, John Milton? This is one of our best cells." The men grinned at each other.

Wincing in pain, Milton gasped, "I understand. Bread Street. My father is a scrivener in Bread Street. He can pay." He gritted his teeth against the pain.

"Thank ye, sir. I will send me son round on the morrow."

"I had silver." Milton tried to talk without inhaling or exhaling.

The bulldog face changed, and added the smile of an insincere shark. "I'm sure you did. But you see, by the time you arrived here, there was none to be found. The soldiers that captured you in Kent must have taken some—for expenses, you understand. And then there was the wagon to bring ye here, and then the bridge tolls, hay for the horses—it adds up quickly, and there is never any left for us when the prisoner arrives. Sad, but it always seems t' work out that way."

"But don't worry," Wilson said. "Ye probably won't be 'ere long. None of the others were 'ere long...before they was beheaded." Wilson and the shark-toothed bulldog laughed loudly, and clanged the door shut behind them.

✧   ✧   ✧

"John, can you hear me?"

John Milton was stirred from a light sleep by his father's voice, and tried to inhale. The pain in his right side wrenched him awake, and he moaned. He felt hands turning him and gritted his teeth against the pain.

"What have they done to you, John?"

John gasped. The pain of simply trying to breathe was tremendous.

"Father, what have they done to him?" John recognized the voice of his younger brother Christopher, who had recently begun studies for the bar. "Is he injured?"

"John, can you hear me? Son, what did they do to you? Tell me."

"Kicked . . . Ribs . . . ohhhh . . ." His hands clutched his side.

"Dammit. Christopher, he has broken ribs. We must get him vertical. He'll die of congestion of the chest if he's allowed to lie here like this. Help me get him up."

Christopher and the senior Milton picked up John as gently as possible, pushed insect ridden straw into another corner, and used it to prop him in a sitting position. Both visitors retched at the smell of the floor.

"You have got to stay vertical, John. Otherwise you might catch a disease of the lungs and die. Do you understand me? You must sit upright!"

John managed a slight nod, but a wave of nausea came over him. He moaned slightly.

"Bastards!" Christopher exclaimed. "You've done nothing to deserve this. No crime has been committed. This is injustice at the highest level, total disregard of the law—"

"Shush! None of that here. Be quiet, boy. There is a time and a place for such talk. And this is neither. We're here for your brother. No sense in all of us being locked up. Hush, or return home."

Christopher glanced over his shoulder at the closed door of the cell, looking for signs of an eavesdropping guard. "I'm sorry, Father. I shouldn't let my feelings get in the way of our immediate needs."

The elder Milton nodded grimly. "And those needs are great, if we are to save your brother's life. The beatings should stop now we have paid the guards, but what remains? That concerns me, Christopher."

John finally produced a rasping voice. "Will somebody please tell me what the *fuck* is going on? Wh—" He stopped and licked his lips. "Why am I here?"

"Give him some brandy, Christopher. Then some bread," his father said.

Christopher nodded and began digging into the knapsack he was carrying, brushing a semi-clean area on the floor where he could sit in front of his brother. His father lowered his voice. "You got our letter in time at the cottage in Hammersmith, I assume?"

Milton nodded.

"We understand they caught you in Kent?"

Milton nodded again. Christopher gave him some brandy to drink, and he sipped it carefully so as not to cough.

His father sighed. "We have learned some things since that time. This all goes back to that accursed Grantville, landed in the Germanies. Apparently the king, in that history, was beheaded. The whole thing was there in the books of the town. There were lists of who was on what side in the revolution—who was a royalist, and who was not. Most of what would have occurred would have happened in a few years. So, in truth, nobody has done anything yet. Except the king, who is having nearly everyone on that list brought in for questioning. And anyone who signed his death warrant is put to death."

Christopher jumped in, fuming. "Have you heard of John Bradshaw? He was a fine legal mind, and mayor of Congleton in Cheshire. The rumors say that he was taken from his home and executed in front of his young wife. No trial, no hearing, just summary execution. Outrageous."

Father continued. "He was apparently the Chief Justice at the trial where they found Charles guilty." He paused and shook his head. "To kill a man in front of his family for something he has not done, nor likely will ever do! It makes me ill to think of it. Once we heard of what was going on, we were afraid—everyone was afraid, but we did not appear on any lists, at least so far."

John blinked at them in disbelief, and then became thoughtful. "Am I on that list? Is that why I am here?"

"Thank God, no."

Milton steeled himself to speak, softly. "I am a student. A poet. That is what I do. There is no secret to that." He paused, and tested a deeper breath, and winced. "You're right, Father, it's better if I am upright."

"John, you have always been a proud and strong willed young man. Brilliant, yes. But contrary. You know what happened at Cambridge. You were nearly thrown out—"

"That man was an imbecile." Milton's outburst sent him into a painful cough. When his coughing stopped, Christopher offered him more brandy, and a small chunk of bread. John nodded gratefully.

"Nonetheless," his father continued, "you jeopardized your academic career because of pride and stubbornness. You are a man of principle, John, but not always the greatest of judgment. When we heard that you were involved with this government that killed Charles, we believed it. It sounds like something you would do, quite frankly. With so many legal minds being taken—did you ever meet Oliver Cromwell? He was the leader of the rebellion. He is in the Tower, awaiting what fate I do not know. Others have disappeared. And many of them are young. Thomas Grey, son of the earl of Stamford, only eleven years old, was dragged away from his mother by soldiers. We do not know what has happened to him. A ship's chandler by the name of Okey here in London . . . simply disappeared. We think he's dead. There are many others. Sir John Danvers, MP for Oxford. Did you know John Hutchinson at Cambridge? Many others. We just don't know."

Christopher said, "I was able to get some word out to you because I heard of it—*you*—at Lincoln's Inn. We occasionally handle paperwork for Whitehall, and thank God for serendipity. I tell you John, this was a grave mistake on the part of the king. To kill men who have done nothing, and up to now were either innocent children or loyal subjects . . . I tell you it has set the courts on their collective heads. And several of the men taken were practicing before the bar, or were sons of Lords, or were members of Parliament—if it ever meets again. 'Tis tyranny, simple and pure. I have never seen so many learned and respectable men so angry. It's infuriating to anyone with a sense of justice. I truly do not know what will come of this."

"But what of me," John whispered. "Where do I fit into this insanity?"

His father looked worried. "We truly do not know, John. Apparently you were known for your poetry in the future world. That is comforting, I am sure. But why would a poet be the object of this sort of persecution? We are still hoping to find out. Perhaps the Americans in the Tower would help us, if we can speak to them somehow. You must take care until we understand what is happening. We will do our best to discover why, and get you out of this. There are many who will help us."

"What should I do?"

"Stay alive, John Milton. Stay alive until we can do something."

He had no Plato, no Homer, no quill, ink or paper. It was the boredom, killing him a little each day. Once a week, his father or brother were allowed to visit, briefly. This week, it was his brother.

"I'm sorry, John. They found them—"

"My mind has been honed sharp for the last five years! To be imprisoned here, held here with no stimuli, no challenge worthy of my mind, is—is maddening! I feel as if I am falling into atrophy. Do you understand, Chris? Atrophy! I can feel my brains and heart and soul shriveling like dried fruit. I may as well be dead."

They were sitting next to each other in the small cell, on a recently acquired pallet for a bed. Christopher looked down at the floor, embarrassed. "I was too ambitious, and they found the papers on me, John. I was trying to bring you more than last time. I—I am sorry, John. Sorry."

John stood and began pacing around the small cell, frustrated. "I have been here nearly two months with not much news, and even less to read. I must have stimulation, Chris, or I shall go mad, surely as I stand here. Stark-raving-foaming-at-the-mouth mad." He quieted and turned to his brother. "I tell you, I have never felt so dark a time such as these. I want to write about it. Yet I am *unable* to write about it. That makes things darker still."

Christopher looked up, nodding in agreement. "I do not have your mind, brother. I cannot profess to know what it is like for you. Some can survive this sort of thing better than others." He smiled, with a bit of mischief in his eyes. "But. I have brought you something. Something that is quite legal." He opened a cloth and pulled several small pieces of chalk from the folds. "You cannot have pen and paper, but there was no order against chalk. You have the walls and floors to write upon. It is an advantage to have a lawyer in the family now and again. Parsing rules is our specialty."

John could feel himself stepping back from the abyss, where his mind had dwelled of late. He could not hold back the tears.

✧   ✧   ✧

"Norton. Sir Gregory Norton. Looks as if we are to be cell mates for a while. Pleased to meet you. And you are?" The tall gangly man with an affable face extended his hand.

"John Milton." John shook hands, standing up from his pallet, still wincing a little.

"Quite a nice cell, I suppose. Nicer than where I was at the Tower. Odd decorations though. Are these your writings all about?" Sir Gregory squinted at the tiny writing, in Latin and Greek, on the walls. One wall was completely covered, each stone a page.

"It is my way of remaining sane. At least as sane as one can be in this place."

Sir Gregory coughed a little. "I had no such problems, Milton. I'm a patient man by nature. Not too bad a thing for a man to bear, if you are strong. How long have you been here?"

"Two months, Sir Gregory."

"What have you heard?"

John eyed Sir Gregory carefully. His father's voice sounded in his mind. *Trust no one.* "Almost nothing."

"Damn. I was hoping you knew something. I've been locked away and not able to hear any word from the outside. I do know there are all sorts of men missing from across the country, and it has something to do with some plot against the king. Quite extraordinary. I was taken prisoner on the first day, and have been in the Tower since. Then they moved me here . . . Quite disconcerting. I know nothing of my family. Nothing of what is happening. Do you know why I have been moved here? Placed with you?"

"No idea." John regarded the man. He had a subtle Irish lilt to his speech, and what seemed to be a genuinely sunny disposition, despite his recent hardships.

"Not much of a talker, are you, Milton? Please excuse, I have been talking to myself for almost two months, and I am quite ready to talk to someone who will return my conversation. Talking to one's self becomes rather predictable after a while."

John looked at the man with a small smile, hiding his suspicions. "You don't appear to have been beaten, Sir Gregory." John turned his face so Sir Gregory could see the scar, cut into the side of his face the first day at Gatehouse.

Gregory looked startled. "I say, sir. That looks nasty. They did that to you in here?"

"That's not the half of it. Three broken ribs too. Fortunately, my family is allowed to visit."

Sir Gregory stepped closer, and looked at his face in the only light that came into the room, through a small slit near the stone ceiling. "Oh, my."

"The guard Wilson did it. I have since learned he welcomes nearly everyone like that, especially if the new guest has money. You may want to be ready."

"Certainly that would not apply to me. I'm a baronet of Nova Scotia. I can't imagine a man like *that* treating a man like *me* in that manner. I was well liked at court before this idiocy occurred. I think it is a test of my loyalty, an obscene joke of some sort."

For the entire world, Sir Gregory seemed sincere. Not too bright, true, but sincere. Milton's narrowed his eyes. "Are you aware that Nova Scotia, or New Scotland as some call it, has been given to the French?"

Sir Gregory's eyebrows knitted into a single bundle on his forehead for a moment, as if in deep thought. The eyebrows then went up to the top of his forehead, and he started laughing. "That is a good one, Milton. Very funny. You had me going for a moment. Ha!"

"Very well, Sir Gregory." Milton sat on his pallet. "There's some clean straw. It's changed every other day for an outrageous sum, but does keep the lice down a bit. Sleep on it for tonight. You'll need to make some arrangements soon, for your own comforts."

"Very good of you, Milton. Very good. Thank you."

"You are welcome, Sir Gregory."

John watched this new man. Was he here to spy on him for some reason? John had never seen him before. The man seemed so unconcerned. So innocent. And not the sharpest quill on the table. John shrugged, then lay back. He would watch the man carefully, listen carefully, and tell him as little as possible. He didn't want to let his captors know of the effort being quietly put forth by the London legal community in the investigation of what was now called Charles' Purge.

The next morning they were awakened before sunrise by Wilson and his bulldog supervisor, along with another man and a priest. They came into the room, motioned for Sir Gregory to come with them.

Wilson stayed behind and grinned. "'Tis his turn."

John was puzzled. "Turn for what?"

Wilson drew his finger across his throat and made a slicing sound. "Off with his 'ead. And you're the guest of 'onor. Come along."

He grabbed John's arm and steered him down a narrow corridor that opened onto an enclosed courtyard. There was just enough light to see in the gray predawn. The guards and the bulldog supervisor tied Sir Gregory's hands behind his back, and were leading him to the chopping block that stood in the corner of the yard. Sir Gregory had just started to figure out what was going to happen, and he began to struggle.

"This is ridiculous. There must be some kind of mistake. I am Sir Gregory Norton. You can't do this. There has been no trial. Is this a test of my loyalty? Is that it? Some kind of a test? Certainly there can be no doubt? I have done nothing. Nothing!"

The priest began his low prayer, and another two guards came to hold Sir Gregory, and force his head to the block.

"I don't understand! Why are you doing this? *Why?*" He began to sob hysterically. "Please tell me why . . . please?"

The executioner came from behind a door in the courtyard, tugging at his black hood, and carrying his axe. As he drew closer, Sir Gregory began to scream. "*No! This is not happening! No-no-no-no!*" The executioner knelt in front of the priest for a moment, and received a blessing. He then rose, and knelt on one knee before Sir Gregory. Gregory stopped sobbing, as the executioner quietly spoke to him. Milton could barely hear the executioner, who was a skinny and wiry man.

". . . Keep still, sir. This is inevitable 'tis, sir. You don't wa' me t'miss and 'ave to take two or three swings, now do you? Let's jus' do this quick and get it o'er wit. Ye needs t'be brave now, sir . . ."

The calm speech of the black-hooded man seemed to quiet Sir Gregory. The executioner swiftly stood, then stepped back to swing. As the heavy ax came down, Gregory flinched with surprising strength against the men holding him, and the axe hit the top of his head, glancing off and taking a lot of scalp with it. Milton could see the gleaming white of his skull. Gregory fell back on the block, stunned, and the executioner swung again. That swing was rushed, and only half of the neck was severed. Sir Gregory gave a gurgling shriek. The executioner took his time with the last swing, ignoring the pitiful sounds of Gregory, and chopped the head off clean. It rolled to the ground and toward Milton. When it stopped, Milton saw the eyes flick back and forth and the jaw seemed to be gasping for breath. Then it was still.

"You must excuse me for being so late. I have been extraordinarily busy these past months, and I have not had the time to visit you as I hoped. I trust your accommodations are satisfactory?" Thomas Wentworth, the earl of Stafford, was smooth, professional, mature and polite as he spoke.

John smiled coolly. "We got off to a rather poor start, but things have improved."

"Good." Wentworth stood with his back to the door, and Milton stood in the corner. Wentworth had a small book under his arm. "It is odd, but I thought you would be older. I know when you were born, of course. After reading so much of your work I just assumed I would be talking to an older man. You are quite famous, you know, in the future. We found out a lot about you, what you wrote, your biographies, analysis of your work, criticisms. Fascinating, really. There was more information on you than on many of the vastly more important people of our era." Wentworth let the last phrase hang in the air for a moment.

John ignored the jibe. "I've heard that's the case, although I have not been allowed any books or paper during my imprisonment."

Wentworth's eyes began to travel slowly around the walls of the cell, now nearly covered with chalk writings, and he smiled bemusedly. "I will be more specific in my orders next time. You came from a family of lawyers." He squinted at a couple of writings. "Nothing treasonous I assume."

"Of course not, milord." John tried to guess the man's motives. His several month imprisonment had given him time to think, to guess what it was that Wentworth was going to do. John had several ideas, and he discussed many with his father. But now, it looked like Wentworth was about to start putting him into play. It was time to discover the game.

"It is curious," said Wentworth, "one of the most famous poems ever written was written in this very prison, in the shadow of Westminster Abbey. And not by you, I might add. In that other future, when Cromwell became a king in everything but the name, many royalists were imprisoned. One who was imprisoned here wrote a poem:

Stone walls do not a prison make,
Nor iron bars a cage;
Minds innocent and quiet take
That for an hermitage.

"Of course, the man who wrote that is only a lad of fourteen or fifteen today, so it is unlikely he will ever write such a verse. I wonder how that will make him feel? What do you think, John?"

"I cannot say. I have not yet read anything I have written from the future."

"I have brought something for you to read."

John desired the book under Wentworth's arm. His eyes flicked quickly to it, then back to Wentworth's smiling face. Wentworth's smile went a little larger. John was determined not to speak first.

"Aren't you curious about what I have?" Wentworth asked after a pause.

"It is something of mine, something a future version of myself wrote in that other world."

"Indeed, yes. It is something I personally picked out for you, although it is not poetry. Some of your poetry I have read, by the way. Overrated, I thought, but then I am not a poet. I am a practical man, above all else." Wentworth held up the book. "This is a political tract. This I understand." He looked briefly at the small book, changed his grip, and held it in front of him, looking at the binding. "It argues first against prelacy, and then a second article is written as an apologist tract, defending the regicidal government of Oliver Cromwell."

Milton waited patiently once again for Wentworth to continue.

Wentworth smiled again, and nodded. "Very well, John. Since you appear to show no curiosity, I will simply tell you what I wish. But first, I want you to understand the futility of the wrong course of action, so something terrible does not happen to you." Wentworth tucked the book back under his arm.

"Is that why you put Sir Gregory in my cell for a night? So I can see firsthand these consequences?"

Wentworth shrugged. "No sense in letting an inevitable execution go to waste without being instructive to someone. Otherwise, what has it done except to kill one man?"

"That man had done nothing!" Milton spat in anger. "Nothing!"

Wentworth casually held up the book in front of him. "Exactly,

John. He had done nothing. You have done much. These books precede you, and are overwhelming evidence of treason. And yet a man who had done nothing, as much as it grieves me personally, was put to death by order of the king. Where does that put you, John Milton?"

Milton's mouth went dry. Fear and anger surged in his gut. He fought to regain his emotions. He was surprised how quickly Wentworth had drawn out his fear. He swallowed and tried to remain calm.

"In a very precarious position, Milton. Very. Sir Gregory could do nothing for himself. He had no special influence or talents. The king's orders sealed his fate, and his best use was to serve as an example. You have done greater injury to the monarchy, yet are still alive. The difference between you and Sir Gregory is you are famous, and the 'greatest English poet,' at least according to the history books. Sir Gregory was a minor baronet, of a land that now belongs to France. That is not to say that there haven't been calls for your head. There have been several, including suggestions by the king. But so far, I have been able to convince others you can be more help to us alive on our side than dead and a martyr. Martyrs can sometimes become a problem."

"I have no side. I have done nothing. Not that it matters any longer."

"Well then. It is answered. You will refute these tracts. In exchange for that, you may escape the axe."

Astonished, John looked at Wentworth. The man was smiling as if he had just asked a simple favor, not served up a life or death decision.

John swallowed, trying to keep his voice calm. "I—I will consider it. I need reading and writing materials, obviously. I will need to do research."

Wentworth smiled broadly. "That can be arranged. As a matter of fact, I will allow you full access to materials, even your own writings."

"Why would you do that?"

Wentworth's face became polite, officious, and an unreadable mask. "Do not look a gift horse in the mouth, Milton." He extended his arm, showing the book.

John reached for it, and at midpoint hesitated, then drew back his hand. "Odd," he said. "Since I have been in this cell, and learned about the existence of my work in the future, I have been struggling with what I would do when faced with it. Would I read it? Or would I not? Would I reject the old works, and create new works? Fresh words, rooted in fresh soil? Pride is a very strong thing, Wentworth." He sighed. "I think I would have read them eventually. I would like to think not, that I could go on with my life and become a poet without comparing myself, but I am not so strong as that. I'm a poet, not a God."

He held out his hand and Wentworth gave him the book. John took it and let the hand holding the book fall to his side.

"'Tis better you get started now, rather than later," Wentworth said. "Now, if you will excuse me, I have another meeting." He turned and rapped on the door, and one of the guards opened it. He turned back. "Is a month sufficient time for you?"

John nodded.

Wentworth smiled. "Very well." He pointed to a few of the stones on the wall. "You may want to wipe some of those away before someone else visits here, John. You are in enough trouble as it is." He nodded a slight bow, and turned.

The cell door closed behind him, leaving John with the book in his hand. He stood for quite a long while, staring at the closed door. Eventually, he turned and sat on his pallet, opened the book, and began to read his own writings.

For three weeks, he paced back and forth in his cell, reading in his own voice words that were familiar, yet not. His "collected works." Some of the poems written in college he considered sophomoric. He remembered writing those but never imagined they would be reprinted three centuries later.

There was a selection of criticisms that accompanied his writings. When the embargo of paper and writing materials was lifted, he finally had access to the library his father and brother accumulated during his incarceration. The library of materials was impressive. The books from Grantville were meticulously reprinted, then smuggled with great risk to England. Milton's writings were outlawed, on pain of death, by order of the king.

He especially enjoyed his essay on censorship "Areopagitica" in light of the present situation.

John understood one thing almost immediately. He had succeeded. His life's goal was to become a . . . No. Not "become a," as in one of many, but to become *the* master of the English language. His desire was to write the most important works ever written, for the glory of God and England. For as long as he remembered, that was his goal. Lofty, to be sure. But he always believed. To meet that goal, he had sequestered himself away for as long as it took, cultivating his mind for the task ahead. From the looks of the publication dates, he had stayed in his father's house for several more years, doing little else except study. So much so that his eyesight began to fail. Study. Study more. Study until he was ready. Ready to write. To write the definitive poems of the English language.

He achieved his life's goals.

He looked at the thin book with the original two articles Wentworth gave him. He did not want to refute them. They were right. A tyrant is not a worthy leader, whether it be Charles or Cromwell. To recall a tyrant from power is a right all thinking men should have. He sat with a blank pad of paper in his lap, and tried to write a refutation to his articles. He tried sketching notes. He tried to outline his arguments. He tried writing them in Latin, then German, then French. He tried to argue them through in his head, but he always came back to the same conclusion. After some hours of this inaction, he tossed the book aside.

There was a rattling of keys in the hallway, and the door opened. Wentworth entered, smiling. John rose and bowed stiffly to his captor, who bowed in return. Wentworth's eyes flicked to the book lying on Milton's pallet, then quickly to the walls and their writings, and then back to Milton. "How is your refutation coming, John? Well, I hope."

"It's coming along. It is difficult to refute oneself, especially when one has been so eloquent. It presents unique challenges."

Wentworth nodded and began to look at the other books collected in the cell. "You have everything? All of your works?"

"Near as I can ascertain. I am frankly embarrassed by some of the early works. But there they are, for the entire world to read."

"One should be cautious about what one writes, John. You never know how it can be interpreted in the future." Wentworth pulled one of the books from a makeshift shelf and looked at it with a wry smile. "Or the past, for that matter." He slid the book back, and turned to Milton, looking him directly in the eyes. "Do you know why you are still alive, John?"

"To refute these two articles."

"More than that, John. I want you on my side. The king's side."

Milton's face remained impassive. "Go on."

"I would rather have your powers of persuasion and writing on my side, than have them wasted by removing your head. It would seem such a loss. A manageable loss, yes. But still a loss." Wentworth paused, his focus burning into Milton's brain.

Milton was quiet for a moment. He looked past Wentworth, staring at the lock on the cell door. He had come to the conclusion that he had achieved his goals. He had written the definitive poems of the English language. He had said all that needed to be said. He had soared to heights unimagined, even by him, with his poetry. What other works could he possibly write? What else could he do?

It was grossly unfair, he felt.

On the other hand, how many men know their work will live for hundreds of years? He sighed a long heavy sigh, and finally made his decision. His father would not be pleased, nor would his mother. But he was his own man, and understood the consequences. He took a deep breath, broke his stare at the lock, and looked Wentworth in the eye. "I—I cannot refute them. I will not refute them. My life is already written." He broke eye contact and laughed. "What a dilemma, eh, Wentworth? A real Calvinist dilemma. It will have theologians arguing for centuries as to what predestination really means." He stopped his laughing, and a smile lingered as he again looked at Wentworth. "I strove for great things, and I achieved them. That was my destiny. The proof is all around you, in these volumes. But what am I to do now? My destiny is achieved. Should I continue to live? Am I an anomaly of God? And you ask me to go against everything I have done, every word I have written, and every argument I made? You want me to ignore my life's work, as if nothing had happened? How can you—"

"You are a *coward*, Milton. More of a coward than I thought. Disgusting." Wentworth turned to the door and raised his hand to knock.

"What do you mean, a coward? I am not a—"

"But you are, Milton. Why did you think I gave you all of your works to read?"

John stopped for a moment to think. He shook his head as

if to clear a fog. "I thought it a mistake on your part; you were being over generous to me for some reason."

Wentworth's mask broke slightly and he looked exasperated. "You must give me more credit than that, Milton. Really."

"Then why?"

"If you just refuted this book..." He picked up the first volume of the arguments and waved. "...then what would have happened when you were allowed out into the world, and discovered the presence of all of this writing?" He swept his hand around the small cell. "It is simple, Milton. You would have failed me. Publicly." His tone changed from that of a chastising father, to a seemingly loving one. "I need *all* of you, John, not just part of you. I need a *tower* of literary strength." He shrugged and continued. "I am not that sort of a man. I am efficient, I serve my king well, I have my mind—a political mind, that keeps me in power. But I lack—what do the Americans call it? Ah, yes. P.R. I lack P.R., Public Relations. Good press."

John looked at the older man incredulously. "I will not do it. I cannot do it."

"You disappoint me with your cowardice."

"Cowardice! How can you call me a coward, I have just walked into certain death in an act of defiance. How can that be cowardice? You are a fool, old man."

"No, John Milton. You are fleeing from your future. You think you cannot match these works. So you choose to become a martyr. A coward. You cannot face what you might become. A mediocre poet."

There was a pause as John stared. Wentworth met his gaze with unfathomable confidence.

John's eyes wavered under the fierce stare, hesitated, and finally looked at the ground. "Get out," he whispered. "Just get out."

Wentworth changed to a softer tone. "You have three days until the deadline, John. Use your time wisely. You have a choice. What will it be? Cowardice?" Wentworth gestured with the original volume towards the bookcase. "Or will you be a Milton who achieves more than this one dreamed of?" He paused a moment then spoke softly. "The Puritans tend to look at the world in two colors, John, like their clothing. Black and white. Right and wrong. Our earthly existence is not that simple. The world has many shades and colors to it. Messy. Unpredictable. Marvelous."

He turned and rapped on the cell door, and then looked back. "I hope you do not choose to be a coward, John. It would sadden me." Wentworth tossed the volume onto the end of the pallet. The door creaked open, Wilson ushered Wentworth into the passage, and the cell door closed.

John slept little that night. He finally nodded off for what seemed like a short blink of the eyes, before waking again. Faint light streamed into the slit near the stone ceiling. He lay on his pallet and looked around, staring at the volumes on the makeshift bookcases. The work in the volumes was impressive. The poetry soaring. His pride at what he had done filled him with tears in the semi-darkness. The books around him told of a life, a life of unhappiness, pain, self satisfaction, insight, brilliant radical thought, deep religious beliefs, blindness, and marriages. What a life it was—*would* have been—*might* have been—*could* have been—*should* have been. He buried his face in his hands and mumbled to himself.

"The question is: can you do better, John?"

He rolled over and sat up, feet on the floor. The dry straw rustled beneath him. "This man was a giant," he whispered. "Do you really believe you could do better? Is it possible?" He spent the next hours praying, hoping that God would give him some sign. Point him in a direction.

But God was silent that morning, as He had been since the Ring of Fire. There was no message from Him, other than the miracle itself. The miracle that put a young man in this place, with this knowledge. He looked at the books again, and felt empty inside. Blank, like an unwritten story.

His eyes then fell on the book from Wentworth. Impulsively, he picked it up. He held it closed, between the palms of his hands, as if praying. He set it down on the floor in front of him, stood, and walked away from it, nervously. He turned toward it, took a step, and then stopped. "You are a man whose heart Anubis is weighing, only you are alive," he whispered. "What an amazing thing." He crouched down closer to the book. "Alive. There is the heart of the matter. Refute this, and you live. Live to become... someone." John continued to look at the book.

"Are you afraid of death, John Milton? Are you as afraid as poor Sir Gregory? Is that why you are even considering writing for Wentworth?" He slowly eased his hand forward, as if the thin book were a poisonous snake. He snatched it up suddenly. Standing, he opened it to he first page, started to read, and then quickly slammed it shut. "Damn that man!

"That John Milton will never live! No matter what I choose, he is dead!" He used the book in his hands to point to others in succession. "I am a different person than this one. Different from this one too. At each age, I wrote in a different tone, a different timbre, with a different mind."

He sat heavily onto the pallet. "The second question is: can you live with who you may become? Who you *will* become. *What* you will become." Bile rose in his throat. "Traitor." He coughed the word, and his throat burned. He swallowed and cursed silently to himself for a while.

He then stood and looked defiantly at the bookshelf, as if it were another man in the room. "Will I be a traitor to you? To me?" He paused as if listening to the answer from the shelves. "You cannot judge me, old man. Not now, not ever. Great works. Epic works. Can I do it again?"

He stopped, puzzled. "What was it that Wentworth said? Shades. Colors. A man who can see different colors?" He noticed he was still holding the book and had an impulse to throw the cheaply bound folio against the wall with all his might. He could almost see it splashing against the stone, pages flying.

But something held him back, stayed his arm.

His frustration flowed out of him like a river, leaving him dry.

He eased himself to a seat on his pallet.

Perhaps, one day he would be able to define what it was that stayed his hand. Define the moment when he decided he should live. Perhaps he could write a great work, discussing the nuances of human thought and rationality, fear of death. Yes. He would do that, some day, when he was older.

But for now, with his quill in hand, John Milton began to write.

To End the Evening

Bradley H. Sinor

Barnabas Marcoli gingerly ran his fingers up along the side of his head. Dried blood had already matted his hair into clumps, around a lump half the size of a small goose egg.

This was definitely not the way he had planned to end his first evening free in nearly two weeks.

Barnabas sagged back against the wall of the tavern and closed his eyes. From the far end of the room he could hear voices speaking a variety of languages—Italian, mixed in with a flurry of German and something that sounded vaguely eastern European—the sort of mixture that could be found in most places like this in Venice.

Someone pressed a mug into Barnabas's left hand; his fingers closed around the pewter surface automatically. He hesitated for a moment, and then downed the contents in two quick swallows. The wine was sharp and bitter, not the kind that he normally preferred to drink, but at that moment he didn't care.

"Easy lad; take a few deep breaths and see if you can get your wits about you before you tear into any more of this miserable excuse for wine."

Barnabas found himself looking at a tall, lanky man, several years his elder, dressed in plain, slightly worn clothing with a sword hanging at his waist. The stranger had a neatly trimmed mustache and dark hair. From his accent there was no doubt that he was French; his Italian was good but not quite good enough to hide his origins.

"Can I ask a stupid question?" said Barnabas. "What in the hell happened to me?"

"Oh, that." His companion chuckled. "Seems a pair of ruffians wanted to relieve you of your purse and weren't too picky in the way they did it. I'm glad I happened along at the right time."

Barnabas nodded. He remembered how he had been cutting through a narrow alley just east of the American embassy when a man had appeared in front of him and demanded money. Before Barnabas could react, someone else struck him from behind. Everything after that, until this stranger had guided him into the tavern, remained something of a blur.

"Damn," Barnabas muttered as he reached inside of his shirt but found nothing there.

"Would this be what you might be looking for?" A small burgundy coin bag slid across the table.

Barnabas let out a long sigh. It was true that there wasn't much money in it, apprentice metal workers weren't rich, but it was *his* money. Not to mention the fact that Barnabas knew full well that his cousins would not let him forget it if they discovered that he had been robbed.

"I thank you, sir. My name is Marcoli, Barnabas Marcoli. I owe you not only my life, but my dignity. I will pray for you at mass," he said. "And who might I name as my Good Samaritan?"

"D'Artagnan, Charles D'Artagnan."

Barnabas stared at the man for a time.

"I have the feeling that I know of you, sir." Something about that name was familiar, but the throbbing in Barnabas's head didn't help his concentration. He repeated it over and over in his mind; the memory was there, and close, infuriatingly close, but he could not bring it to the surface.

"I think not. I am new come to Venice. Before the little altercation with those ruffians, had you dined?" When Barnabas shook his head, D'Artagnan smiled and motioned for the tavern girl. "Good. Neither have I."

A few minutes later they had plates of chicken, cheese and bread set in front of them.

"I hope you ordered enough for three."

Barnabas turned with a start and found a small man dressed in brown sitting next to him. The newcomer looked like he could only be five foot one or two. He had an ordinary looking face with nothing on it that would have distinguished him from anyone else on the streets of Venice.

"I wondered when you were going to show up," said D'Artagnan.

The small man shrugged, motioning for the serving girl to bring him something to drink. "I was working. After all, we do have a reason for being here besides wenching and drinking."

"Pity," laughed D'Artagnan. "Barnabas, let me introduce you to my traveling companion, Aramis."

"Aramis? D'Artagnan?" Barnabas cocked his head at both men; suddenly feeling very pleased with himself. "So where are the other two?"

"Other two?" said D'Artagnan.

"Obviously, he's read the book," said the small man called Aramis, switching from Italian to English.

"Indeed I have," Barnabas responded, somewhat unsure of his English, but wanting to use it now, nonetheless. "*The Three Musketeers* was only one of several novels that Frank Stone, that young man my cousin Giovanna has been making eyes at, lent me. He said they would help me learn American faster. So are you really the one in the book?"

"I suppose I really should to get a copy of that book sometime," muttered D'Artagnan. "Yes, I am the one that book was about."

It occurred to Barnabas that there were several things that might be interesting to ask the Frenchman about concerning the events in that book, but the look on the man's face suggested that this might be a good time to let those questions lie.

"I obviously owe you my life, Monsieur D'Artagnan. If there is any way in which I can repay you, do not hesitate to say so. Had you not come along I suspect I would have ended up face down in the canal," Barnabas said.

"Think nothing of it," said D'Artagnan.

"Actually," said Aramis, a thin smile on his face, "I think that you can help us."

"I take it you have a plan?" D'Artagnan said in a whisper to Aramis.

In the time that D'Artagnan had known Aramis, he had learned that the small man had a sharp sense of strategy and planning, not to mention the ability to think on his feet. That skill alone had saved both of their lives on more than one occasion.

They spoke quietly because while their newly acquired Italian companion was most probably Catholic, they definitely did not know his political bent. So the fact that the two Frenchmen were in the service of Armand Jean du Plessis de Richelieu, Cardinal Richelieu, the first minister of France, was a piece of information best kept to themselves.

"It isn't a plan, exactly, just a way that young Marcoli can be of assistance," he said. "Most of it we will have to make up as we go along."

The two Frenchmen had been in Venice for just over a week. In that time D'Artagnan had begun to feel somewhat frustrated. He preferred direct action; give him a sword in his hand and an enemy to face, and that was the best of all possible worlds. Aramis, on the other hand, preferred to wait in the shadows unseen, until he was ready to act.

Three months before, D'Artagnan had been summoned, late one evening, to the Louvre by the cardinal. Once there he found himself waiting near the door, while at the far end of the gallery that served Richelieu as an office; the churchman spoke at length with a woman in dark colors who had a Spanish look about her. D'Artagnan presumed that, given the circumstances, she was another one of Richelieu's agents rather than a supplicant come to beg some favor from the most powerful man in France.

When she departed the woman smiled briefly at D'Artagnan, but had not spoken. As she passed him, D'Artagnan had inclined his head toward her and said simply, "Good evening, milady."

"When necessary, that woman can be quite as dangerous as you, my young friend," said Richelieu.

"I shouldn't doubt it," D'Artagnan said. "If there is one thing besides the use of the blade that my uncle taught me, it was to be wary of certain women and I think her one of them."

"Indeed. He sounds like a most wise and practical man. I think you may take after him in some ways," said the cardinal. Richelieu had made use of the young swordsman several times since, on impulse, taking him into his personal guard. While the results had not always been what he would have preferred, D'Artagnan's performance had been enough to keep him keenly aware of the young swordsman.

"That is why I am going to trust you with a most delicate mission, one that I think will fit your skills quite well."

"I am at your disposal, Your Excellency."

From a drawer in his desk the cardinal pulled out several sheets of paper and passed them to D'Artagnan. One of them was a travel warrant, giving the bearer priority access to transport anywhere within the boundaries of France. The other bore a highly detailed sketch of a face. This was followed by two small bags of gold; expense money no doubt, speculated D'Artagnan. There was one thing that came with working for Richelieu; he was definitely not ungenerous with the state's money.

"You are to go to Italy. Venice, to be exact. I need you to locate the man whose face is on that paper. His name is Ramsey Culhane. He is the nephew and principal heir of one Jameson Culhane, an Irish Catholic gentleman whom I would appreciate having in my debt," said Richelieu.

"I take it he is not in Venice of his own accord."

"Indeed not. There is a matter of a rather large sum of money owed to one of the trading houses in the form of a gambling debt; I don't have the specifics as of yet. They've demanded payment from his uncle or they will kill the wastrel. Under other circumstances I would just pay the ransom myself; however, there are certain alliances that might be put in jeopardy if that were discovered. So we must resort to your unique skills, Lieutenant."

"It shall be done, Your Eminence. If you have no objection, I will take Aramis with me."

"Take him. He is useful but at times gives me a headache," said Richelieu. As D'Artagnan left he saw the churchman spreading several maps of the French-Spanish border areas across his desk.

A goodly portion of the far western districts in Venice were devoted to docks and warehouses. In the time since he had come to the city to apprentice as a metal worker with his uncle, Antonio Marcoli, Barnabas had become quite familiar with the area.

From the shadowed corner where the three men had stopped, Barnabas could see lights from a few torches and lanterns that marked where some people worked, even now.

The streets were never completely empty, even at nearly midnight. It was just quieter as businesses awaited the coming of the tide to bring more cargo in, and daylight to guide transports that would carry the contents of the warehouses away.

The urge to repay his guardian angel had faded in Barnabas

the farther they had traveled from the center of the city. Now a small portion of his mind wondered if the two Frenchmen would turn around and help *themselves* to his purse and pick up a few extra coins selling his body to a medical school.

"I have a feeling that my uncle may not be all that pleased at my involvement with whatever you have in mind," Barnabas said. "Tell me truthfully, is this thing you want me to do legal?"

"Truthfully, no," said D'Artagnan. "It is also more than likely going to be dangerous. But I say this without a doubt; should we succeed it will not cause any harm to the reputation of the Marcoli family."

From under his jacket the tall Frenchman produced a single-shot pistol that he passed to Barnabas. The weapon weighed no more than a few ounces. Barnabas had fired muskets while hunting, but never at another person. He was more at home with the long knife that hung on his belt, although he preferred not to use it unless there was no choice in the matter.

"I hope that I won't find a need for this," he told the Frenchman.

"True, but isn't it better to have something and not need it than to ..."

"...need it and not have it. You sound like my cousin, Giovanna."

"The one whose friend gave you the book about me? A wise woman," said D'Artagnan.

"Barnabas, do you know this place?" Aramis said, pointing at a small two-story building just down the way. Barnabas stared for a few minutes. Just down from it were the burnt remnants of another warehouse. According to some of his cousins, the place had been set afire four years ago under rather odd circumstances; and, just as oddly, no one had taken over the property, even though, because of its location, it was quite valuable.

"Yes, I do. As far as anyone knows it is supposed to belong to Roberto Salvatore. But according to my uncle, old Salvatore sold the place a few months back to the Kurtz brothers. They're Austrian, I think, and may even have some Russian connections," said Barnabas. "What are we here for?"

"Nothing too difficult," Aramis said. The small man had a slight smile on his face as he spoke that gave Barnabas a chill. It occurred to him that this was the sort of fellow who could as cheerfully slit your throat as share the latest gossip with you. "I just want you to get us inside by telling the men behind that door exactly who you are. The Marcoli name carries weight, even at this ungodly late hour. With any kind of luck that should get us inside the place without things getting too messy."

As outrageous as it sounded, Barnabas could actually imagine that sort of bluff working with some people. He'd more than once seen his uncle push his way through situations by doing just exactly that.

"You did say," he repeated, "that this whole matter would not reflect badly on my family."

"It shouldn't, if things work out, but you never know," Aramis said. "Besides, if things go wrong there is a chance that none of us will have to worry about who gets blamed, since we might all be dead."

Barnabas was overcome with an urge to run, but he blocked that by reminding himself that he did owe his life to the tall Frenchman. Instead, he drew a deep breath and headed toward the warehouse, moving quickly in order to not give himself time to think of reasons why he shouldn't be involved in this whole matter.

Things had already gone wrong when Barnabas reached the warehouse's main door. It was open and there was no sign of any watchmen or other sort of guard. From the look on his two companions' faces, Barnabas was certain this was a discovery that neither of them had expected.

Once they were inside, a short narrow hallway led into the main part of the warehouse. The smell of the canals and the sound of splashing around the warehouse pilings mixed into the darkness.

There were several dozen bales of cloth blocking off one corner of the room where a table with bottles of wine and mugs sat, along with a bowl filled with cheese and a half loaf of bread.

A movement to one side of the room caught Barnabas's attention. A moment later a man emerged from a door and came charging forward with a large, rather nasty looking ax in his hand. Barnabas attempted to step backward but found his feet tangled among a couple of chairs, and it was only a miracle that kept him on his feet.

D'Artagnan came from one of the bales of cloth and threw himself hard against the stranger. That was enough to make the man drop his weapon and give the Frenchman a chance to fire two quick blows to his opponent's stomach and chin, putting an end to the fight and the man on the floor.

"Do you always attack a man with an ax with only your fists?" asked Barnabas, not even sure that he had seen what he had seen.

"It worked, didn't it? Do you know this fellow?" D'Artagnan held his lantern close to the unconscious man's face.

Barnabas stared at the prostrate form for a moment. "Yes, I believe I do know him. I think his name is Brouila, Mordaunt Brouila. He works for the Quinniaros; they are rivals of the Kurtzes."

"I wonder if they discovered that the Kurtzes were holding Culhane and decided to cut themselves in on the matter. The ransom that the Kurtzes were demanding was going to be a tidy sum," said D'Artagnan.

"Possibly. There are two bodies over at the other end of the warehouse, and given the circumstances I suspect they work for the Kurtzes," said Aramis. "I'm guessing that the Quinniaros got what they came for, meaning Culhane. This leaves us at a loss of where they have taken him. Unless our friend there would be willing to give us the information we need. It is possible that if we can wake him up he can be persuaded to tell us where they went."

"I would presume," said Barnabas, "that we are not going to be informing the authorities of what has happened here."

"Indeed not," said D'Artagnan.

"Wait, we might not need Brouila. Wouldn't they want to get off the streets as quickly as possible?" Barnabas asked. The Quinniaros had interest in several ships but that was all that Barnabas knew for certain. But he had heard that they had an interest in a nearby business.

"That would be what I would do," said Aramis.

"Then I may have an idea on where to find them," said Barnabas.

Barnabas and his companions found their way through the streets of Venice quickly. Their goal was a building only a few streets from the docks. Sandwiched between two warehouses, it looked like nothing more than offices for the various businesses that operated in the area. Were it not for the single lantern hanging in front of the heavy oak door, it would have been easy to not even notice the dark green door.

"Welcome," said a woman dressed in emerald and crimson velvet, her long hair hanging in ornate curls, after the three men were admitted.

That she was mistress of the house there was no doubt. She was not young, and according to the tales that Barnabas had heard, Madam Paulette and her establishment had been a fixture in Venice for many years. Her careful makeup and the room's lighting took at least a decade off her age. The serious look in the woman's eyes showed that she was no common street whore, but rather a woman who had learned to make her way in the world and cater to a taste for finer things.

D'Artagnan rubbed his chin and studied the place. That it was a brothel was obvious, but Barnabas had already told them that. The windows were masked with heavy curtains. In spite of the hour there seemed to be a brisk business going on, some sailors and a mixed lot of workmen. There were perhaps a half dozen men there, some with drinks in their hands, others talking to women in revealing gowns.

"You would be Madam Paulette?" said Barnabas.

"Indeed, I am. What can I do for some fine gentlemen like yourselves?" she said. On Madam Paulette's shoulder was a highly intricate butterfly brooch; the stones on it reflected different colors each way that she turned. D'Artagnan suspected that while it looked valuable it might be nothing more than paste. On more than one occasion he had seen that skill and craftsmanship could make paste look like the most valuable jewels in the world.

"I suppose it is your years of experience that tells you we aren't just sailors out moving from one tavern to another, seeking various entertainments," said D'Artagnan.

"I've learned to recognize those who are in need of the services that we offer here. I do have customers from the lower decks of many of the ships that make port here, but also the ranks and officers have been known to hang their hats in my parlor. From the look of you, your manner and attitude, in spite of the plainness of your dress, you are gentlemen," she said. "So how may I help you? I presume you are interested in some female company this evening?"

"Were the evening ours, I am certain that passing it in the company of one of the young ladies you employ would be quite enjoyable," said Aramis. "However, the night is not ours to do with as we would please. Instead, we are seeking some...acquaintances we think might have arrived here in the last several hours."

Madam Paulette smiled, suppressing a slight laugh. "You would have to be a good deal more exact about who it might be that you are looking for. Business has been good this evening; a number of gentleman callers have come through the door.

"Besides, why should I tell you anything about who has come and gone? My customers, even the lower ranking ones, expect a good deal of privacy. They certainly don't expect to have their names shouted by the crier in the town square."

"And they will not be, Madam Paulette," said Barnabas. "I know that there are members of my family who might grateful for any aid you might render us."

"And your name would be?"

"Marcoli. Barnabas Marcoli."

The woman arched her head slightly to one side as she weighed the possibilities.

She turned and headed toward a door at the side of the room. From the smells that were coming from that direction, Barnabas suspected that there might be kitchens somewhere close. Once they were away from the parlor, she turned to face the three men, staring at them and then looking upwards toward the ceiling for a moment before she spoke.

"Gentlemen, I'm sorry to say this, but there is nothing that I can do to assist you in this matter. I run a quiet house; I and my girls try to stay out of anyone else's business. I can think of seven reasons that should remain true. I trust that you can find your own way out. Please convey my respects to your uncle, Signor Marcoli."

With a turn she vanished through the door into the back part of the house.

It bothered Barnabas that Madam Paulette seemed to be more familiar with his family then he had expected. He sincerely hoped that in the months to come he would not regret telling her his name.

"This is no time to linger," said D'Artagnan as he motioned for the others to follow him up a stairway at the end of the hall.

Two lanterns lit the narrow hallway, and from behind several doors D'Artagnan caught the sounds of moans and other noises that proved the rooms were being well put to use.

"I should think...this one," said D'Artagnan, as he came to a door at the far end of the hallway. Barnabas noticed that it was the seventh door.

That was when they heard the sound of something crashing onto the floor from inside the room.

D'Artagnan's sword slid into his hand, a dagger in the other. Then he kicked the door open. The wood cracked under his heel with a sharp sound, but it was almost masked by the sounds within.

"Stay here," the tall Frenchman said over his shoulder to Barnabas, who was only a few steps behind him. "Let no one pass."

Barnabas let out a sigh; with his heart pounding wildly in his chest, Barnabas was more than happy to obey the Frenchman's instructions.

In the dim light D'Artagnan could see two large apparitions, one wearing a cape and the other a long jacket. A smoking pistol was in the hand of the first man, the other had his arms around a smaller struggling man with sandy hair, who was presumably Culhane. An overturned chair with ropes twisted around it suggested that he had managed to free himself, to the surprise of his captors.

The Frenchman let fly with his dagger. It creased the head of the man holding Culhane, gouging his ear and sending blood flying. The man responded with a yelp and a string of curses equal to those of some sailors.

The other man threw himself at D'Artagnan, using his empty pistol as a club. The Frenchman twisted, hit his opponent in the stomach, and then drove his knee into the fellow's crotch. Before the first man had gone to the floor, D'Artagnan whirled about and sent the pommel of his sword slamming square into the other man's face, the sound of a nose breaking confirming its effectiveness. Two more blows with the same part of his sword put the man on the floor at D'Artagnan's feet.

Like most fights, this one was over quickly, almost before Barnabas could be certain of what was happening. He looked quickly one way and another down the hallway, expecting intruders seeking to discover the source of the disturbance.

The first man rose from the floor with a start, grabbing one of the broken pieces of a chair and diving for D'Artagnan. The blade at Barnabas's belt came into his hand and went flying, to bury deep into the man's left eye.

"I'm not sure if Madam Paulette is going to be pleased with the condition you have left her room," said Aramis, who had several of the house's bouncers standing behind him. D'Artagnan couldn't help put notice that the little man also had a pistol in one hand and a bottle of wine in the other.

"No doubt she will vehemently vent her vexation about the matter. She can bill the Quinniaro family. However, I'm sure they paid her well enough to let them keep him here. Besides, I'll lay you even money that she has more damage than this on any given Saturday night," said D'Artagnan.

"More than likely," agreed Aramis.

"You stupid bastards," yelled the man with the sandy hair as he struggled up from the floor, his Irish accent heavy in his voice. "You almost got me killed! Do you have any idea of how easy it would have been for him to snap my neck? You call this rescuing me?"

D'Artagnan covered the distance between himself and the man in three steps, then grabbed him by the collar of his dirty and stained shirt and slammed him hard against the wall. He lifted him up several inches above the floor.

"Is your name Culhane? Ramsey Culhane?"

"Y-y-yesss!" the man stuttered.

"Well, listen well, Monsieur Ramsey Culhane, and know this. You live because of me and my friends. It would have been very easy to leave you in the hands of these men who would as soon slit your throat and dump you into the canals as listen to your so-called righteous anger.

"Quite honestly, I suspect it is your own fault that these men were threatening your life. Of course, it may not have been, but then again I don't really care. When you see your uncle again, just remind him that he is now in the debt of Cardinal Richelieu for having you alive. Do you think you can remember that?"

"Yes, I do." Culhane managed to push the words out of his throat between gasps for air. "I'll remember it."

D'Artagnan let Culhane down to the floor, holding the man's arm to keep him steady. They had taken a couple of steps before he pushed the man up close to the unconscious form of the man in the long leather jacket.

"Remember something else, my ungrateful friend. Your uncle owes the cardinal a favor for the saving of your sorry hide. But it is you who owe *me* your life. Someday I may come to you and demand that you pay back that favor, and you will," he growled.

"I understand," Culhane stuttered before passing out.

D'Artagnan dropped a leather pouch on the table in front of Barnabas as the two men sat at a small table in Madam Paulette's parlor. The thud when the bag hit the table showed that it was full. The younger man picked it up and spilled out the contents into his hand; mixed in with the silver were a number of gold coins.

"It seems that our adversaries had been paid in advance, and they didn't spread the wealth around all that much," said D'Artagnan. "But far be it from me to criticize the house of Quinniaro over their financial dealings, especially when it works out to our advantage."

"Our advantage?" asked Barnabas.

"I gave Madam Paulette a portion of it, to pay for damages and her silence. Half of what is left is yours. Call it payment for your services this evening and also your silence; the spoils of war so to speak."

Barnabas stared at the money for a moment; this would more than double the amount of money in his own purse.

"I did not do this for money, but because you saved my life. It was a matter of honor."

"Quite true, and you've more than repaid that debt, not only by helping Aramis and myself. But when you stepped in and saved my life, the scales were balanced. There is no reason you should not get a reward," said the Frenchman. "Personally, I would suggest you use some of those coins to make some arrangements with one of Madam Paulette's ladies."

"Then you are planning on staying?" asked Barnabas.

"Indeed; the soonest we can get passage will be another day or so. The Quinniaros are tied up in Madam Paulette's cellar and Aramis will stay with Culhane to prevent him from wandering away. Since it is doubtful that the Quinniaros will send others, this is an excellent place to hole up. I suspect I may make an arrangement or two with one of Madam Paulette's employees myself."

Two young women, one in green velvet and the other yellow, had entered the room, taking seats on a chaise longue near the door.

Yes, it seemed to him that D'Artagnan had the right idea. Remaining here might definitely be an excellent way to end the evening.

Cap and Gown

Jack Carroll

On the Ely road
Summer 1634

It was when he heard the split-second hiss of Nathan drawing his sword that Richard realized he was in a bad spot. He was down on one knee in the road. He broke off searching for whatever had gotten into his shoe, and flicked his eyes upward. Nathan was a few yards away, pivoting to face two men rushing from a thicket with knives in their hands.

Richard didn't need to be a soldier like Nathan to grasp the geometry of the tactical situation. These were robbers, and they were separating, trying to catch Nathan between them.

Richard swept back his coat from where it had fallen forward, and frantically snatched at the pistol on his belt. There was no way to get a clear shot at the farther attacker, but Nathan was turning toward him and stepping forward to strike first with his longer reach. The nearer man, though—no time to aim properly. The instant he fancied that his gun pointed the right way, he fired. The man cried out, and spun around to charge Richard. Richard barely had time enough to get his pistol up to eye level in a two-handed grip. He aimed it roughly at the middle of the man's chest, as he'd been taught, and fired again. The man staggered, but didn't fall. Not yet. Richard thumbed the hammer back and was about to fire a third time, when Nathan struck his adversary from behind and ran him through.

Richard glanced behind Nathan, to see what had become of the first robber. He would never threaten anyone again. He was lying in a heap. Richard turned his weapon aside and carefully lowered the hammer.

Nathan did no such thing. Without a moment's pause he freed his sword and whirled to face the bushes again, poised to thrust or slash at need. He snapped, "Let's be away, Richard. There could be another in hiding."

Richard leapt to his feet with his traveling bag in one hand and his gun still in the other, hurrying to keep up. Nathan was watching over his shoulder as much as he was looking at the road ahead. Finally he slowed after a couple of hundred yards, where the view was open on either side. He looked over to Richard.

"That wasn't badly done, for a cloistered scholar. I think perhaps you saved my life just now."

"You saved mine, for certain. It seemed to me that you drew before those men even appeared."

"I did. I misliked the place. Those bushes were too thick and too close to the road. There was that stretch of mire we'd just passed, where we couldn't have run with any sort of burden. It seemed a perfect spot for an ambush. So I put my hand to my sword. Then I heard a sound from within the bushes. I didn't wait to see what would come out."

"And so you ambushed them instead."

"We were unreasonably lucky. They were stupid, and they were most likely new to this game. They should have run when they saw my sword at the ready."

"Perhaps they were afraid you'd follow them into the thicket and take them from behind."

"Then I'd have been the fool. There was no way to know whether I'd run straight into more of them. And that one you kept from my back should have known that a good many travelers carry pistols that can shoot more than once, leaving aside that fancy little German revolver you carry.

"And, Richard?"

"Yes?"

"You won't stop beside any more such places, will you? Whatever poets may imagine, soldiers really don't crave such excitement. After three years in the Germanies with hardly a scratch, it would be embarrassing to be killed by a pair of clumsy louts like those."

"No, Nathan. Learning lessons is what I do."

"I'm profoundly relieved to hear it. Well, it's not over five miles from this place to my family's home. Perhaps you'll stop with us for some moments before you go on to Cambridge. I think my father would be most interested to hear the things you've been telling me, and he could surely find some wine that would be to your liking."

Nathan led the way around the side of the warehouse to the office door. As he and Richard entered, old Edmund looked up from some papers he was frowning over.

"A good day to you, Edmund!"

Edmund Blake stared over his spectacles. "And you are?" He paused. "Young Nathan! Well, not so young any more! You were clean-shaven when I saw you last. A moment, I'll call your father." He stepped through the inner doorway. "Master Brantley! Nathan has come."

Sounds of heavy things being moved came from within, followed by rapidly approaching footsteps.

"Nathan! It's good to see you, indeed! And who is this you've brought? A companion from the German wars?"

"No, Father. I present Scholar Richard Leamington, of Trinity College. We met on board the boat from Lynn, and traveled together since. Even so, we lately became comrades in arms, after a fashion. Richard, this is my father, Master Mercer Jeremiah Brantley."

"Welcome, Scholar Leamington. Edmund, I'll take these two hungry-looking fellows to the kitchen. Dinner is past, but no doubt Cook has some odds and ends that will serve."

"Why, Father! I'd think on such an occasion you'd bring out some of the best."

"What? The best we have cost a pretty penny, and it had better fetch a pretty penny, or we won't be in business for long. Drink it ourselves..."

He seemed to catch sight of the corners of Nathan's mouth, turned up beneath his mustache, and the crinkles at the corners of his eyes.

"Arrr! You always were one for a straight-faced jest. Well, if you don't have the soul of a merchant already, you'd best grow one quick. I'll be relying greatly on you."

"Yes, Father. Of course."

✧　　✧　　✧

With bowls of thick stew set before the young men, Jeremiah poured three glasses. Nathan took his up and tasted, and smiled. Nectar of the gods it most certainly was not, Jeremiah well knew, but it was a respectable wine. Entirely respectable.

"I believe your mother will be home shortly, Nathan. She's gone to deal with some matter with a greengrocer, which Cook wasn't able to settle. Daniel is occupied with business in Cambridge. We can expect him this evening. He's been looking forward to your return as well. Though, it may be it's as much because he's eager to enroll for the Michaelmas term as from any brotherly affection—he could hardly be spared from the business without you to take his place."

"Yes, well, as things have come to pass, it's for the best, for all of us. With the French so thoroughly undone, the army was happy enough to let a good many of us go. I'll not miss campaigning in all weathers, either. These new generals believe in giving the enemy no rest, but that gave us little rest either."

"Speaking of fighting, what was the import of that remark about you and Scholar Leamington here?"

"Oh, that. A pair of robbers set upon us a couple of hours ago. He kept one off my back while I dispatched the other."

Leamington said, "And then you dispatched him as well."

"I merely made sure of him. I doubt he'd have lived more than a few heartbeats longer. That is, if he'd still had a heart to beat, which I don't believe he did after you shot him the second time."

Jeremiah considered, then turned to their guest. "So, you stood by my son at the moment of need. Shall we count you a friend of the family then, and speak as such?"

"I'd be honored. Just Richard, then."

"I'm also honored, and grateful as well. Jeremiah." He reached across the table to shake hands.

"Father, Richard and I had leisure for much conversation on the boat. He told me many things I think you'd find of considerable interest. He's just come from two years of studying mathematics in Grantville."

"The notorious town that's confounded all and sundry? Has it upset the world of scholarship as well?"

"The world of scholarship has hardly begun to feel the upset as yet. You might say it's been tipped up on edge a little, with the great overturning still to come."

"I've heard somewhat from Mistress Chapman's report, and through acquaintances in trade. I'd have thought you'd still be there taking stock, you scholars being what you are."

"Indeed, I could happily have stayed years longer. I could have stayed a lifetime. Leaving was hard, and not only because of the glories of the mathematics they brought with them. I made many friends there. But, Cambridge is my own university. It's past time to come home and teach as much as I can of what I've learned, having come to understand the great benefits that learning brought to the England of the other history."

Nathan nodded. "This is what I wanted you to hear. But perhaps we might do Richard the courtesy of letting him clean and reload his pistol while we talk."

"Of course. If you like, Richard."

"I thank you. Best to get it done before returning to the road." He reached down into his traveling bag for his cleaning kit, and unrolled the cloth wrapping. Laying his pistol and the partly fired cylinder on it, he extracted the full cylinder and laid it aside. Jeremiah eyed the well-made parts thoughtfully as they were laid out before him.

Richard was obviously marshaling his words as he removed the copper caps and prepared the cleaning rod to swab the bore. Jeremiah put down his empty glass and watched him expectantly. Suddenly Richard's right hand trembled slightly, and he nearly dropped the cleaning rod. Then he seemed to recover. Jeremiah wondered—it seemed odd, in someone who had just fought so well. But he hesitated to inquire into personal matters on such short acquaintance. Nathan's eyes narrowed momentarily; clearly, he'd noticed too. After perhaps half a minute Richard spoke.

"How to put into a few words what I found in Grantville? I went to study the mathematics they brought to our time, and came to understand the roots of their power and wealth. They teach a most learned profession called mechanical engineering, which is essential to understanding and creating their many marvels. It rests on the science they call physics, which is a form of natural philosophy accumulated by centuries of careful experiment. Both rest on mathematics for their expression and system of reasoning. I came to a new understanding. At Cambridge we're accustomed to study mathematics to shape the mind. They learn it to shape the world."

"We have many mechanicians who create most artful devices, though."

"To be sure, but often with great difficulty and many false starts. The difference is in the depth and completeness of understanding. A mechanic may make what has been made before, or by a series of trials work out how to make a new thing. But the mechanical engineer has no need of the many trials, or not nearly as many. He calculates, and reasons out what to build. Think of the difference between a printer and a philosopher. The printer can make great numbers of copies of a book, but the philosopher is needed for the knowledge to go into the book. In like manner, what the engineer designs, the mechanic makes."

"What manner of things do they make by such learning, then?"

"Surely you know of the ship Admiral Simpson sent into the mouth of the Thames, that swept aside all opposition as if it were gossamer when it brought away the people from the Tower?"

"Yes, of a certainty. It was said to move as it would, with little regard to wind or tide, and no broadside could be brought to bear against it before it moved aside."

"Well, it was driven by steam, as you've likely heard. I know some of the folk who designed that engine. They had never worked on one like it. Simpson wrote to them saying what his ships required, and within days they were making precise drawings of the necessary parts and sending orders to the foundries and machine shops. I don't mean to say nothing needed to be corrected, but those engines were completed and sent to the shipyard in mere months. There was never any question that they would work.

"England could have ships like that, and steam pumps for the mines, and even things the Grantvillers lack, such as spinning machines and powered looms to comfortably clothe even the poorest of us. We could teach all of their learning at Cambridge and then carry on beyond it. It only needs enough scholars and enough time to publish what they have in their libraries and private collections."

"They allow this? They don't keep the knowledge to themselves?"

"They reason that would place them in greater danger than publishing it freely. If it's everywhere, it can't be lost or suppressed."

"Tell me then, if you would, what such learning in England might mean to the trades in wool and wine, as those are our business. You spoke of mechanical weaving and spinning?"

"Ah. Yes, those greatly changed life in England in that other history..."

✦   ✦   ✦

It was nearly time for Hall. The light slanting in through the windows was turning golden. With so many undergraduates and fellows returning for the start of the term, the buzz of conversation had risen greatly over the last few days. Richard approached the table where he'd often sat before, and smiled to see John Rant concentrating fiercely on a book tipped up before him, very much as he'd often done when Richard last saw him two years earlier. John turned at the approaching footsteps and came to his feet.

"Richard Leamington! Of all people! You look well. Have you completed your foreign studies so soon, then?"

"No, John, but things have changed. You know it was always my plan to master mathematics, then teach it?"

John nodded.

"Well, there's far more to master than I ever imagined, but if I'm to teach here at all, I must begin."

"How so? Places in the university are always in short supply, but surely, with all you must have brought back from that place..."

"Oh, there was no difficulty gaining a lectureship, even without an M.A. It's my time that may be limited. No, I'm not well at all."

John looked stricken. "What's the matter, Richard?"

"Some months ago I began to have moments of dizziness and headaches. At times the sight in my left eye would blur. I went to see one of their doctors."

"I've heard tales of them. Supposedly they do near-miraculous things for all manner of ailments. And so?"

"All they could do for this malady was name it. It's called multiple sclerosis. Treating it is entirely beyond them. Curing it would have been beyond the most eminent physicians even in their own time, and all they are is a few country practitioners, doing their utmost to pass on what they know while they can.

"It causes a gradual worsening of health, and is invariably fatal in the end. There's no knowing how fast it may come on. They know of people living twenty years or more with it, but that's uncommon. So, I decided it was time to bring this new mathematics home, as much of it as I could, and teach for as long as I have."

"Oh, Richard, I'm so sorry. But, this seems to leave room to hope, at least. Perhaps you might live as long even with it, as you might have otherwise."

Richard walked around to the other side of the table and settled down. "Perhaps. But let's speak of something more cheerful. What's that you were studying as I came in?"

John took his seat again, and picked up the book to show the cover.

"Isn't that the same calculus book that went around in Latin translation before I left? I'd have thought, with your passion, you'd have gone a good deal further by now."

"Oh, I have. A transcription of a textbook on complex variables has reached us, in English. Fascinating notions, though the use is still obscure. I'm just reviewing a few points before returning to it. But what do you have in that leather case? It looks big enough for a book, perhaps two."

"Ah. You must see this. It arrived only today."

Richard laid the case on the table and opened it. He took out a flat contrivance of wood and metal, and unfolded it. Then he took out one of several thin packages, extracted a modest-sized sheet of stiff glossy paper from it, and slid it into the rear part of the device. He handed it to John. "Hold this up to your eye. Look through the glass lens on the front, and stand so the sunlight falls on the paper at the back. You can slide the sheet holder left and right, and up and down. Turn this little knob here for a clearer view."

John took the device, and moved it side-to-side while fiddling with the adjustment. He stopped.

"Printing? So small that it needs this glass to read it? Most artful, but why? It must be formidably difficult to do." He slid the paper sideways, looking for the beginning. He read aloud, "Modern Probability: Theory and Its Applications. By Emanuel Parzen of Stanford University. Stanford University?"

Richard gestured, palms-up. "A parched and empty hillside in our era, so I've been told."

"So it must be." John slid the holder around some more. "By the symbols, this appears to be some form of mathematics, but not of a kind I've seen or heard of."

"Yes, it is. An advanced topic, used for many important things in science and commerce. I've recorded a notice to scholars at the state library in Grantville, that I will translate it into Latin, and our university press will publish it in the original English, and then the translation. As to why, this method of making a copy is a temporary expedient. It's done with optics and chemistry, I don't know precisely how. Much less satisfactory than reprinting the book itself at full size, but good enough for the typesetting and translation work, and far faster and cheaper than transcribing by hand. They made this in three days. And with each sheet holding the images of four pages, or four images of anything else for that matter, a whole book adds but little to a traveler's burden—and they hope to put twelve or sixteen to a sheet soon. The actual printed book is safe in the private collection of the husband of one of my fellow teachers."

John lowered the viewing device and looked at Richard in surprise. "*Fellow* teacher? I thought you went there to study. You taught there?"

"Yes, it was how I supported myself during my studies. The Ring of Fire left a good many of their teachers behind. And now there are many more students than before. As soon as I arrived at the library and inquired in English after books on mathematics, the principal sought me out and asked if I could teach. So for two years I taught geometry and trigonometry in the high school, while helping with translations. Meanwhile I studied complex variables, probability, differential equations, and other manner of things. They greatly value our English university men, there."

"They must have been sorry to see you leave, then."

"Mrs. Reardon and her busy crew of volunteers did try to persuade me to stay longer. They have great plans. But John Pell arrived recently, and he has taken my place. He'll serve them well, better than I could, really. I learned much from him in my undergraduate days."

"Pell? I thought he'd gone to Horsham to teach school."

"He did, but it didn't last. But while he was searching for a new situation, word reached him of what was to be found in Grantville, and it drew him."

John handed back the viewer. "So, there's another place of high learning in the world. But, what was that you said about a notice of some kind?"

"Yes, a notice to other scholars that I intend to translate this book. There was the most fearful uproar after three translations of the same book on steelmaking came out within months of each other, all three scholars working unbeknownst to each other. After that, the library agreed to keep records, so that everyone can know which books are already being attended to."

"And what will you teach now? This probability? Would I understand it?"

"You would, but I won't teach it until it's published at least in English so that every student can obtain a copy. I intend to give regular lectures on complex variables at first, since that follows directly after calculus, which is already taught here? Yes? And also an introductory course in physics, which they teach in Grantville at the same time as calculus, so there are many here such as your good self who could follow it. There will be laboratory demonstrations to illustrate the principles and give evidence of their truth."

"Oh, so? You follow our own Francis Bacon in this, that the nature of the world cannot be known by reasoning alone?"

"To be sure, and Master of Arts Charnock Fielder of Grantville High School as well, who I've heard to say in two sentences what the learned Bacon required entire books to convey."

"And that is?"

"'In science there is no authority. There is only experiment.'"

Richard wasn't accustomed to being awakened by Doctor Comber. But then, the distinguished Thomas Comber—Doctor of Divinity, Master of Trinity College, past Vice Chancellor of the university, and Dean of Carlisle besides—wasn't known to make a practice of waking mere lecturers, or even to take the trouble of ascending to a third-floor room.

"Good morrow, Leamington. The dean of the chapel has informed me that Master Ramsey just now went to practice at the organ, and encountered a student of yours asleep beside a guttering candle, by which he was fortunately able to see a large cannon ball on a cord swinging from the ceiling. Would you care to explain that? To the dean? And arrange to have it removed before the morning lectures?"

"Uff? Asleep? At once. My apologies, Dr. Comber." He scrabbled for his clothing. Under his breath he muttered, "I hope he got the data."

"And, Leamington? Attend me in my rooms after the second lecture. There are matters we must discuss."

Richard knocked on John Rant's door. In moments there was a stirring within, and the door opened to reveal a very disheveled and confused-looking B.A.

"Richard? There's light in the sky! I wasn't called."

"Indeed. I've just now been told that Tom fell asleep during the experiment instead of calling you at midnight to take your turn recording the data. We are required to remove the apparatus at once. Dress and join me in the chapel, if you will. If we're quick about it, we may even have time for some breakfast."

"Yes, of course. I'll be but a moment."

Richard left at as rapid a walk as the dignity of a lecturer allowed.

During the first hour Richard attended a lecture. By ironic chance it was on musical scales, and the lecturer was Master Robert Ramsey, the chapel organist. He made no remarks beyond his recent inquiries into the startling notion of an equally tempered scale, in light of the ancient Greek modes, but his displeasure was clear enough by his posture and the dark glances he periodically cast toward Richard. Still, Richard managed to keep his mind on the subject at hand. Mostly.

The second hour went to giving a private lecture on vector calculus to several post-graduate students, who had made considerable inroads into the fragments of new mathematics that had reached the university during Richard's absence. It was somewhat easier for Richard to keep his mind on that.

And then it was time to call on Dr. Comber in the master's lodging at the north side of the Great Court. Richard knocked, then entered to see him seated at his writing table, by the big windows.

"Take a seat, Richard. I just want to capture one thought before it escapes . . . There." Dr. Comber put down his pen and straightened in his chair. "Richard, you've annoyed two fellow members of this college for no good reason. The dean was most upset that you and your students hung that heavy ball in the chapel and set it swinging without saying anything to him first, or indeed to anyone who had reason to go into the chapel and could have walked into its path unaware. He's responsible for keeping the place in good order and fit for services, lectures, and everything else that takes place there. He needs to know what goes on in his domain. As for Master Ramsey, he had a moment of fright, seeing that thing rush toward his ankles in the gloom."

"I'm sorry for that, Dr. Comber. Still, no harm was done."

"No, no harm, except to your own reputation. And that's concern enough. You're no longer some raw undergraduate, whose

inevitable transgressions are to be corrected with stern admon-
ishments and suitable penalties, and then forgotten. You're well
known throughout the university now, and there are those who
look up to you. Your actions have real consequences—some mistakes may not be so easily undone. I had to assure the dean and
the organist that you and your students were conducting some
serious lesson, and not a midnight jape. I was correct, wasn't I?"

"Yes, of course. It was a teaching experiment in physics, demonstrating the validity of certain mathematical predictions."

"Good, as I expected. What, exactly, was this demonstration?"

"It was the Foucault pendulum. It's one of the two classic
demonstrations of the rotation of the Earth."

Dr. Comber dropped his hand to the writing table in front
of him and stared wide-eyed at Richard for a heartbeat or two.

"A *demonstration* of the rotation of the Earth? A *classic* demonstration?"

"Yes, first performed in public by the French physicist Léon
Foucault in the other history, in 1851."

Dr. Comber leaned forward with his hands flat on the table
and gave a distinct impression of a bulldog. "*Do I understand you
correctly?* Is this a tangible demonstration that apparently settles
the controversy between the Aristotelian and Copernican world
models at one stroke? And you did this without telling me, or
any other officer or senior fellow of this college? Which will now
circulate by rumor, because we don't tell students not to talk about
their studies? And cause all manner of upset to scholars who've
spent their lives studying this very question?"

Richard froze.

"Exactly. You didn't think. You considered only the mathematics
and natural philosophy, and how to present it to your students.
Not altogether a bad thing. But now you need to think about
your colleagues as well. You've told me and the fellows of your
hopes to bring whole new fields of learning here. You wish others to take up these studies, and make the university greater in
consequence? For that, you need not merely the acquiescence of
your fellows, you need their wholehearted support. You won't get
it by discourtesy."

Dr. Comber sat back, thinking furiously.

"What must be done now is to present this in a proper and
respectful scholarly manner to the whole university, and quickly.

But before any announcement, I need to fully understand it myself. I would like you to explain it to me. Completely. Now, I understand your time tonight is to be taken up preparing a lesson?"

"Yes, Dr. Comber."

"And I'm heavily occupied for the next two days. Can you come here after Hall on Friday?"

"Yes, certainly."

"Good. Come then with your notes and whatever else is needful to make this clear. I think I may ask Thorndike to join us; he's spent a good deal more time on this new mathematics than I've been able to."

Richard's right hand trembled slightly. He told himself it wasn't from nervousness; after all, he was a seasoned teacher long since. He sat up straighter and looked around the chapel. Nearly time. The seats were filling rapidly with fellows and undergraduates from all over the university. There were at least three heads of colleges. Well, the pendulum was rigged and secured at the start of its arc ready to release, and it wasn't as if he'd never presented this material before.

The bell overhead rang the hour. Dr. Comber rose and walked to the lectern.

"Masters and presidents, fellows, and scholars, there has been considerable talk of late concerning the knowledge conveyed here from Grantville, in particular a demonstration that took place in this chapel a few nights ago. I've asked Scholar Richard Leamington to repeat that demonstration today as a university lecture. I believe this will be of great interest to many of you. Scholar Leamington, if you will."

Richard went to the lectern, where his notes already rested. He was glad to grasp the side with one hand and steady himself; this was no time to look shaky, insidious malady or no. He straightened, faced the audience with level gaze, took a full breath, and began.

"Thank you, Dr. Comber. Thank you all for coming. As you've heard, this will be a demonstration of the Earth's rotation, by means of mathematics and modern physics used together. Since many of you are able to stay only for the hour allotted to the lecture, we'll start the physical demonstration first and let it run. I will explain the reasoning while you observe what occurs." Richard turned slightly and gestured toward the pendulum. "You see before you a weight, suspended by a cord from as high up as the hall allows. As you can see, it's free to swing in any direction. Notice the sewing needle attached to the bottom of the iron ball with sealing wax, the degree circle marked on the large sheet of paper lying directly beneath the point of suspension, and the narrow ring of sand on the paper. Each time the needle crosses the ring, it will sweep aside a few grains of sand to mark the place where it crossed. The whole apparatus together is called the Foucault pendulum.

"As you can see, we have a clock already running. This is a very accurate laboratory instrument, made in Grantville. Scholar Crosfield will start the pendulum for us now."

Thomas Crosfield was awake enough today, and blessed with steady hands as well. He stepped forward shielding a lighted candle behind his hand, and gingerly knelt by the pendulum, taking care not to breathe upon it.

Richard fastened his eye on the clock as it came up to the minute. He called out, "Five. Four. Three. Two. One. Loose."

On that word, Tom brought up the candle and burned through the thread holding back the pendulum. The ball swung away in a stately arc toward the sand ring, while Tom stepped back and blew out the candle. There was the faintest of sounds as the needle flicked through the sand. He returned to his seat and took up a lead pencil and paper.

"Scholar Crosfield has written down the time the pendulum started, and the angle where it first crossed the degree circle. He will continue to do this periodically. By this we will be able to measure the rate at which the plane of oscillation rotates.

"As the pendulum moves, it's acted upon by the forces imparted by the motion and gravity of the Earth. Starting with the Newtonian equations for these forces and the resulting acceleration of the moving ball, we can show by mathematical proof that at the latitude of Cambridge the plane in which the ball swings must rotate by two hundred and eighty-four degrees per day relative to the stars, or two hundred and eighty-five relative to the sun, just under twelve degrees per hour." He turned to the movable blackboard standing near the lectern, already filled with the first part of the accompanying derivation. "We begin with the equation for the force of gravity..."

✧   ✧   ✧

Today Richard had no lectures to give or attend. John Rant had arranged to call later on, to ask his advice regarding the best way to present a seminar on proof by infinite series. For now, though, it was a perfect time to immerse himself in correcting the latest sheaf of typeset proofs for the English edition of the probability textbook. It wasn't a large batch today; there should be plenty of time to make progress on the translation work as well. In truth, he was happy to be able to spend most of the day seated. Well, perhaps he'd feel more like visiting one of the taverns tomorrow, or just walking by the river. He glanced out the window at a few students hurrying past the great fountain in the court below—it was just as well to be inside in any case. He took up his pen and set to working steadily through the stack by the watery light from the late autumn sky.

Shortly before the midday meal Richard finished the proofreading and set it aside. He was the picture of an absentminded professor as he hurried across the court toward the dining hall, in spite of being far below that exalted rank. He didn't seek company at dinner today, being occupied in considering the practicality of constructing the apparatus for the measurement of the universal gravitation constant—without sending to the piano makers in Grantville for a length of fine-gauge music wire. Could it be done with a common lute string? Perhaps some testing might reveal the answer.

He returned still deep in thought to his room, and settled in to rendering probability theory clearly and concisely in Latin, a satisfying challenge. The tingling in two fingers of his right hand faded from his notice. He wrote in the spare up-time style, with no classical allusions, metaphors, or digressions beyond the bounds of mathematics itself. Richard wrote, crossed out, wrote again, made editing marks, wrote again. After a time the weather became typically English. Rain, sun, overcast, wind, at twenty-minute intervals. The sky abruptly turned fair with an unseasonably warm breeze, and Richard thought to air out his room while he had the chance. He opened the windows and the door to the staircase.

He went back to his translation. *Hmm, what would be the best way to express the concept of expectation?*

There was a soft caress against his ankle. He looked down at orange fur and blue eyes. Nan was looking up at him. He reached down to stroke her side. She leaped to his lap, and from there to the table. She sniffed at the inkwell and brushed her upraised tail against his nose. Richard lifted her aside, off his rough draft, and began scratching her behind the ears to tempt her to stay where she was. She settled down with one paw draped limply over the edge, purring and swishing her tail from side to side. Richard was a little too distracted at the moment to remember whose cat she was, but it hardly seemed to matter to her anyway. His hand continued moving, back and forth, as his mind returned to pondering the problem. *Perhaps . . .* He weighed alternative constructions, as they took shape in his mind. After a time footsteps sounded on the staircase. Richard listened with half an ear for a moment, but he didn't recognize the step, and it was early for John. He wrote another sentence.

There was a knock on the door frame. Richard looked up. "Oh, Dr. Comber." He started to rise.

Dr. Comber waved him back down. "Do you have a few moments, Richard? I have some questions."

"Certainly." Richard waved his hand toward the second chair.

As Dr. Comber drew it up to the other side of the writing table and settled down, Nan opened her eyes. He reached out his hand and she leaned into it, while he gathered his words. His gaze swept across the stacked page proofs and the scattered manuscript sheets on the table. "How does it go, then?" Nan rose to her feet at the broken silence, jumped off the table, and sauntered off to parts unknown.

"Very well. There should be only one more batch of page proofs after these, before the English edition can go to press and I can think of offering a course of lectures. There are already inquiries for copies. As to the Latin manuscript, it's nearing the halfway mark. The Latin lexicographers helped me greatly in devising suitable terms for the new principles before I left Grantville, and they've added them to their technical dictionary."

"Excellent. But I was asking after your health, more than the work."

"Not too bad." He reached for the cane leaning against the bookcase and held it up. "I have this, but seldom need it. The special candle lamp with the focusing lens and mirror that I brought for the microprint viewer helps me work after dark."

"You didn't need that cane at all, earlier. Perhaps we'd better find you quarters downstairs for next term. I'll say a word to the bursar and see what might be done. More difficulties seeing, too? You have my sympathy. I'm thankful to have spectacles, these days. But you're able to continue teaching? I know how greatly you wish it."

"Yes, and it gives me greater satisfaction to aid others in taking up the work. I could never bring such a body of new knowledge to Cambridge by myself. No man could, alone."

"Indeed. And so we come to my reason for calling on you today."

John Rant appeared in the doorway. "Oh, Dr. Comber, I didn't know you were with Richard. Should I come back later?"

"No, stay, you might have some thoughts to illuminate the discussion, with all the time you've spent together in study and inquiry."

Both chairs being occupied, John leaned against the wall beside the door and folded his arms, an expectant expression on his face.

"Richard, I've been much occupied with many matters, but you've spoken before of what new learning this university might offer to our students. I would like a more thorough understanding of what it consists, and how large a body of knowledge it might be."

"You're giving consideration to this, then?"

"It's far too soon to say that. Before I can consider anything, or usefully speak of such things with the fellows and officers, I must understand the meaning of these subjects you say are studied now in the Germanies, and as well the numbers of those to do the instructing. Particularly the latter. Do you know, this university has been trying for years to get an endowed chair of mathematics?"

"No, I didn't."

"Well, it has. With no success. But it seems you made a deep impression on your merchant friend Jeremiah Brantley, who is well known in commercial circles and among other notables of the town. He and the mayor unexpectedly called on me yesterday. He's apparently made inquiries overseas and consulted with others, and is now engaged in raising subscriptions all over the shire to found such a post. From merchants and town officials! With relations between the university and the town always in a delicate state, this is to be marveled at. It's also to be approached with great caution, so as not to upset matters."

He brought his hands together and interlaced his fingers.

"So. Pray tell me, what exactly is mechanical engineering,

why are the merchants and local notables so convinced of its value to them that they're willing to contribute to the university on its behalf, and if this institution were to carry on a course of instruction to that end, how would it be done? I wish to be thoroughly prepared to listen and speak of this question, before it arises again."

"Oh. Well. I would define it as the use of mathematics and scientific knowledge to design mechanical devices. Its uses are beyond counting. As to why the merchants are interested, I think they're looking first of all to the rapid movement of people and goods. The sooner and surer the arrival, the sooner and surer the profit. That's what Master Brantley said to me. They see steamships, railroad trains, aircraft on the continent, and they want them here. Then there's mechanical spinning and weaving—he was most fascinated by that possibility, being a wool merchant. Now as to the curriculum, I have some notes here, which one of the physics teachers in Grantville allowed me to copy down."

Richard turned in his chair, and pulled a commonplace book from a shelf. He laid it on the table and flipped through the pages, then turned it so his visitor could see.

"Here, a list of courses for the degree in mechanical engineering, at the great California Institute of Technology. Calculus in multiple variables, linear algebra, differential equations, probability, motion and gravity, electricity and magnetism, the theory of relativity, particles and waves, quantum mechanics, theory and experimental practice of chemistry, biology of viruses, statics and dynamics of rigid and deformable bodies, thermodynamics, engineering design methods, fluid mechanics, technical and scientific writing and speaking, mechanics of materials, control theory, and practical mechanical laboratory sessions. Humanities as well, of course."

Dr. Comber's face was a study in consternation as he stared down at the list. "If all those completely unknown fields of knowledge are of similar scope and effort to the few I have at least heard of, it seems a most ambitious curriculum for a doctorate."

Richard hesitated.

"It doesn't seem so to you?"

"Ah...that's for the bachelor's degree. Bachelor of Science in Mechanical Engineering, a four-year curriculum. The advanced degrees dealt with research, original contributions to the field, and sometimes the leadership of projects and enterprises."

Dr. Comber sat up again and stared at Richard straight-on. "The *bachelor's* degree, forsooth! All that is what those mechanicians studied? And what we would have to teach, and find faculty and endowments for, were we to attempt such a thing?"

John broke in. "Richard, you've mentioned that place to me before. You did say Caltech was one of the most formidable engineering colleges in the world, didn't you? A place for untiring near-geniuses to turn themselves into the leading lights of their profession? Out of all that, how much would be essential to do worthwhile work in our world?"

"Now, there's a thought. Perhaps half could be put to immediate use. Of that, perhaps half is truly essential to do the beginnings of practical engineering work, while continuing formal studies. The Grantvillers call a student at that stage an 'engineering trainee.' Perhaps a little less than that. Thermodynamics is the key, for steam engines, and steam engines are practically the gateway to an industrial revolution. That comes about mid-way. So, a quarter perhaps."

Dr. Comber sat back and folded his hands in his lap. He nodded gravely. "A quarter. So. A faculty of how many to teach such a reduced curriculum? Have you given thought to that question?"

"I'm uncertain. The Grantvillers were wrestling with it when I left, and hadn't reached firm conclusions. But I think perhaps, if we considered only the minimum at first, and if some courses were given only in alternate years, and if we selected students for their ability to study independently, it might be done with eight or so. Perhaps."

"Before Pan and Janus, Leamington, do you have the faintest idea of the magnitude of what you propose? It amounts to adding an entire new faculty to those we already have—medicine, law, theology and philosophy. Not only new academic seats, but new rooms—you said laboratories? Acquiring teaching devices such as your pendulum? Novel statutes for the university, I don't doubt. And more students, likely as not. It's like to founding a new college. And who would pay for all that? Who could, in these times?"

Richard sat, thinking.

"Put that way, I can't dispute it. It reminds me of something one of the engineers said to me, in a moment of desperation. 'If you have a mountain to move, and only a teaspoon to do it with, move the first spoonful. It's a spoonful you won't have to move later.' "

"I suppose that's what you're doing here, teaching what you've brought back, and translating this one book of mathematics into proper Latin? Carrying away a spoonful from the mountain you beheld?"

"I think what they brought to our world was a mere wheelbarrow full. A wagon load, at most. The mountain was left behind. But, yes. And were you to bring us that one professorship through your well-regarded diplomacy, I would rejoice for it, and not complain of the fish not caught. It would be another spoonful."

As they sat contemplating that thought, John took a thick packet from under his arm and laid it before Richard. "I'd thought to give you this earlier, before other matters intervened. There's a letter for you. It's from John Pell, in Grantville."

Dr. Comber looked up. "John Pell! Is it private, or is some of it meant for the university?"

Richard said, "We'll soon see." As he opened it, a small, beautifully printed sheet of cream-colored paper fell free from the rest. He picked it up, and smiled. "Well! A birth announcement. Deborah Lucille Reardon was born on November 17 to Landon Reardon and Sarah Beth Cochran Reardon. So Mrs. Reardon has been safely delivered. Good news, indeed, in many ways. The Reardons have been much in my thoughts."

Dr. Comber was eyeing the corner of a glossy sheet of paper poking out of the stack. "Is that a photograph?"

"It looks to be. A black-and-white one." Richard pulled it out and laid it on the table. John came closer, to see over their shoulders.

Two figures were seated on a brocaded couch. There was a large picture of a saddle horse in a pasture on the wall behind them. A tall, graceful woman with long dark hair sat on the right, wearing a flowered print dress and a single string of pearls. On the left was a husky man with lighter hair, wearing an up-time business suit. They faced half toward the camera, and half toward an infant sleeping in her lap. They were holding hands.

"It's a Reardon family portrait. A new one, obviously."

John mused, "A beautiful woman."

Richard let slip an involuntary snort of amusement. "Indeed, and a most persistent and determined one, into the bargain."

Dr. Comber raised an eyebrow. "Oh, how so?"

"You'd need to know the Cochran sisters. They have a long-standing reputation for letting nothing stop them, once they decide a thing must be done. There's a story that Sarah stayed at the school well past her usual time one day, to deal with a student discipline problem, a boy on the edge of getting himself into serious trouble. By the time she and the guidance counselor were done ramming some sense into his head, the grocery stores had all closed. Nevertheless, she put dinner on the table that night. With a squirrel rifle."

"Remarkable."

"Not by their standards. She's no better or worse a shot than a thousand others. Well, let's see what Pell has to say."

He held up the first page where the light from the sky could fall on it. "He sends his best wishes to all of us and hopes that we are well. Manfred von Ochsendorf has joined the high school faculty, and finished his translation of the second volume of the Resnick and Halliday physics series—that's introductory electrodynamics, the course after the one I'm giving now. The University of Prague was clamoring for it before I left. Oho! He reports that President Piazza has nominated Sarah to the state board of education. That can only mean big things are in the offing over there."

"How so?"

"For close on a year now, she's been the de facto leader of a small group arguing that the Grantville schools must better manage the teaching of mathematics and the sciences, to the end that they may concentrate their efforts toward educating a new generation of engineers and scientists with all possible speed. She argues that their survival requires re-creating the essentials of an engineering college of their own era. They've been consulting, planning, and persuading among the teachers, the citizens, the public leaders, and anyone else who will listen or speak to them. She once asked me to address the city council regarding the state of mathematics and experimental science here in England.

"The thing is this. Piazza was formerly the principal of Grantville High School. He's acutely aware of the place education holds in their world. If he's put forward her name, it means he's convinced himself of four things. First, that the proposal is sound. Second, that its importance justifies the expense and talent it will demand. Third, that he can rely on her to bring it to fruition if given the authority. Fourth, that Congress will confirm the appointment. For that matter, that Sarah herself will accept the challenge, and the citizens will agree to the public expenditure."

Dr. Comber leaned back and clasped his hands behind his head. "You know these people, Richard. Your opinion? Can they carry off such a thing?"

Richard chuckled. "I think every bit of progress will be a struggle, full of unexpected delays and difficulties. To misquote one of their sayings, no plan survives contact with reality. But they've already shown a talent for bending to reality—you'd hardly believe some of their educational expedients. With the state government standing behind it, I think they'll make it work, one way or another."

Dr. Comber stroked his chin, gazing pensively out at the few scholars taking advantage of the sudden fair weather to read beside the fountain. "A very different set of difficulties from ours, for certain. So they would turn necessity into iron resolve?"

"They have before."

John looked over, from where he'd resumed his place by the door. "That's—very interesting. It may present a solution for us as well."

Dr. Comber cocked his head. "How so? I see no prospect of royal favor for a similar thing here, nor donors in the offing wealthy enough to endow a small faculty. If we can gain a professorship of mathematics, we'll be doing well."

"I mean, their college itself may be an answer for us. If all we can teach toward this curriculum is a few courses in mathematics and physics, it doesn't mean our efforts are wasted for not completing the whole. Students could begin here, and go on to finish their studies there, for as long as it takes us to catch up. And soon there would be Englishmen with degrees in engineering and experimental sciences, who could return here to work and teach."

"Move the first spoonful, eh?"

Richard tapped his fingers on the table. "I think that might well be an answer to one of their great difficulties as well. They're practically crippled, when it comes to giving instruction in Latin. It handicaps them, and remedying that will take many years. And where in the world can they find able scholars, who can rapidly absorb abstruse knowledge printed only in English, and who are accomplished in Latin?"

"Ah, of course. Where else but here? If there's one thing a Cambridge M.A. knows how to do, it's learn difficult material quickly."

"Exactly. They've already welcomed Pell and me. They'd be ecstatic to receive more."

"So, you two describe a way forward that might fall within our means. Ingenious."

"You're considering it, then?"

"As I said at the beginning, it's much too soon for that. But I believe what I will do now is open a correspondence of my own with John Pell. I need a feel for what's happening there. I wonder if there's anyone there from Oxford? Probably. Perhaps I'll write to this Mrs. Reardon as well." He shook his head. "Women in the colleges. New mothers founding them. Well, we must get accustomed to the idea, it seems. It's a strange world." He came to his feet. "But we must continue this later, as time for Hall approaches. For now, I'll leave you to your discussions. I thank you both for your thoughts."

John moved to close the windows as Dr. Comber left. The brief warm spell was over.

John Rant was feeling like a fish out of water. This was his first time at a meeting of the major fellows of the college. Dr. Comber hadn't really explained why he wanted him there, but presumably it would become clear in due course. He listened closely and kept silence.

James Duport was holding forth. "Yes, I know he's a fine scholar, and well regarded. But he hasn't completed the scholarly work we expect of a candidate for the M.A. and makes no pretense of doing so. How can you possibly speak of giving it to him?

It would devalue the university's name, besides flouting our statutes."

Herbert Thorndike's posture and tone dripped exasperated patience. "Not the ordinary M.A. The honorary one. A case like this is the reason we have it in our statutes."

"The sheepskin given to the favored by unwritten royal command? I know of no such interest in Leamington's case."

"No, the honorary degree conferred by the grace of the master and fellows of Trinity College. To recognize scholarly achievement outside the ordinary course of things. Don't say it's unheard of. It's just seldom heard of. You do understand why he's chosen not to pursue the M.A., I hope?"

"His ill health? I sympathize, but that doesn't alter the case."

"That, and the simple reality that one more scholar intimately familiar with the abstruse minutiae of Aristotle's cosmos would make very little difference to the world, while the same time spent in teaching advanced calculus and experimental physics will be of enormous value to our future. Logically, Newtonian mechanics fills the same place in the curriculum as astronomy. In fact, Newton's laws are chiefly the harvest of the last century's astronomical measurements. I venture to suggest that our curriculum itself may soon come to greatly resemble Leamington's studies. Or at least it should."

"Aristotle's works are the very core of a Cambridge education, Thorndike. They have been since the earliest days."

"As I recall, you were present at the Foucault pendulum demonstration. You can still say that, after seeing that effect? As if that weren't enough, the experiment to measure the gravitational constant should have driven the final nail into Aristotle's coffin. It showed universal gravitation in the most direct and unmistakable manner. It demolished any need to imagine crystalline spheres to carry the planets around."

"Well, there was no public demonstration of that. Just an exhibit of the apparatus and the reading of a report. And why was the supposed experiment done in the middle of the night? Eh? Tell me that."

"*Why?* Because we were measuring minuscule forces! The ground vibrations from a passing oxcart would be enough to disturb the torsion balance. What, do you think John's technique was faulty, or that he couldn't compose an accurate report of what happened during the experiment? If you think that, come into what we laughingly call a laboratory and run the damn experiment yourself! We can put the apparatus into your hands in an hour."

Dr. Comber raised his hand. "Heated words will do us no good. The question is whether we shall pass this grace."

Thorndike took a deep breath. "Your pardon. I apologize for the outburst. But I stand by the invitation. As Leamington continually reminds us, science progresses by repeatable experiment. The proper way to challenge a scientific result is in the laboratory. Any conclusion may be challenged in that manner."

Duport wasn't done. "Speaking of that, I believe I heard it said that it was you and Rant who did all this, wasn't it? Leamington had little or no hand in it? So why are we discussing an honorary degree for him?"

"Rant, and the others who were in the class from the beginning. I've only audited physics since the pendulum demonstration, and joined the probability lectures. John did most of the design of the apparatus, and supervised its construction. It was he who made the decision to send for piano wire, and Thomas Crosfield who devised the adjustable fluid damper. But, Leamington is a teacher, wouldn't you agree?"

"Well, yes."

"So what was he supposed to do, carry on everything himself, or teach others to do it?"

"By that reasoning, to teach. Certainly."

"And has he?"

Dr. Comber cleared his throat. "Thank you. Let us return to the main business. The donors are growing impatient. They question whether we can make a firm commitment to a regimen of mathematics and science on which an engineering curriculum could be built. There are veiled hints of endowing a chair of physics at Oxford if we don't satisfy them soon, rather than a chair of mathematics here."

Thorndike snorted. "I wish no ill to our brothers at Oxford, but you may readily guess my preference between those alternatives." That brought a few dry chuckles from around the table. "If we confer the honorary degree, we do two things. We do justice for meritorious scholarship, and we take a clear public stand. We commit ourselves to the future instead of the past."

Thomas Randolph spoke for the first time, chin propped on interlaced fingers, in measured cadence to match. "There is a tide in the affairs of men, which, taken at the flood, leads on to fortune; omitted, all the voyage of their life is bound in shallows and in miseries."

"A quotation from Shakespeare is something I'd expect from you, though not necessarily that one. But I couldn't imagine anything more apt. Much hangs on what we do now."

"I merely amused myself paraphrasing your words."

Duport had been staring at his hands. Now he looked up again. "You witnessed this gravity measurement, Master Thorndike? You vouch for the report?"

"Of course. I followed the design of the apparatus from the beginning, and checked the math myself. Not that there's anything complicated about it."

"Very well. I'll take your word for it."

Dr. Comber favored him with a wry smile. "No, I don't think

you should do that. The essence of science is repeatable experiment, as we've heard often enough. I would have you reach a conclusion by your own hands and eyes, rather than give grudging agreement to the opinions of others. Please, do the experiment. John, how long would it take to prepare?"

John snapped to full alertness at the question. "I should think three or four hours for Master Duport to read the report and familiarize himself with the plan. The mathematics is within the grasp of any B.A. The apparatus is still in place in the porter's storeroom, so we only need wait for the town to become quiet before we can start a run. Some time after eleven should be suitable. Say, four hours to take the measurements and reduce the data."

"So it could be done this very night. Good. We can convene again at noon tomorrow and finish this debate without putting off the donors any longer. James? Will you do it?"

"Since you ask in such a way, how could I refuse?"

"I thank you." Dr. Comber looked over sharply at John. "You appear to have something else on your mind. Say it."

"Er, I'm not a major fellow yet."

Thorndike laughed. "We all know how your disputations went. You will be in three weeks, short of slipping a doxy into our sacred precincts." There was a flurry of snickers around the table at that absurd thought.

"You won't like it."

Dr. Comber still had his eye fastened on him. "It seems to be my duty increasingly often of late to listen to things I don't like. Speak."

"Well, then, a number of the undergraduates and B.A.s are starting to ask why they should continue to study Aristotle's cosmos. They object to having their time wasted."

Duport erupted. "We all studied it. Why should they be excused?"

Thorndike shot back, "That was before it was discredited."

The decision hadn't been unanimous, but in the end the fellows had passed the grace, much to John's relief. Thankfully, Duport was among those assenting. Now a large part of the university, with families and friends, was gathered in Great St. Mary's Church for the commencement. Dr. Henry Smyth was officiating, he being vice chancellor this year. John had been placed at the end of the M.A.s, so that he could assist Richard. He leaned over and whispered, "Don't worry. Thorndike and I are being scrupulously careful with the proofreading. The text will be printed as you wrote it."

"The index and the table of contents, though? I've done no work on them."

"A couple of sizars are compiling them as we speak. John Stay and Edward Lucy. They're good lads, and it will benefit their educations more than waiting at table. Besides, Thorndike and I will check every entry. All right, it's time for us."

John stood up, then gave Richard his hand. They walked to the front, Richard leaning on his cane with one hand and John's arm with the other.

Dr. Smyth stepped down from the platform as they came toward him, in consideration of Richard's infirmity. He announced, "John Rant. Master of Arts." He presented the diploma to John's free hand. "Richard Leamington. Honorary Master of Arts, by the grace of the master and fellows of Trinity College." Richard let go of John's arm long enough to take the diploma, then passed it to John to carry for him as they returned to their seats, to scattered clapping.

There were two other honorary degrees given, both by royal influence.

Then two men ascended the platform and went to stand beside Dr. Smyth. John had seen the mayor of Cambridge before; the other must be Jeremiah Brantley. He looked toward Richard. Richard nodded.

The mayor had a document in his hand. Holding it out before him, he addressed the assembly in a ringing baritone. "The towns and merchants of Cambridgeshire named here now present the endowment for a chair of mathematics at this university, to be called the Cantabrigian Chair." It took him a solid two minutes to read all the donors' names. "The duty of the Cantabrigian Professor shall be to act in all ways to promote the knowledge and use of mathematics for the public good, foremost by teaching. We give this with the condition that the holder shall not be required to take holy orders." He handed it to the vice chancellor. "Dr. Smyth, will you confer the insignia?"

"Yes. Master Herbert Thorndike. Cantabrigian Professor of Mathematics." Thorndike stepped forward, and Dr. Smyth draped a colored band of cloth over his shoulders and shook his hand. "The professorship of mathematics shall encompass physics as well, until other arrangements may be possible."

✧   ✧   ✧

It looked to be a decent day. There'd been enough of a rain shower overnight to lay the dust, and not enough to turn the roads into a muddy obstacle course. Raindrops still sparkled on the wildflowers by the roadside.

Nathan watched as James Bright brought the wagon around to the warehouse door, then went to stand by the horses, calming them during the loading.

Nathan and Jeremiah bent to lift a keg into place. "Father, it's well that I heeded Daniel and went to call on Richard yesterday. He needs us now. We must bring him here. I could go with James now and we could carry him back in the wagon. There will be room enough."

"Why so? I regard him highly, but aren't they caring for him at the college?"

"Yes, but that care threatens to take a perverse turn. He's growing feeble, and his speech is slurred at times. One of the medical faculty has been badgering him unmercifully to allow bleeding and purging. You know how arrogant and headstrong some of that fraternity can be. If he can no longer make his wishes understood forcefully..."

"Well, a professor of medicine, though. Don't they know what's best?"

"I think we can safely say that nobody in England knows as much about multiple sclerosis as Richard. If he says there's no treatment, there isn't. Opiates for times of pain, but that's about all. Not to mention what the army's new field medics taught us about first aid. Loss of blood helps nobody, and sterile technique has yet to be taken seriously at Cambridge. Such practices are as likely to carry him off with a raging fever, as bring any other result. And can you imagine anything more miserable than purging a man who must be helped on and off the chamber pot? Not to mention that we owe him once again for Daniel not being caught up in that mess some time back."

"No argument there. What could have possessed him to associate with such a pack of wastrels?"

"The fallibility of all mortals, I suppose, though anyone with the least experience in business matters should have known better. But it's well Richard found out before anyone else did, and him not even a member of the same college, and made Daniel's ears burn. And so Daniel was where he belonged, attending to his studies, when the inevitable happened. For which reason he was neither sent away nor gated. I don't imagine he enjoyed it much at the time, though."

Jeremiah chuckled. "I don't imagine so, either. But what can we do for Richard here?"

"We can take care of him for what little time he has left, and allow him to die in peace, without anyone battering at him with useless unpleasantness. There's no more that anyone can do."

"That has merit, as a Christian act. Still, before bringing in a house guest, especially an invalid, your mother must have her say."

"True enough. I'll ask her, then."

"No, I'll ask her."

A step sounded by the office door. "Ask me what, Jeremiah?"

Supper was long past, yet in high summer there was still plenty of light coming through the windows of the bindery. Rant and Thorndike were doing what they could to speed things along, putting the last few signatures of the body of the book into proper order, and passing them to Master Higgs and his two journeymen to sew. Daniel Brantley came through the open door.

Rant looked up from his work. "What word, Daniel?"

"The last sheets of the index are on the press now. They tell me three hours until they're dry enough to carry here. They advise slip sheets, if they're to be bound tonight."

"Good. You'd best wait there for them, lest they wander away in that time and forget to let you back in. I would very much regret Richard passing from us without holding the completed work in his hands and seeing the words he has wrought. I didn't like the account you gave of his breathing this morning. We leave for your house the moment the work is finished; the moon will be up by then. You have something to study meanwhile, don't you?"

"Yes, Latin grammar seems to be inexhaustible for that purpose."

John grinned at the memory. "Good enough. Until your return."

Daniel left again for the print shop.

It was one thing after another. Inexplicably, two entries in the index had their page numbers transposed. Fortunately, Daniel proofread the thing while the ink was still wet, and the pressman made the correction. Still, it wasted time. The pressman ran off the corrected sheets, several sets for good measure. Daniel was off to the bindery, and the pressman closed up. The first attempt to collate the last signature was done too soon, and it smeared. It was good that there were extra sets, but they had to wait longer for one to dry sufficiently. With everyone tired, Thorndike got the signature collated wrong. The journeyman sewed it, but Master Higgs had seen everything that could possibly go wrong in bookbinding at one time or another in his long life. He caught it before it went into the binding. They took it apart and put it right. Finally it was done, but the sun was already up when Daniel and John Rant reached the Brantley house.

As Daniel led John in, the family was at the breakfast table, except for Daniel's mother, who was coming down the stairs. Father looked up and asked, "How does he fare, Abigail?"

"Poorly. His breathing hesitates, I can hardly hear it. He was able to take some small beer, but none of the porridge. I take it you've brought the book, Daniel?"

John laid down his bag by the door. "I have it." He reached in and produced it.

"Best you take it to him quickly." She turned and went back up, the others following.

Richard was propped up, several pillows supporting his back. The morning sun through the window fell where his hands rested on the coverlet. He turned his face toward the door and saw the book in John's hand. "'s that...?"

"Yes, your work, finished and in print. Here it is." He held it out as Richard raised his hand to take it. Richard got it propped up in his lap, then opened it about three quarters of the way in and flipped pages. The sun fell full on the book.

"Ch'ter eight. Ne'er saw't in print b'fore." He began reading. After five or ten minutes his hand began to tremble heavily.

Nathan looked over to John and Daniel, and said, "You go down and have something to eat. I'll stay and hold the book for him."

As they left the room, a horn sounded from the river. Father glanced out the window, then turned as well. "I must go down and receive a shipment, it seems."

Once again the sun was above the horizon. The morning light and the stirrings below awoke James Bright in his chair by the bedside. Everyone who could read Latin had assisted Leamington at one time or another the previous day. It mattered not that Bright had none; he'd taken his turn keeping company with the sick man while he slept.

It came to him as his head cleared that he heard nothing but the birds outside and the family below. He looked, and could see no movement, not even an irregular rise and fall in the man's chest. He hesitated but a moment, then called out, "Master Brantley! I think he's gone."

Nathan was the first up the stairs, but everyone else down to Cook and old Edmund was close behind. He'd seen death enough in the wars. He looked at the gray of Richard's face, and the unmoving partly open eyelids. It was hardly necessary to feel for a pulse in his neck or listen at his chest, but he did anyway. He straightened up and sighed. "You're right. He's dead, Jim. An hour, perhaps."

"What now, then?"

"He really has no family but the college itself. They'll see to him. You have a delivery in Cambridge today, if I remember correctly?"

"Yes, that's right."

Daniel said, "We can take him in the wagon, then. I'll go with you and give the news to the dean of the chapel. He has the arrangements in hand, and awaits only the word and Richard himself."

Nathan asked, "And the book?"

John answered that. "This first copy will go to the university library. All of us who worked on it have autographed the flyleaf, Richard included. I think it will remain in print for a great long while. And now, after I offer a prayer for Richard's soul, I must gather my things and be on my way to Lynn."

"You'll breakfast with us first, certainly. But won't you stay for the funeral?"

"No, I'm overdue in Grantville. I've put them off as long as I decently could, finishing this work. I must meet the faculty as soon as may be, and set to work preparing my lectures."

Daniel looked at him. "What are you to teach at the high school, then?"

"Not the high school, the college. You haven't seen John Pell's latest letter to Dr. Comber, posted in the hall?"

Daniel shook his head. "No."

"He tells us that the combined faculties have fulfilled the conditions Congress imposed for the founding of the college. They were required to prepare a complete set of examinations in the subjects required for at least one technical degree. They accomplished this for the Bachelor of Science in physics. One Eve Zibarth, a student of the late Charnock Fielder, has passed. Accordingly, the state vocational school was renamed the Thuringia-Franconia State Technical College with a greatly increased curriculum and added faculty. It conferred its first diploma at the founding ceremony.

"As for me, I'm to teach advanced calculus, in Latin. Possibly in English as well, but that's still to be decided. And I intend to carry my own studies as far as possible. I expect there will be examinations offered by the time I'm ready to sit for them. I hope to return in a few years with a Bachelor of Science in mathematics."

Nathan gave him a thin smile. "Mm-hm. Did I see a certain familiar weapon in your bag when you took out Richard's book?"

"Yes, he gave it to me some months ago. He said he could no longer use it."

"No doubt. The question is, can you use it? Have you practiced with it? Do you know what to do with it, and how to keep it in good order?"

"I've done some shooting with it, and cast more shot. I can hit a target."

Nathan snorted. "At leisure, on the shooting range, I expect you can. Stay the day with me, and I'll give you a concentrated session of army training. The roads have been quiet these many months, but I'll feel happier if you know how to fight with that fancy toy. Call it my last debt to Richard."

Author's note: Except for Richard Leamington and Daniel Brantley, the university characters are historical. Their actions are fictional, though extrapolated from available biographical information. The remaining characters are fictional.

A Relation of the Late Siege and Taking of the City of Yerevan by the Turk Including an Authentic Narrative of the Death of the Persian Commander and an Account of the Destruction Wrought by Terrible New Engines of War

Panteleimon Roberts

Mir Arash Khan looked out at the trenches of the Ottoman army and marveled at his enemy's industry. It had been scarcely seven days since the Ottoman cavalry had arrived and chased all his soldiers inside the walls, and already the city of Iravan was surrounded by their works. The Ottomans had moved with astonishing speed, appearing just five days after his spy's first report of their advance from Sivas had reached him. The messenger had nearly killed his horse carrying that report—no army Arash had ever heard of had been able to march so quickly. He had been confident when he was appointed by Shah Safi to defend the city the locals called Yerevan and that the Ottomans had called Revan until Shah Abbas had recovered it thirty-one years ago, but the suddenness with which a force of thousands of Ottoman cavalrymen had appeared had shocked him. He had expected at least a week after the warning arrived to prepare for the arrival of the Ottoman army. That had been a costly mistake—his troops outside the walls had been scattered bringing in supplies or working on extensions to the fortifications. Many of those close to the city had made it inside the walls, but he had lost almost five thousand men on that first day. Of course, that had still left him with over thirty thousand—nearly three times the usual garrison. Indeed, his men were packed so tightly inside the walls that they were all but walking on each other.

He had so many soldiers because the Ottomans had been expected. The shah's English friends had shared with him information about Murad obtained from the magicians from the future who had appeared in the Christian lands. They had said that Murad would attack Iravan this year. Murad was supposed to have refused to believe in the stories told, indeed, to have refused to believe in the magicians, but Shah Safi had clung to the predictions. As a result, he had decided to reinforce Iravan. He had also decided to execute Tahmasp Quli Khan, the man who, in the magicians' histories, had commanded the city and who had yielded it to Murad. The execution had been an excruciating affair, the sort of thing that left one with disturbing dreams. Arash knew this because, when he had been plucked from obscurity to command the defense, he had been forced to witness it as an encouragement to do his duty. Of course, if he surrendered to Murad, there would be little Safi could do to him, but his family had remained in Esfahan. And on that first day, watching as the *sipahi*s had ridden his men down, he had feared that even his best efforts might be to no avail. The second day had been no better, as the Ottomans had rapidly dug a network of trenches and begun to raise gun platforms, and his watchers had reported seeing flashes of the distinctive headgear of the janissaries in the trenches. When the tents of what could only be Sultan Murad's pavilion had been erected, tantalizingly just out of reach of even guns laid by his best gunners, he believed his worst fears had been realized. But on the third day, he had begun to wonder. The guns in the Ottoman emplacements seemed to be awfully light for siege artillery. Indeed, opposite this gate they seemed to have only a single cannon mounted on an odd high-wheeled carriage and to be using a sort of fireworks rocket to try to fill in. The rockets were a bit frightening, and dangerous to anyone near when they burst, but they seemed to need a long time to set up—so far the shortest interval had been five minutes apart—and they were not any danger to the walls.

And then there were the empty trenches. He had sent out raiding parties to try to disrupt the progress and perhaps gather in a prisoner or two to get a better feel for what faced him. They had not brought him a single prisoner. The men who returned said that, when they reached the first line of trenches, they were empty. It was only as they explored them that they ran into sudden ambushes. This experience was repeated on the next two nights. It was possible, of course, that the Ottoman commander was withdrawing his men as Arash's men approached in order to lead them into ambushes. Certainly it seemed to be an effective tactic—only about three in ten of his men came back. But to detect all his raiding parties in time to carry out such a withdrawal (for there had been no sudden firing along the front to suggest that any of the parties were annihilated at the first line of trenches) stretched credulity to the breaking point.

In fact, he was beginning to suspect that the force surrounding him might not really be the Ottoman army at all. Mir Arash Khan was increasingly convinced that what faced him was only the vanguard of that army. Murad was young and inexperienced. He was also supposed to be confident of his physical prowess, his skills with weapons, and his horsemanship. It wouldn't be the first time a man had let ability in one area convince him he had ability in all. And to a young, strong, and impetuous man, the allure of the glory that could be attained by dashing ahead with his cavalry to try to seize the city could have been overwhelming.

If he was right—if all that Murad had with him was his cavalry and a few soldiers who had run along with them—then it was possible that glory would go to Mir Arash Khan for ending the war by defeating—perhaps even killing or capturing—the Ottoman Sultan. The English had taught his men how to stand against cavalry on an open field, and he had more than enough men to mount an assault on the trenches if all the soldiers available were the mounted troops Murad could have mustered. If he acted decisively before the bulk of the enemy army could arrive, then his chances of victory were great.

And so he had planned a counterattack. The plan was simple. He would send five thousand of his men out this largest of the three city gates against the Ottomans. Fortunately, the works he had constructed immediately outside the gates had not fallen on that first mad day, and so he still controlled enough ground to allow a substantial force to be assembled. He had put his best guns and gunners on the gun platforms that had been built flanking the gate. He had had many to choose from—if all the guns that had been brought into the city were fired, they would use up all the gunpowder in a day—and he knew that they could keep the Ottoman cavalry from interfering with his troops as they formed up. They would also be able to keep the Ottoman artillery and musket men from being effective against his men as they formed up—the few guns the Ottomans had in place might have sufficed to break up a small sortie, but against an attack of the scale he planned they would be useless even if allowed to fire unimpeded. In fact, the works the Ottomans had built opposite the gate were just strong enough to fend off the sort of small attack usual in sieges. Only one real cannon, although there were some odd-looking assemblies of what seemed to be musket barrels on high-wheeled carriages like that of the cannon—and the fireworks, of course. It seemed his opponent had decided to concentrate his men and resources in accordance with an Ottoman plan of attack. Another sign of inexperience, not thinking that one's enemies might not act in accordance with one's plans.

Today was the day. He turned and gave the order, the horn was sounded, the gates swung open, and his men began running out to form up on the open space just behind the ditch while the men with ramps laid them over it. Arash felt a smile tugging at his lips as he saw signs of frantic activity in the Ottoman gun emplacement. Apparently they hadn't even kept their cannon loaded against the chance he would send a raiding party out of the gate. His own guns began to fire—the Ottomans' entrenchments would protect them, but only if they kept down. His men would have plenty of time to form up and move on the trenches. And the volume of matchlock fire coming from the trenches suggested that they were held by a few hundred men at most. Today would be a glorious day.

As he watched the Persians spill out of the gate, Kemal gritted his teeth in frustration. For eight months, ever since he had been assigned to the rockets, he had put up with the "friendly" insults of his fellow gunners. He had been told that it was a great honor that one so young had been chosen—but he knew he had been assigned to the rockets because he was junior to the others and probably also because he was from Anatolia—there was always a prejudice against Turkish gunners. Fireworks master, they called him. He had laughed, and reacted by working to truly become the master of the rockets.

He had expected that he would have a chance to make them swallow their mockery on this campaign. But Ahmed Pasha had seemed not to understand the potential of his weapon. He had refused to allow them to be used in any of the skirmishes they had already fought and, when setting up here, he had placed insane restrictions on them. Kemal had not been allowed to fire more than one rocket at a time, and had had to wait at least half an hour before firing from the same launch rack a second time. It had taken him nearly three days to get all the racks properly ranged. It should have taken less than an hour to ready all thirty racks.

Now, today, he had a perfect opportunity to show what they could do. It would take moments to launch the full battery, and that would surely send the redheads scurrying back into their hole. Yet the command to loose did not come. He looked back toward the commander, who sat on his horse calmly watching the Persians form up to attack and doing nothing else.

Ahmed Pasha, sometimes called Küçük—Little—Ahmed, watched the Persians forming up before the gate. His men were eager to get at them and he hoped he could hold them back long enough. He had allowed musket fire at them—it would have been impossible to prevent and would have made the Persian wonder if his men had done nothing. The gunners had wanted to fire too—he had had to have one of his guards knock the match from the hand of one of the gun crew—for good measure he had had the cannon tipped forward and the ball drawn out. Now the gunners were racing to reload it.

The sultan had ordered him to fix the Persians' attention here at Revan for at least a month. Today would decide if he could do it. He knew from captives that the Persians had more men and more guns than he had. But he also knew that he had stunned the Persian commander by the ferocity of his initial attack. Now, it looked like the Persian had gotten over his initial shock. If the Persian succeeded, even in a small way, today, Küçük Ahmed knew he would lose. The Persian would swamp him using his huge garrison, and he would have to retreat too early.

Küçük Ahmed was not a good loser. He planned to stun the Persian again. But to do that, he knew he had to hold his men back until the perfect moment. The moment when he could do the most damage to their confidence. Which was coming up ... now.

Kemal saw the Pasha suddenly turn his head to where the signalmen waited. Then—at last—the flags moved, signaling the time had come. He turned and slashed his hand, and his men bent to light their fuses.

Mir Arash Khan looked down with satisfaction. His men had formed up. The Ottoman musketeers had caused a few casualties, but not nearly enough. It looked like the gun crew he'd been watching had finished loading their cannon, but that would not be enough to stop—or even slow—his attack. He heard an odd noise, like a piece of cloth tearing, and looked back toward the Ottoman trenches. They had fired one of their rockets. Those toys wouldn't stop the attack either. He watched it as it headed toward his troops—some moved to avoid the place it looked like it would fall.

Kemal cursed. There was always one fuse that burned differently than the others. This one had been fast. But at least it hadn't misfired. And there went the rest—first the five that had been left in the rack that launched the first, and over the next seconds the others. One hundred seventy-nine rockets followed their premature brother toward the ground he had so slowly been allowed to range. As soon as the last left its rack, he waved the men forward to begin reloading.

Arash looked up as the odd tearing sound was repeated and magnified. Suddenly the smoke trail left by the first rocket was obscured by what seemed to be hundreds more. His troops began to scatter.

Kemal spared a glance toward the Persians as the sounds of his rockets bursting reached his ears. It had been perfect. Not one rocket had veered off course, not one had stayed in the racks. Now let them joke about fireworks.

To Arash's ears, the sounds of the explosions seemed quieter than he had expected, a bit muffled. A part of his mind concluded that each probably carried no more than two or three times the powder of a grenade. Under ordinary conditions, grenades were a danger the men could deal with. But so many grenades never came at once. The sound of the Ottoman cannon firing was a sharp punctuation to the rockets. Arash looked down. A cloud of smoke covered a long section of the center of his line. As he watched, a man emerged, staggering back toward the gate, seeming covered in blood.

"Hurry. Hurry." Kemal knew his men were working as quickly as they could, but still he felt he had to drive them on. He took a moment to look at the Persians. His rockets had cut a hole in the center of their line, and the troops on the flanks were looking shaken. Men were falling back by ones and twos to the gate, some making a pretense of helping wounded comrades, some simply heading for safety. Fewer men were leaving the Persian left, though. A brightly clad officer was moving about, clearly steadying his men. That simplified Kemal's next decision.

"Shift right two turns." He repeated the instructions a half dozen times, with variations in the degree of shift, moving down the line as his men finished reloading. He heard a curse from Mustafa—his crank had jammed. Mustafa and his loader bent down and lifted the back of the rack, manually turning it.

"Tell the gunners to concentrate their fire on the part of the trenches the smoke trails came from," Mir Arash Khan instructed the runners. The launchers were completely hidden behind earthen embankments, but having cannon balls bouncing near them should at least slow them down. Given how long the rockets seemed to need between shots, with any luck his men could be on them before a second volley could be launched.

He looked at his troops. The smoke had cleared. It wasn't—quite—as bad as he feared. They were among his best troops, after all. There was even a small group in the center that seemed to have reformed and looked ready to step off. And the left flank, where Aryo commanded, looked as ready as though nothing had happened. He ordered the signal for the advance to be raised.

And then he heard the sound of cloth tearing again.

Kemal watched his rockets fly toward the Persian lines. This launch was less perfect. Two rockets had left their racks on trajectories that were completely random, and Mustafa had shifted his rack too far—all his rockets would miss. But it would be good enough, he thought.

A ripple of explosions covered the Persians in smoke. He started to turn back when a flicker of motion caught his eye. Impossibly, the brightly uniformed officer ran out of the enveloping smoke. He was followed closely by two of his men, then four more, then... then nothing. A ripple of musket fire kicked up the dirt around the men running toward the Ottoman lines. They did not slow. A burst from one of the volley guns cut them down. Behind them, the remaining Persians were crowding the gate.

He felt a hand on his shoulder and whipped around. It was one of Ahmed Pasha's runners, his red cap slightly askew on his head.

"Ahmed Pasha commands you to put one more volley of your rockets on top of the walls."

"I can put a dozen more volleys there."

"Ahmed Pasha said to tell you one more, and only one more, if you said something like that. He also said to tell you that you have done what he needed, and done it well."

Mir Arash Khan sat in his hall, occasionally touching a cloth to the cut on his head. It was small, but seemed not to want to stop oozing blood. He had returned to his residence after the gates had been closed. The Ottomans had not tried to storm them despite the confusion created by the third volley of rockets, and all his men who lived had been brought inside the walls.

After the disaster of the morning, the day had passed quietly. The Ottomans had dug more trenches, but there had been only desultory exchanges of fire.

His commanders had pressed him to try again. They pointed out that only one man in eight had been lost—not so many for an attack on a fortified position. They ignored the fact that the attack had not even started. They argued that the fact the bombardment had stopped after the third volley meant that the Ottomans were out of the deadly rockets. They ignored the losses among his best gun crews, and his own near death.

Perhaps they were right. But Arash had been fooled once already. He had thought the Ottomans were weak and would fall before him. The bodies before the gate provided a refutation of that belief.

No, his orders were to hold the city. He would follow those orders. He had been led astray by pride, by a desire for glory. Never again. He would hold his position and let the Ottomans smash themselves against his walls if they dared.

✧   ✧   ✧

Arash smiled as the scribe left the room. The man had obviously been confused by his reaction. He had come to tell his Khan that they needed to ration supplies, that at the current rate they had only enough food for three more weeks. Whatever reaction he had expected, it was clear that Arash's peal of relieved laughter had not been it. It was also clear that he had expected a much larger reduction than Arash had ordered.

But then the man did not know what Arash did. After the disaster of yesterday, Arash had expected nothing but bad news. But it was clear that much of the food that had been planned for had been delivered and had made it inside the walls before the Ottomans had attacked. The scribe thought they had to plan for an indefinite siege, at least three months, perhaps more, before winter would force the Ottomans away. But Arash knew that Shah Safi was probably already on his way to break the siege.

For all that he had heavily reinforced Iravan, Shah Safi had not completely trusted the words of the magicians—Shah Safi did not completely trust anything—and so he had not placed his forces in front of Iravan at places where the Ottomans could have been ambushed before even coming into sight of its walls. But he had created a mobile force that he himself led and had positioned it so that it could move toward any spot that was threatened.

Despite the chaos of the day the Ottomans had attacked, several messengers had been sent and even if all had been caught, the failure of his usual weekly report to arrive would have caused the alarm to be sounded. In fact, by now, the shah's army was probably marching to his relief. It was, at most, a four-week march away. If they forced their pace, they might even arrive before he would have needed to start rationing.

Better to be safe, of course. And cutting rations would actually be good for morale—the men would expect it as part of how things were done in a siege, and if any were captured, they would tell the enemy what he expected to hear. He had ordered the rations cut by enough to make them last six weeks. If he dug into what the inhabitants of the city had hidden away for themselves, he could probably stretch it to eight weeks. But long before that became necessary, he had no doubt that he would see the Ottomans crushed between the hammer of the shah's army and the anvil of the fortress of Iravan.

✧　　✧　　✧

Ahmed looked down at the map. He wasn't sure if he liked these new maps—to be sure, they showed the geometry of the area with great precision, and the terrain—where it was shown—was accurate as well. But the old maps, despite their inaccuracies, had given him a better idea of how long it took to go between places, even if the actual distances were sometimes off. Still, if what the messenger his scouts had captured had told them was true, then the Persian relief force was at least a three-week march away. He could count on at least three days warning from his *deli* scouts or the Tartars who had spread out from Revan. So all he had to do to accomplish his goals was keep the Persians bottled up until he was told the relief force was close by, and then he could fall back on the positions being prepared by the *sekban*s who had followed his strike force. With any luck the Persians would chase him and he would get a chance to bloody their noses.

He looked at the man who had brought the report. "You are certain he said it was the shah himself who led the force?"

"Yes. He was emphatic about the vengeance that would soon fall on us."

"Interesting." He sent the man to get himself a meal while he thought about the possibilities. Shah Safi had a reputation for being . . . erratic. With such a man in command of the opposition, there might be opportunities.

Arash had much to be pleased about. The Ottomans had not advanced their trenches significantly, nor was there any indication that they were trying to undermine the walls. They seemed content to stand off and shoot at him—their bombardment had been continuous, yet the guns they were using were definitely on the light end of the scale for siege weapons. They were able to chip away at his walls, but the rate at which damage was being done meant that the walls were unlikely to fall in the next few months.

Yet, as he looked out over the Ottoman trenches, Arash fought an unhappiness that he knew was unreasonable, even ridiculous. Today had been, by his calculations, the first day it would be reasonable to expect the arrival of the relief force. And they had not come.

It didn't help that he was accompanied on his walk of the walls today by Bestam, one of the shah's loyal circle who Arash was convinced had been sent to spy on him. Bestam commanded only a thousand cavalrymen, all also fanatically loyal to the shah, but nevertheless he behaved as though it occasionally slipped his mind that Arash was in command. But the major reason that Arash would have preferred not to have him along was that Bestam insisted on always wearing his "Haydar's crown," the tall hat whose traditional red color had given the Ottomans their nickname of redheads for the Persians. It attracted attention that Arash would have preferred to avoid.

In fact, as he stood looking out over the field, his eye was suddenly attracted to one of the Ottoman guns. Its crew seemed to be working with great diligence to train the gun right where he was standing. He drew back, to Bestam's apparent amusement. Arash was briefly tempted to let the man stand there. Instead, he waved him down.

An instant later he had the satisfaction of seeing Bestam's face lose its amused look as the Ottoman's ball sent stone fragments flying over the walkway. For just a moment he felt a bit of kinship with the man as Bestam tried to cover his loss of composure.

"It's a good thing they didn't think to bring along any of their real siege guns. Our walls would collapse in a few days if they had."

"Once they got the range, anyway. This place is so small a real gun would send its ball over it—or through it."

"Where do you suppose their big guns are? They've always brought a few along in the past."

"I don't know…" Arash hesitated. Something bothered him about this, and he felt that he was on the edge of an answer. But before he crossed that edge, Bestam decided to demonstrate his loyalty.

"Perhaps the shah sent someone to destroy them. They could have been far back, given how quickly these people arrived—a raid in their rear would have surprised them."

Arash saw the men near them—who had been ostentatiously not listening to their officers' conversation—straighten a bit at that. He knew that that wasn't where his thoughts had been headed, but it was a possibility. Better yet, it was a possibility that would hearten the men. So he stopped trying to find his answer and contented himself with saying loudly enough to ensure he was overheard, "It could be."

✧   ✧   ✧

The footsteps of the messenger woke Arash before the man could speak.

"What is it?"

"Music," the man was clearly flustered by the question from a man he had thought was sleeping. "We can hear music from the walls."

Arash's look spurred the man to further explanation, "Our music. Not the music of the Turks."

Arash moved with a speed that he wouldn't have believed himself capable of the day before. As he came out into the road, he heard the music. The sound was distinctive. It could only be from a band accompanying the relief force. It was distant, but the drums especially carried easily through the quiet that came just before dawn.

The quiet. The Ottomans had not allowed it to remain quiet for more than a few minutes at a time since the siege had begun. A basic tactic, aimed at denying the defenders rest. But it was quiet now.

"When did they last fire a cannon at us?"

The messenger who had followed him out into the twilight looked confused.

"I don't know. Not since I woke tonight."

They have good scouts—they would have known the relief force was coming. They must have waited for night to withdraw.

He grabbed the messenger by the shoulder.

"Go and tell my deputy to rouse the garrison. We must get ready to welcome the shah."

The dawn sun shone on walls lined with men waiting to greet the army that had driven the Ottomans away. Arash looked out on the Ottoman trenches. It was clear they had left in a great hurry—they seemed to have abandoned all their heavy equipment in place and here and there in the trenches he saw furtive stirrings, as though men forgotten in the rush to get away were trying to move unnoticed. Arash supposed he should have someone fire on the stirrings, but he was so happy that the siege was at an end that he was inclined to be charitable and let the stragglers escape if they could.

Then the music swelled and the band came into view. The men began a cheer that stuttered away as the music changed abruptly into an Ottoman martial tune and the trenches that had seemed empty suddenly filled as the men who had been lying in them stood up and began to insult the defenders.

The delegation of his soldiers had been respectful, but firm. They knew how low the supplies were, and the Ottomans had made it clear that their relief had somehow been stopped. Breaking out was clearly impossible. If Arash wouldn't negotiate he would be replaced by someone who would.

Now Arash looked out the new hole in the wall of his official residence—the Ottomans had punctuated their jeers with an artillery barrage that had reached inside the city—and prayed for a solution. He could hold on for two weeks, perhaps four, before food ran out. If the troops were willing, he could go further, but the troops had made it clear that they weren't willing. But then... if word of a surrender reached Esfahan, whether he or his men acting for him had made it, his family would pay.

He had summoned his deputy Behmanesh and his watcher Bestram and told them that they needed to play for time. Behmanesh was to go and attempt to negotiate with the Ottomans. He pointed out to Bestram that, as long as they thought he was negotiating, the rest of the men would continue to resist, if only in the hope of improving the terms. After Bestram left, muttering that it would be better to kill the members of the soldiers' delegation to remind the others where their loyalties should lie, he told Behmanesh to negotiate as though it was real, and get the best terms possible. And then he had spoken in a way that had clearly puzzled Behmanesh.

"You have no family, do you?"

"No. They were taken by the plague two years ago. Only I am left."

"In these times, that can be a blessing. May Allah go with you."

Ahmed Pasha had felt content. It wasn't often that God made it so clear whose side He was on. When a Tartar messenger had brought word that the Persian army had stopped in the middle of the day while it was still a three-day march away—one day before he would have ordered his own forces to begin to fall back—he had concluded that he was no longer a distraction. Less than twelve hours later his conclusions were verified when another messenger had brought word that a newly captured prisoner had explained that

the sudden halt was the result of word reaching the army that Sultan
Murad had besieged Baghdad and that the army was now going
to retrace its steps and go to relieve that city. He had immediately
sent messages—and some of the *sipahi* cavalry—to ensure that the
Persians would be harassed at every opportunity, and then turned
his mind to his new task of ensuring that the garrison remained
bottled up and unable to follow the relief force.

He'd wanted to do more than just keep them bottled up, however.
Sooner or later he would have to end his siege, and that would leave
the Persians with an intact army. He wanted to inflict more casualties on them. Destroying small raiding parties and picking men off
the walls were just pinpricks. But aside from that one attempt, the
Persian commander had offered him no real opportunities.

Then that troop of Tartars had ridden in with the instruments
they'd taken as plunder after falling on a Persian band that had
found itself left behind when the Persian army had changed direction. It had been too good an opportunity to pass up. Now the
Persians knew their relief force wasn't coming and, since prisoners
had told him that their food was running out, that meant the
commander would have to do something other than just sit there.

Yes, Ahmed Pasha had felt content. The feeling had lasted almost
six hours. Then he had received word that the Persians had sent
a delegation to negotiate with him. That was unexpected. It was
clear that the Persians had almost as many men in the city as he
had outside of it. Of course, he had been at some pains to keep
them from realizing that. Now he would have to take even greater
pains. The only thing to do was to offer such unreasonable terms
that the Persian would have to refuse them.

But, just in case, he would have some of the *sekban* troops
that had been preparing his fallback positions move up. After all,
they had been sent along to garrison the city if he did manage to
capture it. And letting the Persians see fresh troops arriving would
help keep them from realizing how closely matched they were.

Behmanesh was downcast as he spoke.

"He was completely unreasonable. We are offered our lives as
slaves to the Ottomans, nothing more, if we leave the city with all
stores and weapons intact and only if we accept immediately. It
was all I could do to get an extra day for us to consider the offer."

Arash found himself relaxing. His course was now set.

"Well, I will talk to him tomorrow. Perhaps I can convince him to soften things a bit."

Ahmed was hard pressed to hide his astonishment. Not only had the Persian returned for further talks, he had brought along the commander of the city. Their situation must be worse than he had thought. Against any reasonable expectation, it might just be that he could actually take the city. Perhaps a concession or two might be in order, although he would have to avoid anything that would let the shah get his garrison back.

When the Persians were ushered into the tent that had been set up for the talks, Ahmed found himself confused by the demeanor of the commander. Mir Arash Khan had sat through the initial round of diplomatic pleasantries giving every impression that his mind was elsewhere.

The Persian's first words, spoken very softly after the pleasantries were over, were also a bit off key.

"Your sultan is not here then?"

"I am who you must deal with. My sultan has more important matters to attend to."

"Of course. I meant no insult."

The Persian seemed to be trying to bring his mind back from wherever it had strayed.

"Your terms are quite severe. We are to march out unarmed, leaving all intact, and become your slaves. And we must agree by today."

"That is so," Ahmed temporized, his mind racing. How to soften it so that the man would throw open the gates. He could get no feel for what the man wanted. Offer him something for himself and something for his men and see which he went for.

"Of course, I would be willing to offer safe passage for yourself and your family, and," a nod to the Persian's deputy, "some of your senior officers as a token of my respect for your determined resistance. And, of course, any of your men who should choose to abandon their false beliefs might well be freed to serve in our ranks."

Interesting. The deputy had shown irritation at the first offer and started to object when he made the second offer. But Arash simply gestured to stop whatever objection Behmanesh was going to make.

"My men are urging this course of action..."

An astonishing admission.

"...and I cannot know what they will do, although you may find fewer who will abandon the truth than you think. As for my family, they are in Esfahan."

Those last eight words were the key. The words themselves, written down, would sound like defiance—a claim that his family was safe from Ahmed. But the tone in which the words were spoken was one of despair. And then came a shock.

"Very well. I will accept those terms with one stipulation. As a matter of honor, I and my personal guard must be allowed to ride out under arms to make our surrender."

The deputy had a look of confusion on his face. Ahmed agreed with it—he had never heard such a proposal before—but he elected to ignore it.

"How large is your guard?"

"One thousand men."

Ahmed looked at Arash. And what he saw in his eyes convinced him.

"It is agreed then."

Arash was not surprised when Bestam strode into the hall, hand on the hilt of his *shamshir*.

"Is it true? You are surrendering? Wasn't it made clear to you what would happen?"

Arash looked at him for a moment and then said, "Yes. Yes. And yes."

Bestam froze. Apparently he had been prepared only for denial.

"I received very good terms for myself. I have even secured permission to leave the city accompanied by my personal guard under arms."

"What? What are you talking about? You don't have a personal guard."

"Of course I do. You command it."

Bestam seemed unsure whether he was being offered some sort of a bribe or just dealing with a madman. Arash pressed on.

"Think! If we try to assemble for an attack, they simply shoot fireworks at us, and use their new volley guns to kill those the fireworks miss. But tomorrow we come out in an orderly fashion and start to come toward them at the walk..."

Light dawned, "...we get out of the place they have their fireworks aimed for, then we can make a charge. I guess I don't need
to kill you. Perhaps I will get to kill Murad instead."

Arash hesitated. That possibility clearly justified his actions to
Bestam. Only Behmanesh had heard him ask the question, and
Ahmed hadn't—precisely—said that the sultan wasn't here.

"Perhaps."

Bestam had moved his men to the gate the night before, replacing
the soldiers who had been on duty there so that they could complete
their preparations without anyone realizing what they were doing.
Arash's own preparations had been simple. He had gotten dressed,
handed Behmanesh with a letter naming him commander in his
stead, and given him a final command: "Whatever happens, once I
am gone, wait an hour and then do what you think best."

And now Arash was riding over the ground that had seen
the failure of his first attempt to sweep the Ottomans away. It
was a remarkably pleasant day, with a slight breeze and a few
fluffy clouds in the sky. He found that he was easily distracted.
Fortunately Bestam was occupied with the business of getting his
men in position.

Bestam had given a lot of thought to getting outside the area
that the rockets had swept. He had had bridges built to let the
horses cross over the ditch and had had the one placed in the
center weakened so that it collapsed as the second horse walked
over it. This gave an excuse for the cavalry to spread out and
present a wide front outside the ditch, while the excitement at
the center explained why the troop didn't close up again quickly.
Still, it took a while for a thousand men to get into position.
Arash didn't mind.

But eventually they were all across the ditch and Bestam gave
the prearranged signal. Arash didn't like the man, but his men
were good at what they did. As one they turned and began their
charge. Arash simply tried to keep pace with Bestam.

Kemal had watched with growing concern as the horsemen
had crossed the ditch unmolested. He had been told it had to
be allowed by no less a person than Ahmed Pasha himself. He
had also been told that he would have to be ready to break up
any charge that might be made. When he had pointed out that

once they were outside the ditch, they would be inside the range at which the rockets were intended to work, he had simply been told to find a way.

He had quickly concluded that increasing the angle at which the rockets were launched was probably a bad idea. The horses would be moving fast, and he wasn't sure just when he would be ordered to send them at their target. Calculating the right angle as cavalry closed was not a task he wanted to try. Instead he had lowered the angle. The rockets would be sent nearly horizontally at the Persians if they decided to attack. He had picked a place a little over halfway between his position and the ditch as an aiming point because it looked like a place where any attackers would have to bunch up.

He had also personally picked out the rockets they would use, avoiding any that seemed in any way imperfect. There had been some unpleasant surprises, including a rocket that had exploded before it had left the rack, killing the luckless Mustafa. Oddly, the explosion seemed to have fixed the launch rack—the adjusting crank no longer jammed.

He had also trimmed each of the fuses himself. The rockets would launch almost in the instant the fuses were lit—the men lighting them would have just enough time to leap away.

Then he turned away from the Persians and looked toward Ahmed Pasha. The commander had positioned himself a bit farther back and higher up, with two of the men with the new long barreled "rifles" and two men with traditional bows. As Kemal watched, he pointed at something back where the Persians were. The four men all shifted, clearly concentrating on what the Pasha had pointed to, but Kemal kept his attention on Küçük Ahmed. He didn't want to chance even a second's delay once the Pasha gave the order to launch.

Suddenly and within a heartbeat of one another the riflemen fired and the bowmen loosed their arrows. At the same moment the Pasha looked at Kemal and made a slashing gesture. Kemal didn't wait for the formal signal, but turned back to his launchers, and for a moment his voice froze in his throat. The Persian cavalry was closing the distance incredibly quickly. "Light them, light them," he screamed, running toward his launchers as if he could somehow make the rockets launch sooner by his presence.

✧   ✧   ✧

Arash found himself on the ground looking up at the clouds. He had had the wind knocked out of him when he was shot off his horse, but somehow it no longer seemed important to try to breathe. He knew he had done everything he could. If God willed, it would be enough to save his family.

He didn't hear the sound of cloth tearing.

Ahmed Pasha looked out over the ground where the bodies of the Persian cavalry lay. It had been an hour since a single volley of rockets had broken their charge. Even trained warhorses didn't like the noisy flame-spitting rockets, whether or not they were hit by them. The cavalrymen trying to control their mounts had been defenseless against his cannon, his volley guns, and even his men with their old matchlocks. He had not lost a single man.

The stories that would reach the redheads about the fall of Revan would terrify them. Terrifying the sultan's enemies was a good thing and Ahmed felt no regrets about doing it. If this new way of making war did not terrify the Persians into making peace, then Ahmed would urge the sultan to let him pursue them with the new weapons until they were utterly annihilated. Not because he hated the Persians. He didn't. If they made peace, so much the better. But the day was coming when the Ottomans would be facing men who also fought war in this new way, and when that day came they could not afford to still be fighting the Persians. He didn't hate those men either. The men who claimed to be from the future. The men from whom the knowledge of the new gun carriages and the new rockets and the new design of volley gun and, most importantly, the best ways to use them had come. He didn't hate them, but he knew he would have to fight them. And they would be harder to terrify.

But now he had to deal with the Persians in the city. They had signaled that they wanted a truce. He would act angry, but in the end let them have the same terms. This attack would give him a reason for having them come out in small, easily controlled groups. His past experience told him that many of them would offer to forgo their false beliefs if it would save them from slavery. That would be good—even if they secretly continued in their errors, their allegiance would not be tested in the fight to come—these men from the future were all true infidels. And some of those who were adamant in their allegiance—perhaps a hundred—could be sent back to their shah with the body of Mir Arash Khan. A gesture of respect for a brave enemy, he would call it. That might make peace easier. And perhaps it might save some innocents in Esfahan.

Zaynab held her daughter and watched her son, who sat between her and the door. They waited in silence and near darkness. They had exhausted all possible diversions in the week that had passed since they had been confined after word had arrived of the fall of Iravan.

Zaynab was torn. She loved her husband. She had wanted Arash to return. But if he lived, and perhaps even if he did not, she knew she and her children would pay the price for his failure to prevent the loss of that city.

Beyond the fact that the city had fallen, she knew nothing. The servants who brought the plain food every day didn't speak, and the guards that accompanied them also ignored her questions. All she had been told was that she and her children would be confined until the situation was clarified.

The sound of the bolt being drawn seemed to echo. It was too early for the meal. Rustem stood up, still facing the door. His stance said he intended to defend his mother and sister as well as a nine-year-old boy could do.

The door opened. Light spilled in, blinding her so that she could not make out the face of the man who stood in the doorway.

"Your husband has fallen in the service of the shah. Go home and mourn him."

𝔉𝔯𝔶𝔦𝔫𝔤 𝔓𝔞𝔫

Anette Pedersen

Part 1

Rostock, the harbor, 31 October 1634

"This is a cold evening, young man. Would you care to keep me company for a drink?"

Lasse had noticed the thin man eyeing him for a while, and wasn't surprised when he finally spoke. Instead Lasse turned with his sweetest smile and the twist displaying his elegant legs that he learned during the year he'd spent as Otto von Quadt's plaything.

"Gladly. I seem to have missed my ship." Lasse tried to hide his lowborn Swedish accent, and imitate Otto's upper-class German, but knew it wouldn't quite work.

"Ah, are you a Dane?" The thin man opened the door to the half-timbered tavern, and stood aside to let Lasse enter first. Lasse considered accepting the man's suggestion—anything to throw Otto off his trail would be fine—but decided to stick a bit closer to the truth.

"Only sort of. I'm from Norway." Lasse wasn't, but his grandmother had been, and had left just ahead of a witch-trial. It was the silver that the old harridan had earned from her herbal remedies and abortifacients that had enabled Lasse to buy an apprenticeship with the cook at the Oxenstierna manor house. The cooking she

163

taught him had let him rise to junior cook in the household of Princess Kristina. But it was the poisons she taught him that let him escape from Otto's house here in Mecklenburg.

Lasse sat down on the bench by the rough trestle table near the fireplace and wondered how to suggest something to eat as well. The landlord, happily, made that suggestion when the thin man ordered a bottle of Rhenish wine. Lasse knew how dangerous it could be to display any kind of weakness, in case the thin man turned out to have more in common with Otto than a taste for pretty young men. The last of the money he had stolen from the corpse of Otto's comrade had run out yesterday, so he accepted an offer of a few slices of meat pie.

"My name is Friedrich Messer, silversmith," said the thin man pouring the sweet, white wine into the clay mugs, "I've just arrived from Copenhagen and must continue on to Magdeburg tomorrow. Prince Ulrik of Denmark commissioned a set of silver goblets from me as a betrothal present for Princess Kristina. They are of course being guarded by my man in my room, so I find myself eating quite alone tonight. A state that I really dislike." He looked at Lasse with what was probably supposed to be a knowing smile, but which actually made him look like a leering skull.

The mere mention of the princess made Lasse want to scream in pain and anger, but Otto had trained him well, so he made sure to smile back, while looking Herr Messer deep in the eyes. Two years ago Lasse had been so proud of his promotion into the royal Swedish household. It had been no secret among the servants that the queen didn't like her daughter. She had even tried to do her harm before the king had given the princess her own household and ordered the queen to stay away. Lasse still had no idea whether accusing him of trying to poison the princess had been the queen's attempt to get back into the king's good graces, or Otto's way to get Lasse into his power. What Otto had said during the months he had sent Lasse through hell could certainly not be relied upon. Or perhaps it had been yet another skirmish in the ongoing power struggle between the queen and Axel Oxenstierna, who had recommended Lasse for the position as the princess's junior cook. All Lasse really knew was that within minutes of the queen shouting poison, he had found himself being beaten senseless and thrown into a stinking hole of a cell beneath the castle. His attempts to protest that he really hadn't noticed the hairline crack in the pewter had been ignored, and once he regained consciousness he had quickly become so terrified by the jailor's talk of torture and execution for treason that he had barely felt the pain and humiliation of having the man rape him. This was repeated several times during the next days, alternating with new beating and threats of what the jailor would do to Lasse if he told of the rape during the process—even though no one would, of course, take the word of a traitorous servant over that of a respectable, church-going married man.

"Do try the egg pie as well." Herr Messer pushed the brass dish towards Lasse. "It really is outrageous the prices farmers demand for food these days, but the political situation does open many new opportunities for a master craftsman."

Lasse nodded in agreement, but in his mind he was seeing Otto coming to take him away from the cell in Stockholm. Otto had looked like the Savior himself in the flickering torch-light, with his handsome face and silver-embroidered white silk, taking Lasse away from the cell, promising that his hardships were over, and that Otto would keep him safe in his castle in Mecklenburg. Otto was the son of one of the queen's ladies-in-waiting from her youth in Germany. Immediately on his arrival in Stockholm, his beauty, wit and charm had made him the queen's favorite. He had used his position quite ruthlessly to amass wealth and remove rivals, but that was business as usual for a courtier. Lasse had known nothing about the games Otto played for his pleasure.

Looking back Lasse could see that Otto had deliberately set out to break his will by gaining his love and trust, and then breaking it, over and over again, in a devil's circle of betrayal and hope, abuse and excuse. And something had broken. It just hadn't been Lasse's will. Lasse wasn't sure exactly what it was that was gone, but three weeks ago when he had stood looking at what was now the corpse of the most recent "friend" Otto had told him to entertain, he finally realized that the bright, young Swedish boy who had made such beautiful pies and sauces was now gone forever. He still planned to go back to Sweden, but his vague idea of seeking out Oxenstierna, exposing Otto's schemes and crimes, and getting his old job back, could never work. Even if Oxenstierna believed him, he would be like a gutter rat set in the place of one of those caged songbirds in the queen's garden.

On the other hand, there was now very little—if anything—Lasse would stop at doing to remain out of Otto's power. Dragging his mind back to the present where Herr Messer droned on about his royal connections, how important he was, and how Lasse should really come to his room to see the goblets, Lasse laid his plans.

Shit! The bastard was a beater! Lasse twisted to break the silver chains binding him, as the whip hit him again. He hadn't liked the chains, but Herr Messer's explanation about liking to see a beautiful body wrapped in the work of his hands had seemed innocent enough, and it wasn't until Herr Messer had suddenly tied a gag over his mouth that Lasse had realized his danger. Ignoring the pain from the whip, Lasse concentrated on twisting a kink in the chain. He had been tied before, both for real and with the purpose of letting him think he could escape, and knew that the chain would break easier at a kink than if he just pulled.

At last the chain broke, and when the whip came down again Lasse rolled off the bed and got hold of his knife from his doublet on the chair. Herr Messer stood frozen for a moment before shouting and running for the door. Before he could reach it, Lasse grabbed the fleeing man and with a hand over his mouth, cut his throat with a single stroke. Only when the blood stopped spouting did Lasse let go of the corpse. He held the knife ready to strike again, when the door in front of him began to open. The intruder was a short, rather skinny, young woman that he vaguely remembered seeing in the taproom. Seeing that she was also holding a knife in her hand made him pause.

The woman looked down at the corpse, then looked up at Lasse, smiled and leaned against the door-frame. "I thought I heard a noise I recognized, but you seem to have taken care of the problem yourself. He's quite dead. They always are when they've bled like that. Why don't you grab your pants and get out of here, before your customer's valet comes to see what's happened? He looks like he might like to listen at the door."

Lasse nodded, ripped the gag from his mouth, and dressed quickly, hissing as his shirt slid over the welts on his back. As he bent to take Herr Messer's purse, he noticed the velvet bag containing the goblets and stuffed those inside his slightly too large doublet as well.

"Quick," said the woman turning towards the stairs.

"What goes there? Help! Thieves!" Herr Messer's valet shouted and blocked the narrow staircase. Lasse heard the sound of chairs turning over and heavy feet stamping in the taproom below.

"Damn! They think I'm with you. This way." The woman grabbed Lasse's arm and pulled him toward the other end of the narrow corridor and down an even narrower staircase.

"Stop them! They're getting away! Go around to the stable!" Lasse recognized the voice of the tavern keeper as he hurried down the dark stairs. From his wanderings during the day he knew that a passage led from the stable yard to the maze of old, and twisted alleys between the harbor and the Maria Church. If he and the woman could get there, they could quickly rid themselves of their followers, but three people were running to cut them off. The stable boy, waving the pitchfork he had grabbed, probably wouldn't use it unless he was directly attacked, but would the woman be able to take out one of the men, while Lasse fought the other? That question was quickly answered as she kicked one man in the balls—seemingly without breaking her stride—and shouted "*Herauss!*" at the boy so furiously that he dropped the pitchfork and stepped back in fear. That left only one man for Lasse to deal with, but more were coming down the stairs behind them, so he made a feint with his knife towards his opponent's eyes before copying the woman's kick, and following her out in the alley. He stopped only to cut the purse strings of both the groaning men.

"Let's stop here." The woman stopped and pulled Lasse into the shadow beneath a stairway. During his time with Otto, Lasse had developed a strong dislike of having anyone touch him, but for some reason having this young woman pull him around seemed natural, and didn't bother him at all. Once out of the stable yard they had quickly slowed their run to a walk to avoid catching anyone's attention, but after ambling around for a while, the woman started heading south along the hill, as if having a specific goal in mind.

"Now, I don't need to ask what was going on in that tavern, but what are—or were—your plans, boy?" The woman folded her arms, and leaned against the wall in the same position she had assumed in the tavern.

"I was planning to go back to Sweden, but needed the money for the passage. I have that now." Lasse shrugged. "I've sold the horse I arrived on, but I could walk to Warnemünde in the morning."

"You'd better disguise those pretty looks of yours before trying to leave town." She pulled a small knife from somewhere in her skirts, and started using it to clean her fingernails. Lasse smiled. He had absolutely no doubt the woman could be dangerous, but seeing her imitate the ways of a bully boy was still kind of cute.

"And you? How much did I damage your plans?" he asked.

She shrugged but looked a little worried. "We'll have to abandon our belongings, and Viktor will not be pleased."

"Your pimp?"

"Oh no, we don't have to sell our body these days." She stopped seeming a little surprised at her own words, then nodded and went on. "Viktor is an arms dealer, and I work as his clerk. We don't normally work out of Rostock, and didn't use our real names in the tavern, so there's no big problem."

"Good." Lasse's smile felt a lot more genuine than normal these days, but then he really didn't need an angry pimp to deal with as well.

The woman looked up and down Lasse with a speculative look on her face. "You're rather good with that knife, boy." She paused. "And you look completely harmless. Viktor wouldn't have any use for you in bed, for himself or for others. He doesn't work that way. But if you'd be willing to gather information, and perhaps be the unexpected guard to his back, he would look after you in return. Probably not hire you full time, but pay for any job you do. And he pays well."

Lasse lifted an eyebrow in surprise, but before he could answer, the young woman stepped away from the wall and walked toward two men who were crossing the square. Judging from her gestures she was telling them what had happened as she led the men back toward Lasse.

"I am Viktor and I have no use for a useless pretty boy, especially not one that has cost me money." The bigger of the two men grumbled with a strong accent while folding his arms and leaning against the wall in exactly the same pose and place that the small woman had just left.

"I am deeply grateful for the lady's help, and I apologize for costing you and your people the belongings left in the tavern. On the other hand, I don't think anybody could reasonably expect you to pay your bill." To his horror, Lasse could hear that he hadn't quite managed to keep all his amusement out of his voice, but the big man didn't seem offended, and just gave a grunt as response.

"Viktor, I really think it would be worth it to take the boy along. I like the way he thought to snatch up the purses of the two men we kicked down." The woman paused and seemed to relax and soften a little now her friends had arrived. "In fact, even Brigitte was impressed by his behavior tonight."

Lasse didn't understand the last remark, but it seemed to make Viktor accept the woman's recommendation.

"As you wish, my dear Tat'yana. Boris, give the boy your hood, and let's find Vladimir's taproom. We can spend the night in his back room, and get some disguises tomorrow. What's your name, boy?"

"Lasse." Lasse pulled the old-fashioned hood with the big collar over his head and followed the others across the square. He had no intention of finding himself in anybody's power again, but then Otto would not be looking for Lasse in a group of travelers.

"And do you have any other trade but your looks?"

"I used to be a cook." Lasse couldn't hear any emotions in the big man's voice, as if he not only didn't judge Lasse for making a living as a catamite, but actually didn't care very much.

"Can you do poisons?"

"Yes."

"And would you?" Viktor stopped and looked over his shoulder.

Lasse was about to just answer yes, but stopped to think. Would he? Granny had taught him how to make portions for just about anything, including death, but poison was difficult to control. He would gladly have poisoned the wells at Otto's estate, killing everybody in the household, but he could not imagine doing the same at Oxenstierna's estate, or even at the royal castle.

"Not for everyone or everywhere. Besides, strong sleeping draughts are usually just as useful, and much more forgiving of mistakes."

"Hm. Cannot deny that. You can come with us. We operate out of the Vulgar Unicorn in Stralsund."

Part 2

Stralsund, 30 April 1635

"Why do you spend so much time at the harbor?" The voice of Nicolaus Montanus sounded tired and old, and judging from the black circles under his eyes he had spent the night on his knees in prayer again. Lasse closed the door to the small study and went to the young man he had been living with for the past four months.

"I'm not fishing for customers if that's what you think." For once Lasse didn't smile or try to be graceful as he sat on the second chair at the writing desk.

Nicolaus shook his head and sighed. "I didn't think so. I was just wondering." He paused. "Lasse, I love you. It might be a tainted love according to the laws of man and God, but it is love, not just lust. I've been in lust before—and dealt with it. This is something else. I alternate between wanting to lean on the strength you hide behind that pretty surface, and protect you from the darkness I sometimes see in your eyes when you're not aware that I'm watching. I want you beside me for the rest of my life, and yet, when I reach out to you, I feel like I'm reaching for a shadow in a mirror. As if you're not really here or not quite real. What are you, Lasse? A mirage, like the sailors tell of? Or some kind of darkness from my own soul?" Nicolaus' usually soft voice had grown in intensity until it was almost grating.

Lasse sighed and put his legs up on the heavy crossbeam beneath the table. Nicolaus wasn't just a customer, but he also wanted more from Lasse than just a body and an agreeable surface. And Lasse didn't feel anywhere near ready to trust anyone with his heart and mind again. Not after Otto. On the other hand, he also didn't want to leave Nicolaus. Lasse liked the ardent young priest, and wished their life together wouldn't hurt Nicolaus so much. For Lasse, it didn't matter. He didn't desire anyone, not even Tat'yana or Nicolaus. As long as it paid, did him no damage, and didn't hurt too much, it was all the same to him. The money he earned from his jobs for Viktor actually meant that he hadn't needed to accept any customers lately, but of course those jobs might be even more difficult for Nicolaus to accept than what had happened to Lasse in the past. After all, Lasse had then been a suffering victim, something he wasn't any more, and was determined never to become again.

"Did you know that evil is real?" Lasse kept his eyes fixed on the candle in the heavy pewter candlestick on the table rather than looking at Nicolaus. He couldn't take the young priest completely into his confidence, not even as much as he had told Tat'yana, but he supposed he did owe Nicolaus some kind of trust. "I've been touched by such evil. *No!*" Lasse raised a hand when Nicolaus sat up, suddenly alert. "I'm not talking about evil from the devil, but about evil in a man. Something delighting in destruction and betrayal, but entirely of this world."

"But my dear Lasse, such are the signs of the devil." Nicolaus was now smiling and looking a lot happier.

"No. I don't agree. There is evil that is entirely in man, and that we cannot blame on the devil." This was the first time Lasse had ever argued with Nicolaus, or showed any kind of disagreement, and the young priest's smile was growing broad enough to split his face. "But let us take that discussion another day, Nicolaus." Lasse hesitated, wanting to be honest, but not really sure how far it would be safe to go. "Back when I was a cook . . . I've never told you that, but I was and I was good at it. Back then I used to be quite fond of one of the young maids, who'd smile at me and call me Cookie. Right now I don't suppose I'm really interested in anything but survival and revenge against the man who turned me into what I am today. But the point is that I'm not certain I could ever love a man. Not like you love me. Do you think—" Lasse suddenly had to stop and swallow. "—Do you think you could possibly settle for some kind of friendship instead?"

Nicolaus, with his smile still in place and his eyes filled with tears, said, "My dearest Lasse, I'd be absolutely delighted."

"I suppose the sea means freedom to me. Getting away and leaving the past behind. Including the past me." Lasse smiled wryly, and looked at the sunlight glittering on the water across the harbor.

"To me it's just frightening. I have no intentions of ever sailing if I can avoid it." Nicolaus was looking at him rather than at the sea. Things had actually gotten a lot better between the two of them since they had stopped sharing a bed. Nicolaus still took delight in teaching Lasse all kinds of things from his beloved books, but he no longer spent most of his nights kneeling in prayer, and joining Lasse for his daily walk around the harbor had given him brighter eyes and a better appetite. "What frightens you, Lasse?"

"Frightens?" Lasse started walking again. "Well, the mere thought of falling back into the power of Otto von Quadt is enough to scare me out of my mind, but aside from that? Being helpless, perhaps. People with the power to hurt me."

"The worst hurt can come only from the people you care for."

"If that was true, I'd fear you and Tat'yana more than Otto. And believe me, that is not the case."

"Who is Tat'yana? A Russian?"

"A friend here in Stralsund. She's from France. She used to wear another name, but if you meet her you better call her Tat'yana, that's what she calls herself these days. You might hear her call me Cookie."

"Is she the maid you told me about?"

Lasse stopped and looked at Nicolaus. "No, the maid is back in Sweden. Tat'yana is a clerk. When I disappear on those occasions that I refuse to explain, I'm usually with her. We work for the same man."

"And what do you do for him?" The tension in Nicolaus's voice showed that he knew he was intruding more on Lasse's privacy than ever before.

Lasse stood for a while, looking at the water again before answering. If he wanted Nicolaus's friendship, he'd have to take a chance and tell his something of his life. "I kill."

"What! Is that a joke?" Nicolaus looked ready to faint.

"No." Lasse dropped every bit of the polished surface he usually wore as a mask, and knew Nicolaus was facing empty eyes in a stonelike face. "Nicolaus, there are three things that I can do well enough to make a living. One, I can cook, but taking a place as a servant would mean placing myself in somebody's power, and I cannot do that. Two, I can be elegant and desirable enough for wealthy people to pay me for sex. And I'll do so if I need the money. Three, I can kill. I'm good at it, and I feel nothing in doing so." He hesitated. "Except, once or twice, a slight regret."

"Once or twice?" Nicolaus almost whispered. "But how many have you killed?"

"I don't know. Twenty? Thirty? Less than a hundred. I've never tried to count."

"But...but how? Why?" Nicolaus seemed even more shocked than Lasse had expected.

"Preferably with a knife." Lasse shrugged and looked into the young priest's eyes. "Would it help if I told you that most of them deserved it and would in fact have been hanged if their crimes had been exposed in a court?"

"I don't know." Nicolaus shook his head and sat down on a wooden post, ignoring the horse tied to the post even as it knocked off his hat and started nibbling at his hair.

"You must have guessed that I had to kill to escape Otto, and Viktor is an arms dealer. Part of my work for him is as a bodyguard, and many of the people he does business with are not nice people."

"But you are so pretty. And so young."

"And therefore anyone targeting Viktor is going to concentrate on the more obvious threats." Lasse smiled slightly. "Eh, Nicolaus. You really don't have so much hair on your head that you should feed it to the horses."

Nicolaus put a hand to his head and looked around to stare at the horse. "I think I better go home." He got up from the post and stood a bit, wobbling.

"Do you want me to come with you?" Lasse kept himself from reaching out to steady Nicolaus. If Nicolaus couldn't accept what Lasse was and how he made a living, they'd better stop it now.

"No. Thanks. I'm fine. I just need to think." Nicolaus gave a rather wavering smile and set off more or less in the direction of the small house he'd rented near the St. James Church.

"Hello, Cookie. Did you tell him you were pregnant? He looked that shocked."

Lasse turned with a smile to answer Tat'yana. He had spotted her during his talk with Nicolaus, but she was in her tavern doxy persona today, and the few people going in and out of the small shops would have wondered at Nicolaus talking to her. The area around the Church of St. James was still partly a ruin after being destroyed by Wallenstein seven years earlier, and Nicolaus' scattered colleagues had simply accepted Lasse as an old friend of Nicolaus from the university in Rostock with an occasional taste for low company. With the exception of a widow well known for her pretty young male servants, Lasse had been very careful to select his customers entirely from the travelers staying in the harbor area, and of course there was no overlap between the clerics of St. James and Viktor's people at the Vulgar Unicorn.

"No. I told him that you were, and that you were going to claim him as father," said Lasse.

Lasse and Tat'yana both stepped aside as a man came out from the fishmonger with a brace of dried cods over his shoulder and untied the horse. He hesitated, looking at the well-dressed young man and the whore in the stained red dress, but when Lasse raised a questioning eyebrow the man just shook his head, mounted, and rode on.

"There's been questions asked." Tat'yana sat down on the post Nicolaus had just left. She kept a bright smile on her face as she looked up on Lasse, but her voice was dead-serious.

"Who and what?"

"One is addressed as von Werle. I don't know about the other two. They are staying in the house of Herr Buchman, who has ordered his servants to give his guests absolutely everything they want, and who practically genuflects every time he meets them."

"I don't believe I know Herr Buchman."

"He's a major merchant living in the big new brick house by the market square. Viktor has occasionally rented space in one of his warehouses. The three men are searching for a runaway Swedish servant who is also a thief and a murderer. They have a drawing that two of them show around in taverns. One of the children I sometimes hire saw it and came to tell me it looked like you. It's only a question of time before someone either tells them where you live, or that you often walk around the harbor."

"I'll go grab some belongings. Will you ask Boris to buy me a horse and meet me at St. James Tower? I'll send Viktor my address if I'll settle down in a place where I might be useful."

"I'll have Viktor lend you his big roan horse. It's faster than any for sale right now. Anything else?"

"No. And thank you, Tat'yana."

Lasse quickly made his way among the potholes and rubble surrounding the partially rebuilt St. James, but stopped immediately as a rat ran past him down the hill. Rats ran away from—not toward—people. Nicolaus didn't like the shells of the abandoned houses that once had housed his neighbors, so he always went straight to and from his home. It might of course be nothing more than a hunting cat that had scared the rat, but with Otto in town Lasse preferred not to take any chances.

By leaving the cleared path and moving carefully through the ruins, Lasse made his way to the small yard behind the house, but stopped at the sound of a whining voice coming from the study next to the kitchen.

"I want to take him along. Surely a priest as sacrifice at a Black Mass would produce a spectacular result." Black Mass? Lasse paused to listen. Had Otto taken up Satanism or was this something entirely different?

"No, Wilhelm." The sound of Otto's voice not only answered Lasse's question, it also made him break out in a cold sweat. "We came for Lasse, not just to grab anything that came our way. You really need to show more discrimination. Lasse is a work of art. Perhaps my very finest. And I want him back to see what new possibilities this small taste of freedom has opened up. This rather pathetic little priest isn't even pretty enough to keep around for amusement."

So they had Nicolaus in there and he was still alive. Lasse turned to head for Viktor and Boris, only to see a man standing among the ruins with a gun in his hand.

"So, we meet again, Lasse. Why don't you go inside? All this sunlight really isn't good for your complexion." The man came closer and Lasse recognized Johan, one of Otto's oldest cronies. Johan had never shown any interest in Lasse and had always withdrawn early from the excesses of Otto's parties. Johan had probably been concentrating on the political aspects of Otto's schemes. Not that this was likely to be of much help right now. Whatever Johan's deal with Otto was, it was highly unlikely that Lasse could offer the man anything better.

"Open the door, and go say hello to Otto. He has been talking a lot about you since you left, and I think you'll find that you have escaped from the frying pan, only to find yourself in the fire."

Lasse took a deep breath and went inside, then turned to slam the door behind him, and close it with the thick bar he had installed himself. Three quick steps brought him across the tiny kitchen and into the study.

Nicolaus was sitting in his usual chair behind the table, but across from him, where Lasse usually sat, was Otto. Right beside Lasse stood an unknown man, gaping in surprise.

"Ah, Lasse my dear, do come join us." Otto turned his head with its gleaming curls to smile at Lasse, but kept his gun pointing straight at Nicolaus. The man to Lasse's right closed his mouth and started turning his gun toward Lasse. Lasse grabbed the gun with his left hand while sliding his knife into the man's stomach and jerking it upwards. If Otto shot Nicolaus there would be nothing Lasse could do. Once they lost the advantage of surprise they would have no chance against the armed men, and Nicolaus would certainly die anyway.

Lasse pulled his knife from the man sliding screaming to the floor, and swung the gun around to shoot Otto, only to see Nicolaus turning over the heavy table. Nicolaus leaped over the table with the heavy pewter candlestick in his hand. He swung it toward Otto's head. The candlestick connected with a sound like a dropped egg, just as the bullet from Otto's gun buried itself in the heavy oak table.

"Keep down. There's one more man outside." Lasse tried to listen for any sound of movement, although the screaming of the wounded man interfered. There was nothing to be seen through the thick bubbled glass of the window, and there was no air movement suggesting that Johan had opened a door. There would have been time enough for the man to get around to the front door or even break open one of the windows.

Nicolaus was kneeling in front of Otto, staring at the man he had killed. No help there. Lasse glided toward the front door as silently as he could. It was neither locked nor barred. Slowly he pressed down on the handle and stood aside to let the door swing open. Nothing. Outside was silence. Inside, the screams had faded to a whimper.

Lasse waited. This was the kind of situation where impatience would get you killed. Then a slow shuffle outside. A horse? Lasse chanced a quick glance out the door. Viktor's big roan horse was walking slowly past the door snatching at the weeds growing along the path.

"Boris! Are you there?" Lasse shouted.

"Yes, with friends! All clear?"

"All clear in here, but one man outside."

"He's no longer a problem," the gravelly voice of Viktor sounded from beside the door. "Brigitte is quite protective of you. She insisted we all come. Who's the hurt one?" Viktor came through the door with Tat'yana close behind.

"I've no idea, but I spilled his guts. I'll go clean it up." Lasse would have liked to give the woman a hug, but judging from her flat watchful eyes her Brigitte persona was still in control, so he'd better just leave her alone until it faded. Tat'yana was in many ways even more damaged than Lasse, but she had dealt with her problems in her own way, and usually managed to balance her various personas quite well. Still, when Brigitte was in control, you'd better be careful.

Nicolaus was still kneeling by Otto's corpse, tentatively reaching out to touch the bloody curls.

"He's quite dead. They don't look like that if there's any chance they'll wake up." Tat'yana had gone forward to squat beside Nicolaus, who looked up at her with unseeing eyes. "How do you do?" Tat'yana held her hand out almost into his face, and he took it by reflex. "You must be Nicolaus. Lasse has told me about you. I'm Tat'yana."

"Yes. Yes, I'm Nicolaus. Lasse, what are you doing!"

Lasse stood upright. "Nicolaus, no one recovers from that kind of wound. It really would have been no kindness to let him live." He paused. "Or did you want to shrive him? Give him a chance to confess his sins? I really don't think that would have helped his soul. Providing he still had one. I heard him wanting to sacrifice you at a Black Mass."

Nicolaus shook his head and looked away. "This is a nightmare," he whispered.

"No, my dear friend. This is encountering and fighting evil. You've done nothing wrong." Lasse pulled Nicolaus up from the floor. "Come say hello to my friends. Tat'yana you have already met, but this is Viktor and Boris is outside, probably preparing for getting rid of the corpses. These are very good people to have along if you jump into fire."

All God's Children in the Burning East

Garrett W. Vance

1630, Kingdom of Ayutthaya, Southeast Asia

The setting sun floated like a red paper lantern in the darkening sky, casting the golden temples and palaces of Ayutthaya in crimson and bronze, as Nishioka Yoriaki paddled his small wooden boat lightly down the Menam river. Today the tides ran out to sea, making his journey home easy. Sometimes he stole a glance backward at the fantastic scene, surely a glimpse of Paradise although he would never admit to thinking such a thing to the Dominican or Jesuit fathers. He crossed himself quickly to clear his mind of such fantasy.

He had done well that day, selling his Japanese style *bento* lunches and snacks to all kinds of folk as he made his journey around Ayutthaya's island stronghold, the paragon of Siamese civilization. It seemed Moor and Malay, Chinese and Portuguese, Dutch and Cochin all relished his wife's cooking. Even a silk-clad seneschal of the highest Siamese nobility had sent a servant down to the water's edge to purchase six lunches! Soon after, a group of gaily clad rich young Siamese women waved to him as he passed by their waterfront gardens. They each bought a bento, opening their banana leaf wrappings right then and there to see what the day's treat may be, in this case grilled catfish. "Tell your wife we should like shrimp tomorrow if she can manage it!" they told him in the musical tones of their language. He managed to

179

answer that he would do so, his tongue tripping as he blushed at the attention of such fair and noble women.

As he mumbled his shy thanks and paddled quickly away, Yoriaki thought that such as these were lovely indeed, but to him his wife Momo was still the best. She was as pretty as the peach she was named for. He had to admit to himself that part of the reason he had become a Christian was to get close to the Nihonmachi Christians' daughters, who were mostly pure blood Japanese. Certainly the Siamese, Mon, and Lao girls that most of the samurai and merchant class married were beautiful, with their large smokey eyes and slender figures, but to Yoriaki they couldn't match the pure radiance of a *Yamato no deshiko*, a perfect flower of Japanese womanhood such as Momo. Upon their marriage he had left behind the warrior life to become the simple man he was today, and was much happier for it.

Yoriaki knew that Ayutthaya was one of the few places in the world where people from Asia and Europe mixed so freely. That was certainly a large part of the kingdom's financial success. He had been lucky to end up here, considering that when he left Japan he had no idea where he was going, content to board any ship that promised to sail far from his homeland. Yoriaki smiled to himself but his mood fell as he sighted the spire of the Portuguese Dominican church down the river's west side. It was a modest piece of architecture compared to the fantastic designs of the Siamese temples, but with a quiet beauty of its own in the rosy light.

Through the course of Yoriaki's daily travels, he had learned to speak and understand the basics of the many languages found in the cosmopolitan realm of Ayutthaya. Everyone said that he had a gift for tongues. As he sold his delicacies he heard many things and lately not many of them had been good. On the last Sabbath after attending holy mass Yoriaki, who had become nearly fluent in Portuguese since embracing the Christian faith, had overheard several of the good fathers discussing rumors from the Siamese court in hushed tones. They feared the new king, Prasat Thong. He had formerly been the regent or *Kalahom* appointed by the boy's father, good king Song Tham on his death bed to look after his son and successor, fifteen-year-old King Cetthathirat. There was no doubt the scheming *Kalahom* was responsible for that boy's untimely death and had certainly gone on to murder

Cetthathirat's younger brother and successor as well, poor little King Athittayawong, who had been just a boy of ten. Although all feared to say it aloud, Prasat Thong was an ursurper with blood all over his hands. To make matters worse, he had managed to remove the only possible obstacle to his plans, Yamada Nagamasa, who to everyone's horror seemed fooled by the usurper's lies and had allowed himself to be sent to the south, safely out of Prasat Thong's way. Upon hearing such discouraging words from the fathers, Yoriaki slipped away home then, feeling ashamed that his people's revered leader in this distant land had been tricked by the *Kalahom*, no, "king."

Yamada Nagamasa, trained as a samurai for a war that would never come, had left Japan to become a man of great influence in Ayutthaya. He'd been a favorite of the old King Song Tham and well loved by the court for his skill and courage in battle. A successful merchant with a knack for trade, he had also become the leader of Nihonmachi. Their "Japanese Town" on the eastern shore of the Menam, just south of the city, produced the highly respected Japanese Royal Guard, a force rightfully feared by the kingdom's many foes. Nagamasa had been the Guard's commander and Yoriaki had served under him for two years after his arrival here as so many *ronin* did, masterless samurai seeking glory no longer possible in Japan. They had fought the Burmese together and brought great honor to themselves in the eyes of all those who made Ayutthaya their home. Now those days were gone and Ayutthaya was left without its hero.

Yoriaki now let his boat drift along slowly with the various flotsam and jetsam that spotted the busy river, his thoughts darkening with the waning light. How could a man as great as Nagamasa not see what even a simple ex-samurai turned food vendor could? It was widely suspected that the new king, well practiced in sycophancy, had appealed to the ego of the otherwise noble Nagamasa, offering him rulership of Ligor province far down the east coast almost to the lands of the Malays, the chance to be the first Japanese to hold such a position outside of Japan! It was surely a trick of that creeping cobra Prasat Thong but it had been too tempting for him to resist and the people of Ayutthaya and particularly Nihonmachi, watched him leave with heavy hearts. "Who?" they asked, "Who would protect us now?" While the new leader of their enclave was a good enough man he was no Nagamasa. Yoriaki had heard unsettling rumors that the Japanese welcome in their adopted kingdom wasn't nearly as warm as it once was.

A whistle from the west shore rousted Yoriaki from his brooding. The dock bosses in the Dutch area just north of Nihonmachi were calling to him—he had almost forgotten them and would have drifted right by! Replacing his somber expression with the wide smile that sold his wares so well, Yoriaki paddled over to the float beneath the pier they waited on, his small craft dwarfed by the big Dutch merchant ships tied nearby.

"Have you anything left for us today, Yo-san?" one of the Dutchmen asked, a plump fellow called Blom whom Yoriaki had grown quite fond of. He was jesting, of course. Yoriaki had been selling to these gentlemen for several years now and always made sure he had a few of the leaf-wrapped bento meals tucked away for them at the end of the day.

"Yes, yes, here you are, my friend!" He had learned enough of the Dutch tongue to banter with these fellows, who were a jovial bunch. As he passed out the meals (Blom bought two) and collected the lumpy metal *Pot Duang* coins that the Europeans referred to as "bullet money," Blom's usually smiling face took on a thoughtful cast. The beginning of a frown formed beneath his rosy cheeks and plump nose.

"Yo-san, have you heard the news?"

"I hear much news, being as how I float all over the place like a leaf riding the stream." Yoriaki tried to sound lighthearted but his dark eyes met Blom's bright ones with fierce interest. This was the most serious he had ever seen the man, so the news could not be good. A knot was already tying itself in Yoriaki's stomach as he waited for Blom to go on.

"I think you haven't heard this news yet. Look down the river toward your home." Blom raised his heavily fleshed arm to point toward Nihonmachi lying about half a mile downriver from them. Yoriaki turned to see a very large ship docked there, one of the great red seal junks that traded between Japan and the rest of Asia. His eyes widened to see that it belonged to Nagamasa!

"Yes, you see. They must not have heard that your former leader is now a king in the southlands and came straight here thinking to find him. I fear they have made a mistake." Blom's sea-blue eyes narrowed and he leaned down close to Yoriaki. "Something is up. Our employers have been conferring in their offices all afternoon, ever since that thing got here. They have doubled the watch for tonight. I like you, Yo-san, you are a good fellow. Have your eyes and ears open tonight and keep that pretty little peach of yours close by. There is contention over who owns that cargo and I fear there may be blood shed over it this night." With that he clapped Yoriaki companionably on the arm, then gave his little boat a gentle push back out into the current before he could be questioned further.

"Thank you, Herr Blom, I will do so. You have my thanks! Go with God!" Yoriaki called back to him. With his usual friendly wave the Dutchman and his comrades headed home to eat their meal. It was nearly dark now, but the Nihonmachi docks were aglow with lanterns where the brightly painted ship with its cargo of goods from far off Japan was berthed. From the dock behind the ship's massive bulk he heard the raucous sounds of loud argument in both the Siamese and Japanese languages. There was definitely a fight brewing; the choice of words was less than polite. Yoriaki quickly paddled farther out into the river than he usually would so as not to be noticed by the growing crowd on shore. In the distance the Islamic calls for prayer from the Moorish and Malay enclaves began, their eerie wail skirling above the cries of angry men. This drove him to paddle faster and faster, sweat growing cold on his back despite the humid warmth.

Any semblance of good humor left to him from a successful day at work was long gone now, replaced by a rapidly growing worry. Yoriaki paddled as fast as he could, passing up his usual place under the docks, tying his boat instead to an old tree growing out over the river at a stretch of grassy shore. The spot was not far from his house in the town's quiet, mostly residential southern section. He and Momo sometimes enjoyed picnics together in its cool greeness. Yoriaki left his paddles and the few leftover bento behind in the boat. No one would bother them there and he could always retrieve them later. Trying not to break into a full run, he hurried to his home along the cobbled path, his light cotton *yukata* robe flapping above his softly clacking wooden *geta* sandals. Around him the houses all perched high on stilts taller than a man by half again to keep them safe from the occasional flood, a feature that sometimes made him feel as if he were shorter than he really was, a child dwarfed by adult-sized buildings.

Other than their unusual foundations, the houses of Nihonmachi mostly resembled those of Japan: rice paper screened windows glowed a mild white from the lanterns and candles within, peaked roofs pitched a few feet higher than in the old country in order to wick away the heat, but still crafted in the Japanese style. Most of these were thatched with grass like a Siamese house but some sported fired clay tiles of glossy red and blue. Despite its oddities Nihonmachi felt like home to Yoriaki now after seven years, but behind that feeling of warmth and belonging there was a cold fear growing, an anxiety that would not be ignored. Something was indeed up on what would otherwise be just another night in Ayutthaya, the bustling crossroads of the East and West. Something bad.

Yoriaki slipped through the row of trees that marked their modest plot, taking a shortcut through the small garden in back where Momo grew the Japanese vegetables that she used in her cooking. Despite his hurry he stepped carefully around the heads of the long, white *daikon* radishes and bunches of savory *shiso* beefsteak leaves. Reaching the front walk he charged up the steep wooden steps to his front porch three at a time, kicking off his sandals with a clatter. He burst through the door with such a wild expression on his face that it startled his wife Momo so much she dropped the tea she was carrying in from the kitchen. The ceramic cup bounced harmlessly off the springy *tatami* floor, woven from durable rice stalks, but its spilled contents spread across the golden fibers with a red darkness.

"Husband! What is the matter!" Her oval face was pale and her eyes wide with shock, their liquid darkness reflecting the lantern light in two bright points, making her seem like some graceful forest creature caught out in the hunter's path. The silver cross hanging at her neck made a third point of light, flashing as it moved with each of her rapid breaths.

"Momo! Where are my swords? Get them out, now!"

His wife paused only for a moment before she ran to the massive teak wood *tonsu* chest of drawers they kept their few precious belongings in.

"What is going on?" she asked again plaintively, as her deft hands searched the deep bottom drawer.

"I'm not sure. Hopefully nothing, but I have a terrible feeling. The men around town have been talking that we Japanese are no longer welcome here now that Nagamasu is gone and we are left with that devil, Prasat Thong. He has no love of us, despite his pretty words." By the time he had finished speaking Momo had thrust a heavy bundle into his arms which he carefully unwrapped. He took his scabbarded longsword, his prized *katana*, and shoved it snugly into his waist sash. The smaller but equally deadly *wakizashi* shortsword he handed back to his wife, who gripped it gingerly by its red lacquered sheath. "Take it! I have the boat tied up at the big tree. I want you to go there now and wait for me. Get in the boat and paddle out a few yards, then anchor. If any Siamese come, row farther out. Do *not* come to shore unless it's me or someone you know! Trust no Siamese, do you understand? Do you?"

Unlike him, his wife had been born here and spoke the Siamese language as fluently as if it were her own tongue. The idea of running away from a native of this land was utterly foreign to her. She stared at him for a moment as if he were a lunatic but then straightened herself up and answered, "Yes, husband, I understand! I will do as you ask."

Seeing his beautiful and stout-hearted wife standing there holding his *wakizashi* filled Yoriaki with an overwhelming combination of pride and fear for her well being. He swiftly took her in his arms and kissed her. The herbs she used to wash her long sable hair filled his head with their sweet scent. She kissed him back fervently. Savoring her for as long as he dared, Yoriaki gently pushed her back.

"I must go down to the docks and see what is happening. Nagamasa's red seal ship is there and I heard men arguing as I went by. Prasat Thong will want whatever that ship brought back from Japan whether it is his by rights or not. Blom the Dutchman thinks it will end in a fight, and judging by the curses I heard I fear he may be right. We must be ready for anything."

"But, dearest, it is not your fight! You are no longer a soldier, you gave that up when you let Christ into your heart! That ship doesn't matter to you!"

"My dearest, it's not the ship that I care about, don't you see? I fear this may be the excuse Prasat Thong needs to make a move against us, against all of Nihonmachi! I need to go over there and find out what's going on. God willing, it's not serious. Even so, I will not take a chance with you." Careful to not use too much strength in his excitement, he took her by the arm and led her to the door. "Humor me, Momo, go down to the boat and wait. If I am not there with you by midnight, paddle across to the Portuguese side and wait at the Dominicans' church. You should be safe there."

"What about my mother and father? What about my friends? We must warn them, too!"

"Your parents' house is on the way. I will tell them to go to their fishing boat and meet you at the tree. If things go badly we may not be able to come back here."

Momo nodded. "I will prepare our traveling clothes and what belongings I can manage."

"No! There is no time! I can't tell you why but I feel the worst will happen! Nothing is more important than your precious life, my love. Please, just go now!"

Momo looked at him, true fear spreading across her gentle face. "Very well. But I will not leave without at least taking this!" Breaking loose from her husband's nervous grip she ran across the room to grab a round clay pot sealed with wax hanging by a leather strap on the wall. "These are the seeds of all we grow here!" she told him in a tone of reluctant defiance. "If we take nothing else, at least these will give us a future!" Yoriaki nodded his agreement. His wife was as wise as she was lovely.

Stepping out onto the porch, Yoriaki slipped into the pair of deer skin boots he had worn as a guardsman. This was no night for wooden sandals. He made Momo put on her most sensible foot-wear and practically carried her down the steps. Their part of town was farthest from the docks and still quiet, but he could hear loud voices coming from the north. He took Momo's shapely hands in his, folding his larger fingers over hers and the *wakizashi* she held.

"If anyone tries to hurt you, you will use this sword. You know how, I have taught you. Do you understand me?"

"Yes." But her voice was very quiet now.

"I love you, Momo. Now, go! Pray tomorrow we both are laughing at a protective husband's foolishness!" He gave her his usual silly grin to which she responded with a laugh despite the overriding tension of the moment. Yoriaki was about to push her in the direction of the river when, with a sigh, she turned of her own accord and broke into a run, something he rarely saw her do. He watched as her brightly floral patterned summer kimono caught the light from a nearby porch, then faded away into the shadows. It was always summer in Ayutthaya, but tonight he was chilled as if he stood high in the mountain snows. Yoriaki turned toward the docks. The voices had grown louder still.

On his way, Yoriaki swung by Momo's parents' house. Her father, old Mori, a kindly gentleman who had fled Japan twenty years before when the persecutions of Christians had begun in his district, was standing out on his porch looking toward the docks. His wife Kiku, younger by some ten years, stood in the doorway, an expression of fear on her softly lined face. They looked down at the panting Yoriaki in surprise.

"Father! Mother! Something is happening!" That was all he could get out before he had to pause for breath. It had been a long time since he had done much running himself.

"Yes, Yo-kun." Momo's father called him by the honorific a father might use for a son or younger male relative, the older man being very fond of his son-in-law. "I fear there will be a fight at the docks, they grow hotter by the minute. But why are you headed there?" His eyes dropped to Yoriaki's waist to take in the sword sheathed there.

"I need to see what's going on. There has been a lot of talk lately, all around the city. Today a Dutchman, a friend, warned me that something really bad might happen tonight and this last Sunday the fathers were worried about what the new king is up to. I fear he may move on us now that Nagamasa is gone! I am afraid and I have sent Momo to wait in our boat where I left it by the big tree near our house. Please, Father, take Mother to your boat and go join her!" He patiently waited for their response despite the urge to continue on his reconnaissance.

The old couple looked at each other for a long moment and then came to the kind of unspoken agreement only possible to those long married.

"We will do as you say, Yo-kun. You are a good son and we know you are wise to the ways of the world. We will join our daughter downriver."

Yoriaki let out a long puff of relief, not realizing he had been holding it in. "Good, that is good! But please hurry, don't bother packing anything, there may be very little time! Just put on your shoes and go to the river! Please, I implore you to go to safety right away!"

Momo's parents nodded, then dutifully began to put on their shoes. Satisfied, Yoriaki gave them a deep bow and started to leave.

"My son!" Momo's father said before he could break into a run again. "Please come back to us safely. We need you." Behind him his wife burst into tears.

"I will, Father. I promise!"

Somewhat relieved that his small family was on their way to reasonable safety, Yoriaki slowed his pace somewhat. It would not be good to arrive all out of breath. As he came to the docks, he saw that the crowd had swollen to a very large size, mostly Japanese men but also many of Nihonmachi's women. These hung farther back, talking amongst themselves nervously in a patois of languages. Beyond the crowd Yoriaki could see two groups in a face-off around the gangplank, which was guarded by the mixed race crew of the ship loyal to Nagamasa along with a party of Japanese samurai who had remained in Nihonmachi for their own reasons when Nagamasa left with his troops. A few of these had become Christians much as Yoriaki had, but those now stood in solid ranks with their Buddhist and Shinto countrymen. In front of their line stood a cadre of enraged Siamese soldiers and officials. Both sides continued to shout threateningly at each other and it showed no sign of letting up.

Yoriaki arrived near the back of the crowd and found a familiar face, a man named Hiranaka, a retired samurai he had served in the guard with, now turned ceramic maker. Hiranaka was not a Christian, but choice of religion was usually of small import among the Japanese of Ayutthaya in their dealings with each other. Ayutthaya was remarkably a very free and tolerant society and these concepts had soon been embraced by the Japanese who came here, nearly all of whom had been persecuted in some way by the stifling social constrictions they had left behind in Japan. Here they could do any job, marry any person and worship any god they wished. Unfortunately, Yoriaki thought such freedoms might be coming to an end.

"Hiranaka-san! What's going on?" Yoriaki asked him.

"Ah, Nishioka-san! Well, it's quite a kerfuffle. That ship is Nagamasa's and it came here thinking to find him. Now that they have learned he's not here anymore they want to take their cargo to him down in Ligor. The problem is, King Prasat Thong has other ideas. He has sent this group of Siamese soldiers to claim it for himself, but our fellows aren't letting them on board. Right now it's a standoff, they are all just yelling at each other but I fear it may come to blows. A while ago several of the Siamese were sent running back to the city, and it is likely they will return with reinforcements." Hiranaka pulled back his *yukata* to expose a *katana* tucked beneath. Yoriaki did the same and they both shared a grim smile.

"Looks like I'm not the only ex-samurai who had a bad feeling this evening," Hiranaka said wryly. "We may have left the warrior's life behind but it seems we retain our instincts. I sent my wife and children to the river and told them to board whatever boats might be available..." His eyes raised the question to Yoriaki.

"I have done the same for my family. I do hope we are wrong."

The confrontation at the dock was reaching a climax. Yoriaki and Hiranaka began to push their way past the women in the crowd, ordering them as they passed by to leave the docks for the safety of the shore farther downriver. Some did as they were told but others stayed anyway, entranced by the excitement. Just as they reached the front of the crowd the situation arrived at its boiling point. The thirty or so Siamese soldiers gathered there made a lunge at the ship's guard, who were outnumbered but ready to defend their prize with their lives. The battle had begun. Swords clashed in an angry din.

Now that fighting had begun most of the crowd fled to a safer distance, but there were many such as Yoriaki and Mori who were ready to join the action. These latecomers quickly closed ranks with the men guarding the ship so that now it was the Siamese who were outnumbered, facing well over a hundred men. Their officers bawled at them to fall back, which they did, reluctantly. The Japanese held their position, the clash ceasing for the moment.

"Go tell that child-killing king of yours that he may not have that which is Nagamasa's!" the Chinese captain of the ship bellowed in accented Siamese.

The city official leading the Siamese contingent shrieked back, "How dare you speak disrespectfully of our blessed ruler! Remember that you are but guests in our land. The welcome you had under dead Song Tham has come to an end. Just wait, you shall see!" And with that the silk-clad and bejeweled man laughed shrilly, his heart as black as the ursurper he served. Just then a bell began to toll, the bell of the Buddhist temple of Nihonmachi, a plain structure compared to the great gleaming towers of the Siamese *wats*. The official laughed even louder, joined by his men. This made the Japanese take a step forward, more than ready to put an end to their impious gaiety, but now shouts came from the road that ran north to south along the east side of their enclave. A handsome male youth of mixed race, one of the many children of unions between the Nihonmachi men with local women, came running from the road yelling in Japanese.

"Soldiers with torches are coming from the north, hundreds of them!"

There was a brief silence while the men of Nihonmachi looked at each other, their faces full of dread. The Siamese they had briefly clashed with began to laugh again, which turned out to be a mistake on their part, their last such on this earthly plane. The Japanese moved through them like an avalanche through pines, cutting down their tormentors long before their reinforcements could arrive. Yoriaki slew two himself; he hadn't intended to come fight but Hiranaka had been right, the instincts were still there. He saw the boy, a lad of no more than thirteen, still standing there, staring at the carnage.

"You, boy!" Yoriaki called to him, "Run through town and shout your warning to all, tell everyone to flee to the river, then do so yourself. Go!" he commanded. The boy bowed quickly and did as he was told, shouting the alarm at the top of his lungs. Doors opened and lantern light fell across his path as he made his way down Nihonmachi's narrow streets. Yoriaki turned to where the men were making a quick battle plan. A man called Ishida, one of the town's highest ranking samurai, an officer recently retired from the palace guard, had stepped up to take charge due to his experience and the respect they all held for him. He was in his late fifties but there was no doubt his sword arms were still strong. No one knew where their town's current leader was and no one asked.

"You, Captain, sir." Ishida turned to the ship's master. "Untie your ship and be ready to push off, but first I ask you to take on as many of our people as you can until you must go," he said in Chinese. Yoriaki understood that language fairly well and was impressed by Ishida's fluency, no doubt the result of years of trading.

The captain agreed to this request. "I will do as you ask, sir, we would save as many as we can. We will take the refugees with us to Ligor." He then spat on the ground and said in heavily accented Japanese. "That stinking bastard king has ruined the peace of this great city, may he burn in Hell forever!" In answer came a murmur of agreement and darkly muttered oaths.

Many of the noncombatants who had made up the crowd were already hurrying onto the great red seal ship, looking over their shoulders with mounting fear as they climbed aboard.

"The rest of you men, listen now." Ishida's voice was calm and full of confident authority, the voice of a man who had commanded troops before in his long career. "They are coming to burn the town, there can be no doubt. We can't possibly win against such numbers. I say we let them have Nihonmachi and live to fight again, I have no doubt Yamada Nagamasa will want revenge for this treachery and I plan to march on Ayutthaya with him!"

That brought a round of cheers from the gathered men.

"So, here's what we must do. We will make a stand at the road until we can't hold there any longer. From there a fighting retreat, slowing them down long enough to be sure that all our women and children can get to the river. Once they have got clear we fall back to the shore ourselves and make our own escape. Let those two-faced sons of dogs burn this town, we care not—one day it will be *we* who live in those pretty palaces on that island! I say 'Death to Prasat Thong!' What say you?"

As one, the men of Nihonmachi made their battlecry, "Death to Prasat Thong!" Following Ishida they sprinted to the road, forming a line across it at the north edge of town. The Siamese were close now, marching confidently, carrying a single edged *daab* sword in one hand, a torch in the other. Most Siamese fought wielding a *daab* in each hand with considerable prowess. Many now lay their torches down by the side of the road to draw their other sword before engaging the Japanese. There was no doubt that the Siamese soldiers were a force to be reckoned with. There was another moment of quiet as the attackers paused not five yards away from the defenders, waiting for the order to attack. They could hear each other breathing. Then the order came, with a deafening clash of blades the two forces slammed against each other in the soft red sand of the road.

The Japanese held their line, cutting down wave after wave of charging Siamese. The Siamese were powerful warriors indeed, but the men of Nihonmachi were more highly skilled, having undergone rigorous samurai training before seeking their fortunes in this far off land. It was widely considered that the Japanese were the most feared of all fighting men in Asia; certainly they were the most fearless. These men, facing an overwhelming force, had one thing in their favor the Siamese did not—they were fighting for the survival of their loved ones. The longer they held out, the longer their women and children had to flee what would surely be carnage to come. Still, they were not invincible and inexorably some samurai fell to lie beside the slain of their former allies in the blood-drenched dust.

"Look! Some of them have gone around through the rice fields, they're crossing the road into the south part of town!" one of the men cried out.

"Fall back, follow the plan! Those that can get free quickly run and head those bastards off!" Ishida commanded.

Yoriaki was engaged with a man who he was acquainted with from his time in the royal guard. He had been trying to only wound the fellow and put him out of the fight alive, but his opponent didn't seem to recognize him and fought savagely. "Sorry, friend," Yoriaki told him in Siamese, then with a lightning fast swing of his *katana* he beheaded the man. Freed up from the melee, he instantly ran to the south end of town, joining some twenty or so others. They cut the town at an angle so they could get between the Siamese and the beach. Yoriaki saw flames shooting up; the Siamese were pausing to torch the houses. Good, that would slow them down and let him and the other men form a line. Yoriaki saw his own home beginning to burn as he ran by, the man who held the torch turning to go light the next. He lost his head without even seeing Yoriaki coming.

Suddenly five more enemies appeared in the path from the road, a row of houses blazing behind them. Their work done, they were now headed toward the water to make what mischief they could amongst the fleeing townsfolk. Yoriki ploughed into them, gutting the first three before they had time to react. He was in full fighting fury now, his weapon and body working as one, his mind focused only on the killing. Of the remaining two, the senior and more skilled forced an engagement, skillfully bringing his sword into close quarters with Yoriaki's, the blades ringing in a furious dance of death. Yoriaki saw the second opponent was going to try to get behind him. Wielding his longsword one-handed temporarily, Yoriaki's free hand snaked out to grab that one by his wrist, snapping the bones with a well-practiced twist. The man's animal-like cry caused his companion to pause for a split second, leaving his belly exposed. Yoriaki's sword flashed as it passed deeply into the soft flesh with a single upward slice then continued in an arc to enter the disabled attacker's neck behind the ear. Both men went down in twitching heaps on the cobblestones. Pausing for a moment to catch his breath after the intense encounter, Yoriaki heard shrieks coming from behind him, the cries of women.

Yoriaki ran faster than he ever had in his life, the breath pumping in and out of him with the force of a blacksmith's bellows. He arrived to the beach to find three men of Nihonmachi facing three times their number near the shore, behind them several families were wading waist-deep into the water, women and children crying in fear. One of the women (Not Momo!) hadn't made it, she lay folded up on the beach in her blood-soaked kimono like a crumpled origiami sculpture discarded by a careless child.

So far Yoriaki had fought nearly without emotion and simply out of necessity; although terrible to be sure the night's tragedy was not something their opponents had any choice about, they were following their orders. He had killed without hate, having fought at the side of these Siamese in the past and regretted being pitted against them because of one evil man's greed. But now that he saw they didn't intend just to burn Nihonmachi down and cast its people out but were bent on slaughtering the innocents as well, Yoriaki felt a rage build in him. With an inarticulate scream he dove at the Siamese soldiers, his blade a wet, red whirlwind gleaming in the glow of their burning homes. One, two, three Siamese fell before him in a row, the fourth had time to block his blow before the next slew him. Yoriaki's onslaught gave the Japanese the advantage again, the savageness of his attack inspiring them to redouble their own. Shortly Yoriaki and his three comrades stood over the corpses of their enemies.

"They are trying to kill our families now," one of the men said, one Nakagata, who was still technically employed by the Siamese king but had taken a few days off to get over a cold. "That bastard Prasat Thong, I'd like to cut his head off myself."

"You may get your chance," another answered. "We will have our revenge for this."

Yoriaki, pausing to catch his breath, watched a boat come near the shore manned by several of the holy fathers from the Portuguese side of the river. They helped the wading women and children clamber in, then began to paddle away, looking for more in need of rescue. One of the fathers recognized Yoriaki and silently gave him a blessing with a pale, trembling hand. Suddenly Yoriaki felt a spear of ice go through him. "Momo!" he cried as he turned south to look farther down the beach. The big tree stood some twenty yards away. His boat was there but he couldn't see anyone in it. Nearby, a body lay obscured by the tall grass. "My wife!" Yoriaki broke into a sprint, behind him he could hear the others following.

Half out of his mind with fear he arrived under the tree to find that that the body was that of a Siamese soldier, not his beloved wife. He scanned the boat to see if she was lying within but it was empty. Before he could call out her name another band of Siamese appeared, chasing a young girl of fourteen, the daughter of Yoriaki's neighbors, a paper screen maker and his Laoatian wife. The girl sobbed in terror; her sticklike arms dripped blood from small cuts where they had toyed with her, torturing the mouse a bit before landing the final blow of the claw. As one Yoriaki and his comrades moved inland. As the girl ran through their ranks, Yoriaki ordered her to get in his boat and cast off, but he wasn't sure she even heard him such was her terror.

Now the four of them faced an even greater number, a full twenty Siamese. Even so, the enemy slowed down and came to a stop some yards away from the samurai. Yoriaki, in the grip of a terrible wrath, was surprised to find himself speaking.

"What has happened to this fair and lawful kingdom?" Yoriaki challenged them in their own language. "What has happened to the brave and noble warriors of the Siamese who fought at our sides like men? How can it be that they have turned so quickly into a pack of rabid curs, cowards attacking their neighbors in the night at the order of a pretender king? How have you come to such a low pass?"

"Shut up, you scum. You're no warrior, just the man who sells lunches along the docks," their chief officer snarled back, but Yoriaki knew his words had stung. "How can you dare judge the will of great King Prasat Thong? He is wise, our benefactor and protector!"

This made Yoriaki laugh. "I can guess how this has happened. He must have paid you well to turn on your truest allies. Your honor was bought with coin from the child killer, what price did it take to make you his dogs? I may not be a warrior any more but I have money. I make a good living, perhaps I can buy you myself. How much? Name your price, you sons of bitches!" Yoriaki's comrades began to laugh. One of them pulled a bag of silver coin from his belt and threw it so that it spilled out across the enemies' feet. Yoriaki did the same, joining in the laughter. "There it is, just lick it up off the ground, dogs, the same way you lick Prasat Thong's feet for favors."

That last jibe was more than enough to push them over the edge. The enraged soldiers came running forward haphazardly, forgetting their discipline. This made it easy for Yoriaki and his three allies; they cut down the first eight of them nearly effortlessly, making a pile of severed limbs and heads between them and the remaining force. The officer bellowed at his remaining men to get back into a formation. They men listened then, awed by the sight of their slaughtered comrades, but still brave and offended enough not to retreat. Yoriaki's heart sank to see another ten men arrive behind them; having no more houses left to burn they had come to the riverside to join in what they thought would be the massacre of fleeing civilians. Yoriaki felt a grim pride that they had prevented the worst of that. He gripped his *katana* tightly and prepared for the next round of battle. The Siamese grinned smugly now at their superior numbers and began a slow, methodical advance. Yoriaki stole a glance at the men with him. Silently they agreed; they would make their stand here. The four of them formed a square, ready for the Siamese to surround them. As one they backed toward the river's edge, knowing the water would impede anyone who came at them from behind.

The enemy saw what they planned and pressed forward, but the Japanese were ready for them. The four samurai stood their ground at the water's edge, their superior swordsmanship holding back the Siamese onslaught. There was no doubt the Siamese were fearsome warriors, they simply weren't as disciplined as the samurai. Still, the four of them were taking a terrible beating, as soon as they cut down one man another jumped in to take his place. Yoriaki's muscles were on fire, he had not practiced with his weapon for several years and he suffered for it now. His blade grew heavy, feeling as if it had been alchemically transformed into lead, but he kept on, never slowing his ever-changing patterns of attack and defense, slaying one enemy after another. Behind him he heard a gasp; out of the corner of his eye he saw Nakagata fall, pierced through the heart by both of his opponents' dual wielded *daab* swords. His killer was having difficulty pulling one of the blades back out of the dying samurai; Yoriaki helped him by cutting that arm off at the elbow before turning back to his own foes.

All along the beach similar scenes were taking place, small bands of samurai holding the king's soldiers back from the shore as women, children and the elderly swam or boated their way to what safety they could find. Stealing a split second's glance, he saw more boats had come, mostly Portuguese but some Chinese junks as well. Apparently they were not alone in their darkest hour; the Siamese may have let a madman rule them but the other peoples who called Ayutthaya home felt pity for their long-time friends and neighbors in Nihonmachi. This made Yoriaki smile. The Siamese chose that moment to fall back to regroup, making ready to finish off Yoriaki and his two remaining warriors. He took that opportunity to search the river for Momo again. Farther down the beach he saw a Christian Japanese, no samurai, just a merchant, holding off several soldiers with nothing but a garden shovel while his family fled into the water. The brave man went down beneath the Siamese swords as his loved ones screamed. Yoriaki saw with horror that the soldiers were now wading out after the women and children, who were clumsily trying to swim away now. Snarling with renewed rage he took a step in that direction but the enemy at hand had returned and he was forced to hold his ground.

The fresh troops came in hitting hard and Yoriaki felt his body begin to falter. The mind could only control the matter so long before it had no more to give. A lucky blow from a young Siamese warrior cut him across the belly, not too deep but he felt a tide of blood seep down his abdomen. In return his *katana* skewered the youth through the mouth, then thrust down through the chin, slicing open the neck all the way to the clavicle. Blood sprayed like the waterfalls he had once meditated under in the cool mountain forests of Japan. As that one fell, another stepped in to take his place. Deep within Yoriaki's mind he began to pray to Lord Jesus that his wife would be spared and taken to safety. There wasn't much time left to him so he also asked for forgiveness before his imminent exit from this world. He would die with honor, protecting his people from treachery, and he hoped the Heavenly Father would not judge his many sins too harshly. Just as he felt his sword had at last grown too heavy for another swing, there was an ear-rattling explosion from a few feet beside him. The face of the Siamese who was closing in on him for the kill disappeared in a pall of smoke, leaving behind a broken mess of shattered flesh and bone. There was another such explosion and the next man fell as well, a gory, smoking hole where his stomach had been.

Momentarily free from attack, Yoriaki turned to see Blom reloading first one massive pistol, then a second. The mustachioed Dutchman looked over at him and grinned. "Ah, Yo-san! How nice to see you again! Great bento, by the way; the grilled fish was perfect!" Having finished reloading, the plump fellow stepped forward with a pistol in each hand to shoot first one Siamese full on in the chest, then another. As Blom paused to calmly reload, again more blasts were heard and Yoriaki realized the plump Dutchman wasn't alone. His usual mates were beside him and several more of what looked to be sailors, all cheerfully mowing down the Siamese with their blunderbusses and pistols. The battle was over a scant few seconds later, the Siamese swordsmen being no match for the barrage of Dutch firepower. Of Yoriaki's fighting companions one was badly injured and being helped toward a longboat by the Dutch sailors, the other stood unsteadily on his feet beside Yoriaki, nearly overcome with exhaustion. Yoriaki felt a tear in his eye, a tear of glistening joy that a merciful God had sent these good Christian men to their aid.

"Thank you, Lord Jesus," he whispered in Latin. He turned to Blom, who shoved his pistols into his belt in order to take Yoriaki gently by the shoulders to steady him. "My wife. Momo. I can't find her." Yoriaki's voice a croak, rough with fear.

"She is safe with us, my friend. She and her parents were out in the middle of the river directly offshore from here; they were all crammed in her father's little fishing boat. I hardly think they would have made it out to sea in that, so we brought them aboard the *Groenevisch*. She is the one who sent us to your aid; she knew right where to find you." Blom carefully put pressure on Yoriaki's left shoulder, turning him gently and then leading the exhausted man toward the water. "See that fellow there?" He pointed to the dead soldier Yoriaki had found earlier. "Your wife's work. She told us she slit his gut with that nasty little shortsword she had. I hardly think he expected that. She's a pretty peach but I wouldn't get her angry for any reason! Now, I better bring you to her or she'll have my hide. I promised her I'd fetch you!"

Yoriaki looked at the dead soldier with a mixture of horror and pride at his wife's fierce courage. She had cut him open in a neat slice up the abdomen just like she would a dinner catfish. "She has many talents," he managed to say as the world begin to swim blackly before his eyes. Too weak to go further himself, he let sturdy Blom lift him up and load him into the longboat. "Thank you, Blom, you are a true friend," he managed to say before drifting into a scarlet-tinged unconsciousness.

He came to on the deck of one of the Dutch merchant ships he had seen earlier. Around thirty Japanese families were there, too, some wounded and being tended by a Dutch doctor and his assistants, but most stood staring at the conflagration that had once been their home. He heard a woman's wordless cry come from nearby and then he was nearly knocked down as his wife hugged him fiercely with a tightness that was painful to his combat-tortured muscles. He felt the handle tip of the *wakizashi* blade she still clutched in one hand dig in painfully beneath his shoulder. "My love, please put down the blade. You may kill someone," he breathed in her ear, managing a weak chuckle. She let him loose then and, both of them bloodstained and bedraggled, they looked long into each other's eyes.

"I fear I already have," she confided in a hushed tone.

"I know, I saw. Well done, wife, well done." He gently took the crimson stained *wakizashi* from her tremblng fingers and slid it into his sash next to his battle scarred *katana* before he took her in his arms again.

Dawn found them headed south in a fleet comprised of all manner of vessels, now approaching the mouth of the Menam where it met the Gulf of Siam. There were two Dutch and three Portuguese merchant ships, a Chinese junk and a variety of smaller seaworthy vessels that were owned variously by Japanese and their former foreign neighbors. They all followed the massive and well-armed red seal ship, with its cargo of goods brought from Japan still onboard and unmolested, bound for Yamada, Nagamasa's new kingdom in Ligor on the east side of the long peninsula that eventually became the lands of the Malay. All in all, some six hundred of the thousand or so who had inhabited Nihonmachi were making their escape to the holdings of their former leader. The rest had either been killed by Prasat Thong's forces or were in hiding among the Portuguese or other folk who might be sympathetic to them. Yoriaki prayed for their safety and was grateful that so many had escaped what could have been a horrendous massacre. Along the way they sighted several Siamese warships but were given a wide berth. It seemed that not all of the kingdom's military cared to persecute their former neighbors and allies.

After a few days sailing on fair seas, they reached Ligor and were welcomed by the people there, albeit a bit coolly. Yoriaki, his wife and in-laws were given a simple mud brick cottage to stay in and were brought food and a change of clothing. For the next two days meetings went on between their host Nagamasa and the higher ranking citizens that had escaped Nihonmachi, such as Ishida. Yoriaki, being a retired samurai who had chosen the life of a Christian commoner, was not invited, nor did he care; he was simply grateful to be alive with his loved ones.

Meanwhile, the two Dutch and three Portuguese merchant ships who had come to their rescue waited around in port to see what the fate of the Nihonmachi refugees might be. Yoriaki visited Blom daily and learned the Dutch ships belonged to Blom's uncles, men who were very sympathetic to the Japanese with whom they had a long and profitable relationship. The Portuguese ships were temporarily under the will of the holy fathers, their captains hard pressed to leave so many Christians to an uncertain fate and so they waited alongside the Dutch to see if further transport was needed.

Yoriaki and Blom both shook their heads in sad wonder at the violence Prasat Thong had ordered against them, a foolish move surely driven by fear for his ill-gotten power, since it would not be at all profitable for a new Siamese king to ruin his relationships with both Ligor and Japan. Eventually the Shogunate would learn of Nihonmachi's fate and would likely be immensely displeased at such treachery against other Japanese, even those who had chosen a life so far away from their island nation. Another day later, a stone-faced Ishida called a secret meeting of Nihonmachi's surviving men and the sympathetic Dutch and Portuguese who had brought them here.

"Yamada Nagamasa has heard our tale. We implored him to lead his army along with our surviving warriors against Prasat Thong, but he will not. He has a consort now, a woman given to him by the ursurper king and she whispers poison in his ear. He is not the man he once was; he has grown weak and complacent. He had many chances to kill Prasat Thong as that devil murdered the boy kings, but he didn't act. Now he has no will to face him, preferring to sit here in his little kingdom and do nothing. He won't be swayed. Worse yet, I don't think we are safe here. No matter what we say, he will listen only to his serpent bride. It is with a heavy heart I tell you that Yamada Nagamasa can no longer be trusted."

."What should we do? Where should we go?" the men cried. "You samurai and merchants might have a chance, but we can't possibly return to Japan. They will surely kill us if we do," one of the older Christian men said plaintively.

At this point Father Nixi, a Japanese Jesuit well loved by the Japanese Christians and one of the few of their community to enter the priesthood, stood up to address those gathered.

"My friends and brothers in Christ, I know of a place where we may go. I can lead us there. There are many Portuguese and a few Japanese Catholics living in the Khmer Empire just across the gulf to the east. I am sure they would welcome you, especially since you may now be considered enemies of Prasat Thong who is their most hated foe. I correspond regularly with my brother Jesuits there and though it lacks the riches of Ayutthaya, you could live safely."

"What of those who are not Christians?" Ishida turned to the Jesuit and asked in a respectful tone. "Have you some place we can go? I left Japan never to return, a masterless samurai who made a life for himself here in this part of the world. There are some hundred more like me here, and their families. Have you a place where we may live in peace?"

The Japanese Jesuit nodded. "You are brave men, sir, and when war came to Nihonmachi you fought side by side with the Christian men. We owe you our lives. The Khmer worship the gods of India just as the Siamese do; I see no reason why you Buddhists would not be welcome there. Please, let us all go together. You have survived a terrible ordeal, we can all sail from these accursed lands to find peace among the Khmer." The priest sat down then, giving them time to consider his offer. The room was full of quiet discussion for a time.

After a while Ishida again rose to face the crowd. "I and those samurai who follow me have decided to go with Father Nixi to Khmer. Any who join my men and I, of any religion, will have our swords to protect them, this I swear. Who will sail with us?'

It was nearly unanimous; most of the Nihonmachi refugees would travel to Khmer. Ishida turned to the Dutch and Portuguese captains.

"Fine sirs, can we prevail upon your good graces once more? It seems we need to cross the Gulf of Siam and have no vessels capable of such a journey of our own. We humbly beg your assistance and will repay you as best we can."

The captains conferred for a few minutes, the holy fathers browbeating the Portuguese captains while Blom was cajoling two older gentlemen who must surely be his ship-owning uncles to "do the right thing." At last the captains turned to the crowd and agreed to transport them all to Khmer. Their kindness was met with a chorus of joyful cheers and blessings. It was decided they would sail at dawn, better not to give their unpredictable hosts much warning in case they should choose to try to stop them.

The next morning Yoriaki and Blom once more stood at the rail of the *Groenevisch,* which was Dutch for "green fish" and had something to do with a lucky catch one of the uncles had made in his youth. Yoriaki grinned merrily as they left the feckless Nagamasa and Ligor behind, bound for the eastern side of the gulf.

"What will you do now, Blom-san?" Yoriaki sometimes added the Japanese honorific to his friend's name even though he spoke in Dutch. "Will you go back to Ayutthaya?"

"Well, I could, but we may not be too popular there for a while. Still, that greedy little king likes Dutch money, so I have a feeling he will forgive and forget. But it doesn't matter to me. I've decided to travel with my uncles and learn their business. Now that I'm at sea again, I find I've missed it. Being a dockmaster was safe and had good pay but it was a bit boring, and after all, I'm still fairly young. I have a few more adventures left in me.

Besides, I'll have to come check on you and that little peach of yours once in a while to make sure you are getting along in your new home."

Yoriaki thanked him and wished him good luck and the blessings of the Lord in all his ventures. When they arrived at the mouth of the Mekong from where they must take smaller craft upriver to Phnom Penh, they said their fond farewells. Yoriaki wouldn't see Blom for another five years.

1635, Phnom Penh, Kingdom of Khmer, Southeast Asia

Yoriaki hated his new home. The Japanese, who had until recently been so closely allied to the Ayutthaya kingdom, had been welcomed with suspicion by the Khmer and it was probably only the earnest pleas of the Dutch captain, Father Nixi and the Portuguese fathers that had convinced the Khmer not to simply have them all killed. As it was, the last five years had been an exercise in misery.

In their first year Momo had given birth to their daughter, little Hana, a blessing in their lives who was healthy and hearty enough, if a bit too thin. She had only gotten to know her grandparents a short time, they had passed away last year from one of the many wasting diseases that the filthy Mekong teemed with. First Momo's mother went, followed not two months later by her father, who Yoriaki was sure had been getting better. Yoriaki knew in his heart that old Mori had actually died from missing his wife of so many years but said nothing of it to grieving Momo. His beloved wife, although still lovely at age twenty-seven, had also grown thin and seemed to have lost the peachlike flush on her cheeks. The oppressive heat and general filth of Pnomh Penh was stealing what was left of her youth.

They made their living much as before, he and Momo getting up early in the morning to prepare the day's bento lunches, then Yoriaki paddled up and down the river along the docks while Momo tended the little garden next to their very modest house on the city's outskirts in what passed for their new Nihonmachi, a pale shadow of their former town. Momo complained bitterly that most of the seeds she had brought with her simply wouldn't grow in this climate, or died before producing any crop. She grew what she could of the heartier species and found some suitable replacements among the strange vegetables grown by the Khmer, but her cooking suffered for it, no longer quite reaching the level of perfection it had in Ayutthaya.

Phnom Penh was definitely no Ayutthaya; there was little money here as the Khmer kingdom was squeezed between two more powerful neighbors, their long time enemy the Siamese and the Quinam to the west. With no seaport, merchant ships had to travel up the Mekong through Quinam, a costly and unpleasant voyage according to his customers, and impassable to larger boat traffic in certain seasons. Still, there was always some trade to be found on the Mekong and where there was trade there were hungry men, but he sold less than half of what he had back in prosperous Ayutthaya. The locals were, by and large, not friendly to him. They were poor and regarded him as competition for their own vendors, so he mostly sold his wares to the Europeans he could find. The rule of law was not always in evidence, gangs of bandits roamed in daylight and he kept his *wakizashi* on his person at all times. So far he had killed seven such scum who had attacked him on his rounds; now it seemed he had a reputation and he went about unmolested. Momo and Hana were never never to leave the confines of Nihonmachi without his attending presence.

Of the six hundred souls that had fled Ayutthaya just over four hundred now remained, mostly comprising the Christians who couldn't return to Japan. Ishida was still with them, though, and some fifty of his samurai, most now converted to Catholicism. They found work as hired guardsmen and made a living, but they too suffered in the poor economy. The Siamese, Mon and Laotian wives they had brought with them lived in constant fear of the Khmer, who were their people's sworn enemies. Many of them also became Christians so they would not have to visit the temples outside the borders of their sad little Nihonmachi, looking to the mercy of Lord Jesus to protect them in a hostile land, just in case their Japanese husbands could not.

When Yoriaki ran into Ishida now and again, the older gentleman always swore that one day he would lead them all back to Ayutthaya and have revenge on Prasat Thong. Despite his adopted faith telling him to "turn the other cheek," Yoriaki secretly wished to join him if he ever really did go. The years in this subtly menacing and uncomfortable place had made him bitter. Cutting off Prasat Thong's head and sticking it on a pole at the mouth of the Menam would be most satisfactory. One thing was sure, he had not allowed himself to grow rusty in the way of arms again. He spent at least two hours of every day (except the Sabbath) drilling with his swords. His wife watched him and said nothing against it; the activity had her silent approval now that she had seen with her own eyes that allies and neighbors could turn into deadly foes without warning. She had a long dagger of her own now, and Yoriaki had given her further lessons, just in case. When Hana was a bit older she too would learn to carry a knife, Yoriaki had on occasion witnessed the awful fates of children around Phnom Penh captured by bandits and sold into bondage. Either his daughter would kill any who laid a hand on her or kill herself, Christ have mercy on her soul.

One bleary morning as Yoriaki began his day of paddling his little boat up and down the docks of the filthy Mekong he came around the bend to find a surprise. There, tied to one of the piers, were two very familiar looking Dutch merchant ships. Yoriaki blinked his eyes and shook his head to clear his vision. There could be no doubt. Letting out an exceptionally rare whoop of pleasure he began paddling as fast as he could, coming up astern of the big ships, wondering how they had even made it so far upriver; obviously the work of master pilots. A young Dutch boy who stood watch on the back deck of the vessel to the left turned and made a loud whistle. Thankful to the Jesuits for teaching him his letters, he was soon close enough to read the names, rejoicing to see that this was indeed *Groenevisch* and her partner *Vlissengen Tuin*, the Vlissengen Garden. These were really the ships belonging to Blom's uncles, here in Phnom Penh after five long years!

"You are late! I haven't had any breakfast yet and am holding out for one of those bentos!" the familiar voice came down from the deck. Yoriaki looked up to see Blom, a little thinner, a little darker and more wrinkled of skin, but still with his great, cheerful grin.

"I have just what you need, sir, see me on the dock!" Yoriaki secured his boat tightly, loaded ten of the banana leaf wrapped lunches into a hemp sack, then clambered up the pier's rather dodgy ladder as ably a boy of twelve climbing a garden willow. Seeing his friend after so long filled Yoriaki with so much joy he found himself embracing the man as if he were a long lost brother, to hell with samurai discipline! The larger man embraced him back, squeezing him in a suffocating bear hug until Yoriaki flailed feebly for release.

"You missed me then, Yo-san. I am so glad! I thought maybe you had forgotten your old friend. I am sorry it has taken me so long to come back."

"Never mind!" Yoriaki reassured him. "I am so happy to see you, Blom-san, truly I am. Here, your lunch," he said thrusting the sack into Blom's meaty hands. "Don't even think about trying to pay me for it, I owe you far more than a meal, or even two! I know your enormous appetite, I've put in a few extra, some for later or to share with your mates. Thank the Lord you are still alive and standing before me, it's a blessing!"

"I feel the same way, my friend, besides, it's been far too long since I've had any food as good as your little peach's cooking. Is she well?"

"Yes, she is, well enough. The climate doesn't agree with her and truth to tell I don't care much for it either. Oh, we have a daughter now, Hana, which means 'flower'! You must meet her, she will sit on your big tummy and pull that mustache of yours until you cry for mercy!"

Blom laughed heartily and gave Yoriaki one of his jovial yet gentle claps on the back. "That's wonderful, a little girl. I'll bet she's as pretty as her mother! Why, does she even know she has a fat old white-faced uncle? Won't she be surprised. I'll bet I have something pretty for her from my travels. Here, let's get out of this blasted heat and have a good talk. We need to catch up. I have much to tell you, Yo-san, much to tell."

The two of them repaired to *Groenevisch* where they found some shade beneath the reefed sails and sat on a couple of handy barrels. Between bites of grilled fish and rice, Blom told him of the many journeys he had made with his uncles and polished off one bento and then a second faster than Yoriaki had ever seen anyone else manage to.

"The reason I took so long to get back to you, Yo-san, is that we sailed all the way to Europe. Once there I had quite a bit of business to attend to, family matters and such, and my uncles needed time to straighten out their own affairs and find new cargoes to bring back here to Asia. But all that's neither here nor there, what was interesting was the special expedition we took to the Germanies, the lands that run east and south of my own Netherlands. Something happened there and it's rather odd." Blom paused, his jovial face having taken on a very thoughtful expression. "You probably won't believe me, a good Christian like yourself, but I swear it all to be true."

He paused again, finally prompting Yoriaki to ask, "What, what did you see there? I'll believe anything you say now that I've seen you eat two bentos in the time it takes most men to have one bite!" This made the two of them laugh, and Blom seemed to relax.

"All right, then. My uncles and I visited a town, a very strange town like no other in any corner of the wide Earth, and I've been to most of the corners. This was a town...from the *future!*" Blom's eyes were sparkling with wonderment, like a child's on his first visit to the pageantry of a Christmas mass. Yoriaki studied him for a moment and knew that whatever Blom said it would be true.

"I believe you. Tell me more," Yoriaki said, moving his barrel closer in anticipation.

When Blom was done it was nearly noon. Yoriaki tried to imagine the ground vehichles that moved without horses, not to mention those that flew with men inside them through the very heavens! But more than wonders such as those he pondered a society in which men were free to choose their own religion and to live as they pleased without caste and station, so like the Ayutthaya that had been lost to them.

"It sounds like a kind of paradise on Earth," he murmured to Blom, who having finished his tale was fortifying himself with two more bentos.

"Well, wouldn't call it paradise. It's still in the Germanies, you know," he said between bites. "But it is a good place, a place where people have freedom and rights. Plus, it's a boom town; it has riches and opportunities that make Ayutthaya look like poor Phnom Penh here." He looked around at the depressed city. "What a shit-hole! Anyway, I wanted to tell you about Grantville for a good reason, not just to entertain and amaze you, which it appears I succeeded at doing, by the starry-eyed look on your face."

Yoriaki gave his friend a confused look. "Yes, it was a wonderful tale, I am very enthralled. But what is this 'good reason'?" Yoriaki asked him with great curiosity.

"Simple! I think you should move there."

"Move there." Yoriaki blinked at his friend in the light of the merciless midday sun that had shifted in the sky to catch them out in its blaze as they were engrossed by Grantville's tale.

"Yes, move there. To live. *All* of you."

"All of us?"

"By my uncles' beards, is there an echo here? Yes, Yo-san, all of you who fled Ayutthaya to this sweltering outpost of Hell! This place stinks!" With that he got up and slid his stool back into the dwindling shade beneath the mast, Yoriaki doing the same.

"Look, I talked to some people there, including some Catholics. I didn't tell them exactly who you were and where you were from, but I said you were Catholic refugees who had been persecuted, numbering a few hundred looking for a safe home. They just about tripped all over themselves to tell me you would be welcome there, you poor darlings, and if you came they would do whatever it takes to find you homes and get you started. I must say, these Americans are nice to the point of almost seeming ridiculous, but I can also say they really mean it, I saw their charity with my own eyes. Come, Yo-san, think on this. Surely you aren't happy here. I'll wager none of you are."

Yoriaki shook his head solemnly in agreement. "Yes, Blom-san, you are right. We all despise this place, but there has been nowhere else for us to go. The Khmer, although not kind by any means, at least leave us alone and so far no one has tried to burn down our houses. Please, give me some time to think on this and discuss it with the others. I will call a meeting of our men this very night. May we hold it here on your ship? It would be best if the women didn't hear of this yet."

"Absolutely, you are all welcome!" The big Dutchman grinned widely, very pleased with himself.

"Blom, if we should decide to do as you suggest, how will we get there? We are so poor."

"Not to worry. My uncles are big-hearted fools just like me. It's already been decided. You will ride on these two ships. It will be tight but we can fit you all, plus we are a bit short on crew anyway, so you can help sail. We are bound back to Europe next, with only a few stops along the way. In any case, we shall consider your future success in Europe as an investment, and in my uncles' case, a little Christian charity might be just what it takes to keep them from ending up in a place like this when they die." The two of them laughed long and hard. Yoriaki grinned like a fool all the way back to their settlement, dreaming of a new faraway land full of freedom.

By that evening Yoriaki had whispered in the ear of the Japanese men, all of whom agreed to come listen to Blom's proposal. They remembered Blom as a hero and benefactor during their time of trial and would hear his words with open hearts. Arriving two hours before midnight as planned they sat on the deck of the *Groenevisch*, enjoying the wine that the Dutchmen passed around along with what fitful river breezes cooled the muggy night. When Blom began speaking, Yoriaki acted as his translator, swearing from time to time as he went that he was absolutely sure his friend was sincere and telling the truth. The Japanese listened silently until the very end. For a long time after Blom finished no one spoke. Finally Yoriaki, himself convinced through and through that they should take this offer, spoke to them.

"Men of Nihonmachi, please, what do you say? Surely this is an opportunity the likes of which we may never see again!" Yoriaki implored them in excited tones.

Ishida stood up and walked over to where Blom and Yoriaki stood, giving them a brief but polite bow.

"I have a question. If these Americans have changed the tide of history with their arrival, how did they do it? You said they landed in the middle of such a terrible war, why weren't they slaughtered along with the rest of the unfortunates in the region?"

Blom answered him, Yoriaki translating quietly as he spoke. "Ishida-san, not only do they have amazing vehicles and lights that burn without flame, they also have weapons of incredible power. They have guns that can shoot a hundred times, nay, a thousand times faster than any we of this century possess, and other, larger weapons of unbelievable destructive force. With their superior firepower, they were able to turn the tide of the war quickly in their ally's favor and have affected to some degree the politics of the entire continent. You have seen that we Europeans are a powerful people in this world. What these Americans of Grantville can do dwarfs our achievements. They are feared by all who stand against them and loved by all who stand with! No one has ever seen anything like it."

Ishida listened carefully, his face a stony mask. He then nodded once, looked straight at at Blom and said in passable Dutch, "Thank you, sir. I shall come with you." Then he turned to the crowd of Japanese gathered on the deck and proclaimed, "Men of Nihonmachi, I say that we follow this man to Europe. I believe all he has told us, and I believe this is our chance to leave this terrible place forever." Ishida's voice rose, taking on the cadence talented leaders have used to spur on their people since language began. "Ever since that accursed night when we fled Ayutthaya I have felt a great destiny awaits us, that we have been biding our time until our next move appears. Now I say it has arrived, thanks to our great friend, Blom! I have heard the wisdom in his words and am absoluely certain that Grantville, this town from the future, is where we may at last achieve the greatness that awaits us! Let us sail, let us sail yet again to a faraway land and meet our destiny without fear, we, the courageous men of Nihonmachi! What say you?"

As one, all leapt to their feet and cheered at the top of their lungs:

"Grantville! Grantville! Grantville!"

Do It Once and Do It Again

Terry Howard

Wietze Oil Field, August 1635

"Hannsi, I'm telling you, you're sitting on a gold mine," Hermann said.

"And I'm telling you, you're crazy," Hanns replied.

"No, I'm not."

Hanns was dressed no better than, if as well as, a prosperous farmer. Hermann was dressed in a color-fast, light mud-brown—what the Confederates called butternut and others called khaki—long-sleeve, button-down, collared shirt, like the up-timers wore. A local seamstress was selling them as fast as her sewing machine could turn them out. The oil workers wanted to look the part and that is what they decided the part should look like. The two men sat drinking at a table in the Wild Cat Bar and Grill, which had just changed its name to reflect the mood and vocabulary of their up-timer customers, and they had just expanded to better serve the Wietze oil field community. The owner overheard a conversation once. Once was enough.

"This place needs more tables."

"Yeah, but where else, close by, can you go?"

"Well that's true enough for now. But, I'll tell you this, if he doesn't add on it won't be true for long."

✧　　✧　　✧

The oil worker waved a hand at the south wall, beyond which the oil works lay. "Hannsı, you've seen what they're doing out there."

"So? What has that got to do with me?"

"Look, you're the one who owns grandfather's rights," Hermann said.

"Just what are you going on about?" Hanns asked.

Hanns and Hermann both were thoroughly familiar with their grandfather's "rights" and all of the circumstances that surrounded them. They were fully aware of the fact that downward mobility was much more readily available to the nobility than upward mobility was to the commoner. Not that grandfather had been all that high to begin with. At this point in time there wasn't a whole lot left.

Three villages' worth of land was leased out for ninety-nine years or three generations, whichever came first. But grandfather had mortgaged the rents. His second child, a daughter, was, to use an up-time expression, drop dead gorgeous. He spent money he should have put elsewhere to send her to the court of Henry Julius of Brunswick, duke of the principalities of Wolfenbuttel, Göttingen and Calenberg, where she could be seen. The investment paid off. She married well above her station to a widower. Before the investment could be capitalized the daughter died in childbirth.

The third child, also a daughter, was even prettier than her sister. Having done it once, Grandfather knew he could do it again, so he mortgaged the rents to send her to court, where she caught the eye of a young visiting *Hochadel*. She claimed he was a prince. Before the fairy tale could unfold the *graf* was thrown from his horse and broke his neck. It happened on the day she told him she was with child. Home she came in disgrace with an unacknowledged, unsupported bastard in her belly.

When the manor house caught fire, grandfather died rescuing something that he valued as much as life itself. To say that the first child, a son, rebuilt the manor house is misleading. He tried, but the replacement was a pale reflection of what the old house had been. The son, Hanns' father, supported a wife and four children, of whom only Hanns and one sister survived, along with his sister and her whelp, in what might graciously be called genteel poverty. The manor, along with a lot of hunting, barely kept them fed. Anything of value went for cash, as cash was needed from time to time, while the family waited for the leases to lapse so the sold rents would revert. The right to a tithe of the grain the villagers sent to be ground in the mill on manor lands helped feed the family, after a miller was paid, of course. The wood lots were watched very closely to see to it that only those who had a right to cut wood did so and then only in the allotment that fell to them, and the tenants knew better than to even think about hunting the game. The right to hunt belonged to the landlords, and the family in the manor spent a great deal of time watching every right like a hawk, in order to collect every last half-copper coin they had coming.

There was no going to court for Hanns. There was no going to a university either. His education ended with what he learned at the local grammar school in the nearest village. A tutor for even one season was out of the question. Hermann received the same scant education his cousin did. In better times Hermann might have gotten a better education and made a life as an officer in the military. In better times, without an education, he might have raised a mercenary unit and made his way in the world. But outfitting a company took money. In better times he might have joined someone else's outfit as an under-officer but equipment took money. In better times he could have scrounged old equipment out of the attic and gone off as a mercenary but what survived the fire was long gone for cash.

"The axle grease seep." Hermann said in response to his cousin's question.

"Hermann, there isn't that much of it. Besides, the village has the right to harvest anything that comes up. You know that every bit as well as well as I do."

Hermann smiled a smile that forced his ears further apart. "Exactly!"

"What do you mean by that?" Hanns asked.

"They can harvest what seeps to the surface. The family still owns anything deeper than a plough can turn."

"So?"

"Oil, Hannsi, it is all about the oil. The family is sitting on a gold mine and you own it."

"Oil?"

"That's right! Oil! We will sink a well over the grease seep."

"Hermann, the village is not going to let us drill a well and pump out oil without making a fuss."

"Hannsi? How are they going to stop us? We own the land. We own what is on it and what is under it. The tenants hold a lease. They have leave to farm the land and build in the village. Someone else owns the rents. But the family still owns the land," Hermann smiled. He knew there was something a bit odd about the terms of the *Lehen* the family held.

When their ancestor was given the fief ages ago, in return for his knightly service at arms, he thought there might be something worth mining on the land. So he asked for and got the right to mine. The family figured the Herzog gave it to him because the then "His Grace, the duke" knew there was nothing there. They owned the mineral rights free and clear in the face of any custom to the contrary and they could prove it. Hermann's grandfather staggered out of the burning manor house with his arms wrapped around an iron-bound chest to die a slow painful death from horrible burns. The chest held the family papers. Some were so old the parchment was brittle. "I told you, you're sitting on a gold mine."

"So, maybe I have a right to the oil? But the tenants have the use of the land." Hanns was skeptical.

"Hannsi, they have never cropped that portion. They have never run stock on it to graze. They don't harvest the grease anymore." Hermann was sure of this because they always checked anytime they hunted through the area. If they were harvesting the grease a toll was due the family. "They are not using it, they haven't ever used it other than years ago to collect any grease that came to the surface and they can still do that. It is like the wood lot next to it, if it isn't technically part of the wood lot anyway. They do not have the use of the land other than the limited right to harvest the grease, just like there is a set portion of the trees they can take."

"Still, Hermann, we don't have one of those things that goes hiss and thump."

"You mean a steam driver?"

"Whatever you call it. We don't have one and we can't afford to hire one. We couldn't even get one to the seep if we did. There is no road back there, only a path and the only bridge is a log across the creek."

"Don't need one. All a steam driver does is push enough steam under the hammer so the weight goes up then the steam escapes and the weight comes down. Ten men with a rope can do the same thing."

"Hermann, you're not listening to me. We don't have the money. We can't afford to hire ten men."

A stranger turned from the next table turned to face them and said, "Excuse me, I don't mean to intrude. And I wasn't meaning to eavesdrop on your conversation. But you weren't being particularly quiet about it. Do I understand correctly that the only thing between you and an oil well is capital to hire labor and buy materials?"

"No," said Hanns.

"Yes," said Hermann.

"Let me introduce myself," the short, blond, blue-eyed stranger said, pulling his chair up to their table. "My name is Adolph Holz." He faced Hanns. "You have a grease seep?"

Hanns looked at the short man with ice blue eyes and blond hair that was almost white from the summer sun and formed an opinion. He was probably a small-time merchant or a younger son of a larger merchant house. His clothes were not rich, but he was not a laborer by a long spell. Hanns decided he could trust the man to be reasonably honest as long as he kept an eye on him and counted the change. "Yes. But there isn't that much of it and the tenants have a right to what there is," Hanns said.

Herr Holz turned to Hermann. "You are convinced that you can get oil out of it?"

"Absolutely! I work on a drilling crew and we've sunk three wells in or next to seeps just like it. I can do the same on family land. All Hanns has to do is turn loose of the money and I can make the family rich again!" Hermann glared at his cousin.

"Hermann, you're crazy. Besides I haven't got enough money to do it. And anyway, I wouldn't let you throw it away even if I had it." Hanns glared right back.

"My good fellows, please, there is absolutely no cause for family to turn against family here. Now, Hanns, I gather it is not the idea of trying for an oil well that you dislike but the thought of spending the money?"

"I don't have the money!" Hanns replied.

"Yes he does! He just won't turn loose of it!"

"And if Hermann could do this without you having to invest any money in it, then would it be all right for him to try?"

"I guess so. Yes, if the tenants don't object and if the rent holder doesn't object, and I don't really see how they can do anything other than grumble, I can let him drive a well on the land, it should be all right. After all, it is our land. Yes, as long as he pays for it and it doesn't cost me anything then he can drill his well."

Hermann sneered. "You know I can't raise that kind of cash."

Holz smiled. "But if you had the cash you are sure you can bring in an oil well?"

"Sure I can!"

"Then the solution is simple." He looked at Hanns again, "I will put up the money, Hermann will organize and run the project, you will provide the land and we will split the income three ways."

"Fine," said Hanns.

"No way!" said Hermann.

"What?" Hanns was truly shocked.

"That oil is ours. I'm not giving away one third of it just because you are too cheap to pay for the drilling."

"Hermann, I really don't have the money!"

"Then we will find it somewhere else."

Adolph Holz saw his chance at a life-changing dream slipping away. "One quarter?" He offered, while waving to a bar maid and making the hand down circular motion that the Wild Cat patrons had learn meant another round. The patrons and staff now accepted it as a way of saying, "Bring another of whatever anyone in the group is drinking."

In the end, they agreed it was a loan and Adolph would get one half of the output until the loan was paid back, then, a hard-bargained seven percent of the profits after that.

"Why are you doing this?" Hanns asked the stranger.

"I have the money." Which was true. Even if it wasn't his money, he did indeed have it. "I like to gamble." This too was true. "This sounds like a better bet than a game of cards." This, though, was a cold blooded lie.

"Hermann, why didn't you hire a steam hammer?" The brawny fellow, who was sweating away, stripped to the waist, in the August heat, asked his friend.

"Johannes, we've been over that before. It would have been too much trouble to get it here and it cost too much! We would have had to build a road and a bridge just to get it across the creek. This way all we had to do was build a derrick and the trees for the lumber were already here."

"If we have to go very deep this is going to take forever."

"When I was child the crude was practically bubbling up out of the ground. It looked just like that last seep we sank a well in before we quit to come here," Hermann said for the fourteenth time.

"Quit your grousing and pull," was all Adolph Holz had to say on the topic. Once he put up the money, Holz wanted to be involved in every step of the project. On the first day, when he tried to sit and watch, work ground to a halt. It wasn't like his name was von Holz or something. So he was bending his well-dressed if scrawny back to the rope along with Hermann and the hired help. Hanns, of course, claimed he could not free up the time to work on the project. "Hey, I'm providing the land and the lumber you want to cut for the scaffolding. Don't ask me to waste my time on top of that." There had been an argument about the lumber until it was pointed out that it would still be there when they were done and it would be cut and ready to be dragged out.

Once the derrick was up they started driving. They had been at the actual process of picking up and dropping the hammer for four days. Late in the day they took a rest from the backbreaking labor. Hermann, as always, dropped a lead weight on line down the pipe. When he pulled it up the last two feet were dark, slimy and stinky. Hermann's shout of sheer joy brought the tired crew up from the ground on the bounce.

"Well, we still have to build a road and a bridge to get the crude oil to the river," Johannes said, "unless you want to wait until winter and move it on sleds."

Adolph heard him and quickly snapped, "No." Then in a calmer voice he said, "Oh, we'll need the road and the bridge but not for the crude. We'll refine it here and only ship out what we sell. The rest can go to surfacing the road."

"We can't get a cracking tower in here, even if you are willing to pay for one. It will have the same trouble we would have had trying to bring in a steam hammer. It is just too big and too heavy," was Hermann's comment.

"The cracking towers are new, aren't they? Do we really need one?" Adolph asked. No one wondered why or how Adolph knew so much theory and history of the oil fields while having little or no actual experience. Watching and talking about the up-timers, and what they were doing, was a major pastime in the Wietze community.

"Hermann," Johannes said, "you didn't start working in the oil fields as early as I did. I helped sink the very first well. You don't need a cracking tower to get started. You need a still."

"You mean like they use to make brandy?"

"Yes, but bigger. And you can make it out of iron, not copper. Because after the first still, which, I think, they actually did get from a brandy distiller, they built the next one out of iron. Instead of a coil it fed into a forty-foot-tall cooling tower."

"The cracking towers aren't that tall," Adolph objected.

"No, they're not," Johannes said. "But they're all metal and they operate under pressure. This was just two layers of ironbound wood with catch basins at different points. You see, the heavier oils won't go as high when they're vapors. So the gasoline is collected near the top of the tower, there is only one basin higher, and the asphalt collects at the bottom. What gets cleaned out of the boiling pot any time the system goes down is good for road work too."

"Iron bound wood? You mean like a barrel? Can we get the cooper in the village to make it for us?" Hermann asked.

"Why not?" Johannes answered. "That's who they got to make the first one at Wietze; the local cooper built it for them."

"We're going to need a steady supply of barrels anyway," Hermann said, "We might as well hire the cooper full-time if we can. His son should be able to handle their farm." The cooper and his family were half farmers. They did not have the right to cultivate enough land to make a living so they made barrels when they weren't working the land.

"Yes, but even if he can build us a barrel that tall, we would have to know where to tell him to put the catch basins, and we would need valve cocks to drain what is caught," Adolph objected.

"Herr Holz, the latter are just oversized barrel spigots," Johannes tapped the side of his head, "and where to put the basins is all right up here." He was part of the crew that put the first one together and he could reproduce the gaps between the basins in terms of how many body lengths it was between taps and where the taps fell on his body when he was standing next to it. In other words he could place them within a few inches of where they needed to be.

"If it was that easy, why did they go to the all metal high pressure cracking towers?" a skeptical Adolph asked.

"They could get more of what they wanted out of the crude that way. But we can sell the gasoline and the kerosene and the fuel oil to whoever wants it, what comes out under the fuel oil and over the asphalt base we can sell to the refinery at Wietze and they can crack it."

Adolph looked at Johannes. "If you know so much about it, why don't we just build a cracking tower?"

Johannes laughed softly. "Because the first cracking tower took forever to build; then it took even longer for them to get it to work right. It kept springing leaks. When they got it tight they had to install bimetallic strip temperature gauges and a lot of other claptrap I never had anything to do with, don't understand and can't do. But I can build a condensing tower, if you can get a blacksmith to set up a forge out here and a cooper to work on site, then a week from now we can be hauling refined oil off to Wietze."

Adolph look at Johannes and smiled. "Let's go talk to the smith and the cooper and see if we can get 'er done," he said, using a fashionable up-time phrase.

"Herr Holz, are you sure you want to do this? We can sell the crude to the refinery in Wietze. Right now all you've got tied up is a week's labor for the crew, some tools, the drilling head, pipe and the metal parts for a walking beam to pump it out of the ground. We can turn a clean profit in short order."

"Yes, but we can make a lot more selling to the end user instead of a middleman." Holz gave Hermann an explanation that made sense, even if it was far from the whole reason. "I've got the money, and shouldn't we get a steam engine in here to run the pump?"

"I suppose we should so the well can pump around the clock and not just when someone is walking the beam. It's okay with me, if you want to spend the money. I'll get the crew started on the bridge across the creek," Hermann said. "That's just labor and lumber and Hanns can scream all he wants to about us cutting trees."

"Why don't you start by rough splitting forty-foot barrel staves out of one of those big old oaks?" Adolph asked, pointing to the stand of oaks on the ridge overlooking the seep. Some of the trees were well over a hundred years old and the oldest were over a hundred feet high. Each and every one of them was accounted for. If one fell in storm then the tenants had the right to cut it up for firewood. If they wanted structural lumber it would have to be paid for.

"I can hear Hannsi screaming now." Hermann grinned from ear to ear.

"Is that going to be a problem?" Aldoph asked.

"No, we'll go ahead and get started on it." Herman replied. "Hannsi will okay it when he figures out it means more money in the long run. You tell the cooper the rough staves are waiting for him. Then after you are through in the village, go see Hanns and tell him he needs to settle up with the tenants and the rent holder for widening the path into a road. You can mention that we are building a cracking tower. I'll deal with him over cutting the tree when he comes out to see what a cracking tower is."

Johannes was a bit overly optimistic in his estimate. It took two weeks before the first run came pouring out of the tower and into barrels. It was three and a half weeks before the oxen pulled the first stout tanker cart the cooper and wheelwright put together, full of heavy oil, over the new bridge across the creek to start its journey to Wietze. It took that long to get the paperwork settled with the tenants and the rent holder for the road across the leased land.

Hanns, Hermann, Johannes and Adolph walked into the field office and told the receptionist they wanted to talk to Jerry Trainer.

"Can I ask what you wish to see him about?" the clerk asked.

"Yes," Hanns said. "We need to know if he wants to buy our full output or just our heavy oil for cracking?"

"What are you talking about? All of that is settled before they send in a drilling crew."

"Well, they didn't send in a crew, we drilled it ourselves. We've got fourteen barrels of heavy oil in a tanker cart outside. You can pretty much dictate the price on it, but if he wants the gasoline, the kerosene and the fuel oil, then he's going to have to give us the full market price on it or we'll sell it ourselves."

Jerry Trainer walked through the open door of his office. He looked over the four men standing there, made eye contact with one of them and said, "Johannes? I heard you went wildcatting. We were wondering whether you had any luck or not. You've got a cart of crude outside?"

"No, Herr Trainer, we have a cart of heavy oil. We cannot crack it so we thought to sell it to you. Of course, if you do not want to buy it we can burn it to distill the next run."

They would have to use part of the last run to boil the next one anyway. Hanns made it clear that he was not about to let them cut any more firewood without paying for it. Fortunately the trimmings off the trees that went to build the derrick more than met their needs so far. But that was it. Hanns was adamant. Even the trimmings from the timber cut for the bridge and what the cooper didn't use was now set aside to wait for an itinerant charcoal burner to come through. The charcoal burners preferred to work with well-seasoned small branches. The firewood was corded up and shortly would be on its way to the manor house now that a bridge spanned the creek. Until the charcoal burner came, the brush pile encouraged rabbits and other small game, which Hanns thoroughly approved of and the farmers truly hated. Even with the prospects of the oil money coming in, the habit of being tight with the resources was deeply ingrained.

"Well, let's go take a look at what you have, shall we?" Jerry said.

Outside, Jerry cracked the wooden valve open just a hair and caught a tablespoon full of oil in the palm of his hand. He looked at the color and rubbed a bit of it between the thumb and forefingers of his right hand. "Yeah, you're right, it's heavy oil. You can sell it for lubricant or we can crack it for gas and oil. Let's see, if you've got fourteen barrels of heavy oil then you should have about—" Jerry ran off a very accurate list, measured in barrels at fifty-five gallons to the barrel, of how much of each type of petroleum they had. "If you don't match those numbers then you've not condensed it correctly. And of course we will do a quality control check on every cart you bring in, but assuming it's okay, then let's see—" Jerry did some quick math and spun off totals and named prices per barrel which were indeed not far below what he was getting for it. Since he ran the only refinery in the world, until now, at least, it would seem he had an effective monopoly on petroleum sales, other than what found its way onto the black market, of course. He would just as soon keep it that way for as long as possible so it made sense to buy their entire output. "How does that sound, Johannes?"

Johannes looked at Hanns, who looked at Hermann, who nodded to Adolph who nodded to Johannes. "Herr Trainer, can we see that in writing, *bitte*?"

"Sure, we can do that. Then I'll give you a sales slip to take to the bank." The Abrabanels had opened an office in Wietze. It was their office that Jerry was referring to when he said "the bank."

At the Abrabanel office Adolph stepped up and took control. They had not discussed what to do, Hanns had assumed they would be paid in cash and they would split the money. "We need to set up three accounts, if you please. Then any receipts coming here will be split between the three accounts. Until further notice I get fifty percent and the other two split the rest. After you are notified, I get seven percent." They had agreed on seven percent of the profits. Herr Holz was claiming seven percent of the gross product.

Hanns of course called him on it. "You are right, Herr Holz, you are entitled to half until the loan is repaid. But then you get seven percent of the profit, which is not seven percent of the output. We will have expenses, there is the rent for the roadway, there is any more wood that is cut, there is the wage for the cooper and the smith and the refiner and his helper. No, after the loan is paid off, we will deposit seven percent of the profit."

It really was small change, but it was not in Adolph's nature not to try and it certainly wasn't in Hanns' nature to let him get away with it.

Hanns and Hermann took their portion in cash. Adolph left his on deposit. Johannes had already been paid by Adolph when he paid off the construction crew. Outside in the street a very happy Hanns was counting his money. Hermann put his, uncounted, in his pocket. He could do that with the paper currency that was now an accepted standard in Wietze. The same seamstress who was making the shirts was also producing four-pocket pants on the blue jean pattern, complete with rivets.

"Buy me a beer, Hermann," Johannes said, "and let's talk about doing this all over again elsewhere, since you've got the money to front us. Or do you want to just sit back and run this one for your cousin? If you do, then I'll have to talk to Herr Holz about investing in another well and tower."

"No, Johannes," Adolph said. "I'm through here. I'm heading home."

"Sure, Johannes, a beer sounds good. Hannsi can hire someone else to run his well for him," Hermann replied.

Paris, October 1635

A short, blond, blue-eyed man was ushered into the office of one Yves Neff. Of Cardinal Richelieu's many clerks, Yves was one of the few who had an office instead of a desk. The nature of what he kept track of required privacy from time to time. This was one of those times.

"M. LeBlanc," the clerk said, "just what is so important that you felt you had to leave your assigned station to share it with me personally instead of putting it in your regular report?"

"I really do think I need to talk to His Eminence."

"Oh? And why is that?" As a bureaucrat part of his job was to act as a filter and see to it that his boss was not bothered with trivial matters.

"If he will secure the mineral rights to the tar pits near the village of Parentis en Born for me, I can start producing the petroleum fuels you know he will need for the research projects that I am sure you currently have ongoing."

"Can you indeed?" the clerk asked with just a hint of a raised eyebrow. "I am afraid," the clerk said, "you have wasted your time in coming to Paris. I shouldn't tell you this but under the circumstances I will make an exception. There is an ongoing oil fuel project. Top people are working with the best and latest information. We even had a man in Wietze watching for new developments until he decided to return to France without authorization. I shall have to recruit someone a bit more reliable, someone who knows how to stay in place and forward timely reports, to replace him with and get the new man to Germany immediately.

"Now as long as you are here, we need to discuss these sizable sums you recently spent."

"I was authorized to buy information."

"And that information is?"

"I now know how to drill a well and refine petroleum fuel."

"You seem quite sure of yourself," Yves said.

"I am. We started from scratch with nothing but an oil seep, and finished with refined fuel which we sold to the manager at Wietze."

The clerk sighed dramatically. "You were authorized to buy 'new' information! We already knew how to do those things. I am afraid that money you spent on your personal education is going to have to be reimbursed, in full and immediately."

Henri paled. He had financed the driving of an oil well and the building of a cracking tower. In return he would get the lion's share of the profit until the loan was paid off. Then he would get a premium for as long as the well was in production. His share in the output of the oil well in Germany would pay what he now owed, but it would be a while in coming. He could end up sitting in debtor's prison until it did. A man could get sick and die doing that. "I don't have that kind of money lying around!" M. LeBlanc objected. "I can pay it back. But it will take some time."

"I understand." Yves smirked. "Why don't you see about raising it and come back at the end of the week?" He knew Henri could not raise the money. What he had in mind for M. LeBlanc was a nasty, unpleasant job that he was having trouble getting a reliable man to do. This looked like the perfect leverage to get it done.

By sheer chance near the end of the day the clerk's supervisor M. DeMille stopped at his small office. "Yves, here is a list of questions about cracking oil we need answered. Get it off to our man in Wietze right away."

"I am afraid, sir, that we no longer have a man in Wietze."

"What happened? Was he found out? Was he killed, imprisoned, did he fall ill?"

"No sir, he is alive and well and returned to Paris without authorization."

"What brought him back? Was he homesick? I can understand that. I have been to the Germanies. The cooking is horrid and the wines are worse."

"No, he thought we would be interested in setting him up to refine petroleum."

"As if he could!"

"Oh, he can," Yves said. "According to his reports, he was involved in every step of the process from drilling a well to carting off the finished fuels."

The clerk's superior dropped the stack of papers on the clerk's desk in excitement. "You are sure he can do it?"

"Reasonably sure," the clerk replied. "But we have a well in production, another one is being drilled, and a team of our best people are working on a cracking tower."

"And failing miserably!"

"What?" a startled Yves asked.

"You heard me. They can't get it to work. It has blown up twice. It has burst and burned twice more. It is consuming money, men, and time at an alarming rate. The money is minor, they can always raise another tax, the men mostly do not matter, the prisons are full enough, but the time is something we cannot spare. The teams working on engines were promised fuel a month ago. They are at a standstill until we get it for them. We've bought as much as we can but the people in Wietze are keeping a close watch on it and we cannot get anywhere near as much as we need.

"If we have a man who has practical hands-on experience in fuel production we need him right now."

"M. LeBlanc says he can do it and I see no reason to question the man's honesty."

"Where is this wonder worker? I want to see him immediately."

"I have a local residence recorded right here," Yves said, picking up M. LeBlanc's file.

"Let's go."

"What?"

"When I said we need that man right now, I meant right now! Let's go!"

"But, sir, now?" It was, after all, very near the end of the day.

"Now!"

Yves knocked on the door. When a toothless old woman answered he asked, "Is this where Herni LeBlanc has a rented room?"

"Well, that was fast indeed. When he moved out this morning he told me he had someone else who would take the garret. Do you want to see it?" She really didn't think they would. They really did not look like the type who would rent such a room up under the eaves.

"No, we do not. You say he moved out? Did he say where he was going?"

"No, all he said was he would send someone else to rent the

garret. If that isn't you, then good day to you." With those words she closed the door.

"How odd," M. DeMille said. "Why would the man move so suddenly and without a forwarding address as if something were wrong?"

Yves looked sheepish. "Well, I was planning on offering him that job in the Caribbean that we are having trouble filling. Since I knew I would need some leverage I told him he had to return some misappropriated funds immediately."

DeMille smirked at his underling's deviousness. Then it filtered through his mind and he realized if the man could not be found they could not use the knowledge the fellow was carrying around in his head. "That is not fortuitous, Yves. Find the man. Find him immediately and get him working on the fuel production problem. If you can't produce him by the end of the week, then pack your bags. I think you would be the perfect man for that assignment in the Caribbean."

Yves paled. He had absolutely no interest in seeing the new world.

By sundown agents and officials all over Paris were looking for one Henri LeBlanc. By sundown the next day only a fast horse could have stayed ahead of the search. The selfsame fast horse carried the word to every port in the country and every way station on the highways and byways to the border and beyond. Henri LeBlanc was a wanted man, a very wanted man indeed.

Behind the closed door an old woman winked at her fair-haired grandson. "Merci, Grandmère," Henri said. "It seems I owe those fellows a lot of money and it will be a while before I can raise it."

"How much do you need?"

Henri named a sum.

The old woman shook her head. "I've saved a great deal of what you've sent home, but not nearly that much."

"That is not a problem, Grandmère. I will have the money by and by. I just need to stay out of sight and out of debtor's prison until it catches up with me."

"Well, you just plan on staying right here, out of sight, for as long as you need to. I will enjoy the company. Besides, the money you've been sending home will see to our needs for a good long time."

✧   ✧   ✧

Three months and a bit more went by. When he had the money in hand Henri LeBlanc went to the offices of Cardinal Richelieu's intendants. At the first desk inside the door he said, "I need to see Yves Neff."

"I am sorry, but M. Neff will be out of the office for quite some time, I am afraid. He is on an assignment in the field."

Henri thought he detected a glint of humor in the voice of the clerk as he explained Yves' absence. "Then I need to speak to whoever is handling his case load while he is gone."

"And you are?"

"Henri LeBlanc."

"Certainly. Please wait one minute, please. Page," the clerk called. When the boy arrived the clerk said, "Take this man to M. DeMille immediately."

At the word immediately the lad hesitated. "Immediately?" he asked.

"Yes, you heard me," the clerk said with a nod. "Immediately."

After what seemed like a very long walk that was surely out of the way they passed two armed men who seemed to be loafing in the room they were passing through. Upon seeing them the page quit dawdling and finally moved at a brisk pace until he stopped and rapped on a nondescript door which he then opened without waiting. Henri walked through and the page closed it behind him.

The mature gentleman setting behind an overflowing but organized desk looked up and asked "And you are?"

"My name is Henri LeBlanc, I worked for—"

Before he could even began to explain what the circumstances were the door opened again and the two guards entered the room with their rapiers in hand.

DeMille spoke to the guards first. "Take this man to M. Devereux at the research station." Then he addressed Henri, "Your absence has cost us three months. I had hoped Devereux would have the cracking tower working by now but he has had no success. Now maybe we can get something done."

"Oh, I am sorry to tell you this, but I've never worked on a cracking tower."

"What? But your reports said you worked every aspect of making fuel from driving the well to selling the finished product."

"Yes, sir. I did."

"Now I am confused. Have you or have you not had experience turning black petroleum into usable fuel?"

"Yes. I have done so and offered to do it again, but M. Neff said I was not needed."

"M. Neff is looking after something in the Caribbean by now because he overstepped his authority. Before you leave please clear up one point for me. You say you have never worked on a cracking tower, how then can you have made fuel?"

"Oh, that is simple. We used an old-fashioned, outdated still and a cooling tower."

DeMille snarled, "Get this man out of here." Then he said, "M. LeBlanc. Understand me and understand me well. If there is not a report on my desk within thirty days telling me that enough fuel for the engine research project is no longer a problem, you may count yourself lucky if you are allowed to join M. Neff in Louisiana."

Les Ailes du Papillon

Walter H. Hunt

1

Walks-In-Deep-Woods looked up through a haze of tobacco smoke to see Strong-Arm standing at the tent flap. Normally Strong-Arm went where he wished; he entered any tent he chose, never asking permission or hesitating—but he hesitated here, at the entrance to Walks-In-Deep-Woods' tent.

Walks-In-Deep-Woods did not speak. He placed his hands before him, as if warming them at the fire; then he touched them to his temples, his cheeks, and his breast. Strong-Arm watched each hand motion, perhaps attributing meaning to the gestures... but Walks-In-Deep-Woods smiled inwardly to himself, knowing that they were for show, like most of what a shaman did.

Just for show, he thought to himself, but did not permit a hint of it to appear on his face. Solemnly (*very* solemnly, he reminded himself) he looked up at Strong-Arm, awaiting the chief's first words.

"You are working some medicine," Strong-Arm said. "I will come back later."

"You are welcome in my tent, mighty chief," Walks-In-Deep-Woods said. "How may I help you?"

He gestured to a seat opposite, upon a blanket that a daughter of a chief had made for him when he was much younger. Strong-Arm seemed to hesitate again, as if unwilling to enter a shaman's tent, but after a moment he entered, bowing his head to come through the tent-flap, and took the offered seat.

"You are working some medicine," Strong-Arm repeated.

"Only the beginning," Walks-In-Deep-Woods answered. He touched his temples and his cheeks again; Strong-Arm followed his gestures, perhaps again attributing some meaning to them. "I am trying to make clear that which is clouded."

"By looking in the fire?"

"In part," Walks-In-Deep-Woods said. "I have seen . . . the trail of our enemy."

Strong-Arm was suddenly alert. "Enemy? You mean—"

"The great servant of the Onontio. Yes."

"He is old now."

"But still cunning, great chief. And still dangerous. For him to be defeated requires great medicine."

"Our medicine has never worked against Champlain," Strong-Arm said, and he picked up a bit of earth from the ground beneath his blanket, tossing it behind him to ward off any curse that might come from speaking the white man's name. "Not in my father's time, not in mine. Can you do what no one has done? Can you do what *you* have never done?"

"I can," Walks-In-Deep-Woods answered, letting his face settle into a thin-lipped smile. "I can."

Outside, in the dark, a night-bird hooted. Walks-In-Deep-Woods thanked the Great Spirit for His timing.

Strong-Arm rubbed his hands together and then spread them before the fire.

"What do you intend to do, shaman?"

"It is Champlain that opposes us, great chief. It is Champlain who makes common cause with the Hurons and goes to war against us."

"Yes, yes," Strong-Arm said. He was clearly uncomfortable that Walks-In-Deep-Woods was repeating the name.

"Then it is clear that he must die."

"You . . . can cause his death?"

"Only at the proper time," Walks-In-Deep-Woods answered.

Strong-Arm looked a bit disappointed.

"But *this* is the proper time," Walks-In-Deep-Woods added. "With the harvest moon in the sky, and the first trace of chill in the air. I will cause the cold to creep into his old white bones and drive him to his bed." He slapped his hands on his thighs, making Strong-Arm jump slightly. "And once he lies down he will not rise again."

"When will you make this medicine?"

"When?" Walks-In-Deep-Woods let himself smile again, but this time he bared his teeth. "When, the great chief asks. *It is already done.* The cold is in his bones already."

Now it was Strong-Arm's turn to smile.

2

Champlain felt his age when he awoke in the morning, when he knelt to pray, when he bent over a map that had once been so easy to see, and when he laid his tired bones for sleep—and a hundred other times during the day.

Whenever he returned to France, his friends and the courtiers in Paris would ask: *why go back, Samuel? Why return to Nouvelle France, where the winters are cold and the nights are long?*

You are not accorded the dignity of being named Governor. While the king and the cardinal—and there was only *one* cardinal, whenever the title was spoken—*grant great seigneuries to everyone around them, you are left humble and modest, with no honors heaped upon you.*

Why go back?

Why indeed, he often thought to himself. But the answer was always the same—when he first set foot upon land it reminded him: the pure, clean air, the incredible variety of colors... Nouvelle France was in his blood. It was here that he first realized what he was meant to do.

And it was here, not in some comfortable *salon* in Paris, in the heart of the world, where he would die. He knew it, just as the cardinal had known it two years earlier at an interview when he had learned of the great extent over which New France was to spread. *All of America north of the Spanish possessions belongs to the crown of France,* Richelieu had told him, and then granted him the title of *lieutenant-general.*

In the spring, seven months ago, a confidant in Paris had sent him a scrap of paper—a sort of engraving, a perfect reproduction of an up-time book, somehow procured from the Americans. It was a page from a great encyclopedia; and it was about *him.*

According to the book of the future, there was a calamity awaiting him—an imminent one. He was to suffer something that the English text termed a "stroke"—his correspondent had translated it as *congestion cérébrale*, an affliction of the head. It was written that the disease lingered for some time, giving him the opportunity to settle his affairs and contemplate, during the time left to him, how he would approach the Lord of Hosts when his spirit passed from the world.

The book had been vague about the exact date of the event, placing it sometime in October though it did state that he was to die on Christmas Day. By his own reckoning, the fate that God had ordained for him should logically take place eighty days earlier: forty days from Ash Wednesday to Eastertide, he thought, and forty days from Easter to Pentecost—eighty days placed the event on October the fifth.

All during the summer, Champlain had made his preparations. Confiding the contents of the scrap of paper to no one, not even his confessor, the Jesuit Father Charles Lalemant, he made a number of revisions to his will, providing a number of additional bequests of cash and property and making provisions for the servants of his habitation, his Montagnais godson Bonaventure, and even the old *greffier* of Québec, Nicolas de Laville. Lalemant took all of these changes in stride, asking Champlain about his sudden decisions... and, to his shame, Champlain dissembled (even under the seal of the confessional; he told his beads many times for those minor sins).

He would face his death with dignity, with his affairs in order, with his mind clear and his debts and responsibilities discharged. God had vouchsafed him an opportunity to do it before the *congestion cérébrale* struck him down.

By the Feast of Saint Michael all was in readiness. There was by then nothing to do but wait.

3

From his own Oneida longhouse to the Tree of Great Peace at Onondaga, the Council Fire of the Five Nations, was six days' travel on foot. Strong-Arm expected Walks-In-Deep-Woods to go with him to speak with the other chiefs about war with the servants of the Onontio, but Walks-In-Deep-Woods declined. It was too far a journey for his old bones, with winter's icy breath following just behind.

"I need your sage advice, shaman," he said to him, but the older man shook his head.

"It is no place for shamans."

"What?" Strong-Arm threw his hands in the air. "Onondaga is *full* of shamans. They are constantly asking questions—"

"And never giving answers, wise chief. I do not wish to be asked so many questions by so many shamans. You... you must go to the Great Fire of Peace and speak bravely, and argue your case so that all of the *Haudenosaunee*, the People of the Longhouse, will go to war alongside you."

"I would have *you* beside me."

"From the brave keepers of the Western Door, the Senecas, to the fierce Mohawks at the Longhouse's sunrise entrance—all will harken to your words, mighty chief. You do not need *me* to make you or your speech strong.

"All you need, great Strong-Arm, is the truth."

So Strong-Arm went alone, following the paths across the lands of the Oneidas until he came to Onondaga, where the great sacred fire of the Five Nations was kept. He carried with him the wampum of the Oneida, so that he might speak on behalf of himself and the other Oneida chiefs. As he traveled he knew that other chiefs, carrying other wampum, were on their way to Onondaga to hear him speak.

At the Council Fire at the heart of the lands of the *Haudenosaunee*, nothing happened quickly. Every meeting of the Great Council, ten hands of chiefs from all of the Nations—Seneca, Cayuga, Onondaga, Oneida and Mohawk, represented according to their might and numbers—began with tale-telling: of Sky-Mother and Earth-Father, of the Peacemaker Deganawidah, of the great Onondaga chief Hiawatha and the sorcerer Tadadaho whom Hiawatha cured with sacred beads and secret words. Almost an entire day from sunrise to sunset was consumed with the recounting of these great stories.

On the second day, a new sachem from the Seneca was welcomed "at the woods' edge" to replace an old one who had died. Strong-Arm stood among the "clear-minded," reciting the sacred words and helping to present the sacred beads to the "bereaved." It was an aid to Strong-Arm's patience that there were no debts of blood with the clan who had lost the sachem: there were no graves to cover, no feuds for the Council to resolve before the new sachem could pass through the "requickening" and take his seat. Nonetheless, the chiefs—and the shamans—were not interested in talking seriously until that ceremony was behind them, and thus a second day passed before the Tree of Great Peace.

At last, in the middle of the third day, when the elderly and distinguished chiefs had all had their chance to speak, Strong-Arm rose before the assembly and spread his arms wide. The members of the Grand Council, perhaps sensing that something important was about to be spoken, became hushed and quiet.

"I am Strong-Arm," he began, "nephew of Red-Feather, nephew of Quick-Deer. Sachem I am, chief among the Oneida, neither the least nor the greatest of the *Haudenosaunee*, yet one of all, who stands before you by right and with privilege to speak." He drew his belt of wampum and hung it on the pole that stretched the length of the great longhouse.

He waited long enough to see if any chose to challenge him; none did, nor had he expected it—but such was the custom of the Council. After a moment he continued.

"The *Haudenosaunee* know well that for many years—in my time and the time of my uncle Red-Feather, we walked in paths of war against the servants of the Onontio, from the white land of over sea that is called France. They have made war upon us, with their mighty weapons and white man's charms—and for many years have been victorious in all their doings.

"But all of that will come to an end. The war-chief of the Onontio will come to an end."

The members of the Council began to murmur.

"He is fearless," said an old sachem. "He has always been fearless. He speaks to the land. He *listens* to the land."

"He is mortal," Strong-Arm said. "He can no more outrun the sun or overcome the pull of the Earth-Father than any of us."

"But as long as he walks the earth—"

"No more," Strong-Arm said, and there was more murmuring. It was impolite to interrupt another member of the Council when speaking. Some of the younger chiefs shifted in their seats, as if they wanted to interrupt *him*.

Rise and challenge me, Strong-Arm thought, crossing his arms in front of him. *Come. I will wipe the tears from your eyes.*

There was an extended silence. The clear-minded observed quietly, while the bereaved sought to determine whether they were prepared to intervene.

"Death-medicine has been laid upon the war-chief of the Onontio," Strong-Arm said at last. "We will walk in the paths of war, and he will not be there to lead the white soldiers against the *Haudenosaunee*. My shaman has pronounced it, and so it shall be."

The old sachem stood slowly, his hand grasping a polished maple staff. He made his away between the other members of the Council until he stood before Strong-Arm.

"I am Swift-As-Deer, nephew of Fishes-In-Deep-Waters, nephew of Climbs-High-Mountain, of the Mohawk Nation at the dawn door of the Longhouse. Though I must say to you, young chief, that most deer I see these days are far swifter than I am.

"You speak with bold words, Strong-Arm nephew of Red-Feather. Thus did your uncle speak when he was a member of the Council. When I was younger I walked in the paths of war against the war-chief of the Onontio, the one called Champlain. He is cunning and wise—and not easily killed, not by axe or fire-stick or death-medicine. Who is this powerful shaman that claims to have done it?"

"Walks-In-Deep-Woods."

Swift-As-Deer looked at Strong-Arm from head to toes and back again, and then let out a loud whoop of laughter. The longhouse shook with it as it spread to the rest of the members of the Council.

Strong-Arm's hands formed into fists.

"You are mocking me, Swift-As-Deer."

"You?" Swift-As-Deer lifted his arms, turning his staff in his hand as he held it in the air. "No, Strong-Arm nephew of Red-Feather. I would not mock you. But as for Walks-In-Deep-Woods—oh, I would mock him from sunrise to sunset.

"He is a fake, brave Strong-Arm. He is a cheat, a speaker of false words. He has no death medicine, not now and not ever. Whatever he told you was a lie. He wants nothing but to eat your food and make love to your women."

Swift-As-Deer turned away from Strong-Arm, making the younger man tense in anger—but Swift-As-Deer was an elder sachem, not a youth he could challenge for the slightest public offense.

Such scores were settled elsewhere, at other times.

"Speak, wise Brothers," Swift-As-Deer said. "Who knows of this dog Walks-In-Deep-Woods? Bring light to my Brother Strong-Arm, the brave and wise chief of the Oneida people. Tell him that there is no sense in risking the lives of the people of the Longhouse in a war based on the advice—and the false death-medicine—of this *fraud*."

As Strong-Arm watched, several of the members of the Council shifted in their seats, as if preparing to speak. Before any actually rose, however, the newest sachem of all stood and walked to the center of the assembly. Without speaking he drew a long belt of wampum from over his shoulder and laid it next to Strong-Arm's own.

Then he walked to stand before Strong-Arm and stared at him for several moments, still not speaking.

"What—" Strong-Arm said, but the other man held up his right hand and Strong-Arm fell silent. No one in the Great Council spoke, or shifted position, or made any other noise.

"I want to look in your eyes," the other chief said at last. "I want to look into your soul."

Strong-Arm did not understand what he meant, but answered, "what do you see?"

"Bravery."

Strong-Arm did not know how to respond to that either.

"I am Born-Under-Moon, son of Red-Spear, come to you from the land of the Seneca, new among you. I have heard great speeches and wisdom. And now—when a brave chief calls for the People of the Longhouse to walk the paths of war...I must sit in quiet and have an old man tell me of his *fear*?

"Is that what the *Haudenosaunee* have come to? Is that the blood that courses through our veins? Is that what we have become—playthings of the white men? Is that all we are? I do not believe what I hear."

Born-Under-Moon turned and stared fiercely at Swift-As-Deer. The Council remained silent.

"I went to war when I was younger than you," Swift-As-Deer said. "Many brave warriors fell in battle against this captain of the Onontio. But even if he is old—or dead"—he glanced at Strong-Arm for a moment—"the servants of the Onontio are dangerous. I understand the need for a young warrior with blood coursing hot in his veins to seek glory in battle. I ... understand it very well. But this is not a decision to be taken lightly."

"You think this is a whim?" Born-Under-Moon said. His voice was laced with anger. "Is that what you think, old man?"

Swift-As-Deer did not answer. Strong-Arm noticed a curious expression on the old sachem's face: not anger, but rather weariness—as if he had heard this accusation before and did not want to have to answer it yet again.

"He has walked the paths of war more times than you, Born-Under-Moon," Strong-Arm said into the quiet. "His is a voice to which we listen carefully. Even if this is the time to strike, we must take heed of the wisdom he speaks."

"He is afraid of the old war captain. He is a—"

Strong-Arm held up his hand and the younger chief halted, as if unwilling to finish the sentence.

"Do not let that arrow fly, Born-Under-Moon. If you believe—as I do—that we should go to war with the servants of the Onontio, then making war with the eldest and wisest is not the correct course. It gains you nothing, and it loses you the friendship of many in the Council.

"Including me."

Born-Under-Moon looked as if he did not understand Strong-Arm's reasoning: but he had already spoken of the other man's bravery, and could hardly reverse himself.

"There are many reasons we should take this course," Strong-Arm said. "If you are ready to listen, friend," he continued, "I shall tell them to you."

4

On Monday, the fifth of October, Samuel de Champlain rose and prayed as he had always done. After a brief and spare meal he dressed and went for a walk in the settlement of Québec. He remained in plain sight.

He was waiting for the *congestion cérébrale*.

The day passed without event. Night came, and still nothing. When the sun went down he returned to his *habitation*, partly relieved and partly disappointed. He did not want the stroke, but knowing that it was coming he felt that he had made his peace and was ready for it to come.

On the next day he rose and did the same.

And the next day after that.

On the fourth day, Father Lalemant fell into step beside him as he walked along one of Québec's muddy streets. Lalemant was spare, almost gaunt—it had been clear to Champlain from the time he met the Jesuit Father that Lalemant had been very attentive to his spiritual exercises.

He kept up with Champlain's long, steady strides.

"Father?"

"Monsieur," the Jesuit said. "You are troubled," he added a few steps later.

"Do I look troubled, Father?"

"To be honest, monsieur, you do. I think—" they both stepped around a small pile of refuse—"I think there's something bothering you. As your confessor, I feel it my duty to ask you what it might be."

"You are an acute observer of mankind, Father."

"That remark neither confirms nor denies my observation."

Champlain stopped suddenly; Lalemant took two more steps and had to turn around.

"I have many things that trouble me, not least that my spies tell me that the Iroquois—particularly the Mohawk—have gone on a war footing. But I sense that you mean something else. What is more—" he lowered his voice. "What is more," he added softly, "this is not the confessional. I do not wish to discuss personal matters in the middle of the street."

"That is just as well," Lalemant answered. "You aren't saying anything in the confessional these days."

Champlain's years of training and experience as a leader had given him the ability to stare down native sachems, *grands seigneurs*, and, when necessary, Jesuit priests.

"I beg your pardon," Lalemant said, but to his credit, stood his ground.

"You have a certain right to pry, Father," Champlain said after a moment. "But there are limits."

They began to walk again. Champlain began to make his way back to his own house.

Champlain spoke first. "I am expecting something to happen," he said at last, without looking at the Jesuit. "I have received . . . a message."

As they sat in the study of Champlain's *habitation*, Lalemant turned the thin sheet over in his hands, marveling at it. "This is amazing, monsieur."

"I was alarmed myself."

"No," Lalemant said. "I meant—the quality of the paper."

"Oh, for the love of God," Champlain said, snatching it out of the Jesuit father's hands. He waved it at Lalemant. "I was referring to the *contents*. This is a reproduction. A . . . what was the word that the cardinal used? '*Photocopier*.' A machine picture, some magic the up-timers can perform."

"It's about *you*."

"Yes, I know. I can read. It tells me when I am to die—and how."

"Thank you, monsieur. I, too, can read. This paper says that you are to suffer some sort of attack, sometime this month." A look of understanding came onto his face. "This explains much," he said.

"I am waiting for this to happen. Indeed, I expected it to have already happened—and yet I still live. And walk, and speak."

"Perhaps you miscalculated. And perhaps—"

"Yes?"

"It is possible," Lalemant said carefully, "that it may not happen at all. This paper, this book, speaks of a malady and the death of a man named Champlain—but it may not be *you*."

"I fail to understand. It describes Samuel de Champlain, born in Brouage 1567 . . . 'French explorer, acknowledged founder of the city of Québec 1608, and consolidator of the French colonies in the New World. He discovered the lake that bears his name in 1609 . . . ' Unless I am mistaken, Father Lalemant, that man sits before you."

"Monsieur," Lalemant said, "in some Eastern philosophies, they say that when a man steps into a river, both the man and the river are forever changed. Four years ago, the *Grantvillieurs* came back in time to the Germanies, and from that moment onward, the world was changed. In large ways . . . and small."

"There are no *Américains* here. I do not think that there are any Germans or any Swedes or . . . but how could they change anything here?

"I have never met an up-timer. No—no, wait. In Paris I was once introduced, in passing I confess, to a man named Lefferts. He seemed to know my name. But I fail to understand—are you saying that meeting *him* changed my future?"

"No, no," Lalemant said, shaking his head. "It has nothing to do with this one up-timer you met. In fact, it probably does not matter if you met him or not.

"As soon as the *Américains* came into our present time, things began to change. Things completely unrelated to actions and reactions. The up-timers even have a term for it: *les ailes du papillon*. The wings of the butterfly—also known as the 'butterfly effect.'"

"And thus..."

"And thus, monsieur, renowned explorer, founder of the city of Québec, *et cetera*, it may be that in this world, at this time, God the Father does not ordain that you should die."

Champlain sat back in his chair, contemplating.

"Who else knows of this... *photocopier*?"

"I have shown it to no one else. But there is someone else who knows of its contents, though I am not sure how. I presume that he saw the book of the *Américains*."

"Who is that?"

"The Dutch trader. Bogaert."

"Oh," Lalemant said. "*That* one. A strange fellow. There is something—something about him that bothers me."

"I admit I don't much like him either. He spoke to me privately and asked me if I was feeling well."

Lalemant began to respond, then stopped and looked thoughtful. "Bogaert trades with the Iroquois, monsieur."

"He seemed surprised that I was hale and active," Champlain said. "I dismissed it at the time, but... do you think he has traded *this* with the Iroquois, Father?"

"I am inclined to use William of Ockham's principle of economy when examining events," the Jesuit answered. "The Iroquois Nations have remained peaceful even through the time when the English occupied Québec—indeed, they have caused little trouble to New France during your entire time here. Why? They fear and respect you, monsieur."

"They fear and respect the musket and the arquebus, Father."

"The gun is only as good as the hands that hold it. It is *you* whom they fear. If they believed you were dead..."

"They might go to war."

"Indeed they might. Perhaps you should have words with Monsieur Bogaert."

Champlain slapped the arm of his chair, and uttered a word one does not normally speak in front of Jesuits. "I believe he has gone upriver, perhaps to trade with the Hurons. He is no longer in Québec, in any case."

"Then, monsieur...if you believe that he has indeed spread word of your illness to the Indians, and is no longer here to confirm or deny the truth of it, I suggest that you use that information to your advantage."

5

Of all of the Nations, the Mohawks felt themselves most aggrieved by the Onontio and his servants. Therefore, though it was Strong-Arm of the Oneida who had brought the idea of war to the Great Council, it was the Mohawks who led the way.

Despite the calumnies against Walks-In-Deep-Woods that had been spoken by the sachems, word from the Montaignais and others who traded at the great fort of Québec brought word that, over the last moon, the great chief Champlain had taken to his bed; he was afflicted with some illness, or the weight of great age, or both. No one had seen him in the streets or in the fortress, nor traveling upon the river.

Strong-Arm began to believe that Walks-In-Deep-Woods' death-medicine was truly effective, and other chiefs believed it too. For all of the time he had been chief in New France, Champlain had been respected for that quality that the Hurons called *orenda*: the vital spirit, the thing that made a man do good or evil. The *orenda* in Champlain was very strong.

But he was very old. Strong-Arm's uncle Red-Feather had known Champlain and fought with the Mohawk against him at Sorel, twenty-five summers ago—only a few escaped with their lives when the French attacked. Red-Feather spoke of an arrow-shot that had nearly killed Champlain: but instead of sticking in his throat it had creased his ear—the white man escaped death by the width of a butterfly's wing. Even wounded, the Frenchman had been fearless and deadly. His *orenda* was strong enough to move many men—that, and the weapons they carried.

Old men who lay down sick did not rise again.

They moved through the forest, swiftly and quietly, as the days grew colder. The Mohawk warrior-leader, Hawk-Brother, had chosen the first target of their assault: the place that the French called Trois-Rivières, downriver from Québec.

"That will come in time," Hawk-Brother said to the assembled chiefs and warriors. He was young to be a warrior-leader, but at Sorel so many Mohawks had been killed and captured—including Hawk-Brother's own father—that it was as if an entire generation was missing. Hawk-Brother had tended the fire of his revenge since he was young.

Once again, Strong-Arm wished that his shaman had come with the war party to cool the heads of the angriest warriors—but neither Walks-In-Deep-Woods, nor any of the other shamans from the Great Council, had traveled with the war-party. Neither had Swift-As-Deer, or his Seneca warriors. They did not believe in the death-medicine; they did not believe in the rumors.

Trois-Rivières was a fur trading post on the river. It was surrounded by a wooden palisade to defend against attacks from hostile natives. But at this hour of the afternoon, the gates were open to permit traders to enter with their skins to sell or barter.

While the main force crouched in concealment, Hawk-Brother and Strong-Arm and three warriors, along with Born-Under-Moon and two of his Seneca brothers—the only Seneca among them—approached the gate with bundles of beaver pelts slung on their backs. Two men were there, wearing metal cuirasses and pot helmets.

"They are wary," Hawk-Brother said quietly. "They do not usually defend the gate so strongly."

"Perhaps we should wait," Strong-Arm said.

"Wait? No," Hawk-Brother answered. "If we wait, the wind might change. Warriors might decide that their campfire is more pleasing. I will not show weakness—now that we are so close."

"I hope you are not losing your nerve," Born-Under-Moon said to Strong-Arm.

If Born-Under-Moon had been Oneida, Strong-Arm might have

cuffed him—or taken out his hatchet and struck him down. But he did not wish to explain the matter before the Council Fire, nor cover the grave for the Seneca. So instead he did not answer, and focused his attention on the gate.

"Halt," one of the guards said in French, and then added more words that Strong-Arm did not understand.

Hawk-Brother did the talking in the white man's language; he spoke it haltingly but seemed to make himself understood. He gestured to the pelts that the five warriors carried, and seemed to bow with great respect. Born-Under-Moon looked disgusted; but Strong-Arm understood: the object was to get inside the settlement, not to keep up appearances.

It seemed to take forever, but at last the two guards permitted the eight warriors through the gate.

Strong-Arm had fought many times—raids against tribes outside the Five Nations, rather than fights against Europeans, but battles nonetheless. Whenever he went to battle, a calm settled upon him: it was as if he was in a forest and everything was quiet—no bird or animal noises, no footfalls, no sighing of wind, just the beating of his own heart.

The calm had descended now. There were a dozen people in sight, but Strong-Arm could not hear their speech, or the sounds of the animals, or the sound of the wind. Only one noise pierced this soundless state: a high-pitched whistle by Hawk-Brother signaling the beginning of the attack.

At the same time:

Strong-Arm dropped his bundle of pelts and drew his tomahawk, running at the trade house;

Born-Under-Moon and his two brothers turned and attacked the guards at the gate;

The rest of the warriors outside emerged from cover and began to run at the gate, shouting war-whoops;

Hawk-Brother and his Mohawks ran toward the armory—

And a series of shots rang out, shattering Strong-Arm's silent calm. He watched as Hawk-Brother dropped to the ground, his hatchet skittering out of his hand to land several feet away. Born-Under-Moon crumpled as well; someone concealed on the roof of a building found his mark.

Thirty feet in front of him, in front of the trade house toward which he was running, he saw three Frenchmen in metal cuirasses and breastplates. They held muskets in their hands—or possibly the more complicated arquebuses. Strong-Arm knew two things almost at once: first, the three guns were pointed at his chest and they could almost not miss; and second, his tomahawk was not going to have any effect on the metal armor the Frenchmen wore.

Suddenly, he realized a third fact—and it made him stop short rather than hurl himself forward to a brave death.

Without doubt—because he could see the torn ear that was so well known among the Iroquois—the man standing in the front was none other than Samuel de Champlain. He was not an old man lying in a sick bed: he was armed and armored and aiming an arquebus directly at Strong-Arm's chest.

Outside the settlement, Strong-Arm could hear shots being fired, and the howls of his Iroquois brothers as the bullets struck them.

"We have a word for this," Champlain said to Strong-Arm, who stood before him unarmed, his wrists bound behind him. He spoke excellent Iroquois. "It is called an *embuscade*. Friends among the Montaignais told us that a war-party was headed for Trois-Rivières—and so we simply waited for you to arrive."

Strong-Arm did not answer. He was the only chief from the advance party still alive; Born-Under-Moon and Hawk-Brother and four of the other warriors had been killed at once; most of the warriors outside had fled when the Frenchmen on the palisade opened fire.

"Tell me," Champlain continued. "Is there a reason I should not have you put to death?"

"I do not fear death."

"That is your shame," the Frenchman answered. "You have not accepted the light of the True Faith—so an afterlife of torment awaits you. Yet I would spare you this."

"I do not believe in your True Faith," Strong-Arm said. "What can your God do that mine cannot?"

"My God has preserved my life more than once," Champlain said, and exchanged a glance with a black-robed priest who stood next to where he sat. The priest scowled at Strong-Arm; he stared back, unafraid.

"Why do you break the peace that my king has made with your Council?"

"We avenge past wrongs," Strong-Arm said. "We wish to take back what is ours."

"This is not yours. It is *ours*, by sacred treaty. You anger both your peoples and mine to break that treaty. The sachems of the Great Council would not think ill of me if I hung you by a rope until you were dead for violating that trust.

"But I will not do that," Champlain said. "Much blood has been shed here. I will set you free, and send you back to your people to tell them the story of what has been done here. They will think me generous for having granted you your life, and will think me strong for having defended the place belonging to the Onontio. They can take that as a warning not to do it again." He gestured, and a soldier stepped forward and cut the bonds that held Strong-Arm's wrists.

Strong-Arm rubbed his hands to give them back their feeling, then took a single step forward. Three soldiers immediately stepped in his way, but Champlain waved them aside.

Orenda, Strong-Arm thought.

Warily, the soldiers stepped back. Strong-Arm took another step and reached out his hand to touch Champlain's severed ear.

"Your God saved you at Sorel," Strong-Arm said. "My uncle told me of this."

"Tell your people that my God is strong, and that the Onontio is strong. And soon, with God's help, he will be yet stronger. The other kings across the Great Water have yielded to ours, and soon there will be no others to trouble you."

Strong-Arm stood straight and crossed his arms over his chest. "How do I know that you tell the truth?"

"I have never lied to the people of the Five Nations," Champlain said. "Unlike some who have come among you... spreading that which is false."

"Such as?"

"Rumors of my death," Champlain answered. "You went to war because you thought I was dying."

Strong-Arm again was silent, but he began to understand. Someone had told Walks-In-Deep-Woods that Champlain was on his deathbed, and the wily old shaman had taken credit for it.

And Strong-Arm had believed it. Brave warriors lay dead because Strong-Arm had believed it, and had not heeded the words of the wise old chief Swift-As-Deer.

"I will bring your words to my people," Strong-Arm said at last. "I will say to them what you say to me."

And I will say more, he thought to himself. *I will say much more.*

6

Strong-Arm did not hesitate this time before entering the tent of Walks-In-Deep-Woods. The shaman sensed his anger and looked alarmed, but did not attempt to get to his feet.

"How may I be of service, mighty chief?" he asked, touching his thumbs to his forehead.

"Stand and walk," Strong-Arm said. "Walk out of this camp and do not turn back."

"I do not understand."

"Understand *this*, you snake," he said. "I shall burn this tent, and everything in it—including *you*—if you do not heed my words. You will leave the Oneida. Go wherever you wish. But if your shadow is seen in Oneida lands again, I will kill you. Slowly."

Walks-In-Deep-Woods scrambled to his feet, perhaps realizing for the first time that Strong-Arm's anger was genuine—and dangerous. In his haste he disturbed the blankets in his sleeping-place, and Strong-Arm saw something peeking out from under it: a bundle of paper, hidden among the other bits and pieces of the shaman's art.

He pushed past the shaman, nearly knocking him off his feet, and picked up the bundle. "What is this?"

"It is—well, you see—"

"This is white man's work." He touched the pages in turn: there were many letters, and a single picture—of a man with the hair and beard of a Frenchman, next to a pattern ... something familiar ...

A banner. With the flowers of France.

"Can you read this? Is this your—your death medicine, old snake?"

"No. Yes. I—please, mighty chief!" he said as Strong-Arm grasped the necklaces at his throat and twisted them tight.

"You sent us to our *death*," he said, and shoved Walks-In-Deep-Woods onto his back. The old man looked genuinely terrified now.

He took the papers and tossed them into the fire, then turned his back on Walks-In-Deep-Woods.

"Run," he said. "Or burn. I do not care. I must go and tell my people the words of the great chief Champlain."

"Champlain," Walks-In-Deep-Woods managed. "He—he lives?"

Strong-Arm did not favor the old shaman with an answer, but left the tent.

After a moment, Walks-In-Deep-Woods could see the light of torches coming closer.

And the Devil Will Drag You Under

Walt Boyes

Georg Schuler groaned. He screwed his eyes shut, trying to still the pounding and stabbing inside his head.

"Aaaaah!" he groaned.

He opened his eyes, closed them again, and slitted them open. All he could see was a gigantic horse turd that his face was pushed into. He raised himself up on his arms, and slowly levered himself into a kneeling position. He had been lying face down in a puddle of slime and a large pile of horse manure, relatively fresh.

Worse, yet, it was morning. And from the noise from the street at the end of the alley, he was late for work. Georg staggered to his feet, and wound up braced against a wall. He wiped the manure off his face with his hand, and wiped the hand on his already sodden shirt.

"I smell like shit," he muttered aloud, "which is just *wunderbar*, and I feel like it, too."

Georg waited until the world stopped spinning, and then walked unsteadily to the mouth of the alley. The bright light from the sun caused him to stop, close his eyes and wait until they adjusted. His head throbbed.

"Let's get it over with," he announced to the uncaring passersby who were giving him wide berth on the street.

"Schuler! *Komm hier, schnell!*"

So much for sneaking into work, Georg thought. He turned and walked to the office door from which the bellow had come.

249

"*Ja, Ich komme*," he said to the tiny office's occupant. "Yes, boss, what did you want?"

"The innocent act won't wash, Schuler," Gerhard Mann said, looking him up and down. Mann was a huge man, well over six feet, and brawny. He had been a blacksmith until he read about up-timer production techniques and realized that one of the biggest needs in Magdeburg for a long time to come would be nails. Mann just barely fit behind the desk, and as he stood, he knocked some papers to the floor.

"You're hungover, you're still drunk, you're covered with horse-shit, and you are full of it, too. This is the third time in a week you've showed up late like this. Here's your final pay. You're fired."

Mann threw some coins at him, and Georg scrambled to pick them up off the floor. He didn't bother to argue. Besides, Mann was right. What did the up-timers say? What was their word? Loser, Lo-oo-ser. That's it. Well, I am.

Schuler headed out the door, turned down the street, and looked for the nearest *Bierstube*. Ah, there was one. Since he had money, he might as well drink it.

He walked into the place, and went up to the bar. The tavernkeeper looked at him, as he walked down the bar toward Georg.

"You stink. Let's see your money."

Georg slapped a coin on the bar.

"There. See, I have money! *Bier, bitte!*"

"Fine, but you stink too much to have in here for long. I'll give you one beer. After that you leave." The tavernkeeper palmed the coin, and moved to a tap. He filled a stein and set it down in front of Georg.

"Drink up, and then get out." The tavernkeeper turned away, moved to the far end of the bar, and began drying drinking cups.

Georg upended his beer, downed it, and turned toward the door. There was a commotion outside, and what sounded like music. Georg headed outside, and stopped stock still.

Across the street was, well, something. It was a small group of people dressed alike, with a kind of uniform, and musical instruments including the largest drum Georg had ever seen. There was a large bearded man to go with the drum and he was beating it to a rhythm that made Georg's head pound. There was a trumpet player, who, as far as Georg could tell through his headache, was not very good. There was another one of the uniformed people playing really energetically on what Georg thought was a kind of *guitarra*. The rest of them, three or four, were singing loudly. Georg spent a few seconds trying to figure out what they were singing, then it penetrated his drink-fogged and hungover brain.

"*Ein feste Burg ist unser Gott...*" they sang. "A mighty fortress is our God..."

Georg shook his head, trying to clear away his headache. What next, he thought. Lutherans in uniforms on street corners. What are they doing?

"*Ach*, who cares?" He shook his head again, and immediately wished he hadn't. Things started swimming around again. The noise from the Lutherans just wasn't helping. He held onto the building wall as he moved away from the *Bierstube*.

Georg woke, muzzily, at first unaware of his surroundings. Slowly, he focused, and realized he was in bed in his tiny rented room. How he got there, he wasn't quite sure. He had a headache, but it wasn't as bad as it had been. There was light coming in the small window that was high on one wall, and he was naked. His clothes were in a smelly pile near the door.

He stood up, grabbed his clothes and quickly headed out the door toward the community bathroom. Thankfully, it was empty and he was able to wash himself, and brush most of the horse manure off his clothes. He wished he had another suit of clothes so he could have these cleaned. He hadn't had a new suit of clothes since he was in the army.

Georg dressed and went back to his room. How much longer it would be his room, he couldn't say. Without work, he wasn't going to be able to pay rent, and with the number of people coming to Magdeburg to help with building the new capital and rebuilding the city, his landlord wasn't going to be very willing to let him stay on until he could pay. Well, he thought, it isn't like I have much to move.

Georg sat on his pallet and thought about what to do next. Obviously, he needed to find another job. That shouldn't be too hard, he thought. As he was getting to his feet, he heard a clink noise from under his pallet. He reached under, and found a stoneware jug. It was not large, and it wasn't full.

"*Ach! Ginever!*" Georg grinned as he pulled the cork. "Dutch Courage! I forgot I had this!"

He lifted the jug of gin and took a swig. It went down hard, but the liquor felt pleasantly warm in his stomach. Even though his stomach was empty, he started to feel better. "Dr. Silvius' fine tonic," he said. "Just what the doctor ordered. It shouldn't be hard to find a job again, so I'll do it later." He took another swig. And then, another.

He was feeling just fine as he slipped from his pallet onto the floor. But he wasn't feeling so well when he woke up a couple of hours later.

"*Mein Gott in Himmel!*" he shouted, and then grabbed his ears as the sound of his own voice made the inside of his head ring.

Georg coughed. The smoke was beginning to be very thick. He coughed again. "Stupid idiots! First you pillage, *then* you burn!" There were few houses in Magdeburg that weren't burning now. This was really going to cut down the amount of plunder. *Sheiss!* Georg stumbled through the smoke, hacking.

Suddenly the smoke cleared and he saw he was standing in front of a house that hadn't yet been touched. Lots of loot, maybe!

Three of Tilly's pikemen came up and Georg drew his hanger and waved it. "Mine, you bastards! This one's mine! Beat it!"

He wasn't sure why, but they turned and ran away. Maybe he just looked crazy enough to take on all three of them. He turned and kicked at the door. It didn't move, so he kicked it harder, and it began to splinter. He used his hanger to cut more of the door apart, and then with a final kick it blew apart. Georg raised his hanger and went through the door.

It was dark inside, so he kicked open a shutter and let both light and smoke in. He turned to see what loot there was, and he heard a noise. He raised his hanger and advanced to the back of the front room. He kicked the door in, and saw a woman on a bed. She had a big cavalry man's horse pistol, and it was cocked. She raised it in her shaking right hand, and fired. As she did, Georg threw himself forward and severed her hand, dropping the pistol to the floor amid a shower of blood.

"Nooooooo!" There was a scream behind him, and he turned, sweeping his hanger around. He couldn't stop in time, as his blade cut a small child in half.

Georg dropped to his knees and vomited. He stumbled out of the room, and out of the house into the smoke filled street. He vomited again.

All he could hear was the little girl screaming, "Noooooooo!"

He woke, as he always did, screaming and shaking. He felt waves of cold and hot flashes and he was sodden with sweat. It was the damn dream again. It was the dream that had made him leave Pappenheim's cavalry. It was the damn dream.

Georg wondered what was wrong with him. He used to be able to drink like a fish. He used to be able to put away much more *Ginever* than that with no trouble, and be completely functional the next day. But since that day, he couldn't do it anymore. Maybe it was the judgement of the Herr Gott for what he'd done, killing a mother and her child.

He made it to the chamber pot and puked. He crouched there shaking. *I've got to get myself together,* he thought. After a few moments, he thought he could stand up, so he slowly got to his feet.

"I've got to get a new job," he said to himself. He took a few half-hearted swipes at his grimy, smelly clothes, and walked out the door.

There was a makeshift labor hall near the old moat where they were rebuilding the city walls. Georg stood in line until he was called to the table where the job broker sat. The broker looked him up and down, and handed him a piece of paper with a number on it. Georg looked at it. It was 351.

"This is your number," the broker said. "As soon as we have some labor for you to do, your number will be called. If you don't come when it is called, the next number will be called and you will lose your place."

"*Ja, Ich verstehe,*" Georg said.

The broker pointed to a big group of men standing at one end of the hall. "Go there. You will be called. People are busy. You shouldn't have much of a wait."

Georg walked over to the group. He looked the men over, just as they were looking him over. They mostly looked like him. Dirty, down on their luck, ragged and poor. Just like him.

At first, nobody said much. A little fat man came bustling importantly over and called out, "*Nummer zwei hundert sechs, sieben, acht, neuen, mit gekomm, schnell!*"

Georg turned to the man closest and said, "Two hundred nine! And I am three hundred fifty one! Will there be work for my number?"

"Probably, maybe," the man said. "It is still early. If you want a low number, you have to get here when the hall opens at dawn. I come an hour before usually, but I had a problem last night."

"Ah!" Georg said, noncommittal.

"A problem I think you may have had," the man said. "I got drunk and didn't wake up."

"Yes," Georg said. "I've been known to do that. Last night, in fact. And the night before.

"*Ich heisse Georg,*" he said. "Georg Schuler."

"Pieter," said the man. "Pieter Doorn."

"Ah, a Hollander!" Georg said.

"Yes, but I have not been home for many years. And you, where are you from?"

"Originally, Bavaria," Georg said, "but I've been around here a few years now."

Just then, the officious man returned and called out quite a few more numbers.

"Ah, that's me," Doorn said, "Good luck!"

"Thanks," Georg replied.

Doorn moved off with the group of men whose numbers had been called.

It got later. More numbers were called. But they were nowhere near 351. It got later still, and still no work for Georg. Finally, the little fat man returned and said, "That's it. No more work today. Come back tomorrow."

Georg crumpled the piece of paper and threw it on the floor. He thought he should feel disappointed, but in truth, he wasn't feeling much of anything. It was just the way things kept happening to him. Ever since the army. Ever since that day.

He headed home. Ha, he thought. A little rented closet in a rickety fast built house is home. He put his hand in his purse, but it was empty. He'd spent all his coin getting drunk after being fired. He couldn't even get a beer.

The next day, not being hung over, he woke before dawn. The small window high in the wall of his room was not quite dark. It was that time before dawn that sentries slept, and surprise attacks were made. His eyes went wide at the thought. Ah, you can take the man out of the army, but you can't take the soldier out of the man.

He rose and put on his smelly jacket and his broken-down shoes. Then he headed off to the hiring hall.

This time, his number was lower. Even though he'd gotten there before dawn, there was still a line of men outside the hall waiting for it to open. Somehow, he was unsurprised to see Pieter Doorn standing a few places ahead of him in the line. Doorn turned, and nodded at him. They both got called at the same time.

"What are we going to be doing?" Georg said to Doorn.

"Probably moving rocks. They are rebuilding the city walls."

"Why are they doing that?" Georg asked.

"The burghers have contracts with the people who live about and around the city to shelter behind the city walls in the event of danger. No walls, no contracts," Doorn said, shrugging.

"That certainly didn't happen in 'thirty-one," Georg said. "It didn't protect anybody."

"That's true," Doorn said, "but now this is the new capital, and the Swedish king has new weapons and allies."

"Ah, so..." Georg said.

Doorn proved right. The group was taken a short distance away, and was put to work loading stones into carts. The work wasn't that hard, and the sun was out. Pretty soon, Georg was feeling better than he had in a while. It was like the sun and the work were sweating the alcohol out of him.

"Oh, yes," she said, "my husband is one of the supervisors on the project to rebuild the walls, and also is helping to design the new water system."

"And where did you come to Magdeburg from, Frau...?" The woman was clearly one of the new elite and it showed in her clothing. She was wearing over her dress a jacket of the new up-timer material called blue jean that was probably worth a year's pay to her husband.

"Schuesslerin, Katerina Schuesslerin. My husband is Friedrich Wahlberg, who works for Herr Gericke."

"Otto von Gericke is my husband, Frau Schuesslerin."

"*von* Gericke? Oh, my!" Frau Schuesslerin turned bright red and lowered her eyes. "My deepest apologies, there was no intent to offend!"

"No offense taken. It is still very new. So new in fact, you must not have heard. His Imperial Highness has read in the encyclopedias that in the future, the Holy Roman Emperor would ennoble my husband, and since that is not likely to happen now, His Highness decided to make my husband a noble now, in honor of his work rebuilding His Highness' new capital."

"Ah. My felicitations to both you and to Herr von Gericke," Katerina said.

She paused, and then she said in a rush, "This is the first time I have been invited to a 'movie' and I don't really know what they are."

"It is an up-time thing. They had the ability to record things like plays so we can watch them long after the performance was done with. They call these recordings movies, and what we will see tonight is a movie that is from what they call 'musical theater.' It is much like a masque. This one is called *Guys and Dolls*."

Katerina said, "They are starting to go in, now. Thank you for your help, Madame von Gericke."

"Not at all."

"Oh, Friedrich, it was wonderful!" Katerina said, "I could not believe that the people in the 'movie' weren't alive right there in the theater with us all!"

"Um...hmmm."

"The story appeared to be about a group of men who were interested in a gambling game, and one man, Nathan Detroit, trying to avoid marrying his mistress."

"Um...hmmm."

"There were some excellent songs, too. There was one that was sung by a men's chorus and one of the main actors called 'Sit Down You're Rocking the Boat.' It was very good. It had a refrain that stuck in my head."

"Um?"

"It went, 'and the devil will drag you under by the sharp lapels on your checkered coat...sit down you're rocking the boat.'"

"Ah?"

"But a very interesting part was the Save-a-Soul mission. It seems that there was an army dedicated to saving souls."

"Eh?" Friedrich Wahlberg looked up from his textbook. "An army for salvation? That is an interesting idea. We have plenty of armies. We have the Protestant armies, the Swedish armies, the French army and the Imperial armies. But even though they say they are fighting in the name of religion, they don't seem to care about the souls of the people they kill and maim." Wahlberg shook his head. "It is too bad we don't have an Army of Salvation."

"Maybe we shall."

"What?"

"I have been looking for something to do here in Magdeburg. You are so busy with your engineering, and we have no family here."

"Hmmm. You know, we are having a real problem with the workers on the wall and drunkenness. It would be good if there was some way we could stop them from getting drunk and not being fit to work the next day. Do you think your Salvation Army might be able to do something about that?"

Katerina thought.

The next morning she went to get an appointment to see the abbess of Quedlinburg. To her surprise, after a wait of perhaps an hour, she was ushered into a sitting room, where the abbess awaited.

Getting straight to the point, Katerina told the abbess what her husband had suggested, and said she wanted to make it come true.

"I want to start an Army of Salvation. My army would not carry weapons. We would be like the mission in *Guys and Dolls*, have you seen it?" she said.

"Yes, I have," the abbess replied. "An interesting story, was it not?"

"Yes, especially the mission. I looked up the Save-a-Soul Mission in the up-timers' books, and found out that it was actually called the Salvation Army. I want to have a Salvation Army, a *Heilsarmee*, here in Magdeburg."

The abbess gestured for Katerina to go on.

"Particularly we would work with the workmen who are building our new city. My husband tells me they have terrible problems with drunkenness and absenteeism. We have to help these poor men!"

"I like it," the abbess said, after some thought. "We must see how this can be done."

"Did you know, Frau Schuesslerin, that there is a long tradition in Magdeburg of street singing?" Friedrich Spee said. "The university students sang for Christian charity on street corners."

"I had no idea," Katerina said. "I am not from here originally. I followed my husband who works for Herr von Gericke on the construction."

"Yes," the Jesuit said. "In fact, it is said that even Dr. Luther sang on the street with his fellow students. But why have you come to me?"

"I wish to start an army," Katerina said. Spee's eyes widened and his eyebrows rose. "But my army will not have arms. It will be a Salvation Army."

"Ah, like the up-timers, I see," Spee said.

"Not exactly. That is why I have come to see you."

"Ah . . . ?"

"We have Catholic armies and Protestant armies. What I want is an army for everyone. So I have come to you. You are close to the cardinal, and you are also a musician and hymn composer of some note. I want to have Catholics *and* Lutherans in my army." Katerina folded her arms and waited.

Spee smiled. "What would you have me do?"

"Georg, you cannot keep coming to the hiring hall later and later," Doorn said, as they were sitting on the lip of a ruined stairway eating their lunch. "Sooner or later, they will tell you to stop coming."

"I'm not sleeping well, Pieter," Georg said, rubbing his palms over his temples.

"And you are drinking a lot, *ja?*"

"Not any more than always."

"You need to stop."

Georg looked at Doorn.

"What do you mean, I have to stop? You have been known to get drunk, too!"

"Not anymore."

"What?"

"I have put myself into God's hands, and I have stopped drinking."

"Come to think of it," Georg said, "We haven't been to a tavern together in quite some time. What do you mean, you have put yourself into God's hands?"

Doorn looked directly at Georg.

"I have found some help, and I am living one day at a time," he said quietly.

"What help?"

"I have been going to a meeting in the basement of St. James," Doorn said.

Georg looked at him and sneered. "How can going to a meeting in a church make you stop drinking?"

"I have had to look at my life and see that it wasn't working," Doorn said.

"And you do this at a meeting?"

"No, I do it in my life. I am doing it now. But I learn how at the meeting."

"So some priest preaches at you until you stop drinking, eh?

I thought you Hollanders were all Calvinists anyway. I've never had a priest tell me anything that made me better. All they do is tell me how I am going to go to Hell."

"The priest isn't even there most of the time. There are a group of us."

"Well, I don't understand how this would make you quit drinking," Georg said.

"I could explain it to you, Georg, but I won't. When you are ready, let me know and I will bring you to a meeting. You will understand better there."

Doorn levered himself upright. He stretched his shoulder muscles. "Time to go back to working," he said as he walked off.

Georg stood staring at Doorn's back.

Georg turned. He was back in the house in Magdeburg. The woman was keening, holding her blood-spurting wrist. But strangely, the little girl was standing, staring at him, holding her body together with one hand. He was holding the bloody hanger. The little girl said, "Why?" and blood came out of her mouth in a gush. "Why?" Her eyes stayed on Georg's as her body fell away in two pieces.

As always, Georg woke shaking. His eyes were wide open and gradually, he became aware of his real surroundings.

He went to work that morning as if nothing had happened. He was shaky, though, and his friend Doorn noticed quickly.

"Georg, are you all right?" Doorn said.

"Ja, of course... No, I...am not all right."

"Can I be of help?"

"I...I would like to hear more about this meeting you were talking about."

"Of course. There is likely to be one tonight. We use a program that the up-timers knew about. It is called 'twelve steps.'"

"What are the steps?" Georg asked.

"In the first step," Doorn said, "we admit that we are powerless over alcohol."

"Well, that's certainly true enough," Georg said.

"There are eleven more steps," Doorn said, "that lead us to recovery and the ability to live a good and sober life."

There were chairs in a circle. The meeting had started already when Doorn and Georg came in. After a few people stood up and spoke, it was obvious how to participate. After one of the speakers paused and sat down, there were some people who were looking at Georg expectantly. He stood up.

"My name is Georg Schuler. And I am a drunk."

"Schuler, come in, come in!" Friedrich Wahlberg said, rising from behind his desk and coming around with his hand extended. "Thanks for coming in!"

"What can I do for you, Herr Wahlberg?" Georg was concerned and a little nervous.

"You've been doing well, now, for a couple of months, Schuler," Wahlberg said. "And we need steady workers. I'm going to put you on permanently, if you wish."

"No more day labor?" Georg said.

"No more day labor."

"When do I start?" Georg said.

The word got around quickly on the jobsite. Georg kept getting congratulations on his good fortune all day long. At quitting time, his workmates suggested that he come to the *Bierstube* with them to celebrate his new status.

"Georg! It is time to go, my friend," Pieter Doorn said, coming up to the group.

"I'm sorry, fellows," Georg said, "I have a meeting to go to."

At the meeting, the leader said, "Tonight we are going to look at steps two and three. 'We have come to believe that a power greater than ourselves can restore us to sanity' and 'made a decision to turn our will and our lives over to the care of God, as we understand him.'"

Georg raised his hand. "What does that mean? Is this a church? Are we Catholic or Protestant?"

"Neither, Georg. We are not a church, either Catholic or Lutheran or Calvinist. We are open to all. That's what it means to give ourselves over to the care of God as we understand him."

"This is something that came from the up-timers?"

"Yes, but you do not see any up-timers here. Anyone can use these steps, anyone. We just call it the meeting. But up-time, they called this thing of ours Alcoholics Anonymous."

One of the other attendees chimed in. "It's like that new army that they are organizing. The Salvation Army."

"The what?" Doorn said, eyebrows raised.

"That's what they call it. It is an army aimed at doing good, while all the other armies are aimed at doing harm. It was started by a woman named Wahlberg. Both the Lutherans and the Catholics are in favor of it."

"Both?" Georg said, unbelieving.

"Both. The Lutherans are supplying funds, and the Catholics are as well. The cardinal and Father Spee both have been seen singing with the Salvation Army on streetcorners."

"Oh," Georg said, "I think I have seen the Salvation Army. There were some people in uniforms playing music and singing '*Ein feste Burg*' the other day on the corner across from the *Bierstube*."

"*Ja!* That was them, or some of them anyway," a middle-aged man, who looked like he'd been through a lot, said.

"So it doesn't matter what faith we follow," said the leader, "as long as we turn our lives over to the higher power."

"Well, it is certainly true that I cannot control my drinking on my own," Georg said.

Georg continued to attend meetings, stay sober and work through the steps. One day, Wahlberg called him in again.

"I wish to promote you to being a work-gang boss. You have shown that you are responsible and we have need of reliable supervisors. Do you accept?"

"Of course," Georg said, "and thank you, Herr Wahlberg!"

Georg's friends were waiting for him and they carried him, protesting, all the way to the ale house and pressed a jack of beer into his hands. Before he knew it, he'd downed the beer and was on his second and then his third. He'd fallen off the wagon, and by the time he stumbled out of the *Bierstube* and headed home, he'd fallen hard.

That night, the nightmare returned for the first time in several weeks.

In the morning, he went looking for Pieter Doorn, who was not only his friend, but had been serving as his sponsor in AA.

"I got drunk last night, Pieter," Georg said. "I fell off the cart, hard."

"That was last night," Doorn said. "Today is a new day. We have to live our lives one day at a time. Sometimes it winds up being one minute at a time."

"But I..."

"What?"

"I have done some horrible things. I do not think God wants me to give him my life."

"I think," said Doorn, "that God forgives us our sins. But, as the steps say, there are some things we must do, in order to make ourselves worthy of forgiveness."

"What should I do?"

"What religion are you?"

"I was a Catholic, but now I don't know. We did vicious things in the name of the Catholic Church."

"You know what the next steps are?"

"Not really," Georg said.

"Well, next, you have to make a searching and fearless moral inventory."

"Oh, I know what I've done, and what a horrible mess I've made of my life."

"Have you admitted to God, to yourself, and to somebody else, the exact nature of your wrongs?" Doorn said.

"I...no. I've never told anyone else what happened. God knows, of course, and I do."

"What did you do?"

"It was during the sack. I was in Pappenheim's troop, and we had a sector of the city to loot. I...I killed some people."

"You were a soldier."

"Not like that. I..." Georg stopped.

"What? You have to spit it out, Georg. Tell me."

"I killed a woman and I killed a little girl. They haunt me and I have been drinking to forget what I did." Georg sagged with relief that he had finally been able to tell someone what he'd done.

"I cannot judge you for what you did during the sack, Georg," Doorn said. What you did is between you and the people you injured and God. Have you tried to make amends?"

"How? They're both dead, and I don't think I can even find the house again since the sack. I quit the army. I've been drunk most of the time since. Things are very different now. Nothing is the same, except for the Dom and St. James' church, you know."

"Then you are going to have to figure out how to make amends indirectly," Doorn said. "You will be in deep danger of losing your sobriety, and maybe your soul."

"I think I've lost my soul already, Pieter," Georg said.

✧   ✧   ✧

"Can you sing?" that night's meeting leader, who went by the name of Hans, asked Georg on the way out of the basement of St. James' church.

"Loudly," Georg said.

"But not well, then."

"Nobody has asked me to be a soloist at the new Opera House, if that's what you mean," Georg said. "Why do you ask?"

"Well, the woman who is in charge of that new Salvation Army is looking for some singers. Some bandsmen, too. Do you play an instrument?"

"No."

"You might talk to the Army, anyway, Georg. You need to start taking care of the eighth and ninth steps."

"I..."

"Just think about it. You have shared about your background in the meeting, Georg, and I think it might be what you need."

"I don't know," Georg said. "I feel like I'm being pushed around. I don't have control, and I don't know when I will slip off the cart and fall into the mud again. And for me, it isn't mud. It is always horse shit." He laughed bitterly.

Hans held out his hand. "You take care on the way home. There are footpads now, I hear. Magdeburg is the very model of a modern city now."

"I will," Georg said.

"Just remember, trust God, Georg."

"Here, Georg, have a beer."

Herr Wahlberg had taken to having a dinner for his supervisors every month or so, and Georg had finally gotten invited.

The men milled around in the Wahlbergs' front room. There were some finger snacks, and there was, of course, beer.

"*Nein, danke*," Georg said. "I don't drink anymore."

"How did you do that?" Wahlberg asked him, "if you don't mind my asking?"

"I have placed my life in God's hands, Herr Wahlberg, and I live one day at a time," Georg said.

"I've heard that before, somewhere," Wahlberg said. "Ah, yes. One of the people that my wife works with in her Army of Salvation says it."

"Your wife started the Salvation Army?"

"Yes. She did. It keeps her busy, praise God!"

Georg felt as though he was on the receiving end of a message from God. He had been seeing the Salvation Army musicians playing on street corners for a while now. Hans had told him that he should talk to the Army. Now, his boss's wife was the actual creator of the Army of Salvation.

"I . . . Herr Wahlberg, I thank you for inviting me to your home. I must be going now," Georg stuttered, "I have a meeting to go to."

Georg walked up and down across the street from the nondescript storefront. The sign on the building said "Die Heilsarmee"—the Salvation Army. He kept stepping off the sidewalk and stopping, going back to pacing. He knew that he was making an important decision. He didn't know what he was going to do. Now that it had come, he was having trouble committing to doing it.

He recited the first steps to himself. "I have realized that I am powerless over alcohol—and that my life is unmanageable. I have come to believe that a Power greater than myself can restore me to sanity. I have made a decision to turn my will and my life over to God . . ."

He squared his shoulders, took a deep breath and marched across the street to the storefront. He put his hand on the door.

"I have made a list of all the people I have harmed, and I am willing to make amends to them all."

He turned the doorknob, and went inside.

Pieter Doorn watched as the *Heilsarmee* Marching Band played its first concert on the steps of St. James' church. For months now, they had been playing on streetcorners and in their store-front mission. Today, they were playing selections from *Guys and Dolls* as well as the hymns, both traditional and up-timer, that they were becoming famous for.

When they got to "Sit Down You're Rocking the Boat," Doorn heard Georg Schuler's voice. Georg was certainly the loudest, if not the most melodious, he thought to himself. But then they did "Amazing Grace," and Schuler sang with tears streaming down his face.

"Amazing Grace," Georg sang as the band played, "how sweet the sound, That saved a wretch like me. I once was lost but now am found, Was blind, but now I see."

Salonica

Kim Mackey

**Salonica, Ottoman Empire
Spring 1635**

"Atesh!"

Once again the volley of rifle fire tore into the ranks of the bandits. It was more ragged this time. The defenders had taken casualties of their own since the attack on the inner walls of the gunpowder factory.

"To the wall! Forward!" Mustafa bin Kemal shouted. He looked at Sampson and grinned. "Well done, my friend. Those wonderful grenades saved us. Any left?"

Sampson Gideon reached over his shoulder into the grenade pack and held up a "potato masher." "Last one, Mustafa. We'll have to use dynamite from now on."

If we had any dynamite, Sampson thought. He'd sent the last batch to the Sidrekapsi silver mine yesterday. Opening up new shafts at the mine took priority over grenades, by order of Melek Ahmed Pasha himself.

He and Mustafa were at the wall now.

Unlike the inner walls, the outer wall was incomplete and stood less than three feet high. The forest around the factory had been cut back, but it was still less than a hundred yards away.

"What now?" Sampson asked.

"Now we prepare for their next attack, my friend." Mustafa said.

The *bash cebeci*—head armorer—turned to his men along the wall. "*Süngü tak! Süngü tak!*"

Sampson felt the hair on the back of his neck stand up. *Fix bayonets? Oh, God, we're going to die.*

The words from the head enlisted man of the Essen military team, Senior-sergeant Duncan MacGregor, came back to him. "Better pray these Turks never need to use their rifles with the new bayonets, Mr. Gideon. They'll carve you up like a chicken right quick with the bayonets in their hands, but they get too excited to use them on the rifles and just turn it into a club in the heat of battle."

Sampson stopped Mustafa as he came down the line of men. "Fix bayonets? Mustafa, they don't know how to use the bayonets."

Mustafa smiled. "Of course not. But we are almost out of ammunition, and at least the sight of the bayonets will put fear into our enemies. How many rounds left for your pistol?"

"Two cylinders. Twelve rounds."

Mustafa shrugged. "Use them well. We surprised these rebels. They will be more organized with the next attack. It is obvious they are not simple bandits or brigands. That has to be why we have seen no reinforcements from the *orta* in the new training grounds."

Sampson could hear men shouting off in the forest.

"What are they saying?"

"Officers exhorting their men." Mustafa tilted his head to listen, then laughed. "Calling them shit-eating sons of motherless donkeys. If they have any courage left, they will be shamed into another attack soon. Make ready."

"Mustafa! Look!" An armorer pointed back toward the factory. *MacGregor!*

The senior-sergeant pulled up his horse and saluted Mustafa.

"Bash Cebeci, we have two cannon, at your service."

"Essen cannon?"

MacGregor smiled. "Of course. The fifteen pounders. With fifty rounds of canister each. The Chorbaci sends his regards and says reinforcements will be here in fifteen minutes. A diversionary attack hit the encampment."

Mustafa nodded and turned his head to look at the outer wall, then pointed at a bend in the wall a hundred yards away. "There. Put your cannon there. You'll have good enfilade fire."

"As you command." MacGregor winked at Sampson and galloped off.

Once again Mustafa moved down the line of his men. He clapped one on the shoulder and shook him. When he reached Sampson he fixed the bayonet on his own rifle.

"They are coming, Sampson. If Allah wills, we will be victorious. If not..." Mustafa shrugged, then smiled. "We will meet each other in Paradise."

Sampson took a breath. "I'm not ready for Paradise just yet, Mustafa."

Mustafa laughed. "Then victory it is. A good slogan." He turned to the men along the wall. "For the sultan. Victory or death!"

"Victory or death!" the men shouted.

Sampson grabbed Mustafa's arm. "Here they come!"

A wave of riders and infantry charged from the forest.

"Close, Ismail, too close indeed. If the rebels had reached the magazines..."

Melek Ahmed Pasha, governor-general of the new expanded *sançak* of Salonica, closed his eyes and imagined the battle that had taken place at the gunpowder factory. He had been too young to see the end of the Habsburg war in 1606, but there had been plenty of wars with the Persians over the past thirty years.

Hopefully, Melek Ahmed thought, *that will be ended this year when the sultan takes Baghdad.*

But it was not Persia that was the major threat to the empire. As had been revealed by the histories from the miracle city of Grantville, it was the Austrians and Hungarians who were the real threat to Ottoman rule, especially in the Balkans. And the Russians, of course. But they would be later. Much later, God willing.

"It was fortunate you arrived in time with your reinforcements."

Ismail bin Abdullah, chorbaci and commander of the new regiments training with the weapons provided by the Republic of Essen, shook his head.

"The battle was nearly over by the time we arrived, my Pasha. Mustafa bin Kemal and the Essen technical expert, Sampson Gideon, rallied the armorers once the local janissary infantry company was routed."

"Mustafa bin Kemal? Is he not the nephew of Evrenos Bey?"

Ismail nodded. "And his maternal grandfather was a Bektashi *pir*."

"Ah? I assume he is mastering the new mysteries of the pious foundation we have established in Salonica?"

"So I have heard," Ismail said. "The fate of the Bektashi and the other Sufi orders will be much different than in the universe from which Grantville came, God willing."

Melek Ahmed nodded. Bektashi mysteries were just that to many members of the *ulema*, the religious leaders of the empire. The conservatives had no interest in them and even dismissed them contemptuously as nothing but heresies. So it was unlikely they would investigate an unusual mystery in a Bektashi lodge in a newly minted province, despite the fact that increasing numbers of Bektashi dervishes were visiting to learn about the latest knowledge.

Unless the Kadi decided to investigate. "You still think the Kadi, Ebu Said, is behind this attack, Ismail? I find it hard to believe. What would his purpose be?"

Ismail shrugged. "He is a *Kadizadeli*, my Pasha. Your reforms in Salonica alone would be enough to incur his ire. But he is also Albanian and milk-brother to Yusuf Bey."

Melek Ahmed felt his lip curl. "Yusuf Bey. Too wealthy for his own good. If Yusuf Bey is behind this attack..." He looked down at another rebel body on the ground. "Were any prisoners taken?"

"Half a dozen," Ismail said. "No officers. They have been taken to the Red Tower."

"Good. Let me know immediately if any useful information can be extracted from them."

"As you wish," Ismail said. "And Mustafa bin Kemal? Without him the factory would have fallen to the rebels."

"A reward. Two *kese*. That will also make Evrenos Bey happy, as some of the honor will reflect on him. And a *kese* as well for the Jewish Englishman, Gideon, when he recovers from his wounds. This explosive he has manufactured for us...what is it called?"

"Dynamite."

"Yes. The 'dynamite' has allowed us to open new shafts in Sidrekapsi and increase production by twenty percent."

Ismail smiled. "The sultan will be happy to hear that."

"Indeed. And he will need that extra silver if he expects to attack Vienna after Baghdad. Never have two campaigns been planned so close together. Will your new regiments be ready?"

"They will," Ismail said. "The gunpowder factory will have two

hundred tons of the new powder within a year, and the next supply of weapons from Essen should arrive this summer."

Melek stroked his beard. "The sultan has given me great power
in this *sançak*. But if Yusuf Bey and Ebu Said stand against us, we
will need plentiful evidence to have them removed from power.
Find me that evidence, Ismail."

"I will, my Pasha. On the grave of my mother, I swear it."

Lara was just beginning to prepare the mid-day soup when
Hannalica Castro entered the kitchen.

"They can't do this. They just can't!" Hannalica cried. "The
inspection of my trousseau is tomorrow!"

"Who can't do what, Hannalica?" Lara asked. She tasted the soup.

"Him! That Englishman, Sampson Gideon. They've put him on
my bed. Mine!"

Lara felt herself go still. Hannalica's bed was the most comfortable bed in Don Diego's household. There was no reason to put
Sampson on Hannalica's bed unless . . .

"He is injured?"

Hannalica nodded. "There was a battle at the new gunpowder
factory this morning. He's been shot. Not badly, they say, a minor
head wound, but still . . . what if he gets blood all over my bed?"

"Then we'll clean it up, Hannalica. Don't be such a spoiled child."

Hannalica stomped her foot. "I am not a child. I am fifteen
and about to be married into the most important family in the
Aragon congregation." She lifted her chin and looked at Lara.
"Not that I would expect a Ukrainian slave to understand that."

"Don't get snippy with me, Hannalica," Lara said. "Or have
you forgotten who made the poultice to fight your night terrors
when you were ten? Or the amulet to guard against the evil eye
of the girls you think are jealous of you?"

Hannalica lowered her head. "I'm sorry, Lara. Truly. But why
couldn't they have taken him to the hospital?"

"Would you want to go the hospital?" Lara asked. "Yes, it's light
and airy, but it's also in the middle of the cemetery. Tombs for
tables and chairs. Señor Gideon will be much more comfortable
here."

"But what about my trousseau? Where are we going to put my
things? Doña Gazela doesn't like me already, I know it. If she
sees even the least thing out of place tomorrow. . ."

"It will be fine, Hannalica. The weather is good. We'll put everything in the courtyard. We have plenty of room since your brother Raphael and his family moved to Izmir."

Now, if she could just keep her sister Lina from finding out that her secret love was injured...

Lina came running into the kitchen. "Lara! Sampson's been hurt!"

Oh bother.

"He is so handsome. Don't you think so, Lara?"

Sampson Gideon kept his eyes closed. He knew that voice. Who...his memories returned like a wave rushing in to the shore.

Ah, Lina. Sampson felt himself squirming inside. He'd been attracted to the red-haired Ukrainian slave in Don Diego Castro's household from the first time he had seen her in the kitchen. And her older blond sister as well. At first it had made him uncomfortable that such beautiful women were actual slaves (and possibly concubines) in a Jewish household. But Issac Castro, the Republic of Essen's consul in Salonica and Don Diego's cousin, had assured him that the use of slaves in the houses of Jewish notables was a normal practice. Slavery in the Ottoman Empire was a much more fluid concept than the slavery in Brazil, Issac had told him. Many slaves were manumitted after their years of service and those who converted to the religion of their owners often became an integral part of the household and the community.

"Handsome enough, I suppose." Sampson heard amusement in Lara's voice. "Let's get this over with before he wakes up."

It was the clucking noise that made Sampson open his eyes.

"What are you doing, Lara?" Sampson asked.

Lara stopped rotating the rooster over his head.

"Don't stop, Lara, finish!" Lina said.

"I have to start over or it won't work, Lina. It has to be done all at once."

Lina put her hand on his arm. "Be still, Señor Gideon. This will make you feel better. Truly. Lara is a healer. Your pain and injury will pass from you to the rooster."

"I see. In that case, please finish, Lara."

Do not *laugh, Sampson*, he thought. *Don't!*

Lara smiled down at him. Then winked. Ah, now it made sense. This was for Lina's sake, not his.

Lara rotated the rooster three times over his head, then neatly wrung its neck.

"You will feel better soon, Señor Gideon," Lara said.

"Thank you, Lara," he said. He looked at Lina. "And you too, Lina." He tried to sit up and his head seemed to swim. Once again he felt Lina's cool hands on his arm.

"Careful, Señor Gideon. You will not feel truly better until the ritual is complete."

"Ritual?"

"The *Kappará*. Sacrifice." Lara said. She held up the rooster and stepped to the door. "The rooster must be eaten by the patient and his family. Since Don Diego and his household are the closest thing to your family here in Salonica, we will put the rooster into the mid-day soup. Chicken broth is good for the health and soul anyway."

"Stay with him until the soup is done, Lina," Lara said, shaking the rooster at her sister. She walked out the door.

"I'm perfectly fine," Sampson said. His head began to swim again. "Well, maybe not. Lina, can you help me lie down?"

Lina's hands were strong and firm now. They cupped his cheek as his head settled back on the pillow. Her fingers brushed lightly over the bandage on the left side of his head.

"Once the soup is done, I will bring you a big bowl, Señor Gideon. Lara has put fresh vermicelli in it as well. It is very tasty." Lina licked her lips and smiled at him.

Sampson found himself squirming again. He couldn't help wondering how tasty Lina's lips might be.

Issac Castro watched from the doorway as the two slaves fed the soup to Sampson Gideon. It was difficult not to laugh out loud as the two young women fussed over him.

They are as infatuated with him as he is with them, Issac thought. *It is probably good that he has had to spend all his time at the gunpowder factory.*

Issac cleared his throat.

Lara and Lina looked up at the doorway.

"Is he well enough to carry on a conversation?" Issac asked.

Lina looked disappointed.

"Of course, Don Issac," Lara answered. "We were just leaving. Lina, get the soup bowl."

"But..."

"Now, little sister." She turned toward Sampson. "We will bring you dinner this evening, Señor Gideon. I will have Lina go to the market to get the fruit you want. That should go well with the meat dish I have planned. Something to give you more strength."

Both women left and Issac nodded towards the door as he approached the bed.

"They seem to be taking good care of you, Sampson."

Sampson smiled. "Excellent care, Don Issac." He chuckled. "I woke up with a rooster over my head."

Issac nodded. "The *Kappará*. The Jews of Salonica have a number of interesting superstitions. It may take some time getting them to think in a more scientific fashion about health. But at least Melek Ahmed Pasha seems amenable to taking preventative measures against disease in the city. If only the rabbis were as easy to convince."

"Apparently Melek Ahmed sent his protégé, Evliya Chelebi, to Grantville to investigate the rumors of a city from the future," Sampson said. "I think I actually met Evliya at a chess tournament in the summer of 1632."

"Speaking of Melek Ahmed," Issac said, "the pasha has rewarded both you and Mustafa for your defense of the factory. Two *kese* for Mustafa and one for you. That will be a nice bonus to take back to Essen."

"Take back?" Sampson's voice seemed to rise in tone.

Ah ha, Issac thought. *As I suspected. He wants to stay. A pity*.

"That was much too close this morning. If that musket ball had been an inch to the right...your father would never forgive me. It's time for you to go home, Sampson."

"But, Don Issac—"

Issac held up his hand. "You yourself have told me that Mustafa is more than competent now, have you not?"

Sampson nodded. It seemed a reluctant nod to Issac, but still verification of the essential truth that the principal job for which Sampson had been hired was over.

"Good," Issac said. "Once you're well enough to travel, say in a week or two, we'll get you on a ship to Livorno and then home."

Sampson crossed his arms. "But, Don Issac, I don't *want* to go back to Essen!"

Issac smiled. The young man had the same stubborn expression on his face his own sons held when they didn't get what they wanted.

"I understand. Salonica has been an adventure. Exotic compared to Amsterdam or Essen. But every adventure must end, young man. I'll give you a month. No more."

"He can't do this to me, Mustafa," Sampson said, sipping his coffee. "He just can't!"

Mustafa laughed and took a sip of his own coffee.

The coffee shop they patronized was less than two streets away from the busy thoroughfare of the via Kalamaria. Still, it was a tranquil place with a fountain in the small square and several Roman era columns to lean against.

Mustafa shook his head. "I'm sorry, my friend. I should not laugh at you. But you cannot fight the tide. Issac Castro pays your salary. And Melek Ahmed Pasha will not want to upset the consul of the nation providing him with rifles and cannon for the regiments he is forming. Unless..."

Mustafa's look turned speculative.

Sampson felt himself lean inward. "Unless what?"

"You know what," Mustafa said. "We have discussed this before."

Sampson sighed. He knew what Mustafa was talking about. Conversion to Islam. If he converted to Islam Melek Ahmed Pasha would reward him with money and a government position at the gunpowder factory.

It was tempting. He'd never been a pious Jew, despite his mother's wish that he become a rabbi. His interest in science had been a great disappointment to her and they had not spoken in years. He'd thought about conversion for months, especially as he had learned more about Mustafa's Sufi sect, the Bektashi.

Unlike Judaism and the Counter-Remonstrant version of Calvinism he'd known in Amsterdam, Bektashi doctrine was much more tolerant and pantheistic. Many of its rituals seemed similar to Christian ones and unlike more mainstream adherents of Islam, they allowed the eating of pork, drank wine, and incorporated dancing as part of their faith. But the most appealing part of their doctrine, especially after what he had experienced in Grantville, was their attitude toward the education of women.

What had Haci Bektash said?

"Mustafa, what was that quote by Haci Bektash you told me about?"

Mustafa smiled. "Which one? There are hundreds."

"The one about the education of women."

"Ah. 'Educate your women,' Haci Bektash said. 'A nation that does not educate its women cannot progress.'"

Sampson nodded. "That's it. And in the thirteenth century yet. I was just thinking what the rabbis of Amsterdam or Salonica would think about that."

"Probably recoil in horror at the thought."

But could he give up his Judaism so easily? What would his mother say? His father?

Sampson shuddered. They would not understand. If he converted to Islam, he would be dead to them. He did not care about his mother. They had been estranged for years. But his father . . .

He sighed.

"I don't know, Mustafa. My heart feels torn in two. I was born a Jew. But I have no faith. Bektashi doctrine excites me. It feels right. But . . ."

Sampson put his head in his hands.

After a minute he felt Mustafa's arm around his shoulders.

"Come with me. I know what you need."

"What?"

"Mohammed once said, 'if your heart is perplexed with sorrow, go seek consolation at the graves of holy men.' I have a friend who is the *hodja* at the Casimiye mosque. He will let us pray for guidance at the crypt of Saint Casim, he who once was known as Saint Demetrios. Perhaps he will even build an amulet for you that will help you make your decision. Come."

"What good will this do?"

Mustafa shrugged. "It cannot hurt. And many people have been helped by praying at the crypt of Saint Casim, including my father. Have faith, my friend."

The chapel containing the crypt of Saint Casim was dark and cool.

"Your name?" asked the *hodja*.

"Sampson."

"Sampson," the religious teacher repeated, holding the knot in the candle flame. "It does not burn. That is good." Again he held the knot in the flame.

"The name of your father and your mother?"

"Jonathan is my father. Rebecca my mother."

Again the *hodja* held the sacred knot in the flame, then placed it in a small packet along with one of the silver coins Sampson had given him. He added a few bits of soil from the tomb and handed it to Sampson.

"This will ease your anxiety and help you make your decision. Carry it close to your heart for a week."

Outside the mosque, Sampson shook his head.

"Just superstition."

Mustafa smiled. "Is it?"

Wasn't it?

For whatever reason, Sampson felt better once he put the amulet inside his vest pocket. *Close to the heart, Sampson. Keep it close to the heart.*

Yusuf Bey motioned the slave girl away and turned toward Ebu Said.

"An excellent meal, as always, milk-brother. But enough. What news from the Red Tower?"

"Excellent news, Yusuf. There was only one man captured who knew anything about your relationship with the rebel fighters. He has quite mysteriously strangled himself before he could be interrogated. A mystery that I, as Kadi, must investigate, of course." Ebu Said laughed. "At least we may get something out of this disaster."

"And a disaster it was," Yusuf said. "Melek Ahmed has used this incident to increase his grip on the city. The landowners' advisory council is backing him fully on his proposal for a city police force. They have also acquiesced to his use of prisoners to sweep the streets and clean up the filth. Sanitation measures, he says."

Ebu Said nodded. "We have lost this round, Yusuf. But a fight does not end with a single blow. We have just begun."

We have, have we? Yusuf thought. Perhaps his milk-brother had. But he was already feeling the pressures from the other landowners, especially Evrenos Bey's friends and relatives. And a banker must be careful of his reputation or he will soon have no customers, especially with the Jews eager to lend money. One more disaster and he would have to cut his losses.

"So?" He asked aloud, "what do you have planned next?"

"I think it is time to drive a wedge between Melek Ahmed Pasha and the Jews who seem so eager to help fund him. If we can show that he cannot protect them, they will complain to Istanbul. Let me tell you about the upcoming wedding of Hannalica Castro."

Yusuf Bey leaned toward Ebu Said.

The applause and cries of welcome echoed around the courtyard of Don Diego's house as Hannalica Castro walked through the gate.

"She doesn't seem as happy as I thought she would be," Sampson said.

Lara smiled at him. The courtyard was crowded with the friends and relatives of the Castro family and Sampson, Lina, and Lara were standing at the back near the door to the kitchen.

"I know why," Lara said. "Hannalica hates being immersed in water. She almost drowned when she was three. But the ceremony at the baths requires she submit to the *tebilá*, the triple immersion ordained by rabbinical prescription."

"And if Doña Gazela forgot to cut one of her nails, she'd have to do the immersion again," Lina said. She bumped into Sampson.

Sampson felt his face flush when Lina's breast pressed against his arm.

She's doing that on purpose! Be calm, Sampson. What was the phrase they used in Grantville? Deep, cleansing breaths.

"But I know another reason she's unhappy," Lara said.

"*Pelador?*" Lina said.

"Exactly." Lara saw him looking at her and touched her eyebrows.

"The absence of eyebrows is considered a sign of beauty among the Jewish women of Salonica, Señor Gideon. *Pelador*, a depilatory paste, adheres to the skin and can be removed only with a great deal of force. Quite painful, I am told."

"Good," Lina said. "She deserves it after the way she's treated us the past few days. She's been horrible!"

"She's been scared witless," Lara said. "She's fifteen. About to leave her home and become the wife of Hayyim Molho, future rabbi of the Aragon congregation. And before the night is done she will be a virgin no more. You can only lose your virginity once, little sister, as you well know."

Lina bumped into Sampson again. "Sorry, Señor Gideon, it is so crowded in the courtyard."

Sampson looked around. There was no one within three feet of them.

"Of course, Lina. I understand perfectly." Her hand pressed into his and gave it a brief squeeze.

Well well, Sampson thought. *Perhaps I will have as interesting a night as Hannalica.*

"So what is your role with the wedding, Señor Gideon?" Lara asked, watching Hannalica and her entourage enter the house. "You did not attend the groom at the baths."

"True," Sampson said. He patted the pistol under his coat. "I'm a guard for the wedding party, at Don Issac's request. There have been rumors that bandits would attempt to kidnap Hannalica. Since I am a *Franco* protected by Ottoman regulations for foreign delegations, I am one of the few Jews in Salonica permitted to carry a firearm."

"How exciting," Lina murmured. "You must come back after the wedding and tell me what happened."

"It will be quite late, Lina. First the wedding, then *la tadrada,* which lasts three or four hours. By the time I get home I am sure you'll be asleep."

Lina leaned closer and whispered in his ear. "Perhaps not, Señor Gideon."

"Lina! Stop embarrassing him."

Lina jerked away from Sampson.

Sampson smiled. "I'm not embarrassed, Lara. Truly."

Lara sniffed. She scowled at her sister. "Then perhaps you should be. I assure you that my sister will be fast asleep when you return from the wedding reception."

Lina scowled back at her sister and then walked away.

Lara looked around and then leaned closer to Sampson herself.

"But if Don Diego does not require my services tonight, I am sure *I* will be awake." Lara smiled and turned to follow her sister.

Sampson's breath seemed to catch in his throat.

An interesting night indeed.

Sampson rubbed the back of his neck.

"Tired?" Don Issac asked.

"Just a bit, Don Issac. Do we have much longer to go?"

"Just the banquet," Don Issac said. "But first we have the ritual to prepare the wedding couple for their future life of intimacy." He nodded toward the bedroom that Hannalica and Hayyim Molho had just entered.

"They're not going to consummate their marriage now, are they?"

Don Issac laughed. "Oh no. First we sing, then we open the door and rush in and take the plates of sweets around the room. Then we sit down at the banquet tables." He pointed at the tables around them.

Sampson sighed. "Another song?"

Don Issac nodded. "And you may find this one quite, uh, rowdy, young man."

The door to the bedroom closed and the two dozen other guests around them started to sing as the three musicians began to play.

Avridme, galanica, que va amanecer.

Open up, my little chick? Sampson thought. Rowdy indeed.

The guests had sung only two verses of the song when a loud feminine scream came from the bedroom.

No one moved.

It was the second scream that galvanized Sampson into action.

He burst through the door and saw Hayyim slumped over on the bed. At the window two men were struggling to force Hannalica out of the room.

"Stop!"

One of the men snarled and raised his wheel lock pistol as Sampson clawed to get his revolver out of its holster.

The barrel of the wheel lock lined up on his chest.

No!

Instead of a loud bang, there was a fizzling hiss from the wheel lock.

Misfire!

Sampson raised his revolver and fired twice at the gunman's chest. He fell.

The second kidnapper turned and forced Hannalica in front of him. His knife was at Hannalica's throat. She was at least six inches shorter than her attacker. Good.

"Drop the pistol, or I kill her!"

A flash of an image from a Grantville television program popped into his mind.

"I choose door number three," Sampson said. He raised his revolver and fired.

"You have placed men to discourage Ebu Said from wandering too far?" Melek Ahmed Pasha asked.

Ismail nodded. "I have. And Yusuf Bey is being most cooperative in providing the evidence we need to have Ebu Said removed as Kadi. Naturally Yusuf is shocked at what his milk-brother has done."

Melek Ahmed smiled. "Of course. I am sure that pressure from the other landowners was a factor in Yusuf Bey's decision. And once again it seems that Ebu Said's plans were foiled by Sampson Gideon. An interesting young man."

Ismail nodded. "Even more interesting than we had suspected. After the incident at the wedding reception it appears that Sampson Gideon has made up his mind to convert to Islam. Apparently he believes an amulet given to him by the *hodja* at the Casimiye Mosque caused one of the kidnappers' pistols to misfire, saving his life and allowing him to kill both of the kidnappers and save Hannalica Molho's life as well."

"Excellent! Allah be praised. Once he has converted bring him to me. He has shown great courage and deserves to be rewarded. Perhaps his fortitude will encourage others to emulate him."

"As you command, My Pasha."

"But Lara, Sampson is a Muslim now!" Lina wailed.

"So? He is a Sufi, one of the Bektashi. That makes all the difference in the world."

Lina rubbed her eyes. "It does? But I thought you said being the slave of a Muslim was worse than being the wife of a Jew. And being the wife of a Jew is—"

"Worse than being the slave of a Jew." Lara finished. "Yes, I know I said those things. That is why we never converted to Judaism. But being the slave of a Sufi, especially a newly converted Bektashi like Sampson, will be much better. In fact, if we please him, he may marry us. And to marry us, he will have to free us first."

"He will?"

"'May,' I said. We will have to please him. As well as Roxelana pleased Suleiman the Magnificent."

"And how am I going to do that?" Lina asked. "You've kept me out of Don Diego's bedroom for years."

"It was for the best, little sister. Don Diego's desires have changed since his wife died. He even—" Lara leaned over and whispered in Lina's ear.

Lina's eyes flew open. "He didn't! He wouldn't!"

"He would and did," Lara said. "But do not fear. I will teach you what you need to know before we move to Sampson's household."

"But Lara, if we convert to Islam, how will that help us? How can we make Don Diego sell us to Sampson?"

"Once we convert to Islam Don Diego will have no choice but to sell us. Jews cannot possess Muslims as slaves. While Melek Ahmed Pasha is liberal in some things, in that he is as firm as the sultan himself. As for why Don Diego will sell us to Sampson—" Lara smiled. "After six years in Don Diego's bed, I have learned enough secrets about him to twist his mind on such a minor thing."

Lina shuddered. "Are you sure? It would be horrible if we were sold to someone else. Horrible."

"Trust me."

Mustafa bin Kemal walked through the doorway of Sampson Gideon's new house and nodded. "A magnificent residence the governor-general has given you."

Sampson smiled. "It's not much. Six rooms. A small courtyard. A third the size of Don Diego's house."

"And Don Diego is one of the richest Jews in the city," Mustafa said drily. "And where are these new slaves that I've heard so much about?"

Sampson waved towards the entrance into the house. "Getting my bedchamber ready."

Mustafa chuckled. "Really? I think you will have a pleasant time tonight, my friend. But I am here on an errand from the governor-general himself."

Sampson motioned to the chairs and table in the courtyard. "What is it?"

Mustafa sat down and looked around the courtyard. The table was under the shade of several pomegranate and jujubee trees. The two ancient Roman columns that supported the gate into the house were covered with the vines of jasmine and their perfume mixed with that of the roses along the wall.

"Mustafa?"

"Sorry," Mustafa said. "The beauty of your courtyard made me lose the path of my thoughts."

"Melek Ahmed Pasha? He sent you on an errand?"

Mustafa snapped his fingers. "Of course. The governor-general has a request. Your new slaves may be a problem."

"A problem? What kind of problem?"

"The more conservative landowners suspect that the selling of the slaves once they converted was some kind of plot to keep them under Jewish control. Especially given the circumstances of your previous relationship with Don Diego."

Mustafa held up his hand as he saw Sampson's face turn red. "I know, I know. Ridiculous. But to ease those suspicions, Melek Ahmed requests that you marry your slaves, if that is your desire, or sell them to him. That will ease the criticism he is getting from the *Kadizadelis* in the city."

Sampson smiled. "Anything to please my patron. You may tell Melek Ahmed Pasha that I will marry the slaves."

A lilting, seductive voice came from the house. "Oh master, your bedchamber is ready."

Sampson leaned closer to Mustafa. "But we don't need to tell Lara and Lina just yet. Agreed?"

Mustafa laughed. "Agreed, agreed. My lips are sealed."

𝔗𝔥𝔢 𝔖𝔬𝔲𝔫𝔡 𝔬𝔣 𝔖𝔴𝔢𝔢𝔱 𝔖𝔱𝔯𝔦𝔫𝔤𝔰: 𝔄 𝔖𝔢𝔯𝔢𝔫𝔞𝔡𝔢 𝔦𝔫 𝔒𝔫𝔢 𝔐𝔬𝔳𝔢𝔪𝔢𝔫𝔱

David Carrico

Grantville
December 1633

The music came to an end. Atwood flipped a switch on the board and leaned forward to the microphone on the table.

"And that was the beautiful 'Nimrod' movement from Variations on an Original Theme for Orchestra, Opus 36, called the 'Enigma' Variations, by Edward Elgar. That was a foretaste of things to come. We will play the work in its entirety some time next month. I think you will like it."

Atwood had a smooth bass voice, and he had put it to use over the years from time to time serving as a radio disc jockey. He'd never expected to be doing it in this situation, however, over three hundred years before he had been born. But he'd been assured that there were plenty of crystal radios out there in Thuringia to tune into his show, so he'd agreed to do it.

He looked down at his notes. "To close out this evening's program, we're going to play a very different piece of music in a very different musical style. It's what we call 'bluegrass' music. Those of you who listen to Reverend Fischer's morning devotionals have already heard music like this. This particular piece features an instrument that wasn't invented for close to another two hundred years, called the banjo. This is 'Foggy Mountain Breakdown.'"

283

Atwood cued up the CD. After a moment the music began to sound. He leaned back and just listened to Earl Scruggs' picking. Atwood could play the banjo, but it wasn't his best instrument and he enjoyed hearing it played by a master.

All too soon the music was over, and he leaned forward again. "That was 'Foggy Mountain Breakdown,' and I hope you enjoyed it.

"Thank you for being with us this Sunday evening for *Adventures in Great Music* on the Voice of America Radio Network, sponsored by the Burke Wish Book, where you can order anything you need or want. I look forward to joining you next Sunday evening.

"I'm Atwood Cochran, and good night."

A few weeks later

Lucille Cochran turned from the front door's peep hole. "It's for you, dear."

"How do you know?"

"Well, there's only one of him, he's a down-timer, and he's carrying something that looks like one of your old gig bags. He doesn't look like a lawyer, so I don't think he came to see the probate judge. That leaves you."

Atwood levered himself from his recliner, muttering something about people coming around on Saturday evening when a man should be able enjoy some peace and quiet. He opened the door. "Yes?"

"Herr Cochran?" The man on the doorstep was short, dark-haired, dressed in reasonably fine but not new clothing, including a large hat with a bedraggled feather. And he did have what looked for all the world like one of Atwood's old soft-sided guitar gig bags on his back. Atwood guessed it had a lute in it. The man appeared to be in his forties, and by his accent he was not from the Germanies.

"That's me."

"I am Giouan Battista Veraldi. I was in Magdeburg when I heard your radio program with the music of the...banjo?" He pronounced the last word with care, as if he wasn't sure how it should sound.

"Come in, Signor Veraldi." Atwood opened the door wider. The Italian beamed at the up-timer's recognition and stepped through the door. Lucille appeared in the door to the kitchen, wiping her hands on a dish towel. "Dear, this is Signor Giouan Battista Veraldi...did I get that right?" The still beaming Italian swept his hat from his head and made a very courtly bow to Lucille. "Signor Veraldi, this is my wife, Lucille."

"I am very pleased to meet you, Frau Cochran."

"So, at a guess you would like to know more about the banjo." Atwood's curiosity was piqued.

"Yes, please." Veraldi's smile widened.

"Come with me, then." Atwood led the way through the kitchen and opened the door into what used to be the garage. Veraldi sniffed in appreciation as he passed by the stew simmering on the stove. Atwood followed his guest down the step into his studio.

The late afternoon light flooded through the windows at the end of the room. There were posters of famous guitars and famous guitarists on the walls. The room was furnished with a couple of stools and music stands, plus a table under the windows and another at the other end of the room. There was a black cabinet in one corner, and leaning up against it were several odd-shaped cases.

"Where are you from, Signor Veraldi?"

Atwood gestured to one of the stools, but the Italian stood looking around with eyes wide. After a moment, he started and replied, "As you guessed, I am from Italy originally, but I was a lutenist at the Swedish court for a number of years. I left not long ago. The pay was good, but the weather..." He shivered, and they both laughed. "I have been working my way back to Italy. I'm not in a hurry, but it will not be long now before I am back in the land of fine music and olives. I miss olives..."

Veraldi's German was better than his own, Atwood decided. His accent gave it a lilt that neither up-timers nor native down-timers gave it. "It is always good to return home," Atwood said.

"True; and I have been gone for a long time," Veraldi replied. His eyes had by now gravitated to the open case lying on one of the tables. "Such a large *vihuela* I have never seen," he breathed.

"*Vihuela*?" Atwood asked.

"Do you know *guitarra,* or *guiterne*?" Veraldi replied without looking around.

"Oh, guitar. Sure. It's a classical guitar."

Veraldi caressed the guitar with his eyes, then turned to Atwood. "May I..."

Atwood gestured in reply. Veraldi set the instrument bag he was carrying down on the table and picked up the guitar. He held it up to the light and peered at it closely, then ran his hand all over the body. At last he plucked a string, and his eyebrows rose at the strong resonant sound. With a sigh he replaced the guitar in its case.

"Very fine *vihuela*; very fine guitar."

"Thank you. Please, have a seat." Atwood waved at one of the stools and sat on the other. Instead of doing so, Veraldi opened his bag and took out a lute, which he handed to Atwood.

Atwood hadn't handled a lute since a class in Renaissance instruments during his college days. He received it gingerly, holding it in his two hands as if it were a baby. It was a beautiful instrument. The spruce sound board was unvarnished and had darkened a bit from its original white. The ribs of the bowl-shaped body gleamed with a satin patina. And the neck—now there was a joy. The neck was short and wide, supporting ten courses of two strings each. The head bent back from the neck at right angles. He plucked a string, and nodded at the sound. Not as deep and resonant as the guitar, but louder than he had thought it would be.

All in all, it was an excellent example of the luthier's art. And it was a living instrument with signs of use on it, but nonetheless lovingly cared for. Veraldi's pride in it was obvious.

"Very fine lute," Atwood said, handing it back.

"Thank you," came the response. "It was made for me by Master Matteo Sellas, of Venice. The Sellas family are the finest luthiers in Italy."

"It is a fine instrument," Atwood repeated. "Would you like to see the rest of mine?"

Veraldi nodded with eagerness, wiping his hands on his pants.

Atwood started pulling cases out of the stack and opening them up in the tables. "Steel string guitar, twelve string guitar, and of course," opening the final case with a flourish, "the Gibson Les Paul electric guitar."

His guest looked around with a dazed look on his face, not understanding what he was seeing.

"Sit, sit," Atwood said, pointing to the stool. Veraldi sat. The up-timer picked up the classical guitar, and thought for a moment about what to play. After a moment, the perfect song came to him. He wrapped himself around the guitar, and played the opening bars to "Hotel California."

Veraldi was intent, watching Atwood's fingers, drinking in the sound. The delicate tapestry of the music wove through the air of the small room, seeming to bring light with it. Atwood stopped at the place where the vocals would have begun.

The Italian sighed. Then he pointed at the other instruments. "Please?"

Atwood smiled. "Sure." He set the classical back in its case and picked up the steel-string guitar. He settled back onto the stool, then played the same piece of music. Veraldi's eyes widened at the difference in timbre between the two instruments, so similar in size and shape.

The performance was repeated with the twelve-string guitar. This time Veraldi's eyes closed, but Atwood could have sworn he saw the man's ears twitching in time with the music. He smiled a little at the thought.

Once again the excerpt drew to a close. Atwood set the twelve-string back in its case and turned back to his guest.

"You will not play the other guitar?" Veraldi pointed to the Gibson.

"Later," Atwood laughed. "That one takes a different song. But there is one more for you to see." He closed a couple of cases, then set another on top of them and opened it. "This is a banjo."

Atwood picked the banjo up and handed it to Veraldi, whose eyebrows immediately shot up to their limit at the sight of the round flat body. He turned it this way and that, peering at it closely as he took in all the details. After several minutes, Veraldi sat back. "I do not know what I expected to see, but it was not . . . this. This almost looks like the bastard child of a *vihuela* and a *tambour*."

"You're not far off," Atwood laughed. He took the banjo back, and cradled it in his arms. He'd already decided what to play here, so he took off with "Herod's Song" from *Jesus Christ Superstar*. The rollicking beat made it a fun song to play.

When he finished, he looked up to see Veraldi smiling. "Yes," the Italian said, "that is what I heard through the radio in Magdeburg. That sound; that very unique sound. How can I get a banjo? I must take one back to Italy with me."

"Well," Atwood replied, "I won't sell mine. And there's not very many of them in Grantville. However, Ingram Bledsoe might have one or two. I'll check with him tomorrow."

"Then may I return tomorrow?"

"Tomorrow afternoon, certainly. Say, middle of the afternoon."

Veraldi stood from his stool and held out his hand. "I will return then," he said. "Thank you for your time, Herr Cochran. It was very good to meet you."

Atwood ushered his guest to the front door, where they shook hands again and exchanged good evenings.

"Well," Lucille said, coming out of the dining room, "dinner's ready. What did your Signor Veraldi want?"

"Mostly to talk about instruments," Atwood said. "I have a feeling that we're going to be seeing a lot more of him. I suspect he's going to want to drain me dry of everything I can tell him."

Giouan muttered to himself all the way back to the hotel. Mother of heaven, what he had just discovered. The banjo alone would be a prize to take back to Italy, but the up-time *vihuelas*! The sounds they could make. He knew he had had only a taste tonight. He must hear more. He must learn more. He must find a way to take these things home with him.

The next day, Sunday

Atwood opened the door. "Signor Veraldi, come in." He led the way to the studio. He turned the stereo down, then waved at one stool as he took his seat on the other one. "So, how has your day been? What do you think about banjos now?"

"My day has been good," Veraldi responded. "And I would very much like to have a banjo. Have you been able to speak to your friend Herr Bledsoe?"

"Yes, I have. The good news is that he has two banjos, a four-string and a five-string. He says he might be willing to sell the four-string. The bad news is it's somewhat beat-up and he wants three hundred dollars for it."

"Three hundred dollars." Veraldi pulled at his mustaches. "How much is that in pfennigs or groschen?"

Atwood thought for a moment. "About a hundred and ninety pfennigs, maybe. You'd have to convert them at the bank to find out for sure."

The Italian's mouth twisted. "He is proud of his banjos, Herr Bledsoe is."

"To be fair, I was surprised he had any. As of right now, I only know of four in the entire Ring of Fire. I have one, Bucky Buckner of the Old Folks Band has one, and Ingram has the other two. There might be one or two more in closets in town, but I wouldn't count on it. Banjos weren't very popular up-time. People thought they were hard to learn to play. Ingram's going to keep one to be a model for the designers and workers in his factory, so that leaves exactly one to sell. I'm really surprised some musician hasn't come along and bought it from him. If I had anybody wanting to learn banjo, it would probably have sold already."

"You teach, then?" Veraldi cocked his head to one side.

"Oh, yeah." Atwood laughed. "I teach music at the junior high school. I taught in another town before the Ring of Fire. Afterwards, it was just natural for me to keep teaching here. Plus I give lessons on guitar. Anybody under the age of thirty-five in this town who plays guitar probably learned from me. That's why I have the studio." He waved his hand around at the room.

Veraldi pulled at his moustaches some more. "Do you teach . . . older students?"

"Like yourself?"

Veraldi nodded.

"Sure. I once had a sixty-year-old grandmother who wanted to learn the guitar. I think I can teach you." Atwood smiled, and saw it returned.

"How much do you charge?" Veraldi asked.

"Ten dollars for a half-hour lesson."

Veraldi spent a moment in thought. "So, perhaps five pfennigs. And how many lessons could one such as I have during a week?"

"Well," Atwood began, "I normally do one lesson a week for each student, but for you, at least two, maybe three, possibly even four. You would rate as a proficient student."

"Thank you." Veraldi frowned. "I would like lessons on both the banjo and the guitar. Please tell Herr Bledsoe that I would like to buy his banjo. I simply must determine how I can pay for it."

Atwood thought that if Veraldi didn't stop pulling at his mustache, it was going to come out in his hands.

"Are there guitars that can be bought? Up-time guitars, here in Grantville?"

"Probably," Atwood said. "I'll look around for you. They'll be easier to find than banjos, that's for sure. Now, when do you want to do your lessons? Sunday and Wednesday night are out. I have commitments with the church and with the Voice of America Radio Network. Saturday I need for myself. Monday, Tuesday, Thursday or Friday, your choice."

"Twice a week, you said," Veraldi responded. "What about Monday and Thursday evenings, then?"

Atwood pulled out his schedule book. "That will work. What about seven in the evening both nights?"

Veraldi nodded.

"Good. Well, I'll see you tomorrow night, and I should have something to tell you about guitars then as well." Atwood looked up at the clock. "Oops. Gotta go. I need to get to the radio station. My program goes on in an hour." He stood and shook hands with Veraldi.

Three hundred dollars! Giouan almost beat his head. That wouldn't take all his money, but it would take enough that he wouldn't be able to stay long in Grantville. If he took lessons as well, that would shorten the time available even more. But if he got the banjo, he would need the lessons in order to get the best out of the instrument.

Giouan walked along, kicking at rocks on the sidewalk. Three hundred dollars. One hundred and ninety pfennigs. He stopped, and took a deep breath. Did he want the banjo and the guitar if he could get them? Absolutely. That desire went to the bottom of his soul and curled around its foundations. The question now was how could he get everything he needed if he bought the instruments?

That question occupied his mind for hours that night. He wrestled with it non-stop—explored every possibility—and in the end there was one way he could think of, one path open to him: the last resort of any good musician. It tore at his heart, but he saw no other way to get what he wanted.

Monday

Atwood looked up from his guitar when Lucille ushered Veraldi into the studio. "Ah, good, right on time." He continued playing until Veraldi sat on the stool opposite him, then set the guitar aside.

Veraldi looked like a wreck. There were deep bags under his

eyes, which were bloodshot. From the looks of it, he was either hung over or he hadn't had much sleep the night before.

"You've probably already learned that we Grantvillers are a pretty informal people," Atwood began. "Since we're going to be working together pretty closely for some time to come, I'd like you to call me At, and if I may I'll call you John, which is what your name translates to in English. All right?"

Veraldi's eyes opened wide. "That is ... improper for a master and student."

Atwood snorted. "I'm not a master, John. Oh, I'm a good guitarist, and a passable amateur singer, but I'm not a master, not in the sense of your meaning, and not in the standards of our people either. I'll teach you as much as I can in the time that you have, okay? But leave that 'master' stuff out of it."

"Okay," Veraldi responded, "but if I call you Master At, please do not berate me. This is a hard habit to break."

"I think I can live with that, John. So, where do you want to start?"

Veraldi swung his bag off of his shoulder. He held it in his hands for a long moment, then looked up at Atwood. After a hesitation, he said, "Master At, do you know anyone who would be willing to buy my lute?"

Atwood was shocked. "John! You can't sell your lute."

A determined expression came over the Italian's face. "I do not want to. She has been my life and livelihood for years, a part of me." He swallowed. "But lutes are common, Master At. Banjos and up-time guitars are not. I must seize the opportunity before me. To do so means that I must sell my lute." He looked down again. "As much as I have taken this instrument for granted over the years, I find that the thought of losing her is very painful." He squared his shoulders and looked up. "Nevertheless, it is what I must do. I have been to your bank and have learned about money here in Grantville. I think she is worth five hundred of your dollars—a fair price for a master class instrument made by the Sellas family."

Atwood's thought whirled. "I see. Let me make a phone call."

After a couple of rings, the phone on the other end was picked up.

"Hello, Ingram? At Cochran here. You know that four-string banjo we talked about? Well, consider it sold. My new student John Veraldi has an excellent lute that he's going to sell and he'll buy the banjo out of that." There was a burst of conversation from the other end. "Yeah, it's really fine. Made by the Sellas family in Venice. Supposed to be top-drawer craftsmen." More conversation. "Yeah, you talk to old Riebeck and see what he says. I imagine we can work something out. Okay. Good. See you soon." Atwood hung the phone up and turned to the Italian.

"Okay, John. Here's the deal. I'll buy that lute from you for your price. I'll give you three hundred dollars cash, plus in exchange I'll give you a month's free lessons and this." He opened a closet door and pulled out a guitar case. It wasn't as nice as the cases his personal guitars were in, but from the look on Veraldi's face it didn't matter. He set it on the table and flipped the lid open. Veraldi slid off his stool and reached for the guitar with hesitation, but at length grasped it with a firm hand and took it out of the case.

"That is a classical guitar, John. It belonged to a student of mine who was left up-time. I was making a small repair to the tuners when the Ring of Fire happened."

Atwood looked at Veraldi, trying to hold the guitar in the way he had seen the up-timer hold his. "This type of guitar was a standard design in the up-time." Atwood picked up his own guitar. He held it up beside the one the Italian was holding. "See, almost identical in size."

"Is yours a better guitar than this one?" Veraldi asked, looking at his guitar with hungry eyes.

"Yes, it is."

"It is fitting that the master have a master class instrument."

"Well," Atwood chuckled, "mine isn't exactly master class." Veraldi looked at him with questioning eyes. "The real master class instruments up-time were made by hand using techniques almost identical to those used by down-time luthiers today. It takes a long time to make an instrument that way, and their very best instruments commanded prices in the tens of thousands of dollars. Only the true master performers could or would afford those kinds of prices." He sat down and cradled the guitar. "No, this was assembled in a factory, using a lot of hand labor, true, but the goal of those making it was not perfection, it was 'get it as good as you can for the material we use and the time we let you spend on it.' I'd call it maybe high journeyman work. This was made by the Takamini company, and it cost me about eight hundred dollars several years ago."

"Are all your guitars like that?"

"Umm-hmm."

"If these sound so good, it is to be wished that a true master class instrument could have come back with you." Veraldi sounded wistful. "I would really like to hear such."

"Sorry," Atwood chuckled again. "Nobody in the Ring of Fire— including me—would have dreamt of spending as much on a guitar as they would have spent for a car or a house, even if they'd had the money to spare.

"As I was saying, this is a classical design guitar. Almost anything that can be played on a guitar can be played on this one, but it was customary to play certain types of music on the classical and other types on the other guitars.

"So, shall we get started?"

Giouan felt as if he were walking on air. He had a guitar, and he would get his banjo tomorrow, after meeting Master Atwood at the bank at noon. Things were working out so well.

It indeed pained him to leave his lute behind, but if he had to leave her, he was glad that Master At had taken her. In the master's hands she would be safe and valued as she should be.

He looked down at the guitar case he was clutching. In his own hands he held the future. With this guitar, and with the banjo, his fortune and his reputation would be made in Italy.

Days passed. Giouan had a facile memory, and his speed of learning surprised Atwood, who kept giving him more and more information and more and more music to study and learn. Veraldi acted like a man dying of thirst and hunger who had just been placed at a feast. Atwood didn't focus on just musical technique in his teaching of Veraldi; he also spent some time on musical theory. Every bit of musical knowledge Veraldi was presented he consumed. He even parted with some of his precious silver to have some of the high school students copy music for him, music that he didn't have time to learn right then. But above all, he practiced.

Giouan would always remember the smile on Master At's face that day.

"This is not only a good piece of music, it's also incredibly fun. It was originally written for solo guitar with an orchestra interlude by a man named Mason Williams. Another guitarist named Edgar Cruz arranged it for solo guitar only. I love it, and I want you to learn it. It's named *Classical Gas*, and it's a bit of a showpiece, as you'll see."

And yes, Giouan saw. It was indeed a showpiece, one that he also fell in love with at first hearing, watching Master At's fingers flash on the strings. When it was over, he heaved a deep sigh.

"What's wrong?" Master At asked.

"Yet another piece that I must learn," Giouan replied. "One more piece in the list." Then he smiled.

Atwood wasn't sure how many hours a day Giouan practiced, but he knew it was more than any other student he had ever known, even when he was in college.

Giouan watched as Master At connected a cable between the Gibson Les Paul guitar and the black cabinet in the corner, then flicked a switch on the cabinet. Master At was going to show him what the electric guitar could do. A slight hum filled the room. "This is a little piece called *Pipeline*," the master said. A moment later, he flicked a string and a howling tone was generated that went sliding in keeping with the master's hand on the neck of the guitar, sliding down to an almost thunderous low pitch. He began plucking a fast rocking rhythm, then began overlaying a strident melody atop it. The song didn't last that long, but Giouan was breathless by the time it was over, feeling as if he had just run up a tall mountain.

Veraldi's skill progressed by the week, sometimes seemingly by the day. Atwood knew he shouldn't be surprised. The man was an accomplished musician, after all. It was not long before he reached a level where Atwood wanted him to begin performing in public. He hinted at it, only to find his hints ignored. He put forward stronger hints. They were politely declined.

Atwood was bothered enough by this that one Thursday evening he forced Veraldi to accompany him to the Thuringen Gardens.

"Here, take this." Atwood placed a mug of wine in the Italian's hand. "Let's find some place to sit down."

They wandered through the Gardens, looking for chairs, but the place was busy. It wasn't until Marcus Wendell hailed them that they found seats at the table he was sharing with Giacomo Carissimi.

Atwood had seen to it that the two Italians had been introduced some time ago. Even in Sweden Veraldi had heard of the composer, and he had been very glad of the introduction. They chattered back and forth for a few minutes while Marcus and Atwood discussed a school program. The two conversations dwindled down at about the same time, and Atwood seized the opportunity.

"John..."

Veraldi hurriedly swallowed a mouthful of wine and set his mug on the table, looking to Atwood with expectation.

"John, you know you're doing well. You've learned a lot of notes in the last few weeks. I think you're ready to play some of that music in public. You could play with some of the other musicians here in town. You could even play here in the Gardens and make some more money to pay for your stay. But every time I mention it, you put me off. Why?"

Veraldi said nothing for a long moment, just looked down at his mug and ran his finger around the rim over and over. "Master At," he said finally, looking up, "the fourth day I was in Grantville, I went to the library. When the attendant asked what I was looking for, I gave him my name and told him that I wanted to know what the books from the future said about me. Several hours later, I had my answer." He lifted his hand from the mug and snapped his fingers. "Nothing. To the future, I am nobody, nothing. I, Giouan Battista Veraldi, who have played before kings and been rewarded by them, I am not worthy even to be mentioned in any of the books of the future."

Atwood watched as Veraldi resumed circling the rim of the mug with his finger. "I already had my guitar and banjo by then. But that night I resolved that the future that was would not be repeated. I will be more than a memory that fades from the air when the people who know me die. So my plans take on more urgency—I will take the banjo and the up-time guitar to Venice."

"Venice, huh?" Atwood responded. "What's in Venice?"

"*Maestro* Monteverdi, and *Maestros* Matteo and Giorgio Sellas, the leading composer and luthiers in Venice, in all of Italy. To them I will bring what I have learned, in the hopes that they will take that knowledge and advance the cause of music in Italy. I will beg *Maestro* Monteverdi to take up the banjo, to write music for it that will catch the ears of the patrons and make a place for me. To the Sellas family, I will offer the opportunity to measure and analyze the instruments, to make more and make them popular. I will go down in history as the man who brought the banjo to Italy, maybe even to the world."

Atwood could see Carissimi nodding. He understood what his countryman was saying. "Okay, I can understand that. But what does that have to do with not playing here in Grantville?"

"I am a professional musician, Master At. Setting aside all humility, I am probably the best performer in Grantville right now."

"Right now," Marcus interjected, "that's true, but only because our best performers have moved to Magdeburg."

Veraldi made a seated bow to the band director. "Yes, I know, but my point is not that Grantville is deficient in performers, but rather that I am very proficient. I do not need the practice of performing in public. I have been a performer for well-nigh thirty years now. I know how to perform. Nor do I need the practice of performing with other performers. Again, that has been part of my life for thirty years.

"What I need to be is focused. What I need to be is committed. What I need to be is single-minded. I will learn everything I can possibly learn in the time I have left. If I take an hour to perform here at the Gardens, then with the time to walk here and walk back, the time to talk to others, the time I would spend in preparing myself for the performance, I would lose at least three hours. That is enough time to learn over a minute's worth of music. I begrudge that time. I will not spend it thus. And I will especially not repeatedly spend it thus."

Atwood absorbed everything his student had said. "But can you learn what you need without having to earn extra money?"

"I think so. If not . . ." A very Italian shrug. ". . . I will do my best."

Maestro Carissimi leaned forward. "Master Atwood, you will not change his mind. I recognize this . . . mind-set, I believe the word is. It would take an act of God to bend him from his purpose."

"I'm beginning to see that," Atwood said. He turned back to Veraldi. "John, from now on, no payments for your lessons."

"But Master At," Veraldi exclaimed. "It is not right to do this. The master is worthy of his fees."

Atwood laid his hand on the table, palm up. "I don't teach guitar and banjo to make money. Truth is, most of the time I'd be happy to do it for nothing, just to watch kids learn to play and know that I had a hand in it. But I have to charge something, or they won't think the lessons are worth anything. So I set the fees just high enough to make the kids feel like the lessons are worthwhile, and to make them work at it because they're paying for it.

"But you, you're the kind of student every teacher wants to have, a talented student who wants to learn. So think of it as my contribution to your dream. Who knows, those few dollars may just make the difference in you achieving your goal."

"Your master gives you a gift, Signor Veraldi," Carissimi said. "Be gracious in your acceptance of it."

Veraldi stood and made a formal bow. "As you say, Master Atwood, so shall it be."

"I have a gift as well," Carissimi added. "When you are ready to leave, advise me, and I shall give you a letter of introduction to *Maestro* Monteverdi."

Veraldi stammered. "Th-thank you, *Maestro* Carissimi. That is very generous of you, and will be of inestimable value to me."

Carissimi waved a hand. "It is nothing, mere words on paper. If it helps you on your way, it is worth it. But see here," he pointed a finger at Veraldi, "if, despite the generosity of Master Atwood, you find yourself short of silver, come to me. You are from Venice, I am from Rome, but we are both Italians, and we must stick together in these cold northern countries, eh?"

The evening ended in a round of laughter.

More time passed. Atwood, true to his word, made no more attempts to get Veraldi to play in public. And he was also true to his word in that he refused to accept lesson fees from his student, even though Veraldi tried to press them on him several times.

It was both inspiring and humbling to watch Veraldi, Atwood decided. He had never personally worked that hard at anything, not even when he was in the air force orchestra with a solo in an upcoming concert tour. The only person he'd ever seen work as hard as Veraldi was one semester when he was an undergraduate—he'd had a friend who was a Ph.D. candidate who had both a dissertation defense and a doctoral level recital scheduled in the same semester. He swore the man lived on coffee that semester. He knew he lost enough weight that he looked unhealthy.

Veraldi didn't seem to be losing any weight, but he was definitely burning the candle at both ends. Some days his eyes seemed to be peering out of tunnels bored deep into his skull.

Giouan counted his silver frequently, even though he knew to the pfennig how much he had. At least once each week he recalculated how long he could stay, how long he could continue learning, when he would have to leave.

That day finally came.

Giouan knew he had to leave. He didn't want to, not by any stretch of his imagination. He wanted to stay at Master At's feet until he had learned everything the master had to teach, and then stay some more just to work with the master. But it wasn't possible. He had to leave, he had to get home to Venice, for only there could his knowledge create the reputation he needed, only there could he build the relationships that would help bring the new music to his land.

It didn't take long to leave on Saturday. Giouan had already collected his letter of introduction from *Maestro* Carissimi. He packed his clothing that morning, and slid the instrument cases into the oilcloth bag he had had made for them.

He paid the hotel keeper for the last time. His horse was waiting for him when he arrived at the stable, where he tipped the stable boy generously for taking excellent care of his mount. He tied his packages onto the back of the saddle, then headed for the familiar house of his master.

"So," Atwood said, "the day has arrived when you have to leave. I'm sorry to hear that, John."

"I'm sorry to have to say it, Master At. But my money has dwindled to the point where I dare not stay any longer. I have enough to make it to Venice if I start now, but if I stay much longer I won't."

Atwood saw the resolution in his student's eyes, so he didn't try to argue. In truth, he was surprised Veraldi had stayed as long as he had.

"Do you have everything you want?"

"No. Nor do I have everything I need. But I have enough to begin. If God allows, I will return."

Atwood held his hand out. "Good luck, John. Go with God. Write to me when you can, come back if you can."

"I will, Master At." Veraldi took his hand, then snatched him into a close embrace. A moment later, he was walking down the sidewalk.

Giouan swung up and settled his feet in the stirrups. He looked around one last time, felt a lump rise in his throat for Master Atwood, then reined the horse around and nudged it into motion.

Coda

From *The Fall of Fire: The Coming of Grantville and the Music of Europe*

Charles William Battenberg, B.A., M.A., Fellow of the Royal Academy of Music, Schwarzberg Chair of Musicology, Oxford University

1979, Oxford University Press

Chapter Eleven—There Came Sweet Strings

Not all musical advancements from the knowledge of Grantville were made via the road to Magdeburg...the knowledge of the advanced mature instruments, as has already been noted, began to spread out very soon...

With the exception of the piano, no other stringed instrument made as great an impact as the banjo...considered a humble instrument by the up-timers, in the hands of Monteverdi and others it quickly joined the ranks of concert instruments along with the mandolin and guitar, which had supplanted the lute in much quicker fashion than it apparently did in the up-time... down-timers had no knowledge of the banjo, as it had been developed well after the Ring of Fire period of history...

The rise of the banjo was due in no little part to the efforts of one Giouan Battista Veraldi. Little is known of the man. By his name, musicologists assume that he was born in northern Italy, but exactly where has not been determined. It is known that he was a lutenist in the royal court of Sweden for some time. But he enters the Ring of Fire stage in 1634, when he became the student of Atwood Cochran. Therein began the partnership that lifted both the mature guitar and the unknown banjo...

...Veraldi arrived in Venice with guitar and banjo in hand, and addressed himself to Maestro Monteverdi and to the masters of the Sellas family, foremost luthiers in Italy... saw the innovation immediately... Monteverdi's "Sonatas for Banjo and Continuo" were published within the year, and swept through Italy and southern Germany almost by storm... The literature for banjo began to expand almost exponentially... Veraldi's "Etudes for Solo Banjo" are part of the standard repertoire...

The Sellas family had received an almost incalculable advantage... samples of the mature instruments were in their hands for weeks as they measured... far in advance of the Voboams and other luthiers of France and Spain.

After a few years, Veraldi began returning to Grantville to visit his teacher. Before long, he was bringing other students with him... a school developed... students from all over, but especially from northern Italy... Master Cochran was the head, but *il primo* Veraldi was the driving force... The journals of several musicians who later became of note record seeing Master Cochran in his eighties playing together with Veraldi... loved a piece named *Dueling Banjos*, and played it with great glee... significance of the title is unknown, since by all accounts Master Cochran would play a guitar in these performances... unfortunately the music has been lost in the passage of time...

Stone Harvest

Karen Bergstralh

May 1635

Flagged iron stakes dotted the slope above the village of New Hope. Along a section of stone wall, red flags marched. Patterns of green and yellow flags flanked the wall and two lone white flags fluttered in the near distance.

"The red flags mark the walls we've found," Mike Tyler said proudly. "Each yellow flag shows what we think is the interior of a separate room or structure. Green indicates open areas between structures."

"What then do the white ones mark?" asked one of the men standing beside Mike. Ernst von Weferling's face showed real interest. He had sought out Mike the week before, asking questions about up-time archaeology and about a tour of the dig. That's when things started getting complicated.

To von Weferling's right stood short, plump, and unhappy Oscar Clausnitzer. The man reminded Mike of a garden slug, oozing discontent in place of slime. Bruno Glasewaldt, as thin as Clausnitzer was plump, fidgeted next to Clausnitzer. Glasewaldt hadn't said much this morning beyond complaining about how early the tour was.

Two days before, Glasewaldt and Clausnitzer had introduced themselves as antiquarians. Having heard about the upcoming tour they expressed their eagerness to join in. This morning, when Mike

301

appeared with the hotel's surrey instead of an up-time car, their enthusiasm had waned but they still insisted on coming along.

The fourth man, Leopold von Alvensleben, stood slightly apart, frowning. Despite his professing to be a collector of antiquities he looked, dressed, and acted more like a general surveying a battlefield. Mike knew nothing about the man beyond his polite request to join the group going to the site this morning.

"The white flags mark features we discovered but haven't examined yet. So far we think that this site has been occupied by two distinct groups." Mike walked to the nearest set of flags. This section of wall stood roughly two feet tall by six feet long. A wooden box sat on top. Mike took several potsherds from the box and presented them to his audience. "We found these here, in what was probably a kitchen. These red pieces might be Roman dinnerware. Expensive Roman dinnerware." He held out half of a shattered bright red ceramic bowl to the men. "This site isn't Roman, but it's possible that a collector of curiosities lived here."

"Not Roman?" von Alvensleben snarled. "Who would bother if it isn't Roman?" He paused for a moment, peering intently into the excavation square. "Gold! You have information about coin hordes. Where are the coins?" He drew himself up, face flushed; the riding crop in his right hand beating a tattoo against his boot.

"We haven't found any coins and I don't think that we will," Mike protested. "We're digging here because no one knows who built these walls."

"Do you think we are stupid? If this isn't a Roman ruin," Clausnitzer growled, "then the only reason to dig here is that you know of other valuable items buried here." The little man glared at Mike and added, "Who do you mistake us for?"

"He mistakes us for fools," Glasewaldt said. "To be taken in by a few pieces of broken pottery he's picked up from a village's trash pit. Show us what you've really found. If not coins, perhaps marble statues?"

Mike's temper rose. Yesterday they had seemed to understand that archaeology was about knowledge, not finding treasure. These broken bits of pottery told him more about the inhabitants than a gold coin could. He fought to keep his voice even.

"There aren't any statues or gold coins or anything of monetary value here. If there ever was anything like that. Anything valuable was taken when this place was abandoned."

"Don't think that you can fool us. Herr Clausnitzer has the right of it. Either this place is Roman or there is something of value hidden here. You must have secret knowledge about this place," von Alvensleben snapped. "I see nothing more than a pile of rocks pulled from the fields. An old house or barn, perhaps. What sources do you have? How did you know that there was Roman treasure hidden here?" The whip continued its staccato beat on his boot.

"I said it *isn't* Roman. The stone work on the remaining walls does look like Roman work, but we're well outside the area that the Romans controlled. The original builders might have had some contacts with the Romans." Mike offered the red bowl again. "This Roman pottery indicates that at some point there was contact or trade with the Romans."

"Trash! You've shown us nothing but bits of worthless trash!" Von Alvensleben reached out and knocked the remains of the bowl to the ground. His booted foot smashed down on it, shattering it into tiny pieces.

"Get the hell off my site," Mike snarled. His temper rose and his hands curled into fists. Inside he was amazed at himself. He knew that he'd grown over the last three years—from the smallest boy in his classes to one of the tallest—and that work in his mother's garden and on this dig had widened his shoulders and added muscle but...Memories of being repeatedly pounded into the ground by the Colburn twins made him avoid fights. Looking at von Alvensleben Mike realized that he topped the man by two inches and at least twenty pounds. At this moment he wanted nothing more than to wipe the sneer off the man's face. Redfaced, von Alvensleben stared at Mike, then whirled and strode off toward the hotel surrey. Clausnitzer and Glasewaldt exchanged glances and hurried after him. Ernst von Weferling stood calmly, looking slightly amused.

The surrey's driver frowned at Mike. Five men had ridden out from the hotel and he was expecting four to ride back. He was probably hoping for additional tips. Unhappy passengers were unlikely tippers.

"Sir," Mike addressed von Weferling politely. "Do you wish to go back, too?"

"Certainly there is a horse I can rent in the village." Von Weferling smiled tightly. He waved the surrey away and watched as it moved off. He turnd back and said, "I'd like to have you explain more about this archaeological site without the extraneous commentary from the ignorant and ill-informed. Clausnitzer and Glasewaldt have little learning and less Latin. Alvensleben is a complete fraud." Von Weferling paused and looked around. "How certain are you that this isn't a Roman villa? Their writings indicate that they were hundreds of miles from here but if you've found Roman pottery..."

"The style of stonework looks like pictures I've seen of Roman walls and I'm pretty sure that the red pottery is Roman. However, as you said, there aren't any records that show Roman settlements in this area. It could have been built years or centuries after the Romans. The Roman bowl might have been traded for or part of a collection of curiosities. Ask me again in a couple of years and I might have an answer." Mike shrugged. There was so much that he didn't know, so much information that had been lost. So much had to be relearned.

"Up-time," he continued, "they could figure out who had lived in a place at different times from the pottery."

"My researchers tell me that you have only bits and pieces of archaeological knowledge. I've read a précis of the theory of identifying pottery but I understood that there are only a few pictures of identified pottery in the library."

"Yes, sir. But we lucked out on the Roman stuff. Back up-time, one of my girlfriend's cousins visited Germany. She toured a well documented excavation—a Roman *villa rustica*." Mike grinned widely. "It had been partly restored as a museum. Lannie picked up a couple of brochures and saved them. Along with pictures of the stonework there were pictures of Roman pottery. We have to rebuild the pottery databases but we aren't starting completely from scratch. At least not for the Roman stuff. For now we save every pottery sherd, document where it came from, measure it and try to match it to other sherds to see if we can figure out what the whole piece looked like. If it comes out of the same level or is close to a piece that we think is Roman, we mark it as possibly Roman. Or at least possibly from the Roman period. Someday someone will know if we've gotten the designations right. For now, your guess as to who built this place is as good as mine. Ten, twenty, or a hundred years from now someone may figure it out from the pottery."

"Ah, you are looking years ahead. That is good. I've a cousin at the university in Jena who might be interested in discussing archaeology with you. Now, that pair of green flags, do you think that might have been a gate?'

"It seems to be in the right location for one. We haven't managed to trace the wall completely so we don't yet know if it encloses the site. That's one of things I'm trying to establish. Whenever it was built and whoever built it, it looks like it was a farm complex. The location's wrong for a fort and the layout so far seems to follow that of a *villa rustica*. If that's right then there should be a house, a couple of workshops, at least one barn, and quarters for slaves and servants—all enclosed by a wall."

"How did it go today?" Rob Clark handed Mike a cold bottle of root beer. "Try this while you tell me."

"One out of four listened and seemed to understand." Mike smiled sardonically. "Not a great start for the establishment of real archaeology as opposed to pot and treasure hunting." He sat down on the porch swing and took a swig. "Not bad, Rob, not bad at all. Tastes kind of like the way I remember A&W did. Is it a new product?"

"One out of four is a far better ratio than I've had trying to convince people that training horses does not require the extensive use of whips. Part of our problem is our ages. It's hard for anyone to accept that we could know more about a subject than the older folks." Rob sipped his root beer. "Yeah, this is by a new brew master in town. He's looking for something different. We've got to have twenty, maybe thirty guys brewing beer. One more doesn't stand much of a chance against that kind of competition."

"So you set him up, huh?" Mike leaned back, holding the cold bottle against his face. "What else is he trying?"

"Root beer's the start. Got the recipe from an old cookbook somebody gave the library. I figure just the root beer alone should do well."

"Ultimate goal is Pepsi?"

"Coke!"

"If your brew master comes up with any acceptable cola he'll make a mint." Mike finished off his bottle. "I never much liked root beer but this is, um, a taste of home."

"Yeah. Beer's not bad but I'd rather not walk around with a

buzz on all day. Especially not working with the horses. They can be dangerous enough when you're stone cold sober." Rob pulled another bottle out of the cooler beside his chair and handed it to Mike.

"You and Lannie ever finish that list of all the ways a horse can mess you up?"

"No," Lannie Clark's voice answered from behind Mike. "It was rather pointless. How'd your show-and-tell go?" She sat down heavily beside Rob and held out her hand. He put a root beer bottle in it.

Mike sighed. "Three of them accused me of holding out on them because I didn't show them piles of gold. Or Roman statues worth fabulous sums."

"They sound like up-time pot hunters and illegal art collectors." She sipped the root beer, leaned back against her husband and groaned. "Thank you, honey. You finally found something I could drink without worrying about the baby."

"Sorry it took so long, my dear." Rob bent down and kissed her forehead.

"So this isn't a plot to satisfy the cravings of all the up-timers?" Mike teased.

"Just wait until you get married, Michael Tyler, just wait." An evil grin was plastered across Rob's face. "See what hoops you jump through to keep your wife happy!"

"Especially when she's nine months pregnant." Lannie's smile had a Mona Lisa quality to it. "I'm being so-o-o-o-o mean to him."

The next morning Rob saddled one of the young horses he was training. The blood-bay filly was a four-year-old daughter of his Spanish stallion and an up-time quarter horse mare. Her siblings had brought top prices in the spring horse fair at Jena.

It was a fine morning with just a hint of clouds on the western horizon. The filly behaved herself, eyeing the sheep grazing along the road but doing no more than snorting. He traded greetings with the girl watching the sheep. Five donkeys in the last pasture got more of a reaction from the filly and Rob stopped her, making her stand and look until the donkeys went from scary to boring.

Rob checked the condition of the pastures as he rode past. When the last fence gave way to open fields his attention turned to the crops. The barley was doing well and the oats on the other side of the road looked good, too. Closer to the village he could see people working in gardens.

"Good morning, Herr Clark. What brings you to us today?" Heinrich Strelow, the mayor of New Hope, greeted him.

"Good morning, Herr Strelow." Rob dismounted, then paused. The mayor's young daughter, Katerina, shyly stepped forward and took the reins of his filly.

"Thank you, Katerina. If you could unsaddle her and brush her a bit..." The girl smiled and led the filly off.

"It's good of you to let her care for your horse." Heinrich sighed and gestured after his daughter. "Ever since her mother was killed she comes alive only around the horses."

"Any time she feels up to it she can come up to the ranch and work with my horses. They respond well to her touch. When she's older she'll make a good trainer."

"Come, come to the inn. You must see the progress we've made. I trust you didn't ride down here just to let my little girl brush your horse." Heinrich guided Rob toward a two-story building that had scaffolding around it. "Lutz and his crew finished the walls last week. The roof was finished two days ago and the windows are being put in. It is the last of the village buildings to be finished." The mayor's pride was evident in every word. "Never would I have thought that we could rebuild so much so quickly. Without your help it wouldn't have been possible."

Inside the smell of raw wood and fresh whitewash was strong. Rob noted that while there were several long tables with benches, groups of smaller tables and chairs were also scattered around. The mayor led him across the room to an alcove featuring a semi-circular padded seat surrounding a circular table. The seat was upholstered in red leather and he'd swear that the tabletop was Formica. It reminded him of a booth in a 1950s style diner.

Carl Bieber, the innkeeper, bustled up with a pair of beer mugs. He set them down, then took a rag out of his apron pocket and wiped the table. "Beautiful, isn't it, Herr Clark? Just like in an up-time cafe." The innkeeper bubbled with pride.

"Um, yes, Carl." Rob admired the table for a few moments and then turned to the mayor. "Heinrich, I'd like to have Carl join us for a bit, too. What I want to talk about concerns the whole village."

"Should I call out the rest of the council, too?" Heinrich asked.

"No, not yet. My worries may not be real. If you think that they are, you can pass on my concerns." Rob paused, drank some beer and put his thoughts in order. "I'm concerned about the safety of the people working up at the dig site. Talking to Mike Tyler yesterday I realized that some people think that they are digging for buried treasures. One man mentioned stashes of gold coins."

"And the whiff of gold or silver brings out the worst in men," Heinrich said. "This could be a serious threat. Do you want to call out our militia?"

Rob stroked his mustache. Was he jumping at monsters in the closet or was there a real threat?

"I don't know . . . Three of the men up there yesterday were convinced that Mike had already found treasure or knew where it was hidden. They could be nothing more sinister than men briefly overtaken by gold fever."

"Those men could be respectable, but they may have acquaintances who are not." Heinrich nodded, a thoughtful frown on his face. After a few moments he looked up and continued. "The militia needs practice. We can have three or four men practice each day by guarding the dig. I'll tell the men who are working there to go armed, too. We will see that nothing happens to the dig or young Tyler." The man gave Rob a shrewd look. "When my grandchildren are my age that dig will be famous all over Europe. Scholars will come to see where up-time archaeology was first done."

"Not just scholars, but, what is the term—tourists?" Carl added emphatically. He thumped the tabletop. "They will stay in this inn and the village will grow rich off their money." He leaned forward, enthusiasm showing on his face. "Erik Wiess was saying just last week that we should build a place to show off and explain what they dig out of the ground. A museum, he said."

Heinrich frowned and shook his head. "It would be nice but it will be years before we have enough money to build it."

Mike had somehow convinced these folks that their history was valuable enough to protect and display. Given the number of up-timers who didn't understand, Rob hadn't expected Mike would succeed.

Archaeology had always fascinated Rob. Up-time he'd made it to most major museums in the U.S. and a number in Europe. For all that fascination Rob knew he lacked the patience and passion to devote his life to recreating the science of archaeology. Mike had the passion needed. So far he'd also had the patience it required.

Three years before, when Jo Ann Manning first dragged Mike to a family dinner, his passion for archaeology had overcome his shyness. Since then he and Rob had talked many times. Two years ago Rob made the decision to support Mike's vision however he could. Here was another opportunity.

"Decide where you want to build your museum. Mike will have ideas about what it needs. I'm sure he'll want room for laboratories to work with the artifacts. And we have to remember that our dig is just the first. When you have something worked up, come and talk to me. I'll fund it as far as practicable."

Heinrich and Carl stared at him, speechless. Finally Heinrich spoke.

"Too generous, Rob. That's too generous. We owe you and your aunt so much already."

"No, it needs to be done. Someone needs to lead the way. Why shouldn't that be the people of New Hope? Name it for my aunt and run it right—that's all I'll ask."

"The Helen Bennington Clark Museum. We shall set standards that the professors in Jena will envy!" Carl clapped Rob on the shoulder.

Heinrich looked thoughtful. He leaned forward and grasped Rob's hand.

"We'll do it. It will be a fitting honor. She gave us refuge and helped us reclaim our land. Speaking of which, Herr Hartzschorn was here yesterday. He's found the last claimant for the woodlot."

It was Rob's turn to nod. He'd talked to the lawyer two days before. "I've authorized him to negotiate for it. Once we get the paperwork signed I'll turn the landrights over to the *Gemeinde* on the same terms as the rest of the leases."

The two men relaxed and smiled. Rob's aunt had set those terms before she died. New Hope was the result of the survivors of two villages destroyed by the war combining forces. Before the Ring of Fire, the villagers had managed to build five houses and plant gardens but they hadn't been able to pay their leases for several years.

Sliding Rock Farm lost the far end of the valley it sat in to the Ring of Fire. Now the steep slopes of West Virginia hills opened out into a gently rolling vista. While the Clarks lost about a third of their property, the German farmers lost closer to three hundred acres. It took Rob's aunt a month to find Ernst Hartzschorn, a down-time German lawyer, among the refugees crowding Grantville. She'd set Hartzschorn to work finding a way to settle the mess fairly. Before her death she'd charged Rob to finish the job.

A noise from outside interrupted Rob's thoughts. As he realized he was hearing a car engine Liz Manning burst through the inn's door and stumbled against a table.

"Rob! Hey, Rob! It's the baby! Lannie's water broke and Aunt Maggie sent me down to get you."

The room was quiet. Minutes before, Maggie O'Reilly and the midwife had finished cleaning up and gone downstairs, chatting amiably. Lannie slept while Rob gingerly cradled his newborn son. He looked down at this tiny bit of humanity. Love, joy, wonder, awe, fear, and guilt all bubbled within him blending and mixing until he couldn't say exactly what it was he felt. The baby opened his eyes and stared up at him.

"Scary, isn't it?"

Rob looked up to see Ev Parker standing in the doorway. "Yes, sir." Rob sighed and smiled down at the child. "Guess it's starting to hit me just how scary parenthood can be. Horses I know. Business I know. With him I don't even know where to start…"

"Like anything else, son. You start at the beginning. For now you love him, feed him, diaper him, and do your best to keep him safe. Later, as he grows, you love him, teach him, discipline him, show him how to behave, and worry about him." Ev eased down into the big old rocking chair. "You're a good man, Rob. You'll do fine."

"Thank you, sir. Would you like to hold him?"

"I surely would. He's my first great-grandchild, at least as far as I know." Ev's voice was soft and he cradled the baby gently.

"Did you tell Grandpa what we named him?" Lannie asked sleepily from the bed.

"Not yet. Why don't you tell him?" Rob leaned over and took his wife's hand.

"Coward." Lannie smiled up at him.

"No, just a bit overwhelmed."

"Hey, buster, I'm the one who did all the work." Lannie squeezed Rob's hand and looked over at her grandfather. "Grandpa, meet Everett Henry Clark."

The light from the bedside lamp glistened off the tears that rolled down the old man's cheeks.

September 1635

Mike Tyler slid off his horse, staring around. The slope in front of him was pockmarked with holes. Anger burned across his mind. He took a deep breath, closed his eyes, and started counting. By the time he reached thirty-seven he had to open his eyes.

Calmer, he surveyed the hillside again. The damage wasn't as bad as it first appeared. Holes did litter the dig site but there were only about ten of them.

He could hear voices coming from the far side of the shepherd's hut he'd been using for storage. He strode toward the hut, trying to catalogue the damage. Four days ago this had been this universe's second scientific archaeological dig. Now his carefully laid out grid of stakes and string was gone. The straight sides of his three-meter square test hole were gone, collapsed, and in the center was a ragged hole. Pottery shards were scattered in the dirt piles. The holes weren't completely random. Whoever had done this had used Mike's site map. The biggest hole was where he had guessed the main house might be.

When he stepped around the hut two men nodded warily at him. His assistants from New Hope, Carl Heimpol and Peter Matz, stood next to a pile of newly dug dirt, leaning on their shovels. Carl tilted his head toward three figures uphill of them and shrugged. Mike recognized the loud voice and rotund figure stuffed into clothes more suited for town than a German hillside. Herr Martin Schuler was holding forth at full volume.

The two listening to Schuler were Rob and Lannie Clark. Mike didn't have a clue why those two would be standing in the middle of his dig, talking to Herr Schuler. Lannie saw Mike and smiled. She called out as she walked down to meet him.

"Glad to see you." Lannie gave him a brief hug and a peck on the cheek. Very quietly she added, "Keep quiet and let us handle Schuler."

Mike swallowed hard, glad to comply. He didn't trust himself to speak to Schuler just now. Linking her arm with his, she tugged him up the hill.

Rob shook Mike's hand, quirked an eyebrow and tilted his head toward Schuler. Mike returned a slight nod. Whatever was going on, he'd let Rob and Lannie do the talking.

Herr Schuler frowned, apparently unhappy to see Mike. A week before, when Mike said that he was going up to Grantville for a few days, Schuler had reminded him that Mike had been hired to conduct this dig, not run around the countryside. The man had complained so much that Mike had cut his trip short and returned two days early. It was one more puzzle. A happier thought struck. Maybe Schuler wasn't mad at Mike. Maybe he was just unhappy to have the up-timers' attention shift away from himself.

"Now, Herr Clark," Schuler began. "As I was saying we will find wonderful things here. Many wonderful Roman marble statues await discovery. Of course, it would be easier and faster if I could have one of the, ah, mechanical diggers—one of your wonderful oxdozers, perhaps." There was an anticipatory gleam in the man's eyes. His fingers played with his belt purse. "Sadly, because of recent business reverses, temporary to be sure, a small sum to support the workers will be needed. But think of the opportunities to own a piece of art that belonged to Caesar Augustus! Perhaps we will find a gold necklace or two to adorn your charming wife's neck."

Mike's temper rose. He'd repeatedly told Schuler that this wasn't a Roman site. He'd told Schuler that as often as he'd told him that at best they might find a few lost coins. What was the man up to? Glancing at Lannie, Mike caught her frown. He shook his head and remained silent.

"If I want Roman statues I'll have one of my agents in Italy buy them," Rob drawled. He dropped an arm across Mike's shoulders before continuing. "I am willing to support a proper archaeological dig organized and run by Mr. Tyler. I do not and will not lend support to wild goose chases or treasure hunts."

"Whatever would I do with another gold necklace?" Lannie said. "Rob's aunt left me dozens." She grinned maliciously. "You know, I was in Germany in 1998. This place looks like the dig I visited. The only statue they found was a battered old sandstone head. Come on, guys, the innkeeper promised me veal schnitzel for dinner." She started off down the hill with the men trailing behind her. Schuler sputtered and followed, protesting all the way.

A road meandered along the base of the slope. Near it a number of horses stood in the shade of a grove of trees. As the group approached, three men started slipping bridles on the animals. After a moment Mike recognized them. He had heard Rob use the term "battered old fireplug" to describe the shortest man. It certainly fit Wilf Jones. The second man was Dieter Wiesskamp, four or five inches taller than Jones but as solidly built. Christian du Champ's whip thin build and disapproving face rounded out the three.

They were horse traders and good friends of Rob and Lannie. Before becoming horse traders they had been mercenary soldiers. Something very odd was going on if these three were pretending to be servants.

"I'm looking forward to dinner," Rob said as he swung up onto the horse Christian was holding. "I'd like your opinion on some wine the innkeeper has."

"We've stopped there before," Lannie added. She let Wilf assist her onto her horse. "The innkeeper has added several up-time style suites and a private dining room."

Mike's suspicions rose further. Lannie and Rob needed help onto their horses the way a bird needed help flying. He'd save his questions until dinner but it had better come soon. Herr Schuler joined them, puffing hard. It took the combined efforts of Wilf and Dieter to get the man onto his horse.

Belatedly realizing that he'd left his own horse up the hill, Mike turned around. He nearly knocked Carl Heimpol down.

"Brought you your horse, Mike," Carl said nervously, handing over the reins. Under his breath he added, "Sorry about the holes, but Schuler..." His words trailed off as he glanced at Herr Schuler's back. His look should have dropped Schuler to the ground, dead.

"We didn't want to leave until we talked to you," Carl said. "Not until we could explain."

"Thanks, Carl." Mike smiled at the glum man. "It's okay. He was paying the bills so you had to do what he wanted. He's wrecked our work so we'll pack up and leave. Let him hire somebody else to dig random holes. Did he ever pay you? Do you guys have enough money to get home?"

"Yes, die Parkerin gave us more than enough."

"Go home, then. We should have a few weeks of decent weather. Might be a good time to check for the northern run of the wall at the New Hope dig."

"Sure, Mike." Peter Matz joined the discussion. His face was serious and his eyes darted nervously toward the woods along the ridgeline. "Watch yourself. There are a couple of men lurking in those trees on the ridge." A grin flitted across his face. "I don't like the looks of Herr Clark's 'servants,' either. They remind me of a disreputable bunch of horse traders we know. The ones that always find trouble."

"Yeah, but if these three are down here..." Mike smiled. "...I bet we can guess who the men on the ridge are." He shook hands with both men and swung into the saddle, his confusion deepening. What the heck was going on? He had the same nagging feeling that he got when he read a mystery story and found at the end he'd missed half of the clues.

Carl's face split into a wide grin. "At least if trouble comes it will find these servants are war dogs, not sheep."

"And with them around I'll be as safe as can be."

"Still, don't let Schuler or any of his people get you alone." Peter said. "He's not happy with you. The man thinks you owe him treasure."

"Man, that was the best dinner I've had since the last time I saw Grandma." Mike leaned back in his chair and lifted his wine glass to his hosts. "Thank you. Thank you for paying the guys, too."

"No problemo, sport," Lannie said. "Cora cooks a mean pot roast but I think she'd be hard pressed to match this meal."

"I don't think you'd better tell her that." Mike mopped a last bit of sauce with a piece of bread. "Is this a good time to ask what the heck you two are doing here?"

"Told you he's no dummy." Lannie poked her husband.

Rob threw his hands up in surrender. "I've never thought he was. Sorry, Michael, but I wasn't certain you knew what was going on around you."

"I know that I don't."

"We didn't either until Jo Ann told us about the invitation from Schuler to check out his 'Roman' site. She thought there was something fishy about the whole thing. She was right."

Mike felt his world turn upside down. He'd already knew that Schuler thought the site was Roman and remained convinced of that no matter what Mike said. Today, at the site, he'd come to the conclusion that Schuler also was convinced that treasure was buried there. As bad as that was, something in Rob's tone and the look on Lannie's face said there was more.

"I've got an extensive set of business contacts and Schuler's name keeps popping up in odd places." Rob's face was set. "Schuler has a partner, one Conrad Uller. Things happen around those two. Not so nice things. When Jo Ann brought her suspicions to us I did some more digging. Then I talked to Major Stein. Turns out that the authorities in several cities have suspicions about Uller and Schuler."

"They're con artists, among other things. It looks like you were intended to be a front for one of Uller's cons," Lannie added, patting Mike's hand. "He apparently planned to have Schuler show the site and a couple of Roman statues to suckers and then squeeze them for money to continue digging."

"Uller's name's been mentioned but he's never come around when I've been there," Mike said, his tone matching his glum mood. "I told Schuler that the site isn't Roman. All we've found are bits of stone walls and they don't look anything like the pictures of Roman stonework. They don't look like the New Hope walls, either. What I told Schuler was that there might be some Roman influences at the site. That we might, just might, find odds and ends of Roman pottery and possibly a mosaic floor. All I know right now is that there are several stone walls." What Lannie had said about Roman statues sunk in and he asked, "Where's this guy Uller getting Roman statues?"

"He isn't depending on you finding any." Lannie shook her head. "He's got a nice little set-up in Bamberg doing bad copies of Roman statues from photographs. Your men said that he was out to the site twice while you were away for your grandfather's birthday party. Probably figuring out which hole to stash the fakes in."

"I'd bet that he's counting on his suckers not knowing what a real Roman statue looks like," Rob said. "If you ever actually found something, it would be gravy."

"Why all the holes, then?"

"For show." Rob gave him a sympathetic look. "Your nice, controlled square isn't very impressive. Got to show the marks that you're looking."

"Schuler may seriously think that there is some kind of treasure buried there," Lannie added thoughtfully. "He gave me that impression today. Maybe the con artist has conned himself."

There was a soft knock on the door. Wilf stepped in and carefully closed it behind him. Mike got a glimpse of Christian leaning against the wall outside.

"There were three men, heavily armed, waiting in the trees at the stone bridge we crossed," Wilf reported. "Reichard's, ah, talking to them."

"Only three?" Lannie asked.

Wilf shrugged. "Three were all Reichard found. He says the signs show only three at that spot."

"Reichard would know." Rob's grin was feral. "That's one of Uller's other little sidelines—kidnapping for ransom. Nobody has been able to find proof he or Schuler are behind it. Schuler's well connected so the authorities' hands are tied without evidence. Major Stein volunteered Wilf and the guys to find some evidence. Lannie and I are the bait. Did they really intend to kidnap us?"

"Looks that way. There was a farm cart hidden in the trees. It was loaded with bags of vegetables." Wilf pulled an extra chair up to the table. He made a crude map with several forks and a couple of spoons.

"It's a nice spot for a snatch. The bridge is narrow and the road makes a sharp turn, parallel to the stream just the other side. If it were me, I'd wait until the party I'm intending to grab cleared the bridge. One man could slip in between them and the rest of the party. Give him a musket or pistol and he'll have no trouble holding off a gaggle of servants. The rest then slide out of the trees and grab bridles. Hustle the victims off to the waiting cart, tie them up, toss them aboard, rearrange the sacks, and off we'd go. If I was running such a show I'd make sure that my Judas goat was also snatched to throw off suspicions." Wilf's grin matched Rob's.

"Schuler insisted that we go across that bridge first. We were suspicious and ready." Lannie didn't smile but she did pat the fanny pack at her waist. Mike knew she kept an automatic in that pack along with extra clips.

"He kept glancing into the woods along the road. He must have been greatly disappointed," Rob added.

"Aye, Reichard and Klaus got there first. The three kidnappers were eager to throw themselves on the mercies of the authorities. Hopefully they are equally eager to inform on Uller and Schuler." Wilf pulled an empty wine glass over and poured himself some wine. He took a careful sip. "Good wine. The stuff they give servants here is horse piss."

"Our part of the job is done, then." Lannie took her husband's hand. "You and I need to get home. We have responsibilities. We have a baby who needs his mother and father at home, not off adventuring. Besides, Grandpa is spoiling him rotten while we're gone."

"We can leave early and be back by late afternoon," Rob said reasonably. "Grandpa Ev can't spoil Little Ev too badly in that short a time. Can he?"

"Just wait, buster. Just wait and you'll see how fast Grandpa can spoil a kid."

"Mike, can you be ready to leave by seven tomorrow?" Rob asked.

Rob's question interrupted Mike's thoughts. Finding out that Schuler really was working some kind of a con made him feel like an idiot. He felt like when he was eight and his brother Aaron explained that Santa Claus wasn't real—unbelievably stupid for having believed for so long. If he couldn't tell when he was being used then his dad was right and he was just a dumb kid. Maybe he should give up trying to reinvent up-time archaeology—leave it to someone smarter.

Mike sighed and looked up. "Sure, Rob. I've got a room at the Black Boar. I'll meet you here in the morning." Tonight was not the time to decide anything. He was tired and confused. As Gramps was fond of saying, he'd need to "think on it."

Dreams stomped through Mike's head. Weird dreams of jolting, bumps, someone yelling words he couldn't quite make out. Then there was the nausea. He didn't think that dreams should include nausea or the bad smells assaulting his nose. The sound of church bells made even less sense.

His eyes opened. He was on a lumpy bed in a small room. There was a single, small, many-paned window on the wall across from the bed. Had he gotten drunk? Had the innkeeper hauled him in here? His pounding head and heaving stomach supported that scenario.

Mike managed to sit up. His right leg felt heavy and he ached all over. Maybe he'd been in a fight or was coming down with the flu. A clanking noise barely registered. He grabbed the empty chamber pot sitting next to the bed as his stomach lurched. After dry heaving a couple of times his stomach settled for on and off protesting in place of open rebellion.

The room was smaller than he'd first thought. The wall the bed was on was little more than six feet long and the brick side walls stretched no more than eight feet to the wall with the window. There was a door in the wall to his right. The bed itself seemed to be a straw-stuffed mattress over a badly strung bed frame. Near the bed sat a small table with a chair under it.

Some of the odors, he discovered, came from the filthy blanket on the bed. The rest of the smell came from him. His clothes were as filthy as the blanket. Smells of sweat, dirt, manure, urine, and blood blended into an indescribable reek. What he could see of his shirt was stained to match the aromas wafting from it.

Mike felt his upper lip and the side of his face. The only places on his face where he could grow hair were his side burns and upper lip and he'd shaved them both yesterday. His stubble said it had been two or three days since the razor's touch.

Church bells reclaimed his attention. Through the wavy glass panes he could just make out a bell tower. From the bells he guessed that today was Sunday. Damn! He must have gotten massively drunk to lose three days. He dropped his aching head into his hands and tried to think. He remembered having dinner with Rob and Lannie Clark at their inn. That memory brought up another; he'd left them and gone to the Black Boar, a cheaper inn, where he had a room. He must have started drinking there.

Something about that bell tower bothered him. Something wasn't right. Part of his brain insisted he needed to pay attention. The Black Boar wasn't on the town square. It was off on a side street two blocks away and there were several taller buildings between it and the town square. There was no way you could see the church's bell tower from any of the inn's windows. He must be in a different inn. But that table and chair next to the bed didn't belong in any inn room Mike had seen. Admittedly, he hadn't been in that many inns, but he thought that the smelly bed indicated a really cheap inn. The table and chair were too nicely made to fit with a cheap inn.

Mike stood up, intending to get a better look through the window. The clanking sound came again and his right leg stopped abruptly, throwing him to the ground. Stunned, he stared at the iron cuff around his right ankle. A stout chain stretched from the cuff to an eyebolt set in the wall. He tugged the chain but the eyebolt remained securely set. The cuff was held shut by a large brass padlock. Mike giggled in disbelief. This was like a bad movie, one of those really bad horror movies.

Sounds from outside the door resolved into footsteps and someone talking. Not wanting whoever it was to find him sprawled on the floor, Mike stood up. The first man through the door was large, rough looking, and held a flintlock pistol in his hand. That pistol was pointed at Mike.

"Sit on the bed," the man commanded.

Mike sat, disinclined to argue. Not that there was any way he could dispute the command. His chain leash was too short, his head hurt badly, and his stomach was revolting again. His mind, though, was working overtime.

The second man through the door was Herr Schuler, who carried a large roll of paper. A third man, a servant from his dress and demeanor, slid through the door and put a tray on the table. The tray held a stein, a bowl of what looked to be thin soup, and several slices of bread. When the servant left, Schuler placed the rolled up paper on the table beside the tray. Several things clicked into place in Mike's mind.

"Let me guess," Mike said in a sarcastic tone, "You drugged me, kidnapped me, and imprisoned me because I couldn't tell you were to find vast hordes of gold."

"Now, Herr Tyler, you should have been less greedy and more reasonable." Schuler's mouth was smiling but his eyes looked cold, snakelike. "Here is your 'site-plan.' All you need to do is mark on it where items of value will be found."

"I told you before, I can't do that. Your site isn't a Roman villa." Mike crossed his arms. His hands were shaking and he didn't want Schuler or his goon to see how scared he was. "Besides, there's not much information about the Romans in Germany. There is 'they were here and there and they built these roads,' not 'look here for buried treasure.' The records just aren't there."

"Ah, yes, that seems to be true about the books in the main library. However, my sources tell me that you have special knowledge about Roman villas. My partner has verified this. You boasted about it on a private tour of your diggings at New Hope."

"If your partner actually talked to Herr von Weferling he'd know that I have a pair of brochures about *one*, count 'em, *one*, Roman villa in Germany. The one Mrs. Clark mentioned. I showed the brochures to Weferling. He can tell you what was and wasn't in them. The only thing that came close to your 'marble statues' was a broken, crudely carved sandstone head of Athena. Oh, yeah, there were a couple of copper coins from later, much later, around the year 1796. No gold, no statues, no silver. The owners packed up all the valuable stuff when they moved out. Anything that the Romans might have left is long gone, sold or carted off by their German descendents. Anyway, your 'Roman villa' is nowhere close to the area the Romans colonized."

The smile disappeared from Schuler's face. "Don't try your lies on me, boy," he hissed. "If there is nothing of value you wouldn't spend time digging. A wealthy man like Herr Clark isn't paying you to harvest stones. Don't waste my time prattling on about your sacred archlogy."

Mike sighed and tried again. "It's archaeology, as in the study of archaic things. Your sources in Grantville should have told you that archaeologists don't dig looking for gold. They dig looking for knowledge from everyday items."

The goon stepped forward, sneering, and pointed his pistol at Mike's face. "Give me ten minutes with him, he'll spill everything he knows."

"No," Schuler said firmly, "not yet. I'll let him think about it for awhile." He glared. "Sooner or later you *will* give me the information. Or you will give it to Klaus."

Schuler started out the doorway. The goon picked up the bowl of soup and flipped the liquid into Mike's face. "Herr Schuler doesn't like people who don't do what he wants." Then he followed Schuler out, slamming the door behind him.

Luckily the soup was only lukewarm. Mike found a relatively clean corner of the blanket and wiped his face. Moving slowly, he rose, pulled out the chair, and sat on it. His chain let him, just. He needed to think.

Mike had been sitting at the table for an hour or so. His stomach was managing to keep down the bread and a few sips of beer. His head and body still ached but his mind was clearer. Marking up the site plan might buy him a few days while Schuler checked it out. When they found nothing Schuler would probably have Klaus the goon kill him. Or, once he had the marked plan, Schuler could decide that Mike was a liability and kill him immediately. Mike scratched his chin. Not marking the site plan could buy him either a couple of days or an appointment with Klaus the goon. He still couldn't decide.

The chain and ankle cuff had to go. He shifted his attention to the wall and the mortar around it. The mortar looked new and it felt slightly damp. He kneeled next to the eyebolt, took a length of chain in his hands, and began to jerk it back and forth. A minuscule gap appeared around the eyebolt. The chain was cutting into his hands so he grabbed the blanket, wrapped it around the chain, and tried again. Some time later he leaned back and examined the results. There was a definite gap around the shaft of the eyebolt and with each jerk he had felt a tiny bit of give.

At the rate he was going it could take days to pull the eyebolt out of the wall. Mike didn't think he had days. He looked around the room. The mortar might be soft enough to dig out but he needed something to dig with. Remembering the spoon that had come with the soup, Mike started to get up. A bit of color under the bed attracted his attention. In a moment he retrieved it.

Schuler was an idiot. Or maybe it was Klaus the goon who was the idiot. Someone had chucked Mike's backpack under the bed. He dumped it out. The pack had been searched. Mike's gun and ammo were missing as was his folding knife, but his trowel was there. The trowel's edges were nearly knife sharp. It would be awkward to use but he had a weapon. Peeling back the Velcro from an outside pocket he found the soft, rolled up leather pouch that held his dental picks. Mike took several deep breaths, struggling not to shout with glee, and then went to work on the padlock.

"Getting the chain out of the wall would be nice," he crooned to the padlock. "But that leaves me with six feet of chain attached. Hard to sneak away from the bad guys with all that iron clanking. Get rid of you, my lovely, and I'm free as a bird."

Mike had picked padlocks before. His brother had showed him how years before using paperclips and other bits of stiff wire. The dental picks, as fragile as they looked, were all top quality steel. Normally he used them for delicate excavation work, but they also made excellent picklocks. This padlock was huge compared to the ones Mike had practiced on, but he figured that the principles were the same. After some fumbling there was a click and the lock fell open.

Gently, Mike removed the padlock and opened the cuff. Pain flared and he saw that the cuff had chewed through his sock and into the soft flesh above his boot. He opened another pocket on his backpack, found his first aid kit and cleaned the wound thoroughly. Luckily there was a clean pair of socks in the backpack, so he put them on. His shirt and pants were awfully fragrant, enough that dogs wouldn't be necessary to track him, not the way he smelled.

There wasn't any water to wash with but clean clothes from his pack should lessen his stink. When he got out he'd need to find the city guard. With any luck, the clean clothes would make them at least listen to his story instead of tossing him in jail as one more drunk.

Finally feeling halfway decent, Mike stuffed his gear back in the pack. He picked up the trowel, walked to the door and listened. Silence. A look out the window confirmed that he was high up, on a third or fourth story, and there wasn't a hint of a ledge. He went back to the door and eased it open. The hallway ended to his left in a staircase. Three other doors along the hall stood open, showing rooms like his. Only the room directly across from his showed any signs of recent inhabitation. Below him he could hear muffled sounds of someone yelling.

As quietly as he could, Mike descended the stairs, praying that none of the treads creaked. The next floor presented two doors, both closed and another stairway at the far end. Mike passed on investigating. He wanted out of this house. The next flight down brought him into an empty kitchen. Probably not empty for long, since something bubbled in a pot hung over the fire. Candles hung above a table provided a surprising amount of light.

He froze in place; only his eyes moved, searching for a way out. There should be a door into a yard or alley; he hoped for an alley. His eyes found a door in the right place. More odd noises came from the front of the house. Now was not the time to stick around.

Mike muttered a quick prayer that this wasn't the cellar door, opened it, and slid through. For a moment he thought he had found the cellar. The alleyway was narrow and the houses on the other side blocked any sunlight. Waiting for his eyes to adjust he tried to determine if anybody else was in the alley. He heard someone enter the kitchen behind him, talking loudly. Spurred into action by thoughts of recapture, he dashed down the alley, and slammed head first into Klaus the goon. The impact knocked Mike down.

Klaus didn't have his pistol but he did have a knife on his belt. Growling, the goon reached for that knife. Mike smashed his boot into the logical target. The man's hands flew his crotch and he moaned. Mike rolled away, grabbed the trowel, and staggered to his feet. Klaus the goon was bent over, clutching himself and groaning.

"Nicely done, Michael. Nicely done!" The high tenor voice came from the darkest part of the alley. Reichard Blucher stepped out, grabbed Klaus the goon by the hair, and slammed the man's head into the wall of the house.

"That will take his mind off his other pain."

Mike straightened up and gave a sigh of relief. The cavalry had arrived. "Where are Rob and Lannie? Are they okay?"

Reichard smiled. "They're fine. When you didn't show up Thursday morning Wilf insisted that they go back to Grantville. We came looking for you." The big man clapped Mike on the shoulder. He kicked the groaning Klaus. "You're turning into a regular Indiana Jones, young Michael."

Wilf Jones walked out the kitchen door and into the alley. He looked from Mike to Klaus the goon and back.

"Glad to see you're in one piece, Michael. Schuler will be, too. When we didn't find you in the house Christian started to lovingly describe the 'death of a thousand cuts' to him. The head of the Bamberg city guard is in there, suggesting additional, cruder measures."

Jo Ann was snuggled tightly against Mike on the sofa, firmly holding his left hand. They were sitting in the Clarks' comfortable and familiar living room, listening while Wilf and Christian finished up the story of finding Mike.

"Michael saved himself. We just came along and cleaned up the mess he left." Christian smiled and winked at Mike. "Reichard saw him in action and was impressed with how he handled himself."

"Aye," Wilf agreed, "impressed enough to suggest that we take him along the next time we go horse trading."

Mike blushed, pleased at the compliment and half-appalled at the thought of the kinds of trouble Wilf and his friends attracted.

Jo Ann squeezed the hand she was holding. "Mike's heard from Jena. They want him to teach archaeology."

"Well, not really teach." Mike's blush deepened as he explained. "I won't be a professor, more like a guest lecturer. It's kind of weird. I'll be a student but they want me to present some lectures on up-time archaeology, too." The doubts he'd felt earlier were dying down. The letter proved that his efforts to reinvent up-time archaeology weren't wasted and that there were smart people who didn't think he was just a dumb kid. Even his dad had been impressed.

Lannie nudged her husband. Rob stood, excused himself, and left the room. He returned shortly, holding something behind his back.

"In light of your recent adventures," Rob said, "and especially your new status as a college lecturer, we thought these additions to your wardrobe were appropriate." Rob held his hands out. The right held a brown leather jacket; the left a brown fedora. "You'll have to provide the bullwhip yourself."

Fn Eye Opener

Kerryn Offord and Linda Davidson

Spring 1635, Magdeburg

"I hear business is slow."

Ursula Sprug finished securing the door of her optometry practice before turning around to face Cathy McNally. "What makes you say that?"

"Your receptionist told me. He's worried you'll have to close your practice." Cathy grinned. "I think he likes you."

"Thomas is just happy with his new glasses."

"But business is slow?"

Ursula sighed. Slow didn't describe the near total lack of customers. "Yes."

"Well then, why don't you take advantage of your friends?"

"I don't know many people in Magdeburg, and those I know don't need glasses."

"I don't mean you should try to fit your friends with glasses. I mean you should ask them to help you. For instance, I bet there are dozens of girls at school who need glasses. Talk to Casey and Staci. See if they'll let you examine their students."

"They'd never let me take the girls out of school to bring them to my office," Ursula protested.

"They might, if they felt the girls might benefit, but what about just using an eye chart and doing a simple screening test at the school? If you find any girls need glasses you can let Casey or

Staci know and they can contact the parents recommending a proper examination and the purchase of prescription glasses.

"You could also offer to give the students a little talk about the different problems people can have with their eyes and how important properly fitted glasses are. Dad and Dr. Shipley would certainly approve of that."

Ursula thought about Cathy's suggestions. Dr. Shipley and Mr. McNally, the Grantville optometrist and optician who trained her, would definitely approve of her educating people about eye health. And Casey and Staci were, well, more than just teachers at the new Duchess Elisabeth Sofie Secondary School for Girls. They were part owners and could talk to Lady Beth Haygood, the principal. "How much can I charge though?"

"Well, just to get them interested, I'd suggest doing a screening test of the current pupils for free," Cathy suggested.

"Free? Dr. Shipley said I should charge for examinations."

"Hey, it's not as if you have a lot of paying customers. And you might want to prepare a handout for those little talks. Those girls all have families, you know. The more people know, the more likely they are to want to do something. Think of it as preparing the ground for seed. Anyway, it's a way to get your foot in the door. I know of at least a dozen girls who wear those funny down-time glasses, and I bet they would benefit from a decent pair."

Cathy certainly had that bit right. Her father was pretty scathing of the quality of the glasses the local spectacle sellers peddled. At best they had lenses of equal power, when very few people who needed glasses needed the same prescription in each eye. At the worst, well, Jim McNally considered them more damaging than going without.

"Okay, I'll talk to Casey or Staci."

"Tonight! After class."

Ursula glared down at Cathy. "Yes, tonight."

"Don't forget."

Ursula had a feeling that if she did forget, Cathy wouldn't. "I won't forget."

Karickhoff's Gym

The dancers were pulling on their outdoor clothes after a hard session under the eyes of Bitty Matowski. Ursula was pulling a brush through her hair when she felt Cathy's eyes boring into her. In the mirror she could see Cathy nodding suggestively toward Casey Stevenson who was just about to leave the changing room. She glared back at Cathy before thrusting her hairbrush into her bag and scrambling to her feet.

"Casey, could I have a word?"

Casey turned from the door and smiled. "Sure. Can you talk while we walk? I'm supposed to be going to the American Kitchen with Carl."

"Thanks." Ursula took a deep breath. "I was wondering if I could do screening eye tests on the pupils at your school?"

"What does that entail? We can't afford the time to take them to your office."

"I was just thinking of using a room at the school and doing a simple test using an eye chart. For most of the children it wouldn't take more than five minutes."

Casey nodded. "And how much were you planning on charging?"

"Cathy suggested doing the tests for free."

"Can you afford to do them for free? I hear you haven't had many customers since you opened your office."

"What? Where did you hear ... Oh. Cathy's been talking?"

"Yes, Cathy's been talking. You really should have spoken up earlier. Come on, there's Carl. I bet Kelly Construction would be interested in having their work force screened for vision problems."

Ursula skipped home with a new spring to her step, and after an hour and a half of barre and center work under Miz Bitty's eye, that was saying something. She might not have any guaranteed customers, but Carl had promised to talk to the guy who doubled, or tripled, as health officer at Kelly Construction about scheduling screening tests, and Casey had promised to bring up the idea of screening tests and talks on eye health with Lady Beth. Surely some of the tests would result in customers.

She used her key to open the door of the boarding house where she had a room and made for the kitchen. Everyone knew she went to dance class after work, so there was usually something left simmering on the range for her.

She bounced into the kitchen, and froze. Sitting back at the kitchen table working her way through a bowl of stew was the landlady. "Hi, Elisabetha. It's been a fantastic day, hasn't it?"

Elisabetha Schmelzer smiled. "Did you get a customer?"

Ursula flushed. Did everyone know that she'd barely had any customers? "Not yet, but I've arranged to do screening tests at Kelly Construction and the new girls' school."

"What are screening tests?"

"It's just a quick and dirty way of determining whether or not someone needs a proper examination. I can give you one now if you like. I just need to get a chart and tape measure from my room."

Elisabeth shook her head. "No need to rush. Get something to eat, and then have a soak. There's still plenty of hot water. How much are you charging for these screening tests?"

Ursula found a clean bowl and, after filling it with stew, collected some bread and joined Elisabeth at the table. "I was planning on doing them free."

"Have you thought about offering free tests at your office?"

"No."

"You might want to try it. A lot of people see the fancy office and think they can't afford to see you. If you put out a sign offering free examinations...well, it'll be a foot in the door."

Ursula blinked. There was that phrase again. "Have you been talking to Cathy McNally?"

"No. Should I have been?"

"It's just she used that exact same phrase when she suggested I talk to Casey about screening the girls at Duchess Elisabeth Sofie."

"Ah, well, it's probably a common up-timer phrase. My Tommy uses it a lot."

Ursula grinned. "And which door is your Tommy talking about putting his foot in?"

Elisabeth waved her finger at Ursula. "That's enough of that, young lady. Just you finish your dinner and I'll run you a bath."

Glowing inside, Ursula set to cleaning her plate. She'd do what Elisabeth suggested and advertise free examinations. It would, as everyone seemed to be saying, get her foot in the door.

Two weeks later

It was after noon before Ursula returned from the latest series of screening tests at Duchess Elisabeth Sofie. She walked up to the reception desk to check if any mail or messages had arrived while she was out.

"Two parents called about you seeing their daughters. They were on the list you provided me and I've scheduled their appointments." Thomas smiled. "At this rate you'll be able to afford to pay your receptionist this week."

Ursula poked her tongue out at him before copying the appointments into her appointment book. Thomas' services as receptionist were provided to the tenants as part of their rent. "Thank you. I'll be in for the rest of the day."

"Do you want me to put your 'Free Examinations' sign out?"

Ursula checked her schedule for the rest of the day. There were just three appointments over the next five hours. "Yes, please."

The sign caught Juliane Lortz's eye. The enormous glasses showed the shop sold glasses, but it was the word "free" that held her attention. She wasn't sure exactly what was being offered, but it wouldn't cost her anything to ask. She tugged at the hand of her daughter. "Come on, Anna. Let's see what they are giving away."

The man manning the front desk was wearing glasses just like the ones on the sign. She approached him. "What are the 'free examinations,' please?"

"The optician does a few simple tests to determine if you need glasses or if there is some other problem with your eyes that needs to be addressed."

Juliane glanced down at her daughter. Surely her eyes shouldn't be turning in like that. "Could I have one for my daughter, please."

"Of course. The optician is in. I'll give her a ring."

Behind one of the doors was the gentle tinkle of a bell in response to the cord the receptionist pulled. The door opened and . . . a very young female came out. Juliane swung round to question the receptionist, but didn't get the chance before he spoke.

"Fraülein Sprug, this lady would like you to examine her daughter."

"Of course. Would you please come this way?"

Ursula studied the woman and child as they approached. Their dress suggested "poor but proud." The daughter's clothes looked like they'd been made out of material from her mother's old clothes. The mother's clothes had few obvious repairs, but they were heavy wear for the current weather. If she had to guess, Ursula didn't think she'd be able to afford the full cost for glasses.

"What's the patient's name?" she asked the mother.

"Anna."

Ursula wrote that down. "And how old is Anna?"

"She'll be four in August."

Ursula added the age to her notes, then pulled out the booster seat that would raise the child to a comfortable working height and placed it on the examination chair. "If you'll just seat Anna, I'll be right with you."

While Juliane lifted Anna onto the booster seat Ursula took her first really good look at the little girl. She had to bite her tongue to stop herself crying out. Both eyes were turning in. She'd seen this condition in patients during her apprenticeship back in Grantville, but not this bad. She took a small paddle from her work table and did a simple cover-uncover test. She knew young Anna had a definite problem when her eyes swung back and forth. Fortunately, the condition had been caught early enough that it should still be treatable ... if the family could afford it.

Ursula selected the special child's eye chart and proceeded to do the best she could to determine whether there was more wrong than just the eyes turning in. She started by pointing to the largest picture on the chart. "Can you tell me what that is, Anna?"

"A horsie?"

"Very good." It was actually a man on a horse, but at least Anna could make out the horse. Ursula pointed to an image on the next line down, a hand. "Now, how about this one?" Anna shook her head. Ursula pointed to the next picture on the same line. "What about this?" Anna shook her head again.

Ursula repeated the procedure with Anna's left eye, regularly glancing at Anna's eyes. They didn't turn in as much when Anna was looking at the chart. Ursula added that snippet of information to Anna's notes. Finally she turned to the mother.

"Anna has a definite problem, but it is treatable. Unfortunately, the condition that is causing her eyes to turn in is beyond my current ability to assess. She really needs to see Dr. Shipley in Grantville."

"Grantville! We can't afford to go there. And a Grantville doctor? We can't afford the kind of fees they charge."

Ursula nodded in silent sympathy. She knew all about the

fees Dr. Shipley charged. "I believe Dr. Shipley intends coming to Magdeburg for Fourth of July Arts Week. I can probably get him to examine Anna free of charge then."

"Why would you do that?" Juliane demanded.

"So I can learn how to do the examination myself." Ursula was proud of that statement. It even contained a grain of truth. It would be a useful learning experience, but she'd probably have to pay Dr. Shipley's fee herself.

Ursula watched the woman wrap her arms protectively around Anna, and tried to reassure her. "The examination won't cost you anything, I promise. However, Anna does need prescription glasses, and they could be expensive."

"How expensive?"

Ursula mentally compared what she could afford to subsidize with how much a new pair of glasses cost. "About three hundred dollars."

"Three hundred dollars? For glasses for a child? You can buy a pair from a peddler for a fraction of that."

"Yes, you can buy a cheap pair of glasses from a peddler, but Anna's problem won't be helped by them. And if you don't do something soon, her vision could be permanently damaged."

"Permanently? You mean Anna could go blind?"

Ursula hastily shook her head. "Not blind, just beyond our ability to correct. Come on, let's get Thomas to take down some contact details and I'll be in touch as soon as I hear back from Dr. Shipley."

July 1635, Magdeburg

It usually took about half an hour for the atropine eye drops to stabilize a child's eyes enough for him to examine, so Dr. Ezra Shipley spent the time explaining the importance of good eye health to the mother. Eventually he was happy with the dilation of Anna's eyes and turned his attention to his patient.

"Anna, I'm not going to do anything that will hurt you. I'm just going to shine a light in your eye and put some lenses in front of it, like this." He knew that a demonstration helped calm any apprehension a child might have. It even worked on some of his more highly-strung adult patients.

He selected a lens and held it in front of Anna's eye and shone the light from the hand held retinoscope through it. The reflection of the retina still showed movement, so he tried another lens.

"Ursula, come try this. I want you to see how when I move the beam from the retinoscope across the pupil the reflex moves the same way as the light and how it moves faster at the forty-five degree angle than the hundred thirty-five degree angle. It's really easy to see here, because the difference is so great."

He gently coached Ursula through the steps to neutralize the refractive error in the right eye, and after checking for himself, fitted the selected lens into the trial frame before repeating the process on the left eye. With two lenses selected, he passed the loaded trial frame to Ursula and crouched down so he was at Anna's level.

"Now Fraulein Sprug is going to hold this funny-looking thing in front of your eyes. It's called a trial frame. And we're going to try some more lenses."

With Ursula holding the trial frame, which was too big to fit Anna comfortably, Ezra used cylindrical lenses to correct both eyes for the other meridian with the same method.

"There. Now that wasn't so bad, was it? Let's see what you can see on the chart."

In a few minutes Ezra finished measuring Anna's vision through the trial lenses. She was now seeing 20/30. Or more correctly, she was reporting 20/30. Young children had an unfortunate tendency not to want to reply when the pictures got very small. Not great, but probably the best they could do with purely objective measurement. In a couple of years' time, when Anna was old enough to give reliable subjective feedback, Ursula could refine the prescription closer to 20/20. However, there was still the matter of convincing the mother to purchase glasses she might not really be able to afford. He glanced over at Anna. She was a sweet little girl. She didn't deserve to be condemned to a world permanently out of focus just because of a few dollars.

"Frau Lortz, your daughter needs a high prescription. As Miss Sprug has already told you, if we don't correct her vision now she will have blurred vision later in her life that we will be unable to treat. It is imperative that we fit her with glasses as soon as possible. Now, you're probably worried about how much they'll cost. Because they're for a child we can make them up for..." He glanced at Juliane's worried face. Ursula had warned him about the price she'd quoted and why. He might have gone lower, but Ursula had also commented on the poor but proud appearance. "Three hundred dollars."

The mother reached out a hand to run it gently over her daughter's head. She looked at the eye chart and back to Ezra. Then she reached under her jacket and pulled out a crumbled piece of paper, which she handed him.

Ezra flattened out the paper and read it. It wasn't cash, but it the next best thing, a note from the local branch of Boot's Bank saying that Juliane Lortz had the ability to pay Ursula Sprug up to three hundred dollars for glasses for her daughter Anna. He passed it over to Ursula. "I'll get onto Anna's new glasses as soon as I get back to Grantville. Ursula should have them inside a week."

"Thank you, Doctor."

"You're supposed to be running a business, not a charity."

"I know, but well..." Ursula sighed.

"Yes, I know. You can't condemn a child to an out of focus world just for the sake of a few dollars. But you have to earn a living. Can you afford to subsidize Anna's glasses?"

Ursula nodded. It would be hard, but not as hard as knowing that Anna would continue to live in her out of focus world.

"It's good to see you're not in the business just for the money, but just this once, I'll carry the cost."

"Thank you, Dr. Shipley."

"Now, about that sign outside your shop...you're not going to tell me you're performing free examinations, are you?"

Ursula shuffled her feet and bowed her head to break eye contact. "I had to, Dr. Shipley. Hardly anybody came in for an eye examination when I was charging for them. Now I have half a dozen or more examinations every day, with most of them leading to orders for glasses."

"You're making up for the examinations on the glasses?" Dr. Shipley shook his head in disgust. "You're putting the profession back decades, Ursula."

"What? Back decades? I thought what I can do was supposed to be years ahead of the general standard of optometry."

Dr. Shipley grinned. "Back up-time it took the profession decades to make the practice of hiding the cost of examinations in the price of glasses illegal."

"Why make it illegal? Why would people pay for an examination if they didn't know they needed an examination? Quite a few of my customers didn't think they needed glasses, but they wanted to take advantage of something that was free."

Dr. Shipley opened his mouth as if to reply, then slammed it shut. He glared down at Ursula and gently shook his head. "It's not professional."

A week later

Anna stared at Ursula from her position high on the examination chair. "The man hurt me. You're not going to hurt me, are you?"

"No, Anna. I'm sorry the eye drops hurt, but Dr. Shipley had to use them so we could check your eyes. Now, I just want you to look at the eye chart." Ursula covered Anna's right eye and pointed to the man on the horse on the on the top line. "What am I pointing to?"

"Horsie."

"Very good. Now let's try going down a line." She pointed to the hand.

Anna shook her head.

Ursula repeated the steps with the left eye covered with similar results.

"Right. Now I'm going to put on your new glasses and we'll try again." Ursula removed the spectacles from their case, checked them for dust and finger prints, and then gently placed them on Anna's face. She had to make a slight adjustment to the nose piece to position them properly, but soon she was happy.

She pointed to the hand on the second line. "What is this shape?"

"It's a hand, and below it is a duck, and a fish, and a hand, and a man on a horsie."

"Very good, Anna. What about this?" Ursula pointed to the cat on the fourth line.

"A cat."

"*Very* good." Ursula took Anna down the chart as far as she could go and then checked the other eye. It looked like Anna was now seeing at 20/30, just like Dr. Shipley had said she would. "That's very good. Now, I want you to take very good care of your glasses. I'll give your mother instructions on how to care for them." She walked over to Juliane, leaving Anna to look around the room.

"Look at all the birdies."

Juliane turned to see where Anna was pointing. There were sparrows pecking at something on the ground nearly thirty feet away. Anna had never noticed anything smaller than a horse that far away before.

"There are people riding on that wagon, Mommy."

Juliane felt a lump in her throat. Anna was looking around and pointing at things as if she was seeing them for the first time. She looked around the street and tried to imagine what it must have looked like to Anna before she got her new glasses. And to think she and her husband had almost decided they couldn't afford glasses for Anna.

She crouched down and hugged Anna. "Yes, darling. There are people in the wagon. What else can you see?"

Anna's tiny hand reached out and brushed the eyebrows above Juliane's eyes. "What are these?"

"They're eyebrows. Feel above your eyes; you have them as well."

Anna brushed a hand against her own eyebrows. "I do too."

Juliane rose to her feet. The change in Anna already was astonishing. It was reward enough for the economies they would have to exercise to pay off the debt to the bank. Surely Joachim would be pleased for Anna.

Anna let her mother take her hand again. She didn't really notice where they were going; she was too busy examining the new world that her glasses had opened for her.

They walked up to their home. Anna was able to recognize some things, but there was so much that she had missed in the past.

There was a man standing at the door. Anna walked up to her father, studying every detail. "Your eyebrows are bigger than Mommy's."

Make Mine Macramé

Virginia DeMarce

Prologue

Magdeburg, November 1634

"Bernhard is," Mike Stearns said, "*your* brother. You might want to keep your tendency to view with alarm within pretty strict limits on this one, even if it did happen on my watch."

Wilhelm Wettin looked at him sourly.

"We were preoccupied with the League of Ostend. I admit it," Mike offered.

"Southern Alsace," Wettin said. "Not only the Franche Comté, which is the problem of the Isabella Clara Eugenia and the king in the Netherlands rather than the USE, but all of southern Alsace, except for Strassburg itself."

"Not all," Francisco Nasi interjected. "Strassburg is a USE city-state and has managed to annex a considerable rural hinterland in the midst of all the confusion. Not to mention that it was Bernhard's pulling his cavalry back to the line south of Strassburg last spring that permitted Nils Brahe to annex the Province of the Upper Rhine for the USE."

Duke Albrecht, who usually stayed home to run the Wettin family's day-to-day business, so to speak, interjected, "He also had enough sense not to annex Mömpelgard—Montbéliard, as the

French call it, when he took southern Alsace. That is a Württemberg exclave, you do realize? The young dukes are Gustavus Adolphus' allies. And they are Lutheran! That's one major potential point of contention that Bernhard had sense enough to walk away from."

"He isn't insane," Philipp Sattler said. "He also left Mülhausen alone—Mulhouse, the French call it. Trying to annex a city that's been an allied Swiss canton for over a century, even if it's not geographically contiguous to anything else in the Swiss Confederacy, would stir up a hornet's nest. Better just to pass it by."

Wilhelm Wettin frowned and kept counting his youngest brother's offenses on his fingers. "The Sundgau, formerly Austrian—Tyrolese to be more precise. The Breisgau, formerly Austrian—Tyrolese, to be more precise. Innumerable *Reichsritterschaften* and petty lordships. And in regard to those, he has the gall to say that he has done nothing different from what your own State of Thuringia-Franconia has been doing in Franconia."

"Ah," Mike said. "Actually, that last is pretty close to the truth, as far as I know."

This did not seem to mollify Wettin at all.

Mike continued. "Also, he did leave the Basel border and has pulled his troops out of southern Swabia into the Breisgau, at least for the winter, which means that Horn can also go into winter quarters in a more favorable location than right on the northern border of Switzerland. And, as far as I know, the margrave of Baden-Durlach, as USE administrator of the proposed Province of Swabia, from the perspective of his headquarters in Augsburg, is not totally dissatisfied with the current situation."

Wettin stopped counting off his fingers and examined his fingernails. "It is a lot to ask. I don't make this request as the leader of the loyal opposition. We have come together to ask as his brothers. We have dealt with Bernhard all our lives, you realize."

Duke Albrecht continued to sit quietly. Wettin, apparently, was not capable of continuing his request to the end.

Albrecht leaned forward. "Please," he said. "We would like to have a copy of the ambassadress' report. Frau Jackson's report. We would like to know how she persuaded him to go away from Basel. Nobody else has ever managed to persuade Bernhard to do anything that he did not want to do."

"By the time Diane was finished," Mike said, "he no longer wanted to threaten Basel's borders, at least if I understand Tony

Adducci's report correctly. It involves a map that Lee Swiger sketched, and all sorts of arrows that Diane drew on it, following lines that Archduchess Maria Anna had marked with her finger. In short, she illustrated that he is going to have enough on his plate for the time being dealing with the lands you just listed—so much on his plate that he should not be suckered into any more distractions on the right bank of the Rhine. He was convinced that he should focus on protecting his core territories, if he really wants to keep them. That wasn't the purpose of the map, but that is how Diane used it."

Duke Albrecht raised an eyebrow.

Mike cleared his throat. "Well, ultimately, Diane said she recognized the problem almost at once. Your brother never went to kindergarten. Therefore he never learned the lessons of *Everything I Ever Really Need to Know, I Learned in Kindergarten*. She's been giving Bernhard a 'back to the basics' course on prudent and proper sandbox behavior, so to speak. With flannel boards, cutout figures, and everything."

"There should be a hiatus for a few months," Nasi said, his tone placating. "Bernhard is going to be preparing and entrenching, organizing and making plans to deal with the plague epidemic 'scheduled' for Swabia in the spring and summer of 1635 according to the history books."

Stearns nodded. "He's already hired a nurse out of Grantville. He's got three well-recognized down-time plague doctors coming in from Franconia right about now—the Padua men that Claudia de Medici, the regent of Tyrol, loaned our administrators in Bamberg to deal with the outbreak in Kronach. I think he's smart enough to know that a ruler is a lot better off with living subjects than dead ones."

Wettin's face was still sour. "'Dumb' was never one of our touchy, overambitious baby brother's problems."

Chapter One

Bolzen, Tyrol, January 1635

"Those progress reports from the plague physicians we sent to assist Bernhard of Saxe-Weimar last November complete the old business on the agenda." Wilhelm Bienner, chancellor of the County of Tyrol, closed one folder.

Claudia de Medici inclined her head at the members of her inner council. "The next item on the agenda is unannounced. I wanted to avoid the premature spread of gossip." Her steely gray eyes fixed on a couple of her advisers, but she forbore to make any additional comment. "For the remainder of the meeting, I will have present additional persons whom I have recently seen fit to add to my staff."

She signaled to the doorman. He exited into the antechamber, returning with, obvious to anyone who looked at them closely, two up-timers and a down-timer.

"Your Grace, is this...?" The questioner's voice dwindled away into a mumble.

"Yes," Claudia said. "It is wise." She looked around the table. "Does anyone *else* doubt that it is wise?"

If anyone else did, he found it prudent not to say so.

The regent smiled like a cat. "Gentlemen, may I present to you Don Francesco de Melon, formerly the imperial/Bavarian military commander of the fortress of Kronach in northern Franconia." She waved.

De Melon bowed.

She waved again.

He took the designated chair.

"Also, from Grantville, in the Ring of Fire, Herr Matthäus Trelli, formerly commander of the State of Thuringia-Franconia's military forces during the recent siege of Kronach. Prior to the Ring of Fire, he had studied the subject of Medical Lab Technology for two years at Fairmont State University in West Virginia. This study required two more years, but Herr Trelli informs me that because of financial problems, he had left the university and was working at a 'clinic' in the same time to earn sufficient money to complete his professional preparation. He is personally acquainted with the famous Professor Thomas Stone who is now lecturing in Padua." The ritual of waves and chairs followed.

"And Herr Trelli's wife, whom he married just this past month in Würzburg, the gentle-lady Frau Laura Marcella Abruzzo." Claudia's voice firmed. "Lady Abruzzo, before the Ring of Fire, was also a student at this same Fairmont State University in West Virginia. As you may have heard, if not believed, this 'co-education' was common up-time. Lady Abruzzo had completed three years of a four-year course of study in the subject of Civil Engineering Technology. We have been informed that not only nobles but also commoners educated their daughters well."

Turning to Bienner's clerk, who was taking minutes, she pointed. "Take a memo. Dr. Bienner is to write yet once more to both Quedlinburg and Prague, asking them about women's colleges. I will not have Tyrol lose its preeminent economic position because it fails to modernize."

The clerk made a note.

"As to Lady Abruzzo. Since the Ring of Fire, because this university in Fairmont, West Virginia, was not included within the Ring of Fire, she has spent two years apprenticing to the experienced partners who founded USE Steel in Saalfeld to become certified by them as a fully qualified engineer."

At the mention of the word "steel," several of the previously unhappy faces around the table transformed themselves. Their current expressions might be described as mollified.

"I am delighted," the regent said, "to welcome these up-time fellow Italians as they join the administrative staff of the County of Tyrol." She waved.

Marcie Abruzzo did not curtsey. Like the men, she bowed. Then she took her seat.

"Begin as you mean to go on," her Grandma Kovacs always said.

"Fellow-Italians," Matt said to de Melon. "The Trellis came from somewhere around Venice, I think, but my mom is Irish. Dad's mom was Irish. Marcie's dad's family immigrated from Sicily, but her mom's Serbian."

Marcie Abruzzo laughed. "Talk about an exercise in résumé inflation. The archduchess certainly has the routine down pat."

She paused. "She *is* an archduchess, isn't she?"

"Her late husband," de Melon said, "was an archduke. Her

father, however, was Grand Duke of Tuscany, so by birth she is a grand duchess. Her first husband was merely a duke."

"How do those stack up against each other—an Austrian archduke and an Italian grand duke? Is one higher than the other?"

"I am a soldier, not a diplomat. However, I think they would be about equivalent, since the families intermarry and the spouses are considered to be of equal birth."

"How come she didn't run through your résumé, de Melon?" Matt asked. "The one I got for you when I asked Grantville to send me something was pretty impressive."

"I am very sorry," Francesco de Melon said with impeccable courtesy, "but I sincerely believe that your researchers in Grantville were mistaken." The former imperial/Bavarian military commander of the fortress of Kronach assumed an expression that indicated he felt mildly apologetic.

"Umm," Matt Trelli, formerly de Melon's opposite number on behalf of the State of Thuringia-Franconia during the siege of Kronach, asked, "how?"

"Part of this information they sent you . . ." De Melon picked up a piece of paper. "Part of this is me, I, myself, the person who is sitting here in your presence."

Matt nodded.

"I believe, though, that most of it belongs to another person with the same name, or a similar name. More precisely, it appears to belong to two or more other persons with the same name, or similar names. One of them was a poet. The other was a count. I am flattered, of course, to have so suddenly acquired both outstanding literary abilities and a rank of high nobility. However . . ."

De Melon sat there, across the table from Matt. Young. Straight black hair, dark eyes. Not overweight, but a little jowly. Heavy eyebrows, prominent nose, mustache.

"Well," Matt said. "I guess we at least have to give the folks at the National Research Center credit for trying. It's not as if anybody in Grantville could speak or read Portuguese before the Ring of Fire. Well, Ms. DiCastro was in Grantville as an exchange teacher. She's from South America, so maybe she could. She didn't work for the Research Center, though, so it probably doesn't make any difference whether she could or not. She was teaching Spanish at the high school."

Marcie Abruzzo, so recently married to Matt that they still

counted as honeymooners, asked, "Why did you 'fess up? When you realized about the mix-up, I mean?"

De Melon smiled. "Not from any outstanding amount of abstract virtue, I assure you. I just felt sure that if I kept that résumé after I accepted the regent of Tyrol's invitation to enter her service, at some time, unavoidably, I would meet someone acquainted with one of the other men."

"A letter from the emperor of the Austro-Hungarian Empire," Chancellor Bienner's clerk said. "It just arrived."

Claudia snatched it.

She read.

She frowned. "Ferdinand says they are considering the possibility that Vienna might offer the Archduchess Cecelia Renata as a wife for Bernhard of Saxe-Weimar, as a means of maintaining the Habsburg interests in Swabia."

"But he's Protestant," Bienner protested.

"It appears," Claudia answered, "that Leopold's young cousins in Vienna are—how would Marcie put it?—thinking outside of the box. How would such a move affect the position of my sons? The historically Habsburg lands in Swabia do not belong to Vienna. They belong to Tyrol. Perhaps I should think outside of the box as well, before Ferdinand steals a march on me."

"If a leak occurs before I am ready for this initiative to become public," the regent said, "heads will roll."

No one at the table doubted that she meant this statement in its most literal sense.

"After study of the situation and consultation with Dr. Bienner, taking into account some proposed actions on the part of Our cousins in Vienna, having within the fairly recent past taken advantage of Our commercial connections with the manufacturers of the 'Monster' to visit both Venice and Magdeburg, We have concluded..."

Claudia de Medici paused and stood up. She had called this meeting for the specific time in the morning when the sun would come through the windows of the conference room and shine on her titian hair. She had a talent for the dramatic.

"No, no." She waved as all the others scrambled to push their chairs back. "Retain your seats."

She had frequently thought that although proper protocol required that the highest-ranking person in a room sit, while all others stood respectfully unless given permission to sit, this was counterintuitive. She was tall, true, but when seated, she could not tower over anyone else. If they sat and she stood, however, she could achieve a more intimidating effect. A truly satisfactory intimidating effect.

It was definitely time for some changes in Tyrol.

"It is Our intention to extend exploratory feelers to the United States of Europe as to what terms We could obtain if We were willing to bring Tyrol, voluntarily, into it."

"As one of its provinces?" someone asked.

She shook her head decisively. "No. As a 'state.' They may say that the status of the State of Thuringia-Franconia, legally, is no different from that of the other provinces, but, still, 'state' is a distinguishing term. There are nuances to be considered. The word has connotations tied to its history. A 'state' in the English language, I have learned, was not only one of the component units of the 'United States of America,' but also could be and was often utilized as synonymous with 'nation.'"

She suddenly grinned impishly, looking a decade younger than her thirty years. "See how useful it is to have up-time advisers. Marcie had a friend at the university who majored in 'marketing.' First impressions are always important. 'State' is much better than 'province.'"

"'Marketing,'" one of her council asked dubiously. "The up-timers went to a *university* to learn to sell things?"

"I have been talking to young Matthäus," someone answered. "Their merchants no longer offered traditional apprenticeships. They appear to have paid money, called endowments, to schools of higher education, where would-be young merchants were trained by academics, many of whom had never been traders themselves. The result was called an MBA. A 'Master of Business Administration.'"

The sheer horror of this concept caused a gloomy silence to descend on the conference room.

"You now have heard the essence of what I am proposing. Dr. Bienner has prepared a 'position paper' that I want each of you to read. We will reconvene tomorrow. Keep the desirability of a direct connection between your heads and your necks firmly in mind."

✧   ✧   ✧

Wilhelm Bienner had discovered bullet points and the Joy of the Executive Summary.

- Both the USE and Venice are seriously interested, for good sound economic and commercial reasons, in having a land bridge between them; while air transport is a boon, it will not dominate the exchange of goods and people for some decades. Tyrol's entrance into the USE would meet this need (see projections, Appendices I-IV);

- Maximilian of Bavaria isn't the most stable of next door neighbors to have just at this moment (see retrospective from mid-summer 1634 to the present, Appendix V);

- At a time when Tyrol could really use a strong archbishop in Salzburg, the Holy Spirit in its wisdom has chosen to give Us Paris von Lodron. Even if his publicists represent him as being "as cautious and wise as Pericles," what that means for Us is that he's huddling like a turtle in its shell; he may be expected to defend the territories of the archdiocese as strongly as he can, but it is not probable that he will assist Us if Maximilian gives Tyrol problems (see further analysis, Appendix VI);

- Our cousins in Vienna are preoccupied with setting up a new administrative structure for the Austro-Hungarian Empire. They cannot ignore developments in Bohemia and the Balkans; Ferdinand feels he must support the Poles if Gustavus should be imprudent enough to push his eastern campaign that far next summer (see further analysis, Appendix VII);

- If the setting up of a USE "Province of Swabia" goes through as it was proposed at the Congress of Copenhagen the previous June, Tyrol will lose many of its current possessions that are scattered all the way through Swabia to the Rhine (see copy of the relevant portion of the proceedings, attached as Appendix VIII);

- If Tyrol comes in voluntarily as a unit, We can probably negotiate much more satisfactory terms.

Essentially, that was it. With footnotes, legal references, and supplements, the position paper ran to sixty-seven closely written pages. That was not counting the appendices.

Matt Trelli read the point about Salzburg and muttered, "Three cheers for the Paraclete."

De Melon looked at the size of it, calculated the number of clerks who must have been pulled in to make copies for each council member, wondered why the chancery had not yet invested in a Vignelli duplicating machine, and muttered, "If there isn't a leak before the regent is ready to make this public, I will be a very surprised man."

Marcie commented, "That capitalization of "We" and "Us" and "Our" always gets to me—really gives me the shivers."

"I seriously believe," de Melon told the regency council, "that you can anticipate that the leadership of the USE will respond to such a proposal reasonably. Certainly, my experience with the SoTF officials in their handling of the surrender of Kronach last autumn left me persuaded of the essential rationality of the up-timers. Their provision of assistance to the city and fortress during the plague epidemic even left me persuaded of their essential good will. This was not a conviction that came to me easily."

"The USE is not the only party of concern," Chancellor Bienner pointed out. "There is also Bernhard of Saxe-Weimar to consider. The Breisgau. The Sundgau. The Swabian jurisdictional claims of his, ah, new and still developing principality overlap with those of Tyrol in some localities."

"Our aim," the regent said, "is to retain all Tyrolese possessions in Swabia as an inheritance for Our sons. Ferdinand Karl is six. Sigmund Franz is barely four. They are not old enough to speak for themselves. We must be tenacious on their behalf."

She stood up.

Chancellor Bienner winced. He was learning that it was not a good sign when the regent stood up when she was at the head of a table.

"As I think about it," Claudia said, "I believe that I have urgent reasons to visit Besançon, or, at least, to visit wherever Bernhard has his working headquarters at the moment. There is often much to be gained by a face-to-face meeting of the principal parties involved, rather than leaving discussions to ambassadors and envoys."

There was no possible disadvantage associated with this project that her advisers left unexplored. Plague. Horn's regiments. You Name It.

"We shall go," the regent said. "We will do it. Let the matter be arranged with Bernhard. Let the matter be arranged with the people who fly the 'Monster.' Let it be done."

Chapter Two

Schwarzach, January 1635

Once Friedrich von Kanoffski arrived from Freiburg im Breisgau, where he was *locum tenens*, the informal but closely associated group of Bernhard's associates who called themselves *Der Kloster* because of their working headquarters at the "requisitioned" Abbey of Schwarzach, was complete. Once everyone else had extended to the Bohemian their congratulations and felicitations on the safe delivery the previous month of his wife Anna Jolantha Salome, *née* Stump, the daughter of a Freiburg patrician, of a healthy son named Johann Balthasar, they got down to business on the general theme of "Well, what next?"

"You're still officially in the employ of France," Caldenbach said. "It may be the result of incredible bureaucratic inertia, but you are. In spite of everything that happened last spring, Richelieu is still sending money to Besançon."

"Not much," Rosen pointed out. "Not very regularly, either."

"Insurance," Bernhard said. "Louis XIII is very short on regi-
ments at the moment. Richelieu will not formally break the contract as long as he can imagine even the most unlikely 'just in case' scenario in which he might need to call on me. In case you're wondering, I have that directly from a plant on Mazarin's staff. There's no such scenario on the horizon."

"At the moment," Sydenham Poyntz added.

"Next." Bernhard had little patience for meetings.

Johann Faulhaber, the engineer from Ulm who was supervising the military construction at the new national capitol in Besançon, presented a very satisfactory progress report.

Johann Ludwig von Erlach, a Swiss from Bern who was moving up very rapidly and showed every sign of becoming Bernhard's lieutenant in general as well as lieutenant-general, had some things to say about management of the fortress at Breisach. If anyone else felt stirrings of envy when Bernhard named him as governor of the Alsatian territories as well, he didn't say so. Erlach was a flamboyant man. Silver plate was not good enough for the general. His had to be gilded. He currently maintained three households simultaneously—one in his Swiss castle at Castelen, the second in Breisach itself, and the third in camp whenever he took to the field.

Johann Michael Moscherosch, poet and public relations man, outlined his latest campaigns with words, designed to lure a public he considered all-too-gullible into believing that their new ruler was also the cherry filling in their torte.

"I wish, though," Moscherosch said, "that you would decide for once and all what you want to call yourself. There are only so many circumlocutions, euphemisms, and ways to dance on my tiptoes available."

Von Rosen licked his lips. "Besançon is the capital, but the Franche Comté, the old County of Burgundy as distinct from the once-upon-a-time Duchy of Burgundy in the Netherlands, *is* only a county, after all. You are already a duke (not to mention that your older brothers are also dukes, with the exception of Wilhelm, who was a duke). Certainly, you will not demote yourself to become a a mere count, will you?" he asked a little anxiously.

Kanoffski laughed. "Does it bother you that there is more prestige in being employed by a duke than in being employed by a count?"

"Well," von Rosen began. "No, I suppose not. But still..."

"When it comes to sitting around tables, conducting diplomatic negotiations," Poyntz remarked to the ceiling, "dukes are seated well above counts and get to speak first. These things do matter, Kanoffski."

"With the new new additions last year, Burgundy, our Burgundy, is powerful," Caldenbach said. "Bernhard now holds more land than all of the Ernestine-line brothers together, as dukes of Saxe-Weimar, did before the Ring of Fire. He should assume an equally splendid title."

Bernhard was feeling the first rumblings of the indigestion that was his constant companion. "I'll give it some thought," he said. "Move on."

With the one exception of Moscherosch, the men who constituted *"Der Kloster"* were military officers, hard-bitten, experienced, and tough.

Still, it was Moscherosch who said, "Heirs."

Bernhard raised one bushy black eyebrow.

"Heirs, Your Grace," Moscherosch said firmly. "There is no point to all this if you do not produce heirs. Your efforts will amount to spitting into the wind."

Kanoffski nodded. "I have a list of suitable Protestant possibilities."

Elizabeth of the Palatinate? Maybe, but she was in the Spanish Netherlands.

"And," Bernhard said, "she has just turned sixteen. I find that I have little appetite for becoming a father on the same day I become a husband. Rearing a child-bride strikes me as a truly tedious job."

"Well," Caldenbach said, "that lets out Frederik Hendrik's daughters. They are even younger."

"Much too young," Moscherosch said. "Not even of childbearing age. Keep the purpose in mind. Heirs as soon as possible."

"Marguerite de Rohan? She's a little older. Almost eighteen, I think."

"She's in Brittany, on the goddamned other side of France. Plus, Henri de Rohan, for all the respect I have for the man and what he has done to advance the Huguenot cause over the years, will want to control her husband. He wouldn't refuse me. In fact, he's suggested the match already. I turned it down."

"Why in heaven?"

"The *duc* de Rohan wants to buy a competent general for his daughter and heiress, to fight his wars now that he's aging. I have no desire to become a puppet hanging on strings that another man is manipulating."

"What about Christian IV's daughters?"

Der Kloster regretfully dismissed the daughters of the Danish king as not only the products of a morganatic marriage, but apparently extremely self-willed. Poyntz brought up stories about Eddie Cantrell and Anna Cathrine that were making the rounds of European courts, to general hilarity and multiple rude and obscene comments.

Bernhard gritted his teeth. "That one, the oldest one, is the same age as Elisabeth of the Palatinate. The rest are even younger. Did you hear me? They are *too young*. The next of the Danish king's daughters after Anna Cathrine is exactly *half as old as I am*."

"Your Grace," Kanoffski said politely. "Wilhelm of Hesse-Kassel is not likely to die conveniently so that you can marry Amalie Elisabeth."

"I would," Bernhard said. "If she weren't already married, I would snatch Amalie right up. She's interesting. She's intelligent. She's politically astute. I like her a lot."

"She's too *old*," Caldenbach squalled. "She's older than you are, Your Grace."

"Only two years older," Bernhard said mildly. Then he smiled. The smile was not mild. It was wicked. "She's a magnificent breeder. They already have six children living in addition to the four who died. Anyone want to bet me on how many more children she will give Wilhelm? I'll wager ten thousand USE dollars on five more. Two thousand at each birth."

Chapter Three

Magdeburg, late January 1635

"What do you think, Ed?" Mike Stearns tipped his chair back. "I'm really glad that I caught up with you before you left. All this campaigning has left me getting up in the morning not sure whether I'll be going north or south or east or west before the day is out."

Ed Piazza steepled his fingers. "First, to be honest, I'm just surprised. I can't say it's the last thing that expected, because it wasn't on the list. The possibility that the regent of Tyrol might do this never even crossed my mind."

"Do you see any disadvantages?" Francisco Nasi asked.

"From the perspective of the SoTF? Hell, no. It would be great for us. But, then, again, it's no skin off our noses to add another mainly Catholic province to the USE. Wettin and the Crown Loyalists may not be so happy, given that one of their themes is 'narrower citizenship' and another, slinking along under the ground with the anti-Semitic agitation, is still 'we're here to defend Protestantism against the forces of the anti-Christ on Earth.' How's Gustav reacting?"

Mike pantomimed a cat pouncing upon a bird. "I doubt that he's ever seen a piece of real estate that he didn't classify as a desirable acquisition. He tends to stop and think about the complications offered by the inhabitants after he's taken that irreversible first bite. If he can acquire it without expending any of his military resources, it's 'Roll over, Beethoven' or 'Full speed ahead. Damn the torpedoes.'"

"There will be complications," Nasi said. "Swabia..."

"Every time somebody shows up to talk to me about Swabia," Mike grumbled, "I think I understand what Shakespeare said better—that bit about dying a thousand deaths before you die. Not that I would want to call myself a coward, but when it comes to thinking about the geography down in the southwest, I flinch. Clearly, my hopes at the Congress of Copenhagen were premature. To say the least."

"My darling," Rebecca said. "I doubt that you will ever understand how things work in the southern portions of the Germanies. You would love to have one villain—Duke Maximilian. You could fight him. Perhaps, you could even endure his having a limited number of allies. You could fight them. But, truly, outside of Bavaria, which is fairly good sized, mostly in Swabia all you will find is that you are being bitten to death by little, almost invisible, ants."

"Up-time, we said, 'Nibbled to death by ducks.' Or, sometimes, by fishes. 'Better to be snapped up by a crocodile than nibbled to death by minnows.' It depended on the context."

"What do you think?" Hermann of Hesse-Rotenburg asked. The USE secretary of state fiddled with his pen. "Perhaps we can ask Basel to take this on."

Frank Jackson shook his head. "Don't listen to him, Mike. Diane is swamped with Swiss affairs, with Baden and its problems, and with the possibilities of what Bernhard of Saxe-Weimar might do next even though he doesn't show any sign of doing it right now. Tony Adducci—young Tony—is a big help to her, but he's just an assistant. Besides, she's assigned him to the anti-plague preparation team. Anti-plague prevention team. The team that's supposed to prepare to prevent the plague. Whatever the hell they're calling it."

Hermann fiddled some more. "Somebody needs to go to Tyrol, or else the regent needs to come to us. Face-to-face discussions. Radio is wonderful, but not for something this complex."

"She's been here before," Nasi pointed out. "She flies on the Monster. But she says that she can't, right now. Something has come up."

"So pick someone. Send someone," Mike said. "Have done with it."

This time Hermann twirled his pen in a circle on his tablet. "Who?"

"Philipp Sattler," Nasi said. "That's one of the reasons Gustavus picked him as his personal liaison to the USE administration. He's from Kempten, right down in the middle of that Swabian chaos."

"If things come up that are higher than his pay grade?"

"It's hard to get much higher than the emperor's personal liaison, Hermann. Not unless you go yourself."

The secretary of state gave one of his rare smiles. "I can always ask my brother Wilhelm if he's willing for Amalie to undertake an occasional mission for the government. After all, it's customary for women of high rank used as diplomatic negotiators. She and the regent might like one another."

Chapter Four

Schwarzach, mid-February 1635

Schwarzach was in the Rhine river bottoms. The "hill" on which the ancient Romanesque cathedral stood might better have been described as a modest hump.

"Gee whiz," Matt Trelli commented as he climbed out of the Monster after the more senior members of the delegation had already descended. "If they grew corn as high as an elephant's eye around here, the top of the corn and the top of the hill would be just about even with each other."

Marcie nodded. "It's about as big a change from the Alps as we could have found."

Kanoffski presented the members of *Der Kloster* to the regent.

De Melon presented the members of the Tyrolese delegation to the duke.

Dr. Bienner made a gracious speech and adumbrated the issues that were to be negotiated.

Bernhard's chancellor, hauled up from his customary and ordinary duties in Besançon for the occasion, replied. Then he presented the representative from the USE embassy in Basel to the regent and the duke.

The senior delegates retired to their quarters in the episcopal residence to prepare for a diplomatic reception.

Even though Tony Adducci was five years younger than Matt, thus separated from him in the up-time by the yawning generation gap described as 'not in high school when I was,' they were so delighted to see one another that they started wrestling in the antechamber. Marcie made them stop.

The reception was meant to be quite preliminary to the serious negotiations. It proved to be momentous, although nobody but the principal parties noticed. More precisely, the observers didn't notice it that same evening. In the minds of those principal parties, however, the looming issue of "the bride" was settled almost at once.

Duke Bernhard absentmindedly made etiquette-appropriate

chitchat with Dr. Bienner and eyed Claudia de Medici. He expected to found a dynasty. Until tonight, his expectations in regard to what that project might involve had been rather vague. His associates of *Der Kloster*, volubly and vociferously, expected him to found a dynasty. They had hitched their wagons to his star; they expected due rewards, not just now, but for their children and grandchildren.

He had read the briefing papers; here, right in front of him, was a good looking titian-haired widow who in two marriages had successfully given birth to six children, five of whom were alive and flourishing, two of whom were male. She was three months older than he. Both of them were thirty. If she remarried she could—and very probably would—give birth to children for another dozen years.

Five or six children would be plenty, especially if Frau Dunn, the widow of the traitor Horton, could do things to prevent smallpox and plague, reduce fevers, rehydrate cases of infantile dysentery by using a mild saline solution . . . He had received numerous lectures on the reduction of childhood mortality in the last few months. He had been somewhat annoyed, wishing that the woman would pay more attention to training "medics" for his regiments. Suddenly they seemed relevant.

Why risk his undeniable need for heirs on any of the untried virgins who had been recommended to him as wives when a woman with a truly spectacular track record was standing right in front of him? Not to mention that she clearly understood politics and economics or she would not have proposed the current negotiations. Tyrol held colorable title to significant territories in Swabia, a couple of which he had already annexed. This was—always with the exception of Amalie, of course—the most interesting female that he had ever met.

Well, with the exception of the terrifying, tiny East Indian who was the USE ambassadress in Basel. "Interesting" was a very inadequate term to describe Diane Jackson. However, she was not only married, but well beyond childbearing age. Regrettable.

Not that he had met many women. He had gone from home at thirteen, when his mother died, to the university of Jena under the supervision of a strict tutor, to the army at eighteen. His only sister, born a few months after his father's death, had died at the age of three. He barely remembered her. Aside from Aunt

Anna Sofie, the intelligent, strong-willed widow of Count Ludwig Guenther's older brother in Schwarzburg-Rudolstadt, who was childless, committed to educational reform and social welfare, and Amalie, he had almost never sat down and had a conversation with a female. His recent encounters with Frau Jackson in Basel excepted. Mentally, he shrugged. Women had been in short supply in his life. There had been passing encounters, of course, but he had never kept a mistress. He had no bastards that he knew of.

Everyone told him that the regent of Tyrol was strong-willed and intelligent. Why would a busy man want to bother with any other kind? Bernhard was not averse to strong-willed, intelligent women. Particularly red-haired ones. He squelched that thought firmly and returned his mind to his conversation with Philipp Sattler, who had somehow taken Dr. Bienner's place while his mind was wandering.

Claudia, standing on the other side of the room and conversing politely with the abbot of Schwarzach and the mayor of the town, eyed Duke Bernhard. He was a man who was *not* an ex-cardinal. How refreshing. Considering that her father had been an ex-cardinal, her second husband had been an ex-cardinal, and now poor Leopold's cousin Maria Anna had married another ex-cardinal, she could only consider a man who was neither an ex-cardinal nor one of her subordinates to be an interesting variation in the category "male human being." It would be interesting to have a man in her life whose official portrait did not depict him in a cassock. She mentally dismissed all consideration of her first husband, the obnoxious duke of Urbino to whom she had been married off when he was fifteen and she was sixteen. Horrible boy. The nicest thing that Federigo Ubaldo della Rovere had ever done for her was die. Not that she was sufficiently deluded or self-centered to believe that the assassins who murdered him had done it to make her life easier, but, still, she made it a point to remember them in her prayers. Leopold had been much nicer, but he had also been nearly twenty years her senior.

Duke Bernhard looked fairly healthy. Athletic. Superb horseman. The briefing papers said something about chronic indigestion, but he had enough sense that he had hired an up-time nurse.

He had already demonstrated that he was one of the best generals of the age. He clearly had ambition. She would not have had any reason to initiate these negotiations if he didn't. Perhaps, with encouragement, he would help her pry her daughter from her first marriage out of the clutches of her grandparents. Letters from Italy indicated that Vittoria, now almost thirteen, was...not pretty. That, alas, she bore an unfortunate physical resemblance to her late father, the unlamented duke of Urbino. Under the circumstances, she would need her mother's guidance if she were to achieve a happy future.

She had the absolutely irrational thought that Duke Bernhard was taller than she. How unusual. How...irrelevant. She squelched the thought firmly and returned her attention to making social conversation with the local worthies.

Five days later, the negotiations came to a satisfactory conclusion in the form of a preliminary prenuptial settlement. The details remained to be worked out, of course. Still, it would be a match firmly based on substantial mutual advantages, not to mention a shared appreciation of the value of real estate.

True, Bernhard was Lutheran, while Claudia was Catholic. Still, as she pointed out, the Vienna Habsburgs could scarcely complain, considering that they had been approaching the point of offering Cecelia Renata as an option. Given the religious situation in the lands they would be governing—in a real sense, the disparity of cult might even be counted as an advantage. As for the children, they would simply follow the normal arrangement—the girls would be baptized in her faith and the boys in his. That made no problems for Tyrol—Claudia's children by Leopold were the heirs there.

"Your Grace," Matt Trelli said. "Marcie and I really think that it would be a good idea for you to leave us—well, me, at least— here in Swabia. From what Tony Adducci says, the main thrust of the plague will come here in the southwest, not in Tyrol. We just—well, after Kronach and everything, I just feel like I need to be part of the prevention team that the Swiss and Duke Bernhard are putting together."

The regent looked at him. "You work for me and you will return in accordance with your employment contract. You signed it voluntarily."

Matt backed out of the room.

De Melon hurried after him. "Don't do anything rash. She intends to place you as the head organizer of the plague fighters in Tyrol. This is something I have heard. It is not unimportant there. Given the heavy, constant, overland commercial traffic, it will be a challenge to maintain the quarantine without damaging the economy."

"Matt, listen to me," Marcie said that evening. "Okay, I get it. She didn't explain her reasons. That's sort of how people who were born to run things work. They don't know that they have to explain. Actually, they don't have to explain. They might get more cooperation if they did, but—honestly, Matt. They're just not up-timers. You can't expect a down-time aristocrat to run her bailiwick the same way Steve Salatto managed things in Bamberg. Anyway—think of it as sort of like being in the army. You couldn't have backed out of that, either, just because you didn't like some order Cliff Priest gave you."

Chapter Five

Besançon, late February 1635

The air was crisp. The sky was blue. The Doubs river wended its twisty way below the city. Bernhard looked down from the site of his future, still incomplete citadel. It was here, above the imperial city itself, which was now his capital city—his—not inside the medieval walls, that he would assume his new title. His residence was in the *Palais Granvelle* below. He had requisitioned it. It was a gorgeous palace, much better than anything the Wettins had owned in Weimar. The Granvelle family had gone bankrupt long since, in any case.

Most of his garrison officers were quartered across the river, in the *Quartier Battant*, below the Griffon bastion, in the Champagney mansion, which Nicholas Perrot de Granvelle had built for his widowed mother as her dower seat. Fleetingly, he thought about the latest projected cost estimates that Faulhaber had provided for his new citadel and wondered if constructing the luxurious mansions had contributed to the Granvelle bankruptcy.

Besançon was not just defensible. It was beautiful. Residing here would be a pleasure. There were worse reasons for choosing the site of a national capital.

Bernhard glanced around, thoroughly enjoying the pageantry. Even a general could take a day off, now and then.

"Grand Duke of the County of Burgundy?" Kanoffski said to Poyntz. "Now, that's a truly gemlike combination of words."

"Why not, if it makes him happy? I understand that he set a lot of genealogists to work. It appears that he is legitimately descended from someone named Jean de Nevers who was count of this region a couple of hundred years ago."

"Ultimately," Kanoffski answered, "we all descend from Adam. How many other people now alive descend from this Jean de Nevers?"

"Dozens, if not hundreds. What difference does it make? None of the rest of them have a garrison in Besançon."

"None of them are marrying a Tuscan grand duchess, either.

Grand Duchess and Regent of the County of Tyrol. What odds will you give me that he picked it because he wanted to bring a title at least equal to hers into this marriage?"

"I'm putting my money on saying he picked it because it's more grandiose than his brothers' titles. A thousand USE dollars, if we can find some actual written evidence of what went into his decision, one way or the other, of course."

"The time has come," Bernhard said that evening. "Considering that one of my brothers is now the prime-minister elect of the USE and another is still Gustavus' regent in the Upper Palatinate, it seems a propitious moment to see if I can pry an apology out of the old goat and get him to recognize my title and my conquests."

"Apology? From the emperor?"

"I hear rumors that he apologized to John Hepburn, nearly two years ago. Shrewd move. The encyclopedias say that in the other world, Hepburn was so insulted by what Gustavus said about his Catholic faith that he switched over to the French also. In this world, though, he's garrisoning Ulm for the USE. If Hepburn can get an apology, then so can I."

Kanoffski wrote "apology" on the list he was making.

"If I am to concentrate on the challenges coming at me here in the southwest for the time being, which I think that I must, I need a, a *modus vivendi* with the USE." Bernhard raised a bushy, nearly black eyebrow. "Not that I intend to let Gustavus guess that I need it. The whole matter must be presented as if I were doing him a favor."

Kanoffski nodded and wrote *modus vivendi* on his list.

"I want de Melon present when we're working out our offer, since Claudia left him behind to work out the details of our own agreement. I want that finalized—signed, sealed, and delivered—before I show my hand to Magdeburg.

"Then, I think, we need to talk to Sattler again. See if you can get him down here."

Schwarzach, March 1635

"I can't see that the assassinations in Grantville will have any direct impact on our concerns," Bernhard said. "The up-timers I hired were very upset about the deaths, though. They requested permission to hold a memorial service. The chancellor radioed me for approval. I told him to go ahead, and make it a good one. Claudia's up-time hires are all Catholic—not just Trelli and Abruzzo, whom she brought to Schwarzach, but all the rest—so they did a requiem mass in Bolzen with Urban VIII's dispensation, but none of mine are Catholics. Still, I have to say that the Papists know how to put on a good show, so I got her to radio to the 'Cardinal Protector' in Magdeburg and obtain permission for the chancellor to roust them out in Besançon. The city got into the spirit of things. They produced chants, a procession, cloth of gold vestments, and waving banners for those two old Presbyterians."

Poyntz snorted.

Moscherosch nodded. "Excellent publicity."

"Next."

"Brahe, and the SoTF forces from Fulda, are chasing through the Province of Upper Rhine, in pursuit of Butler, Devereux, Geraldin, McDonnell, and their dragoons. Ferdinand of Bavaria, the archbishop of Cologne, ran out of funds to pay them. Duke Maximilian has hired them for Bavaria, to replace Werth and von Mercy. They have to get across Swabia to reach Bavaria."

The bushy eyebrow went up higher than usual. "So?"

"Horn has suggested coordination. He doesn't want to see them reach Max. Neither, I presume, do we."

"We don't. Send Raudegen to Horn, with powers of attorney to act on my behalf. Make sure that the powers-that-be in Magdeburg are aware that sweetness and light are overcoming the powers of darkness in this matter."

Von Rosen smirked.

"Tyrol insists that the Vorarlberg and other Habsburg possessions of Vorderösterreich are not negotiable. Additionally, at Grand Duke Bernhard's death, if he and Claudia de Medici do not leave mutual heirs of their bodies, male or female, the Sundgau and Breisgau, now in possession of the County of Burgundy, will revert to her sons by the late Leopold von Habsburg, archduke of Austria and count of Tyrol."

De Melon's voice was calm, but insistent.

"Agreed."

De Melon looked surprised.

Bernhard shrugged his shoulders. "What's the point of trying to hold on to the lands I have gained if I don't leave children? Wilhelm's a commoner now. He has three healthy sons and Eleonore is pregnant again, but he has declared that even though she has chosen to keep her birth title, their children will take his rank and be commoners also. Little Wettins. The up-time encyclopedia says that Albrecht's marriage in the other world remained childless; he went ahead and married Dorothea in spite of that. Ernst will inherit much of Saxe-Altenburg's property when he marries little Elisabeth Sofie. If they go overboard and have eighteen offspring in this world, as they did in the other, I can only say that they will *deserve* to have to find a way support that many children themselves."

"What about a sweetener?" de Melon suggested. "Throw in the agreement of both parties that if the two of you leave no surviving children, aside from what reverts to Tyrol and will thus be an integral part of a USE state anyway, the County of Burgundy as a single entity will become a USE province."

Bernhard raised that eyebrow.

De Melon spread his hands wide. "Hey, it was just a suggestion."

"It's a damned good one," Kanoffski said. "Carrots with your sticks, Bernhard. We'll all be dead by the time it might happen. Offer Gustavus some carrots."

Magdeburg, late March 1635

"*Modus vivendi*," Mike Stearns marveled. "Four months ago, who'd'a thunk it?"

Wilhelm Wettin just shook his head. "Not I."

"It's a genuine offer," Sattler said. "I sat in on almost all of the discussions, as did de Melon. Including their reiteration of the point about carrots."

Frank Jackson snorted. "Right now, Gustavus is simply slavering at the thought of carrot stew."

"Is there any point," Hermann of Hesse-Rotenburg asked, "in mentioning to the emperor just how *remote* the possibility is that the County of Burgundy would ever revert to the USE? Claudia de Medici has an established reputation for fecundity. Bernhard's parents produced eleven sons."

Sattler shook his head. "Not, I think, when the emperor's

succession is entirely dependent upon one rather small girl, with no prospect for more heirs."

"So." Mike looked at Wettin. "Your brother, your call. You're the incoming prime minister. Rebecca insists that I say this. If you absolutely can't live with this proposal that Bernhard has made, for whatever punctilious points of honor that seem to be so important down-time, tell me now."

Wettin put his hand flat on the table. "Follow it up."

"All right, then. Sattler, you and de Melon go back to get this finalized. Stop by Bolzen and get the Tyrol proposal finalized, too. TEA has put the Monster at your disposal. Not as an act of charity, I regret to say. I hope the budget office is really into heavy short-term investment for the prospect of long-term solid gains."

Bolzen, March 1635

"If We do not even try for more," the regent said, "then We certainly will not receive it. We have not observed that the USE is in the practice of distributing bonuses or free gifts. Moreover, if one perceives the matter properly, it could almost be said that We deserve this."

Even Dr. Bienner looked skeptical.

The regent persisted. She was nothing if not tenacious.

"There is no precedent for this in the organization of the USE provinces," Sattler protested.

"Make one."

"There is no provision for this in the USE constitution."

"Amend it."

"I am far from certain that Prime Minister Stearns will, under any circumstances, consent to the admission of a state which has a *hereditary* governor's office, settled on your children and the heirs of their bodies, independently of whether or not titles of nobility should at some future date be abolished."

"Who runs the USE? The prime minister or the emperor?"

Sattler didn't feel like pushing the point just then. He was fully aware that in the view of Gustavus Adolphus, his desk was the one that held the sign that proclaimed "The buck stops here." He was equally aware that Stearns was not fully with that program.

He was tired of starting to think in up-time terms and phrases.

Overall, he would find it a relief when Wettin took office in June.

✧   ✧   ✧

"The threat of a plague epidemic has weakened the governments of many of the smaller entities along Swabia's border with Bavaria. We fear that Duke Maximilian might come creeping in. We have already extended Tyrol's protection to Irsee, to Ottobeuren, to Füssen, to Mindelheim, to Roggenburg. We would have been happy to do the same for the prince-bishopric of Augsburg, but Margrave Georg Friedrich of Baden forestalled Us by doing the same first."

Claudia paused, a dissatisfied expression on her face. She hadn't thought that the old man was still capable of carrying out a preemptive strike.

"Having thus sheltered them from foreign dangers, We feel it is only reasonable that they be incorporated into the new 'state' of Tyrol rather than into the Province of Swabia that was proposed in June 1634 at the Congress of Copenhagen."

Philipp Sattler, on behalf of the USE, somehow did not see the matter the same way. He particularly did not see it the same way when she offered to extend Tyrol's "benevolent protection" to his home town of Kempten.

Sometimes, even Claudia de Medici did not get everything she wanted.

"God be thanked," Matt Trelli said to Marcie in the privacy of their rooms. "I didn't go to all those little abbeys and manors and things to snitch them up for Tyrol. She told me that I was going to organize the local authorities to be in a better position to cope if plague passed the quarantine lines. I don't want to go down in history as a lackey of the imperialist forces. The damned woman's a shark."

Eventually, however, Sattler completed the commission with which he had left Magdeburg. Signed, sealed, and delivered. Tyrol and Burgundy, both. He had even managed to sneak a few protective provisions into the document establishing a new Tyrolese regency council for Claudia's sons.

"So far, so good," he said to de Melon as he packed his briefcase for the return to Magdeburg. "But if you ask me, she'll be back. This won't be the end of it. Not tomorrow and not next year, but that woman could play the starring role in some story, perhaps one of these 'movies,' that Herr Piazza was telling me about. "The Tomato That Ate Cleveland," I believe was the title. I am not certain why Herr Piazza refers to the regent of Tyrol as a tomato."

Epilogue

Some Months Later

Rebecca and Amalie Elisabeth contemplated the newest map of the area that would have become a nice neat USE Province of Swabia if real life had not intervened.

"It looks like knotted fringe," Amalie said. "Down at the bottom of the map, all the way from the Rhine to the Bavarian border, like a table runner hanging over the edge."

Rebecca shook her head. "No. I think it's more like up-time macramé. I saw some in Donna Bates' house—the woman whose daughter has married Prince Vladimir—back the first year or so after the Ring of Fire, when I was living in Grantville. The maker starts with a lot of strings fastened to a dowel or rod. She brings them down and knots them, over and over, to make a pretty design."

She shook her head again. "Poor Michael."

Upward Mobility

Charles E. Gannon

June 1634

"We are almost at the border of Grantville, Herr Miro."

Estuban Miro tried to nod an acknowledgement, but the motion was lost amidst the greater swayings and jouncings imparted by the wagon's passage across yet another set of muddy ruts. Miro had heard of the wonderful roads in and around Grantville, of their many improvements, but this was not one of those major thoroughfares. Political unrest in Franconia had peaked in the past few months, prompting the regional teamsters to give it a wide berth. Ultimately, that had meant a final approach on this narrow, twisting pike that pushed into Grantville out of Hersfeld, well to the west.

Despite the presumed safety of the route, the driver had been slightly more alert the last few miles. Just south of the light forest that hemmed in this modest lane, the road from troubled Suhl wound its way north into Grantville. Indeed, according to the driver, even along this pike, recent reports of—

There were sudden, sharp noises in the brush. Cracking branches and the unmistakable rustling of rapid, even violent motion. Miro's hand went to his dagger, a move which prompted the driver to scrabble for the rude ox prod *cum* cudgel that he kept at his side.

As Miro tracked the approaching noise, he noticed a small glade just beyond the treeline to the east. This was an excellent ambush

point for bandits, particularly since the slight dogleg in this stretch
of the road hid it from both its east and west continuations.

The low brush seemed to burst outward at them; Miro drew
his dagger, went into a crouch—and froze. A small, wooly ram—a
merino?—leaped out into the roadway. Right behind it—generating
a much larger explosion of sundered underbrush—was an equally
immature ram of much less prepossessing appearance. The horns
of both animals were small and ineffectual, but evidently spring
had awakened their nascent rutting aggression. Or at least it had
so affected the pursuer, who made up for his lack of comeliness
with an inversely proportionate allotment of spunk. Charging
stoutly, he routed the other ruminant eastward. Then, with what
seemed a singularly defiant—and self-satisfied—glance at the
wagon and its occupants, the unbecoming ramlet trotted further
westward along the road.

Another commotion in the underbrush augured further drama: a
boy—perhaps nine years old—broke free of the clutching foliage in
a thrashing tumble of leaves and limbs. He jumped up and swore
vehemently: "*Heugabel!*" Ignoring the wagon and its occupants,
his searching gaze found the young ram's receding rump. The
boy's mouth opened wide; invective streamed out: "*Ess-oh-Essen,
du verdammten scheisskopf! Komm' doch hier! Schnell!*" And, the
sound of his further exhortations dwindling along with his spare
form, the boy—and his wooly charge—were lost to sight.

The wagoneer shook his head. "Here, around Grantville, ist all-
vays trubble. Even der rams are *rebellisch*... 'rebelyus,' I tink ist
die Englisch wort." He shook his head again. "All-vays trubble."

Miro shrugged and carefully resheathed his dagger. Trouble, he
supposed, was in the eye of the beholder. Miro had begun his
journey to Grantville by debarking upon the shadiest wharves of
Genoa, then heading north to begin his transalpine journey via
Chiavenna. That newly open city had been tense: still patrolled
by various Hapsburg detachments, this gateway to the Valtelline
had lately become a hotbed of suspicion and intrigue.

Of course, Italy in general was tense. The anti-Spanish restive-
ness in Naples was increasing steadily. Rome had been simmering higher as Philip of Spain became increasingly impatient with
Urban VIII's "irresolute stance" toward heretical faiths. And with
Galileo's much-anticipated trial approaching... Estuban Miro had
simply been glad to leave Italy when he did. As a *marrano*—a

"hidden Jew" of Iberian origin—any region in which both Spanish truculence and religious intolerance were on the rise was a region he preferred avoiding.

His transalpine journey had been slow (as he had been warned), but not particularly arduous: the light, intermittent snows of spring had been far less trouble than the run-off from the post-winter melt. The passes weren't the only messy parts of Switzerland, though: tariffs, tolls, and other administrative pilferings mired every border between the cantonments. Once beyond the alps in Konstanz, his travel choices had been either an armed caravan through still-embattled and bandit-ridden Swabia, or a barge up the Rhine and over on the Main to Frankfurt. And thence by wagon, and occasional cart, to—well, to this very spot on the road.

The trees diminished on either side of the lane as it neared a more substantial east-west road. The driver pointed to the northeast, where the land seemed to jump up with an eerie suddenness: the famed rampart that was an artifact of the Ring of Fire. "Grantville," he announced. And with a shake of his head, he predictably amended, "Trubble."

Miro smiled. For the driver, the growing cluster of strange buildings and strange customs would certainly define "trouble." But for Estuban Miro, it simply meant "new and different."

And that, in turn, meant "opportunity."

July 1634

Don Francisco Nasi rose and proferred his right hand as Miro entered. The reputed spymaster's shake was not perfunctory, but it was brief.

Sitting in unison with his host, Estuban noted that this office, like every other he had seen in Grantville, was spartan by Mediterranean standards. Indeed, it was austere by any standards of the world outside the borders of this strange town, even considering that this small room was merely Nasi's occasional "satellite office": his duties were now in Magdeburg.

Don Francisco evidently eschewed small talk: "I'm sorry we could not meet earlier. My work for the Congress of Copenhagen was quite time consuming. Tell me, how are you enjoying Grantville, so far?"

"It is full of wonders, mysteries, and puzzlements. I had heard the tales, of course, even seen some of the books. But it does not prepare one for . . . all of this."

Nasi almost smiled. "Yes, it can be a bit overwhelming. Perhaps that is why you have not yet called upon my brothers or cousins? After all, it is not every day that a relative from the Mediterranean arrives in Grantville."

Miro managed not to smile: Nasi was tactful, but wasted little time. "It would not have been appropriate, Don Francisco. It was best that I made my presence generally known in town so that you might—assess me—first."

"'Assess you'?" Don Francisco repeated mildly.

"Of course: to determine if I am whom I claim to be."

Nasi spread his hands in dismay. "But you could no doubt furnish us with letters of introduction from your many commercial contacts. Or from your own father, my father's nephew—" and he stopped when he saw Miro's widening smile.

Miro shifted into Hebrew as he asked: "My father is your father's *nephew*? Hmm: shall I trace the entwined branches of our family trees, *Reb* Francisco? My father is your father's first cousin once removed, not his nephew. Joaquin Nasi is your grandfather through his son—your father—Mendo. Joaquin is my great-grandfather through his daughter Ana, my grandmother. But this proves little: any clever impostor would think to memorize our family tree."

Don Francisco smiled, responded in the same language. "Perhaps—but not many could recite it so concisely and certainly as that, cousin. And I doubt any impostors would be able to mimic that Mallorquin accent so well, as well as the small linguistic quirks of Palma's *xuetas*."

Miro answered Nasi's smile with one of his own. "You have a keen ear, Don Francisco." Even other *marranos* usually failed to discern his origins as a son of Mallorca's Jewish—or *xueta*—community. Even when Estuban allowed his home dialect to emerge.

Nasi leaned forward, all business again—but now, with a decidedly sympathetic undercurrent. "So tell me: why do you have no letters of recommendation? As I hear it, you have contacts in Venice—"

Miro waved a negating hand. "Impossible. Seeking their attestations would have compromised my family in Palma."

One of Nasi's eyebrows elevated. "How so?"

Miro shifted to Spanish, and adopted the bearing and diction of a true *hidalgo*. "Don Francisco, I was not just any *marrano*. No one outside of the *xueta* community in Palma knew I was a Jew. No one. The *marrano*s I dealt with in Portugal thought me a Spaniard. And I never undertook any action, or entered into any relationship, that connected me with other *marranos*—including my own family. That is why I have not been back to the Balearics in eight years."

Don Francisco leaned back, and despite his legendarily imperturbable demeanor, his mouth hung open a little. "Eight years?"

Miro nodded. "I went on my first trading voyage when I was seventeen. My father decided I had a gift for commerce and for navigating the various social complexities that it implies for us *marranos*. So at nineteen, it was decided that I was to be withdrawn from activity beyond the *xueta* community. I disappeared, insofar as the outside world was concerned."

Don Francisco nodded, understanding. "So you could emerge with a different identity, six years later, groomed to pass as a *hidalgo* and to operate as one in all regards, down to the smallest detail. And all the records of your community's hidden holdings, accounts, contacts—?"

Miro tapped his temple. "All up here. Never written down, not one bit of it."

"And your credentials were never questioned?"

Miro kept his shrug modest. "Why would they be? I never attended a court, I never went to a ball, I never proposed a joint family venture, I never wooed a gentleman's daughter. My purpose—and my activities—were purely business, and my demeanor and speech were my *bona fides*."

"So, given your extreme separation, how did you manage to function as a factor for the *xuetas* in Palma?"

"By working as a cargo broker only, and by making sure that my terminal clients in the Mediterranean were non-Jews who had a record of preferring to do business with the *xuetas* of Palma. I was able to impose terms on most transactions which made it inevitable that they would be brought—advantageously—to my community. Whose merchants would know, by a variety of codes, that it was I who had sent the deal to them. The money I made as a broker and speculator was, however, the source of our greatest gains, and I funneled both my profits, and my community's, into separate accounts in Venice. My family and friends access theirs through a lawyer who specializes in handling confidential transactions in the Rialto."

Nasi frowned. "And you left your position—why?"

"Firstly, many excellent opportunities in the Mediterranean were compromised when the Nasis departed *en masse* from the Ottoman Empire." He allowed himself a smile at Don Francisco's raised eyebrows. "I do not criticize your decision; indeed, have I not made the same one myself? But the regional consequences were undeniable: the *marrano* business networks that you managed in the Mediterranean faltered when your direct control dissipated.

"Besides, the trade in the Mediterranean is changing and as it does, it attracts new scrutiny. Any determined attempt to track where my trades ultimately resolve would reveal a suspiciously high percentage of them ending quite favorably in the hands of the *xuetas* of Palma. Not that I am particularly worried about the Spanish government: Olivares' hordes of auditors and investigators have troubles enough without worrying about small fish such as myself. Besides, they would only discover that I am facilitating trade upon which they grow ever more dependent, as their failures in war and diplomacy mount."

Nasi nodded. "So, since exposing your past did not threaten you personally, your primary fear was for how it might impact your community."

"Exactly. I was particularly worried by a group of broadly inquisitive Portuguese nationalists that I knew: they would have found me extremely useful against their Spanish occupiers. Even though attempts at directly extorting me would have been fruitless, the related knowledge of how we *xuetas* have been manipulating trade would been decisive leverage against my community."

Nasi steepled his fingers. "Our old Ottoman masters might have seen a similar advantage in coercing you to become their confidential agent—and not just with regard to the Spanish, but all the European nations of the Mediterranean.

Miro nodded. "So, to protect my community, I left my life as a broker quickly, unannounced—and with no time or opportunity to access my own funds in Venice."

"And now you hope to go into business in Grantville?"

"That is my hope. Although I am open to opportunities involving an official position, as well."

Evidently Don Francisco heard the subtle inquiry; he shook his head—sadly, Miro thought: "Had you arrived two years ago..." Nasi shrugged. "But now, if I tried to—to find a place—for you, there would be strong accusations of nepotism. And let us speak truth: what credentials, besides your claims of who you are and what you have done, do I have of your abilities and accomplishments?"

"None whatsoever." Miro smiled and stood. "My regards to your family."

August 1634

While he waited for the bank's chief officer, Señor—no, "Mister"— Walker, to finish guiding an elderly lady through a lien agreement, Estuban Miro considered his unusual situation. He was, by any reasonable assessment, a relatively affluent man, yet all his money was trapped in a Venetian bank. Radio was, unfortunately, no answer to his predicament. Even if access had not been highly restricted, no responsible bank would transmit or receive confidential instructions through these devices, since their nonofficial operations were expressly excluded from any assurances of secrecy.

So he would have to endure the to-and-fro tedium of exchanging bonded letters with Venice. The first several would be necessary to establish his identity, achieved through a multi-tiered set of codes and checks. Next would come detailed financial instructions, and finally, the actual transfer of credit to the bank here in Grantville. Even if he was fortunate, it would be at least four months before any of his assets—other than his emergency stash—became available.

So here he sat, waiting to see if there was a way to parlay his remaining travel monies into real estate. If the bank was willing to extend him any credit whatsoever, it might allow him to buy a humble property in which he himself could live while subsisting upon the meager rents generated by boarders. The plan elicited a small grin: the price of his newfound freedom was, evidently, a life of penurious humility. His old, Talmud-spouting neighbor in Palma would have found much to appreciate in this pass of events.

However, it wasn't the frugality of the investment that irked Miro: it was the *wrongness* of it. There was a new kind of business booming here in Grantville, which was the epicenter of an expanding trade in information and credit-based (or as some called it, "liquid") finance. In all the known world, only Venice and Amsterdam had possessed primitive precursors of this kind of fluid commercial network. And of course they—and so many others—had now assiduously studied and selectively adapted the vast array of up-time financial instruments for the specific needs of their rapidly altering markets.

These trends were spawning a peculiar kind of economy, particularly in Grantville: here, the power of the up-timer bourse was not vested in traditional accumulations of common goods, coin, and land, but in a far-flung network of high-value, and often rare, equipment, information, and expertise. Interestingly, many of the most lucrative contracts involving the transfer of these "new goods" resembled the contraband trade. The freight was extremely low-volume, high-value, and required maximum security: the most common examples were bonds, contracts, bank notes, correspondence, research, copied up-time books, sometimes gems and specie. And in addition to safe transport, these objects also wanted rapid transport: it seemed that a constant challenge in this new economy was that its crucial assets were always needed in too many places at precisely the same time. And that, Miro knew, was the key to a whole new kind of wealth: anyone who could figure a way to swiftly and safely move these key resources from one nexus of need to another would become a very rich man, indeed.

But how to do it? Airplanes possessed the obvious, needed characteristics—but, just as obviously, were not a practical answer at all. Regularly chartering airplanes was as completely out of the question as was owning them. Those few that existed were already overtaxed, and those in private hands seemed to spend half of their working hours commandeered by the government or its confidential agents. Furthermore, the airplane's need of specialized infrastructure—airfields, prepositioned fuel and maintenance caches, repair personnel and ground crew—made the establishment of a broad, commercial network based upon these rare and complex vehicles something far beyond his capacity for investment, even if all his Venetian resources were at his fingertips...

But they were not, and that lack echoed the very problem he sought to solve: if only there was a faster way to transfer the funds, to access his remote capital for a timely local investment...

Miro caught movement from the corner of his eye: Coleman Walker was finally heading his way, the banker's elderly customer now being escorted to her safe deposit box by a teller. However, before Walker crossed half the distance, his subordinate—an eager, but somewhat disheveled looking fellow named Marlon Pridmore—rose and snared his manager with an eager, urgent phrase. Behind, the elderly lady reemerged from the vault, evidently in some dither of uncertainty, her eyes scanning intently for her implicit savior, Mr. Walker.

Miro, sensing a further delay in the offing, edged closer—and heard Marlon Pridmore gushing: "So we've got the burner running at peak efficiency now, even with alternate fuels." Walker, facing slightly away from Pridmore, rolled exasperated eyes as his employee burbled on: "I tell you, Coleman, that balloon of mine is going to soar..."

By which time the little old lady had returned: she scooped her desperate arm through Walker's, who allowed himself to be drawn away with an apologetic glance.

Which Miro hardly saw. All he could see was the radiant glee of the ballooning enthusiast who stood before him, albeit now somewhat sheepishly.

"Sorry, sir—I just get carried away when I'm talking about the balloon I'm building." Pridmore looked away guiltily. "Other folks can get pretty tired hearing about it."

"Not me," Miro averred flatly. "Tell me more."

Pridmore did just that. In excruciating detail. Miro estimated that he had understood about one third of Pridmore's discursis, possessed a vague conceptual appreciation of a second third, and was absolutely baffled by the rest. But he also knew that none of that mattered: what mattered was that Mr. Marlon Pridmore—an indifferently skilled bank officer—might be able to construct a working balloon. Or, in Estuban Miro's mind, a commercially viable form of air transport.

Pridmore was wrapping up: "I'm actually amazed you can follow all this, Mr. Miro, particularly without any drawings or models to show you. Understanding a blimp is easier when you can see it."

"Well, then: may I see it?"

Pridmore, like a proud father being asked to display his newborn child, beamed mightily. "Why, sure you can! Whenever you want."

Miro rose. "How about now?"

The ride to Pridmore's house was not long, and was the first Miro had ever taken in an up-time automobile. But he almost failed to notice the marvels of this conveyance, so focused were this thoughts.

Balloons. He had read a little about them in the library already. They were not fast in terms of absolute velocity—certainly not in comparison to airplanes—but, like airplanes, balloons recognized few obstacles. Because the sky was their home, they flew as straight as the crow, rather than crawling as crooked as the tortoise. And for them, airfields were not required: a network of the simple support facilities would be easy enough to set up in communities located at the right intervals. And the operation of a blimp was, in comparison to piloting an airplane, almost laughably simple: it was the difference between manning a rowboat on a fishpond and steering a three-masted merchantman through treacherous reefs.

And bandits and toll collectors could only stare up and wonder what small treasures might be nestled in the gondola above them, seemingly close overhead, but for all practical purposes, as distant from their greedy hands as the wealth of Prester John's fabled kingdom.

Pridmore's balloon turned out to be a surprisingly simple device. Large when inflated—it would measure 150 feet in length, and 60 in girth—it became so small when deflated that it would easily fit in its own, longboat-sized, wicker gondola. Two engines—up-time devices once used to propel small, two-wheeled vehicles—provided the motive force that pushed the floating lozenge through the air. Close beneath the bag—or "envelope"—of the vehicle was what Pridmore called a "burner"—a special torch which sent new hot air upwards to keep the canvas inflated. Miro found himself deeply impressed by the elegance and practicality of the whole vehicle.

Or at least, of its many unassembled pieces: they lay about the master ballooner's small barn in what almost looked like disarray, the envelope itself still a pile of unsewn strips. Miro gestured toward the gear: "It seems that you have a long way to go before your airship is ready, Mister Pridmore."

Marlon—who was also called "Swordfish," for reasons having to do with an obscure pun on piscine nomenclature—nodded sadly. "Yeah, got a ways to go with this ol' girl. Just me and Bernard doing the work. A few other folks pitch in—when they have the time."

"Can you not hire more workers?"

Pridmore stared sideways at him. "On my salary? Not hardly. I'm lucky to have a week where I get twenty hours to work on her." He sighed and stared longingly at the somewhat chaotic collection of airship components. "Not like I haven't had offers, though."

Miro turned to face Pridmore. "To what offers are you referring?"

"Well, there was a bunch of Venetian fellows who came out here just last week. Said they had come all the way from Italy just to learn how to build aircraft—any aircraft. But none of the airplane firms wanted 'em: they've got more staff and apprentices than they can pay, right now, and these Venetian fellas didn't have any prior experience with up-time machines. So they wound up coming here. They were plenty interested but couldn't stick around: said they needed a salary more than knowledge, so they left. Can't say as how I blame them. Last I heard, they were trying to scrape enough dollars together just to get back to Venice."

Miro began walking to the barn door; Pridmore looked up, surprised, and trotted after. "Where are you goin', Mr. Miro?"

"If you would be so good as to drive me back to town, Mr. Pridmore, I have some new business to conduct there."

An hour from closing time, the tubular door chimes sounded, causing Nicolo Peruzzi to look up from securing the display case in the front room of Roth, Nasi, & Partners, Jewelry Sales and Lapidary Services. His first instinctual hope was that it might be a customer, but one glance made him conclude otherwise.

He had seen this fellow before—a handsome, saturnine man of about thirty years with a hint of the *hidalgo* about him. And today he seemed more Mephistophelean than usual. Perhaps it was because he entered the store alone, and Peruzzi was—uncharacteristically—without nearby employees. Perhaps it was because of the fellow's careful backward glance into street, as if checking to ensure that he was neither followed nor under observation. Or perhaps it was because of the long, straight dagger he produced as soon as the door had closed behind him.

Peruzzi's hand went to the large button under the rear lip of the display case and remained there, quite taut. Was this fellow—named Miro?—really going to rob him? In broad daylight? It was known that, although Miro was a wealthy man, he was struggling financially, still separated from his funds in Venice. But had he really become so desperate? And so stupid? Did he really think he would get more than a mile from the store before the police—?

But Miro smiled at Peruzzi and pointed with his finger—not the dagger: "May I borrow that small—do you say, 'screwdriver'?—please?"

Wordlessly, and now as thoroughly baffled as he had been terrified, Peruzzi complied.

Miro used the screwdriver to wedge up the brass band that secured the narrow neck of the pommel to the end of the dagger's grip. Then, exerting pressure in the opposite direction, he levered the pommel off the hilt. As it fell into Miro's hand, Nicolo saw that it was hollow—and that, nestled inside, were two rubies and an emerald, the latter of a most prodigious size.

Sometime later—seconds? minutes?—Nicolo Peruzzi realized that he had been staring at the green stone, and that his jaw had been hanging slack. As he closed it with an embarrassed snap, Miro smiled faintly and said: "I am told that up-time gem-cutting techniques can dramatically increase the value of these stones. What share of the emerald would you charge to undertake this service for me?"

The Venetians were not hard to find in the Thuringen Gardens. In the first place, there were nine of them. In the second place, they had obviously been nursing well-watered wine and a few pretzels for a very long time. In the third place, they wore the morose expressions of the underemployed.

Miro sat down without invitation. "May I buy the table a round of drinks?"

From that moment on, no invitations were needed. Nor credentials. Nonetheless, Estuban Miro provided a (strategically edited) review of his assets, prospects, and immediate interests: to wit, constructing an airship. He ended by staring hard at the one who seemed to be the group's leader, a fellow named Franchetti. "Can you build it?"

"What? Signor Pridmore's airship?" Franchetti shrugged. "Our conversation with him never went so far. After all, we came here to build air-o-planes."

"Airplanes," Miro corrected him.

"*Si*: air-o-planes. But we learned that we did not have the skills for that work. Or the knowledge. And for every up-timer who could teach us, there are a hundred, maybe a thousand, down-timers who want to learn. And it is a long process—made longer if one does not read English."

"Or does not read at all," grumbled his beefiest partner.

"*Si*: this is true. The balloon—that would be easier. But Signor Pridmore, he does the work himself; he has no way to pay us. And we must eat."

"And, I fear, go home," added another sadly, watching a bevy of jeans-clad young women, recent high school grads, swaying past, the denim evidently painted on their hips.

Miro kept his eyes upon Franchetti's. "If Signor Pridmore were to let you watch him at his work, and explain his procedures as he did so, do you think you could learn to build it?"

The Venetian shrugged. Among the French, that gesture would have meant, "it simply cannot be done." Among Italians, it meant "of *course* it can be done." His words matched the motion: "Yes, the balloon is not so difficult, I think. We have the right kind of skills. Sails, wheel locks, ships, dyes, even clocks—one or more of us have had a hand in crafting all these things in Venice. The work we saw Signor Pridmore doing—the physical tasks—appeared simple enough. But what to do, and why, and in what order?" He shook his head. "Of this, we have only a small understanding."

"Or no understanding," put in the beefiest one again. Miro decided that this large brooding fellow—apparently named Bolzano—could not be a bad sort: he was too forthright about his own cognitive limitations.

The wiry leader went on. "But together, we could learn to copy what he does. Particularly if he will take the time to explain each action and its purpose."

Miro allowed himself the luxury of a small smile. "That, I think, can be arranged," he said, producing a purse that attracted the eyes of the Venetians like a magnet attracts iron filings.

October 1634

Marlon Pridmore clapped an encouraging hand down on Franchetti's narrow shoulder. The Venetian foreman nodded gratitude and withdrew to study the burner yet again. "They're clever guys, most of them," Pridmore averred with a nod as he came to stand beside Miro. "Hardly need all the tutoring you're paying me to give them. They'll build you a fine balloon, sure enough."

"They have an excellent teacher."

Pridmore looked abashed and very, very proud. "Aw, I jus'—"

"You have taught them as no one else could. Their progress is extraordinary." *Yes,* Miro added to himself, *so extraordinary that they are already outpacing you, Marlon.* Not that there was any surprise in that; a handful of part-time enthusiasts were no match for nine artisans working full time. But that speed of construction had a price—nine salaries worth, to be exact. So Miro had to use his limited funds as efficiently as possible, which gave him no choice but to complete his own airship before Pridmore's. But one particular difficulty had begun to loom large: "Mr. Pridmore, I am concerned about our engines."

"What about them? Don't they work?"

"Yes—I mean, I believe so. But they are not the same as yours. They are—what is the term?—'lawn-mower' engines. And this is where the understanding of my men is so very limited. Is there any chance that they could receive some special tutoring in regards to these engines? That, for an additional consideration, you might guide them through—?"

"An additional consideration? Don Estuban, your weekly fee for my services is plenty enough as it is. But I'll tell you what: some of the real small-engine experts are over at Kelly Aircraft. And Kelly always needs extra money. So if you could push a few hundred at him—"

"It will be as you say. And if you will be so kind as to be my intermediary to Mr. Kelly, I believe it is only right that you receive fifteen percent of the fee I will give him. This is your 'finder's fee' principle, yes?"

"Well, yes—but maybe you could help me with something else, instead."

"If I can, I will."

"Well, it's like this: to make the canvas really hold the air, I need to coat it with a blend of different substances. And one of them is pretty hard to get, up here."

"Oh? And what is that?"

"Gum arabic. I'm telling you, with a few gallons of that stuff, I could—"

"I believe I have a connection for that substance, Mr. Pridmore. And I think he owes me enough old favors that it can be made available at a very reasonable price."

Pridmore's gleeful expression made his answer redundant. "Not a problem, Don Estuban. Hell, I was worried that I might not be able to afford enough—or maybe *any*—gum arabic. So this is great news, just great."

"I am happy to be of service," said Miro with a small bow, and a smaller smile.

"Not as pleased as I am for your help, Don Estuban."

Staring at the engines, Miro straightened and let his smile expand. "I assure you, Mr. Pridmore, the pleasure is all mine."

December 1634

Francisco Nasi watched Piazza reading the report. "Miro's airship is already closer to completion than Pridmore's. Much closer."

"Mmmm-hmmm," Piazza subvocalized.

"He's very good at what he does."

"Pridmore?"

"No: Miro."

"You mean, building airships?"

Nasi sighed; every time he made one of his brief returns to Grantville, Piazza seemed to take a subtle delight in becoming marginally more obtuse. "No, Ed: I mean Miro is very good at getting information, managing relationships, coordinating disparate operations and drawing upon widely divergent resources."

Ed put down the report. "What are you saying?"

Nasi shrugged. "I'm saying that you might want to consider Miro's capabilities in the context of a more—permanent—relationship with this government."

"You mean, as a spy?"

"No. As an intelligence officer. Maybe even chief of intelligence, eventually."

Piazza put aside his glasses: it was an exasperated gesture. "Francisco, we've already got one of those." He stared meaningfully at Grantville's resident spymaster.

"For now, yes. But Mike anticipates that when his time as prime minister is over, he is likely to relocate, and my own interests might take me in the same direction."

"Oh, so we're back to the imminent Prague exodus again...."

"Ed, I understand you don't welcome the thought of it, much less the actuality, but I have a duty there—not just to the USE, but to my people. Sooner or later, I must—" He sent a desultory wave toward the east. Toward Prague.

Piazza made a sound that resembled "Umhh-grumpff" and looked at the reports on Miro's airship project again. "So you think he could do your job?"

Francisco shrugged. Was it his merchant's instinct not to "hard sell" Miro—or a sense of pride—that kept him from simply answering "yes"? Instead he said, "His mind is nimble, highly adaptive, but also capable of sustained focus. He speaks and writes six languages. He is a trained observer of nuances, including social ones—such as those required to construct and to live an assumed identity for almost ten years. He has extraordinary knowledge of one of our most urgent intelligence areas, having unparalleled familiarity with waters, ports, and markets of the Mediterranean. And he learns very, very quickly."

"So you've been watching him? And he's reliable?"

"Yes, to both."

"Do you think he knows you're watching him?"

"Of course he knows. As I said, he's very good at what he does."

January 1635

Marlon Pridmore walked around the large barn that Miro had rented, staring at the neatly arranged airship components at its center.

"You know, I would have been happy to do this without the extra—"

"Mr. Pridmore, please. It is the least I could offer. Your presence here is of immense help to us."

Pridmore snorted out a laugh. "Really? Hell, I wish my shop

looked so good—or I was so far along." He started walking again, eyeing the rows of empty fuel tanks professionally. "Giving yourself a lot of operating range, eh?"

"Or more payload over shorter distances—and at higher speeds."

Pridmore stopped. "How high a speed?"

"It is our objective to be able to operate at thirty-five mph."

Pridmore started, then glanced back at the envelope. "Thirty-five mph? Then you're building it wrong."

Miro felt a stab of panic deep in his bowels, but gave no sign of it. "Wrong in what way?"

"Well, you need a keel and a nose-frame; you can't just have an unsupported bag."

Miro's response was the most routine sentence he used when discussing balloons with Marlon Pridmore. "I don't understand: what do you mean?"

"I mean, if you try to get an unsupported hot air envelope up to 35 mph, it's going to deform on you."

Miro felt an incipient frown and kept it off his face. "Can you explain that to me . . . erm, visually?"

"Oh, sure. You've seen soap bubbles, right?"

"Yes."

"And they stay round as they float through the air, right?"

"Yes."

"But what happens if you blow too hard on them—either with the wind or against it?"

Miro thought for a second, then nodded. "Their shape begins to stretch, to warp. They can't really be pushed very hard without, without—"

"We would call it 'being deformed by atmospheric drag.' It's the same with a loose-bag blimp; there's only so fast you can go before the 'nose' of the bag starts dimpling and buckling: the air inside can't hold the shape against the pressure generated by the air friction on the outside."

"So you need a . . . an 'internal skeleton' to help it keep its shape."

"Right. In this case, you don't need more than a keel and a nose-cone—sort of like a spine with an underslung umbrella at the front."

"I see. And you would know how to make this?"

"Why, sure. And Kelly will have some good tips for you, too. Better, maybe."

"This is most helpful: please, let me compensate you for your advice."

"You already do compensate me for my advice. Damn, your money is helping me far more than my advice is helping you."

Miro smiled as he opened his purse. "Trust me when I insist that you are quite mistaken in that assumption, Mr. Pridmore; quite mistaken, indeed."

March 1635

Despite the bitter wind that drove the cold rain sideways into every pedestrian's face, Francisco Nasi waved broadly at Miro and crossed the street toward him.

Miro waved back and smiled. He had not seen much of Nasi over the last five months. Mike Stearns'—and Ed Piazza's—spymaster extraordinaire was usually in Magdeburg, often closeted for marathon meetings, and sometimes "traveling on business" to places about which only one thing was known: they were far away from Grantville. In consequence, Miro had had few opportunities to converse with Nasi again—and whenever he did so, Miro sensed—what? A shadow of guilt? A hint of regret?

Miro took Francisco's extended hand, noted the same slightly melancholy smile. "How are you, Don Francisco?"

"I'm freezing, so my senses still function. And you, Don Estuban?" Nasi's use of his full, correct title was code, but its message was quite clear: Nasi had learned that Miro's Venetian funds had finally arrived, were more considerable than even he had guessed, and—most importantly—were the proof positive that the *xueta* was exactly who he had claimed to be almost eight months earlier.

"I am well enough, Don Francisco. And my project is nearing completion." *As if you didn't already know that.*

"Excellent. But it must be very absorbing. We don't see much of you in town."

"But how would you know if I'm in town, Don Francisco? Your presence here seems much rarer than mine."

"*Touché.* But I have much family here, and they are my eyes and ears. On the streets, in the restaurants, elsewhere—"

Elsewhere. By which you mean, "the synagogue."

Nasi looked up the street at nothing in particular. "I have

regretted that the circumstances of your arrival made it impossible to—to welcome you, as was proper. As is traditional."

Miro proferred a small bow. "You had no choice, Don Francisco. Your official responsibilities must trump all other considerations."

"Yes. But only for as long as they must." Nasi put out his hand to say farewell, opened his mouth, waited a long moment before speaking. "You have no family here. And a *seder* alone is no *seder* at all." Then Nasi smiled faintly, released Miro's hand, and, hunching over, hurried off into the cold.

Miro looked after him: it had not been, strictly speaking, an invitation. But that would no doubt change when Estuban Miro made his appearance in the almost-repaired synagogue this coming Shabbat.

He trusted that the spitting rain hid any other moisture that might have made his eyes blink so quickly. To sit and pray in a synagogue once again. To share a *seder* once again. To hear and speak Hebrew. To be a Jew in something other than name and memory only. To reclaim his life after nine long years.

Estuban stared up into the cold rain and felt suddenly warm, felt his soul rise with the promise of his almost-ready airship.

April 1635

Franchetti angled the props upward a bit, driving the blimp toward the ground. Then he cut the engines, and pulled hard on the lead ground line.

The forward bow of the gondola pushed into the soft loam, and the night-time noises hushed; the moon stared down, bright and indifferent.

As the rest of the Venetians swarmed the craft—affixing new lines, tossing in some ballast, opening flaps—Franchetti hopped out, followed by Bolzano, his beefy assistant in all things. "I am an aviator!" Franchetti cried. "I have flown like the birds!"

Miro smiled. "Excellent work, Franchetti—and you must not breathe a word of it."

"But Don Estuban—"

"This is as we agreed, Franchetti. Would you take away Signor Pridmore's joy at being the 'first' to fly in a balloon? After all he has done to help us build the *Swordfish*?"

Franchetti looked like a truant child. "No, you are right, Don

Estuban—but did we not finish first? Long before him? And look at her! Is she not beautiful?"

Now sagging slightly in the moonlight, her abbreviated ribs showing, Miro thought the airship looked more akin to an emaciated maggot. "She is beautiful indeed, Franchetti—and I promise, in the future, you will be able to tell everyone that you were the first test pilot—for the *next* airship we build."

Franchetti stared at him. "The next—? So we are not done? Then why did you say that this was our final week of pay?"

"Because now we change how you will be paid, Franchetti. I have been thinking that the master craftsmen who build my airships should also have the option to have part ownership in them. Of course, not all will want that. However, for those who do—"

But Franchetti was out of the gondola in a single leap and, landing with his arms around Miro, planted a sweaty kiss on each of the *xueta's* well-shaven cheeks. "I will be an aviator!" he shouted loudly into the night sky.

So loudly that Miro harbored a faint worry that Marlon Pridmore might have heard—and might have lost the joy of thinking himself the first to fly one of the airships he had designed.

May 1635

Francisco Nasi's desk was almost bare, and the contents of his "courtesy office" were now mostly in boxes. Nasi was bound to depart within a few months, and the process of relocation was already underway. But right now, his attention was very much riveted on the report in front of him. "I notice that President Piazza's agents picked up this man Bolzano just a day after you passed word to me that we keep an eye out for him, heading south. What I'm wondering is: why?"

"Why what, Francisco?"

"Why you wanted the local authorities advised to pick him up. And how you knew he was a confidential agent for 'other interests.'"

Miro shrugged. "The answer to the second is also the answer to the first. Bolzano started out as self-deprecating, unskilled illiterate, only worried about securing a salary. But during the process of constructing the *Swordfish*, he proved to be a quick study, dedicated, resourceful. And when I offered extended contracts with better terms to all my workers, he demurred, pleading urgent business in Padua. Nonsense. He had to return south to report to his real employers, and so had to decline the permanent position—which was wholly out of character for the role he had opted to play up here."

"Well, you were right—although it seems he was not working directly for any government. Only a factotum for parties unnamed. But why did you recommend that President Piazza hold him in custody, Estuban?"

"Firstly, Francisco, I suggested it to *you*."

"Yes—and my responsibilities here are finished. I no longer have power in this matter."

Miro decided not to look as dubious as he might have. "Yes— that's what all the official documents say. But it seems to me that President Piazza has asked you to, well, 'watch over' me this far, so I surmised that he might ask you to oversee this final related incident. Just as a means of ensuring a smooth transition, of course."

Nasi did not blink or move for five full seconds. Then he said, almost without moving his lips: "I have certain—discretionary allowances—regarding the resolution of your current project. But let us return to the topic: why did you request that Bolzano be held?"

"First tell me this: why have you elected to do so? My suggestion certainly isn't justifiable grounds for detaining a foreign national, is it?"

Nasi shifted uncomfortably in his chair. "You know it's not."

"Then I was right to guess that—for a little while, at least— Grantville's own intelligence 'brotherhood' would like to keep my balloon a secret."

"Well...yes. So far as it's possible, since the Venetians spoke openly about what they were doing. But most everyone thinks they are still building the first balloon, not the second."

"Yes; that was why I suggested you find and detain Bolzano. Not to protect the knowledge of how to make an airship; that will be common knowledge, soon enough—particularly since this design is so simple. But Bolzano might also have informed others that we already had a working balloon."

"Yes, about that—"

Estuban let himself smile. "It's about Italy, isn't it?"

Nasi's face became completely expressionless. "How do you know?"

"News like that travels quickly; by tomorrow at the latest, every-one in Grantville will know that there will soon be an anti-pope,

and that Urban is missing." Miro smiled wider. "Or is he? Because
if Urban *isn't* missing—if, instead, someone wanted to fly him out
from a spot where there was no airfield, or fly in a special security
team and their equipment—I suspect it might be very helpful to
have a balloon to expedite that kind of mission."

"So you can do it? You can fly to Northern Italy?"

"I can lift three thousand pounds over the Alps and arrive in
Brescia four to eight days after we start out. The journey would
be in four legs. Leg one is to Nürnberg. Then to Biberach. Then
across the Bodensee up to Chur in the Grissons cantonment. Then
south over the Valtelline and onto the Northern Italian plain.
Each leg is a three-hour trip, give or take. Assuming that we must
arrange support at the endpoint of each leg, we should be able
to make a flight every two or three days. If the support could be
arranged ahead of time,"—Miro looked through the wall in the
direction of the radio room—"we could perform a flight a day."

"So we—that is, President Piazza—could have a team on-site
in four days?"

"If you consider Brescia 'on-site,' then, yes: if the weather permits, four days. Assuming that President Piazza—or even higher
authorities—can arrange the necessary support."

"And what kind of support will you need?"

Miro wondered, given the carefully rehearsed diction of that
question, if it had been originally anticipated by Nasi, or Piazza,
or Stearns—or maybe all three. "At each endpoint, we need a
place to store the balloon—which, given its segmented keel, folds
down to fifty feet long and twenty wide. And we need enough
fuel on site—ethanol, methanol, lamp oil, fish oil—for the balloon's next flight."

"Sounds simple."

"Oh, it is—which is why I already have twelve transport contracts for when I begin commercial flights."

"Twelve? Already?"

Miro nodded. "Six out of Venice, one from Lubeck, two from
Amsterdam, one from Prague, two from Brussels."

"And you are carrying—?"

"A fair number of passengers, particularly diplomats and special-
ists. Lots of documents: data, research copies, bonds, certificates,
and contracts of all sorts. Some specie, some spice, some lenses,
even some gemstones and pearls. Low weight, high value. My

rates are steep, but the transport is fast, safe, and almost entirely tariff- and toll-free."

"And could you carry a—a 'special cargo' for President Piazza, first?"

"Of course; here's the rate sheet."

Nasi studied it, blanched, and then looked a bit like a penniless farmer confronting a burly *amtman*. "Estuban—I can't—I don't think the government here can pay these charges."

Miro nodded, watching Nasi closely: another second and the spymaster might start mentioning how President Piazza might need to "nationalize a key asset—such as your balloon—for the duration of the crisis." Probably not, but why risk having the deal move in that direction? By claiming poverty, Nasi had inadvertently given Miro the initiative: "Let's keep the operating expenditures equal to my costs, Francisco: just have the president—or your successor—pay for the fuel and the crew. Besides, what's more important to me than your government's money is your government's political influence."

"What kind of influence?"

"The kind that would allow my airship company to become a government partner in bulk purchasing and shipment of various kinds of fuel. The kind of influence that would help us get support facilities established in the cities we'd be servicing directly. The kind of influence that reduces or eliminates certain tariffs or taxes. In short, nothing that needs to come out of a president's— or a spymaster's—always overburdened operations budget." And Miro smiled.

Francisco smiled back. "To quote a fine, if sentimental, movie I just saw, I suspect that President Piazza may consider this 'the beginning of a beautiful friendship.'"

Miro nodded. "*Casablanca*. See? I'm acclimating. And none too soon, for today I am truly embarking upon the American Dream."

Francisco frowned. "What do you mean?"

Estuban feigned surprise. "Why, I have attained what every person in Grantville is pursuing! Today, as my financial prospects promise to rise with my airship, its seems that I have literally achieved 'upward mobility.'"

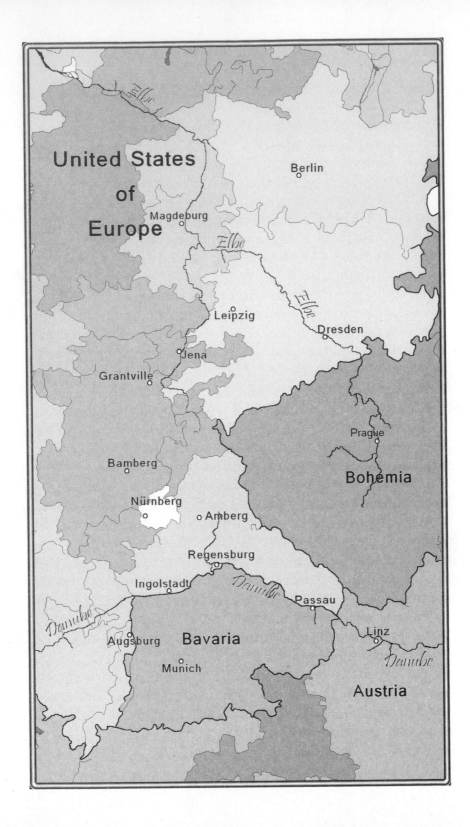

Four Days on the Danube

Eric Flint

Chapter 1

The first notice Rita had that something was amiss was on the startling side. The front door to the small apartment in Ingolstadt's military headquarters that she and her husband Tom had just finished settling into was blown in by an explosion. A splinter from the door sliced open her left arm just below the shoulder. Another splinter flew into her side and stuck there like a pin, just above the hip.

The blast itself sent her stumbling back. She tripped and fell into the fireplace. Where her dress caught fire.

A man came through the door on the heels of the explosion. He had a wheel-lock pistol in his hand which he leveled at her and fired.

That was pretty much the low point of the evening. Luckily for Rita, the door hadn't been completely blown off the hinges. Half of it was still hanging in the entrance and a jagged edge caught the man's sleeve as he brought up the gun. His aim was thrown off and the bullet went into the fireplace instead of Rita's chest.

Squalling with fear and anger, Rita scrambled out of the fire-place. She started slapping at her dress to extinguish the flames licking at the hem. Then, seeing that her assailant was bringing out another pistol, she left off trying to extinguish the flames and

391

turned instead toward the mantelpiece. Her husband Tom kept his shotgun up there.

She wouldn't make it, she realized despairingly. By the time she—

Another crash drew her head around. Tom had burst in from their bedroom. The front room of the apartment doubled as a dining area. Tom disarmed the gunman by the simple expedient of driving the dining table across the floor into the man's hip.

Tom Simpson was a former football lineman. If anything, the years since the Ring of Fire and his military service had put still more meat and muscle on his immense frame. And he certainly hadn't lost any strength. The table smashed into the assailant like a battering ram, smashing his hip and slamming him into the door frame. His eyes rolled up and he slumped into the room unconscious.

Now that he was out of the doorway, Rita could see another assailant coming right behind. This one had a pistol also.

"Watch out, Tom!" she shouted, as she brought the shotgun to bear.

Rita had been raised a country girl, the daughter and sister of coal miners. She'd been handling firearms since she'd gotten a .22 rifle for her eighth birthday and had been hunting pheasant and quail with a shotgun since she was ten.

That had been a 20 gauge, of course, suitable for a small girl. But she'd graduated to a 12 gauge long since.

Tom had the gun loaded for war, not hunting. The heavy slug punched the man back with a hole in his chest. If he wasn't dead already, he would be soon—and either way, he was out of the action.

A third man stood behind him in the corridor, a look of surprise on his face. He had his dying companion half-supported with one arm while he tried to bring his own pistol to bear with the other.

Rita pumped in another round. Since she didn't have a clear shot at the man's center mass, she aimed at his head instead. Later, she'd realize that she could have taken the much easier center mass shot. At that range, a solid slug fired from a 12 gauge would have blown right through the man standing in front. But this was her first gunfight—and it was a mistake even experienced gunmen probably would have made.

The head shot missed, not surprisingly. But the man she'd fired at, who was also not thinking clearly, frantically pushed his dying comrade aside so he could bring up his own pistol and fire.

And miss. The shot went completely wild, in fact, striking the wall of the corridor and never even making it into the room Rita was standing in.

Now she had a center mass shot. She pumped in another round and fired.

And missed. Her intended target, at least—but the shot went high and struck her opponent on the side of the head. A chunk of his skull was torn off and the corridor was splattered with blood and brains all the way to the outside entrance another fifteen feet further down the corridor. The man spun completely around, dropping his pistol, and then collapsed on top of his companion.

Rita jacked in another round. The next thing she knew, she was doused with cold water.

"Hey!" she squealed, spinning around to face this new attack. Just in time, she managed not to point the shotgun at her husband.

"Don't move, dammit," Tom growled. "You're on fire." He had the faucet running in the basin and the saucepan under it. A couple of seconds later, he threw half the contents over her dress.

Looking down, she saw that there were still some flames flickering along one edge.

And her leg hurt. She'd been burned, she realized.

"Ow," she said.

Tom took the time with the third panful to lift up the hem of her dress and carefully pour the water over the still-burning and smoldering spots, instead of just splashing it on her.

"You'd better see to your wounds and change clothes," he said, setting the pan down on the table he'd used to disable the first assailant.

Who, for his part, issued a groan.

Tom leaned over, lifted the man to his feet with one hand, slammed the back of his head against the door jamb again, then let him slump to the ground.

This impact was far more savage than the first. The man would be unconscious for hours. If he wasn't dead—Tom was in a quiet fury and he was very strong.

"I've got to go see what's happening, hon," he said, reaching for the jacket of his uniform hanging by the door.

For the first time, Rita realized there was a cacophony of shouts and gunfire coming from outside. It sounded like the whole city was under attack.

It finally dawned on her that this hadn't been a house invasion by criminals.

"What do you think...?"

Now, Tom was buckling the holster with his sidearm around his waist. He'd had that hanging by the door also.

"At a guess, the Bavarians are attacking."

"But how'd they—"

"Get in? Treachery, I figure. Has to have been, as many as there are from the sounds of it."

His gun holstered, Tom stepped forward, reached out and plucked out the splinter above her hip. That was her first realization that it was there.

"That's probably nothing to worry about," Tom said. "It's hardly even bleeding, from the looks of your dress. But you'd better see to your arm."

For a moment, he seemed to be dancing back and forth, obviously torn by indecision. Rita shook her head.

"I'll be fine," she said. "Go see to your men."

A moment later, he was gone. After giving the corridor a wary glance, Rita put the shotgun back on the mantelpiece and drew her left arm across her chest to get a better look at the wound.

It was bleeding a fair amount, but she didn't think it was really all that serious. The proverbial "minor flesh wound"—except that now it was starting to *hurt*, damn it all.

They had some first aid supplies in a small chest in the bedroom. It was under the bed, since there wasn't much room in the apartment and the kit wasn't something they expected to be needing regularly. She went in, knelt down and looked under the bed. Not to her surprise, she discovered that the first aid kit had faithfully obeyed the Iron Law of Anything Put Under A Bed. By whatever mysterious means, it had migrated to the very center.

So, an already torn, dirty and blood-stained dress got a bit more wear and tear on it, while she half-crawled under the bed to drag out the kit. By the time she got it out, she was worried enough that she almost gave up the effort halfway through. The sounds of fighting from outside were unmistakable now. That was a pitched battle being waged out there, with rifles and grenades—even an occasional cannon shot—not some sort of raid or minor incursion.

With the kit finally in hand, she hurried to the apartment's basin. The military housing had running water, even if it didn't have electricity. Fortunately, there was enough light being shed by the fire and the two lamps in the room for her to start working on her wounds.

The one on her side proved to be minor, sure enough. The dress itself had absorbed most of the impact. But the wound on her arm was a different matter. Once she washed it off and could see the damage clearly, she winced. That gash was big enough and deep enough that it ought to be closed with stitches. But there was no way she would be able to manage that herself, one-handed. She'd just have to be satisfied with a pressure dressing. She wasn't worried about blood loss, as such. But without stitches, she'd wind up with a pretty nasty scar on her upper arm. She tried to console herself with the thought that sleeveless dresses weren't in fashion in the year 1636 anyway.

There was a small bottle of concentrated alcohol in the first aid kit. She used that to sterilize the wound—which *really* hurt—and then started awkwardly wrapping some (theoretically) sterile cloth around it.

Sounds coming from the corridor drew her attention away from the task. She snatched the shotgun off the mantelpiece.

Hearing female voices, she relaxed a bit. There was far too much fighting going on for there to be any enemy camp followers moving around. Then, recognizing one of the voices, she relaxed completely.

"In here, Willa!" she shouted. "I'm alone, and there's no danger!"

She glanced down at the two dead men in the corridor. "Well, no immediate danger, anyway," she added.

A few seconds later, the shapes of three middle-aged women appeared in the corridor. They minced their way across the two bodies, taking care not to step on them.

Their gingerly manner had nothing to do with squeamishness. The nickname given to Willa Fodor, Maydene Utt and Estelle McIntire was "the Three Auditors of the Apocalypse." Tender-hearted, they were not. But they were also no longer lithe and athletic girls, if they ever had been, and the sprawled corpses in the narrow hallway were not minor obstructions.

Fodor was the first one into the room, followed by Utt. As her sister-in-law Estelle came in, Maydene knelt down and checked the pulse of the third assailant whom Tom had smashed into the doorjamb, then reached behind his head.

"Well, he's with the Lord," she announced. "Or wherever. What d'you do? Hit him with a train? The whole back of his skull's caved in."

"Uh... Tom slammed him into the door. He was really pissed."

Grunting, Utt heaved herself back on her feet. She was a big woman. Not fat, particularly, just very heavily built. "Well, I guess a really-pissed Tom Simpson will pass for a pretty good train imitation. Where is he now?"

Rita nodded toward the door. "Out there, somewhere. He left to see what was happening."

By then, Estelle had come up to look at Rita's arm.

"Hold still," she commanded. After a quick examination, she said: "You got a needle and thread in that first aid kit?"

Rita was tempted to say no. Sorely tempted. McIntire was about as skinny as her sister-in-law was hefty, but they shared the same temperament. It was the sort of middle-aged female Appalachian temperament for which phrases like *quit your whining* and *stop being a baby* came trippingly off the tongue. Estelle would sew up the wound without worrying much about minor issues like agony.

"You got medical training...?" Rita ventured, half-hoping she might fend the woman off.

Estelle sniffed. "Who needs medical training for something like this? I've been sewing up torn clothes since I was six." She turned her head. "Mary, give me a hand."

For the first time, Rita realized that two other people had followed the three auditors into the room. The one to whom Estelle had spoken was Willa Fodor's niece, Mary Tanner Barancek. The girl had graduated from high school a year and half earlier and had gone to work in Dr. Gribbleflotz's laboratories in Jena. Some sort of clash with her boss had led her to quit and she'd come down to the Oberpfalz to work for her aunt. She had some sort of dignified-sounding down-timer job title, but she was really a combination gofer and clerk.

The man standing next to her, on the other hand, had a job that actually matched the title. Johann Heinrich Böcler was the private secretary for the Upper Palatinate's new administrator, Christian I of Pfalz-Birkenfeld-Bischweiler. He'd held the same position for the previous administrator, Ernst Wettin, Duke of Saxe-Weimar, before Wettin had been reassigned to Saxony.

Böcler was a certain type of German official, by now quite

familiar to Rita after four and a half years in the seventeenth century.

Physically, he was unprepossessing. He was in his mid-twenties. On the short side, fattish—not obese, just plump—with a pug nose, brown eyes, and a prematurely receding hairline. The hair itself was that indefinite shade of gray-brown that so often signaled a prematurely receding youth.

With respect to his skills, he was very competent. As you'd expect from a man who'd gotten his position because of those skills, not because of any great social standing. He'd been born in a small town in Franconia whose name Rita couldn't remember. His father had been a Lutheran pastor; his grandfather, the down time equivalent of a high-school principal. A respectable family, certainly, but not a high-placed one.

In short, the sort of fellow you'd want at your side to keep track of the complex details of a political and commercial negotiation. Not the sort of fellow you particularly wanted at your side in the middle of a city that was being overrun by enemy soldiers.

While Rita had been contemplating these matters in order to avoid thinking about the proximate future, Estelle McIntire had been preparing that future with Mary Barancek's assistance.

"Okay," she said, "this going to hurt a little."

The needle went in.

"*Ow!*" Rita squealed.

"Don't be a baby. It's just a few stitches."

Again.

"*Owowowowow!*"

"Oh, quit whining."

Chapter 2

Tom found his commanding officer dead in his quarters, just a block away. The door to the apartment had been blown in by the same sort of explosion that had destroyed Tom's own. Colonel Friedrich Engels' body was sprawled across the floor of his living room, half-dressed, with at least two gunshot wounds that Tom could see at a glance. The floor was covered with drying blood. A pistol was lying near the colonel's body that Tom recognized as belonging to Engels. It was a wheel lock and the mechanism hadn't been engaged. Obviously, the attack had come so quickly that Engels had been roused from sleep but hadn't had time to arm the weapon.

Reluctantly, partly because he didn't much like the idea of getting his boots soaked in his commander's blood but mostly because he was pretty sure what he was going to find, Tom stepped over Engels' body and went into the bedroom. As he'd expected, Engels' wife Hilde was dead too. Her body was sprawled across the bed. Her neck had a deep gash in it and the bedding was blood-soaked.

Their year-old daughter, who slept in a cradle against the wall, had also been murdered. Also with a sword, at a guess.

Doing his best to control his fury, Tom hurried out of the apartment. He was now certain that the enemy—whoever it was, but it almost had to be the Bavarians—had launched a well-planned and coordinated assault on the city. There was no way they could have managed something like this without the aid of traitors, including traitors in the military.

Tom and Engels had worried about that, but there hadn't seemed to be much they could do about it at the moment. Tom's artillery unit was the only one made up entirely of volunteers, mostly recruited by the CoCs in Magdeburg and the State of Thuringia-Franconia. The rest of the soldiers in the regiment were the men left behind by the Swedish general Báner when he left for Saxony with most of his army. Those soldiers were all mercenaries except for the *Jaegers* and boatmen—the River Rats, as they were called—recruited by Ernst Wettin while he'd been the administrator of the Oberpfalz. Clearly enough, a number of them had been persuaded to switch their allegiance to Duke Maximilian.

Once he was back out on the street, he could hear the sounds of fighting all over the city. He was sorely tempted to return to his quarters and help Rita make her escape, but he had duties of his own. With Engels dead, Tom was now the commanding officer of the regiment—or whatever portions of it, at least, had not defected to the Bavarians.

The one unit he was sure of were his own artillerymen. He'd have to start there. He set off at a run toward their barracks against Ingolstadt's eastern wall.

"What do we do now?" asked Estelle McIntire, once she'd finished sewing up Rita's wound and had sterilized it once again. "Sit tight here? Go somewhere? If so, where?"

"And if we do decide to go somewhere," added Maydene Utt, "everybody better be really well-dressed. We're in January, not June. January in the Little Ice Age, mind you. Right now, at a guess, the temperature isn't any higher than fifteen degrees out there—Fahrenheit, I don't hold with that Centigrade crap."

Everyone looked at each other, gauging their mutual willingness and ability to brave the conditions of a January night in the middle of Germany. In the Little Ice Age, as Maydene had so kindly pointed out.

They'd almost certainly have to venture out into the countryside, too. Rita had no idea what the military situation looked like, but she was pretty sure it was dire. Tom had told her of his and Friedrich's worries over the loyalty of many of the garrison troops. It looked as if the worst of those fears had come true, and if so she didn't think there was much chance Colonel Engels and her husband could hold the city.

She said as much, ending with, "I don't think we have a lot of choice. I think if we try to hole up here we'll just wind up getting captured. After that . . . well, it's likely to get awfully ugly."

She didn't see any reason to dwell on the details. She and Mary Tanner Barancek were young women. Both of them were good-looking, too, to make things worse—but that probably didn't make much difference if Ingolstadt was sacked. Troops running amok were anything but discriminate. All five of the women were likely to be assaulted. The one man among them, Johann Heinrich Böcler, would get slaughtered out of hand.

Their one chance was the fact that all of them were up-timers except Böcler. Most down-time rulers and military commanders were leery of infuriating Americans for no good purpose, which the brutalization of five American women would certainly do. All the more so since one of them was Mike Stearns' sister.

But...

First of all, the commanders of this attack probably wouldn't even learn what was happening to the women until it was too late to stop it. Troops sacking a city were no more discriminate about getting official permission to commit atrocities than they were to commit them in the first place.

And secondly, Maximilian of Bavaria was one of the exceptions. The duke had made quite clear in times past that he held up-timers in no high regard, to put it mildly.

"I really don't think there's any choice," she repeated. "We've got to get out of the city."

Estelle and Willa grimaced. Maydene, stoic as ever, shrugged her shoulders. "I don't disagree. But we'll need some horses, or at least a wagon. There's no way we can manage for very long on foot once we get into the countryside. We're still hours from dawn. At that, we're lucky there's a moon out."

"What about the *Pelican?*" said Mary.

Everyone turned to look at her.

"Is it still here?" asked Willa uncertainly.

"And even if it is," added Estelle, "would it carry all of us?"

Mary nodded vigorously. "It'd carry all of us—easy. And, uh, yeah. It's still here." She paused, seeming to avoid her aunt Willa's gaze. "Well. At least, it was this morning."

Fodor glared at her. "I told you to stay away from him!"

Even under the circumstances, as dire as they were, Rita couldn't help but choke out a laugh. Fodor shifted the glare onto her.

"Give it up, Willa," Rita said, shaking her head. "Trying to keep nineteen-year-old girls from chasing after boys has been a lost cause since the Stone Age."

"He's not a boy! He's at least ten years older than she is."

"He is not!" countered Mary hotly. "Stefano's only twenty-six."

"Seven years is still too much! Especially when he's Latin."

Maydene looked exasperated. "Is that 'Latin' as in Eye-talian, Willa? Like a lot of the population of Grantville? In fact, if I recall correctly, wasn't your high school boyfriend Matt Difabri?"

"He was Italian-American," Fodor said, defensively. "That Franchetti guy is Italian-Italian. It's not the same thing."

"Can we please concentrate on what's important?" said Estelle. "Worry about Mary's love life later. If that contraption can get us all out of here, I'm for using it."

"Me too," said Rita forcefully. "And there's no time to lose. By now, Stefano is bound to be trying to get up in the air. We've got to catch him before he does."

She gave the apartment a quick survey, to see if there was anything she wanted to take with her. The walkie-talkie radio, of course, which was also perched on the mantelpiece. Hopefully that would enable her to get in touch with Tom, since his unit had a radio also. Beyond that...

There was a fair number of personal items she'd hate to lose, but she sternly suppressed the urge to snatch them up. Besides the radio, there was really only one thing important.

"Mary, give me a hand," she said, hurrying into the bedroom. Once there, she began emptying the chest of drawers against one of the walls. Her clothes got piled onto the bed, Tom's got pitched unceremoniously onto the floor. No one, not even Maydene, was big enough to fit into her husband's clothes.

As she did so, she pointed to a corner. There was an old suitcase there, that Tom had had with him when the Ring of Fire came and had held onto ever since. "Use the suitcase. Skip the underclothes but cram it full of whatever will help keep us warm."

Maydene wouldn't fit into Rita's clothes, and she didn't think Böcler probably would either. But there was no help for it.

Well...

Maydene stuck her head in. "Can I help?"

"Yes. Grab the blankets off the bed and roll them up. We'll need them, I figure."

Less than a minute later, the suitcase was packed and Utt had the blankets over her shoulder. Rita headed for the front door, stopped, and raced back into the bedroom. Tom kept a box of shotgun shells in the drawer of the little table next to the bed. She shoved it into the capacious pockets of the heavy jacket she'd put on and went back into the living room. After stuffing the walkie-talkie into one of her pockets and picking up the shotgun that she'd left leaning against the wall, she went into the corridor. As the rest of the party followed, she took the time to reload the weapon.

"Is anyone else armed?" she asked.

"Me," said Estelle. Looking back, Rita saw that McIntire had pulled a revolver out from somewhere. The gun looked like a small cannon. Rita thought it was probably one of her husband Crawford's guns. He had a big collection of them and was partial to heavy calibers, as she recalled.

The weapon looked too big for Estelle, but Rita knew there'd be no point in saying anything on the subject. Besides, even if the woman lost the revolver after firing it, her first shot would hit the target. McIntire was the sort of person who'd handle killing the same way she'd handled sewing up a wound. If it needs to be done, just do it.

Once they were out in the street, the sounds of fighting were much louder. They seemed to be concentrated toward the eastern side of the city. That was where Tom's artillery unit had its barracks. The unit quartered next to them was a mercenary force, but it was under the command of Bruno von Eichelberg, a young man from a modest noble family in Brunswick whom Tom and Friedrich Engels had been on good terms with. Rita thought it was unlikely that Eichelberg's unit had participated in whatever treachery was underway.

She was tempted for a moment to head that way, but stifled the impulse. She and her party would just get in the way and be a distraction for Tom. The best way she could help her husband under these circumstances was simply to get herself out of the city.

The *Pelican* was hangared just outside the city walls near the northwest gate. She set off in that direction, with her shotgun held at the ready. Estelle came right behind her with the revolver, followed by the three other women. Johann Heinrich Böcler brought up the rear.

The scholar and clerk seemed to be holding up well, a bit to Rita's surprise and certainly to her relief. He was a studious young man, straightlaced to the point of being something of a prig. But he hadn't gotten badly rattled at any point, and had even had the presence of mind to pick up one of the assailants' pistols and the ammunition pouch he'd had on his belt. Rita had no idea if Böcler knew how to use the weapon, but the fact that he'd thought to take it was a good sign in itself.

There was only one incident along the way. As they came around a corner, they found a couple of soldiers breaking into a shop. One of them was smashing in the window with the butt of his musket while his companion watched.

As was more often the case than not with seventeenth-century soldiers, neither of them was wearing a uniform. So Rita had no way of knowing offhand which side they were on. But she figured the act of vandalism and presumed looting was a good enough indication and she didn't dare hesitate for long.

Remembering the wild misses in the earlier gunfight, though, she controlled herself enough to aim carefully before she fired. The man she aimed at was the one watching, not the one smashing the window, since she figured he was the one who'd be able to react more quickly. He was standing perhaps thirty feet away and not looking anywhere near her. She took a breath, aimed, and squeezed the trigger.

He went down as if he'd been hit by a truck. At close enough range where marksmanship wasn't a big issue, it was hard to beat slugs fired out of a 12 gauge. They had all the stopping power of heavy caliber seventeenth-century muskets but without the slow rate of fire.

In a hurry, but doing her best not to move frantically, Rita pumped in another round and aimed again. Luckily, the remaining soldier was either dim-witted or—quite likely—too drunk to react quickly. He wasn't even looking at her. He was staring down at his companion, who was now sprawled against the wall of the building.

She fired. And...almost missed, even at that range. Her shot did strike the soldier's musket, however. The bullet not only knocked the weapon out of his hand but some sort of ricochet struck him in the face. From the minimal damage done, it was probably a small piece of the firing mechanism or possibly just a splinter from the stock.

But the soldier was startled enough to clasp his face with his hands rather than deal with her. She jacked in another round. Not trusting her reactions—she had to be practically afloat in adrenaline—she strode forward a few steps, almost running, until she was no more than six feet away from him.

The soldier's hands came down from a bloody face. His mouth was wide open as he stared at her. She fired. At his chest, and this time the bullet struck where she wanted it to. The soldier was knocked off his feet and back into the window he'd been smashing, taking what was left of the glass mostly with him.

Rita did her best to blank out the horror from her mind as she reloaded. She'd never killed anyone before tonight, and now she'd killed no fewer than four men. She'd never even been in a gunfight, for that matter, except for the escape from the Tower of London. But she hadn't been directly involved in the fighting there.

Maydene came up to her. "You all right?" she asked softly.

Rita nodded. "Right enough." She'd probably have some bad reactions later, but there was no time to worry about that now.

The shotgun reloaded, she set off again. "Let's go, folks."

Chapter 3

Hearing another burst of gunfire, Stefano Franchetti was distracted from his work with the airship's burners. Nervously, he glanced in the direction the gunfire was coming from. Insofar as he could determine the direction, at least, which he couldn't with any precision. There was a three-quarter moon in the sky, but he still couldn't see very far. A line of trees at the edge of the clearing where they'd set up the airship station impeded his view of Ingolstadt.

The State of Thuringia-Franconia had leased one of the blimps built by Estuban Miro in order to carry out a thorough survey of Thuringia, Franconia and the Oberpfalz. They'd wanted Filippo Franchetti for a pilot, but since he was Miro's foreman he'd declined and offered his nephew Stefano in his stead. As it was, Miro was simply breaking even on the operation. The rates he normally charged were far higher than the SoTF would have been willing to pay. He'd cut them drastically in the interests of maintaining good relations with the authorities.

The man placed in charge of the project was Hank Siers, an independent engineer who'd been trained as a surveyor. Three young women who'd recently graduated from the geological survey program connected to the SoTF's State Technical College in Grantville had also come along. Those were Dina Merrifield, Bonnie Weaver and Amanda Boyd.

Stefano heard more gunfire, accompanied by the sound of at least one cannon firing.

Where were Hank Siers and the girls?

No, young women, he reminded himself. American females had odd quirks, one of them being that the older women liked to be called girls and the young ones resented it.

As always with up-timers, there were exceptions to this rule as there seemed to be to all rules concerning them. They were the most perverse people in existence. It was worth your very life, he'd been told, to refer to the famous Melissa Mailey as a "girl" in her presence. He'd also been told—was there *any* coherence to American customs?—that the young up-time women who were most famous for their free-spirited ways like the equally well-known Julie Sims and the rapidly-gaining-notoriety Denise Beasley, apparently had no objection at all to being called girls.

The four Americans had left the airship station that morning to obtain some supplies in Ingolstadt. They'd been planning to spend the night inside the city at one of the inns. They needed fuel, mostly, but they'd also wanted food. The girls—no, women—had quickly grown tired of the staples that Hank Siers had insisted on bringing. So had Stefano. Siers' idea of suitable provender for a geological survey consisted of crackers, dried meat and vegetables which had been subjected to some sort of "preserving" process that didn't bear close examination.

Why? Stefano didn't know for sure, but from idle remarks dropped by Siers it seemed the American thought that an airship survey of Franconia and the Oberpfalz was somehow similar to an expedition to the Arctic. As if Stefano couldn't land the ship almost any time they wanted at any one of the hundreds of well-provendered towns and villages that dotted the German countryside!

Stefano would have ascribed Siers' eccentricities to his advanced age, except that the American engineer wasn't more than forty years old. Bonnie Weaver had told him, a bit sarcastically—well, more than a bit—that Siers was hopelessly addicted to romantic adventure twaddle.

"I've been to his house a few times," she'd told him, "since he likes to hold seminars around his kitchen table. Says it's quieter than the school, which is true enough. Practically every square foot of wall space is covered with bookshelves. At least a third of them hold books about exploration. It drives his girlfriend Mina David nuts."

The thought of Bonnie Weaver provided some distraction from his current anxieties, but only at the cost of raising new ones. It was bad enough for any young man to find himself caught between two girls—no, women—even if neither of them was an up-timer. When *both* of them were American, the situation was one which Hank Siers liked to call "fraught with peril."

The engineer was fond of such florid phrases. Bonnie said that if he wrote anything besides dry survey reports Siers would redefine the expression "purple prose." After she'd explained the term, Stefano had had his doubts. So far as he could tell—keeping in mind that his education was fairly good but mostly informal and oriented toward practical matters—his seventeenth century was the era which had more or less defined purple prose to begin with.

Bonnie ought to know that, too. She belonged to the Baptist church, an up-time sect that she claimed already existed in this world but which Stefano had never heard of until he encountered Americans. Apparently, in this day and age it was still confined to England.

Somewhat against his will—it might be better to say, against his spiritual will but in accordance with his interest in things of the flesh—he had once attended a Baptist sermon with Bonnie, at her invitation.

Purple prose, indeed. Thankfully, his own Catholic church mostly used Latin for such purposes. Latin was a language which Stefano could read, with some difficulty, but the difficulty was enough that he could ignore whatever the priest was saying unless he really wanted to pay attention.

Which he usually didn't. Had anyone questioned him on the subject, Stefano would have insisted he was a pious Catholic. But, in truth, he didn't think much about religious matters.

In that regard, he was closer to the Baptist woman than he was to Mary Tanner Barancek. Bonnie Weaver's attitude toward religion seemed quite relaxed. Mary, on the other hand, while she shared Stefano's own Catholic faith—the odd up-time version of it, anyway—was far more devout than he was. She'd told him that she'd even considered becoming a nun on several occasions.

She hadn't explained her decision not to take that course, but Stefano was pretty sure it was because Mary would have had difficulty adhering to the demands of chastity, and had enough sense to know it. The girl—young woman—was . . . attracted to men. And the reverse was certainly true.

Best to leave it at that, he thought. Stefano was already on perilous ground without adding to the risks by thinking about it.

Another burst of gunfire came from Ingolstadt. Where were the Americans? Stefano's concern was for himself as well as for them. He couldn't get the airship ready to fly on his own. They'd deflated the balloon after they arrived in Ingolstadt, as they normally did when they were stopping somewhere for any significant stretch of time. The sheer mass involved in getting the balloon reinflated was just too much for one person to handle in any reasonable amount of time.

For that matter, even if he could get the blimp aloft on his own he couldn't really handle it safely. The airship was designed to be flown by a minimum of two people, and a crew of three was better.

Where were they?

Hank Siers was lying next to a pile of rubble, from which his companions had just pulled him out. The building he'd taken shelter behind had been collapsed by an exploding cannon shell. His leg was broken and he was unconscious, but he was still alive and otherwise unhurt, so far as Bonnie Weaver could tell.

Of course, that assessment was based on nothing more substantial than a two-week class in first aid that Bonnie had taken a couple of years earlier. For all she knew, Hank was bleeding internally, had all sorts of internal damage, and was even now exhibiting plain and unmistakable symptoms of said injuries that she was too ignorant to recognize.

"How is he?" asked Dina Merrifield. She and Bonnie were the same age, had grown up together, and had been in the same classes in school. In short, they knew each other as well as people in a small town do who are acquaintances rather than friends—but very closely acquainted. Closely enough that Bonnie didn't see any point in pretending to know more than she did.

"I don't really know, Dina, to be honest. I'm sure his leg's broken, although—thank God—it's not a compound fracture. He probably has a concussion, too."

Amanda Boyd came around the corner of the building—what was left of it, rather. She'd gone to see if there were any signs that enemy soldiers were moving around in the area.

"I can't see anybody, except a couple of women hurrying to get into a building. So far as I can tell, the fighting is still at least a quarter of a mile away."

That wasn't really much comfort. A man could walk a quarter of a mile in five minutes. But soldiers in combat wouldn't move that quickly, Bonnie told herself, unless they had specific reasons to know that a target was nearby.

Still, she didn't think they had more than half an hour of safety. That gave them barely enough time to get out of the town and reach the airship, with a wounded and unconscious man to carry.

Hank was no lightweight, either. It would take all three of them to carry him, even if they could jury-rig some sort of stretcher.

The thought of a stretcher concentrated her mind and helped her to control the incipient panic. *One thing at a time. We need something to make a stretcher from.*

As it turned out, Dina had been thinking along the same lines. "There was a wheelbarrow back there, where they were doing construction. And some wood we could make a splint from."

"Fitting a man as big as Siers into a wheelbarrow isn't going to be easy," Bonnie said dubiously.

Amanda shrugged. "I saw a picture once of something like twelve guys who crammed themselves into a VW. And I don't see where we've got an alternative, Bonnie, unless we just leave him here. Ain't no way we're gonna carry this fat asshole."

Amanda didn't get along well with Siers. Partly that was because of her age—she was two years younger than Bonnie and Dina, just shy of twenty—and partly it was because Amanda was edgy and didn't get along with a lot of people. Being fair, although Bonnie herself wouldn't go so far as to call Hank an asshole, he certainly wasn't one of her favorite people, either. He was a fussy and overbearing boss, just for starters.

Dina straightened up. "She's right. I'll go get it."

She was back in less than five minutes. It took them at least that long to fit a splint onto the surveyor's leg. Bonnie, who did the work of setting the broken bone, could only hope she'd done it right. If she hadn't, Hank would probably walk with a limp for the rest of his life. But she was beginning to fear that might be the least of his problems. Hank was still unconscious. Not even the pain of having a broken bone reset had aroused him. She didn't think that was normal, even for a man who'd been knocked out and almost certainly had a concussion.

Then, it took another two or three minutes to get Hank into the wheelbarrow and positioned in such a way that he wouldn't fall out—entirely, anyway; at least a third of him wasn't actually in the wheelbarrow—and enough of his weight was distributed properly so that they could pick up the handles.

At that, it would take two of them, one on each handle, to move him. The third woman would rotate so they'd each get some rest.

They'd need it, too. Bonnie didn't know exactly how much Hank weighed. She'd have said two hundred pounds or so. Now, straining at one of the handles as they trundled toward the gate that led out of the town in the direction of the airfield, she revised her estimate upward.

"Like. I. Said." Amanda was on the other handle while Dina led the way ahead of them. "Fat. Asshole."

Chapter 4

As he got close to the barracks, Tom was relieved to find that his artillery unit was apparently still intact and, judging from the noise, fighting back with considerable spirit. The unit was officially a company—a "battery," in the artillery's parlance—but it was way oversized because the men assigned to Ingolstadt's defensive guns had been incorporated into it. Instead of two hundred men, Tom had almost four hundred under his command. That was more than a third of the total strength of the Danube Regiment.

Not all of them would have been at the barracks when the fighting broke out. But he probably still had close to three hundred soldiers available in his artillery unit, and he'd picked up a couple of infantry companies on his way to the barracks. The companies belonged to the 2nd Battalion, whose commanding officer had been murdered in his sleep also. The two captains in charge of them had no idea where the rest of the battalion was, nor what had happened to the 1st Battalion.

Tom didn't know the answer to that question either. But he was pretty sure the 1st Battalion had defected to the Bavarians. That would explain how the enemy had managed to pour into Ingolstadt the way they had. Units from that battalion had been in charge of several of the city's gates. They would have let in assassination teams first, to target the regiment's still-loyal officers, and then opened the gates for the Bavarian forces who were camped nearby.

Tom and Colonel Engels had both been worried about the reliability of the soldiers in that battalion, but there hadn't been much they could do about it given the political situation. Reliable units in the regular army—meaning volunteers, in this context, not mercenaries—were now mostly in Poland or Bohemia. And with a new prime minister, the few such units which were still stationed in the USE itself were not likely to be assigned to the Danube Regiment.

The officers and enlisted men in the 1st Battalion were Italian mercenaries, almost to a man. Italy provided a large percentage of Europe's professional soldiers. They were valued for their courage and skills—nobody made wisecracks about Italian armies in the seventeenth century—but were notoriously prone to switching sides if presented with the right inducement.

Tom stopped while still just out of sight of the barracks. Behind him, he could hear the sounds of a hundred and fifty men coming to a ragged halt. More ragged than usual. The companies were missing at least a fourth of their men and officers.

The two company commanders came up to join him. "What do you want to do, sir?" asked Captain Conrad Fischer.

Tom had been pondering the problem. With a firefight going on, they couldn't go directly to the barracks. Even with a moon out, the visibility wasn't good enough for the men in the barracks to distinguish easily between friend and foe at a distance. In this dim lighting, the field-gray uniforms of the USE regulars would be hard to tell apart from the more nondescript clothing and gear worn by the Bavarians—even leaving aside the problem that, if Tom was right, a fair number of the enemy were USE defectors wearing the same uniform.

If the artillerymen saw a mass of soldiers charging toward them, they'd assume they were enemies and open fire. And that fire would be pretty devastating. By now, forted up in their barracks and the arsenal which directly adjoined it, the regiment's artillery units would have their cannons in position and loaded with canister. The somewhat desultory gunfire Tom could hear was not the noise produced by a frontal charge. The Bavarians would have tried that once, been driven off, and were now settling down to what amounted to a siege.

It couldn't last forever, of course. Eventually, they'd bring up their own artillery. But at least until dawn, the Bavarians were stymied.

"Nothing for it," he muttered.

"What was that, sir?" asked Erhard Geipel, the other captain.

Tom shook his head. "Just talking to myself. We don't have any choice. We'll have to attack the enemy from the rear—well, more likely the flank—and drive them off. Until and unless we do that, there's no way we can join the artillerymen."

"They'll just fire on us," agreed Fischer. "But we may be outnumbered, sir."

"We almost certainly are," Tom said grimly. "The Bavarians would have sent at least a battalion to seize the artillery barracks."

He was using "battalion" in a generic sense, not the precise meaning that the term had in the USE army. Like most armies of the day, the Bavarian forces were composed largely of mercenaries. A good number of them would be Italians, and not more than a third would have come from Bavaria itself. Mercenaries were organized into companies—another generic term—which were of whatever size their commanders could put together, ranging from less than a hundred to close to a thousand.

Tom was convinced that part of the reason many seventeenth-century armies liked crude formations like tercios was because the rigidity of the formation compensated to some extent for the irregularities of the units that actually made them up. But in a free-for-all melee like this sort of street fighting after a successful assault on a city, he knew the Bavarian commander, whoever he was, would have simply dispatched one of his larger "companies" to take the artillery barracks.

That meant Tom and his two understrength companies were going to be attacking a force that was at least twice as large as they were.

So be it. They didn't have any other option, so far as he could see. Hopefully, the much-ballyhooed "advantage of surprise" would turn out to be all it was cracked up to be.

Seeing motion in the shadows of the street ahead of them, Rita pressed herself against the wall of a building and gestured with her hand to tell the people following her to stop. She could hear the slight scuffling of their feet but didn't think anyone else could if they weren't within ten yards. The motion she'd spotted had been at least twice that far away, just past an intersection.

She tried to figure out what to do. They were now close to the gate that led out of the city toward the airfield. That made it tempting to just charge ahead, and deal with whatever they ran across. But the shadows were very dark. There was only one street lamp in sight and that was next to a door twenty yards or so down a cross street. Rita couldn't really see anything now. The motion she'd spotted had stopped. For all she knew, a whole squad of Bavarian soldiers was waiting in ambush.

Behind her, Mary whispered something. Rita couldn't make out the words but she was pretty sure Mary had asked one of the other women what was holding everything up—as if any of them knew either!

For a moment, she considered firing a shot into the shadows. Just to see what happened, basically. It was quite possible that the motion she'd seen had been nothing more than a street mongrel scurrying for cover.

But that would be insane. The motion could also have been caused by a frightened child.

"Oh, fuck it," she muttered. Rita turned and handed her shotgun to Maydene, who'd been following right behind her. "If anybody shoots me, kill him, will you?"

She turned back around and strode out into the street. In for a penny, in for a pound. She might as well make herself as visible as possible.

In the same spirit, not knowing what else to say, she shouted: "Hey, you!"

A second or so later, she got a response.

"Rita, is that you?"

That *had* to be Dina Merrifield. Nobody else she knew could manage to speak Amideutsch with that much of a twang. Dina was from southern West Virginia, where people's speech had a much more Appalachian accent than they did in Grantville.

"Oh, thank God!" another woman exclaimed. Rita thought that was probably Bonnie Weaver.

A woman came into the light cast by the distant street lamp. As she'd guessed, it was Bonnie.

"Boy, are you the proverbial sight for sore eyes," Weaver said. "We heard you coming but didn't know who you were. We ran across a Bavarian patrol a few minutes ago, but we managed to hide from them. At least, I think they were Bavarian even though their uniforms looked like ours. I don't know who else would be attacking Ingolstadt."

They were probably traitors rather than Bavarians, Rita thought. But this was not the time and place to share her suspicions and guesses on that subject.

"Who else is with you?" she asked Bonnie. "And where's the *Pelican*?"

Bonnie gestured behind her. "It's at the airfield. Stefano should have it ready to fly by now, even working on his own. All we've got to do is get there—but we've got a problem. Hank was hurt pretty badly."

"Can he walk?"

"Hell, Rita, he's not even conscious. We've got him in a wheelbarrow we found, but we're not making much progress any longer. We're pretty well worn out."

Given Siers' size, Rita wasn't surprised. "Well, we can spell you on that chore."

By now, all of her people had come out into the street. So had Amanda Boyd and—sure enough—Dina Merrifield.

Böcler came forward. "I will handle the wheelbarrow. I am not doing anything else and I am not much use with firearms."

Uncertainly, Rita stared at him. The secretary wasn't even five and half feet tall. He had pretty wide shoulders for a man his size, but a good part of his bulk looked to be fat rather than muscle.

Bonnie had obviously been thinking along the same lines. "Ah...Hank Siers is awfully heavy."

Böcler shrugged. "So I will be very tired by the time we reach the *Pelican*. But I will be able to rest then. I am not much use with airships either."

The gunfire that Rita could hear had become rather desultory and all of it was now coming from the direction of the artillery barracks. She was pretty sure that her husband's unit was the only one still putting up a fight. They were probably well-fortified and the Bavarians had stopped trying to take the barracks with a frontal assault. They'd be settling in for a siege and waiting until they could bring up some cannons.

Suddenly the sounds of intermittent gunshots was replaced by a cacophony. That was the sound of hundreds of guns being fired mixed in with the sound of men shouting. Here and there she could hear the clap of grenades, too.

She felt a surge of hope. That might be Tom, leading a charge to relieve the siege of the barracks.

The hope was short-lived, of course. Tom could easily get killed in the next few minutes.

But that thunderclap of battle also gave them their best opportunity to get out of the city. Any enemy patrols would be drawn toward the sound.

"Let's go," she said. Böcler left immediately, heading toward the shadows where the wheelbarrow was located. Rita turned to Weaver. "Bonnie, stay on top of Johann Heinrich, will you? I think he's overestimating his strength and endurance. And you know what men are like in front of a bunch of women."

Bonnie grinned. "Yeah, he'll refuse to admit he can't handle it until he collapses and we've got to carry *two* of the silly bastards. Neither one of whom would ever grace the covers of *GQ* or *Esquire.*"

Rita chuckled. "God, can you remember a world where they published magazines like that? Do you miss it much?"

"Not the magazines. I sure as hell miss the plumbing, though, any time I venture out of Grantville. Wait'll you see what passes for toilet facilities on a seventeenth-century airship."

"Gah."

"You did bring your own toilet paper, I hope. No? Boy, are you in for a treat."

"Gah."

Chapter 5

Tom never remembered much afterward about the assault that drove off the Bavarians besieging the artillery barracks. The light thrown by a three-quarter moon only seems bright when everything is calm and peaceful. In the chaos of a battle, there were shadows everywhere and all colors were leached out. You could detect motion clearly, and that was about it.

That might have been a blessing. Tom still had vivid memories of his first real battle, when he and Heinrich Schmidt had driven off an assault on Suhl by Wallenstein's mercenaries almost four years earlier. The horror hadn't stemmed from the fighting itself. There hadn't been much of that, since they'd been firing at an enemy in the open from behind good fieldworks. The end result had been a lot closer to a massacre than what you could really call a battle. Afterward, the field had been carpeted with bodies. And blood; and intestines; and brains; and some things whose identity Tom had never been sure about and didn't want to be.

There wasn't so much of that tonight. Not because it wasn't there but because you couldn't see it very well. Fighting in the darkness, by the light of a moon and the flashes of gunfire and grenades, all a man had time for was motion. Once an enemy went down, you ignored him. The blood spreading out from his body blended into the cobblestones. Everything was a shade of gray, and blood was no different.

There were drawbacks to that, of course. Twice he slipped and fell, when his foot skidded on something wet—and, in one case, horridly squishy. But who could say? In that sort of melee, the falls might even have saved his life, when bullets passed through space he no longer occupied.

His one clear memory was that of an enemy soldier rising from the street, as he neared the last corner before the barracks. The man had probably slipped and fallen himself. He must have fired his gun and hadn't had time to reload—or he simply panicked. He came up screeching, thrusting his arquebus forward as if it were a spear and catching Tom in the stomach. If the weapon had been a spear, the blade would have sunk into him at least six inches. As it was, the gun barrel just knocked some of the wind out of him and left a nasty bruise.

Not all of his wind, though; not even most of it. Tom's torso was massive, and most of the mass was hard muscle. He didn't feel any pain and didn't even realized he'd been bruised until afterward. He just grunted—a very pronounced sort of "oof!"—and struck back in reflex.

That instinctive reaction was not the best response, all things considered, since he held his pistol in his hand and the blow was mostly delivered by his knuckles. Against a lobsterstail helmet, too, not a mere skull.

That *did* hurt. But as strong as Tom was, the blow knocked his opponent back down onto the street. He was dazed, and his weapon slid out of his hands.

Before Tom could decide what to do, a pikehead came from behind him, thrusting forward just past his elbow. He was almost deafened by the screech of the soldier wielding it, who was now standing right next to him as he skewered the man lying on the cobblestones.

Night battles aren't much suited for taking prisoners. Tom would probably have decided to kill the man himself, in another second or two.

He took a moment to look around, the first time he'd had a chance to do so since he ordered the charge. And was relieved to see that the much-vaunted virtues of surprise had real substance. Everywhere he looked, the enemy was running away.

At least, he assumed they were the enemy. Some of them were wearing the same USE uniform that his own men were wearing. Traitors from the 1st Battalion, he figured. The rest, the ones in more nondescript clothing, would be the Bavarian mercenaries.

He fought down the temptation to order a pursuit. If there were any chance of winning a real victory here, he would have given the order. But even before he launched the charge, he'd come to realize that Ingolstadt was lost.

Tom wasn't the only commander who'd used the factor of surprise tonight. Duke Maximilian of Bavaria had done so also, and done so to much greater effect. Tom had taken a barracks; the duke had taken a city. There was simply no way Tom would be able to drive the Bavarians back out of Ingolstadt with the forces that remained to him. All he could do now was try to lead an organized retreat out of the city and salvage as much of the regiment as he could.

Captain Geipel came up to him, pointing over his shoulder with a thumb. "One of my sergeants says he's established contact with the artillerymen in the barracks. But they're distrustful since they don't know him and—just as you guessed—a number of the regiment's units have turned traitor."

"I'll talk to them." Tom started toward the corner Geipel had been pointing out, with the captain walking alongside him. "You and Fischer get your companies back into order. We're heading out as soon as we can get the artillerymen moving."

"Where to, sir?" Geipel's question sounded a bit apprehensive.

"Don't worry, Captain. I don't propose to attack the Bavarians with what little we've got. We're leaving the city altogether."

Geipel nodded, his expression obviously relieved. He'd never served under Major Simpson before, so he'd had no idea whether the American officer was reckless or not.

Once he got to the corner, Tom gingerly stuck his head out far enough to see the barracks. "This is Major Simpson!" he shouted.

After a moment, a voice shouted back: "What's your mother's maiden name?"

Tom frowned. That wasn't a question a down-timer would normally think of; not, at least, as a security question. Seventeenth-century German women did not adopt their husband's last name when they got married. In the here and now, that custom was mostly restricted to England.

But Tom himself was the only up-timer in the Danube Regiment. There were three Americans in the TacRail unit that had been stationed in Ingolstadt, but they'd left the city a couple of months earlier in order to work on a rail line leading north from Regensburg. So who...

The answer came to him almost at once. In the months he'd been in Ingolstadt, Bobby Lloyd McDougal had made friends with one of the artillery units. He'd probably been gossiping.

The sergeant in command of that unit was David Steinbach. "My mother's maiden name was Forbes, Sergeant Steinbach! Now quit playing games or I'll use you to demonstrate American football! You'll be the playing field!"

He heard a distant laugh. "All right, Major, come on!"

✧　　✧　　✧

From there, things went quickly. The artillerymen were every bit as eager to get out of Ingolstadt as all the other soldiers in what was left of the regiment. The only hang-up was that the heavy artillery units wanted to salvage their twelve-pounders.

That idea was impractical to the point of lunacy. Artillerymen were not entirely sane on the subject of their guns. The twelve-pounders had been taken off their carriages in preparation for placing them as defensive guns on the walls. It would take at least an hour of hard labor just to get them remounted. And then how would they haul the carriages? Guns that size needed to be drawn by large teams of horses. There weren't enough horses in the stables adjoining the barracks for the purpose. In fact, there were barely enough to salvage the six-pounders, which would be a lot more useful in the field anyway.

That would have been true even in summertime. In midwinter, hauling big guns across the countryside would be extraordinarily taxing on men and animals alike. As it was, they were lucky there'd been no large snowfalls for the past few weeks. A moderate snowfall had struck Thuringia and Franconia a few days ago, but it hadn't come this far south. The roads would be icy but still manageable for lighter field guns.

Tom managed to quell them soon enough. In the meantime, artillerymen less subject to madness went about the business of getting the six-pounders ready to go. Within twenty minutes, they were done.

It took another fifteen minutes to load the wagons available with as much ammunition as possible. Begrudgingly, Tom set aside three of the wagons to carry enough food for a couple of days. Three, if he imposed tight rationing. He hated to cut back on ammunition since they might be in for a lot of desperate fighting soon. But it would be foolish to assume he could get any supplies from the countryside until they got a fair distance from Ingolstadt. Once he was well into the Oberpfalz, he was confident he could obtain supplies from local towns and villages. The province was loyal to the USE and hostile to Duke Maximilian. It also had a large and active Committee of Correspondence.

He also decided not to take the artillery's main radio. The device was powerful enough to transmit in voice anywhere in central Europe, at least during the evening window. But it was inoperative at the moment, due to a minor problem of some sort, so he couldn't use it tonight. The radiomen assured him they could get it fixed within a day or two, but the radio was too heavy to carry except in a wagon, because of the batteries, and on the fragile side. It would slow them down and might break again anyway.

They didn't really need it. He'd bring a small Morse-code-only radio that could be carried in a backpack. With one of those radios, he could transmit a brief signal to Bamberg that would tell Ed Piazza and Heinrich Schmidt everything essential. They'd have the bulk of the State of Thuringia-Franconia's National Guard on the march within twenty-four hours.

He also took the company's walkie-talkie. He'd been in such a rush that he'd forgotten to tell Rita to take the unit he kept in their home. He could only hope she'd thought of it herself.

For a moment, his fears for his wife surfaced, chittering for his attention. Savagely, he drove them under. He had no time for that now. The Bavarians could launch a counterattack at almost any time. He was pretty sure the only reason the enemy commander hadn't already gotten one underway was because many of his soldiers were running wild, as often happened when a city was being sacked. Especially in a night attack, where maintaining control was harder than usual.

The inhabitants of the city were going to pay a savage price for the 1st Battalion's defection tonight. But there was nothing Tom could do about that, so he pushed the matter out of his mind also. For now, at least. In the future, hopefully, there'd be a reckoning—and it would be a harsh one, if he had any say in the matter. He had no use for the duke of Bavaria and even less use for traitors who took his silver.

The commander of the artillery battery came over to him. That was Captain Martin Kessler, from the Thuringian town of Langenwolschendorf. He was accompanied by the two infantry captains, Geipel and Fischer, and Bruno von Eichelberg. Tom had been pleased to see that the young captain from Brunswick had remained faithful to his oath. Von Eichelberg's company of mercenaries was undersized, barely a hundred men, but they were veterans. Between them, his artillerymen, and the two companies from the 2nd Battalion, he now had well over five hundred men under his command.

"We're ready to go, Major," said Kessler. "We've spiked all the guns we're not taking and the big radio is destroyed. Are you sure about leaving the food and gunpowder, though?"

Normal practice, in addition to spiking the guns—better still, if they'd been next to the river, pitching them in afterward—would have been to destroy all the food and gunpowder they were leaving behind. But the only quick way to do that was to blow up the powder or set the whole barracks on fire, and the artillery barracks were right inside Ingolstadt. Nothing but city streets separated them from residences and places of business. Tom didn't think the food and gunpowder was important enough to kill citizens of his own nation in order to deny it to the enemy.

If he hadn't been so pressed to get out of the city quickly, he would have had the gunpowder casks opened and the contents spread all over the foodstuffs. Then, for good measure, soaked everything in water, wine and any other liquids available. That wouldn't completely destroy either, but it would go a long way in that direction and certainly create a time-consuming mess for the Bavarians to deal with. But they were just too short of time.

"No, we'll leave them as is." He fought down the urge to look around for himself. Unless junior officers gave you reason not to trust them, you had to take their word for things like this or you'd undermine morale.

Instead, he just nodded. "Let's go, then. Bruno, what's the situation at the gate?"

Shortly after the fighting started, a few squads of artillerymen had seized the nearby gate that led out of the city walls to the east. That had been easy enough, since the gate was held by a platoon of still-loyal soldiers. As soon as Tom had driven off the enemy besieging the barracks, he'd ordered von Eichelberg to send most of his mercenaries to bolster the gate's defenders.

"Everything's quiet, sir," replied von Eichelberg. "According to the last report, at least."

That report would have been carried by a mounted adjutant. There were a handful of them attached to the artillery units. The USE army still didn't have enough radios to provide them to many units smaller than battalions, unless they had special duties like the artillery. Most down-time officers weren't really comfortable with the gadgets, anyway. So almost every unit larger than a company had at least one mounted adjutant ready to serve as a courier.

Tom motioned for the radio operator to come over to him. "Let's go then," he said.

It would take a few minutes to get hundreds of men with their wagons, guns, and other gear moving. Tom had enough time to send a message to Bamberg.

The radioman unlimbered his equipment. Once he was ready to start transmitting, Tom gave him the message:

Bavarians over-running Ingolstadt. Colonel Engels murdered. City cannot be held. Withdrawing what remains of regiment into countryside.

He wondered if there would be ever be a follow-on message. There was no way to know yet. Within a day or two, Tom and all of his men might share the same fate as the colonel who had once commanded them.

Well, no. Whatever else, they wouldn't be murdered in their sleep.

Chapter 6

Once he realized who was coming—that had been a tense few seconds, until he recognized the women—Stefano was immensely relieved. Before they'd even arrived at the airship, he'd already begun deploying the envelope.

Trying to, rather. It really wasn't a job for just one person.

Dina Merrifield and Amanda Boyd hurried over to help.

"Where is Hank?" Stefano asked, trying not to sound exasperated. The help of the girls—no, women—was appreciated, but neither Dina nor Amanda was large. Siers was big and there was quite a bit of muscle under the fat. That muscle would be useful at the moment.

Thankfully, it had been a cold and dry January night, with a clear sky. In damp conditions, the envelope had a nasty habit of absorbing moisture which not only reduced the lift but made it more difficult to deploy.

"He's hurt," Dina said. "Broken leg, we think, and he's still unconscious."

Stefano broke off from the work long enough to look at the other people who were now arriving. A small man he didn't know was struggling with a wheelbarrow, heavily loaded with...

Sure enough, Hank Siers. He looked more dead than alive, although that might be an effect of the moonlight. One of his legs had been bound up in some sort of crude splint.

Bonnie Weaver was with him. Behind them came another group of women. He recognized all of them. The wife of the American artillery officer—she was also the sister of the former prime minister—was bringing up the rear, with a shotgun in her hands and a very fierce look on her face.

Mary Tanner Barancek was there, he was relieved to see. He was less relieved—considerably less—to see that her fearsome aunt was with her, along with the two women she seemed inseparable from. The three of them were something called "auditors." Stefano wasn't sure what the term signified, but he knew that a number of people viewed their comings and goings with considerable trepidation. They were police officials of some sort, apparently.

Mary came over to help also. Within a short time, the envelope was ready and Stefano began the process of filling it with air driven by the fan that would maintain pressure in the envelope during flight. This air was cold, not hot, and would not provide enough lift for the craft to actually fly. But it would fill out the envelope and get it prepared for the hot air to come.

That process was finished in a few minutes. While the envelope was filling out, Stefano used the time to operate the control surfaces and engine tilts to make sure they were functioning properly. Then he lit the pilot lights for the burners.

Now came the moment Stefano had been dreading. As soon as they were ignited, the burners would light up the entire area. The flames would be bright and visible even in broad daylight. At night, despite the moon in the sky, they would be like beacons.

But there was no help for it. They'd just have to hope they could fill the envelope with hot air and lift off the ground before anyone came out from Ingolstadt to investigate.

Slowly and carefully, as a man will when he's worn out, Johann Heinrich Böcler lowered the handles of the wheelbarrow until the weight had settled firmly on the braces. Then, finally letting go, he staggered backward a couple of steps. He might have fallen, except that Bonnie Weaver came up quickly and steadied him.

"Easy, fella," she said. "It's done. Don't hurt yourself now."

He grimaced, thinking of the damage he'd already inflicted upon himself. By tomorrow, his muscles would be aching all over. Böcler was stronger than he looked, but his life was mostly a sedentary one.

The worst would be his hands, though. He dreaded to look at them. He hadn't stopped once during the journey and he was quite sure he had a number of blisters.

Weaver had figured out as much herself. "Let me see your hands," she said. He held them up, unresisting. May as well learn the worst now, he supposed. She took them in her own and gently turned them over so she could see the palms.

He heard a little indrawn hiss and saw her wince. "Let's go over to the light," she said. "I can't see well enough just by the moon."

Franchetti had the burners going by now, and the flames were very bright. Once they got near, Weaver resumed her inspection of his hands.

"Well, I won't lie to you, Herr Böcler. I'll see if I can find some salve and bandages. But even if I can, your hands are going to hurt like the dickens before too long."

The term "dickens" was unknown to him, one of the many English words that slid in and out of Amideutsch according to the whim of the speaker. No German dialect was standard in this day; Amideutsch less than any. But the meaning was clear enough.

He shrugged. The gesture was minimal, since she was still holding his hands. "The problem should only be temporary." He smiled, a bit ruefully. "I was not planning to do any more writing for a while, anyway."

She chuckled. "Writing? I know you have a reputation for being meticulous, Herr Böcler, but I can't imagine there's any point in keeping records for a while. The Bavarians will already be turning everything upside down and inside out."

He shook his head. "I was thinking of my book, not the province's records."

She cocked her head and raised an eyebrow quizzically. "Book?"

Böcler realized he was speaking too freely. He was usually quite reserved, especially in the presence of women, but Bonnie Weaver had a relaxed and friendly manner that invited casual intimacy. Between that and his own exhaustion, he was being less guarded that he should be.

"What book?" she repeated.

He cleared his throat. "I am . . . ah. Well, it is an ambition mostly. So far I have a great deal of notes, but nothing I suppose you could properly call a book."

"That's how most books get written, I figure. What's it about?"

"It's a book on history." He'd hoped he could leave it at that, but the expression on Weaver's face made it clear she expected a fuller explication. "A record of our own times," he added.

"Good luck with that! I remember Ms. Mailey saying in class once that it was impossible to analyze human events dispassionately until at least two centuries have gone by—and not always, even then. Anything more recent than that, according to her, was just current events. She said that with a sniff, as if the term was synonymous with gossip. She didn't teach current events, of course. That was taught by Dwight Thomas, who doubled as our driver's education teacher." She smiled. "They didn't get along real well. Being fair to Mr. Thomas, he was a pretty good driver's ed teacher."

Böcler had no intention whatsoever of asking the formidable Mailey woman her opinion on his book project. Or anything else. She was the sort of person his father and grandfather would both urge him to avoid at all costs. His father was a Lutheran pastor; his grandfather, a school director. Neither was a profession noted for taking risks.

Thankfully, Weaver seemed willing to let the matter drop. Böcler really didn't like to discuss his book with anyone. Some of that was his natural reticence. Most of it was the reluctance of an unpublished author to discuss his ambitions openly. The printing press was less than two centuries old, but it had already been well established that the phrase "unpublished author" was a ridiculous oxymoron.

Johann Heinrich Böcler had a horror of looking ridiculous. In that, as in many things, he was a faithful son and grandson.

Weaver looked away, toward the work being done to ready the airship. The envelope was now beginning to fill out completely, as the hot air produced by the burners did its work.

The moon was almost directly behind her, so her profile was well-illuminated. She had a short, blunt nose, above lips that were slightly imbalanced. Her lower lip was thin; the upper, rather fleshy. Her chin was round, as were her cheeks. Like Böcler himself, Weaver was someone who would constantly tend to be plump.

Her figure, also well-illuminated, was much like her face. Not obese, certainly; but not at all slim, either. She was attractive, in a modest sort of way, but not a woman anyone would consider a beauty. Or even particularly pretty.

Böcler felt a sudden, powerful attraction to the American. He was taken completely off-guard. What had triggered that impulse?

He was a bit alarmed, too. He was only twenty-five years old. A rich man's son or a nobleman would contemplate marriage at such an early age, but someone from Johann Heinrich's modest origins would not be able to sustain a household until he was in his late twenties or early thirties. He had no business getting interested in a woman yet. Any woman, much less an up-timer.

The thought of pursuing a mere dalliance never even occurred to him. A considerable number of people—most people, truth be told—thought Böcler was a prude. But at least he could claim the virtues of prissiness as well the vices. He was not a man who would toy with anyone's affections.

✧   ✧   ✧

Bonnie Weaver wasn't thinking of the man next to her at all. Her concentration was on the man tending the burner that was filling the airship's envelope.

Stefano Franchetti. Slender, dapper in a commoner's sort of way, quick-witted; altogether charming.

He reminded her a lot of Larry Wild. The reminder drew her to him and repelled her at the same time.

Bonnie and Larry hadn't exactly been involved, but they'd been very close to it when the Ostend War started and he went off to fight the Danish fleet attacking Wismar. He'd been killed in that battle, when his rocket boat attacked the enemy ships.

Foolishly, in hindsight, Bonnie had probed hard and long to find out exactly how he'd been killed. When she finally learned, she wished she hadn't. Cut in half—literally, cut in half—by a cannonball. They never found any part of his body. The upper half had been sent flying into the sea, where it would have long ago been eaten by sea life. The lower half had stayed in the rocket boat, but the boat itself had blown up a short time later when it rammed one of the Danish warships.

October 7, 1633. More than two years had gone by since then, but she still had nightmares about it sometimes; even flashbacks to something she'd never actually seen.

The worst of it was that she couldn't grieve properly. It wasn't as if she'd lost a husband or a fiancé or even an established boy-friend. Just...a possibility, forever gone. She still wondered what might have happened between them. Not just from time to time, either, but often. She was beginning to fear she'd developed an obsession over his memory.

Hearing a sound next to her, Bonnie turned her head and saw that Böcler had a tight expression on his face. That had been him, issuing a little hiss of pain. What was she doing, mooning over a dead man and his Italian doppelganger when she had an injured man to tend to?

There was a first aid kit in the gondola, she remembered. She'd never looked inside it, but it had to hold bandages and some sort of salve or unguent. Bandages, for sure.

The problem was that the envelope had been inflated enough to come completely off the ground. Stefano and Amanda and Dina were scurrying around with last minute preparations. This was the worst possible time for her to start rummaging around inside the gondola. She wasn't even in it yet.

Her thoughts must have shown in her face, because Böcler cleared his throat and said, "There is nothing you can do for me at the moment. Once we are in the air, we can see if there are medical supplies in the...what do you call it? The part that looks almost like a boat and hangs underneath the huge balloon?"

"Gondola. It's called the gondola." She gave another smile. "And you'd do better to call the inflated part the envelope instead of the balloon, or you're likely to get a long lecture from Stefano on the profound metaphysical distinction between a dirigible airship and a pitiful balloon, subject to the mercy of the winds."

He smiled back. It was quite a nice smile, she thought. Much less stiff-upper-lip than his personality seemed to be.

Then, again, maybe the smile was the reality and the personality just the appearance. It was always a mistake to judge people too quickly. Whatever else, she'd learned one thing about the short, stout Franconian secretary tonight. He was a very steady man. Reliable in a crisis, and not given to either panic or self-pity. She knew plenty of people with more charming externalities who were a lot less solid.

"We're ready to go!" hollered Dina. "Hurry up!"

You didn't want to dally when it came time to board an airship that used hot air instead of hydrogen. It was lifted and lowered by adjusting the heat produced by the burners, not by dropping a lot of ballast. Each passenger who came aboard added to the weight, which required more heat—which, if you overdid it, ran the risk of lifting too far while another person was trying to climb aboard.

The long dimension of the envelope had been aligned to face into the wind, and there was a bow line anchored to a tree stump that kept the ship fairly steady. But "fairly steady" is one thing, once a person is in a gondola; something quite a bit more challenging, when you're trying to get into it in the first place.

Under normal conditions on a proper airfield this wouldn't be so much a problem, because there would be half a dozen groundspeople who'd be holding the gondola down with ropes. Not to mention that they'd almost always be working in broad daylight.

It dawned on Bonnie that she'd given no thought at all to the problem of getting Hank Siers aboard. The surveyor was still unconscious.

Stefano sprang over the side of the gondola and landed lightly on the ground, by now almost six feet below the rail. He was a lithe and agile man.

Not a big one, unfortunately, nor a particularly strong one. With Willa and Maydene's help, he was now trying to get Hank into the gondola, and...

Was not going to manage it. Bonnie hurried over, with Böcler right behind her.

Once there, she and the secretary lent a hand to the effort.

Still no success. The problem wasn't simply Hank's mass, it was the height of the gondola. Dina had replaced Stefano at the burner—she was more-or-less the expedition's designated copilot— and was trying to lower the airship as much as she could. But, at best, that still meant trying to hoist more than two hundred pounds of dead weight over a railing that was never less than five feet off the ground.

"Use me as a stool," Böcler said. He got down on hands and knees, right beside the gondola. "Quickly, please."

Stefano didn't hesitate for more than a second before he stood on Böcler's back. "Pass him up to me."

As stated, the proposition was absurd. Franchetti was barely more than half the size of Siers. But with four women pushing from below and using Stefano as a combination hoist and ramp— Amanda and Rita were pulling from above, too—they managed to get it done.

Bonnie helped Johann Heinrich back on his feet.

"Are you all right?" she asked. She was genuinely worried. He had to have taken something of a beating down there in the final frenzied push to get Siers into the gondola.

He took a deep breath. A bit of a shaky breath, too. "I have been better, at times in the past. But worse also. It's not as bad as being bitten by a horse. Or kicked by a horse, which is still worse."

She stared at him. Northern West Virginia had been a rural sort of place, especially a small town like Grantville. But the truth was that Bonnie, like many people in the area, didn't really have any more experience with horses than a resident of Manhattan.

Or hadn't, at least, until the Ring of Fire planted them all in

the seventeenth century. But even then, Bonnie—also like many people in Grantville—still didn't have much experience with horses. You could get pretty far by walking, when you got right down to it. And didn't have to negotiate with a creature six or seven times bigger than you were in order to do it.

"You were *bitten* by a horse?"

"Oh, yes. They're quite vicious animals, actually. I look forward to the day when we can all ride in automobiles everywhere and put horses in the zoo. Or, better yet, in the larders. The meat's tasty, if you slaughter the animals before they get too old."

"You've *eaten* a horse?"

"Not often. The meat's too expensive unless you get the flesh from horses slaughtered late in life. And that's no good except in sauerbraten. I've heard the Bavarians make a good sausage out of horse meat too, but I've never tasted it."

It was their turn to get into the gondola, everyone else having already gone aboard. That was an awkward process. Neither of them was slender and Böcler had the further handicap of hands which were now almost useless. But with the help of the people pulling from above and a complete disregard for dignity, they managed the task.

As soon as they were in the gondola, Franchetti increased the output of the burners. At his order, Dina cast off the anchor line. They began rising immediately.

Panting a little from the exertion and half-sprawled on the floor of the gondola, Bonnie went back to staring wide-eyed at the secretary. "You *ate* a horse. Was that, like, a revenge thing?"

Böcler frowned. "For the horse who bit me? And the one who kicked me? Of course not. They're simply brutes, Ms. Weaver. I'd have to ask my father—he's a parson—but I believe seeking to wreak vengeance on dumb animals would be frowned upon by the Lord. Viewed severely, in fact."

He sounded for all the world like a man discussing the temperament of his department boss instead of the Almighty.

So. Steady, solid, seemingly unflappable. Add severely practical to the list, too.

Chapter 7

Hearing the door open, General von Lintelo turned to see who was entering the chamber in Ingolstadt's Rathaus that he'd seized for his headquarters. To his surprise, the officer coming in was Colonel Caspar von Schnetter. He hadn't expected him back so soon.

"Simpson seems to have escaped, sir," said von Schnetter. "His wife also. The cavalry unit I sent to investigate found all three of the men assigned to that task dead. All of them in or near the door, which had been smashed in. Somehow, the Americans must have gotten a warning."

"By their radio?" asked one of the other cavalry officers in the room. That was Major Johann Adam Weyhel von Eckersdörfer, usually known simply as Weyhel.

Von Lintelo had to put a stop to that immediately. Even the Americans' enemies—perhaps especially their enemies—had a bad habit of ascribing near-magical powers to the up-timers' technology.

"Nonsense," he said firmly. "The assassins simply bungled, that's all. What happened to them afterward, Colonel? The American couple, I mean."

Von Lintelo already knew the answer to that question. In light of the latest developments, it was quite obvious. But he was a firm believer in the tried and tested method of reminding subordinates of their flaws and shortcomings.

Von Schnetter hesitated. "Ah . . . I don't really know, General. Perhaps . . ."

"Again, nonsense!" von Lintelo boomed. "It's obvious that Simpson managed to rejoin his artillery unit—which would account, of course, for their success in driving off your attack on the barracks."

The "your" was a collective pronoun, in this case. Von Schnetter hadn't been personally in charge of that mission. In point of fact, none of the officers in the room had been assigned to the mission. But they were part of von Lintelo's staff, the staff had clearly bungled, and since these were the officers present at the moment they would be the ones to receive his chastisement.

The general, a devout Catholic, did not share the Protestant superstitions about Biblical texts. But there was no denying the

wisdom in the Proverbs, one of which was: *He that spares his rod hates his son.* That applied just as much to subordinate officers as it did to children.

Von Schnetter flushed a little. But, of course, made no protest. Timon von Lintelo was one of Bavaria's most prestigious figures, and not just in the military. He was a member of Duke Maximilian's privy council as well as holding the rank of major general. It was a measure of the duke's trust that he had placed von Lintelo in charge of retaking Ingolstadt.

A charge which von Lintelo had not failed, even if his success had a few ragged edges.

Speaking of which . . .

"And where is the artillery unit now, Colonel?"

"Ah . . . They seem to have left the city, General."

"Escaped you, in other words."

Von Schnetter said nothing. After a moment, von Lintelo decided to relent a little. The colonel had not been directly in charge, after all.

"Never mind, Caspar. What's done is done."

"I could lead a pursuit, sir," said Johann von Troiberz, one of the cavalry officers present.

The man's tone was obsequious. Von Lintelo had no objection to that, but in von Troiberz's case the fawning habits were tied to a man in whom the general had no great confidence. If he decided to launch a pursuit after the American officer and his artillery company, von Lintelo would give the assignment to Lorenz Münch von Steinach. Colonel Münch was as much of a sycophant as von Troiberz, but he was also a lot more competent.

But it was a bad idea, to begin with. "They made their escape through the eastern gate, I assume?" he said. The artillery barracks were located very near to it.

Von Schnetter nodded. "Yes, sir."

"In that case"—he looked at von Troiberz—"I have better use for the cavalry. We need to send every cavalry unit available to the north, to Amberg. At first light."

Seeing the expressions on the faces of several of his subordinates, von Lintelo sighed loudly with exasperation. "I don't propose to *seize* the city, gentlemen. Not now, before we've taken Regensburg. But the heirs to the duchy are being held there. They need to be rescued."

He nodded toward yet another cavalry officer in the room, Captain Heinrich Benno von Elsenhaim. "Von Elsenhaim has been preparing the mission. All of you cavalry commanders should discuss the details with him. Now, please, there's no time to lose. Colonel Münch, I'm placing you in charge of the expedition."

The cavalrymen began collecting around von Elsenhaim in a corner. The general turned back to von Schnetter. "Are there any other problems I need to be made aware of?"

"Ah..." Whenever he thought he might have bad news to report, von Schnetter seemed incapable of speaking without that annoying preliminary noise.

"What is it now, Colonel?" The general made no effort to disguise his irritation. He rarely did, when dealing with subordinates.

"Nothing specific, sir. But... We don't have as much control of the troops as I'd like."

Von Lintelo stared at him. Von Schnetter had been an officer long enough—more than long enough—to know the realities.

"Of course we don't," he snapped. "They're in the middle of sacking a city—which, I remind you, I gave them express permission to do if they succeeded in taking Ingolstadt. The legitimate spoils of war."

"Yes, I know. But..."

Another officer came into the chamber. Also an unexpected one—Captain Johann Heinrich von Haslang, whom von Lintelo had sent to find out what had happened with regard to the airship. That hadn't been more than five minutes ago! He couldn't possibly have any news this soon.

"I think you'd better see this for yourself, General," said von Haslang. He pointed to one of the windows on the northern side of the room. "It's quite visible from there."

Von Lintelo went over to the window and looked down at the city. The chamber was on the third floor of the Rathaus, so he had a good view of the square below.

There was nothing to see, beyond some soldiers plundering a shop.

"Up in the sky, sir. You can see it clearly in the moonlight." Captain von Haslang came next to him and pointed up and to the left.

The general saw the object immediately. Even at what was clearly a considerable distance, the airship seemed enormous. The moonlight glistened off one of its flanks, as if it were a leviathan that had just leapt from the sea.

Von Lintelo had seen diagrams of the things, but had never actually seen one in person. It was ... impressive.

Also infuriating.

"What happened?" he demanded. "My orders were clear. I wanted that airship seized at once."

"Yes, sir."

"Who was in charge?"

"Von der Felt, sir. As you instructed."

Von Lintelo glared at him, and then glared at the airship. He had, in fact, specifically placed Captain Andreas von der Felt in charge. The former Catholic League officer was a reliable man. But he didn't appreciate the near-insolence involved in being reminded of it by von Haslang.

So, he shifted the issue. "What happened?"

"I don't kn—"

"Of course you don't know! I specifically assigned you to find out what happened and here you are, back again almost immediately with no explanation. You won't find out anything here, Captain. Attend to your duty."

After von Haslang left, the general went back to glaring at the airship. There would be no way to capture it now, of course. Or even destroy it. The craft was already at least a thousand feet high, beyond the range of any gun except cannons—and no cannon was designed to fire almost straight up.

That was something that would have to be attended to, as soon as possible. Realistically, there was no way Bavaria would be able to match their enemy's capabilities in the air in the foreseeable future. That would have been true even if they'd succeeded in taking the airship. Von Lintelo would urge the duke to devote resources to developing guns which could strike down aircraft instead. Such guns were quite possible, he'd been told.

The general's foul mood didn't last for long. Every campaign has its shortcomings. Taken as a whole, however, this campaign had succeeded splendidly. Ingolstadt was theirs again.

When Captain von Haslang finally found Captain Andreas von der Felt, he still had no answers. The captain's body was cold—ice cold, as you'd expect in the middle of a clear night in

January—and the first signs of rigor mortis were setting in. He'd
been dead for hours. His body was half-sprawled against the wall
of a shop that had been broken into. A general store, from the
looks, which sold foodstuffs and other items. Von Haslang was
pretty sure the captain had been dragged there from somewhere
else, though, judging from the trail of blood leading out into the
street. That was where he'd probably been struck down.

The cause of death needed no explanation. There was a big hole
in his forehead and the back of his skull was missing. A gunshot had caused that, obviously. From the huge size of the entry
wound, von Haslang would normally have assumed the captain
had been struck by a canister ball. But that was most unlikely.
Who would be firing a cannon in this vicinity? It was almost all
the way across the city from the artillery barracks.

At a guess, the captain—damned idiot—had been breaking
into the shop when someone inside fired on him with an antique
arquebus, the type of huge gun designed to be fired from wagons
or with a forkrest. They were often called by the French term
arquebus à croc. The weapons weren't much use on a modern
battlefield but, passed down generation to generation, they'd serve
a shopkeeper well enough.

Drawing his wheel-lock pistol, von Haslang climbed into the
shop through the smashed window. The shop itself was dark, but
there was a gleam of light coming from somewhere in the back.
He headed that way.

Before he got more than ten feet, he tripped over something
on the floor and barely managed to keep from falling. Squatting
down and investigating in the darkness with his free hand, he
discovered another dead body. He'd stumbled over one of the
man's legs.

After a few more seconds of groping, he found a big arquebus
lying next to the man. That confirmed his guess as to what had
happened. The captain—damned idiot—had led his men into a
plundering expedition instead of attending to his duty; he'd been
shot dead by the shop's owner; his men had fired back and killed
the owner. Then they'd dragged their commander's body out of
the street and placed him against the wall of the shop.

And then what?

He rose and resumed his slow progress toward the light. As he
got near, he saw that the light was spilling from the floor above.

What he'd seen from a distance was the crack in the door that led to the stairwell.

Slowly and carefully, making no sound, he opened the door enough to pass through. Then, waited for a few seconds, listening for any noise coming from above.

Nothing. That he could detect, anyway. There was quite a bit of noise filtering into the shop from the street outside. A city being sacked is anything but quiet. Whatever noise might be coming from above was drowned out.

But von Haslang didn't think there was any. He had a sense for such things, from his years of war. Whatever had happened in this shop was over. The whole place had a dead feel to it.

He went up the stairs, still moving slowly and carefully. Once on the landing, he spent another few seconds listening.

Still nothing. He started moving from room to room. As was often the case with small shops, these were the personal living quarters of the shopkeeper and his family.

The family was all dead, too. A wife, at a guess; two sons of teenage years; a girl perhaps eight years old. The boys had been killed immediately, shot dead. The woman and her daughter would have died later, after much torment. They'd both had their throats cut.

Several empty bottles of liquor were lying about. Those would have been looted from the shop below. The few possessions of the family had also been ransacked, not that there would have been much to steal.

Despite the empty bottles, the killers hadn't been completely drunk. Soldiers sacking a city didn't usually murder the women they raped. Their men, yes, as a rule; but they'd keep the women for concubines. This had been done to eliminate witnesses.

Not witnesses to the atrocity itself. Duke Maximilian and General von Lintelo would be quite indifferent to that matter, and any of their soldiers would know it. But they wouldn't be indifferent to gross dereliction of duty—and these men had been given an important mission. At which they'd failed completely, because of their own lust and greed.

For that, they'd hang—if they were found out.

But would they be? Did anyone besides Captain Andreas von der Felt know which soldiers he'd taken with him? Anyone, at least, whose word could be taken as good coin.

Probably... not. Von der Felt was well-known for committing atrocities, and such officers transmitted their attitudes to their men. Captain von Haslang strongly disapproved, and his reasons were military as well as moral. Units which behaved in that manner invariably became coarsened, and the coarseness spread over time into all areas of their conduct. Who in their right mind would take the word of a murderer, rapist, arsonist and torturer for anything?

Not he, for sure. Not even General von Lintelo would.

So, the guilty men would probably go undetected and unpunished. And an important mission had failed in the process.

The colonel sighed, slid the pistol back in his belt, and headed back down the stairs. He was beginning to get a bad feeling about this whole campaign—and he was a man who trusted his instincts.

Chapter 8

Tom and his soldiers got out of the city without any problem. He even had time to order the gate destroyed, after making sure no civilians would be caught in the blast. That was a pointless gesture, perhaps. By the time the USE army or the SoTF's National Guard could get back to Ingolstadt, the Bavarians would have had plenty of time to repair the damage. But blowing up the gate made Tom feel better anyway.

It made his troops feel better, too. They gave an impromptu cheer when the explosives went off.

"*We'll be back, you bastards!*" shouted one soldier.

And that was the key to it. Destroying the gate wasn't a pointless act of vandalism, it was a statement. A symbol, you might say. The Bavarians had taken Ingolstadt, yes. But they wouldn't keep it.

Now, though, Tom had to make a difficult decision. Where should he take his rump regiment?

There were only two viable options: retreat north to Amberg, the capital of the province, or march down the Danube to Regensburg.

Amberg was the safest destination. The city was garrisoned by a full regiment. The regiment was a mercenary unit, but Tom didn't think there was much likelihood it had been suborned also. Most of the soldiers in Amberg's garrison had been recruited in the Upper Palatinate, many of them from nearby towns. They'd been stationed in the capital long enough to develop ties with the local population, too. The chances that they'd agree to betray Amberg on behalf of the Bavarians were slight to the point of being nonexistent. Duke Maximilian had a reputation for savagery.

Amberg was well-fortified, too. With Tom's men added to the existing garrison, they'd be able to withstand any Bavarian siege long enough for Heinrich Schmidt to come down from the State of Thuringia-Franconia with most of the National Guard.

Regensburg was a riskier proposition. On the positive side, there was no chance at all that the garrison at Regensburg had turned traitor. That was the Iron Regiment, a unit of the regular USE army made up entirely of volunteers, most of them also recruited in this province. It was one of the few such regiments that hadn't been sent into Poland or Bohemia.

Regensburg was also well-fortified, but the defenses had a weakness because the city was right on the Danube. Most of Regensburg was on the south bank of the river, with just a small and not-well-protected enclave on the north. The enclave wasn't even legally part of Regensburg, but was a separate town. Tom couldn't remember the name of it. That town couldn't be held against a large and determined enemy, but losing it wouldn't by itself threaten Regensburg. The Danube was wide enough at that point to require a great stone bridge to get across, and the bridge could be easily defended.

Except in winter. The river froze over, enabling enemy troops to cross without using the bridge or needing the use of boats. Doing so had dangers of its own—no soldier likes to cross an iced-over river against enemy fire—and there were occasional thaws that might weaken the ice. But it made Regensburg's bridge less of a defensive barrier than it was most of the year.

Tom decided he had enough time to try reaching Bamberg on the radio. This was really a decision that should be made by the president of the SoTF and his top officers. They'd known for months that if hostilities broke out with Bavaria again, the brunt of the fighting would have to be borne by the province's National Guard. Between the war with Poland and the domestic turmoil in the USE itself, the only units of the nation's army that would be available were the troops Tom had pulled out of Ingolstadt and the Iron Regiment in Regensburg.

But...

Nothing. No reception at all. Small radios like this one were chancy at any distance, except during the evening and morning windows. Tom could only hope that his original message had been received.

He'd have to make the choice himself. The road they were on, coming out of the east gate, was the road to Regensburg. If he decided to march for Amberg, he had to cross over now to the northern route. He couldn't delay the decision. The next road they'd encounter which would enable them to head for Amberg didn't intersect this road for another ten miles down the river. By then, they'd have covered about a fourth of the distance to Regensburg anyway. They'd do better to just keep going than try to backtrack.

There were several small roads before then, but they wouldn't be of any use. Five hundred men with their gear—even infantry, much less artillery—could not march down narrow country lanes without slowing down almost to a crawl. Tom couldn't afford to dawdle. The Bavarians had cavalry; he didn't. The enemy commander had probably lost control of his troops tonight, but he'd have them back under control by the end of the day tomorrow.

He decided to go for Regensburg. That was a riskier decision for his own forces, but Tom was pretty sure that the Bavarians would try to seize Regensburg before they tried to penetrate further into the Oberpfalz. If they held Regensburg as well as Ingolstadt, they'd control both of the main crossings of the Danube along the border between Bavaria and the USE. They wouldn't have to worry that a sudden attack by the USE would get large numbers of troops across the river that could threaten their own rear and cut their supply trains.

The Iron Regiment would be hard pressed to hold Regensburg on their own against the full weight of the Bavarian army. But with the help of what was left of the Danube Regiment and its guns, they'd have a real chance. They didn't need to hold for long, after all. Tom had been part of the staff planning for this eventuality. General Schmidt could get a full division of the National Guard down to the Danube within a week. Ten days, at the latest, if the independent little principality of Nürnberg got stubborn and refused to let the SoTF march its soldiers through their territory.

He turned to give the order to his immediate subordinates, who had gathered around him once he called the halt to use the radio. To his surprise, he discovered that none of them were paying any attention to him at all. They were all gawking at the moon, it seemed like.

That was annoying. It was just a three-quarter moon, no different from the same sight that came every month. Tom was normally an even-tempered officer, but there'd been enough stress tonight to put him on edge. He was about to make a sarcastic remark when a peculiar gleam caught his eye.

When he looked up at the sky himself, he immediately understood what had drawn his officers' attention. They weren't looking at the moon—in fact, they weren't even looking close to it. They were looking at an airship flying northwest of the city.

That was the *Pelican,* if Tom remembered what Rita had told him. The airship was carrying out a survey of the region and had arrived in Ingolstadt yesterday. He'd forgotten all about it. Luckily for them, they'd obviously managed to get airborne again before the Bavarians could seize their craft.

He cleared his throat. "Gentlemen, if I could have your attention."

His officers immediately turned away from the sight of the airship, several of them with slightly sheepish expressions.

"I've decided to make for Regensburg," he said. "That will almost certainly be the next target for the Bavarians. We and our guns—especially the guns—would be a big help for the Iron Regiment. Does anyone have any questions? Any problems you can see that you'd like to raise?"

Most of the officers shook their heads. Bruno von Eichelberg, though, had an intent look on his face. "Does that airship have a radio, Major? If it does, it would give us superb reconnaissance. We could use that badly, come tomorrow. The Bavarians will be able to send out cavalry patrols everywhere and all we've got to match them are a handful of couriers."

Tom shook his head. "No, unfortunately, it doesn't. I'm not guessing, either. Rita went over to pay a visit yesterday after they landed and spent an hour or two with them. She told me Dina Merrifield and Amanda Boyd were complaining about the absence of a radio, which they thought was plain stupid. Apparently the expedition commander insisted on loading the airship with enough foodstuffs to fly to the South Pole and back, so there wasn't..."

He didn't finish the sentence, struck by a sudden thought. He'd forgotten about the *Pelican*—but what if Rita hadn't?

It was a long shot, but you never knew. He looked around for the radioman and saw him standing ready just a few feet away. Tom had given him the walkie-talkie to put in his backpack.

He held out his hand. "The walkie-talkie, please, Corporal Baier."

The corporal set down the pack and rummaged in it for a few seconds before coming up with the device and handing it to Tom.

"Rita, are you on the other end?" he asked. "Rita, Rita. Repeat: are you on the other end of this thing? Rita, come in. This is Tom. Over."

A few seconds went by, that seemed much longer than they actually were. Then, when he'd just about given up hope, Rita's voice came through.

"Tom? Tom! Is that really you? Never mind, stupid question. Where are you? Uh, over."

"Looking right at you, babe," he replied, almost laughing with relief. "Right up at you, I should say. Me and my soldiers—what's left of us—are out of the city and on the road to Regensburg not more than a mile from Ingolstadt. We can see the *Pelican* clearly in the sky. Over."

Belatedly, it occurred to Tom that he was simply assuming Rita was on the airship. She might be transmitting from the ground herself, after all.

But she didn't correct him, so apparently she was. "*Hold on, I'll look.*" She was off the air for a few seconds. "*No, dammit, I can't see you. The moonlight's just not bright enough and I guess we're up pretty high. Over.*"

"You're not really all that close, either." He hesitated for an instant. "Uh...what are your plans? Over."

"*We don't really have any. Get out of Ingolstadt was about as far as it went. We were thinking about flying to Amberg, but Stefano—he's the pilot—thinks that's going to be a problem. We don't have much fuel because they weren't able to refuel in Ingolstadt, and he says the wind is blowing the wrong way. He's not sure we can make it before we run out of fuel. Then he says we're at the mercy of the winds. Over.*"

Von Eichelberg had that intent look on his face again. "Isn't there gasoline in Regensburg?"

Tom held up a hand to interrupt him, nodding and talking into the walkie-talkie at the same time.

"There's plenty of gas in Regensburg, Rita. They're storing it up for the spring, when they hope to get that ironclad working again."

Working for the first time, would probably be a better way to put it. The small ironclad in question had been designed entirely by down-timers, whose enthusiasm had outrun their experience. The thing was so top-heavy it almost capsized the one and only time it had been put in the river, and was so awkward that the oars which were supposed to drive it through the water couldn't compete with the current. It was lying up in drydock to be fitted with an up-time engine as soon as a suitable one became available. But, hope springing eternal, the enthusiasts had somehow managed to sweet-talk the powers-that-be into providing them with several barrels of gasoline.

"And we could sure use your help while we're trying to get there ourselves," he added. "We've got no scouting capabilities worth talking about and within a day the Bavarian cavalry will be all over the place. Over."

"Hold on a minute, hon. I've got to talk it over. Uh. Over."

She was off the air for about a minute before she came back on. Tom was surprised, actually. He'd figured Hank Siers would make a fuss and it would take Rita at least five minutes to bully him into it.

That she'd succeed, he didn't doubt at all. When his wife wanted to be, she was pretty ferocious.

"Okay, Tom. We're on. Stefano thinks it's a good idea and so does everybody else. What do you want us to do? Exactly, I mean. Over."

She made no mention at all of Siers. Tom wondered what had happened to him. Had the surveyor been killed?

But that wasn't something he needed to worry about tonight. Tom studied the distant airship for a few seconds, wishing he knew more about the devices than he did. How easy were they to land and take off? And what did they need in the way of space and facilities?

For sure, they'd need plenty of space. The *Pelican* was as long as half a football field, and at least fifteen yards wide. There was no way it could land in a small meadow.

Von Eichelberg and his men had been stationed in Ingolstadt longer than Tom himself. So Tom turned back to him.

"Is there any large open area in the next few miles?" He pointed up at the *Pelican*. "It needs to be big enough for the airship to land. Say, a minimum of a hundred yards."

The young mercenary captain pursed his lips thoughtfully. After a moment, he said: "Two, that I can think of. Luckily, the nearest one is the largest."

He turned and pointed toward the Danube. "It's a big clearing alongside the river, perhaps two miles downstream from here. We could be there in an hour."

That was pushing it, Tom thought. In an hour, a man could walk two miles quite easily. Five hundred men, with six-pounders and supply wagons? In the middle of the night, to boot, with just moonlight to guide them? He thought they'd be doing well if they made it within two hours.

Still, that would get them to the clearing before dawn, which was what mattered. The Bavarians wouldn't be sending out any large cavalry force until morning.

He got back on the walkie-talkie. "How much room do you have in that thing? Can you carry another man, with—"

He looked at Corporal Baier, quickly gauging the weight of the radioman himself as well as that of the equipment he carried.

"Say, two hundred and twenty-five pounds, all told. Over."

Rita's answer came immediately. "You're not talking about yourself, obviously. Yeah, I'm pretty sure, especially because we can subtract my weight from the equation. Your guy gets on, I get off. That brings it down to a net gain of less than a hundred pounds. Hold on, I'll check with Stefano."

Tom winced. He'd been afraid she'd come up with that alternative. With thousands of Bavarians running wild, he wanted his wife to stay right where she was—way, way, way too high for the bastards to get to her.

Rita came back on the air. "*No problem, as long as we make the switch. Stefano says the* Pelican *could handle at least two more people—if we weren't low on fuel. But he says we've got enough to land and take off with an additional hundred pounds or so. Where do you want us to set down? Over. No, wait—don't tell me, tell Dina. She's the copilot and she'll double as the navigator. I'll put her on.*" A couple a seconds later: "*Oops. Forgot. Over.*"

Tom would have handed his walkie-talkie to von Eichelberg, since he was the one who'd actually be providing the directions. But he didn't think the Brunswick captain was familiar with the device. He'd show him how to use it after they were done here, but for now he'd keep serving as the intermediary.

While he waited for Dina Merrifield to come on the air, he contemplated some of his wife's personal characteristics. There'd been a good reason he'd thought she could bully Hank Siers within five minutes.

He foresaw some difficult times ahead. In about . . . two hours.

Chapter 9

By the time the rendezvous was made, Tom had figured out
what to do. He and Rita—and von Eichelberg, whenever further
directions were needed—had stayed in regular contact throughout
those two hours. Once she told him about Hank Siers' condition,
the solution to his problem was obvious.

The key was getting enough weight removed from the *Pelican*
to be able to add Corporal Baier and his radio to the gondola
without endangering the airship because of its fuel shortage.

And . . . *voila!* The surveyor weighed almost twice as much as
his wife did. And was useless aboard the *Pelican* because he was
still unconscious. And—could it get any better?—badly needed
medical attention, which Tom could provide since they'd brought
the regiment's ambulance along with its doctor.

True, the doctor wasn't exactly a medical titan. Dr. James
Nichols, he was not. In fact, the soldiers usually referred to him
as "the surgeon"—which was not a prestigious title in the here
and now—because what he mostly did was amputate limbs and
extract teeth. He also served as the regiment's dentist, a trade
whose principal tool in the here and now was a pair of pliers.

But he knew and followed the principles of sanitation and
sterilization, and however meager his skills they were better than
anything they had aboard the *Pelican*.

Well . . . That was pushing it, so he'd better leave that argument
aside. Rita was a very good practical nurse in her own right, and
had quite a bit of experience at it. During their long captivity
in the Tower of London, she'd wound up being the prison's de
facto medical expert. The Yeoman Warders had credited her with
keeping several of their children alive when disease struck, and
they were probably right.

Still, she didn't need to deal with Siers. There wasn't much
anyone could do for him now.

"You want to put Hank in a *wagon*?"
"Hey, hon, it's an ambulance," Tom protested.
"It's a fucking wagon with a red cross painted on it—except
you never even got around to painting on the cross. Don't bullshit

me, Tom. This is just a scheme to keep me on the *Pelican*." Rita turned and pointed at the airship, which was tethered to a tree not far away in the clearing. A number of soldiers were helping to keep it down and steady with ropes.

"You see that?" she demanded. "It's *not* a wagon." Her hand made a gliding motion. "Flies right through the air, as gentle as you please. And you want to take a man with a bad concussion—maybe worse!—off that best-ride-you-could-ask-for and put him in a fucking *wagon*? On seventeenth-century roads? Are you fucking nuts?"

When his wife got agitated, she tended to lapse into the Appalachian patois of her not-so-far-back youth. This ran heavily toward short Anglo-Saxon terms, which perhaps lent support to the theory that Appalachian speech was closer to Elizabethan English than any other dialect had been in the twentieth century.

Or maybe hillbillies just liked to cuss a lot. The habit had been a source of trouble when Rita first met Tom's very blueblood parents.

Rita crossed her arms. Tom was familiar with that gesture. Alas.

"No," she said. "N. O. Absolutely not. Siers stays on the *Pelican*."

A third party intervened. "If I might interrupt..."

Turning, Tom saw that the speaker was the province administrator's secretary, Johann Heinrich Böcler. Tom hadn't even been aware the man was standing nearby. The three middle-aged auditors were with him, along with Bonnie Weaver.

Tom didn't know the man very well, but any interruption was welcome. "Sure, what is it?"

Böcler gave Rita an apologetic glance. "I agree with your wife that Herr Siers should remain on the *Pelican*. Truthfully, it would be much safer for him. But I also think, for the same reason, that it would be foolish for her to leave that safety. She should also remain aboard the airship."

Well. It turned out he was a splendid fellow. Who knew?

Rita was glowering at him. "Why should I be any safer than anyone else?"

Böcler made a face. "Mrs. Simpson—please. You must be realistic about these things." Now he gave Tom an apologetic glance. "Meaning no disrespect, Major, but the key political factor here is that your wife is also the sister of General Stearns. Short of recapturing the two young heirs to Bavaria now in Amberg, Duke Maximilian could have no better hostage than she."

He was right, Tom realized immediately. He hadn't even considered that. Rita was so unpretentious that no one who knew her thought of her as a "big cheese." And like most up-timers, even years after the Ring of Fire, Tom didn't really think of holding people hostage as a political tactic. Kidnapping was just a crime, dammit.

But in the seventeenth century, as had been true for at least a millennium in Europe, holding high-ranked captives for ransom or blackmail was considered business-as-usual.

But then, why...

Rita had seen the same flaw in the logic. "That's bullshit, Heinrich!" she snapped at Böcler. "You came in right after it happened, so you should know. Those guys who broke into our home weren't trying to take me hostage. The first thing the bastards did when they came through the door was try to shoot me."

"That happened in the heat of the moment, when they'd just smashed through the door," countered Böcler. "I think they expected to find you in bed, not standing right in front of them. That first shot was probably fired in reflex. Thereafter, of course, since you were shooting back with the shotgun, they had no choice but to try to kill you."

The secretary spread his hands. "A great deal depends on the instructions the assassins were given, which we don't know. In particular, were they offered a share of the ransom? If they were, then they'd have had a keen incentive in keeping you alive. But Duke Maximilian is just as well-known for his penny-pinching as his ruthlessness. They probably weren't offered any such incentive, so they had no great reason not to simply murder you."

It made sense. Tom had been there himself, and remembered the chaos and fury of that brief gunfight. Unless the assassins had been tightly focused on the goal of capturing Rita, their natural fighting instincts would have overridden everything else.

And, regardless, Böcler's general point remained valid. Rita had no business getting down on the ground where she could be captured.

From the fact that she was now just silently glaring at the secretary, Tom knew that Rita understood it herself. She could be stubborn beyond belief, but she also had a very strong sense of duty.

Still, he hesitated to say anything. In the foul mood she was in, she'd lash out at him if he did.

Thankfully, Böcler stepped into the breach again. "Of course, we do need to lighten up the airship. But I can take care of that problem. I don't weigh as much as Herr Siers, but I certainly weigh more than you do."

At a guess, the secretary probably weighed at least one hundred and eighty pounds. He might even be pushing two hundred. He was on the short side, but thickly-proportioned.

"One—or all of us—could get off also," said Maydene Utt. "There's no use for auditors on board the *Pelican*."

She sounded a bit uncertain. Tom was more than a bit alarmed. He had no use for three auditors either, down here on the ground. He and his troops would be undertaking a forced march over the next two days. Granted that middle-aged Appalachian women were almost invariably tougher than they looked, they still weren't accustomed to that sort of exertion.

Bonnie Weaver stepped into the breach, this time. "That's silly, Maydene. You and Willa and Estelle are almost fifty years old." Fodor started to protest something but Bonnie drove right over her. "And the three of you have been on horseback for the last two years—no, it must be three, now. When was the last time you walked as much as half a mile?"

She made a wry face. "Me, on the other hand, I'm scared of horses. So I walk everywhere. And I weigh more than any of you except Maydene. So we can lighten the airship further by putting me on the ground too. Between me and Heinrich, that more than makes up for adding the corporal and his radio equipment."

Tom was a bit dubious at the prospect of having Bonnie along on the march, but only a bit. Like every military force of the day that had been in one place for a while, the Danube Regiment had collected camp followers. Women, mostly, who were either married to one of the soldiers or pretended to be. They doubled as cooks and laundresses for the unit; and, in some cases, prostitutes. There were at least two hundred of them along on this march, including several dozen children. If they could keep up—which they surely could, with the incentive of staying out of Duke Maximilian's clutches—then Bonnie should be able to as well. She was on the plump side, true. But that was due to genetics, not sedentary habits. She was a vigorous sort of person, as you'd expect from someone who'd chosen to become a surveyor.

"What time do you think it is?" asked Willa Fodor. She was squinting to the east, trying to see if she could spot any signs of the dawn arriving. "My watch doesn't work any more."

Neither did Tom's. He hadn't worn a watch in more than a year, since the battery finally died. By then, four years after the Ring of Fire, silver oxide batteries—the very few that were left—cost a small fortune. It hadn't seemed worth the expense, especially since the new battery would eventually die also. With a handful of exceptions, the only up-time watches that were still functional were old-fashioned wind-up watches. And there weren't all that many of those.

Happily, there had already been a primitive watchmaking industry in Europe when the Americans arrived, which quickly began adapting the designs in up-time encyclopedias. The balance spring and balance wheel designed by Huygens in the late seventeenth century in the up-timers' universe were well within their capabilities. Within two or three years, a fairly large number of pocket watches were available in much of Europe.

They were expensive, of course, and up-timers tended to scorn them. The watches weren't nearly as accurate as the timepieces Americans were used to.

Böcler dug into his coat pocket and came out with one. He flipped open the lid and tilted the watch so he could see the face by the light of the moon. "It's almost five o'clock in the morning," he said.

Seeing everyone staring at him, he smiled slightly. "No, of course I can't afford such a device on my salary. Duke Ernst gave it to me as a gift, when he left for Saxony."

He put it back in its pocket. "I have tested it against American electronic timers. It is accurate within ten minutes every day. I have to keep adjusting it, naturally."

The sun would be rising in a couple of hours, then. They still weren't more than four miles from Ingolstadt. Tom wanted to get five or six miles away before making camp, if at all possible. But he'd stop sooner if they found a good place to set up defensive fieldworks. It wouldn't be long before the Bavarian cavalry found them and they had to start fighting.

The men needed some sleep, too, even if only for two or three hours. And something to eat.

Von Eichelberg had been reading his mind, apparently. He'd make a superb staff officer. "There is a very good place to set up camp about a mile farther down the river, Major," he said. "Thick forest comes almost to the river, creating a bottleneck. With your guns, we could hold off five or six times our number."

Tom nodded. "Let's be about it, then." He turned to Rita. "You're in charge up there, hon. If it looks like you're in any danger of running out of fuel, head for Regensburg immediately. I'm hoping you'll be able to scout for us all the way, but it's not worth the risk. If you lose power, the winds will probably blow you into Bavaria or Austria."

It was tempting to send the *Pelican* to Regensburg right now. They could refuel and, thereafter, could provide the regiment with reconnaissance without having to worry about losing power.

But that presupposed that "refueling" was a simple, cut-and-dried matter, which it certainly wouldn't be. By the time the relevant authorities could consult with each other, wrangle over everything relevant authorities could invariably find to wrangle about—you could get a headache just thinking about it—the regiment would probably have arrived in Regensburg and made it all a moot point.

Rita gave him a quick hug. A moment later, she was headed back toward the *Pelican*. The three female auditors and Corporal Baier followed her.

Tom looked at Bonnie and Johann Heinrich. "Do you two have anything you need to get off the airship? If you do, you'd better move quickly."

The two of them looked at each other, then simultaneously shook their heads.

"No," said Bonnie. "We were in such an all-fired hurry to get out of the inn when the fighting started that we didn't take anything with us." She nodded toward the secretary. "He's been staying in the same inn and came with us."

Böcler shrugged. "I regret not taking some additional clothing, but other than that, there really wasn't anything in my room worth bringing. Administrator Christian sent me here to compile records on a number of routine matters. The Bavarians are welcome to plunder the lot—the very great lot—and take it back to Munich. Perhaps they'll die of boredom as they study the files. I came very close to doing so myself."

So Böcler had a sense of humor, too. Who knew?

Certainly not Bonnie Weaver. The expression on her face, looking at him, was positively startled.

Chapter 10

The next morning, Captain Johann Heinrich von Haslang wasn't any happier than he'd been the night before. If anything, his misgivings about the campaign were growing.

There were a number of things troubling him. To begin with, as he'd foreseen, there would be no serious effort made to track down the culprits who had caused the failure of the expedition to capture the airship. When he'd reported his findings to von Lintelo, the general had shrugged irritably and said, "These things happen when a city is taken. Assign a reliable sergeant to see what he can find out. I have more important work for you."

Assign a reliable sergeant was a meaningless phrase, applied to this task. What was one sergeant supposed to do? If he wasn't from the same mercenary company as the perpetrators, he would have no idea where to start his investigation. If he was from that company, acting essentially on his own, he'd be too wary of stirring up animosity toward himself to do anything but a perfunctory investigation.

So, not only would a vicious crime go unpunished, but the discipline of the troops would degenerate still further. But there was nothing Captain von Haslang could do about it, so he put the matter aside and concentrated on the new orders he was getting from the general.

Those were . . . also not to his liking.

The one pleasant note was that he would be working under the command of Colonel von Schnetter again. He and Caspar were old friends, and got along well professionally as well as personally. So far as von Haslang was concerned, Colonel von Schnetter was the best field grade officer in General von Lintelo's whole army.

The assignment itself was straightforward, too—always a blessing in military campaigns led by generals like von Lintelo, who thought of themselves as superb military strategists. In Johann Heinrich's experience, the phrase *superb military strategist* meant a general whose plans were invariably too complex and intricate and made too little allowance for the predictably unpredictable mishaps that all military campaigns were subject to. There might be some exceptions to that rule, but the Bavarian commander was not one of them.

On this occasion, however, the mission was clear and simple: Pursue the USE forces that had escaped the city, presumably under the command of Major Tom Simpson, and either capture or destroy them.

So far, so good. But thereafter, everything turned sour.

The first problem was that von Lintelo was not giving them a large enough force to do the job properly. All told, they'd have fifteen hundred men to overcome an enemy force that was probably no more than a third that size—but consisted mostly of artillery. Well-equipped artillery, at that. Two of Colonel von Schnetter's adjutants had investigated the barracks and reported that Simpson's artillery unit had taken all of their six-pounders and four-pounders with them, along with plenty of powder and shot. They'd spiked the heavier ordinance and done a surprisingly good job of damaging the rest of their supplies before they left.

They'd have done a still better job if they'd simply blown up the barracks, of course. Presumably, they hadn't done so because Simpson was reluctant to inflict casualties on the nearby civilian population. Many officers might—no, certainly would—interpret that as weakness on Simpson's part. They'd think he was either a pewling neophyte or just too tenderhearted to make war his business.

But Captain von Haslang suspected otherwise. That act of merciful restraint was also what you'd expect from an opponent who was coldly determined to recapture the city someday—and quite confident that he would. The American major's ability to rally his troops so quickly and effectively and lead a successful retreat—one of the most difficult maneuvers of all in war—certainly did not indicate a fumbling, uncertain novice.

Such a commander wouldn't panic, when pursuit caught up with him. He'd position his men behind good fieldworks and take a stand. With the guns he had, he'd inflict a lot of damage on his enemy before he was driven under.

To make things still worse, most of the companies von Lintelo had assigned to them were infantry companies!

For a *pursuit*? In Captain von Haslang's professional opinion, that practically constituted criminal negligence.

Initially, in fact, von Lintelo had assigned them nothing but infantry units. After Colonel von Schnetter protested vigorously, the general had at least given them an explanation—which was unusual for him.

"I need all the cavalry I can muster to send to Amberg," von Lintelo said. "Above all else, we must rescue the heirs to the duchy!"

Rescue the heirs to the duchy. There was another phrase that begged for a coherent translation.

Duke Maximilian was childless himself, so the heir to the throne was—had been—his younger brother Albrecht. But the uproar that resulted when the duke's betrothed, the Austrian archduchess Maria Anna, fled before the wedding, caused a rupture between Maximilian and his brother. Who, with his wife and three sons, had also fled Bavaria.

Or tried to. Duke Maximilian and his soldiers caught up with them and in the fracas that followed, Albrecht's wife Mechthilde and his oldest son Karl Johann Franz had both been killed— Mechthilde at the duke's own hand.

Albrecht had become separated from his two other sons. He eventually managed to escape and had been given exile in Prague by Wallenstein. The tutor for his two younger sons, the Jesuit priest Johannes Vervaux, had managed to smuggle the boys out of Bavaria by a different route. They'd found exile in the United States of Europe; in Amberg, specifically, the capital of the province of the Oberpfalz. There was still a Jesuit school there, where the boys could continue their Catholic education.

Thankfully, the USE's formal stance of religious toleration and freedom was actually practiced in the Upper Palatinate. The province adjoined and was heavily dependent upon the State of Thuringia-Franconia, the province of the USE which, along with Magdeburg, took the principles very seriously. So there was no immediate danger of a forced conversion of the two boys—who, since their father had been outlawed, were now Maximilian's only heirs.

In short, *rescue the heirs to the duchy* meant bringing back to the custody of their uncle two boys who'd seen him slay their own mother and had placed their father under a death penalty. So that one of them could eventually succeed him as the duke of Bavaria.

Such were the established principles of aristocratic and royal inheritance, as ridiculous as the results might sometimes seem.

But what made the project itself ridiculous was that it had no chance at all of succeeding, anyway. So why waste the time and efforts of good cavalry units, who could be put to much better use bringing down Simpson and his men?

Even before the Ring of Fire, von Haslang was skeptical that such a mission would have succeeded. In essence, a large force of cavalry was being tasked with racing to a city at least fifty miles away, measuring as men and horses travel. In midwinter. They could not possibly arrive in less than a day and a half, and more likely two or three.

Then, upon arriving, they were to assault a well-fortified city garrisoned by a full regiment—with no artillery at their own disposal—in order to reach and capture two boys being held in a school within.

Not...impossible, in the old days. But very close to it.

Today? Almost five years after the Ring of Fire? Did Duke Maximilian and General von Lintelo think there had been no radio in Ingolstadt? Or, even if the attempt to reach Amberg had failed initially, that the retreating artillery unit didn't have a portable radio with them with which they could try again?

And even if by some near-magic luck the cavalry did manage to reach Amberg before a warning arrived, what then? They couldn't possibly break into the city in time to prevent the boys from being spirited away again. Von Lintelo was sending no more than five thousand cavalrymen to Amberg. The capital of the Oberpfalz was not a small town, and the surrounding terrain was hilly and wooded. There was no chance they could encircle the city and invest it tightly before any number of people could escape.

That would be true even if the means of escape were restricted to horse and foot. But they weren't. For the love of God, von Lintelo had *seen* the airship in the sky over Ingolstadt last night with his own eyes.

Nor was that the only airship at the enemy's disposal. Leaving aside any airplanes which could only land at the airfield outside of Amberg's city walls, the State of Thuringia-Franconia was home to a fleet of no fewer than four dirigibles. They could only hope that all of those airships were out of the province at the moment, having flown somewhere to the north.

Finally—it failed only this!—the one and only cavalry company that von Lintelo had finally agreed to provide them was the one commanded by Colonel Johann von Troiberz. Who was probably the most incompetent field grade officer in the Bavarian forces and certainly the most obnoxious.

✧　　✧　　✧

As it happened, all but one of Estuban Miro's fleet of airships was out of the State of Thuringia-Franconia that morning. But the one that was in the province was right where it needed to be—at the Bamberg airfield, fueled up and ready to go.

"I've got an important mission for you, Estuban," said Ed Piazza, the president of the province. He nodded toward the third man present in his office, General Heinrich Schmidt, one of the top officers in the SoTF's National Guard. "Heinrich and his staff can fill you in on the operational details later. But the gist of it is that I need you—or Franchetti, rather—to take the *Albatross* down to Amberg and get the two young Bavarian dukes out of there. Better bring their Jesuit tutor, too."

Miro looked at Schmidt, and then back at Piazza. "And bring them here? Or take them to Magdeburg?"

He didn't bother pointing out that the boys could be flown just as easily to Prague as to Magdeburg, where they could be reunited with their father. The equations of power were what they were. So long as the USE had custody of Albrecht's sons, they had some leverage over the man who might very well become Bavaria's next duke without having to wait for Maximilian to die a natural death.

"Bring them back here," said Piazza. He didn't elaborate on his reasons for choosing Bamberg over the nation's capital. Given the near-civil war that had erupted within the USE, the SoTF's president probably saw no reason to give up any assets, even if he didn't have any immediate use for them himself.

As a technical exercise, the project was perfectly manageable. Bamberg had an airfield outside the city walls which could handle dirigibles as well as airplanes. But in a pinch, an airship could be brought into the city itself. The market square was big enough to land one of the *Swordfish*-class airships like the *Albatross* or the *Pelican*. Doing so in strong winds would be difficult, though. But the weather today looked good, and Miro presumed that Piazza wanted this mission undertaken immediately.

The news of the Bavarian attack on Ingolstadt had already spread throughout the city, but Miro knew very few of the details. Of course, it was quite possible that no one knew many details yet.

"Do we know if the Bavarians are sending an expedition to Amberg?" he asked.

"Yes, they are." That came from Heinrich Schmidt. The thick-chested young general had a cold grin on his face. "And if you're wondering how we know, you'll be pleased to hear that your *Pelican* escaped the city last night. *With* Rita Simpson on board, as well as your survey crew."

That was a relief. Estuban had been worried about what might have happened to Stefano and the airship.

"They've decided to remain in the area, serving Major Simpson and what survives of the Danube Regiment as scouts, while they try to reach safety in Regensburg."

He didn't bother to ask Miro—who was, after all, the proprietor of the *Pelican* and Stefano Franchetti's employer—whether or not he approved. Estuban was not surprised. He'd already learned that Americans and those like Schmidt who shared their view of things took a very expansive attitude toward the use of private resources in times of crisis. They called it "nationalization." Being fair, plenty of down-time rulers did much the same thing—and the Americans eventually returned the property and recompensed the owners for its use, which any number of kings and dukes neglected to do.

Estuban had already figured out that the smart thing for him to do was to be very cooperative at such times. Indeed, he satisfied himself with simply billing the government for his expenses, not seeking a profit from such work at all.

Not a direct profit, rather. Indirectly, eventually . . . ah, the possibilities were endless. The up-timers also had an appropriate name for that. "Most favored nation status." Estuban saw no reason that term couldn't be used expansively as well. "Most favored company status" had a nice ring to it, he thought.

"In that case," he said, "I think it would be wise to plan on bringing more gasoline to Regensburg. If it's not carrying anything else except the necessary crew, any *Swordfish*-class dirigible can haul five barrels of gasoline in a single trip. We could operate both airships out of the city, with that much fuel. Not just now but throughout the crisis."

Schmidt and Piazza looked at each other. Then, the gazes of both men got a bit unfocused as they considered all the many military possibilities that would open up if the SoTF had what amounted to its own air force.

"Oh, splendid," said Schmidt. His grin widened while somehow not gaining any warmth at all.

"How soon can you leave?" asked Piazza.

Estuban pondered the question for a moment.. "I am tempted to say within an hour, but it might require two. The flight itself, depending on the winds, will take somewhere between an hour and a half and three hours."

The SoTF's president nodded. "Either way, you'd get there well before nightfall. Would you have enough time to fly back?"

Miro shrugged. "Perhaps not. But if the Bavarians are already investing the city—very unlikely, I'd think—and the situation was too critical to wait until morning, we'd simply take off. Then it all depends on the winds. That's what the *Pelican* chose to do last night, after all."

An airship the size of the *Albatross*, even with a minimal crew and all cargo space devoted to extra gasoline, couldn't fly for very many hours without refueling. The problem wasn't the engines, it was the fuel needed to keep the burners going. That was the great advantage of hydrogen over hot air designs, in addition to the greater buoyancy—you could fly much greater distances before having to refuel. Estuban had chosen the more primitive but safer hot air design for his fleet because the ships were only intended for short-distance runs. And it was much easier to stockpile gasoline supplies where needed than make sure hydrogen would always be available.

But if the winds were light and there was no need to reach an exact destination—nor any way to find it easily, in the dark—it was usually possible to keep an airship like the *Albatross* afloat until daybreak. Nothing was certain, of course.

Up-timers often had difficulty accepting that reality. They had come from a world in which air transport was a safer form of travel than any. But this world was in the very dawn of the avia-tion era. Nothing was certain, once you left the ground—and casualties were heavy.

Estuban loved it.

Chapter 11

To Tom's surprise, the Bavarians didn't attack them until late in the afternoon—and then, it was no more than a brief skirmish between a cavalry patrol and two platoons from Geipel's company. From what Tom could tell, the cavalry unit seemed to have stumbled upon the platoons by accident.

"*There's a large force of infantry coming after you,*" Rita told him that evening. "*I figure at least a thousand men. But they've already camped for the night. I don't see how they could catch up to you until tomorrow afternoon.*"

By then, Tom would be within fifteen miles of Regensburg. That distance could be covered in a day, with one long hard march. That assumed they didn't have to stop and fight, of course, which was probably wishful thinking.

"*All told, I think there's another five hundred or so cavalry on your tail,*" she continued. "*They're a lot closer, but they're hard to count because they're scattered all over east Jesus. I can't for the life of me figure out what their commanding officer thinks he's doing. Over.*"

"They're probably foraging," Tom replied. "We haven't been leaving anything behind for them."

He was feeling a little guilty about that, but only a little. His troops were taking all the foodstuffs they could find as they marched down the Danube, and burning everything behind them. That wasn't much, in midwinter, but it was enough to keep his men and—most important of all—their horses going. They hadn't been able to bring much fodder with them when they left Ingolstadt. If they lost the horses, they lost their cannons, and without those guns they didn't have much chance of fighting off a force as big as the one pursuing them.

That was hard on the population, of course. But if Tom's soldiers hadn't taken the stuff, the Bavarians would have. At least the Danube Regiment was passing out promissory notes for it. What was probably more important, from the immediate standpoint of people living in the towns and villages they passed through, was that Tom's rump regiment provided them with an escort. Refugees were now streaming away from the Bavarian onslaught, but these were the only ones who had military protection.

A lot of the refugees were coming out of Ingolstadt itself, according to Rita, some of whom were being savaged by Bavarian cavalry as they tried to flee. Her voice had been tight when she reported that; taut with anger.

Tom's own fury was near a boiling point. It was a near-constant struggle to keep his temper under control. The Bavarians were clearly making no effort to restrain their troops. The reports he got from Rita on the *Pelican* kept reminding him of the horror that the collapse of the Danube Regiment had allowed to spill over the inhabitants of Ingolstadt and stretches of the Oberpfalz near or on the Danube.

Some of his rage was sublimated guilt. Whatever the reasons might be, in the end he and Colonel Engels had been responsible for the regiment. He was by no means blind to that reality. But most of Tom's anger was not directed at himself. It was not even directed at Duke Maximilian. The ruler of Bavaria had only been able to suborn the 1st Battalion because of the political crisis produced in the USE by the actions of the Swedish chancellor, Axel Oxenstierna. So far as Tom was concerned, every murder, every mutilation, every rape, every act of arson and every theft committed by Bavarian soldiers could be laid at the feet of that bastard.

Not that he was giving Maximilian or his commanding officers a pass, either. There was no excuse for the conduct of their troops. The mayhem being inflicted on USE civilians went far beyond the occasional atrocities and excesses that were an inevitable feature of war. These soldiers hadn't simply been set loose, they'd obviously been given the green light to run wild by Bavaria's leaders.

Why? Tom wondered. Even in narrowly military terms, the policy made little sense to him. The Bavarians were not nomadic raiders, who simply intended to return to the steppes with their booty. Duke Maximilian planned to seize the Oberpfalz—as much of it as he could grab, at least—in in order to use its assets. So what was the point of ravaging the area? Of all those assets, the human resources were far and away the most valuable. Leaving aside the people being killed, there was now a flood of refugees heading north, east and west. There were close to a thousand such people being shepherded ahead of them by his own troops.

He hadn't been able to spare much time—no time at all, really— for the needs of those people. Fortunately, Johann Heinrich Böcler had taken charge of that task. Some initial prodding from Bonnie Weaver had been necessary, because Böcler didn't think of himself as an "authority." Partly that was his youth, partly that was his modest origins; but mostly, Tom suspected, it was just the man's personality. The provincial administrator's secretary was one of those people whose natural relationship to the world's affairs was that of an observer more than a participant.

That didn't necessarily mean such people were incompetent, however, whenever they set their minds to a practical task. Often they were not, and in some cases that same detachment made them very good at such work. They were more objective about the decision that needed to be made, and less prone to letting their own aspirations and ambitions influence them unduly.

How good would Böcler be at such an assignment? Tom had no idea. But he was pretty sure they'd know within a day or two. This column of people moving down the Danube might be going slowly, but so did a pressure cooker.

By the time they made camp for the night, Bonnie had already come to a conclusion on that subject. Once again, pudgy little Johann Heinrich Böcler was proving to be a man of greater substance than he looked.

True, he fussed a lot. Unflappable under pressure, steady at all times . . . well, no. He tended to get agitated, he talked a lot, and he dithered back and forth before coming to a decision. But he always did come to a decision, and he didn't dither for long. And insofar as the fussing and talking was concerned, that might well be an asset under these conditions. He was dealing with large numbers of frightened, uncertain and often confused people. His willingness to talk with them, once his authority was established, probably helped to calm them down.

Even in the seventeenth century, Germans tended to be a law-abiding folk. They were not particularly orderly, though—Bonnie had never seen a trace of the automatic obedience ascribed to Germans in the folk mythology of her own universe—and they were quite willing to argue with the powers-that-be. At the drop of a hat, in fact. But that those powers existed legitimately was not something they disputed. They just felt keenly that they had a right to be consulted before they were commanded to do something, and they were always sensitive to issues of fairness.

Böcler's authority derived from his status as the personal secretary of Christian I of Pfalz-Birkenfeld-Bischweiler, the imperially-appointed administrator of the Oberpfalz. The fact that he'd served in the same post for the previous administrator bolstered his status also. Ernst of Saxe-Weimar had been a popular figure in the province. "A fair-minded man," was a phrase you heard often when people spoke of him.

Böcler had that sense of fairness also. Perhaps that was his detachment at work, but Bonnie couldn't do more than guess at that. She still barely knew the man, although working with him in such close proximity and under such severe conditions was drastically speeding up a process that would normally have taken months, given his reserved nature. By late morning, at his invitation, she'd started calling him Heinz. That nickname was not used by many people who knew the secretary.

Heinz would have been a disaster as a politician. Glad-handing, back-slapping—the thought of him kissing babies was downright hysterical—these were not his skills, to put it mildly. But he was conscientious and he listened to people. So, with few exceptions, his decisions were accepted with good grace, even by people who had wanted a different one.

Those were usually people who just wanted to rest for a while, something that Heinz never allowed them to do until the army itself halted the march and began making camp. Then, Heinz chivvied his charges relentlessly, insisting that they had to help the soldiers set up the camp. Not until that was done—yes, that included digging latrines; of course it did!—would he allow the civilians to finally rest.

But he'd been chivvying the cooks and sutlers just as relentlessly, so when the time finally came when labors could cease, there was food ready—and he saw to it that it was fairly distributed. He did not eat himself until he was sure that everyone else had been fed.

He was quite a guy, actually, in his own sort of way. Bonnie realized he was growing on her. And was surprised again.

Captain von Haslang was in a much fouler mood than the American woman two miles downstream, whom he'd never met and whose name he didn't even know. The day's pursuit—by now he was using the term derisively—had been a disaster from daybreak to sundown.

The retreating force was doing a very good job of destroying everything behind them. (So much, if further evidence was needed, for the absurd notion that Major Simpson was a fumbling novice.) In some places, where the conditions were suitable, they'd felled trees across the road. And not one bridge spanning the occasional smaller streams that entered the Danube was left intact.

Worst of all, the enemy hadn't simply destroyed the bridges. The first one that Colonel von Schnetter's soldiers had come across had seemed in fine shape—until they crossed over it and discovered it had been mined. Eight men were killed in the explosion and twice as many badly wounded.

Thereafter, the enemy had simply brought down the bridges, figuring that the surprise wouldn't work twice. But they left other mines hidden alongside the road. Given the hurried manner in which the mines had been designed and laid, the Bavarian troops spotted and disarmed all but one of them before any damage was done. The single mine they missed had been set well to the side and only injured one man when it went off, and him not badly.

But that didn't really matter, because the mines were doing the critical task for the enemy—they were drastically slowing down the pursuers.

The pursuing *infantry*, that was to say. If the cavalry had been doing their job properly, they'd have been constantly harassing the enemy—which would have accomplished the same task of delaying the opponent's movements. All other things being equal, a mostly-infantry force should be able to overtake an enemy that was primarily made up of artillery units.

And why wasn't the cavalry doing its job? Because its donkey of a commander, Colonel Johann von Troiberz, had sent his men all over the countryside—everywhere, it seemed, except in the vicinity of the retreating Danube Regiment.

"Foraging," he claimed. And stubbornly kept claiming, no matter how angrily Colonel von Schnetter demanded that he bring the cavalry units back into the pursuit. The claim was either a lie—nothing but a fig leaf for looting—or, which might even be worse, an attempt to cover up gross negligence or outright corruption.

It was true enough that cavalry—infantry too, for that matter—needed to forage from the countryside if they undertook a long march that outstripped the ability of the supply train to keep up. But that should not be necessary *on the very first day*. Any

experienced cavalry unit with even half-competent officers had enough sense to load their mounts with ten to fifteen pounds of hay and a bit of oats or bran.

It was conceivable that von Troiberz was that much of a bungler. The officers he surrounded himself with were not much if any better. But von Haslang was almost certain that the real reason von Troiberz's cavalry had set out with no supplies for their horses was because their commander—probably in cabal with his top subordinates—had sold those supplies on the black market.

Whatever the explanation, von Schnetter and von Haslang were pursuing a well-led enemy with nothing more than infantry companies. Even if they did manage to catch up with them, the ensuing battle would be ferocious. Without cavalry to threaten and tear at the enemy's flanks, they'd be forced to launch frontal assaults in the face of field guns that would certainly be loaded with canister.

Von Haslang had even considered—it was quite possible his commander had done the same—that it might be wisest to simply slack off a bit in the pursuit. Stay on the heels of the Danube Regiment but let them make their escape into Regensburg. A siege of Regensburg was going to be necessary, in any event. While there was no doubt the addition of Simpson's forces would strengthen the defense, that was a problem for a later day.

A sound from above distracted him. The enemy airship had returned and was again passing over the Bavarian column. It was no more than five hundred feet from the ground, but that was enough to put them out of range of infantry firearms. Effective fire, at any rate. It was conceivable that if a volley were fired at it, one or two bullets might strike the thing. But at that height, even if it struck the small boatlike appendage that held the passengers, it would hardly do much damage.

The contraption made a surprising racket. Von Haslang hadn't expected that. From a distance, the dirigible's flight seemed serene and effortless. But up close, the engines that drove the fans that propelled it forward were extraordinarily loud.

The distraction was brief. Captain von Haslang went back to his grim thoughts and prognostications, now made all the worse for the irritating noise yammering at his ears.

Chapter 12

That very moment, as it happened, Rita was looking down on Captain von Haslang—or rather, at the small group of mounted officers at the front of the Bavarian column, among whom he was riding. At that height, even with up-turned faces not hidden by hats, it was impossible to distinguish individual persons. And it wouldn't have mattered if she could. She'd never met the captain, or, indeed, any of the Bavarian officers.

She'd never met Duke Maximilian either, for that matter. But she could probably have recognized him at close range, because she'd seen a good likeness of him in a portrait.

Not that she'd want to be in close range of the man. By all accounts she'd ever heard, Bavaria's ruler was as cold and deadly as a viper.

The *Pelican* had just returned from its first refueling stop at Regensburg. That had gone quite smoothly, much more so than Rita had expected and certainly more smoothly than she'd feared. Not only had there been no quarrels, but the city's authorities had already had barrels of fuel brought out to the airfield. It seemed that the administrator of the Oberpfalz and the president of the SoTF had both sent radio messages to Regensburg instructing the city's officials to do everything possible to aid Major Simpson and his one-craft air force.

Even that might not have done the trick, by itself. German city officials could set the world standard for narrow-minded parochialism, in Rita's experience. But General Schmidt had also gotten on the radio and explained that:

A. If Regensburg did not provide Major Simpson with sufficient aid and assistance—in a timely and efficient manner—then Major Simpson would almost certainly run into severe difficulties and setbacks in his attempt to save his regiment from the depredations of the Bavarians. Who set the world standard for wickedness, in the general's professional military opinion.

B. That being so, General Schmidt himself—now already marching his National Guard division to come to the assistance of Regensburg—would have no choice but to divert his troops in order to rescue Major Simpson. Who, by then, would be engaged in a desperate last stand against that selfsame Bavarian wickedness.

C. In which case, Duke Maximilian, a man whose wickedness was only matched by his cunning, would immediately launch the most furious assaults upon Regensburg, intending to seize the city while it remained lightly defended. In which project he would almost certainly succeed, since the relieving force under General Schmidt was unfortunately preoccupied rescuing Major Simpson from the predicament he had been placed in by the slothful and selfish behavior of the authorities of the very same city about to fall into the hands of Bavarian wickedness.

D. Which wickedness, he reminded the officials listening to his radio message, had been demonstrated not five years earlier in the unspeakably barbaric sack of Magdeburg, carried out largely by troops on Maximilian's payroll.

So there they were, three full barrels of gasoline, ready to be loaded as soon as the *Pelican* was tethered. With six more barrels, they were assured, already on their way to the airfield.

Rita didn't wait for those next barrels. Stefano told her that they now had enough fuel for the burners and engines to stay in operation another day. So she ordered him to fly back to the location of the Danube Regiment.

That location had moved a few miles downstream, but only a few. Being married to a soldier, Rita had been abstractly aware that large military forces other than cavalry units—and those also, more often than not—simply could not and did not move quickly across a countryside. But seeing the phenomenon for herself at first hand drove home that reality in a way that listening to Tom talking with fellow officers never had.

The problem began with the very term that people used to refer to the process. They would say that an army "marched."

Marched. The word brought up images of parades, or newsreels Rita had seen of GIs during World War II passing through a bombed-out French or German town. No longer in formation, just walking. But unless they were moving carefully because there were enemy troops in the immediate vicinity, they were still making quite rapid progress. A person in good physical condition, like a young soldier, can easily walk two miles in an hour, even carrying a heavy pack, and maintain that rate for hours. They can move fifteen or twenty or even twenty-five miles in a day.

But that presupposed, first of all, twentieth-century macadamized roads. Wide roads, at that. Rita didn't usually think of up-time two-lane country roads as being "wide," but compared to the roads that existed in central Europe in 1636 they were practically boulevards. A standard up-time lane measured somewhere between ten and twelve feet, which made a two-lane road somewhere between twenty and twenty-four feet wide—not even counting whatever shoulders might exist. Half a dozen men could comfortably march abreast on that sort of road. Place them in rows spaced six feet apart—again, a very comfortable distance—and you could fit an entire regiment of a thousand men in a stretch of road that was less than a quarter of a mile long.

And those World War II-era newsreels usually only showed the infantrymen, or perhaps the armored fighting vehicles. They rarely showed everything *else* that was needed to keep an army marching, such as the long line of trucks carrying all the necessary supplies, equipment and ammunition. You saw the quickly-moving teeth of an army, not the massive tail that came behind it—a tail which was itself mechanized and therefore able to move pretty quickly.

None of that applied here. The road that Tom's men and the refugees were traveling on that ran more-or-less alongside the north bank of the Danube was no more than ten feet wide and often narrower than that. It was not macadamized. In fact, it was rarely even a gravel road. Most of it was just a dirt road. Hardened by the passage of many feet and hooves and wagon wheels over the years, to be sure, but still just a dirt road.

And now, in mid-January, very often covered in thin ice and snow. The ice and snow didn't last long, of course, with hundreds of people and livestock moving over it. No, it melted and started turning a dirt road into a mud road, at least in patches.

Things weren't helped any, of course, by the fact that Tom had decided to put the refugees ahead of the army so his soldiers could provide them with some protection from the pursuing Bavarians. But, in truth, that probably wasn't slowing them down all that much. There simply wasn't any way to move some fifteen hundred people and close to two hundred horses, mules and oxen at anything faster than a crawl.

From high in the air, the army and its accompanying crowd of refugees made Rita think of a giant caterpillar inching its way down the Danube. Just as with a caterpillar, the center would expand as the soldiers in the rear pressed against the refugees ahead of them, forcing some of the refugees to move off the road.

Then the officers would order a halt while the refugees were able
to move a little farther, and the whole process repeated itself.

The situation would have been horrendous if the enemy cavalry
had been doing what it should have been doing, moving ahead of
the column and tearing at its flank. But the cavalry was still nowhere
to be seen. Not from the ground, at least. From her vantage point
two thousand feet in the air, Rita could see cavalry units moving
about in the distance. But the closest cluster of Bavarian horsemen
she could spot was at least half a mile from the river.

She wondered why the Bavarian commander, whoever he might
be, was tolerating the state of affairs. If she'd been in his position,
she'd have blown her stack by now.

Colonel von Schnetter blew his stack no fewer than four times
before the sun finally set that day. He kept his mounted adjutants
racing all over the landscape, bearing orders—first, firm; then,
stern; then, peremptory; then, furious and profane—to the cavalry
commander, demanding that he leave off his so-called "foraging"
and attend to his proper duties.

Colonel Johann von Troiberz ignored each and every one of
those orders. He didn't refuse to obey, he simply made no response
at all. He was able to do that because the orders given by General
von Lintelo had not specifically placed von Troiberz under von
Schnetter's command. Most likely, the general had simply assumed
that the cavalry commander would have the sense of a goose—or,
more to the point, wasn't desperately trying to cover up the fact
that he'd sold off his cavalry unit's supplies.

Von Troiberz had done that the day before the assault on Ingolstadt began. He knew that the assault was predicated on treachery
and was primarily planned as an infantry affair. Thereafter, his
cavalrymen would have access to the city's resources and could
surely obtain replacements for vanished supplies within a couple
of days. So he calculated that he could safely sell off the supplies
before the assault began. Who pays attention to such things as
hay and oats?

He hadn't considered the possibility that he might be ordered
into an immediate cavalry action to pursue enemy soldiers who
had managed to escape the city. That had been a tense moment,
when he realized what might be in the offing at von Lintelo's
staff meeting after the successful seizure of Ingolstadt. But von

Troiberz had acted quickly—he was still patting himself on the back for it—and immediately volunteered his own force for the mission. Secure in his knowledge that von Lintelo had an inexplicable dislike for him and always favored one of his pets. So he wouldn't be given the mission anyway.

Then, to his horror, von Lintelo had set forth his intention to send all the cavalry units available on a raid on Amberg. Von Troiberz had simply not considered the fact—perhaps obvious, in retrospect—that the unsettled state of Bavaria's line of succession would result in a cavalry expedition being sent north immediately. He was not, as an up-timer might put it, the sharpest pencil in Bavaria's military box. He was a lot closer to the eraser end of that spectrum.

Thankfully—the only useful thing the annoying fellow had ever done, so far as von Troiberz was concerned—Colonel von Schnetter insisted that he needed cavalry assistance, after von Lintelo placed him in charge of pursuing the retreating enemy. The general had eventually agreed and given the assignment of "assisting" the infantry to von Troiberz.

Such a vague and uncertain word, "assisting." Truly delightful, the way its borders and boundaries wandered about.

It was still a very awkward situation for von Troiberz to be placed in, of course, but far better—far, far better—than if he'd been assigned to participate in a raid on Amberg under the direct command of von Lintelo's most favored officers. He'd have been in trouble almost immediately. As it was, von Troiberz figured he could fend off the pestiferous infantry colonel's demands for at least two days. That would give his men enough time to plunder what they needed immediately from the countryside.

Those so-called "commands" were nothing of the sort, anyway. Given that von Troiberz and the infantry colonel were of equal rank and the fact that the general had never specified the command arrangement, von Schnetter's "orders" were legally nothing more than requests.

Very rude requests, to boot. The man could be quite insufferable.

Night finally fell, on that first day. Tom thought it had probably been the longest day in his life. It had certainly been the most harrowing.

✧   ✧   ✧

Two thousand feet above him, as she tried to get to sleep, his wife Rita thought exactly the same. And she was afraid she'd have the nightmares to prove it. Throughout the day, she'd been getting periodic flashbacks to the gunfights of the night just passed. The most upsetting was the look on the face of the soldier whom she'd shot dead outside the broken shop window.

He'd been young, barely more than a boy. At the very end, just before she pulled the trigger, he'd obviously understood that he was about to die.

That look...

It hadn't been so much an expression of despair as one of sorrow, for the things he would now never see, never do, never know, never feel. Rita was quite certain that she would carry that memory with her for all her days on earth, however many they might prove to be. She could live to be a hundred, and would never forget the man whom she'd severed from whatever days might have been his.

Not far from her in the gondola, on the other hand, Stefano Franchetti and Mary Tanner Barancek were having a very pleasant evening. They were engaged in the sort of lively conversation that young people think is dazzling beyond belief—no greater conversation had been held anywhere on the planet since Socrates questioned his guests—because every sentence, every phrase, seemed loaded with suggestion and invitation.

The conversation was all the more dazzling for the fact that Mary's grim aunt and her two fellow Furies were no longer on board the *Pelican*. They had been dropped off in Regensburg when the airship made its refueling stop earlier in the day. Rita had pointed out that there was really no purpose in the three auditors staying aboard, and the *Pelican* could use the extra lift provided by their departure to carry more fuel. Willa had been reluctant, but finally agreed when Maydene stated—quite bluntly—that there was not much opportunity for premarital coitus in the gondola of an active airship, especially with Rita not more than ten feet away from the youngsters in question. Estelle then weighed in by pointing out—just as bluntly—that even if such activity did take place, the girl was now of legal age and she'd hardly be the first country bumpkin to get screwed by a slick fellow of the Latin persuasion. She'd survive.

✧   ✧   ✧

Bonnie Weaver and Heinz Böcler did not get to sleep until much later in the evening. The secretary stayed up for hours, checking with everyone in the refugee camp to make sure that they'd gotten something to eat and that no one, especially children and the elderly, was going to spend the night in freezing conditions. Those people who were short of blankets or other sorts of bedding got some loaned to them by people who were in better shape. On their own, they might or might not have made such offers, but the combination of Böcler's quiet persistence and his ever-ready notebook turned the trick. No one doubted for a moment that if the province administrator's personal secretary said he would keep accurate records of who had lent what to whom, it would surely be done and done properly.

In the event, Bonnie wound up keeping most of those records. She accompanied Heinz on his rounds and figured out early on that it made more sense for him to concentrate on wheedling people and for her to do his bookkeeping for him. It wasn't that he was a better wheedler than she was. Actually, he was rather inept at it. But he was extraordinarily persistent, long past the point where Bonnie herself would have stalked off in disgust at someone's recalcitrance and pigheaded selfishness.

So, she let him wheedle and cajole and harass and pester, while she wielded the magic pen. That worked because Heinz always introduced her as *his* secretary, which apparently satisfied the proprieties. It turned out that maintaining a clear and precise chain of bureaucracy was every bit as essential in Heinz's line of work as maintaining a clear and precise chain of custody was for police work.

Who knew?

Chapter 13

The second day was a carbon copy of the first, for all intents and purposes. Two small armies kept moving slowly down the Danube. They were of approximately equal size, fifteen hundred people in each. But two-thirds of the leading army consisted of civilians, where the entire pursuing force was made up of infantrymen.

For whatever reason, however, the following army was moving no faster than the one it was pursuing. Hour after hour, now two days in a row, it remained about a mile behind. Close enough to make the fact of a pursuit obvious, but not so close—not once—as to make it necessary for Tom to break off the march and arrange his men into a defensive formation.

That was odd, on the face of it. Very odd, in fact. No large body of people could move quickly under these conditions, that was a given. Still, the pursuing force was made up of men in fit condition—well, mostly—and carrying nothing more than muskets and backpacks, with a supply train bringing up the rear. In contrast, a very large percentage of the fifteen hundred people ahead of them were composed of elderly people, children, the ill—there were two very visibly pregnant women in the mix, even. Not to mention carts and wagons of all sorts including field guns and caissons. You'd think they'd have been able to move at least a *little* bit faster.

By the evening of the second day, when they made camp for the night again, Tom was pretty sure he knew what was happening. And he'd had all day to decide what to do in response.

So, he assembled a war council of his top officers, to which he also summoned the leaders of his (very unofficial) air force.

The suspicion privately entertained by some that he'd done so in order to see his wife again was actually quite unfair—as was proven by the fact that, once the meeting was over, Rita got back into the *Pelican* and flew off.

Stefano Franchetti's uncle Filippo attended the council as well. The *Albatross* had successfully spirited away the two young Bavarian heirs from Amberg the day before. Actually, they'd done it in plain sight at the airfield and in broad daylight because the Bavarian cavalry was still a good two days away. At Ed Piazza's request, once Filippo brought the boys to Bamberg, Estuban Miro had agreed to send the *Albatross* down to the Danube to provide whatever assistance it could to Major Simpson and its sister airship.

When Tom finished explaining his plan, the reaction of his officers was stalwart and supportive. The reaction of the two Franchettis was enthusiastic. That of Rita, uncertain. That of Heinz Böcler, dubious. That of Bonnie Weaver, agitated.

The officers were stalwart and supportive because they were soldiers and, besides, the plan didn't require them to do anything.

The Franchettis were enthusiastic because they foresaw their future fame. Their sure and certain place in the history, since they would fall into the blessed category of "The Men Who First..."

Rita was uncertain because she didn't know enough about the issues involved.

The provincial secretary was dubious because he was a dubious man by nature.

Bonnie was agitated because she'd not only taken some chemistry courses but, in her days hanging around with Larry Wild and his friends, had picked up a fair amount of knowledge on the subject. And because Tom wanted to put *her* in charge of the technical side of the project.

"You need to add styrofoam to the gasoline to make decent napalm," she protested. "Where are we going to find that much styrofoam? I doubt if there's even much left in Grantville, these days."

"You can substitute soap or sugar, can't you?"

Bonnie frowned. "Well... I remember Larry and the guys talking about it. They wanted to try, naturally—boys! But they never got around to it. Besides, I don't know what kind of soap and I think it's supposed to be powdered sugar and that's a lot trickier than it sounds. There's probably enough sugar in Regensburg, now that they're making it from sorghum around Freyburg, but very little of it will be powdered. And it's pretty expensive, no matter how it comes. Who's going to pay for it?"

That last question was silly, and Bonnie knew it. She had a tendency to starting jabbering when she got uneasy. Talk first, think later. In time of war—this happened up-time, too—governments got very heavy-handed in the way they handled critical war supplies. And they got to define the term "critical war supplies" in the first place. If King Louis XIV could proclaim himself the state, any state could certainly claim the status of a dictionary.

Tom waited patiently until the little flood of protest ebbed. "Bonnie, nobody's expecting military-grade napalm. Napalm is basically just thickened, jellied gasoline. The sugar, even if it isn't powdered, is bound to help in that direction. Soap is probably even better, if you liquefy it first. I'd suggest mixing in some fine sawdust, too. The worst that happens is that we get functional firebombs that aren't any better than big Molotov cocktails. For what I want, I think that'd be enough right there."

He turned back to Rita. He'd begun the council by asking her and Stefano a number of questions about the Bavarian cavalry dispositions.

"I'm a lot more concerned about getting the target right. You're sure about that village?"

His wife shrugged. "No, of course I'm not 'sure.' But that's where the largest bunch of cavalry spent last night, and whenever we've flown by there today it looks as if there are plenty of them hanging around. They're obviously planning to spend tonight there also. I think that's where they set up their headquarters. But who knows? They might pack up and leave tomorrow."

The Bavarian cavalry had taken over a village about a mile from the river. It had been a big village, with a sizeable inn and stables. All the inhabitants had already fled, so Tom didn't have to worry about civilian casualties.

Tom stuck a finger under the collar of his shirt and scratched an itch, thinking about Rita's cautions. She was certainly right that nothing was certain, but it was just human nature for people to get attached to creature comforts. It was the middle of January—in the Little Ice Age, no less, as Americans always insisted on reminding everyone. Any soldier, even those in highly disciplined elite units, would prefer being billeted in a village house or tavern room than sleeping on the ground wrapped in nothing better than a blanket.

And everything he'd seen about these cavalrymen indicated they were very far from being highly disciplined elite troops. He was now all but certain that the cavalrymen had been deliberately shirking their duties—and the infantry units had delayed their own pursuit out of sheer anger. Were they supposed to bear all the casualties? Which were likely to be steep if they attacked artillery without cavalry support.

That's what the commander of those infantrymen had apparently been asking himself. And the answer he'd come up with was "no," at least so far. Whether that was because he was a mercenary and those troops were his working capital that he didn't want to waste, or because he genuinely cared for the well-being of his men, or simply because he was peevish, Tom had no idea.

Nor did it matter. All that mattered, for the next two days, was making sure the Bavarian cavalry stayed out of the picture. Two days from now, they'd have reached Regensburg and could thumb their noses at anyone pursuing them.

That Bavarian cavalry wasn't much good to begin with, the way it looked to Tom. So let's see how they'd stand up to this world's first-ever aerial incendiary carpet bombing. Even allowing for the fact that the terms "incendiary" and "carpet" were gross exaggerations, Tom didn't think they'd stand up well. Not well at all.

"We'll do it," he announced, his mind finally made up. "Bonnie, are you willing to give it a try?"

She spread her hands. "Yeah, sure."

He nodded and turned to Böcler. "Heinrich, I want you to go with her."

The secretary started to protest. "But the refugees—"

Tom held up his hand. "They're fine. You've already got things well enough organized there. They can manage on their own for the next two days. The real danger to them now is that we won't reach Regensburg at all."

Böcler frowned. "But why do you want to send me to Regensburg?"

"Because you're a top-notch organizer. Bonnie isn't—no offense, Bonnie, but you're not—and besides, she's got to concentrate on the technical side of making the bombs." A charming analogy came to him, and he couldn't help but smile. "She's Oppenheimer, you're General Groves."

"Excuse me?" That came from Böcler. Bonnie Weaver was staring at Tom as if he'd just grown horns.

"Never mind," Tom said. "Up-time analogy. Something called the Manhattan Project. Bonnie, explain it to him—"

"*Oppenheimer?*" Bonnie demanded. "I've got a high school diploma! With a B-minus grade point average!"

Rita started laughing.

"—when the two of you have a spare moment. The thing is, Heinrich, you're only going to have a few hours to put together a lot of bombs. You'll have to organize people to get it done. Find suitable bomb cases—I figure by now Regensburg has got to have started producing small barrels that can hold gasoline. Big glass jars would work too, if they've got decent lids, but that's probably asking for pie in the sky."

Glassmakers in the seventeenth century could do phenomenal work, but they weren't really set up yet to mass produce things like Mason jars. Such containers in the here and now were mostly pottery. Speaking of which . . .

"See if you can find big clay pots and something to plug them with. That should work too. But probably the trickiest part of the work will be coming up with suitable fuses."

He stuck a big finger almost under the secretary's nose and waggled it in a warning gesture. Then, for good measure, waggled it under Bonnie's nose.

"But don't get too fancy! I don't want to risk having one of these things going off in the gondolas. If the best you can come up with is just a fuse you light at the last minute, when you're shoving the bomb over the side, that'll do."

Böcler was frowning again, but the expression this time was simply that of a man pondering a challenge. "How many bombs do you want?"

"I'm not sure." He turned to Filippo Franchetti. "How many do you figure you can handle in a couple of airships? Figure each bomb will be about this size"—his hands sketched out in midair a roughly spherical object about the size of a two-gallon jug—"and will weigh somewhere around twenty pounds."

"It will be three airships," Franchetti said, almost idly, scratching his chin as he contemplated the problem. "We just got word from Bamberg before we landed. The *Petrel* has returned from Amsterdam. Don Estuban is sending it down to join us tomorrow morning. He told me to tell you the ship is at your disposal for the duration of the crisis, as are the *Pelican* and the *Albatross*."

Apparently, Miro had decided to use the crisis as an opportunity to rack up lots and lots of brownie points with the SoTF's administration. He was certainly racking them up with Tom himself, even though he'd never met the man.

"The problem is not the weight," Franchetti said. "It's the space needed—as well as the need to handle them safely. Two men to fly the ship, two men to handle the bombs, one man to choose the times and the places to drop the bombs."

Stefano cleared his throat. "Some of those tasks do not require men, uncle." He held up his hands in a vigorous gesture, as a man might protest any suggestion of heretical leanings. "Yes, yes, certainly to manage the bombs themselves! But Dina Merrifield and Mary Barancek have already helped fly the *Pelican.*"

He now bestowed a solemn nod at Rita. "And I am quite sure that Mrs. Simpson would make a splendid...ah...what is the term I want?"

"Bombardier," Tom suggested.

"Fucking moron," was his wife's countersuggestion. "What else can you call someone who tosses lit firebombs from a flimsy hot air balloon?"

"Dirigible," said the Franchettis, sternly and simultaneously.

Rita shook her head. "Well, at least one historical question is now answered. Fucking geeks can be found in any time and place."

Tom had learned long ago that when his wife started using Appalachian patois in every other sentence it was time to wrap up the discussion. Before the patois began appearing in every sentence. Then, every clause.

He clapped his hands. "All right, it's settled. Mr. Franchetti"— that was directed at Filippo—"I figure your airship should lead the bombing run. So it's probably best that Rita transfer now from the *Pelican* to the *Albatross*. She's the best person to guide the run and serve as the lead bombardier. Bonnie and Heinrich can transfer into your ship also, since it's your turn to make the refueling run to Regensburg. You can drop them off in the city."

He turned to the young nephew, striving mightily to keep a straight face. "Stefano, that'll leave you with Mary Barancek as your bombardier. I know she's awfully young, but I think she can handle the job."

Stefano beamed. "Oh, certainly!"

Tom was no slouch himself, when it came to racking up brownie points. He turned now to Bonnie and Böcler. "Any further questions?"

They looked at each other. After a moment, Bonnie shrugged. "Probably a thousand. But we'll manage. We work pretty well together."

She thought about that, most of the way to Regensburg.

It was quite true, actually. They *did* work together well. Got along well, too.

The rest of the way into Regensburg, she spent contemplating the fact that for the first time since Larry Wild died, she found herself interested in a man who didn't remind her of Larry in the least, teeniest, itsiest, littlest bit.

That was probably mentally healthy, she figured, although she wasn't sure.

She giggled, then. Böcler, who'd been standing next to her in the gondola throughout the trip, raised his eyebrows. "What has amused you?"

She put her hand over her mouth, to cover the grin. "Oh, nothing," she mumbled. "Just a stray thought."

It *was* funny, but there were too many up-time referents for her to be able to explain the humor clearly to Heinz. Had anyone told her, back in her West Virginia days, that the time would come when she'd wonder where she could find a shrink, she'd have told them they were crazy.

But it was true, nonetheless. Up-timers now even had a saying about it. *The Ring of Fire changed us all.*

Chapter 14

The third day went much like the first two. Two small armies moving slowly down the Danube, keeping the same steady distance. Hundreds of cavalrymen charging hither and yon across the landscape—everywhere *except* where the armies marched— plundering everything they could get their hands on.

Which wasn't much. That landscape had been picked pretty clean. If a cavalry platoon caught a chicken, they deemed it a great prize and a cause for celebration. They would hold the celebration immediately, roasting the chicken on a spit while consuming a bottle of very bad wine they'd looted from a neighboring village. As ravening plunderers went, these fellows were definitely bottom feeders.

By then, although Colonel von Schnetter had said nothing openly to him, it was quite obvious to Captain von Haslang that the infantry commander had decided to let the Danube Regiment make its escape. He would follow them closely all the way to Regensburg, for the sake of appearances, but he would make no effort to bring the enemy to battle. He would not subject his own men to the casualties of a frontal assault on prepared artillery, with no cavalry support. If General von Lintelo broke into one of his tempers over the matter, let him place the blame where it rightly belonged—on the cavalry scoundrels and their own commander, Colonel von Troiberz.

Von Haslang had no objection. Neither to the substance of the issue, nor to the colonel's tactical judgment. Insofar as the substance was concerned, he too saw no reason their own men should suffer because of a general's carelessness and a cavalry officer's dereliction.

As for the tactics...

If Colonel von Troiberz had been one of von Lintelo's favorites, this would be a risky maneuver. The general would almost certainly then bring his wrath down on Colonel von Schnetter—and, the general being the sort of man he was, on von Schnetter's staff as well. Happily, von Lintelo held Colonel von Troiberz in no high regard either. That was the reason he'd given him this assignment, almost as an afterthought, instead of including his unit in the more important mission to Amberg.

So, most likely, von Lintelo's fury would come down on the cavalry, who richly deserved it. But it probably wouldn't be that great a fury anyway, since it had also been obvious that von Lintelo didn't view capturing the escaped fragments of the Danube Regiment as a particularly important matter.

He might come to regret that judgment. Captain von Haslang's own assessment of the enemy commander had steadily grown over the past two and half days. Given that a siege of Regensburg now seemed inevitable, he'd be a lot happier if Major Simpson and his men weren't part of the defending force.

But, like Colonel von Schnetter, he didn't think it was worth the casualties to prevent that from happening. If a man sought perfection, he should find a different trade than that of a professional soldier.

To her great relief, Bonnie found that her new assignment was not as hard as she'd thought it would be. (For years thereafter, whenever confronted with a quandary, she would throw up her hands and exclaim "Oppenheimer!") That was true for three reasons:

First, Heinz Böcler turned out to be far better in his General Groves persona than she was when she tried to imitate a world-class nuclear physicist like Oppenheimer. Within less than an hour after their arrival in Regensburg, he had the city's officials and guild masters eating out of the palm of his plump little hand.

How he managed that was something of a mystery to Bonnie. It was certainly not due to his dazzling personality. Heinz was a pleasant enough fellow, but he possessed about as much in the way of social charm as you'd expect from a man raised by a parson, educated to be a clerk, and filled with the ambition to write a history book.

Her guess was that Heinz fit, to a T, every pompous city official and stuffed-shirt guildmaster's notion of what the personal secretary of a provincial administrator *should* be like. So, oddly enough, it was his very lack of charisma that lent him great authority.

The second factor working in her favor was Brick Bozarth. Bonnie had completely forgotten—if she'd ever known at all, which she probably hadn't—that the State of Thuringia-Franconia had sent Bozarth to Regensburg back in 1634. The man served as one of the SoTF's semi-official trade representatives and consuls to the Oberpfalz.

Bozarth's precise position in the SoTF's bureaucracy was never clear to Bonnie. The middle-aged ex-miner had nothing more than a high school diploma, so far as his education was concerned. In his days as a coal miner, he'd operated a continuous mining machine—a skill that was about as useful, in the here and now, as knowing how to pilot a submarine. She suspected that his main qualification for his post was simply the fact that was a member of the United Mine Workers.

In the period after the Ring of Fire, Mike Stearns had leaned very heavily on the membership of his union local to provide him with a ready-made cadre. Those days were over now. Mike himself had left for Magdeburg and the man who succeeded him to serve as the province's president, Ed Piazza, was not and had never been a coal miner.

By then, though, certain social customs had become rooted in the State of Thuringia-Franconia. The same customs didn't hold much sway elsewhere in the United States of Europe. Being a UMWA member in Magdeburg province, for instance, was certainly respectable—even admirable—but gave a man no particular status in political terms.

In the governing circles of the SoTF and its surrounding officialdom, on the other hand, membership in the UMWA had much the same informal prestige and ability to open doors that being a Harvard or Yale graduate had provided back up-time. That hadn't been due to the supposedly superb education one received at those Ivy League schools, no matter what people claimed. That education was certainly excellent, but so was the education a person could get at MIT or the University of California, or any number of top universities in America, public as well as private. Indeed, in many fields, the education someone could get outside of the Ivy League was quite a bit better.

No, the real cachet that having an Ivy League degree had given people back up-time was social, not educational. Being a graduate of Harvard or Yale put you in the right old boys' networks. Being a UMWA member did much the same in the SoTF.

Thankfully, Bozarth had not taken his post to be a sinecure. Being fair, very few UMWA people did. They might not necessarily be the best person for a job, but they almost always carried out those jobs with the same blue-collar work ethic that they'd taken into coal mines.

So, as soon as Bonnie explained her needs to him, Bozarth knew exactly where, how and from whom those needs could be met. He knew Regensburg very well by now, especially that part of Regensburg that was involved in what he considered "useful work."

Brick defined that term the way coal miners do. If you knew how to make something or fix something or grow something, you were a stout fellow. If you were a parson, you were regarded with respect but otherwise dismissed as being of no practical use. If you were a lawyer, you were automatically under a cloud of suspicion.

The third factor working in her favor was just blind luck. The first item Brick brought to her to try out as an additive to the gasoline was a tub of soap. It turned out that Regensburg had a soap manufacturer—the German term was "Seifensieder"; literally, soap-boiler—and he had plenty of his product available.

The standard soap of the time in the Germanies was a lye soap. You could also find some scented olive oil bar soaps from Italy, but they were an expensive luxury item. The lye soap came in the form of a semi-liquid soft soap, rather than being hardened into bars. In other words, absolutely perfect for Bonnie's purposes.

The first batch of napalm she mixed up worked like a charm. Being a firm believer in the principle *if it ain't broke, don't fix it,* Bonnie saw no point in going any further—to the great disappointment of the commercial factor in Regensburg who controlled the town's sugar supply and had briefly imagined great riches were in store for him.

It was just as well. She found out later from people in Grantville who'd done the experiments back in the early days that sugar was a poor cousin to soap, in the "hey, guys, let's make some napalm!" department.

The bomb cases were easy. The city's cooper could provide her with barrels, but those were too big for the actual bombs. On the other hand, they made great containers to mix the batches. The result, which had the consistency of fresh-made pudding, could then be easily poured into jugs that held about three gallons. There were plenty of such jugs available in a town the size of Regensburg.

The end result was a bomb that didn't weigh more than twenty-five pounds, something that even one man could handle easily enough.

That left the fuses. Bonnie dithered back and forth between using gunpowder fuses and the even simpler device of rags soaked in gasoline. Both methods worked—but which would work best when the bomb was dropped from a height of several hundred yards? She had no way of testing that short of the time-consuming method of taking them up in one of the airships.

In the end, Heinz solved the quandary for her, in his inimitable fashion. For a man whose great ambition was to become an historian, perhaps the world's most impractical profession, he had a surprisingly wide pragmatic streak.

"There is no danger of an explosion, from either type of fuse?" he asked. "If you light it too soon, I mean, and it burns down into the bomb before you want it to."

She shook her head. "No. These things aren't really bombs. They're basically great big Molotov cocktails. They don't blow up, they just shatter when they hit the ground. The napalm goes flying everywhere and sticks to everything—and the lit fuse sets it on fire."

"Then use both," he said. "Stick one kind of fuse on one side of the sealed lid, and the other across from it. Light them both, drop the bomb. One of them has to work."

She gave him a quick hug and set about giving the orders. So she didn't see the look of surprise that came to Böcler's face, followed by a look of pleasure, followed by a look of consternation.

By early afternoon, she had enough bombs to load up both the *Pelican* and the *Albatross*. The *Petrel* had arrived in the area also, by now, but it was flying over the Danube at the moment keeping an eye on the movements of the Bavarian troops below.

Given how easy the whole process had turned out to be, Bonnie decided it made more sense to transfer the final stages of the bomb-making from Regensburg to the field. Tom Simpson and his people were now within ten miles of Regensburg. The airships had found a suitable landing area about three miles farther down the Danube. It was on the north bank, fortunately, since the south bank was in Bavarian territory. She'd bring enough napalm there in barrels to provide the *Petrel* with a full load of bombs. And there'd be enough left over to fill quite a few more jugs. She figured at least one of the airships could carry out a second bombing run, if Major Simpson decided to do so.

So, off they went. By now, Bonnie was starting to take flying by dirigible almost for granted. She was even enjoying it.

Except for the incredible racket. Having four un-muffled lawn-mower engines yammering at close range was enough to drive you crazy after a while. The noise was so bad that whenever they needed to use the radio or the walkie-talkie they had to shut off the engines and just let the ship drift for a while.

But Heinz had thought of that, too. He'd found linen and had it soaked in some kind of wax. Little strips of it rolled up and stuffed in your ears made pretty decent ear plugs.

The airship crews clapped him on the back. Bonnie gave him another hug. Not a quick one, either.

It did not occur to Johann Heinrich Böcler, then or ever, that it was peculiar for a man headed back to a war zone to spend the entire time worrying about anything else.

But, such was his nature. His background, training and personal inclination led him to be fatalistic on the subject of death and dismemberment. Not so at all, on the subject of right and proper conduct.

What was he to do? By now, his attraction to the American woman was undeniable. Indeed, it was getting feverish. He was having thoughts—images, even—that he was quite sure his father would declare unseemly. His grandfather, should he discover, would be furious.

They *were* unseemly thoughts. But he could not stop having them.

If the woman in question had been uninterested, Heinz was sure he could have brought himself under control. Unfortunately—well, also delightfully—she very clearly was not. That last hug, especially, had born no resemblance at all to the sort of hugs one occasionally got from a particularly affectionate and free-spirited sister, aunt or cousin.

The fact remained that he was still too young to consider marriage. These past days had been eventful and stimulating; certainly. He would even allow that they had been exciting. But soon enough, the real world would intrude—say better, return to normal. And he would go back to being a modestly paid secretary who was still some years away from having accumulated enough in the way of assets and income to sustain a household.

What was he to do?

Chapter 15

Tom decided to launch the bombing raid just before sundown. By then, the cavalrymen staying in the targeted village would be settling in for the night. Most of them, anyway. But there would still be enough light for the airship's bombardiers to see the targets easily. Even with a clear sky and moonlight, he didn't think they could do so very well after nightfall.

So, he stopped the march an hour earlier in the day than he'd stopped the previous two days, and spent the extra time setting up fieldworks to guard the camp. He wasn't sure how the Bavarians would react to the bombing. He didn't think they'd retaliate with an attack, because the infantry were the only ones really in position to launch such an attack and they weren't going to be the target of the bombing.

But you never knew. Relying too much on your own assessment of an enemy's intentions was a military error that probably dated back to Cro-Magnon times. *Naw, those guys won't do nothing tonight so we may as well get some sleep.* And so perishes another little band of hunter-gatherers...

He didn't use all of his men for that purpose, though. Earlier in the day, once Bonnie explained her plans to him over the radio, he sent Bruno von Eichelberg and his mercenary company on a forced march down the river. Their assignment was to meet up with the *Pelican* and the *Albatross* at the landing area the airship crews had selected and provide them with a guard unit. Tom didn't know yet if he would want to carry out a second bombing run, but he might. So he'd approved Bonnie's plan to set up an impromptu combination airfield and bomb-making facility.

And, again, you never knew. There was certainly no way that the Bavarian infantry could get down there tonight or tomorrow morning. And he didn't think it was likely at all that a cavalry unit would either. There had always been at least one airship in the sky above them since early morning. They could keep an eye out for any enemy troop movements within miles, and they'd reported no cavalry any closer than half a mile upstream. But you couldn't rule out the possibility that some stray cavalry had gone unspotted and were now well down the river. If even a small number of cavalrymen came across the airships on the ground and unprotected, there'd be an outright slaughter.

And now, there was nothing left to do but wait.

"What do you think, Heinrich?" asked Colonel von Schnetter. He passed the telescope he'd been using to Captain von Haslang. The two of them were sitting on their horses atop a small rise near the river bank, studying the fieldworks the Danube Regiment was putting up a half mile or so downstream. From here, they had a good view.

"Can you think of any reason they made camp earlier today, and are taking the time to create fieldworks?"

Von Haslang didn't reply for a few seconds, while he studied the enemy's activity through the glass. Then, passing it back to his commander, he got a slight smile on his face. He and von Schnetter had known each other for years and this was not the first time they'd worked together. The colonel's use of his given name was a subtle indicator that his friend wanted a frank and private discussion.

"Not really, Caspar. It's not as if you've given them any reason to expect an assault."

Von Schnetter took the eyeglass and slid it back into the case he kept attached to his saddle. He had the same slight smile also.

"No, I haven't. And as I'm sure you're figured out by now, I have no intention of attacking them. That American major—and it's him, for a certainty; did you see the size of the bastard?—has shown himself to be altogether too competent for my taste. Any attack we launched with no cavalry to work at their flanks would be a bloodbath. We'd probably win, in the end, because we outnumber them three-to-one. But that's more of a butcher's bill than I'm willing to pay with good troops who've been left in the lurch by swine and..."

He let the end of the sentence trail off. The "swine," of course, referred to von Troiberz. Von Haslang was quite sure that if his colonel had completed the thought, the "and" would have been followed by a very unfavorable reference to General von Lintelo.

He *had* gotten a good look at the commander of the enemy force. Just now, and also the day before when he and von Schnetter had studied their opponent making camp from another rise in the landscape. The colonel's eyepiece was superb. He'd only been able to afford it because he came from a wealthy family.

It was conceivable, of course, that the Danube Regiment had two officers as huge as the one they'd been looking at. But it was not likely. The Simpson fellow was rather famous, all across the Germanies. So was his admiral father, but in the case of the son the fame came entirely from his physique, not his accomplishments. That would begin to change, of course, as a result of his exploits over the past few days.

It was said that the young American major had engaged in an up-time sport that required immense men. "Feetball," it was called, if von Haslang remembered right. He was not clear with regard to the details of the game. His image of it, had he laid it before an up-timer, would have resulted in smiles, perhaps even laughter. Von Haslang's conception of "feetball" bore a much closer resemblance to mass sumo wrestling than the actual American sport.

But the details were irrelevant. Von Haslang would hate to confront that man in a physical clash, armed with anything but a gun. And now that he'd experienced three days of maneuvering against him, he'd want to fire the gun at a distance.

He and von Schnetter went back to looking at the distant enemy fieldworks.

"Make camp for the night, sir?" von Haslang asked, figuring that the moment for informality had passed.

"Yes, please see to it, Captain. We'll not be launching any attacks."

Colonel Johann von Troiberz was planning no attacks of his own that night, either. Not even an attack on the virtue of the woman sharing his bed, since that virtue had fallen many years earlier. Not to him, but to a different officer.

He thought he was the second Bavarian officer for whom she'd become a concubine. In actual fact, he was the fifth, but the woman in question had never seen any need to enlighten the colonel on the matter. Men were always bothered by such details.

After von Troiberz fell asleep, Ursula Gerisch stared at the ceiling. It was the sort of ceiling that she'd become familiar with, since she'd cast her lot with von Troiberz.

The ceiling belonged to one of the rooms in the sort of inn you ran across in large German villages. "Large," in this instance, was a term partly defined by the mere fact that the village had an inn, that was more than just a front room in a villager's house that provided drink and food purely for the locals.

Needless to say, the room was neither large nor well-furnished. It was certainly not luxurious. There was a bed—not large; not comfortable—and a nightstand, one chair, and a chamber pot.

The chamber pot had not been washed lately. So much was obvious.

She tried to remember how she'd wound up in this state of affairs. She was still well short of thirty years old. She couldn't even claim the excuse of desperately poor origins. Her father had been a tanner in a small town in Swabia—a trade that paid rather well, although you had to put up with the terrible stench.

It had begun with excitement, she recalled. Soldiers passing through town, a handsome young lieutenant. Ursula herself, bored. And she truly hated the stink of the tannery.

To this day, she liked to imagine that first liaison would have worked out well in the end. But the unfortunate young lieutenant had been serving under Ernst von Mansfeld at the disastrous battle of the Dessau Bridge, where the Protestants were crushed by Wallenstein. He'd vanished in the course of that battle. Presumably killed, but you never really knew. He might have just run off and decided to keep running. Whatever had happened, she'd never seen him again.

The second officer had not been exciting at all. A fat colonel in late middle-age, whose wife had died and whose career had stalled out. But he'd been a decent enough man, and she'd been desperate. Then, a year later, the colonel's heart had failed. He'd left no provision for her in his will, despite his promises. Everything had gone to his own children.

Back on the streets again. She'd worked those just long enough to find another officer. Another lieutenant. Also, alas, another unfortunate. In this case, not a casualty of bullet and sword but a casualty of the still deadlier combination of getting stinking drunk and climbing onto a horse.

Then, finally, a stroke of luck. Not much, but some. A captain this time, in his mid-thirties and in good enough health that she could expect some considerable years with him. As a concubine, to be sure, not a wife. The hopes Ursula had once had of eventually getting married and raising a family had died of neglect and malnutrition, somewhere along the way. But the captain was faithful enough that she didn't really fear he'd desert her for another woman or give her some sort of horrid disease.

He was something of a mean bastard, though, with a hot temper. He beat her from time to time. Life was far from perfect.

Worse than the beatings was the temper itself. The day came when he mistook the ease of beating a concubine with beating another officer. Unlike the concubine, the officer had a sword—and, as it turned out, was considerably more proficient in its use than the man who'd struck him.

They buried the captain's arm in the same coffin that held the rest of his body. The cut had taken it right off, after which he'd bled to death.

Luckily for Ursula—well, it had seemed lucky at the time—Colonel von Troiberz had attended the funeral and took it upon himself to comfort the not-exactly-a-widow after the ceremony concluded.

That had been three years ago. Her life had been a slow but steady slide downhill ever since.

The colonel did not beat her. That was his one virtue. So far as Ursula could determine, his only virtue.

Otherwise, von Troiberz was an unpleasant man in every particular. He had no sense of humor, no capacity for joy. He smiled maybe once a week. Laughed, perhaps once a month.

He had no capacity for any sort of pleasure, for that matter, except ones deriving from spite and greed.

Petty spite and petty greed. The man lacked style and verve even in his vices and sins.

Mostly, von Troiberz was a sullen man, riddled with resentments and envies. He drank constantly. And then spent his few sober hours coming up with schemes that might save him from the consequences of other schemes he'd come up with while drunk. She knew perfectly well the reason he'd spent the last three days dragging her around this miserable countryside in January was because he was desperately trying to cover up one of his thefts.

The drinking also made him incapable in bed but that was not a problem, so far as Ursula was concerned. On the now-rare occasions when the colonel did choose to engage in sexual activity, the result was brief and would have left her completely unsatisfied except that she began the coupling with no such expectations anyway. Somewhere along the way, her hopes that sex would at least be enjoyable had also died a natural death. The causes, again, being neglect and malnutrition.

The biggest problem was that Colonel von Troiberz stank, most of the time—and Ursula had begun this life in the first place because she hated bad smells.

He bathed once a year, at most, not counting the occasions he fell into a creek or stumbled into a pond while inebriated. But that didn't help because such bodies of water were usually smelly in their own right, not to mention the result of the time he'd fallen into a latrine.

He was flatulent. He had bad breath.

No, terrible breath. Even the food he preferred was nasty-smelling. His favorite meat was pickled pork, his favorite vegetables were onions, and his favorite herb was garlic.

His favorite drink was cheap korn made from rye taken with cheap beer. When he could afford it, he drank cheap schnapps made from apples. When he was short of money, he settled for cheap wine. All of it smelled bad to Ursula. Being fair to the colonel, all liquor smelled bad to her, even the expensive kind. She herself did not drink liquor except for an occasional glass of wine on celebratory occasions, and then only because it was expected of her.

He had no favorite flower. What was far worse was that he disliked flowers altogether—he claimed they made him sneeze and made him itch—and so he forbade her from putting any in their rooms. Even though she loved flowers and had ever since she was a child.

Lying in the bed staring at the ceiling, Ursula started to weep. No loud sobbing—the last thing she wanted to do was wake up von Troiberz—just tears, oozing slowly from her eyes. Eventually she would wipe them off, but not for a while. She was too tired. She was always too tired now. She could barely summon the energy to cook and do the laundry.

The colonel didn't want much of the first, since he usually ate in taverns, and he wanted almost none of the other. His clothing was as filthy and bad-smelling as he was, and there wasn't much point in her washing them because within a day he'd have them covered again with spilled liquor and food; within three days, vomit; and within a week, the condition of his breeches and underclothes didn't bear thinking about.

Every day seemed to pass in gray colors. She was losing her hopes for simple contentment as surely as she'd lost her hopes for marriage, for children, for joy, for pleasure. She'd begun to think about suicide, from time to time. So far the residue of her Catholic upbringing kept her shying away from the idea. But she thought that eventually her faith would die also. She felt like a walking corpse, stumbling toward a grave that she simply hadn't seen yet.

But she would see it some day, she knew. Probably before she saw her thirtieth birthday.

She knew her birthday, at least. Many people didn't. February 11th, less than a month from now.

She wouldn't be able to celebrate it, though. Von Troiberz disliked birthdays also, even his own. She wasn't sure why. She thought it was probably because the colonel had lost whatever capacity he'd ever had to enjoy a day just because it was a day to enjoy. And so he found it irritating to have others expecting him to celebrate. So might a man who has lost all sense of taste react when people urge him to eat a cake.

If she wasn't too tired, maybe she'd be able to have her own private little celebration. Just by herself. There still wouldn't be any flowers she could pick yet, though. Even the crocus wouldn't come up until March.

She'd often wished her birthday had been in April or May. Maybe then her life would have turned out differently. She liked to think so, anyway. There was still some small, not-quite-dead-and-buried part of Ursula Gerisch's soul that thought most of her life's trajectory had been the result of misfortune and happenstance. Not all, no; she accepted that she bore some of the guilt. But on her best days she thought—well, mostly she just wondered—about someday being able to find a new course for herself.

A peculiar sound coming from somewhere outside finally penetrated her bleak thoughts. Ursula realized that she'd been hearing it for some time but hadn't paid attention. It had gotten quite loud, by now.

She found a clean portion of the bedding and wiped the tears from her face. Then she rose from the bed and went to the window.

The sight beyond, in the glow of sunset—even in January, it seemed warm—was the most wonderful she could remember seeing in years. The one thing in the past three days that had brought some happiness to her was seeing those incredible flying machines in the sky.

They were so big! Yet not frightening. Not to her, at least. Many of the soldiers were scared by them, but she wasn't. Where they saw monsters in the air, she saw gigantic puppies.

She liked puppies. She liked dogs, too. They smelled nice to her, even if some people didn't think so.

She'd have kept a dog except the colonel didn't like dogs either.

And now there were three of them! All at once, in a line, one behind the other. She'd only seen one at a time, up until now.

They were coming in her direction, too—right at her, it seemed. And because they were approaching from the west, the setting sun lit up their huge, swollen bellies. She could easily see the boats that hung below them, with their noisy machines that apparently made them fly. She could even see people clearly, looking over the side of the boats.

They were quite low, she suddenly realized, much lower than she'd ever seen one of them come down before. They couldn't be more than six or seven hundred feet high, maybe even less.

Suddenly, for the first time in years, Ursula was filled with excitement. She had to see them better! From outside, not through a small grimy window. It was a cheap window, too, which made everything look distorted.

She glanced at the colonel. Von Troiberz was sprawled on the bed, snoring heavily. He'd come to bed drunk, as he usually did. Nothing would wake him up except the clap of doom.

Splendid. If he were awake, he'd undoubtedly forbid her to go outside. Moving quickly, Ursula put on her clothes and shoes, wrapped a cloak around her, and left the room.

In less than a minute she was outside. But the tavern door opened into a small courtyard surrounded by buildings. She couldn't see any of the ships from here. So, she hurried through the gate and out onto the village's main street.

But the street was narrow and the buildings alongside it just as tall. Frustrated, she looked around and saw a meadow in the distance, perhaps twenty yards beyond the last building. She could get there in a couple of minutes, if she hurried. The soil would probably be icy, but she had good shoes. It was the one piece of apparel she owned that the colonel had been willing to spend some money on.

✧   ✧   ✧

She got there in a minute and half. Looking up, she saw that the first ship—they were huge, now, *huge*—had come right overhead.

This was so marvelous! For the first time since childhood, she started jumping up and down with glee, clapping her hands.

Then, frowned. Not worried yet, just puzzled. Why were they dropping things from the boats? They looked like jugs or some sort of pottery.

Understanding came, and she made a small moue of disgust. Thank God she'd gotten out of the village! It was going to *stink* in a few seconds.

She was a little sad, though. A little upset, too. She wouldn't have thought that people who could do such a wondrous thing as fly through the air would be so petty and spiteful that they'd drop their chamberpots on their enemies.

Ursula couldn't help but giggle, though—and then realized that might be the first time she'd done that in years, too.

Colonel Johann von Troiberz was in for a rude awakening. He was about to get shat upon by leviathans.

Chapter 16

Ursula was wrong. Colonel von Troiberz did not get a rude awakening.

He didn't wake up at all. The tavern was one of the first buildings hit by the firebombs and it was hit by no fewer than four of them—two dropped by the *Albatross,* and one from each of the airships that followed in the bombing run. Within less than five minutes, the building was an inferno. Von Troiberz had been so drunk when he fell asleep that he died of smoke inhalation without ever regaining consciousness.

Most of the soldiers in that building died. Only five made it out alive, and two of them died immediately thereafter when the eaves of the tavern collapsed on them while they were still in the courtyard.

The very worst casualties were inflicted on the soldiers two buildings over. There were eleven of them crowded into that house. It had been the "party house," where those soldiers went who were in the mood to carouse—and they'd started carousing before noon. Only one survived and he suffered horrible burns that left him badly scarred.

Within fifteen minutes, the entire village was on fire. Almost three dozen cavalrymen had been killed, twice that many injured—and the stables were burning too. Luckily for the horses, a sober and conscientious sergeant had raced about unlocking all the doors in time for most of the beasts to escape.

Having made their escape, though, the horses were in no mood to stay in the vicinity of the holocaust. They scattered across the countryside, leaving all but nine cavalrymen stranded on foot.

In January. In the Little Ice Age. As night was falling. Most of them without having had time to don heavy clothing. A number of them bootless. And with nowhere nearby to spend the night indoors that wasn't smoldering.

Some of the men just wandered off, but most of them gathered together near the village when the fires began dying down. Their commanding officer was nowhere to be seen, and neither were the two captains who had been with them. Of the officers who'd been in the village, only three lieutenants were left.

After some discussion, they agreed that the best course of action was to join Colonel von Schnetter's infantry. Insofar as they knew where that camp was located, a subject on which there was considerable dispute. The lieutenants, in particular, were quarrelsome men. In the end, three different parties went their separate ways.

One of the parties found the camp. Another eventually stumbled across a deserted village two miles away before any of them had died, although some wound up losing toes to frostbite.

The third party died of exposure. The last man went at three o'clock in the morning.

Watching this all unfold from above, Rita was aghast. She'd had no idea—never once imagined—that the bombing run would have such horrific success. She'd thought that most of the bombs would miss entirely, first of all. Some would hit the target, certainly, but few enough that by the time the fires really began spreading most of the men down there would have been able to escape.

She hadn't even thought about the horses. Americans of the eighteenth and nineteenth centuries would have understood how deadly it could be for a man to be stranded in winter without a horse. But she'd come from the end of the twentieth. "Being stranded" meant running out of gas and hitching a ride with the next car to come by. In a rural area like Grantville, people would usually stop for you. Especially in winter.

What had thrown her off, again, had been watching too many newsreels. She'd seen documentary footage that depicted bombing runs from World War II and the Korean War and the Vietnam War and Operation Desert Storm. Planes moving hundreds of miles an hour when they dropped their bombs; the trajectory of those bombs themselves covering a great distance before they finally hit the ground.

It was amazing any of them hit anything they were aimed at. And those bombs had been military-grade high explosives or incendiaries, vastly more powerful than the ones Bonnie Weaver had jury-rigged. By the time of the Iraq-Kuwait war, some of them had been guided munitions. But even as far back as World War II, she knew, the bombers had some kind of superb bombsights.

Her bombsights had been her eyes, looking down over the lip of the gondola, while two of Franchetti's crewmen held a bomb on the same lip, waiting for her signal.

What she hadn't considered, until the bombs started hitting, was that *her* bombing platform was almost stationary. She'd told Franchetti to maintain just enough power to keep the airship from drifting. Both of the airships that followed her after the *Albatross* unloaded all its bombs had done the same.

And none of it had taken very long. Once Rita saw that the bombs really didn't need to be "aimed" at all, she'd told the crewmen to just start pitching them over the side as fast as they could.

Another deadly factor had been her decision to make the run at a much lower altitude that the airships normally flew over enemy troops. At her husband's insistence, the airships had stayed at least two thousand feet high most of the time. They never dropped below a thousand feet.

But Rita had decided, just this once and to hell with what Tom said about it afterward, that they'd come in not more than the length of two footfall fields over the target. That was still within range of seventeenth-century musket fire, technically speaking. But at two hundred yards the fire would be wildly inaccurate. Besides, although Rita didn't know the exact formulas, she knew from things her husband had said that smoothbore round shot lost its muzzle velocity much faster than rifled bullets did. She figured that even if a bullet fired from a musket six hundred feet down did manage to hit the envelope or even the gondola, it probably wouldn't be moving fast enough to do a lot of damage. Barring a really lucky shot, anyway.

In the event, only two cavalrymen shot at them, and both of them used wheel-lock pistols. She had no idea where those bullets wound up going. Nowhere close, for sure.

This was just a massacre. She felt sick to her stomach.

Once she stopped screaming and brought her panic under control, Ursula got up and looked around. She had to get up because in her frenzied race away from the inferno the village had become, she'd eventually tripped on something and sprawled flat on the ground.

She'd come a long way from the village, she realized. At least a quarter of a mile. She wasn't sure. She hadn't been thinking about anything except *get away! get away!*

She looked up. Now, the things in the sky did look like monsters to her. You could still see all of them very clearly, since the sun hadn't fully gone down yet. Its red hemisphere glowed above the western skyline.

She stood there for a while, gasping to regain her breath and trying to figure out what to do. Going back to the village was... unthinkable.

But where else? She looked around, more slowly this time, and realized she was the only person in sight.

She was cold, she suddenly realized. Very cold. The temperature was already below freezing. Within a few hours no one would be able to survive out here without some way to stay warm better than a coat and a pair of shoes. Even a good pair of shoes.

Noise drew her attention back to the sky. The first of the airships had turned and was now coming...

Right at her.

She screamed and started running again.

"What do you think is happening, sir?" von Haslang asked the colonel. Von Schnetter lowered the eyeglass and shook his head. "It's too far away to see much. Something is burning, though. A whole village, I think, as bright as it is even from here."

Both of them now looked above the glow in the distance. The airships in the sky were quite visible, even this far away.

"Do you think...?"

Von Schnetter sighed. "I don't know, Heinrich. But... it could be, yes."

He looked around at their own camp. "Better make preparations, Captain. Just in case we have to move suddenly."

Tom Simpson was even farther away. But because of the radio, he didn't have to wonder what had happened.

What he was starting to wonder about, though, was how much more his wife could take. There'd been a ragged edge to her voice that he'd never heard before.

There were a lot of ways in which Rita resembled her older brother Mike, but other ways in which they were not alike at all. One big difference was that Mike Stearns—as nice a guy as he was, and Tom would vouch for that also had a ruthless side to him. As wide and deep as the Mississippi, sometimes.

Rita just plain didn't. She was the sort of person for whom healing and nurturing came easily and killing did not.

At all.

Tom was starting to worry that she was going to come out of all this with a lot more scars—and a lot worse ones—than the one left on her arm by a splinter from an exploding door.

She hadn't fired the first bullet. But she'd fired some of the ones that came after, including a gigantic bullet that had just taken out dozens of men and the whole village they'd been in.

"Look there!" said one of the *Albatross*'s crewmen. His first name was Luca, but Rita couldn't remember his last name. It wasn't Franchetti but she thought he was somehow related to the Franchettis. Like most up-time businesses had been in a small town like Grantville, seventeenth-century companies were usually family affairs. The families got pretty big, too.

Luca was leaving over the rail of the gondola, pointing at something on the ground ahead of them. Rita went over and looked herself.

At first she didn't see anything. It was now getting dark down on the ground, if not up here where the last of the sun was still visible.

After a few seconds she spotted a flash of movement that drew her eyes. It took her a few seconds to realize what she was seeing.

"It's a woman, I think," said Luca. "Hard to tell from here."

Rita thought the figure on the ground was a woman herself. She didn't know why, exactly. You really couldn't distinguish body shapes from this far up, much less facial features. It was winter, too, when people wore bulky clothing.

But something, whatever subtlety of movement or posture, led her to think Luca was right.

He shook his head. "She might make it through the night, if she can find one of the abandoned villages and get inside. Probably not, though."

Rita stared at him. Then, down at the woman below.

That *was* a woman, she was almost sure now. But even if it wasn't, that person certainly wasn't a Bavarian cavalryman.

"Fuck that," she muttered. She turned to Franchetti. "Take the *Albatross* down, Filippo. All the way to the ground." She pointed to the figure herself. "We'll pick her up. We've got room and plenty of weight allowance, now that the bombs have all been dropped."

"But . . . signora . . ."

"Oh, stop worrying! There's nobody else down there. Not within half a mile, at the very least. We've got plenty of time to get down, pick her up, and get back in the air before anyone'll be able to come at us."

"But ... signora ..."

"Just fucking do it!"

She took a deep, ragged breath. "Please, Filippo." She had tears in her eyes. "I am so sick of killing people."

In the end, what saved Ursula's life was her own despair.

She ran from the monster. Ran and ran for a while. But it kept pursuing her, coming closer and closer to the ground.

Eventually, partly from exhaustion but mostly from too many years of seeing her hopes all scraped away, she just stopped. Then, sat on the ground, holding her knees. Ignoring the cold seeping into her buttocks. Just waited for her death, the way prey run to the ground waits for the predator.

If she'd kept running, she could have escaped the *Albatross*. It was dark now and she could have slipped away into the shadows any number of times, if she'd been thinking clearly.

Rita had almost given up hope herself.

The monster had the face of a young woman. Ursula hadn't expected that.

Quite a pretty one. Black hair, blue eyes. The color was very clear, even in twilight. A slender build, she thought, although it was hard to be sure. She was wearing a peculiar, puffy sort of jacket.

The monster extended her hand. "Come on, girl," she said. "It's time to go."

Some time later, looking out at the moon from the gondola, Ursula finally spoke.

"I'm flying," she said, wonderingly. "I'm really flying."

A while later, she added, "Away."

Chapter 17

On the fourth and final day, the Bavarian infantry made no effort
to close with the Danube Regiment. In fact, by late morning
they'd let the distance between the marching armies stretch to
two miles. By mid-afternoon, to three miles.

Colonel von Schnetter's couriers had come across several survivors of the bombing raid and two of them had been to see the
village ruins themselves. So the infantry commander had a pretty
good idea of what had happened.

The ever-growing distance between his forces and those of Major
Simpson's were no longer due to simple caution, but outright worry.
His infantry was moving more slowly down the Danube because
he needed to be sure, at all times, that he could get the men *away*
from the river if the need arose. Airships that could destroy a village could also destroy a tightly-packed infantry column.

Von Schnetter was no longer concerned about General von Lintelo's reaction to the events of these past four days. First, because
Colonel von Troiberz had certainly died in the fire—and who
better to take the blame for disaster than a man already dead?
Second, because not even von Lintelo was so thick-headed as not
to understand that the introduction of these infernal airships onto
battlefields created many new problems.

And third, because he had better things to do than fret over a general's possible peeves. Such as spend his time discussing new tactical
possibilities with his friend and trusted aide, Captain von Haslang.

It was quite pleasant, actually, that last day's march down the
Danube. Vigorous conversations with an intelligent man were one
of life's high points. Even when the subject was grim.

Twice, Tom almost ordered another bombing run. Not because
of bloodlust, or because he feared that the pursuing Bavarians
posed a threat any longer. They were making it very clear that
they had no intention of fighting before he reached Regensburg.
You could almost call them an escort of sorts, in this final stretch.

No, it was because he too was beginning to consider tactical
options in the light of new developments, and had started discussing them with his own trusted aides.

"It'd be interesting to see," pointed out Bruno von Eichelberg, "how an infantry column marching down a road handles an attack from the air."

Both times, what stopped him was his wife's face. Rita was slender almost to the point of being skinny. Now, though, she was looking downright gaunt.

Every night since the first, the nightmares had brought Rita awake. Sweating, frightened, tight of breath. Always that same boy's face.

This morning, though, she'd been able to look at a woman's face that she thought might start easing her soul.

She could hope so, anyway.

When the Danube Regiment entered Regensburg, they discovered that a parade was expected. Right through the town to the square. Where apparently speeches would be inflicted upon them.

Ah, well. Even tired soldiers respond to applause. And they were getting a lot of it. An awful lot.

"This was mostly Heinz's idea," Bonnie told Rita. They were watching the parade from one of the stands set up on the side of the square. Overhead, the *Pelican* came into view. The crowd in the square burst into cheers again.

"You know what city officials are like," she continued. "I swear, frogs have more imagination. All they could talk about—fuss and fuss and fuss about—was where they would find enough billets for all these additional soldiers. But Heinz set 'em straight. 'First we make them welcome,' he said, and wouldn't take no for an answer. As usual."

There was a certain tone in her voice. Proud, you might call it. Proprietary, too.

Böcler was watching the festivities from the officials' stand. He would have much preferred to be with Bonnie Weaver. Mostly because he liked being around her, but partly because he wouldn't be at the center of everyone's attention. He disliked that rather intensively, he'd come to discover.

He'd also come to understand some things about his former employer, Ernst of Saxe-Weimar, that had been unclear to him before, as well as gaining a better understanding of the advantages that Caesar and Thucydides had had, when they turned themselves to the historian's trade.

The front ranks of the Danube Regiment entered the square. At the fore marched the figure of Major Simpson. Impossible to miss, of course.

The cheers erupted again.

Or Xenophon. Böcler had read the *Anabasis*. But he decided he should read it again. He thought he'd get more out of it now. He was quite sure he would, in fact.

He looked toward Bonnie. She was standing next to the major's wife, and, as it happened, she was looking in his direction.

She waved at him, very cheerily.

Anxiety, in the midst of celebration. Doubt, where certainty also tread.

The cautions were all in the Bible, of course. He'd known that for years, although he hadn't understood them so well until these past few days.

In his own way, he too had been marching upcountry.

And still was.

What was he to *do*?